$\mathcal{V}$OICES OF THE $\mathcal{S}$OUTH

THE WAVE

THE WAVE

EVELYN SCOTT

Louisiana State University Press

Baton Rouge and London

Library of Congress Cataloging-in-Publication Data

Scott, Evelyn, 1893–
    The wave / Evelyn Scott.
    p. cm. — (Voices of the South)
    ISBN 0-8071-2068-5 (pbk. : alk, paper)
    1. United States—History—Civil War, 1861–1865—Fiction.
  I. Title. II. Series.
  PS3537.C89W3 1996
  813'.52—dc20
                                          95-47385
                                              CIP

TO LOLA RIDGE

FOREWORD

In the insertion in this text of the characters of mythical military leaders side by side with those who existed in fact, and in other deliberate inaccuracies of time and place, this book takes a number of liberties with "history." These digressions from the accepted fact were not made, however, until after the acquisition of information from acknowledged sources. Phyllis Crawford Scott, G. S. Fechter, and Lola Catesby Jones, not to be held responsible for this arbitrary interpretation of records, were most generous in assisting the search for the necessary, even if half discarded, background for a wilful narrative. The help they gave is very much appreciated.

There is also a debt to be happily acknowledged to "Mammy" Alice Johnson, deceased, whose personal recollections extended backward to the period embraced herein. Not all the songs she recalled were included, but the reminders of the past which she offered were given with her confident expectation that she would see her name on this page. I hope her faith in a prophesied solution of large issues has been fulfilled, and that her death, before the completion of this book, is no barrier to the satisfaction I have thought she would feel in the fulfilment of her anticipation.

"The water of the ocean is never still. It is blown into waves by the wind, it rises and falls with the tides. . . . The waves travel in some definite direction, but a cork thrown into the water does not travel with the waves. It moves up and down, to and fro, but unless it is blown by the wind or carried by a current it returns to the same position with each wave and does not permanently leave its place. . . . In deep water the motion of the particle at the surface [of the wave] is nearly circular. At the crest the movement of the particle is forward, at the middle of the hinder slope it is downward, in the trough backward, and at the middle of the front slope upward . . . waves have very little effect excepting near the surface . . . when a wave approaches a shelving shore it keeps its form as a wave until it is near the land and then the top falls forward and the wave breaks. This is due in part to the fact that the wave travels more slowly as the water becomes shallower. . . . When the water is deep close up to the shore, the waves, if they break at all . . . appear to throw themselves against the cliff . . . and the water dashes . . . some times to a very great height."—*Physical Geography*, by Philip Lake, M.A.

I

IT was so quiet in Charleston Harbour, that Dickie Ross, working his row-boat out to sea, felt as if half drowned in the tides that he could hear, while they moved invisibly. That was the night, trickling from the blades of his oars; or, if the wind ran along his forehead and lifted his hair, it was the night, too, making his mind vague. Fort Sumter was *there*, however, compelling him to excitement, preventing his enjoyment of the dreamier elation of freedom. He rose, faced forward, and pushed hard, drawing his oars up until they dug into his chest over his heart, which was so large with the very amplitude of darkness as to impede his breathing.

Milt Smith said that President Davis's ultimatum to Major Anderson had been sent. If the government did not surrender the fort at once, the trouble, long awaited, would begin at last, Dickie, guilty in his intrusion upon the quiet, anticipated joyfully, brutally, as though it were a stealthy revenge which he would be allowed to take upon his mother and his sister, that first shot promised to his ears if the Yankees, foolishly, did not give up.

He was far enough from land. His skiff nosed a clot of shadow that was an island, and he sat down suddenly, the oars clattering. The lights on the mainland gave him the impression of veiled signalling. He resented it that his privileged aloofness allowed him no definite sense of what impended. The rocking of his boat lulled, but he rejected the indolence which made daily life bearable. Mr. Wright, his boss, was organizing a corps of volunteers, and Dickie had been one of the first to enlist in it. The gesture had invited Sister Mollie to usual ridicule, and she had reiterated her opinion that Dickie 'never had an idea of his very own,' but that he behaved, constantly, as Mr. Wright suggested.

And why not? Mr. Wright had been in the army previously. He had been to Mexico. He had gone West and knew how the Indians were fought. Dickie felt that it was like a girl to condemn a gentleman because, first, of course, he was a bachelor, and, secondly, because his head was baldish and his nose so big.

He was a cotton merchant, prosperous, but not careful of his appearance, and smoked a corncob pipe. Dickie considered Mr. Wright too modest. The dingy planter's hat, the wrinkled cotton trousers and the soiled cravat produced an effect unrelated to his character. If Sister Mollie could ever hear Wright swearing she would change her notion of him. It exasperated Dickie that Mr. Wright made 'no more show.' Mr. Wright displayed an embarrassment before women with which Dickie did not sympathize. Women were devious, they were contemptible, they were jealous, and they resented masculine prerogatives and liberty because they could not share them.

Only yesterday, Dickie had realized, suddenly, that it was necessary, inevitable, when a man began to think and act upon his own initiative, that he should hurt somebody. On this account he would leave his savings to his mother. He would pay her off. He was nineteen. For three years he had been learning bookkeeping, in order, with his earnings, though he was not much more than an apprentice, to assist Mrs. Ross, who was a teacher in the Charleston *Ladies' Seminary*. Maybe, if he went to war and left her, she would accept the 'offer' tendered her by old Mr. Childers. It was a fact that for ten years or more she had made her son and daughter her excuse for continuing to wear her widow's weeds. "You are just like your papa, Dickie," Mrs. Ross often declared, "and I thank the dear God who has given you to me to take his place." There was something here which the son could not express—why it was that he could not be grateful for her long devotion to him. It must be that he was a 'no-account.' But he was not oppressed by his wicked nature. When there was a scrap brewing, as at present, he was hard, he was cold, he was almost happy. He believed that he did not care 'a tinker's damn' how his mother suffered.

She was a lady, and to see how she had 'come down in the world' should have aroused his pride of family, given him ambition. Well, he was proud enough, if she only knew it, and he reckoned that his impulses, however reckless, were those of an aristocrat. The poor whites, Dickie reflected scornfully, to the heavy lisps of the darkness, will be on the side of the damned Abolitionists.

Why was it so hard to get his mother out of his mind? Her physical presence seemed upon him even here in the harbour. He had an hallucinatory certainty of her large, brown, humorous eyes, filled with a constant doubt of him. She was too thin. For some reason, he was annoyed by this. When, the other day, he had seen her, for the first time, with her black dress relieved by a low-neck and a fichu, he had been revolted. He could endure vulgarities when they were perpetrated by other women. Toward her alone he could not be tolerant. No doubt, he had idealized her. She was old. When he had shown a dislike for Mr. Childers, it had been for her sake. It had distressed him, in the winter, that she had gone to school wearing mended mittens. To look so shabby made her ridiculous. She was so tall, so stately. She taught a little French and the use of globes to her silly schoolgirls. If he should really find that she was not respected, he would cut his throat.

The night kept running by, over his oars, over his forehead. But that was a woman's life, in this silly town, with its silly gossip. He was going to leave it all, shake it off. Getting drunk hadn't done it. The need to think of money, and of propriety, often seemed identical. If Mr. Wright had been a drinker, Dickie might have attempted to carouse more frequently. And then, the next day, there was Mother with the look that you could not escape. She did not reproach. She was silent, she was offended, and very kind. Dickie recalled, without connection, a story he had heard about a man who owned a nigger wench whom he would beat unmercifully when he grew angry with anybody.

The boat floated, carrying Dickie, sightless, with it. He was grounding on the island, and pushed himself resentfully away again. When would it happen? When would it happen? A man had a right to a little excitement. Dickie felt ugly.

In Charleston, things were always the same. He worked a little for Mr. Wright. He went home to dinner. He came back down town again. Or it was late, and he idled in the office window. The streets by the water always stank of fish. He could catch the same smell now in the night. It seemed to him that he envied the doggone niggers who were always happy, who were made to work. It was when he really expected a change to come, that he felt so feverish. When he had earned the commendation of his general, his mother would not silently reprove his selfishness. There were

3

qualities, like courage, which nobody understood. And if he told her that he loved her too much to remain at home, she would not believe him. The hard sensation contracted his heart again. There were times when you could wish that the world would go clean to hell. How say that to his mother, and, worst of all, to his grandmother; to the humped old lady with her clean dry hands, and her clean dry apron, who was always so industrious about the house, who gazed at him more questioningly than even his mother did. Mrs. Kinnibrew, his grandmother, was now eighty-six, and she was dependent upon his mother for everything. She wanted Dickie Ross to love her, so she always listened admiringly to all he said. When he was obliged, in duty, to kiss the powdery cheek she offered him, he often hated her. It was, he said, in defence of his mother. Mrs. Kinnibrew was weak, she was eager, she was mercilessly grateful to him. He had no word for her state.

It was mostly because of her that he nursed lusts. He had a life that she did not recognize. That was his own. He kept it out of the tumble-down cottage by the harbour. He was a man, and they didn't believe it yet. He supposed that, were he thirty, they would still consider that he was growing up.

As Dickie waited, the night seemed heavier. The presage of dawn was withheld almost unbearably. He would do *anything*, he felt, that would hurry the day. He was helpless. It was awful to be as poor as he in a place like Charleston, and with *his* capacities. If the sun would come, if the war would commence, he would be able to explain, by his actions, what his dissatisfaction meant. He despised loose women, but, if he had to seek them at his age, his mother drove him to it. It would even make you feel good if you could let loose in a quiet place like this, and shoot straight into the air. If there were only fish to hear you and *they* would scuttle, it would be relieving. Day itself would be the herald of some precious alarm. When the sky cracked with day, in the early morning, there was always a sense of something to do. The frantic obligation was to be fulfilled. But before it was accomplished, the night, when people went to wasted resting, closed in again. Dickie sometimes grudged the experience of his father, who had died of an accidental wound while on a hunting expedition. Father, smug and liberated, now regarded his wife, his mother, and his son and daughter, from a plush-framed daguerreotype on the parlour wall.

4

He had escaped Charleston. He was dead—like a betrayer. I don't believe I would have got on with Father anyhow, Dickie said to himself.

Shot! The explanation came tardily, long after the noise. There was a glow in the sky. Dickie trembled blankly, and the compulsion to meditate in self-justification passed away. Smell was later, and confirmed conviction. His elation was an illness. A plush-swathed hammer pommeled at the dusky air. His skiff, rocked violently by his uneasy motions, seemed to awaken with him to the aliveness of ruddied ripples that had not existed for him while the world was black. He huddled. He was conscious of his chilled body, and his beaten posture. *Blum, blu-uum,* low in the night behind a curtain; and a rain of ponderous invisible objects sank into the water, as if a million miles beneath. There was a pause, long, utterly hopeless. He began to wonder where the sound had come from, for he could not see the Sumter that his side were firing at.

A disease of incredulity persisted. Then his confused, seeking pupils widened on another faint radiance. *Blum. Blum-bluuum,* full with anticipated echo. His mother and sister would be listening. He longed almost viciously for knowledge that they had been awakened. *Blum. Blum-blum-blum.* He was on his feet again, toppling, staring, looking for Sullivan's Island. Then the accents grew thicker, quicker, as though castanets clicked. A weight splintered on a giant anvil. A dusty sneezing brought a glow that made the harbour deeper and more impenetrable under its flitting skim of fire. Echoes thrashed the passive distant scenes of ocean. It would go on, for years and years. It would never cease. His throat ached with tension, with the realization of some ghastly joy. This was *life.* This was seeing life. A strange cry swelled in him, chokingly. He 'hoped to God' that the damned Yankees would never 'get enough.' What did it matter who was hurt, who died? What did it matter how long the war would take? They would be wiped out, the dad-blamed Yankees, the intruders, the Abolitionists. Maybe they're too cowardly to stand it, he wondered. He was sick, wanting an opponent worthy of his mettle. They would *have* to fight, by God, they would! A man like Wright—why, he would *make* them fight. And there was purification in this sudden frenzy. Dickie felt 'good,' he was glad. His mother must needs acquiesce.

5

It was like the Deluge. It was a calamity demanding 'men.' He wanted to see the niggers run through the Charleston streets. He wanted to have his mother and his sister behold. There were reasons for existence plain to a man which were not included in their vocabulary. He would get down to brass tacks. Life wasn't all smooth and slick and genteel. It *began* somewhere. It began with fighting, it began with keeping niggers in their rightful place, it began with giving hell to Yankees, it began with loyalty to Mr. Davis, to the new Confederacy. Let 'em hurt me, Dickie insisted fretfully. He preferred to be hurt. He wanted to *feel*, at last. This was 'real.'

Metal cards slid in a box. The day broke. Sullivan's Island surprised him, abruptly, by actually *being* there, beneath a smoking, flowery canopy. Now he was sorry that the folks in Charleston knew what had happened. The daylight took his secret from him. There was a woodpecker tapping on the island near him in the underbrush. Behind the spit of sand, the flat-spread claws of the groined palmettos spread their glistered fans. Beyond this stale hostility of green, scrub oaks, vaguely bulky with lilac clouds of Spanish moss, rose occasionally, adding something suffocating to the growing calm of morning. A gull, flying against the rising sun, was as large as an eagle; until, swooping heavily upon the beach and drawing in its wings, it shrank to the dimensions of this usual, this nothing, and, strutting primly, parallel to the skiff, watched Dickie oddly, from its large bright eyes placed too far back in its head.

To the right of him, in the path of the fierce grey light, the garnished ocean exuded mists. The glare's shattered rays revealed the oozy tracks of dragging currents. And there was Sumter, low, with hazy walls, under a slight flag colourless as an apparition. He had expected to see it crushed by the blows that had dinned his ears. Its chill double-image in the smooth, far-off reflecting ripples defied him. The spell which enwrapped him always had not been broken. Things *did* change. They must change. Weakened by his prolonged emotion, he could yet aspire toward Sullivan's Island which was steaming under a dry white cloud above a sea like milk.

Dickie wished to row, to move—but where? Quiet, and the daylight bred new agitations. He was safe here, and, even if he were not safe, he was not afraid. He tried to rest himself in the boat

6

on the elevations of the tide. The small waves, thrown back from the beach, lopped on the hull. A pink crab sidled to the water. Was this a world where even crabs were secure, and would the long days go on and on as always, ignoring him?

There was a burst as of sunny thunder. He breathed. Jesus, let 'em hear it. Let the folks in Charleston hear it. Let Mother waste her time at a young ladies' seminary. The damp-throttled noises were swelling suddenly. The heat, as if concentrated by a burning glass in April, beat on his neck. Energy compelled him. He stood up, teetering, and began to shout—at last, at last, he began to shout whole-heartedly, and to drown out the stealthy rustles of the harbour and the morning, so big and so indifferent to him. "Hurrah for President Davis! Hurrah for the Confederacy! Hurrah for the war, by gum, and playing hell with everybody!"

The sun douched him in a warmth foetid with salt, with fish smells from the swamps and islands, with a kind of rotten quiet. When he had left off 'hollering,' he felt like a fool. But the mortars and cannon kept on. There was no mistaking it now, with the daylight here to prove it. The war had begun. There was something that a fellow could *do*. It was a great age that he was living in. This was a great life. His mother could talk all she liked about brutality. They were in for trouble.

II

Percy was annoyed because he had misdated a letter and Lawyer Burroughts, of *Burroughs, Pierce, and Franklin*, had reprimanded him. The meticulous rewriting of the letter had kept Percy at work in the office after Raeburn had gone home to get his dinner, and Coulter had retired to the back verandah to eat his lunch. There was a calendar on the stained wall flaunting the nineteenth of April above an advertisement of *Arthur's Home Gazette*. Percy, as if to rebuke the calendar, had gone on scratching with a splintered goose-quill long after he had lost a human audience for his assiduity. He hoped that Eva would regret his delay, but he could not be blamed. It was a sticky day, springlike, but too warm and moist. He was conscious of his heavy face, dewy with a kind of greasy sweat, and of the young flies that, in their weak delicate persistence, alighted upon his high forehead repeatedly. As not even Coulter seemed left to observe the degree of martyrdom which duty demanded, Percy at last got up.

He had never called himself handsome, for his bad eyesight and his spectacles embittered his natural shyness. He was reliable and self-dependent, however, he decided, and what he lacked in 'prettiness' was compensated for by his 'character.' He had married Eva chiefly because she had appreciated this.

Percy, wary before a mirror, and careful to be unseen, placed his little flat-crowned hat on thoughtfully. Trousers were very round this season and his coat so short that he jerked furtively at the tail. He would quarrel about the price of a garment, but he was relieved to permit Eva to select the fashion for him. Clothes, as he regarded them, were an investment. It 'paid' to buy only the best materials, whereas Eva was likely to purchase a dress that would show wear and look shabby before she could have it 'turned.' He wished to educate Eva to his precious view of life. He was interested in her management of their cottage home. He was often exasperated by her ignorance of proper cooking, and he would ask the men whom he met daily in the office their advice on sauces. He was penurious, he admitted—if you wished to call it that—but because he was an 'Epicurean,' and enjoyed things well done. Methodical in his employment, he sometimes invited his wife's criticism; but he was satisfied with himself as he was. To be nagged, made him frantic. He was cautious, yet he now and then displayed a childish peevishness to his superiors, and, by imprudent retort to comment, had risked his position. This was one of the mornings when he felt 'fract'ous,' as the niggers said, and only restrained his temper until he could return to Eva where he could find something appropriate to quarrel about.

Nothing was as offensive to him as disorder. And since this talk of war was troubling all his neighbours, disorder threatened. Eva had persuaded him to wear his Sunday clothes to work. It was weakness to listen to her. He would as soon appear in mud-splashed brogues and the corduroys in which, on summer holidays, he took fishing trips. He defied Lawyer Burroughs to object. Was a man paid for his effiiciency, or were clerks chosen for their silky whiskers? Look at Coulter—wretched, cringing little toady. What did he get by it?

Percy, the sulky rage of his expression a just protest against accustomed poverty, strode heavily through the bare hallway on which the offices abutted, and reached the street while under a treasured impression that his dinner would be cold and not fit to eat when he arrived at home. It was a strain to offer, for Eva's adoration, a perpetual spectacle of masculine aggression. There was so much that really did not interest him which she longed to have him care about. Through the winter, he had forgiven her. When he came in tired at evening and saw that his dressing-gown was warmed and his slippers toasting, he felt a mild, depressing love for her. If she would only learn to let him live his life according to his fancy, he would grant her his protection for ever. But today, he was certain, she would be 'at him' again, quoting Great Aunt Phoebe's hope that he would ally himself with the Secessionists. Percy would not be pushed. His conscience as a Southerner was as insistent as a toothache. But he and Eva owed Aunt Phoebe five hundred dollars. Did Aunt Phoebe imagine that, for five hundred dollars, she could buy his freedom of decision, his right to act for himself? Did she keep that debt in the background as a club over him? He left people alone. Let them leave him alone. He had a mind, sometimes, to distress Eva and defend Unionism just to spite Aunt Phoebe. *She* had the slaves and the money. She was deucedly careful that he and Eva should not benefit by either until she was dead. These men who were idling, filling up the streets today, they need not stare at *him* as if they expected *him* to hiss the government. On the other hand, if trouble *did* break out, he was not going to waste his sympathy on Lincoln's soldiers, when the governor and the marshal had joined in a warning, and had been certain beforehand that to send the troops through Baltimore this morning would be an invitation to rioting.

Percy walked quickly along the thronged sidewalk, his gait one of purposed awkwardness. His little brown eyes cast incessantly, through his spectacles, contemptuous glances. He despised alike those of staid appearance and the hoodlums who were gathering. The soldiers must be marching by this route to the depot. Well, let them get out.

On a corner, Percy's way was blocked. He resigned himself unwillingly to the slow pace of a congesting multitude. He wished to cling to his indifference, but that was difficult with his certain premonition that Eva was waiting and would feel abused. It was sultry. The day greyed, as the sun, in the blue, still sky, was buried temporarily in fleecy depths of cloud. Percy fumbled fretfully the soft whiskers beneath his plump chin, and sucked irritably at his bare upper lip. But he could disdain passion. He would be controlled. Eva, though she placated him insultingly, had once gone so far as to tell him that, when his indolent temper was aroused, he behaved badly. He had felt her subtly couched rebuke as a design upon his liberty.

Halted just before Percy, was a little old negro man, in a greenish, shapeless kind of preacher's coat. The glare was beating glisteningly upon his bare head thinly dotted with speckled wool. He was squatting, peering, with a sort of demureness, between the boldly planted legs of some men in front of him. Percy, disturbed, guarding the confidence which he could show to an inferior, said, "What's the matter, Uncle? What are you leering at between those feet? What's happening down the street today?"

The small, shrivelled negro, with a deafness which Percy thought pretence, hesitated to reply, and the interrogation, to bring an answer, had to be repeated. Then the small, old monkey spoke as if to himself.

"Um—um, Mistah. Um—yes-suh, Cap'n. Hit's de Union sojers." His head was cocked sidewise. His eyes glinted moistly, and his information, given with a doubtful chuckle, was like a timid challenge. The crafty satisfaction of his wise, harsh face somehow disgusted Percy. "Dey's seb'n companies come frum de nawthun to de suthun depots. Folks say dey won' let no othah hawse cars pass an' dese has to walk."

Percy, nervously keen to suspect insolent intention, ignored the negro suddenly. Why should *he* care how and when the soldiers came and went? The politicians were a selfish lot at best. It was just as likely that what they wanted most was to irritate a stupid crowd like this. He had told Eva that he and she were going to 'keep cool' and let the 'rabble' fight it out. The South was at fault, and the North as well. For years the South had kept a majority in the Senate, and now the North was jealous, was taking its revenge. A man like Lincoln, an upstart playing for popular favour, was making hay while the sun shone. If the government compromised properly with Southern interests he would forfeit his opportunity for playing a spectacular part. Wars, Percy meditated grudgingly,

10

were an offence to reason. History did not record one just war, one war carried on rationally and not for the gratification of a prejudice.

He was tall, yet he was obliged to elevate his bulky body on his tiptoes in order to see beyond the people who were jostling him. Damp, sun-dazzled profiles, blobbed now and then by the shadows of the jerking, new-leafed trees, filled all the street. This imposition of an absorption which he did not share was maddening. He cursed a thin man under a stove-pipe hat, a fat man wearing a wide-brimmed straw, and, above all, the women, whose bonnets, just exceeding his shoulders, scratched at his cheeks. All at once his perturbation focused on a shocking view of the light-crackling tips of bayonets, and on arresting repetitiousness of uniforms like the crest of a tide. This explained the monotonous, constant shuffling of so many feet.

"The devil take the whole crew!" he ejaculated unpremeditatedly. And it was as if he were being forced to a risky defence of his self-respect. He had anticipated soldiers, certainly, but not so actually; and he saw so many. It was like the 'damned presumptuousness' of military authority to thrust such a martial sight upon peaceful Baltimore. If we don't consider the war our affair, why won't they let us decent people keep out of it! It was as though the United States government had failed utterly to appreciate the steady qualities of those citizens on whom depended the state's security. Percy felt that his own rising choler was the result of 'their' tricks. It was a fact that, after you heard one lot talk, and then the other, your single desire was to keep your mind clear and remain aloof from both. Lincoln says he won't meddle with the slaves, and Aunt Phoebe and President Davis seem sincerely convinced that he is doing so already. Percy wondered why he had drudged in an office for the last ten years to witness chaos acclaimed as the reward of his endeavours. He could feel his ears burning, his face hot. His intensity of indignation was like a proof that he was right, and the others, 'curse their gizzards,' who *wanted* war, were without scruple, without conscience, without any sense of justice. "All this excitement about you worthless niggers," he exclaimed, finding the occasion for reproof still beside him in the person of the elderly darky whom, the instant previous, he had desired to evade. "I never saw a nigger yet who was valuable enough to fight about." Of course it *was* only the niggers, and this

State's Rights altercation just a screen for greed. If people would be satisfied with what they had, there would be no 'question,' and the demand for violent decisions would not arise.

The little black man peered up slyly, and agreed amiably. "Hit's Gawd's truf, Cap'n, we-all niggahs ain' wuth much," he said, with the intonation of one who can afford concessions. He remained crouched, swinging on his hams. "But we doan wan' wah no mo' den yawl does, Cap'n. Ah got a good massa. Mah massa he wone take free hundred dollahs faw me. Whut hez Ah got to go to wah about?"

"Whether you want war or not, you are going to get it," Percy retorted viciously, his despair become a weapon to be directed upon this too-perfect innocence in which he had no faith.

"An' de gov'nah, too," insisted the modest enemy on the side-walk. "He warn de Pres'dent dat dey can't no Lincum sojers pass dis way, but dey's suttenly goin' by all right."

Percy resisted the levelling of interchange. Like a dog emerging from unwelcome waters, he shook himself, pushed with his elbows on a massive back, and tried to forge a progress. His head ached. He was becoming very warm. It must be one o'clock.

Despite resolutions, the density of the shapes intervening between himself and the soldiers made him feel a certain identity with them. They were self-contained, as he wished to be, they were moving, they ignored the populace. It was the 'damned pig-headed city government' that should be rated most soundly. In the pack of beavers, bonnets, and bulging-eyed profiles, his dis-comfort augmented so acutely that the attempt to fix blame exactly became an obligation. His upper lip was cool with nervous heat. His fingers, stroking his chin, were chilled, numbed, and trembled slightly. The sun, a stagnant blot in the cloud-raddled sky, shone down colourlessly. The trees churned their leaves intermittently; but even the breeze, when it came, was no more than torpid. "Why are they doing this? Why is the street blocked? What is it all about?" Percy flung his sudden questions at a young fop in white, strapped trousers, high hat, long-tailed coat, and magnificent cra-vat. The reply to the savage inquiry was a silence more than silence. Percy had drawn to himself the opaque, supercilious stare of an obsessed gaze. Immediately his agitation heightened, became revolt, physical repugnance. He stepped fastidiously from the young man's side. This enforced intimacy with bodies for which he felt aversion was stimulating him to hysteria. He was habitually squeamish, and, in the summer, accustomed to take as many as three baths a day in icy water. If he saw a wart on a man's nose, or a mole upon a pretty woman's cheek, it always made him sick. Eva was not beautiful, but was better looking than he found himself, and he liked her clear skin, her calm manner, the ladylike nicety with which she kept herself. Through his childhood and his adolescence, he had been religious. It was his painful pride that, for the moment, he was 'on the side of science,' and expected scientists to prove for him that the 'truths of the Bible' could be upset. This disillusion with belief left him crushed, with his pride soiled by a sense of fleshliness. It was because he was 'a sceptic' that the mob disgusted him, he fancied, and he found himself an alien here.

Petulant, he began to stamp his feet violently. When his glance roved militantly, demanding a comprehending interchange with some one, he beheld only faces in which was expressed that fixity of purpose which discards recognition of the personal. He was certain, as he glowered, that nobody felt as he was feeling, so he forgave nobody. His involuntary neighbours, with widened nostrils and brilliant eyeballs, displayed the evasive eagerness of animals who receive a scent. A raucous sound of furtive jeering came from some point nearer the marching men. He was fearful, and, as he could not control his alarm, the impression that he was being subjected to unmerited degradation grew. A woman beyond him burst forth unexpectedly with shrill words that cursed the Lincolnites, Percy shuddered and despised her—a 'flat-nosed, common Irish girl.' He had a kind of terror of association with her incontinent speech. If she could realize how she appeared to a gentleman onlooker she might keep her mouth shut. He glared at her hotly. No doubt, if she noticed, she would assume that he was quizzing her admiringly. Was any cause so unworthy that a crowd of geese and fools could do justice to it? Chivalry, such as Eva enjoined, would be wasted here. But that slut had best be thankful he was bred to gallantry and would not break her neck. Just let one of these sweating men bawl out such words. It was not because he condoned a partiality for government soldiers that he was chagrined. You could resist a menace with some kind of dignity.

Several heedlessly elate youths, emerging from an alley behind a row of residences, usurped attention. "Hi, Pat, there they goes. Let's give 'em a dose of the right kind of medicine," the foremost yelled. Percy, sensing an attempt to elbow him aside, stood his ground belligerently, and demanded, with a pugnacious sneer, what the 'row' was about. The eyes of the offenders revealed a self-engrossment which trivial affront could not touch. "Don't ye think we kin git back to the front again," one was shouting to a comrade. "Ye might try a rock." And, from another, boastfully, "Did ye see me git that —— Yankee behind the ear?"

Percy, hoping unreasonably that these adolescent gamins would quail beneath the scorn with which he regarded them, was composing a letter to the newspaper. If peace was to be maintained in the city, let the volunteer guard take care of it. At the same time, pettish behind the screen of his spectacles, he felt curious. What plan were these guttersnipes devising, and what delinquence had sent them running so precipitately from the cluttered alley?

"They ain't gonta grab us when we gits out there?" a marauder inquired doubtfully. "Naw," comforted his companion. "What's throwin' a stone? Did ye see that woman spit in the soldier's face? She done it right."

The boys forced themselves on pantingly, hurrying, kicking at ankles that were obstacles, and digging their elbows in people's backs. Percy, nauseated as he always was by violence, resolved suddenly to abandon a forward progress, and, instead, to retrace his steps, returning to the office through uncongested thoroughfares. Staggering a little, because of the press to the rear, he reversed his position. He was now an insignificant unit, with a feeble will directed to oppose the dozens who had seemed to support him while he submitted passively. Stubbornly, he resisted all this contrary intention. The whiskers of a short fellow lurching against him tickled his face. From a slack mouth between bloated jowls, whisky was breathed into his nostrils redolently. "Let me pass," he insisted.

"Quit that shovin'," was the unrelenting retort his demand received. As he did sidle so as to weave some paces of his intricate return, a few were ready to allow him to squeeze by them. Others, more kindly, in the spirit of a holiday, said, "Let the young man get on." But he soon met a barrier in the persons of two gentlemen—'sic, supposed,' he was snorting inwardly—who, already

14

in wordy discussion with one another, were adamant. "What the devil? What are you tryin' to do, young fellah? You can't act like that. Do you think the pavement *belongs* to you?" And they abandoned argument for reprimand.

Percy used all the lumbering weight of his body to compel their accession to his desire. Saved by their astonishment, a first encounter was avoided through a common distraction. There was a brittle *crick-crick*, as of twigs breaking, and a shriek, thin, metallic, and penetrating as a stiletto, from a woman in the crowd. The populace, as if on the urge of a torrent conveying it, rushed against Percy with such unanimity of motion as to drag him backward, while he clutched feebly, waving his ponderous arms futilely in an effort to retrieve his balance. Concordantly, he heard exclamations of wonder, of protest; until the sounds resolved in scattered murmurs that held notes of triumph. "Somebody has fired a shot back yonder. The dirty soldiers are gonta shoot on us."

Confined by the panic of his neighbours, Percy tumbled, weakly upright, against the glass-surmounted wall of a garden in which pear trees were growing. Suddenly, among the broken bottles above his head, a man's hand appeared, fumbling—a soft hand, nervous with anxiety, amidst the iridescent twinkling of the bottles, shaking jostled pear bloom whitely down. In the bristling fragments of crystal, the hand clung, insanely disregarding hurt, until its grip had lifted, above the parapet, tumbled hair, matted in the drift of displaced petals, a dusty brow, shoulders in a torn cotton coat, and the wild eyes of a stranger who was muttering hoarsely an appeal for succour. Ignoring self-inflicted wounds, the man, important with his own blood, topped the wall, leaped, and was in the street, running, while the crowd, half pleased, half astounded, made way for him. "Lemme by. Lemme by. The soldiers have begun to fire. Turn back, you fools. Turn back, you idiots. They're gonta shoot the lot of you," the man shouted hoarsely.

Then the refugee, like Percy, was submerged, with his terror, in another bewildered advance of the mob. The crowd, with fifty wild voices to encourage, leaned mindlessly upon the forward uproar that attracted it. In a lull, he heard, like a silly bleat, "What did I tell ye? We gonta see some more fun, boys. We'll show the Lincolnites if Baltimore is gonta go Secesh or not." And the youth who cried out, red mouth parted ecstatically, and harsh eyes wide, began to lay about him with his fists, irresponsibly, as in a passion.

Percy, feeling fear of himself mount beyond the threat of his surroundings, cried. "Shut your confounded jaw," holding the boy's thrashing arm in check. They stumbled together, and were torn asunder. Percy, while hurtled zigzag, re-established composure, crooked his elbows like wings, and hurriedly bestirred himself again. Intermittently, he glimpsed his vague vis-à-vis, who exhibited an underlip thick and glossy with blood, and seemed too dazed by his condition to pursue revenge. In the end another man was given the curse and the blow that Percy's ready knuckles had solicited. And this fellow, in his turn, struck desperately at a woman, not seeing whom he hit.

The mob churned agitatedly. Its activity within itself was as if confined by that other steadier noise, the continual shuffle of the soldiers' boots. Somebody, with a random energy, rapped Percy's head, and pain dulled anger and the sunshine, while he recovered. A greasy leaden downpour was drenching the distance. Shouts and calls grew louder. Percy was certain now, from the dim sounds so far away, that the outrageous firing promised had really begun. He could not reconcile remote confusion with the methodical tramp that he could yet distinguish past the corner beyond his own massive group. The glare, with its wilting heat, continued to beat through the frail leaves over the pavement, and to dazzle his vision. The trees were as bright, in their rustlings, as green chandeliers; and again, in the shapeless foldings of the rain-clouds, the sun was vanishing formlessly. Drops, as of dew, dappled him with their chill. The house fronts looked stale, and the blank, refracting windows held dense shimmers. The feeling of a shower about to fall made the tension break. "They're givin' the order to charge on us. Stand back. Stand back, for your lives."

Percy leaped backward. He swayed. He resisted. He was thrown on again as upon a barricade of piercing shrieks which the women's throats cast up.

In a delirium of inanition, he seemed to recognize a brusque military voice, calling: "Stand back. Stand away from the curbing, or our men will charge the whole damned lot of you." His hatred of authority weakened in a peculiar, restless fatalism. He stumbled with his eyes closed. He looked up, and found himself at the corner

16

at last. He was grateful for it when, ejected to the edge of the crowd, and beholding the soldiers unobstructedly, a fresh tingling of animosity revived his useless will. All his life, he had avoided altercation. If he resented wordily, he did so in private, and for Eva's ears. The sight of a drunken rowdy had often undone him. He did not *wish* to fight. He and Eva were poor, but they were very proud. Their independence was valuable. And he swore that murder would be on the heads of this whole multitude and of these —— damned soldiers, if they did not let him quit this gathering quietly. Anguishedly, he stretched out his arms, steadied himself with his spread palms, and his longing for peace and unmolested solitude was so intense that, for an instant, his sicklied imagination almost encompassed it. The din about was, for a second, completely obliterated from his hearing. As in a dream too perfect, his self-respect once more flowed through his veins and heart like an elixir. *Them,* he eschewed utterly. Then he received another cuff from an unknown and his spectacles fell off.

"*Charge* on us," the defiant screeched. "A brave lot of soldiers you-all think you are. Go on and *charge* on us." Murmurs contradicted. A girl's titter ended in a wail. Percy heard a cracked female voice, monotonous with passion, deriding the marchers ceaselessly. The loss of the spectacles left him without the shield of vision. The noises combined more loudly. The horror of being trapped with others became more intimate. His rejection of the scene was a dull, pervasive ache of loathing. His whole body throbbed with this resentful feeling. He was ready to respect those who merited respect, but his rights as a human being and a citizen were ignored. This was a *mob*. He had used the word previously without recognizing it. A mob! A damned fiendish *mob*. Soldiers and private individuals, they were all alike. Hastening, in his subjective twilight, from the advancing troops, he butted the swelling fringe of the crowd, half fell in a gutter which seemed to glide away from him, and regained the sidewalk. He *knew* this street. He had walked along it often. In a silly, bumping current, men and women swept past him loggishly. Percy flung his grip upon two fence posts, and held himself in a dead readiness to resist being jostled onward. Shawls trailed his shoulders, bonnets rasped his cheeks, excited voices stuttered dark words of alarm and misery into his ears. Several persons shouted. His obstinacy had now become quite

17

terrible, and he would not loose his hold on that picket fence though his arms be dragged from the sockets. The soldiers had halted to the flooding of the highway with the human stream. Percy found himself like a man on a lighthouse, and was sustained by a blurred, transient conviction that, whatever the judgment of a Great-Aunt Phoebe, or even an Eva, there was true courage in his passivity.

An unanticipated thinness in the bulk of the crowd surprised him. At the moment when he had imagined himself secure in struggle, he was being left to his victory as to a kind of nakedness. A regular clatter inclined him to turn his head slowly. Good God —the soldiers were coming, marching firmly toward him. The street seemed abandoned, unexpectedly spacious. His enfeebled gaze could pick out, through its distortions, the starkly vivid flash of rainy sun on bayonets.

His wrists were palsied. His impulse was to yield passionately to his incapacity to ward them off. *"Charge bayonets."* The order was brutal with directness. He knew now that the crowd which had escaped him had begun to run. Whoever doubts my loyalty to the South is a dirty blackguard, he thought excitedly. But I never believed that we had to go to war, and anybody who denies that to be the truth can argue over my dead body. I won't give up.

"Clear the streets. Clear the streets." Undecidedly, he listened to the abrupt command, and perceived, with an instinct exceeding his visual feebleness, that the lines of steady soldiers were encroaching upon the sinister emptiness. Indeed, all at once, he was confronted by an inimical and unfamiliar countenance not half a yard away from him. From a ruddied face, a gaze, undeflecting in its antagonism, pushed nearer, nearer: and before the features so unjustly hostile, thrust a bayonet point.

Percy watched. He knew clearly definitions which he could see but doubtfully. In the first second, his defiant sense that he was 'right' replaced uneasiness. Bewilderingly, he waited for the man to turn aside, for the stolid weapon to swerve. The twinkling threat increased to a larger glitter. Its inevitable persistence conveyed to him a deeper, more fundamental sense of insult than he had ever surmised could arise in him. Thought ceased. With the strength of a rebellion which was dear as life, Percy turned quickly, clawed, in a nightmare, a paling he had loosened from the fence, and, lifting it as a missile, struck down the gun.

The soldier stumbled, passed; and, confronting Percy mutely, sprung from the wildness of the sunlight, another weapon, another face replaced the fallen ones. Percy felt eyes that despised his private wretchedness. (You looked at a man. You looked at a woman. You did not stare too long or sharply.) Percy banged at the eyes that would not be deterred, at the bayonet point, with its senseless glisten, which would go on through him unrecognizingly. They *want* a fight, he reflected crazily, and they can *have* a fight, *but I never asked for it.*

He was dealing blows with a numbed impulse, but it remained a necessity to keep it before him, as he shivered blindly, that *they* compelled this gesture. He was afraid, past feeling, but he would not have thrust upon him, with the fruits of havoc, an undeserved responsibility. He longed, as he reeled to wanton impacts, to discover an enemy—*the* enemy. Why were they striking him? Why he striking them? A cold contact against his shoulder revived a repugnance that exceeded the accompanying pain. There *was* no enemy. He had been mistaken. There was only the crowd. It was the bayonet point that would not know him that had pierced his coat, sunk in his flesh. Even as he was wounded, he felt ignored. Again, he lifted his paling. But it dangled, it clattered. When he was stabbed a second time, he sank indifferently into the gutter, and the weapon prodded his sloping back.

He was defeated. The obliviousness of the others had overtaken him. The sun drizzled a callousing heat upon his exposed cheek. His limbs twitched irritably. It was as though the sense of desecration, of defilement, ascended his being along his spine. Spasmodically, vindictively, his hands fumbled for the paling. He could not recapture it. An unutterable, throbbing aloneness had suddenly taken possession of him in the very midst of the street. Feet bruised his ribs. He reached upward and, with a waning malice, attempted to bring a soldier down beside him for companionship. The madness of action flowed on and left him. He defended his liberty. He was a free citizen and born a gentleman. He would not be *made* to fight. But there was a hollow consciousness of being conquered. The shame of pain overpowered him. He wanted to lose awareness, to forget the contempt of the oblivious.

19

He stirred. He muttered. The sun burned black. He lost consciousness suddenly.

III

Henry Clay had once heard Mamma say that Aunt Amanda, 'poor little creature,' was already beginning to have an 'old maid' look. Mamma had remarked, then, that Aunt Amanda's throat was 'stringy,' and Henry Clay had resented it. He had stared. When Aunt Amanda turned her head, slowly, the skin on her neck made little bags. It was the first time that Henry Clay had observed this, and it upset him. He disliked Mamma for having told him. Previously, he had regarded Aunt Amanda as, of course, a 'grown-up' lady, but much, much, and forever, younger than his father and his mother who were married people.

Aunt Amanda wore blue dresses. In the winter they would be brocade and velvet and very fashionably wide, but in the summer, in India muslins and sashes, with the short puff sleeves and the low neck, and the garden hat, she often put off hoops. Then she was like a strange little girl in a long gown. There was something alert and frightened in her expression, which never altered, and Henry Clay, though he loved her, and was sorry for her because she was so very little, would experience just the smallest shiver of discomfort when he met her glance. She was 'like a doll,' with her frizzly blond hair that no amount of bandoline could keep in place. And she was too gay. He understood what it was that he had been trying to say about her when his mother called her 'hystericky.'

Aunt Amanda was Papa's sister. Henry Clay had no little sisters of his own, and he had 'helped Papa' to take care of Aunt Amanda ever since she had come to live with him. But she was not young enough after all, he realized, when his mamma told him sharply she was twenty-eight.

Something to do with the war that had come, had made Aunt Amanda change. And it was the war coming, and Papa going to Richmond to join the army, that had made everybody 'different.' Mamma was 'very nice' to Aunt Amanda, yet spoke of her in a tone of voice which Henry Clay called 'indignant.' And when Aunt Amanda talked of Papa being a 'hero' and an officer, she did so 'crowingly,' as though she had been made glad by it. Mamma was

20

a 'Yankee.' When Aunt Amanda whispered to Henry Clay, softly, that Mamma's brothers in Boston were 'Black Republicans,' Henry Clay waited a minute before replying, then, his heart beating terribly because this was something he did *not* want to know, he answered steadily, "I don't believe it, Aunt Amanda, because I've seen the miniatures that Mamma keeps in her dresser, and they're *not* black."

He was sorry for Mamma because her brothers were Black Republicans. He had to admit, finally, when he understood things better, that a man could be a Black Republican and not look like his own body-servant, Jesse, who would belong to him when he grew up. Henry Clay thought long and secretly before he understood these matters. Papa's army was going to 'whip' the Yankees. Black Republicans, if they were ever found, would receive no mercy. It must make Mamma both ashamed and sad. But Henry Clay would not blame his father, so he blamed his uncles. He considered that it would be a good thing for Mamma if the Black Republican brothers who humiliated her were 'wiped out.' He did not tell her so, directly, but played a game with Jesse in which Jesse was a Black Republican who was to be executed. Henry Clay kept his ideas on safeguarding Mamma entirely to himself. When Aunt Amanda said, "Poor Mamma, Henry Clay—she is in a very distressing situation and we must try not to make it hard for her, not to make her feel it," he glanced at Aunt Amanda cautiously, and, somehow, though her voice was so low and sweet, he did not believe that she was as anxious to save Mamma trouble as she pretended to be. Always, however, when he would be deciding that he simply never could forgive her, she would snatch up the guitar with the white ribbon, draw him quickly beside her upon the sofa, and sing songs to him.

He liked *Gathering up the Shells on the Seashore*, though it was sad, and he was glad when she had finished it and sang *Jim Crack Corn* or something funny. There were pier-glasses in the parlour, and Aunt Amanda, when she played on her guitar, always seated herself so she could see in them. There was a picture of the hill and the river, made by the reflection in the mirror which faced the window. When Papa had gone to Richmond, Henry Clay had left off crying to see the tiny, 'really-truly' boat sail by in it. He had not believed that he could see it, but Aunt Amanda had persuaded him, and, sure enough, through the bare trees, and down, down past the sheep that were cropping the lawn to keep it trim and neat, the steamboat had swum away like a little fish, and the trail of smoke, like a little puff of wool, had floated off, outside the mirror's frame. He had not gone with Mamma to the steamer landing, but it had been much, much more wonderful to behold his papa steaming off to Richmond just inside the pier-glass. The tears had stopped while he gazed. Then he had sprung up from the sofa suddenly, and had been shocked, had been disappointed. It was only a trick after all. There was the river, greasy-looking and white, at the bottom of the garden, and the *real* boat was like a little trail of smut upon it, going out of sight.

When Aunt Amanda sat in front of the mirror, she looked at herself. And when she looked at herself, picking the guitar strings with her little white hand, her little finger crooked so delicately, she would be smiling and smiling in a peculiar manner, as if she were very satisfied with what she saw. She made nice little faces at herself. Henry Clay would notice, and would pretend that he was unobservant. For, if ever she found him looking at her at such times, she would start, become grave, abruptly, and that queer, secret, suspecting gaze would return to her eyes. She was happiest when Papa was about. Then she talked a great deal and laughed too much, and too merrily. But if Mamma entered the room, Aunt Amanda would say: "There, I must leave off such nonsense. Hannah already finds me too frivolous, Gordon."

Aunt Amanda often talked a long time to Henry Clay about his papa. "You must be proud," she would declare, "that your papa is a gallant officer who would give all for the cause that he believes in, and loves the South." Mamma was proud of Papa, too, but it was not agreeable of Mamma to assert so glumly that she had no opinions about the war, and that she would be just as loyal to Papa if he were an Abolitionist. Mamma was a Protestant, and Aunt Amanda was a Roman Catholic, and that made 'friction,' Henry Clay had quoted. Aunt Amanda had one criticism to make of Papa. He was not a 'good' Catholic. He did not do his duty by Henry Clay, who was receiving only his mamma's religious instructions while he was growing up. When Henry Clay's education had been discussed with Papa, Aunt Amanda had 'spoken out.' And Henry Clay had been wretched. He did not see why his mamma should object to having him a Catholic if it would make Aunt Amanda content to see him so. But when Aunt Amanda informed him, surreptitiously, that his prayers were the only thing that could keep his papa safe in battle, he felt angry. He hated them both—Mamma, who came from Massachusetts, and was *not* a Christy; and Aunt Amanda who tried to frighten him unfairly because he did not say his catechism properly.

"Pray hard for us, Honey," Aunt Amanda whispered in her sweet, queer, little breaking voice, when she stole into his room at night.

Henry Clay, in the smudged dimness made by the bedroom candle, did not look at her. Her arm was about him, and her 'smell,' of lavender and orris, was in his nostrils. He shivered in his nightshirt, and his heart grew hard and his body stiff against her. She made him feel like a baby which was what he hated. He wanted her *not* to touch him. If she would stay away from him, he could do it better. But he kept his eyes shut, and repeated hastily the *Our Fathers* and the *Hail Marys*, while she annoyed him with prompting. His hands fumbled for the beads stealthily. Aunt Amanda said: "Don't stop, Honey. We must tell God how much we love dear Papa that he may be spared to us. Your father wants it, Precious. We can't deprive you of the benefits of the Church because your mother's brothers in Boston are scientific men."

Mamma prayed, also. It was a relief to find it out. He heard her, when, his own prayers said, he climbed from the trundle bed and went noiselessly into the hall to fetch himself a drink of water from the pail out there. The door into Mamma's bedroom was ajar, and he spied on her just a little bit. When he 'forgot' and dropped the dipper he was holding, there was a clatter. Mamma, startled, straightened up beside the bed, and he thought that she was as embarrassed as he was when Aunt Amanda would caution him to go on quickly with his *Hail Marys*. He went away before she could come out into the hall. But why was she such a liar? When, the next night, she discovered the prayerbook under his pillow, he said, "Don't tell Aunt Amanda that you found the prayerbook," and he felt desperate, and began to weep bitterly without knowing why. Then Mamma squeezed his ribs tight, and he was glad, and felt he ought not to be, until she whispered, "It's so degrading, Henry Clay—so undignified—but *don't* be a Roman Catholic—please don't be. And don't believe all that Aunt Amanda tells you about your uncles. It's bad enough to have to give up Papa—and we must do our duty."

Henry Clay became silent. He was so still that his mother imagined him asleep.

When she had spread the quilts over him and tiptoed away, the necessity to deceive her ended. He opened his eyes again. His eyeballs felt hot. Horrid prickly feelings came in his stomach and his 'bread-basket.' He seemed to hear, in his head, words that he had listened to *them* saying:

"You know I did it for love of the child, Hannah."

"You teach the child to be ashamed of his mother and his uncles and you call that 'love.' You do this and ignore one of the greatest tenets of your own religion—to love your enemies."

Aunt Amanda's small face, on her thin neck, had gone up. The strange, frightened sparkle had become more brilliant in her pale blue, wide eyes. Henry Clay remembered the two women like rocks, and himself ignored. Nobody loved him. "I won't defend myself, Hannah. I am devoted to my brother, and to your son, too, Hannah. If it is a crime to teach a child to ask God to protect his father's life, then I am guilty. That is the last thing I would deny. If I had known how bitter your sentiments were—but after all you *married* a Virginian and a Catholic."

"If you did not think that I objected, why did you not attempt to convert Henry Clay openly?" Mamma's face, as it came back, was bold and cold, and it was black and white. That made it alarming. Aunt Amanda wore flounces and ruchings that Henry Clay liked, but Mamma was 'plain,' in her grey merino with her stiff white cuffs and collar, and her hair as Papa preferred it, in 'Grecian bandeau,' though Henry Clay did not care for that much. Aunt Amanda called Mamma's severity of dress 'an attitude.' It was adopted, Aunt Amanda reckoned, because Mamma wished to be 'taken for a bluestocking.' Or, Aunt Amanda had conjectured, "It's because she disapproves of me so much."

"I did not anticipate direct interference, Hannah, but I anticipated ridicule. I believe in the Church and in the Miracles of the Church. When I came here, I subjected myself to your flippant comment on matters that are sacred to me. In the future—I will keep hands off the child—unless Gordon—who is as much a Catholic and a Southerner as I am——"

Mamma had interrupted. Henry Clay remembered her face growing 'ugly,' while she smiled sarcastically. "*I* flippant," Mamma seemed to be saying, drawing her breath in sharply. "*I* who have done my duty if ever wife did! And you *dare* to say such a thing to me. *I* flippant."

Henry Clay turned over sidewise in his bed and looked at the moon. The cedar trees on the lawn were like silver bears. Above them, a big gold claw, like the claw on the balls on the parlour furniture, clutched fiercely at its own round shadow. He thought he would like to go to war on Papa's horse. He didn't care about the religious part of it—if Mamma would only let him go to war and wear a Confederate uniform. Mamma was 'mean,' she was 'wicked' when she would not let him talk about the war too much. But if he gave up 'religion,' Aunt Amanda would be 'broken-hearted.'

He tossed. It was troubling here at home. He looked at the moon again, and pretended it was a silver-golden cannon ball that was sailing down to get him. All at once he was frightened, and grew quiet, in the whitened sheets, trembling. He had forgotten about God, and what God might do to his papa if he did not pray enough.

"Mamma?" Henry Clay lifted himself on one quivering elbow, and called to her shrilly, demandingly. Even the sound of his own voice left, in his confused mind, the echo of his own uneasiness. She did not hear him. He gave up. His hot head fell back on his pillow. He *was going* to war, when he got big enough, and if the war hurt people he was glad—*not* sorry. He was a 'mean' boy—almost as mean as a Yankee (and his mother was a Yankee anyhow)—and he *liked* war.

The power and the glory everlasting, it said somewhere. In the silence, he could hear the trees brushing outside the window. It was a creeping, quiet sound. He longed for something that would go off suddenly, and wake his mother up. It was so still in the house. The boards creaked. Jesse was a 'nigger,' and a coward. Jesse belonged to him. He would like to send Jesse to the battle front and *make* him fight the Yankees. It was Jesse who had told him all about the devil, 'wif green eyes gogglin'.'

But the devil was less than God whom you could not see—more insignificant.

Suddenly, Henry Clay began to sob helplessly, coughing, sputtering, his thin ribs racked by his incessant sighs. I wish I was dead. I wish I was dead, he told himself, surprised that this was what he wanted. It seemed so much better, with all this horror around him, to get the worst over with.

After a time, he stifled his agitation in the thick heat of the pillow. He grew, little by little, *so* still, inside his heart, inside his mind, that he wondered, stricken pleasurably by the fancy, if he *could* be already dead. It wasn't true. God had not listened. Mammy Nancy slept in the room behind the nursery, and he could detect her stirring as she left her pallet. She was often restless, and would potter about the house at night.

An owl passed, noiseless, like a cloud of dust, between him and the moon. That round glare bored into his eyes, bored craftily into the quivering exhaustion of his mind. He began to fancy the explosion. He waited for the big *boom,* that would send the silver splinters of the cedars right into his face. If it would only 'crunch' them all. The war was coming nearer every minute, and he wanted the moon to burst so loud, so violently, that his mother and his Aunt Amanda could not argue any longer. Nobody—not a single person in the world—should hear another noise. He shivered. He felt weak and 'wicked.'

IV

"This is where we gona finish the Johnny Rebs, young Charlie." Franklin Rutherford hesitated by a creek, and, for the sixth time that morning, as his friend counted it, filled his water bottle. Charlie, swaggering after him, was more reluctant to invite the disapprobation of the sergeant. The creek emptied itself through a gully, and a cold, mouldering smell flowed out of the wet bushes. In the acrid refreshment of shade, the two dallied a little. Ahead of them, they could hear men splashing, sloshing in the shallows, slipping from the pathway made by the protruding, iron-stained stones, bone-dry, where the sun smote, with the advanced staleness of the day. Above the *throp-thropping* of the sallow crystal current, a dragon-fly bounced stiffly, blue needle-lights refracted from its minute, rigid, metallic body. Franklin soaked his wrists in the

26

water as if in the quiet. Ripples ticked chokingly into the neck of the half-inundated bottle. He lifted it, dripping glaring globules, and, saying, "Hear's a reb hide to you, Charlie," threw back his head and drank, his gratification signified measuredly in the slow undulations of his Adam's apple.

"Fall into the ranks, you men there," the sergeant called defiantly, nervously challenging his subordinates. Franklin took a long time to cork his bottle. His expression remained deliberately stupid, as he always made it when he wished to irritate. "That feller usta be a section foreman on the B. and O.," he remarked under his breath. Charlie, glancing backward from his beefy shoulder, winked cautiously. The wink was to distract Franklin's notice from his own capitulation to authority. In Hutchinsville, Indiana, *he* had never been tardy in suggesting to Franklin the contrived annoyance of those in power. Ashamed, now, that he was the first to move on briskly, in obedience to curses, he tried to conceal his confusion by whistling, *Johnny git yer gun, git yer gun, git yer gun.*

Charlie constantly attempted to provoke Franklin into confirming comradely interests. Franklin responded just enough to tantalize, but was never whole-hearted in acknowledging fellowship. So, having trudged a pace or two, he again halted obdurately for a second sufficiently prolonged to give him opportunity to claw into his forage cap a handful of pinkish, brilliantly noduled blackberries, too young for eating.

"Come on, F. R. You're a sojer, I calculate—or you're pretendin' to be. Your Uncle Abe ain't got any use fer that extra quart o' fruit you're stoppin' to pick."

"Well, I ain't sendin' 'em to Washington," Franklin replied woodenly. "I guess I can take care o' my own bellyaches."

The sergeant bawled more captiously, and Charlie, wearing his bonnet over one ear, and 'h'isting' his bayonet jauntily, reluctantly stumbled into the stream. Franklin followed, holding his gun so that it just escaped the sudsy, leaf-bearing ripples, while, lifting his 'haul' of berries to his face, he tried, like an animal, to nose them toward his mouth.

On the opposite bank, the men mounted through a thicket, tiger-spotted by the steamy radiance that poked among the close foliage. And when they had reached a road once more, those who were to the rear of the column were ordered a respite from marching, so that the advance of the contingent might proceed less congestedly. Other blackberries, on hoary vines jutting rosied thorns through dust-greyed vegetation, sprang, matted, from a rail fence. Franklin, resting his bayonet beside him, resumed his ostentatious pleasure in the green fruit. A bumble-bee, in gross, striped plush, *glum-glumed* around him jealously, flashing staidly the neat, insignificant wings, too small for its bulk; or, falling to rest soddenly, lumbered fastidiously over shedding bloom of an insipid rose.

"This marchin' gits tiresome," Charlie observed. "We got out o' camp early enough. Seems like we been hip-hippin' along all night." An officer, mounted, cantered, on a sweat-darkened chestnut, parallel with the fence. The men had to fall together to permit him to pass. The subduing suggestions of his presence made them all so quiet that the jingle of steel rings on the horse's bridle became abruptly loud. The officer, who was thin and freckled, and wore waxed blond moustaches, overlooked the crowd noncommittally as he went along. Charlie, cutting self-conscious glances from left to right, threw out his fat chest importantly. He was always wondering worriedly if the 'big fellers' who saw him did not pick him out. Franklin, munching hugely was 'too consarned indifferent' to what others thought of him. In Hutchinsville, Charlie had tried to make himself a leader as 'the town scamp.' His career in this rôle had begun at the log schoolhouse when he had compelled one of the younger and weaker boys to do his 'cipherin'' for him.

Franklin was small, with alert, puckered features. When the dusty thump of hoofs had suspired, and the consequential progress ceased to exacerbate the knot of infantry, he smiled as at some-secret joke. That was to stir Charlie's cowardly inquisitiveness. Franklin, his quick, little brown eyes carefully ruminative, flaunted inexplicable reserves that kept his friend 'on tenterhooks.' "What I can't stand is a defeat," he declared irrelevantly. "We got turned back to Centerville the other night without showin' what we could do. You ain't been given your chance, Charlie. If this keeps on you oughta complain about it."

Charlie, with the sly scrutiny that sought a cue, did not retort at once. "Don't criticize the judgment o' yer betters, F. R.," he answered at last, resorting to that bantering tone of an elder brother with which, ever since the two had become acquainted,

28

he had ponderously avoided acknowledgment of Franklin's greater daring and cleverness.

Both boys had taken part in the battle of Blackburn's Ford, three days before, and Charlie, if Franklin had not curbed him, would have been ready to 'brag.' He resented Franklin's interference with his references to hasty prowess. "Was you scared, old fatty, when you heard that there shot?" Franklin had demanded, in wicked innocence. But Charlie, a false twinkle defending his furtive gaze, had kept the presence of mind to call back appropriately, "Was I *scared?*" And to forestall any suspicion that his wit was slow, had added, "I was jest *pet-ri-fied* with enthusiasm, Partner. Why, there was some minutes there when I couldn't even act as smart as you—couldn't even run." And he had thrust out his coarse, good-natured underlip to its full thickness, as he shook his head wisely.

Where they waited, they could still see the sergeant. He was a gawky man, with a black beard, and a perpetual, unnecessary violence of lean gesture. Charlie regarded him contemptuously because he looked 'unhealthy.' The army was no place for a 'feller' who wanted to do 'right' by himself. He'd like to see the sergeant at 'a quiltin' bee.' The 'gals' would know how to make a fool of him, 'you bet.' The sparse maple beneath which the sergeant stood cast imperfect shade, and he was mopping his forehead. Charlie stared at him guardedly, then gave Franklin another puffy wink. But Franklin, purposely, returned the glance opaquely, and with no encouraging contortion of expression. Charlie, Franklin thought, ought to have been a 'show doctor, a patent medicine man.' He was a 'born faker.' With the growing discrimination of maturity, it required an effort to tolerate that smooth, hairless, bulging-cheeked face, that thick, 'calf' neck, with its brand of sunburn, that brow which no meditation could ever wrinkle, and that knowingness of gaze by which so little could be conveyed. Charlie had once been 'the big frog in the little puddle,' and, years before had bullied Franklin. Franklin's revenge, half the residue of discarded timidity, would be to 'fool' Charlie into believing that he was taken seriously. "Maybe in the next scrap, old Squint-Eyes," Charlie was saying to cover the silences with which Franklin could upset him, "the rebs will git that there skinny chicken of a sergeant first." Charlie flung the speech out with a bravado that was a torture to him. He could feel Franklin's long allegiance wavering and must risk something for its continuance.

"Ye're hopeful," Franklin answered.

In Charlie's brick-pink, yokel's countenance, his little pale eyes were self-compelled to the dull sparkle which would denote his 'cuteness.' His pursy cheek muscles were given to respite from a cramped effort to display cunning. When he found himself scrutinized by others, he either stared back at them too intently, or talked loudly in what 'F. R.' called his 'funny strain.' At the log schoolhouse up in Hutchinsville, his 'funny strain' had made his reputation, and he had flaunted it often, with insolent guffaws, to his youthful schoolmistress. Well, he hadn't stayed in that school too long. Brother John, who was reading law with old Judge Sitchel, was the 'smart' one in the family, for Charlie, since he had discarded 'that consarned little blue-back speller,' had spent most of leisure at *The Reputable Saloon.* He had surprised his friends by his enlistment in the army, and their very astonishment had been a revelation of opinion from which his vanity had not yet recovered. The effect of this revived a hateful moment when the 'gal,' who was 'teacher' at the schoolhouse, had called him 'zany.' He loathed her, he despised her spitefully; and it was as if she had deprived him of an outlet for his vague moods of benevolence.

"The worse I git to sweatin', the more my jaw wants to work," Charlie mumbled elaborately, as the men were told to fall again into marching order. "You could put this here uniform through a dish-wringer without dryin' it."

The dust churned up in small soft eddies. The landscape looked 'all crumpled,' the heat standing like a haze in the bushes, the fields glittering with the rapid, constant wings of grasshoppers, the sky as dead in sunshine as blue paper. Uniforms were drily faded of colour. Charlie's bayoneted rifle slipped up and down in his thick, oozy palm. The sweat glided stingingly from his flat brow to his eyelids, and he blinked it to his ruddied cheeks. His insensate feet stumbled. Rain! God, if it would only rain! Charlie wondered what the 'gals back home' would think of this. It had always been incomprehensible to him that he had made so little headway toward their approval. His explanation was that he was 'no dern macaroni,' and *they* lacked 'gumption.' He rather enjoyed their suspicion that he was reckless, though, actually, he was neither a great gambler nor an inveterate drinker. He did not like the feeling of not knowing his 'whereabouts' when he had drunk too much.

The emphatic glare made his brain court blindness. "Where are we, Squint-Eyes?" he interrogated, attempting to compete with Franklin in the casual attitude, but, despite himself, unable to endure uncertainty mutely. "Seven miles east of Manassas Junction, er some sech backwoods place, that feller allowed just now. Anybody got any idea what this part o' the country's like? It wasn't down on no set of globes *I* ever studied." Charlie, lumberingly jovial, vainly solicited the usual heavy interchange of humour. Franklin, marching jerkily beside him, went on, obstinately uncommunicative, with a small grim face. I must be the only feller in this lay-out with any grit, Charlie mused densely, heat heavy in his mind. F. R. kin go to hell when he gits ready if he's gona act like this. I'm a tough customer, if anybody's got the sense to see it, and these—— Yankees got to find it out.

Fearful of the dogged reserves of those around, he yet tried to tell himself that it was 'pretty good' to leave off being 'too golderned independent.' It was his too great independence which had always led him into trouble. He guessed he ought to be 'more modest.' But if you was truthful you couldn't help having a good opinion of yourself. He tried to pride himself on his 'muscle.' When his body, shrimp-pink from exposure, was stripped to the waist, he could double his arms upward, clench his fists, and tighten, for the admiration of comrades, the tense rondures that swelled beneath the too-girlish flesh. That he had no hair on chest or shoulders was his one embarrassment. All them humps come from pitchin' hay, he thought belligerently: and this even though the gossips said he did not work too much. When you 'j'ined' up, 'thank Pete,' you 'was taken care of.' You 'was doin' your duty fer yer country.' You 'was well protected.' All his life, Charlie had suppressed a terror of being sent to the 'calaboose.' Having, for years, secretly cowered beneath the threats of the respectable, he had donned his uniform defiantly, as a child seeking protection at its mother's apron strings. When this war is over, I'll be a vet, you hayseeds back in Hutchinsville. You can't say then that Charlie didn't save the day for you.

Poor old F. R. He must be scared. Charlie was exhausted, hostility lulled. When Bill Jenkins had been shot, in *The Reputable*

Saloon, Charlie, transiently, had been implicated in the crime, and F. R., faithful then, and worshipping, had 'stood by' him. Charlie, in that instance, really blameless, had been strongly tempted to encourage adulation by confessing falsely to astute devilishness. His one brief unearned passage as a hero had brought him disillusion. It was since he had been cleared of the charge brought against him, that F. R.'s infatuation for him had deteriorated. Folks liked excitement, Charlie had decided, but you must have the government behind you when you took part in it. When you took orders promptly, and did your 'duty,' you could do what you liked. Anticipating hidden Yankees in the green and gleaming fields, he gazed about. That slow, sensual, vicious feeling, which was part with his affection when he watched F. R., swelled his chest to a less furtive emotion. He was a good friend. As good a friend as there ever was. But he wouldn't take no 'sass' from F. R. Let F. R. watch out.

Charlie felt that his company must have been marching in a circle. Vague as the heat made him, and with an aversion to the landscape, he could guess that they were inclining toward Bull Run again. From off somewhere, was growing more audible the *pick-tick, pick-tick* of skirmishing shots. Down yonder near the water, in that mystery of windless trees and sound without visible origin, slow smoke sailed its yellowed gloom across the face of the woods. Once, catching the echo of a far-off cry, he interpreted it as the rebel yell, already associated in his mind with menace. His wrists throbbed with his thick, heated blood. Noises, as if unravelled from their source, fell on his ears with an impact as weightless as that of cotton falling on the ears of a deaf man. Over yonder, where a fight seemed to be in progress, was the place, the one they called the Stone Bridge. Higher than the east bank of Bull Run, along which he tramped, rose the steeper western hills, in a rank stillness of scrubby pines. The bushes, appearing flattened by the pervasive glare, were like patches of dark moss clinging to the distant boulders. A bleary immobility was in everything. The rocky blue of the sky was somehow alarmingly pure of the stains of firing. Yet the increasing smoke gave Charlie the impression that he was staring at the sunshine through a window pane. The woods and stubble were suddenly contracted in a circle of dim, yet magnified vision. Now and again his detached tread vibrated to a jealous

32

earthquake which awoke in some remote spot. Upon his intelligence, woolly with fatigue, a faint *blo-ooming* broke gently, in tides of echoes. Compelled to passivity, his gorge rose in the nausea of involuntary protest. Nearer the Run, and as he descended toward it, he was able to discern, painted in feeble flashes through the sunny swell of nearly black trees, inappropriate flames. He looked at Franklin. The same mousy, grudging profile presented itself. Charlie, trapped between his instinctive fears and a rage against his friend's obliviousness, said to himself, Anyhow, I'm no worse off than *he* is. Charlie's longing to trust somebody had come nearer to fulfilment in his relations with his friend than through any other circumstance. Yet this lack of sympathy, of appreciation, seemed what he expected from the human race, inclusively. What was the secret of success? How was it that you 'bluffed' people. Was the government really to be confided in?

He clambered downward to the water, heard the ploshing boots of those who had preceded him, and, missing a rock that should have borne him, sank, in a current of the tint of weak coffee, up to his thigh. The stream, pointed here and there with rays of light, dazzled him. He tried to support his equipment well above the dampness, but it was difficult. His pantaloons were soaked gradually, and he felt, about his hips, the ache of an exquisite chill, a contrast to the burning dryness of his sweat-drained brow. "Good-bye, F. R. See you at supper," he remembered to call surlily, though, already, he was approaching such engrossment in his own security as weakened his perpetual, fretting attention to what others thought of him. The water, lisping with a scummy froth, and drawing leaves and twigs around his armpits, dragged its cold through him, between his legs, and its weight made his plodding heavy. Red House Ford, Red House Ford, he kept repeating to himself, for, though he could discern no building, he had heard that name, and it was like a talisman of security persuading him that he knew where he was going. Franklin had gone ahead of him —Franklin, with a narrow nervous back. It was in the realization that Franklin could not see him, would not know what he was doing, that Charlie felt defeated. A pang twisted his torpid heart. Fortunately, the relief of finding his huge body steeped in that quiet chilly motion of water was beginning to absorb him. Even his fear could not resist the ecstasy of the slow, icy saturation in a

33

sensation which defied the barbed, anguishing sun-rays. He felt no breeze, but his cheeks and forehead cooled. For an instant, he stopped, balkily, as a horse, in a grateful flood, will outwit the rider. Then he realized that his clumsy relief would soon leave him isolated; and, in cumbrous, abrupt panic, staggered on again.

To the last instant, however, he was reluctant of the bank, and he had no sooner emerged among the stones, than his wet feet were constricted painfully by the burning leather of his bleaching boots. Drained, in part, of that lucid, ineffable moisture, his clothing steamed. The nape of his neck was smitten quickly with parching darts. A horse-fly settled on his cheek, and stung him cloyingly, and he was too bewildered by the rush ahead, by the commands which meant he must crouch and fire, to shake it off.

The *pi-ling, pi-ling* of rifle cracks was directly in front of him. *Do what the other fellows do, do what the other fellows do,* his mechanical brain rebuked. For a second, he could hear nothing, and see nothing, but he tried to obey himself. F. R. had disappeared, and it was this absence of an audience which was most tormenting. If he tried to sneak away, would anybody observe it? But he was will-less, he was moving. He was with the others, and 'ducked,' and squatted.

Charlie's comrades crouched, leaped up, vaulted over rocks and obstructions, and mounted the hill. He was maddened by their example of flying in the face of danger. The enormous *bonga-bonga, thump, thump, thump,* which rapped the emptiness, fell on his ears unheeded. He fired, he crouched, he ran on wildly; and found his companions turning back upon him confusedly, as creatures turn in an ant-hill stirred by an unfriendly foot. It was a miracle of unpremeditated valour that brought him, left behind and too cumbersome to keep pace with the temporary retreat, face to face with a young man running—sweating and capless and like himself. There was an instant's common halt, and common hesitation, before each realized in the other an unarticulated 'difference.' Charlie's sensual excitement muffled alarm, but his own readiness of action surprised him. *Bill Jenkins—murder—*but *they'll never be able to pin it on me.* He swung his bayonet viciously out before him and prodded at the young man's chest. The fellow's arms dropped. He swayed. And pain gushed, as in the brilliant dark distension of his pupils, while suffering forced his gaze to seek some hidden spot

34

beyond his enemy. The softness of the body, as it inclined in some unutterable relinquishment of motion, startled Charlie a little. Through the cloudy pandemonium surrounding him he glanced behind him anxiously. Then, in swift reluctance, as he freed his rapid weapon, his comprehension revived. He could not delay to examine the figure now lolling on the grass, but it was a *grey* uniform. He's a reb, he's a reb, Charlie said to himself, as his brain cleared to a vigour it had never owned before, and he began to run again. The heaviness of his intelligence had always laid ambushes, it seemed, for other people to catch him in. That brief, familiar doubt, stirring him as he fled, had to be rejected. Fleetingly, he reviewed the instants preceding, and it was as if the moments were pursuing him. Men in blue, whom he had not before noted, straggled beside him. In the hollow by the water, groups fluctuated. A banner, carried by an unseen bearer, seemed to stalk above the crowd. Still the *rick-tick, rick-tick* of the rifles, and the longer, further, deeper incessance of the cloudy *bonga*. Charlie had done his duty. He tried to keep that straight before him. His flesh tingled with this strange new lust that was affection for his unrecognized comrades. He fought off fear, fought off regret. He was on the right side *this* time, he could tell you, and the 'goshdamned' rebs couldn't do a thing to him. He would tell *that* to the folks when he got back home. It was as if he were casting away, and forever, all the torments of his shaming private sensuality. He could live for something besides himself, you bet he could. He had done his duty. Yet he was not entirely satisfied. Was there anybody you could *really* trust? Would Mr. Lincoln ever notice him if he put his heart and soul in this? Charlie wasn't afraid any more. How could you be frightened when a lot of 'dern good fellers' were 'standing by' you. It was trying to do the thing alone that turned your liver white. He was out of danger in this hollow —but if F. R. would only come along with him, so he could be *shown* something, it would be better.

v

The *Ladies' Aid Society* was meeting in the Guild Room of the rectory. The bare-washed ecclesiastical effect, produced by hook rugs on polished floors between white plaster walls, was a relief to all who had just experienced the brittle heat of glaring summer

35

roads. Country members, arriving tardily, as they came in, loosed their bonnet strings dramatically, and sank, with almost lurid gestures of exhaustion, upon the cool cane chairs. As Mrs. Witherspoon remarked kindly to a neighbour, it was the news of the great Southern victory at Bull Run and Manassas that made all faces bright. Only Mrs. Garvin, peevish because of six weeks passed without news of 'Fred,' refused to consider the occasion one for merry-making.

On the wall by the door which stood ajar upon the yard, hung a lithograph copy of the *Rock of Ages,* and near it a sampler, *In God We Trust,* worked by the rector's wife. When enough donations had been collected, it was proposed to place, in the unadorned spot opposite, a handsome replica of the well-known daguerreotype, *The Beloved President of Our Confederacy, the Pilot of our Galleon through these Times of Stress.* "For no one is nearer the Rock of God," Mrs. Witherspoon had asserted, "than dear Mr. Davis."

There was a pump out of doors, under the grape arbour, the path to it, among the vines, marked with floating shadows of foliage in a mottling so vivid that the grassless ground looked black and white. Mrs. Witherspoon, always complacently kind to everybody, told Josie Kendricks and Annie Byrd to take a pail and the gourd dipper and fetch some water for the perspiring women, who must be refreshed before they could go to work on lint and bandages.

The two girls, bareheaded, one so blonde and tall, and one so dark and plump, ran out gladly, though Josie, as usual, was the more generous in her concern for others. Annie Byrd, recently, had become silent, almost surly, and Mrs. Witherspoon, who would some day be her mother-in-law, did not approve of this new phase. Proud of George, who was 'bravely' fighting for his country, she wished that she might call attention, as confidently, to the 'beautiful, self-sacrificing spirit' of his 'fiancée.' Mrs. Witherspoon indeed, lately, found it difficult to keep her temper with Annie Byrd. It was as though the young woman, who was just nineteen, considered herself unique in feeling painful the hard conditions that the Yankee invasion had forced on all.

Josie Kendricks 'tripped' out, chattering. Annie Byrd followed. And the two figures, in white dresses which the sunlight almost obliterated, grew small down the dappled arbour, until they could be seen halted beside the scaled and rusted pump, which Josie worked energetically while Annie Byrd held the pail.

When they came back, bearing heavily between them the clear, lurching water, Mrs. Witherspoon, a little grim, tried to shed approval upon them equally. Annie Byrd, with that melancholic, resentful glance, met Mrs. Witherspoon's eye, and it was evident to each, embarrassedly, that her scrutiny made the other uncomfortable.

Josie 'gabbled' continually, and today she was full of the new dress she was making, which was grey, like the Confederate uniforms, and would be trimmed with bullion, 'to celebrate Manassas,' as she had been saying. Mrs. Witherspoon condoned frivolity with smiles, yet an unrest not habitual to her made her offer her glance again questioningly to the other girl, whom she could not like, whom she always referred to dutifully as 'George's future wife.' If Annie Byrd had been different—'more frank, more open'—the two, Mrs. Witherspoon was often 'thinking, might have been 'such a comfort' to one another. Schooling herself not to resent silences, Mrs. Witherspoon conjectured, with a pang too deep for malice, that Annie Byrd might be jealous. "Do you know, my little lady, you have been a bit spoiled by your papa, and are a little wayward," Mrs. Witherspoon had remarked sharply, hopeful as she challenged, for, if Annie Byrd was going to remain 'hostile,' it was better that 'the secret out.'

Josie was clasping Annie Byrd's waist and 'rambling' on. It seemed that she objected to the number of enlistments because they had emptied the town, and when the girls had tried to organize a ball for charity, they had found no dancing partners of 'the opposite sex.' Josie was 'indignant' that she had to be a 'man' when waltzing, and made a roguish grimace. She was 'full of life and nonsense,' Mrs. Witherspoon was meditating, as a girl 'ought' to be.

One by one, the ladies, offered the dripping gourd, drank daintily. The slightly bitter chill was like a soothing lotion to their parched throats, irritated already by brisk conversational interchange. The radiant heat swam through the open windows, and it was suggested that Josie draw the red serge curtains to keep out the light. "Oh, for a breeze!" One 'longed' for a flask of Cologne water. Another, with delicate incessant taps, beat her bosom with a fanning handkerchief, and diffused the acrid odour of 'sweet geranium' through the 'stifling' room. Mrs. Pettis felt 'faint.' Mrs. Johnson dampened her 'mouchoir' and pressed it to her pallid mouth. And the girls, before the large deal table, spread out the lint and cloths for making surgical dressings.

Mrs. Witherspoon, rising firmly, had begun to talk. "Ladies," she was suggesting, sonorously, "if I may say a word to you—" Her black merino settled its folds into a stiff sheath about her upright body. With her strong knuckles, she rapped assertively upon the table. But her voice, as she attempted to continue, was slightly tremulous.

The affable chatter did not cease at once. The news of the victory was more powerful than that impression which she usually produced. The ladies, acceding reluctantly to her habitual domineering, lifted, from furtive last-words of exultance, the features of children who are obliged, for an instant, to become decorous at a festival. Interest in what she had to communicate was conscientious, and the gradual silence, for several seconds, was punctuated by tiny, stricken coughs. At last the row of billowing figures in the cane chairs became upright, rigid, and there was only the ticking accompaniment to quiet made by the dozen palm-leaf fans which were swishing unrestingly, when, in a sibilant whisper, a final wayward voice expostulated: "Not at all. The best treatment for anybody struck by lightning is to throw cold water on him."

Mrs. Witherspoon, benevolent, yet relentless, ignored the lagging interruption. "Ladies," she began once more, with the intonation of mild rebuke, "I see that you are all, and rightly, in a holiday mood." The shattered moan of a rooster floated in peremptorily from the rector's chicken coop, and several in her audience started. This noise was followed, first by the steady screeching of a wheelbarrow which somebody was trundling along the grape arbour, then by the soothing caw of a hen. A bee, seeking vainly for a garden, buzzed grumblingly in the curtains. Mrs. Witherspoon— 'Miss Agnes,' as her neighbours called her—saw, all at once, with dim eyes. "The fact that our brave generals, our brave soldiers— officers and privates alike—have given us a victory, must not cause us to lose sight of the responsibilities we continue to bear. The South has reached a turning-point, and has, I believe, by utterly routing the enemy in the first big battle of the opposing

38

forces, convinced her Northern neighbours that she will resist oppression with the last drop of blood that is in her. At Bull Run, near Manassas Junction, our soldiers met the great mass of those misguided ones who have been sent into our territory to accomplish our subjugation. They have not accomplished what they wanted. God has shown us that he hears our prayers. Our faith in Him, in good deeds, in justice, has been rewarded. Let us set to work. Though, in my humble opinion, the war which has been going on for several months will soon be finished, let our motto be work and *more* work. I was going to call this a *terrible* war. I change that. A state of affairs that inspires us to show the best that is in us is not terrible. It may even be sent by God. And it is not our men—our noble Southern gentlemen—bless them—"

She hesitated, her old throat wrinkling heavily as she swallowed several times constrictedly. If Annie Byrd would only stop suggesting doubt. It was 'downright wicked' to be so suspicious of the Lord's plans. All should 'pull together.' *Pull together.* The thought became a dumb cry. Mrs. Witherspoon mumbled her finely gathered lips, and her large eyes, which were brown and were considered 'cold,' warmed faintly with a distant antagonism. She had told no one, in these days, that she did not sleep at night. But at the height of her bravado, her bonnet strings seemed to choke her. Untying them absently, with her bony hands, she swayed just perceptibly, unguardedly. I reckon helping nurse George through his present troubles will make a woman of her, Mrs. Witherspoon meditated hastily. *That* was for Annie Byrd, at whom she would not stare. The force of contempt, however, fell upon 'poor Mrs. Garvin,' there in a front chair and as 'lugubrious as ever.' Mrs. Witherspoon's aged nostrils expanded scornfully. What had she to complain of with the *one* son *she* had given, while the three who were at home were too young for danger?

'Loathing' that 'mewling, sickly mother,' Mrs. Witherspoon, summoning faith ecstatically, defiantly, went on again: "It is not the men alone who will drive the invader forever from our beloved South, but wives, mothers—and *sweethearts, too,* if they are worthy of the devotion of the boys they adore, who, as the man of letters puts it, prefer death rather than ignoble surrender of their high and cherished beliefs. I have two sons in the war. You know this—you have already heard me say this." She paused.

39

Then the tremor, as it passed across her calm, keen, aquiline features, was conquered, and her brown eyes, opaque as wood, resumed inscrutability. "If I had *ten* sons," she reiterated, using an old phrase, but somehow, now, with a more despairing vigour, "I would gladly give up every one of them. What kind of a Southerner—worse—what kind of a mother would I be, if I who thought I was doing my duty when I counselled them and gave them the fruits of my experience in their childish troubles, gave less when they had reached their manhood and faced the storms of life? It would be an insult to faith—to *my* faith, anyhow —to think of such good boys—so conscientious and high-minded— as guided in their present decisions by any hand but that of God. Some of you have been impatient with me because I refused to whine and grumble about this separation. You've had the temerity to imagine that I felt less love for *my* dear sons than *you* feel for your sons and husbands—and sweethearts. But, do you know the lesson this great victory teaches me, and how it was brought about? It was brought about by *faith*, ladies." Mrs. Witherspoon smiled with kind bitterness. "I don't mean to take to myself the credit for the courage shown by our troops in the great battle at Manassas." Her smile waned, and she half closed her eyes, under the concave shadow of the bonnet, while her head went back. "I know well, in the first place, that there are many of you who have shared that faith. Well—we are all here rejoicing. I can't say more." She raised her lids, issuing a kind of stern appeal. "We must set to work. Remember, gentleness is not weakness, and a true gentlewoman in a time of war has a martial spirit. We are going to fight until there *is* no war, and we are going to do it with our threads and our needles and our darning cotton. If all you ladies are unanimous, I move that we dispense with the reading of the minutes of our last gathering. Mrs. Pettis can give us her report on funds before we are ready to go."

The speaker sighed deeply, and sat down abruptly beside the table. Annie Byrd was commanded shortly to distribute materials to the industrious. There was quiet again: or ladies echoed insincerely their agreement with 'Miss Agnes' in her ardour for self-immolation. Some, chagrined to feel their own resolutions imperfect, murmured, subduedly and cautiously, from distant corners, that 'Miss Agnes' liked 'orating.'

The bee, lumbering, sank on the window sill. The wheelbarrow, pushed to and from the garden, screeched persistently. "We must put aside all our sectarian prejudices and follow Miss Agnes's example," Miss Jenny Bates said. "She wants us to combine with the Methodist and Baptist sewing societies and meet with them in the Court House every Monday. After you are through with this, she wants me to talk to you about the bazaar we are planning. Mr. Davis needs a lot of money, and we are going to equip each soldier with—with—" She fumbled vaguely in her reticule, and brought a paper forth. "*There's* the list. Each man must have—one gun, one pistol, canteen, haversack, knapsack—um—let's see—yes—knapsack. Knapsack—each knapsack is to contain a—a fatigue jacket, two blankets, an oilcloth, several suits of underclothing, several pairs of white gloves." And the enumeration continued in a shaking voice.

The war gives Miss Jenny something to do, Mrs. Witherspoon conjectured shrewdly. And added, as an acrid afterthought, I suppose Annie Byrd has it all fixed up that me and Miss Jennie are just alike.

"You sit over there, Euphemia." Mrs. Witherspoon could never keep her tongue from orders. And if she *had* kissed President Davis's portrait when she had seen it out on Mrs. Kendrick's piano, whose business was it? Wasn't the President, in these days, like a father to the boys, watching over them? "Why don't you try cucumber juice for your complexion, Annie Byrd?" Mrs. Witherspoon said, interjecting this remark into a conversation concerning the advisability of bathing the face in buttermilk. That was Josie's idea. But if Annie Byrd feigned not to care about her looks it was just 'contrariness.' George's assertion that Annie Byrd's pride was 'to have no vanity,' did not deceive his mother. It's all right for me, an old woman of sixty-five, to go around like I do in these shabby clothes, but for Annie Byrd to say that the war has made her listless about such things is simple affectation.

Mrs. Witherspoon often suspected that her 'daughter-in-law-to-be' accused her of 'acting.' And indeed the indiscreet Josie had one time hinted it. How could a girl like *that* understand the necessity to be whole-hearted? George and James would comprehend it better. *They* knew their mother. They *knew* her love and courage in emergencies, and could depend on her. She was, of course, more confident of George. James was a 'strange' boy, and had always been. George would be a captain in another month, but James—and she was a little ashamed of his constant attitude of 'self-depreciation'—might not be promoted.

Mrs. Witherspoon, issuing curt, kindly, superfluous instructions, unexpectedly felt herself tired. The whining of the wheelbarrow became too intrusive and exasperated her. She must be growing old indeed if she could let these silly trifling noises so 'put' her 'out.'

"Why, there's Miss Gracie!" 'Miss Gracie' was Mrs. White, a little woman of Mrs. Witherspoon's generation. Mrs. White was a neighbour to the rector, but a Presbyterian, and did not usually attend the *Ladies' Aid Society.*

"Come in, Miss Gracie. Come in, Miss Gracie. Even a good predestinationist like you can celebrate the victory of our troops with us."

Mrs. White, very small and fragile, wore a mob cap, with ruffles, grey sidecurls covering her ears, and a full black dress which no hoops supported. She was fond of 'joking' Mrs. Witherspoon for being 'stylish.' There existed a few months' difference in their ages, and each, with a pang which was concealed by laboured humour, pretended to exercise over the other the privileges of seniority.

Mrs. White, evidently, had 'just run in.' She halted in the doorway, and, behind the friendly keenness of her careful expression, her eyes held a searching, doubtful look. "I *supposed* you'd be here to see that all the ladies behaved themselves," was her jocose preamble. And she moved into the room a step or two. There was a certain air of importance about her, which caused Mrs. Pettis to ask her eagerly, "Have you come here as our Mercurius, Miss Gracie? There hasn't been a telegram the livelong day. Have you any news for us?"

Mrs. Witherspoon, for some reason vexed, stirred, and said: "Of course she hasn't. She doesn't need to *buy* her welcome. We've had enough good news to last us several days, and if she's too young to wake up her mind herself, I'm going to give her orders now to sit right down and get to work with us."

Annie Byrd was bent over a heap of lint, but Mrs. Witherspoon was sharp enough to observe the quivering of the girl's short fingers, and the veiled inquiry with which she glanced, in 'pre-

42

tended' indifference, at the new arrival. There was a little clicking sound of Mrs. Witherspoon's tongue. Annie Byrd really ought to be 'shaken,' she was so nervous. We can't expect the President to send us *special* messages, Mrs. Witherspoon thought derisively. *I'm* satisfied to hear nothing at all after the benefits we have just received.

Mrs. White, nevertheless, revealed some agitation, and, though she continued to smile, ignored the badinage. "I think you are going to swamp the boys with bandages anyway. The fact is that—that I want to speak to Josie for a moment—privately."

Josie, pleasurably astonished at being signalled for attention, in a swirl of muslin ruffles above black slippers, sprang to her feet. "Mind, then, you can keep no secrets," Mrs. Pettis called. But Mrs. White, with her arm pressing Josie's waist, hurried her out of doors.

Politely, the ladies attempted, while they travailed, to maintain the conversation. A few 'senseless' comments on the weather were all they could produce. Mrs. Witherspoon, with a kind of sudden rage in her heart, simply *would* not meet Annie Byrd's seeking eye. Women, halting at their tasks, turned their heads toward the door, and were baffled to discover that Josie and Mrs. White had moved outside the range of vision. Mrs. Witherspoon thought that she would '*murder*' somebody if that wheelbarrow gave so much as another groan. But she was *not* foolish. She was *not* demoralized by the 'hysteria' of the last weeks. When people could doubt, after the completeness of the Bull Run triumph, they '*deserved*' bad news. She understood that the country had gone 'wild' with joy. Her hostile resolve was weakening. She had the sensations of one observed. She looked up, saw that Annie Byrd was staring at her, and felt regret. Mrs. Witherspoon began to hum *Dixie* under her breath. She realized that by her 'droning' she was calling attention to herself, and exclaimed petulantly: "Sing, you ladies. Come on and sing a hymn with me. Why can't you forget yourselves and your troubles and sing when you are happy like the darkies do!"

Beyond a few quavering titters, the invitation brought no response. The disappearance of Josie, with Mrs. White, had produced distracting meditations. Why does she keep us all in suspense, some were reflecting. If she had some ordinary message for Josie, why be mysterious?

Mrs. Garvin, at last, oppressed too much by the false industry of her companions, 'broke down.' "It's something about Fred. She was looking at me just as she came in. I never believed that the telegrams were right about the victory. The Yankees cut the wires these days and we never get things straight." She gazed about, demanding contradiction, her small fat face smeared with uncontrolled tears. The women who watched her, to whom she turned, looked at her coldly, querulously, and as if revolted.

"My goodness, Miss Bessie, pull yourself together! If you can't believe the newspapers, what *can* you believe? I never heard such foolishness." Mrs. Pettis sounded vicious, and spoke with a tight mouth, her lids lowered evasively.

Mrs. Witherspoon, flinging lint and cloth aside, rose, with a gesture of rebuke to all, walked to the door, peered into the heat-whitened yard, and called: "Josie. Gracie. Josie. Gracie. Come here this minute." All waited, all wondered, and all were dimly shocked, resentful of her precipitateness.

Josie, with a face blank with the wretchedness of a predicament, was the first to appear. In the cave of the room, necks were craned, that the beholders miss nothing. But Josie, the rosy colour drained from her cheeks, disregarded them. Especially did she seem anxious, as she pushed into the room, to evade Mrs. Witherspoon, who was blocking the way.

"I want to see Annie Byrd," Josie announced hurriedly.

Annie Byrd rose too deliberately, picked lint from the lap of her muslin frock, and passed Mrs. Witherspoon, as she did so, giving her a glance that smouldered wildly with some unspoken rebuke which the old lady, feeling the look like a blow, could not interpret.

The two girls proceeded out of doors and vanished. Mrs. Witherspoon stood there, shivering, bracing herself with her hand upon the door jamb. Her heart was fluttering uncomfortably, and she was possessed by a queer bewilderment like a premonition.

Her state was not to be endured. Emotion obliterated thought, almost obliterated consciousness. Waves, as of darkness, moved on her mind. The glare stung her eyeballs, but she scarcely realized that she was staring into it. Now and then, a leaf of grapevine, swinging, moved through the morbid dazzle of the sunlight into sudden sight. The twitching of the bold, loose leaves on the arbour annoyed her. Then the wheelbarrow began to sing again, piercingly, monotonously, though she could not locate it.

Mrs. Witherspoon, angry, as if she were being deprived of something that was her right, walked into burning exposure. Josie and Annie Byrd were just returning, while—and the spectacle irritated further—Mrs. White was to be discerned, waiting, motionless, at the corner of the house. Mrs. Witherspoon became, at once, acute of vision. She could distinguish, not only the redness of Josie's eyelids, but, remotely, the clenching of Mrs. White's withered hands, the details of an expression of aversion. Mrs. Witherspoon felt so ill, with all that she knew herself about to hear, that she wanted to die. Yet a stronger emotion was her jealous defiance of their secrecy. What made them all appear about to run away from her? Had she become repulsive, so that they were obliged to treat her like a leper.

She marched forward and caught Josie's dangling wrist. The girl's bare arm, squeezed, reddened to cloudy colour. "Tell *me*," Mrs. Witherspoon commanded slowly, "what the three of you have been talking about."

The heat waves flowed upward from the gravel walk, and a quivering iridescence hung about the yard. The shade under the grapevines was growing contiguous, and some tufts of grass under the edges showed greener again. The wheelbarrow was silent. *Chiluck-chuck-chuck,* came from the rector's chicken-run. A wren bounced from the ground, set its wings out stiffly, and sailed into the emerald midnight of a magnolia tree.

With a movement of capitulation, like one convicted of guilt, Josie freed herself from the clutch on her arm, buried her face in her cupped palms, and cried: "*You* tell her, Annie Byrd. I can't say it. I can't say it."

Mrs. Witherspoon, stupidly, regarded the bowed blond head on which every hair in the thick chignon tingled separately with sun. There was something menacing in its appearance. She wished never to 'lay eyes' on Josie Kendricks again.

Annie Byrd came slightly nearer. Her broad, rather heavy face was dark with a blush of excitement. She looked displeased, unusual —'even out of her head,' Mrs. Witherspoon thought.

45

"George is—he's wounded." Mrs. Witherspoon anticipated information frantically. She might have borne the news from Josie, but that Annie Byrd should bear her tidings, she would not allow. Yet she blinked, and hoped for contradiction. Little dewdrops of sweat broke suddenly from her upper lip. This was the hottest day of the summer. Warm—terribly warm. She must be on the verge of sunstroke. Then she was ashamed that her first anxiety should be for George, and added, "James—James is hurt. Don't keep anything from me."

"Why do you make *me* say it?" Josie wailed.

Mrs. Witherspoon wanted them to be quick. Mrs. White was drawing nearer, and it would be better to hear the worst before she was *here*. It was true that Mrs. Witherspoon could not endure it that her old friend should surprise her in this condition. And besides, where had the information come from? These girls were such 'sensationalists.'

Annie Byrd's eyes glittered somberly in a direct gaze. But she was overcome. She averted her face. "I—I've got to go away, Josie. You *must* tell his mother. I can't."

Mrs. Witherspoon could not tolerate this reference to herself as to something inanimate. "Annie Byrd—look at me. None of this nonsense. If there is anything *you* are strong enough to hear, I can hear it too. Where did you all hear that George was wounded? Why did they tell Gracie White about it instead of me?" She was excited, wondering how long she had to go on like this.

Josie, speaking through her fingers, said: "Miss Gracie had a telegraph. It came for you while you were out, and Aunt Melissa took it to her to find out whether it was important or not."

Mrs. Witherspoon felt trapped. Gracie White was hurrying, and, in a minute, would be able to listen. Mrs. Witherspoon, involuntarily, put out her hands in a shaky indication that she would ward off sympathy. "When are they sending him home? At least they know he has a mother waiting."

Unexpectedly, Annie Byrd came forward. "He's dead, Miss Agnes." The announcement, in that calmed, emotionally vibrating tone, was like an attack. Mrs. White said, "Oh—that's not the way to tell her." And Josie, revealing her face, displayed, unwittingly, the thrill she felt in astonishment.

Annie Byrd's hard speech could not be halted. She talked

46

viciously. "He died like a *hero,* Miss Agnes, at Manassas, but I haven't your consolations. It's not in me to care more for a lot of politics than for flesh and blood." Annie Byrd was panting. Tears glinted in her harsh, staring eyes.

Mrs. Witherspoon's gaze, like that of an idiot, was fixed, past her attacker, upon the still scintillant magnolia tree. Her lips contracted. A pale lustre of defiance spread over her eyes, and, tears blotting her cheeks, her look came back to her accuser. "You're a wicked girl," she articulated slowly. "You're not fit to be the sweetheart of my—my patriot." Her voice quavered flatly. Her spread palms pressed vaguely at the air. Whispering brokenly to Josie, she said: "Let me get home, Honey. Keep those women away from me, Honey. I'm not strong enough to meet them yet."

Annie Byrd watched the indefinite stride uncertainly. Josie said, "*Say* something to her."

And Annie Byrd answered, "There is nothing more that I can say. I hate—her—her *damned* Confederacy."

Instantly she had made this choked utterance, a repentance for which she despised herself, obsessed her. She made a step forward. "Miss Agnes—"

Mrs. Witherspoon halted, swayed, then relinquished herself to Annie Byrd's sturdy support. Her head lolled, inclined toward the girl's shoulder, and she moaned: "You won't try to tell me the war's *wrong,* Annie Byrd. You won't take my only comfort from me. Why, everything I have's wrapped up in it. God wouldn't take my only son away but in His Own cause, would He? The war's *right.*" Her tongue was thick. She found herself talking in a daze. If she could only lie down in the blistering torrent of the sunlight and feel her brain beaten out.

II

THE reverse side of the duplicate was known to me, who am James Witherspoon, because of the heat. As I write this I have a caustic feeling that I am in a military asylum, at least away from Mother. It is understood conventionally, I believe, that hands forget these things, and I was always studious. I was young when the question presented itself to me, do hands forget? Yet my origin and entrance into the world has associated me forever with morbid flesh. That protest against Nature for which I have barely been able to account, assumed paramount importance after that last bloody battle in which my brother, George, was shot. Birth is not the only reality. George and I will be born again.

The books which I find have been written on this subject fail to convey my conceptions of experience. I am a peculiar man. Many here in the hospital attempt to prove me non compos mentis. That they have not been able to adduce insanity is due to the fact that I can show them how joy and ecstasy are arrived at without restraint. I begin by denial. Deny everything, and say plainly that the war is not. From my diverse articles in the local newspapers in the last few years, it will be understood that I have weighed blood carefully and have put myself in the balance for slavery, for freedom troubled me as a too great burden. It has demanded much. Others who are jealously safeguarding their shackles force it upon me. When an old lady dies, in the dry marrow of her adversity, we look for lenience. Or would I were a dog to yap pleasantly at her future nuptials in heaven where the begetter waits. The nurses, libidinous under the mask of their prying undertaking, have not, until this moment, allowed me to put on paper that which outlasts niceties. Without power, the elements confuse. It was my design to go to President Davis, but he also has become iniquitous. Pride is his doom.

This is written before my recovery. Tomorrow, they tell me, I will be better. Thus of fools. An old hatchet and five saw teeth cannot surmount persecution. After I was elected I made no further attempt at suicide. Rather have I been interested in enlarging the net. It is thought only which achieves omnipotence, and man will some day laugh at his aggressor. Inventions prosper. With steam power and the sewing machine, Icarus laughs. An old goat squirting from her bawdy teats down the cannon's throat. The effort to draw truth out of its storehouse and present it, in this world in which nothing lives, is still offensive to me. My madness is sheer malice. There is truth grown by hoarding, and one whisper of the secret dissipates progress. They resent me therefrom. And why? Rachel, after that affair of honour in which only my mother was acquitted, was placed in custody, her qualms of conscience disproved by punishment. A greater soul has no chartered expiation, but must meet the verge in a nightcap. That is why I, who am so many people, insist on being the same person that I always was. The disguise is as complete as Hamlet's. None can penetrate it, nor can I say honestly that I wish it penetrated. As the sun sheds its own light, so the mind knowledge. I am the salvation. My gratitude to the asylum is based on the fact that no one is recognized for what he is supposed to be, but for what he is. This might be the case with Lincoln, Davis, and the members of the Northern and Southern cabinets if they could see sufficiently. There is no truth in our common names for things. Self-exposure is painful to me. I do not shirk duty. I have tried to show myself for what I am without decency which alone prevaricates. The war has a purpose. Calvary was not less than what I felt under the shocked eyes of the nurses who gave back my clothes. They were not women, but souls. I behave foolishly, stick pins in myself, and no one can be persuaded that indignity is part of the lesson. Converting nothing into nothing. I must beat my skull against the stone wall if I would deaden it. The strait jacket was exhausting, too, like the swaddling clothes of my youth. What of it? None guessed the ascetic triumph in which I lay with flanks heaving upon the thick carpet where I was thrown. I have my own plot, however. On some occasion when the doctor is examining me, I will do him violence, provoke recourse, and oblige those who surround me to do the horrid inevitable. My words will convey a meaning which I have not suspected. They have done so before, dominating the printed page of my composition; they

49

have walked through the land. Thus my talent. But no more till Phoebus bids me.

II

"Scuttle along, Mose. There's two reb fellahs goin' down that air trail behin' Ma Gaines's cabin, en they's unarmed, er I'm a liar. Ef they ain't got no more gumption than to sneak through here in broad daylight, we'll git a pot at 'em. Hit ain't patriotic to leave 'em think a secesh sojer kin show hissef aroun' these parts 'thout gittin' picked off."

Dawsy did not speak excitedly, but in the high, whining nasal habitual to him, and he 'hitched up,' furtively, the enormous, collapsing trousers which his sister, 'Miss Hettie,' had bought him at a 'rummage sale' just before she died. Dawsy had approached Mose's doorway in the manner which had inspired the sobriquet, 'Cat-Foot,' and was poking his head stealthily into the single, dirt-floored room of the Elder dwelling, his eyes glittering oddly through his whitish lashes.

Dawsy, on occasion, was a 'preacher,' and a weak, fairly freckled hand, grasping the door jamb, protruded from a lengthy, black, 'preacher's' coat sleeve that had ravelled edges. In the other hand, he grasped a shotgun, which he displayed to Mose suggestively.

It was September, and, in the mountains, prematurely chilly, but Cat-Foot Dawsy, small, thin and anaemic, belonging to the class called 'dirt-eaters,' only a degree above the 'Georgia cracker,' wore no underclothing. His indifference to this lack was emphasized in the exposure of a bony, ribbed diaphragm through the split fragment of a calico shirt, grease-glazed and buttonless. Yet Dawsy was an important member of a secret organization vowed to resist the compulsion of Tennessee mountaineers into Southern regiments. Dawsy felt a general aversion to authority, but, at this time, the advocates of Northern politics had made no effort to coerce him in behalf of their cause.

Dawsy's subdued intrusion had just awakened Mose, who, stretched on a shuck pallet, in a position which allowed him to enjoy to the full the pleasantly enervating warmth of the Indian summer sun, now 'shoved' himself to a half-sitting posture, and stared, with dazed eye and slack mouth open, at the doubtful associate who held such sway of influence over him.

50

It took Mose some seconds to recover his wits from their dispersion in slumber. And, anyway, he wanted to 'gain time.' Mose was fat, he was slow, and he was very cautious. Terror of risking his 'skin' in the fighting line had made him the dupe of one to whom surreptitious deeds of recklessness came 'more naturally.' Mose, at a clandestine gathering at an abandoned whisky still, had vowed under cover of an oath of silence, to fight the 'Secesh' men perpetually, and to spare no enemy life out of mere 'chicken-heartedness.'

Moonlight, masks and ornate ritual had fired his soul to indefinite resolves. But he was already regretful. Dawsy, whom he had before despised—Dawsy the failure and the eccentric—revealing, unexpectedly, the 'born' temper of a criminal plotter, 'pestered' him continually to be 'patriotic.'

Grudgingly, Mose rose from the floor. "Look peert, Mose," Dawsy was whispering ambiguously, "hit's about the fust chance we-all had et any uv them there fien's fer well-nigh a week. Ef you don't act spry and shinny down that gully easy, they'll git away from us."

Dawsy, with continual nervous movements, seemed to dance with animation. Still Mose delayed, in torpid panic to which he could not admit. "Hadn't we better roust out the whole gang to git after 'em?" he asked.

Dawsy would have none of this. "Ain't none uv 'em got you-all's sand? Think uv ownin' up thet Mose Elder's feared to face two gosh-durned unarmed rapscallions uv secessionists. They's moseyin' 'long like they reckoned they wuz in friendly territory. Ain't we sent 'em warnin' not to come up here? You ain't fergot Jeb Trotter, Mose? Bushwhackers come to Jeb Trotter's door one night an' sez, 'Is you-all resolved ter give you-all's allegiance ter Jeff Davis an' yer native state, er ain't you?' En whin Jeb 'lowed he warn't gona be druv to do nothin' his conscience didn' tell him to do, an' fixed fer to go inside so as to shut 'em up, an' turned his back, they turned loose an' fired right th'ough his gizzard, an' he an' his ol' 'oman both got a broadside uv shot. She wuz laid low thin an' thar. Jeb's ol' gal wasn' much loss, but don't you 'member how Hez Dortch offered fair an' square to buy 'em off with moonshine, only when they-all seen where 'bouts his still wuz they sez they'd turn him over to the law uv his own party ef he didn' jine in with the

51

dern Confed'rates fust? He sassed 'em an' tol' 'em to go ahaid, an' they didn't think nothin' uv stringin' him up high as Haman on thet there road to the Gap."

Mose, with five thick, grubby fingers, scratched labouredly in a blond mat of hair. He could persuade himself that he would not be timid of an encounter more open, but these plans, concocted by Dawsy, to dog the footsteps of suspicious 'feriners' and fire upon them from the safe cover of tree or bush on a greater height than the one they traversed affected him disturbingly. As much as he disliked orthodox, rigorous procedure, he respected it. To Blyville, fifteen miles away, Mose had gone with Dawsy, and had heard 'Parson' Brownlow speak. "Parson 'lows thet the whole war come about through the intentions uv slave-holdin' gentry down thar to run the state uv Tennessee ter suit their own notions, makin' slave-holdin' the cornerstone uv the new nation, an' payin' no mind to what hones' po' folks hanker fer." This was Dawsy's explanation of Brownlow's oratory. Dawsy had always been glib of tongue. "Them feriners frum down Nashville way come inter our midst an' begun by scarin' people so they wouldn't be nobody kiragous 'nough to vote down secesh. When they seed that wouldn' work, they-all sets out ter git the vote-payers drunk." Mose knew this to be true, for he himself had fallen as a temporary victim of their wiles. It was astonishing to everybody that Dawsy, considered a ne'er-do-well and, when not 'religious,' a frequenter of easy company, restrained himself to sobriety during the whole epoch of public perversion. For seven months had the war endured, and Dawsy, by 'layin' low,' seemed to have saved himself, and was still 'on top.' As he expressed it, he liked good whisky, but he was not to be 'taken in' by tricks 'as transparent an' easy ter see th'ough' as those of the enemy. "I never set much store by a vote befo," Dawsy said, "but whin them thar robbers lets on how much they prizes votes, I sez to mahsef thet a vote mus' be wuth a whole lot mo' than the nip uv cawn-juice they been offerin' fer it." As a result of his calculations, he had received three dollars in Federal cash from Bud Smith and Dave Waters, renegades who attempted to keep themselves on 'both sides uv the fence.' And, even with the expenditure of so much money, the *agents provocateurs* of Richmond had obtained no evidence against their devious opponent.

Dawsy was 'slickery.' Mellowed by success, throwing back his coat and revealing the shadowy intimation of ribs etched on his bleached flesh below his bony, prominent chest, he would rub his chronically distended stomach, and allow himself a womanish chuckle at the expense of the conspirators against his freedom.

Secretly, Dawsy condemned, with the venom of the envious and feeble, the bolder course taken by John Dean, the blacksmith at the Gap, who had announced himself, without preamble, as a Union supporter. That he was still free to pursue his vocation, Dawsy attributed to his bold presence and his stronger arm. "But he ain't goin' on like that long," Dawsy had prophesied softly. "You keep yere eye on him, Mose. He's sech a gosh-derned fool, he's gona pay fer it."

Mose eschewed association with John Dean and his handful of followers, and was thoroughly convinced that plain speaking was appropriate only for Brownlow and such men of power. Yet it had been a leap from the frying pan into the fire to become almost unwittingly associated with Dawsy's organization of defence.

Murder's murder, Mose's slow mind would quibble. On one other day he had been with Dawsy and Abel Burroughs when a wandering deserter from 'down there where the secesh war is a-goin' on' had been shot by them. And the incident had committed Mose to a future in which Dawsy's little ratlike brain dictated every act. Hit ain't like a feud, where there's some reason to the thing, Mose's alarmed mind had argued stubbornly. But he was trapped. His position as a party to surreptitious crime had been established.

Mose fetched his gun guiltily from the corner where it reclined upright among some skillets, and stepped out of doors, into the placid, tepid clarity of afternoon, uncomfortably. Gazing above the toppling stalks of an old corn crop that surrounded the cabin, he 'spied' to make certain that his 'stepma,' Miss Susan, did not observe his departure. In an aerie, very aloof, on a ledge above the house, was the old lady, minute in her speckled Mother Hubbard and sunbonnet, collecting, from the drying vines spread out around her, heaps of winter squashes. The light glittered, lukewarm, on the dry heights of the mountain. To the east, where she stood, the high boulders and the vegetation looked ruddy, disclosed without the protection of a shadow. To the west the pines rose, murky and unillumined, 'as ef the angel of darkness flew over half the crags and the valleys with his wings stretched out.'

Dawsy 'speculated' that Miss Susan, idling for a moment, was taking her 'drap' of snuff. She leaned on her hoe and stared downward. But there was a vagueness in her attitude which assured those who scrutinized her unmindful figure that she gazed, not at them, but into the windless, prematurely night-drenched valleys so obscure below.

Dawsy coughed—'hacked'—anxiously. "We got to lump it, Mose," he insisted quaveringly, "before them thar rebel fellahs hits mo' open country like." It pleased him to see Miss Susan, unaware that considered disaster was about to overtake two fellow mortals, 'plant' her hoe, and sit down on a stump to 'look around a mite.' The Angel uv Darkness, he meditated, almost blithely, as he shivered, hit's hoverin'. Hit's hoverin'. But he never spoke such thoughts aloud save in a 'preachin' spell.' If he and Mose could 'git' up over Hooker's Point, they'd shoot down on those 'sojers 'fo' they got away, all right.'

Dawsy mildly regretted that he was losing the opportunity to sow alarm. It was a 'seed' with which he had experimented in the 'Lawd's gardenin'.' Dawsy knew that his alert hold on Mose's fancy had been strengthened by the half-invented story of Wallace's Emmeline. It was a part of Dawsy's character as historian that, when he conveyed hearsay, he improved it. Wallace's gal was 'purty high an' mighty.' Dawsy had never liked her 'highty-tighty' ways and her 'pert,' white face. So—it *might* be 'gospel' and it *might* be 'nothin' but a pack uv lies'——but he *had* heard folks say that when the Bushwhackers went up to Wallace's house and surrounded it, the 'whole blame passel uv them fellahs hed their way with Emmeline.' When it 'come' to the 'rapin' an' abusin' uv the women-folks,' there wasn't a 'whiteman in these here parts' who would 'put up' with it.

The story about Emmeline had influenced Mose peculiarly, and, for the time required to hear the narrative, his fatness, his slowness, and his indecision had congealed to make a resolute personality. "I reckon you-all kin tell me about thet happenin' again, Dawsy. I ain't got it straight yit." And Dawsy, mouthing a fresh enthusiasm, had elaborated conjecture into detailed certainty. It was a fact that you could 'git worked up' yourself telling tales like that. The gal hadn't been like a human all summer, and her 'paw' was 'goin' clean offen his haid about it.' "Hit's

54

the Gawd's truth, as my Maker is above me," Dawsy had asserted.

Queer, the concern for women that men like Mose would at times display. Dawsy warily eschewed their company. 'No truck' with women, was his motto, he declared. He had felt crafty and malignant toward the awkward boaster when Mose belligerent, had squared his shoulders, 'tried' his muscle, and looked like a 'fire-eater.' From that time forth, Dawsy, disturbed, contemptuous, was determined to use sensational power to make Mose 'show fight.'

Today that resource was held in store. Mose was capitulating without it, and the two, Dawsy leading, began to climb toward the mountain's summit. They were soon so high that the pines, in their stiff ranks, seemed to grow downward for miles on miles from a hanging sky.

Dawsy, who was leading the Indian file, liked to feel himself 'high up.' He lived the existence of a hunter, his mean hut perched at such an altitude of isolation that few would venture to it, though his reputation as a 'yarb doctor' and 'healer' sometimes inspired pilgrims who, condemning him in the usual relations of life, would seek to utilize his knowledge of 'signs.' He lacked faith in himself, and so connived to deceive, yet he regulated every act by omen, and never neglected to hook his little fingers together and pull 'hard' if, when he was shooting, a strange dog ran across his path. The same credence made him almost choke with fearful expectation if a bird alighted on the crooked sill of the glassless window which aired his wretched dwelling. He felt himself impotent to avert fatalities, but was delighted to see others, harassed, seek his futile aid in their behalf. It was his revenge on them to keep them 'guessin'.' Family affairs and family feuds and troubles, he was excluded from. But he was a hearty harbinger of evil, and was always the excited first to bear the tidings of a 'shootin' scrape.'

Dawsy's insignificant courage invariably grew sufficient as he climbed. His tread was as sure as a goat's, and soundless. In this attitude of seeking prey he felt familiar, for there had been many times when, had he been without his gun, he would not have been able to eat. His veins tingled. He was happy, pleased by this second sinister venture in impartial justice, and by the miserable concurrence of panting Mose whom he had coerced into becoming a permanent accessory to such enterprises.

Dawsy enjoyed a 'good, rousin' sermon.' Yet preaching over-stimulated him, and there was relief and larger rapture in activity. He 'reckoned' he was not more passive in contemplativeness because he did not smoke, or 'dip' or 'chew,' his weak stomach rejecting tobacco. He was without 'vices.' A man's thoughts turn to the Word of Gawd, Dawsy told himself, when he ain't pisined by the weed, er fillin' his stomach, er hangin' round women-folks.

"Quick. Lie down, Mose. You-all kin see 'em now. I'm aimin' et that ther fellah on the left hand side. I'm gona crack him jest above his ear. The low-down skunks an' spies they is. You ain't took the love uv yer own free folks ter heart ef you-all kin set by comfortable an' see them restin' sech a spell in Gillis's woods like hit belonged to 'em."

The fear and the rapture which Dawsy courted were in his tense, blinking-eyed face, as he threw himself on his breast and peered over a rock. Mose squatted, but more to hide himself than to utilize advantage. In the shadows of a path below were two men, bareheaded, in grey dusty coats, reclining with backs against some pine trees, exhaustedly.

"Maybe they's deserters. Maybe they's friendly, Dawsy. We-all agreed to patrol the Gap, but this here is the second time you led me into trouble without knowin' what hit's about."

Dawsy, pressing his shotgun to his trembling shoulder, laid the barrel levelly along the stone. He was angry with Mose who interfered with a triumphant sensation born of beholding, from a point of vantage, the helpless victims of intention, still unmindful they were being watched.

There was a little wind rising. On the bold profiles of the hills, sudden isolate trees leaped into waving prominence. The pines, in the steady, parted sunshine, began to seethe like cataracts. The needles on the rocking boughs sucked the air in and out, in and out, like glassy gills; and Dawsy thought of fish. The path below was like an evening river with green eels moving softly through it.

Dawsy, with Mose beside him at a disadvantage, was quietly joyful. The two capless soldiers were not more than thirty feet lower than the sheltering boulder. Without comprehending what they were saying, he could hear them speak. Dawsy had the feeling that the whole untouched world up here belonged to him. He could take his time to aim. There was not much difference between a

56

coon, a deer, a bear, a man and a jack-rabbit, when you were going to shoot. He thought of the silence—or the cry—that might follow on his firing, and put the moment off voluptuously.

Yet he was 'scared to death.' Dawsy cocked his eye sidewise, and beheld the clumsy, crouching shape of Mose—Mose the handsome, the respectable, the favourite stepson of Miss Susan, who was so raspingly intolerant of Dawsy as an associate. Mose did not even have his rifle lifted. His features were moulded firmly in apoplectic horror. But he was not going to 'raise' any objection to the annihilation of at least one vagabond from the 'secesh' ranks. Mose had been deeply affected by 'Parson' Brownlow's logic, and, as Mose interpreted it, pity had no 'reason.'

Dawsy shuddered, exulted, drew into his meagre lungs the dry, cooling, pine-scented air, and thought: You dern coward. You big fat bragger. You ain't got the gumption of a jay-bird. It's a good thing that the Committee fer Free Rights ain't dependin' on *you*-all to see Tennessee saved. He had 'sighted' perfectly, as he knew he always did; then he closed his eyes, and pulled the trigger.

There was a crackle, followed by a faint *bi-ling* of echo, and the tinkling of some falling twigs which the bullet snapped in its passage. Mose was running. Dawsy let his shotgun slide from his nerveless fingers, avoided the scene below him, and started to his feet to follow Mose's swift, graceless descent down the path they had mounted together. Then he thought better of it.

He began to scramble up the slope. As he approached the end of the rise, haste ejected him into encroaching space. The day was so nearly at an end, and the sky, which had fallen impalpably upon him, dispensed, luminously, a great quiet. He hesitated, halted, gazed about him over a rocky meadow, and, realizing that he had left his gun behind, squeezed his hands together in a gesture half effeminate, while his whole thin body trembled in nervous paroxysms of indecision. Gradually, tension became calm. The mountains would be free of rebel sympathizers by the time he 'finished.' He was aiding the Union. But, more than that, he was aiding Dawsy.

He was on a small upland, almost like a table, and precautions of concealment could not be effectual here. Yet he sank down on his hands and knees again. When he had crawled to the beginning of a declivity, he peeped over. He could see no human, could hear

57

no human sound. The dusking billows of the greening evening trees waved in his face.

Dawsy stood up and began to run, to race, almost to gambol. He trotted to one extremity of his small plateau, and gazed below, carefully, into the great tide of shadows which flowed as from secret sources in the receding valley. He turned his face to the white plaque of bright, enormous sun, from which rays, dartled over miles of upland, no longer pierced his eyeballs blindingly. Then he rushed, on mad tiptoe, back to the first spot from which he had surveyed the watery depths of an untenanted ravine. In giddy moments, impulse overpowered his instinct for reserve. But he was *secure*. He had conquered. He was up here where no one other than himself could think of travelling. Pursuit was not to be longer feared. This world belonged to him. Dawsy was satisfied. At times he was afraid of 'Sister Hettie's ha'nt.' But, for the most part, he was contented in obscurity. He enjoyed the shelter afforded by the contempt of his fellows. He chuckled, but, startled by the queer inappropriateness of his weak, rasped mirth, hushed himself immediately. His thin fingers fumbled his neck. If he could only secure his gun! If he could kill or steal enough food to last over several months, the war 'down thar' in the far-off valleys could come as near as *it* liked.

Anyway, he was no 'slave nigger.' Nobody could trap *him*, or put a ball and chain about him, or make him shoulder a rifle. His nostrils, mobile as a rabbit's, widened, and he smelled the heat of the sun on the dry grass here among the last glittering rocks, together with the dank odours of sodden gorges already in a half-night. Shivering with chill, he turned his head slowly, nervously, exultantly, wishing for some higher peak accessible, to which he could climb, some last boulder nearer the blue endlessness of sky from which the day's warmth was slipping away, leaving, to his alarm that mingled with physical sensations of victory, colder, more ponderable slopes, the bleak fragments of a round moon, and the faint, cracked glow of a first autumn star. How cold it was!

III

It was three o'clock in the afternoon. In a line abreast, the four ironclads under Flag-Officer Foote moved dingily forward, the bows growing steadily so that the whole channel of the river seemed filled by their progress. The two wooden gunboats which Grant knew to be following at a hundred yards were not yet in sight. The wind sawed continually in the ears of the watchers. The mane of Grant's horse lifted and blew out in taut strands from the shuddering flesh, while the horse pawed, 'counting the ears of corn he had eaten.' As the boats steamed largely by, under combining flutters of dun smoke, growing always more dense as speed was accelerated, Grant rejected that slightly intoxicating astonishment induced by a spectacle resulting from his new authority. He was deliberate in bewildering his staff by long silences, but he was determined to conceal himself. Perhaps there was really a change in him. This attack on Donelson, at any rate, would at last provide him with the opportunity to show what was 'in' him. His determination to win was so much more colossal than any previous feeling he had ever detected in himself, that he resisted the confronting of such disproportionate emotion as it provoked. It was an embarrassment to his concentration on the scene and the problem before him, that he could not avoid overhearing every trivial comment made by Major Smithers to Colonel Wood. For some reason, their discreet attitude toward his presence annoyed him, and it seemed their fault rather than his own that he could not ignore them completely. He fidgeted unconsciously, and pressed his short legs, and his feet in damp leather stirrups, against the horse's belly, almost viciously. The 'sentimentalists,' as he called them, to reassure himself, would, he supposed, discover something 'fiendish' in his 'cold-blooded' state. Having been compelled by his father, and for years, to see himself as a 'failure,' he obstinately flaunted, to his own imagination, some of the freshly aroused impulses of his character which, as he realized, he had not the 'slick' tongue and the ready wit to justify openly.

Resentment against 'Fate,' against his parents—particularly against his docile mother's lapses as his champion at home—quickened his blood, and by the time the boats were swerving, and shrinking squatly about a bend in the Cumberland, he had become oblivious to the painful sharpness of the raw breeze.— Dear Ulysses, with the accounts we have had of the esteem in which you are at present held and the great influence you have exerted in . . . 'Father's' letters were all alike, all couched in the same terms, all making the same requests, all filled with demands that the son support recent boasts by supplying positions, in connection with the army, to old family associates. Julia, no doubt, 'bragged a lot.' And Grant was divided between relief in making a good appearance before his wife, and an exasperated anticipation that she would be indiscreet. Julia, particularly since the débâcle of the real estate business, had been inclined to emphasize the fact that it was by the help of *her* relatives and not his own, that she and the children had escaped further hardships. He tried to regard the situation 'humorously.' Now that all had beheld him as he was posed in the daguerreotype he had sent Clara, in his full regalia in a uniform with so much bullion on it, they had been forced, perhaps, to regard him more respectfully. In Mexico, he had 'got the dirty end of the poker,' but the experience had 'taught' him something. Without making another 'damned move' to secure popularity by truckling, he was going to prove that 'horse sense' had a value beyond a mere 'knack' for society. Julia would yet make her essay in circles as 'polite, the devil take them,' as were any frequented by Colonel Wood's wife.

Backwater, overflowing from Hickman's Creek, it was said, vibrated with a chilly twinkle along the lower portions of the bleak shore opposite, and the puddly depths, exposed among bared trees, duplicated the indefinite sunlight. Grant knew that, farther on, between the river and the earthworks of the Confederates, water batteries had been excavated. There was a rumble in the distance, the whole surface of the Cumberland seemed to swell and rise a little. The scene blurred. There must be ten or twelve guns in that lower battery, Grant conjectured, swiftly confident of accuracy, though the position he tried to observe was deep in the fog created by the remote firing. Thirty—thirty-two, he guessed, attempting to gauge, by attention to the volume of sound, what the weight of the shot might be. This talent for measured observation had come lately as an unpremeditated self-discovery, and he exulted, nervously, in its contradiction of his more doubtful measurement of men.

Under the stimulus of those colliding echoes, his mind functioned with a clearness of perception that eliminated all those constant personal confusions. If Donelson was taken—if Donelson was taken — Ignoring deferential companions, he turned his horse, and began to ride slowly back and forth along the river bank. Colonel Wood, who distrusted him respectfully, noted, in the ruddiness of his crude, worn, yet almost handsome face, the abstract glitter of blue eyes brilliant like a brutal adolescent's. The new, old-young commander was what the colonel called 'a caution,' a 'fool' in matters outside the army business, and coldly awkward in social life.

The winter afternoon was waning early. Smoke, like a flood of stained wool, jetted, almost soddenly, over the haze-filled woods, when, unexpectedly, the muffled cannonading ceased.

"Looks as if there's something wrong, General." Colonel Wood announced his misgivings politely, calmly, and, Grant facing him reluctantly, they stared at one another a minute. Grant, with vexation, felt the colonel's gaze 'wooden.' And the colonel experienced a familiar disturbed sense of Grant's adamant defiance of security.

"The *St. Louis* looks as though she's had a knock." Major Smithers, on foot, approached the two riders. He held his glasses in his outstretched hand and now offered them.

Reluctantly, Grant accepted the binoculars and looked at the river. Under the smutted sky, filled with charred reflections, he could make out, against his will, a boat drifting downstream toward him. "Um—we'll have to arrange to make a landing for them below here." Grant's hand, supporting the lenses, was just perceptibly unsteady. But when he desisted from this inspection, his features were taut again in a forced indifference. Strangely, the moment he became uneasy, he realized again the discomfort of the weather. The countryside, in the oppressive quiet, seemed to extend beyond his previous impression of it. And he was grateful for the presence of his orderly, for the presence of a company of infantry, idling restlessly near him in a screen of leafless bushes along the waterside. They helped him, in some way, to resist suspicion of present reality. The Grant he had read about in the newspapers was himself. He affirmed it cautiously. But it was as if, every moment, he must support a myth that might elude him. He glanced at the men. *They* believed. He would be capable of any ruthlessness which would sustain that faith of others in him, and he had endured so much to produce that faith that his sensations intoxicated, lifted him, as a 'leader,' above his own hesitant morality.

With a curt "Thanks," for the glasses, he pushed his horse a little nearer the greasy, scintillant river. There were round stones in the way on which the hoofs of the animal slithered, and Grant caught

61

up the bridle with a sharp jerk. The water was turning green in the dead twilight, and was blobbed and mottled with pallor. A bird shot up from the ground and passed into the upper, travelling fog. The raw odour of the cold, and the coming night flowed out of the wet pebbles. Grant's evaded desperation was like a stern, involuntary conceit. Donelson *had* to fall, by God. There was going to be a good, firm reason for McClernand's flattering jealousy.

IV

In order to escape the constant *bi-lip, blip, blip,* sounding dripping rain, Albert lay flat on his stomach, his arms under his chest, his chin tilted uncomfortably so that, beneath the shaggy, moisture-beaded cedars, he had an oblique view of the muddy, empty road that was the Nashville Pike. He had been hidden there since early morning, and the occasional pedestrians who had gone by had not given him the impression that they were the sort on whom he could call for aid. Yet, with a resolution which now exceeded reason and denied caution, he was determined on getting up North again.

Albert was the more bewildered by the restraints imposed on him, because he had volunteered for the Union, had been with Grant when Donelson was captured, and Clarksville and Nashville taken, and had not then been conscious that the army life interfered with freedom. Charlotte, too, had encouraged him to join the 'colours,' and her attitude, during the final months, had not prepared for him the reproaches contained in the last letter he had received from her. Her mother was ill, she had written, her father most unwell again, and, in despair at the condition of her family, without hope that Albert would ever see fit to return to Broughton-ville, she contemplated marrying Sylvius Cook, though she had refused his 'attentions' for so many years.

Albert, when reading the note in camp, had felt a wave of reproach flow through his mind so intensely that he was near hating her. He had been tired, but in a mood of confidence resulting from the Nashville victory, and had been looking forward to a furlough in the later spring. It was as though, ignoring all he had endured this winter, Charlotte, without any serious intention of becoming Sylvius's wife, had written the letter deliberately just to crush high spirits. It was the first time Albert had ever convicted her of petty motives—'downright maliciousness.'

As he lay in the damp silence under the cedars, he felt sleep and rest his right. But Charlotte's morbid attitude had driven him to take such a desperate step that he dared not indulge in so much as a moment's indolence. The rain had begun to fall more heavily. The twigs rattled and the leaden branches swayed and bent to the steady *pat-pat*. Albert's body was still sufficiently protected, but a chill web, sprayed from the heavy drizzle, netted his rigid features. His teeth chattered. Twice, when under marching orders, and much fatigued, he had thrown away his blanket and his overcoat, and he had long ago reached equality with the old campaigner who can lie on the ground in the rain all night without hut or tent to cover him. Admiration for General Grant had inspired Albert to undergo many miseries uncomplainingly. That made the present situation but the less acceptable to reason. It was not fair to an 'old' soldier, and a faithful fighter, that authority refused to advance six weeks the leave of absence which it had already promised him. Albert had used every 'influence,' every cajolery. And then he had put it plainly to the officer in charge. There was a temporary abatement of hostilities. If Albert did not get his furlough immediately, Charlotte, according to her letters, would be married before he could arrive at home again. Albert now recalled, desperately and viciously, the officer's curt final refusal, and his impassive face. The denial of the privilege had seemed doubly a signal of personal hostility because Lowes, Turner and Bert Wilson had, during the course of the war, gone to Broughtonville twice. It was gossip that General Grant, too officious after Donelson, had been reprimanded. Albert was one of the only six, who, in surreptitious mess talk, had defended the general against spiteful, unimportant critics. If there had only been some way of approaching Grant himself! But Albert had tried. He had attempted to speak with Grant in the Nashville streets, and had been rebuked by Billy Kennedy for the effort to go 'above' somebody's 'head.'

Albert fidgeted stiffly in the soaked deep foliage beneath the trees, and felt an animosity for General Grant, exceeding, for the moment, the painful, all-possessing desire for Charlotte. Yet, rather, was it an intangible enemy who stood between himself and relief from the anxiety that would not permit him to relax at night.

He had given up the effort to find warmth in his clothes, and to lie here stripped of warmth gave a sensation of helpless, almost demeaning nakedness. Then, again, the rain abated. In the increasing glare of midafternoon, the flicker of drops, through the strange, toneless light, became almost invisible. Or, the cracked sunshine caught in the branches glistening as with glassy fruit, and threads of mica were spun in the webs of spiders on the shaking bushes.

His desertion, looked at in one way, was irrational. Seen differently, humanly, while the men were idle—and he had only asked for a week at most—it was 'common sense.' How was it possible that, by this gesture so unmenacing to others, he became a criminal? He had run off once, he had been court-martialed and imprisoned in the guardhouse. He had run off yesterday for the second time, and he knew, with exactitude, that he was being hunted. Why, no man in his senses with a human mind and heart would treat a dog like this.

Albert was conscious of himself, of a fixed obsessed gaze that had come into his own eyes. It was because *they* would not let him see the world the same. Or was he the same, was anything the same? There was a strangeness in this dreary landscape, a strangeness in everything that he was doing, in himself, in Charlotte. He was no longer able to consider Charlotte as he used to know her. She was a mood, a feeling, a peculiar ingredient in an insanity. How was it to be explained—a necessity that nobody else could comprehend? He said to himself, "Charlotte," yet it was as if he addressed, not her, but a possession, an emotion, some part of himself. Often he was forced to conclude that he did not care about her as he had at all. How could he, when she did not know him, when she could even consider marrying Sylvius? What was a woman to you when she could torture you unmercifully, not even realizing that she did so.

He rolled to his side weightily, buried his face in the wet, and made his eyes grow dark. And he said, "Charlotte, Charlotte, Charlotte, Charlotte," like an incantation. It was like a hunger, this state neither of heart nor of stomach, which possessed him unspecifically. At times he would believe that, if anybody *understood* how he felt, the ban on his actions would be lifted. He had tried to tell them, and had failed, because, beyond that constant, "Charlotte," he had no words for it. His mind was heavy. He was stupid. It was as though he longed, not for ardent contact, but for some ineffable indifference which Charlotte's touch and nothing else could convey to him.

In camp, at night, he had caught himself in confident allusions to her. He had talked about her to Billy Kennedy boastfully. Not offensively, or disrespectfully, mind you; but he had felt so certain. There had been even a pleasure in his absence from her. It had been as if, in his supposed security, he had watched the future growing ripe. He had been honestly oblivious to casual other women, because, with them, nothing accumulated, nothing had 'meaning' beyond the moment. Perhaps he had wished to revenge himself on her for the discomforts of separation, and there had been that delicious harshness augmenting in his meditation on her. He was 'not a fool—not by any means a fool.' And he had loved Charlotte. She was small, she was a woman. There were things that he had wanted to do for Charlotte when she should 'belong' to him.

Albert pushed himself to his elbows, stared about him blindly, then rose unsteadily. There was a sound—a creaking sound, not rain, in the road out yonder. There was somebody coming. There was a cart coming. Tonight he would get as far as the Kentucky border. These sensations aroused by Charlotte were directly seated in his brain. And it was the first time, perhaps (since others had not understood him) that any man had felt like this. He was possessed, he was a deserter because of his possession. He was glad, not regretful. Anything to relieve him, anything to keep him moving. He must see Charlotte. He must hold Charlotte against him, closer and closer and closer, forever, so that he need never leave again. Yet the resuscitating of her queerly fading image left him more than ever balked. He hated the Charlotte that his senses could not hold, the Charlotte who evaded him by her intangibleness. He was escaping, somewhere, but not to her. They would never meet again. It was like a sickness she had brought on him. He could not forgive her. When you loved a woman, it was always so—as if you asked for pity. It was she and her 'callousness' that had brought him to this.

Around the bend which cut the road short, the enlarging heads of a pair of oxen had obtruded suddenly. The oxen, brows lolling massively under a double yoke, drew a laggard cart, and it was the piercing, continual whine of the heavy wheels that had arrested

Albert to unwilling heed. Announced by this ceaseless squeak of wooden axle pins, the dark beasts, crowned by vast arcs of bright horn, held his overwrought attention tormentingly. Toward the rear of the cart, walked the loose-boned negro driver, resting a jolted hand upon the tumbled boughs of dry cedar with which the vehicle was heaped. The negro marched somnambulistically behind his charges, his head bent limply, his eyes half shut. Over one lax shoulder, hung the rawdide lash of his dangling whip. He was hatless, ragged and barefooted.

Albert advanced abruptly from his hiding-place. He had discarded the cap and jacket of his uniform, but knew, with a kind of witless exultance, that his status was revealed by his pantaloons and boots. Niggers were shiftless, niggers were treacherous. But Albert had retained a rifle stolen from the guard. If that nigger disobeyed his orders he was going to shoot.

The oxen, their great doleful eyes ignoring him distrustfully through a mist of lashes, dragged on, slowly, rhythmically, their plush flanks quivering; and still the driver remained oblivious. Albert, now almost even with the little cavalcade, could stare directly into the beast eyes that, rolling, without emotion, saw everything. The animals swerved slightly. They were so close to him that he felt their gentle impassive breathing on his cheek. Beneath their narrowed, dusky foreheads, rubbery nostrils pouted in white flexible muzzles, and a dribble of spume was wafted from their steady, mournful respiration.

Albert loathed them. It was as if, between them and himself—they quiescent, and he docile in expectation of a friendlier world—there were something common. The driver was at least half man, and he could hate a man. A nigger was a creature on which the impulse of defiance could expend itself.

"Hey, you darky, halt there or I'll shoot." The nigger stopped, lifted a frightened, astonished face, and stared about him at the rainy, wintry fields bewilderingly. His whip slipped from his arm, slithered to the road, and curled there, fouled in the mud; and though, in a second glance, he had seen Albert, the man was so confused by the unexpected barrel of the rifle, that before replying to the aggressor, he leaned to retrieve the whip.

Albert, resisting the premonition that all he did was feeble, mistook the gesture for one of menace, and fired, wildly. In the second

66

after the shot exploded, he had the feeling that his mind 'went out.'

Again the rain had begun to fall. The cold, eager smell it brought seemed to pervade the still world with a kind of deathly animation. And the negro driver was lying sprawled uncomfortably, with his features buried in a filmed puddle. What Albert could not reconcile with this spectacle was that the oxen were going on, stolidly, carefully, unconcernedly, beyond the dew-feathered cedars, in the fleshy quiet, in the metallic tasting air. It was as if something were closing down invisibly about him, contracting about him. There was an enemy. But if it were not General Grant, if it were not even Major Healy, who had refused the furlough, who was it? You can't tell. You'll never know. You'll not even know why you killed that nigger—for he must be dead. And the feeling about Charlotte *would* come back. Albert wanted it to. He invited it. It was something to hold fast, when he saw her, when he had her, and he would rest and never think more about all these things. Charlotte, Charlotte, Charlotte, Charlotte, like a numbedness, like being dead and buried in something warm. No 'reason' about it, no having to 'figure' it out, though you'd kill her and yourself, too, if you didn't get it, Charlotte, Charlotte, Charlotte, Charlotte.

Then the wave of voluptuous horror, about her, about himself, about his present situation, ebbed. He walked to the 'nigger' and bent above him, 'flopped' him over carefully, so that his face showed, impervious like a mask; and it was disappointingly, frighteningly certain that he was still breathing. Albert wondered swiftly how he was ever to take away the 'nigger's' cotton trousers and put them on. If the darky, though only a darky, would but be certainly lifeless! Albert could not overcome the conviction that the man was suffering as he himself suffered, and it was disagreeable to be once more conscious of the icy rain which fell upon them equally. But why, when '*they*' had forced him to desperation, consider this isolated wretchedness? Albert refused to take responsibility for any matter. He was learning the way this world was 'run.' He fumbled miserably with some pins that held the tattered clothes. The rain came quicker. The light from the sky was morbid, radiant, icy-looking, of a dirty yellow. The rain shuffled in the bushes. And if he could see her, could speak to her, could touch, so that there was nothing about her he didn't know, so that she

67

belonged to him— He was begining to fear her. But that was the army, so impersonal, so uncomprehending. His worship for her was not like his newer admiration for General Grant. He did not believe in the letter she had written. She could not be so faithless. He pulled the trousers on himself, over his uniform. He hastened after the oxen, and the car that was whining far away before him. He had reached the point where the thing he was telling himself had lost all meaning. His feet thumped in the loose mud. He had left his rifle. He couldn't turn back where that nigger was.

v

Will Davis, Will Davis—that's my name. Pinned in the darkness, under the weight of debris, the stars, appearing through the flicker of some glowing signal burning in the ship itself, were like a delicious lacy flouncing—on Aunt Martha's black silk petticoat. Through a skeleton of wreckage, the bitter wind shuddered, but the night sky, brilliant with hurtled brands, with flying embers, with the reflections of the murky water, looked radiant as from the playing of concealed fountains of light. Even if the *Merrimac* had not yet withdrawn, he could lie here on the *Congress* decks forever, eternally, restfully, until he went to sleep again. Sleep and rest, sleep and rest. Upon his aching eyelids, the stars poured glitteringly their cups of snow. The coolness and the silence fell on the sounds he had heard that evening, upon the sights he recalled, upon the emotions that had seemed important to him, when he was told that the *Cumberland*, now somewhere yonder on the depths of swishing ocean, had begun to sink.

His own ship had been run ashore. He remembered that, and it accounted for the present quiet, for the faint rustle of a tide that he could not see, for this stationary feeling of security. But a smell disturbed him. The odor of charred timber was very strong and acrid. And a glare, suddenly lilting brightly against his face, showed him what he had forgotten: the snapped masts still reared up, the scorch-bitten fragments of the damp and fallen sailcloth still flapped in the unreal twilight, with some reddish, tinsel bits of dangling, smouldering rigging.

All at once he comprehended the existence of a body—*his*—and of the numbed torture of an oppressive mass lying on his legs. The ship was burning yet. It was hours since the *Beaufort* and the

Raleigh had run alongside to take off prisoners. But the Union battery on the land had driven away vanquishers who might have brought salvation. Something had happened. The *Beaufort* and the *Raleigh* had withdrawn in silence. The boats of his own ship had been lowered. Somehow he had not been able to follow his mates to safety. He recollected crazy fellows jumping into the water. He had tried to rise. Now, *now*, he must try to rise. He was conscious, unexpectedly, of blackened depths of sea below him. He could still get out. The ticking flames displayed a cloudy land, not distant—or—but for pain he might be already dead—did he imagine land?

There was a roaring in his ears. The girl in the leghorn bonnet walked down the pier. Aunt Martha said no single solitary star shines forth its way to cheer but it must throb with sorrow still and nourish all its care on its own altar and conceal the pangs that linger where boatmen *row*, row, *boat*-men *row*, floatin' down de *riv*-ah, uv de O-hi-*oh-h-h-h-h*, like a siren whistle. Before the fight, the whole fleet was visible at once, and in Boston Harbour when we left the whistles made high moans like iron harps of an-*gels*, because Will Davis's name, though undistinguished, marks peculiarity. Aunt Martha believes in Fate. F-a-t-e, fate, when she adopts a poor, orphan boy, nobody listens. Barges are mammoth drift. Aunt Martha says the girl does not love you they made a Walpurgis evening of the river in Cincinnati. He was ambitious and had read Faust. Because he was ambitious and had read Faust, and there were *storms* of smoke.

The whole ship began to shudder. People were shut up inside, *in themselves*. The sky turned black as a nightcap. When Will Davis saw two persons in intimate conversation, ignoring him, he *had* to know just what they talked about. People seemed to be talking everywhere. He could crawl to the rail and watch the brassy current flowing through the deep silence at the stern. The *Congress* must be floating out. Particles, red like agate, fell on either side of him. Aunt Martha understood his desire, when enlisted, to become a member of the crew on a sailing vessel. And the *Congress* was an 'old one.' This was her last ro-ose o-of *summer*. Not like that ugly little new invention he had hear-rd *a-bout*. The water was full of iron cows mooing. There were deep, snuffling noises from a long way off. But, if he could jump—

He managed to stand, leaning, and teetered, with his face half hanging over the sea of watery fire that glided past. The shore was like a shadow, faintly glistening to the right. He felt that, bending farther, he could stretch his leaden hand to it. It smelled of grass. And it was chilly, peaceful; while the waves were alive with things that moved, that seethed. The current looked enraged. He had always wanted to get away from home, where there was more excitement—like you re-ead, *unconfined*. But that was not war. The steamers, going down the river, used to bellow at night, guttural brays, that dug into your bowels. They carried thin wings of gold, spread stiff over the ripples and never breaking. Decks were on fire with lamps. Compact like houses, coughing silent soot clouds, people went sailing by you, and it was a pleasure to realize that you did not know them, that they were not the people you were acquainted with. The world was so much, much, much, much larger—

Around the *Congress,* where he stood, the ocean drew away, muffled. It was too hot in the fire. There was more and more room in the quiet yonder, if only he dared jump. Maybe people would learn about this in the papers. Yet he was disappointed. There was another place he had meant to go to where the ship was *not* like the burned, gutted shell of an insect, when the *Cumberland* sucked all down with her in the afternoon, that the moon dews with unnoticed drops. It was adventure, sure enough, as he had longed for, but they had played a trick on him.

He came, in his thoughts, to the end of a blind alley all rosy with pain. The planks sent up streamers near him, making blisters on his face. It was the most horrible drought ever imagined. The water slap-sticked plumply under the lowering hull. He could feel the deck listing, water coming up through it, producing in his senses a kind of burning seasickness.

Then there was a tearing reverberation, and before the end happened, his mind, widened to the new sound, felt the obscuring darkness swept away, and the whole Atlantic, clean, like a silvered palm at morning, upon his heart, so it could not beat. The beautiful silver deadness, only imagined, swept across his brain. There were other noises, thumping, blaring reports of the explosion. He heard nothing. He had always wanted to be a sailor. Not just like the ordinary ignorant American. He had been everywhere.

III

*T*HE *most obstinate antislavery man, if fair-minded, will grant,
when he understands the argument, that African slavery is
not the cause, but only the occasion of the Southern protest. The
cause for which our soldiers fight and shed their blood is that once
sacred to all who called themselves Americans—constitutional
right. It is but an accident of circumstance that the right to the
labour of slaves happens to be the issue on which the sacred authority of the law has been assailed. If the North, in its greed and
envy, had not attacked us on this point, there would have been
some other excuse. How can it appear that the aim of the South in
carrying on this war is to perpetuate slavery, unless it be proven
that the aim of Northern aggression is to end that bondage? The
Black Republican Party has expressly declared that it proposes
no interference with slavery in those States in which that institution is an accepted one.*

*"Brethren, I will be criticized for using the pulpit and the altar
as a platform from which to expound my political views. No—I
would have been criticized some time back. I can't believe I will be
now. There is a fight in progress, and I am in the fight. And it is a
just fight, God's fight. He is behind us. So what more fitting than
to fight the Devil here and now? His name, at the present moment,
is Treachery to the Confederate Cause. He hides behind a so-called
liberality.*

*"Brethren, I am not liberal. God's Word is Truth, and Truth
when uttered, has no qualifying phrases. It must be spoken plainly,
and in few words, and the place you all come to, to hear Truth
spoken, is the pulpit in your own church. It does not need a crisis
to justify the expounding of plain Truth by me in this place which
is God's House where Truth ever shall abide. And no fear of the
outrageous Yankees shall ever bridle my expression.*

"The North's policy would not make one slave less in all Amer-

ica, unless by enhancing the misery of the slave's present condition until he is exterminated altogether. Nor would the South's demand that the African race be allowed to labour in the evolving territories, if granted, make one slave more in all America, unless by ameliorating the slave's condition and saving some alive who otherwise will perish. Our enemy has no friendship for the black man, but is moved by the enmity to his white protector. That, brethren, is the attitude of the Northerner, the revelation of his hitherto long concealed pretension to dictate to us.

"Black Republicanism is a system of intense hostility to the African race. It persists in saying that the African is a citizen of the Union, but has refused him the enjoyment of the common territory in any form. Most Black Republicans admit that slavery is the mode best adapted to the present welfare of the negro. Almost every Black Republican State formed out of the national territory has legislated against the immigration of negroes. Black Republicanism always means that the African shall not exist at all on American soil. The uniform shibboleth of this party is the assertion that this continent must belong exclusively to the white race. The proposal universally made by its demagogues—and especially by that ignoramus, that master demagogue, Abraham Lincoln, whom it has chosen to lead its agrarian hordes, is, 'Overthrow the institutions of the South, exclude the negro from its industry and take his place.' As to what would be the destiny of millions of humble God-fearing Africans if the treacherous policy of free-soil should be established, our enemies have no answer other than a sardonic shrug. Others, more candid, have pointed to the fate of the Indian tribes, wasted to nothing before the criminally expended energy of the whites.

"The hideous meaning of Black Republicanism, therefore, is the oppression and enslavement of the humane master for the purpose of exterminating the contented comfortable servant. Black Republicanism has made the war. It is Yankeeism. To the holy cause of defending our land against those contemptuous of the spirit of the old constitution—the Constitution which inspired our revolutionary forbears with the true conception of the duties of a great nation—on which our own Confederate States are based—a beloved leader and general, Albert Sidney Johnston, has just sacrificed his life. Bereft as we are, by the loss, last week at Shiloh, at Pittsburg Land-

72

ing, of this noble man, commiserating as we do all the patient, uncomplaining fathers, mothers, wives and families who are mourning the dead fallen in this battle in which the Federal forces claim themselves victorious, we yet have cause, brethren, for exultance. What appears to the Yankees an occasion for self-congratulation, is really the sanctification of our cause. The flesh is corruptible. But for those who have humbled themselves to receive the true message of Christ, who tells us that the Spirit lives for ever, the vanquisher, flushed with earthly triumphs, is the plaything of his own illusion. Like the blood flowing from Immanuel's veins, the Southern blood shed about that little log church at Shiloh a few days ago, has flowed for us only to make us stronger in our conviction of righteousness. Brethren, the spiritual cause feeds on defeat, or what, to the spiritually unobservant, looks like defeat. Albert S. Johnston, to whose memory all of us incline our heads in spontaneous reverence, shall lead us and our armies to a glory of belief in right and justice never before imagined. Justification? With all the apparent truth that is on our side, we need no justification.

"Any honest man who has been so unlucky as to absorb the perverse dogma which says that the relation between master and slave is unrighteous, will admit that this relation, be it right or wrong, was not instituted by the Confederates, nor at their option, but was forced on them by the greed of the Federal and British slave-traders, when the tyranny of Great Britain thrust slavery upon her unwilling colonies. Since then, it has existed by recognized laws, guaranteed by a Constitution which the people of the North were bound to observe, and it is natural, yea, incumbent on the self-respect of the South to resist usurpation of those Constitutional prerogatives, even by forming a separate confederation of those states in which every citizen, like General Jackson, disdains to argue from the premise that the relation of master to slave is unrighteous in itself. We have been told that slavery here among us makes a human being a chattel. This is false. Every slave law of this state, and of most of our states, treats the slave as a responsible being and not a thing. If the involuntary labour of a human being cannot be property, then every parent, husband, and master of an apprentice in the civilized world is a transgressor. Woe to them who bear false witness against us. It is asserted that slavery outrages

73

the golden rule. Laws oblige the master to render to his servants a liberal return for their labour, and the slave can command of his master a lifelong maintenance of himself and his family, secured against every contingency of sickness and decrepitude—surely, a better recompense than the African could win as a free negro.

"It has been charged that slavery makes the master the irresponsible possessor of the chastity of his female slaves. Can we, who feel beating about us the wings of those fiery spirits who have given all in this mortal life to the refutation of such charges, offer anything less than our all to the cause of defending decent, lawabiding people against the imputation of gratuitous immorality? We know that the law fences around the chastity of the woman servant, safeguarding her even against the possible violence of her own master, and by the same sanctions and the same means that protect the white lady. Even if there were no benevolent government to take her part, however, the negress working for a good Southern master would be amply safeguarded by the function of those traditions which make it second nature for a Southern white man, and a gentleman, to reverence the purity of womankind above all other things. The law does require the servant to accept the chastisement of his master. But does not the wife yield to the judgment of the husband, the child to the parent? Why, it is even said in the North that our laws forbid a master to teach his slaves literature, whereas, actually, as many of our slaves can read, and do read, God's book, as of the agricultural peasantry of boastful England. Shame that it has been published abroad that our institutions forbid the marital and parental relations among slaves. Shame that it is rumoured of us that our laws consign our faithful servants to concubinage. There are instances of barbarity, even of murder, practised against slaves, but they are punished just as similar instances of outrage against free persons are punished. Slavery has civilized and elevated the African race more rapidly than any other philanthropy has elevated any other pagan race in the world. It has brought converts to the Christian religion in numbers which no mission to the savage, heathen portions of the world could ever reach. Three generations ago, all were besotted pagans. If the slave has suffered in slavery, he suffered also in heathendom: but his suffering among us has brought him spiritual profit.

"Christ Himself did not condemn slavery. His apostles admitted

74

slave-holders to the church and exacted no repentance or renunciation from them. Christian slaves, in the old days, were commanded to obey and honour Christian masters. The runaway was remanded to his injured owner. If slavery is a sinful thing, then the Bible is a sinful book, because it supports slavery. Let the Black Republicans answer that. None of the great masters of moral science, classic or scholastic, ever condemned slavery. None of the luminaries of the Church, patristic or reformed, ever condemned it. The condemners of slavery had no mouthpieces until the dogma of modern abolition was born of atheistic parentage amidst the radical cutthroats of France in the Reign of Terror. Moses legalized slavery among God's chosen people, at the very moment he set them aside to holiness. Christ, the Great Reformer, lived and moved amidst its teachings which he approved. When we come before the judgment seat, the testimony of Christians, and not the testimony of Black Republicans with their sop-offering of compensated emancipation, will be listened to.

"Let me give you this last message as if from the lips of your own dead in Shiloh churchyard: Don't give up. Don't be discouraged. Stand by the beliefs of those who are gone, which are your own beliefs. Keep faith with the watchful soul of General Johnston, and with the wakeful human spirit of our President. He who loses his life shall surely find it, and we yet have all the benefits given to those on whom the Holy Ghost has descended with unwritten promises. Let us pray for our dead. Let us pray for ourselves— for courage, for endurance, for humility rather than puffed-up pride, and for an intelligent understanding by which we may know how to obey God's will for us here on earth, and realize the meaning of His Universe. In the name of the Father, Son, and Holy Ghost, Amen.

"Today we are going to forego the usual application of our offering, and anything that you can freely give to us will be turned over to the Ladies' Guild of the Confederate Hospital Society.

"Let your light so shine before men that they may see your good works and glorify Our Father who is in Heaven."

II

One, two, three, four, five, six, seven, eight *sheep*. The room was gone: the ormolu clock on the marble mantel, the chest of

75

drawers, the chair, all faded out. There was nothing but darkness, on which was written, like a message, one red ember glowing steadily in an unseen grate. He turned wearily under the oppressive comforter, and began to count again. The sheets smelled of lavender. It was night outside, and springtime, but the open window, against the blackness of imagined rain clouds, remained unmarked. When he closed his eyes a dimness, like the soft glow of some inarticulated comprehension, pressed on his folded lids. One, two, three, four, five, six, seven, eight sheep. They were pulpy spots. They wavered softly against his stare, and it was as though he were staring at objects under water while a tide pushed fluctuatingly upon his sea-drenched face.

It was more than an illusion. Lately, he had often the feeling that Predestination made his own efforts useless, that the importance of human decisions existed only in man's vanity. He could not adapt himself to the conviction. There was a coldness, a hardness in his nature which refused humility. The audience was 'cheap.' He knew it was 'cheap,' though in the world's sense now, it was big enough. He had not 'got over' his love of 'acting,' that was the truth. He had 'acted' when, as a youth, he had improvised his pseudo-legal speeches. He was acting yet. But there was a fear—he couldn't say just what it was he feared. He wanted to find out something not yet known to him, to 'lay hold' of something. It all slips away—that was the feeling. And sometimes he believed that, at the time Anne died, the 'thing,' whatever it was he sought, had evaded him finally. The fact was he was 'too conceited to take failure.' He never spoke the thought aloud—but he could not bear to be ignored. At home, where God knows there had been no excuse for him, he had always wanted to boast. He had been exasperated constantly by his father's whining confession of inadequacy, and he had admired his stepmother's good sense and patience while resenting these qualities. *You* can do it, was the feeling. Of course as long as you all sit down and accept inferiority there is no help for you. You deserve to be downtrodden. You let folks look down their noses at you. Well, I won't. I'm smart. If any of you fellows believe you can outlast me, be the contest with you of wit or muscle, you've got to show me. I'll never take your word.

I studied hard. I liked to have them think it all came easy to me, but I studied hard. I couldn't stand to have them spouting about a heap of things I never heard of. And when they were mean to the ones who took meanness meekly, I calculated that they would treat me just as bad as that, given the opportunity. There's something cussed in the human animal that runs to bullying.

One, two, three, four, five, six, seven sheep. The white spots grew with a glitter, and moved into strange positions, like the pattern on the hidden carpet. The thought of Anne, after all these years, was not so much the tantalizing recollection of a person lost and gone, as the keynote which revived resentment. That was something I couldn't get over. I had made up my mind I was going to get whatever I set my mind to, and here was a defeat I had to swallow. Death was a little bigger than you, Abe Lincoln.

Yet now, when I have hidden it so long, like shame, why is it sweeter? In the position of a public servant a man has so little left for himself. It is better, I don't know why, to dwell on Anne and pain, than on present glory. Funny, Mary's grief about Willie didn't soften me, didn't bring us together. I guess I was jealous that she took on so much. It seemed to separate us. I wanted to believe that the capacity for grieving belonged only to me. I couldn't give Mary the credit for caring for our child as I did. She never understood how Anne's loss affected me, and I guess I never wanted her to understand. It was the same way when Willie was sinking, and she was standing there in that black lace and satin dress, trying to get the doctor to persuade her that the boy was well enough for her to leave him while the reception was going on. I never let on how I regarded the performance, but I guess I wanted her to go downstairs again. But there is something better in me. There's something in me that I've never shown, that they've never guessed at.

The wind flowed, with vague motions of shadow, into the still room. He pulled off his nightcap, and lay there with his brow turned to the soft, invisible agitation that sucked the curtains in. There was guilt in this mood of self-investigation, self-commiseration. Maybe those who were dead—the many on both sides who died—knew the excuse for him. As he looked at it sometimes, in his bitter moods, there was neither justification nor explanation of his selfishness. An old man, philosophizing for himself, out there in the backwoods, led a life more dignified and reasonable. He

—the other—could live without self-assertion. This desire to have your will with everybody was simple obstinacy. If pride was as big as it ought to be, it could ignore what people said and thought.

Again, discontent like this seemed downright ingratitude to the Deity. And in this appearance of being fair and generous, he indulged himself. He had believed once that, when the time came, he would 'show' them. But the time never came. Was he a fool, to be more discontented than the men in his cabinet with the way the war was going? Stanton, for instance, never repined. He saw practical affairs on one side, and things of the so-called mind-and-spirit, on the other—that is in the most high-falutin' sense. One sheep, two sheep, *three* sheep.

When the raw spring air washed on your face like this, you were obscure, insignificant. Defeat itself was chastening. It wasn't that a mere conquest over Douglas had inflated him. Damn Douglas. Who is Douglas for me to measure myself by him? Who is any man? I have done most of the things that I ought not to have done, but have not lost my self-respect. A man is as he is born. But if the standard is not success in human affairs, what *is* the standard? I have looked at myself fairly and squarely. I'm not setting up pretensions. I will show no mercy to those who display pretensions. Even to know my limitations and my type of bunkum, isn't what I mean. It's even the devil to be too cocksure about being honest. Well, then, have it that way if you want to that I'm never honest. I lie better than the others—that's all. I know I'm a plain, ornery, fallacious human, and I see to it that no other humans set up any condescensions toward me on that account. I'm not a groveller and never will be. Mary wanted to get on, and so did I. I've kept myself out of some of the things she's fallen into, because I've kept my sense of humour. I can't boast of any social finesse and I'm not going to try to acquire any. It's by that sort of trivial hocus-pocus that people create imaginary distinctions and falsify so much justice as there is on earth by dealing out honours to men and women who haven't a profound thought in their heads. I demand that people have some real feeling about something, or that they keep out of my way. The law dinned it into me pretty thoroughly that it is the cutest orator that wins rather than the man with most right on his side, or even gumption of another kind.

And if present power had gone to my head, the way it might affect a man who had not dealt so much with facts, and hard facts, and had not been so impressed by the seamy side of life, I might get the notion that I could overthrow the ideas of society as it is today and reconstruct a better civilization.

He stirred. He was so wide awake now, his eyes expecting the daylight, that it was a pain to keep fixed so unbeholdingly his pupils tensely opened to penetrate what would not dissolve before them. He had to meditate on narrow personal matters to give himself an instant's relief from these pressing problems that nobody could solve. It had been said that he vacillated on the slavery question. It was certainly true that he felt the most acrid antagonism toward the sentimentalizers of the 'nigger.' As a poor white, he *knew* niggers. He had been thrown with niggers in a position lower than equality with them. There had not been many folks 'back home' who owned niggers, thank Heaven, but wherever the hardworking white man had a nigger to deal with he was competing with shiftless, treacherous opponents. Lincoln assured himself that he did not care a 'tinker's damn' what his Southern critics said of his upbringing. Such beginnings offered advantages. As the result of a poverty-stricken youth, Lincoln knew where he 'stood.' And he knew where he stood especially in relation to the nigger, and to effects of slavery and slave labour on the life of the competing whites. He would like to get rid of slavery altogether. But he would also like to get rid of the nigger altogether. As long as the nigger stayed in the country, the program of emancipation would need to proceed slowly. In a way, it was hard to resist the temptation of a lesson to the South, but the truth was, the whole country would suffer disintegration if a group unconditioned for freedom should be suddenly turned loose on the community.

Lincoln wondered, though, if he had any real reason to feel so superior to a nigger; and there were certainly people from the surroundings that had bred him who had not evolved much beyond the nigger's idea of civilization and advancement.

The fire had gone out long ago, but in the dead grate a twig snapped suddenly. His lank body convulsed, for a second, involuntarily. Recently, he had discovered himself in a state of weakness which he would have 'eaten' his 'head' rather than admit to. He was a prey to the most horrible depressions. If anybody ever dared to commiserate him, he always wanted to joke, to 'put them off.' And he was not satisfied until, afterward, he had embarrassed them a little by showing them, lightly, as though it were unimportant to him, his position as a great man. He *did* believe that there was some literary value in his stories. Yet that was not why he told them. It was his inability to talk about himself, directly, that made him speak in parables.

To Anne—Oh, well, he had been as little frank to her, as to any one else. He never could forgo the effort to impress her, even when by no more than foolishness. He had seen many a young fellow in love, and he supposed they all looked forward to the beginning of a new existence with the beloved, and the anticipation doubtless, with the opportunity, did not materialize.

Yet his feeling for her *had* been different. He had that conviction about himself whether or no—that nothing he felt was quite duplicated in the feelings of others. He *might* be mistaken. He did not take to fellows in rôles like those acted by Booth—Julius Caesar or Macbeth. He was not 'cut out for a hero.' He supposed, as he had been told, that he was the ugliest man alive. Despite being the ugliest man alive, he had shown people what he wanted, and, for the most part, had gotten what he wanted—even of women. He had wanted Mary enough at one time, too. And he still acknowledged the attraction for him of a pretty face—though he would rather admire a woman for doing her duty in life than for cutting a swath as a simpering society beauty.

The night was breaking. Beyond the smooth, livid window, he perceived, flowered suddenly, the black blossoms of a budding tree. With this futile dawn, and the shimmer of a growing clarity, making the room that had merged its contours in the same obscurity which lapped his mind, grow disagreeably definite with hostile furnitures, came the sense of wasted hours, febrile exhaustion. And about what? There was enough to obsess him in the daytime. He need not think at night. It would soon be time to rise. Then, as usual, in assuming his daily garb, he would feel that he assumed a cunning, became, in short, what they expected him to be—the man of plain, glib speech, with the ability to twist his audience, to appeal, at the right moment, for popularity. He hated them for considering him that. He had to make them admit he could do what they wanted—but there was always that something more

80

left out. Like Brown—John Brown was a born fool. He got drunk on the idea of reforming and got himself strung up as a traitor. Recklessness is just about the easiest thing there is to indulge. And the idiot didn't see where his own folly was leading him until he got, literally, to the end of a rope. Then it was too late to turn back and he died like a martyr. They would be glad enough—some of them—to give me the same end. If I could fool myself into believing I was accomplishing something I could be a first-rate victim of a popular insanity. Unfortunately, I know myself too well, and know I'm too good for that kind of thing. I could never see how a man could get into the habit of thinking himself bigger and more important than he is. If the complications go on, though, I'll have to save myself somehow. Liberate the darky in the end, I guess, no matter what the result. An emancipation proclamation would certainly be the right answer to some of these libel-sellers. State your baldest opinions to some foreign diplomat and you can be sure he'll read into them some meaning you never thought about.

My God, he was tired. Reflection through the night brought him to the morning with a sense of labour accomplished. When the hour came for breakfast, he was just ready to abandon himself to ease, and to sleep on again. Suppose Grant can be depended on. I began by supporting him out of contrariness, but he is another man without frills who is justifying his existence despite the cultured carpers. And I couldn't stand being licked by the veriest cub in Gentryville.

I'm so tired. It must have begun to rain. The rain was boiling gently in the dawn that was like a colourless twilight. A small empty moon, invisible through the darker hours, now bulged its frail shell in a web of mist. He got up, uneasy in his awkward length of nightshirt, and walked to the window. Milky, as if sunk in moat water, the shell of moon cast its sicklied pallor beyond the White House gardens and upon wet roofs. An icy lemon-tinted streak was beginning to widen over the damp houses. Gutters on cornices had commenced to emit, jerkily, beery gushes of froth. Suddenly, across the dripping distances, the reverberations of a drum bounded, carried above the sounds of drizzle. The din, widening remotely, seemed, all at once, as the tinny glare of day expanded, to fill and crowd the whole green morning. A fife, struggling to achieve exact melody, soared, in irrelevant minuteness, on the waves of incessant, muddied undertone. The shrill, precise notes of the fife stabbed through some numbness of sour discouragement. Tears sprang to his eyes. His body still lethargic after the time spent tossing on the bed, he shivered as with some uncontrollable elation which the pointed tune engendered. There were soldiers passing down the street. In gradual diminishment of rhythm, the drum thumps, underscored by the shuffle of feet, ebbed. The fife notes shattered against the adamant spaces of the city, and the rain again, with its gentle sizzle, in the tonelessly augmenting daylight, became predominant.

With a stubborn instinct of caution, Lincoln resisted that unwilled instant of emotion. Enthusiasms about the justice of the cause were 'not for him.' And who, after all, was to thank him for the responsible attitude he was taking? People liked ornate oratory, the suggestion to act without the consideration of consequences. Who was there to talk to about this matter? Reason, common sense were the most despised of attributes. And yet there *was* a reason—Something, Somebody, somewhere listened to the unspoken thing. He felt too utterly lost to contemplate the continuance of his present existence without the hope, sometime or other, of a new discovery. People speaking in a sophisticated language he was unaccustomed to, just 'provoked' him, drove him to sarcasms disproportionately bitter. It was all as 'plain as daylight,' anyway. They dressed their paucity of feeling in elaborations of a new tongue. Yet, if—if, really—if he could find somebody he could respect completely—even then would he be able to acknowledge that he came to them seeking? No, unless they 'understood' him, unless they happened to be like him at bottom, he would acknowledge nothing that could be 'used against' him. He supposed distrust was bred in his bones. If he could only show them by what he *did*—if only, by the end of the war, there would be discovered, through his efforts, somewhere, greater charity. Because he could respect them only in so much as they respected him, just as he was, born to his faults as they were born to theirs. And he would rather die than bend the knee one iota to anybody, *anybody*. That awful hard sense of compelled inadequacy was coming back with the contemplation of the day's round of office. Maybe it was liver. Perhaps he needed sulphur and molasses. There was something wrong with him. At any rate, he would

82

rather explain himself that way than play the grotesque hero with the broken heart. He would keep his questioning to himself. Let them think he had a bilious turn of mind. Reserve was a curse. A man with a play-actor's whiskers who could talk about himself to ladies, had the best of it. Mary would be on his side. Poor Mary! Yet why in blazes I pity her, I cannot say. Of the two of us, she has made the most success of her life. She has what she wants —with the exception of me. And I'm too derned grandiose to be satisfied with the small part I am capable of fulfilling. Anyway, if I'm a fool, I'll be the first to find it out—the first to laugh at myself, thank God.

III

Melinda gazed, with belligerent ennui, at the thick, toneless water of late afternoon. Oh, this sea, this sea, that had so long stood between her and the gratification of all ambition, that had laid all its unconquered wastes to intervene when she had embarked with her new, young husband on the fateful—now she termed it 'fatal' journey to the California coast! Nine years, nine years of struggle, nine years of what might well be considered 'penury.' Little had she realized her blessings and the comfort of her life with 'Auntie Williams,' back in Mimms. She had been nicely 'taken in,' she felt, by Thomas's self-confidence. He had displayed not a single virtue of the 'bread-winner.'

There he was on the bridge where Captain Dugan had invited him. You could always depend on Thomas to find an opportunity for 'airing his views to every one in sight.' Melinda saw the captain as a man of such hard mercenary sense that she doubted he could have great sympathy for Thomas's 'flights of oratory.' She stared distantly up at the two. Her husband was in profile, yet, even with his features only half apparent in the gilded vagueness of declining light, she detected the expression which accompanied earnest speech. Sensations of shame always overcame her when Thomas became serious too publicly. She was willing to humour his vanity in private, but, when she beheld him 'making a fool of himself before strangers,' it was with faint shudders of repugnance that she observed him. Such 'treasures of heart and mind' as she believed herself capable of offering him, he had never once discovered. If ever, for an instant, he made himself impressive, she felt guilty relief. She was convinced that she had done her best to help him, but that he was too unmindful to appreciate her efforts. There he was, giving a political harangue, when Captain Dugan did not care a thing about the Southern cause, but would be thankful to eliminate it from the conversation. He is blockade-running solely for the purpose of making money, and if the ship is searched and there is any question made about our presence here, he will give us up without a scruple. Captain Dugan was always most polite to Melinda. If Thomas were not always interfering she would, she was certain, be able to 'handle' the commander adequately. Yet this passage from Porto Bello, and by way of Martinique, she had not enjoyed. How different all 'from her anticipation'! And to think that she must confess to 'Sister Donie,' that, while Thomas had been out prospecting, she had kept a boarding-house. Even as a surgeon, he had not made money. In Sacramento he had practised for 'a pittance.' And if he were flattered by a patient, he could be cajoled into rendering all sorts of services for which he would receive no money recompense. Thomas listened to 'anybody.' He wished to be considered generous and, exasperated by her insistence on the responsibility both bore for the two little girls, called her 'nagging,' or 'petty.'

Yes, she might have guessed what was before her. On the voyage out he had spent the very last of the money he had brought from Tennessee in assisting that 'wretched Grainer family.' How well she remembered it all—the shooting scrape in which the little Creole, Blanchard, had been wounded, and the 'horrid Grainer,' the agressor in the brawl, kept down in the hold in chains when the boat put in! The memory was nauseating. At that time she had been 'in a delicate condition.' But Thomas, expanding to appeals for pity, had ignored utterly her dependence on him. She would never get over a feeling that, when their first child, a son, had died in teething, it had 'served Thomas right.' That did not prevent her, however, from feeling sorry for herself. Rising from a bench on which she had been seated, she stared downward, in the dimming glow, at Agnes and Euphemia. She would do all she could to save her little daughters from the miseries almost invariably accompanying 'woman's lot.' Though she supposed that 'Donie,' married to Thomas's 'selfishly' prospering brother, Edwin, did not think about such things. Melinda pursed her lips decidedly. If Thomas volun-

84

teered as an army surgeon, it was likely that she and the children would be obliged to return to Mimms again, and subsist, for a time, at least, on 'hated charity,' in Edwin's house. Melinda did not intend to 'kotow' to her family. She had decided that. It was very possible prosperity had 'gone to Donie's head.' And to think that Thomas had allowed his daughters to be maintained, during the whole year past, on Edwin's money. Melinda had borrowed it secretly, but Thomas, if a 'self-respecting' husband, would not 'drive' her to such measures. When she got back home, and was 'in Edwin's power,' she didn't doubt that he would 'gloat.'

At least she had escaped California. Thomas, of course, in his 'perversity,' would not admit a single fault there. *He* never made mistakes. He would allow himself to 'sink to any depth of folly,' but he was always right. Oh, men, men, men! If it were not for the 'foresight of the wives and mothers' in what a state the world would be! Why, she owed this needed journey to secure the children's 'schooling' to a national calamity. Had Thomas not been convinced that his country could not do without him, California would have been a final resting place for all of them. Thomas had secured a loan for the expenses of the voyage, but only because the 'call of honour' justified him. Dear little Agnes and Euphemia, with no 'cultured advantages'! She would not forgive him. And how she longed to quit this ship with all its dangers, and to press her feet once more on 'terra firma'! Or did she, did she! A return to the 'bondage' of their former poverty would be another misery.

Agnes and Euphemia, fatigued by hours of 'trotting' about the decks were curled up where a blanket had been spread for them beside some rigging; and had gone to sleep together. Melinda thought it 'very pretty,' the spectacle of the two young things, one three and one seven, huddled protectingly against one another, with that abandon of childhood which no maturity can emulate. Their bodies were limp, their lids drooped tightly, and their fat faces were lifted to the evening dews, to the last sombre glitter in the red-ribbed sky.

Was there not, indeed, a certain beauty in all family life? Melinda, resolving that Euphemia resembled her, was flattered to a sudden melting, melancholy tenderness.

Smells of onions frying floated to her from the galley—the very odours of the *Martha Addams*. Her throat constricted. She could

85

not 'rave' about the ocean and the evening. If she did so, Thomas would only listen to her abstractedly. And she felt angry. Her cheeks were hot to the evening wind. The stillness, the emptiness of evening so reminded her of *'life's* emptiness.' Or, as she mis-quoted suddenly, 'after life's fitful fever comes a time like this.' Rest, rest, rest—when the weary are at rest. But she did not wish to rest. Why did Thomas always treat her as if she were already old? She longed to enrage him. She was satisfied when she enraged him. He called her 'nagging,' but, if she seemed to 'carp' at him, it was her rebuke for his obliviousness. She was *not* 'selfish.' She calmed herself. She laid her plump, worn palm upon her breast. 'Abnegation' was her lot. It was for the 'little ones' her heart was always aching. When she was dead, when Agnes and Euphemia were grown, would they know, would they remember all their 'dear kind mamma' had endured for them?

The *Atlantide* veered slightly to port. Melinda noted the changed course, and observed, as well, an unfamiliar heaviness on the horizon line. Land! For how many days had she looked for this! She felt so weak her knees began to tremble. Some one must sup-port her. She was too excited, too unhappy, too filled with doubt, anxiety. She glanced at the bridge where the figures of Thomas and the captain were growing dark and bulky. This incident also reminded her of another sight of foreign shore and ocean, so long ago. She must cry, she must speak, she must wake the children up. She could not bear it. This, she was almost certain, was 'the dear Virginia coast.' A sailor tramped by, and she stared after his rugged back reproachfully. Ah, was she born, in poetry, to misery, to agony! Could a soul be doomed, while in its prime, to everlasting loneliness?

The shore sprang forward. In blurred, rolling trees, it crashed higher on the rosied water. The *Atlantide* swam evenly into a channel marked for sailors, and, on either side of her, the land reared, intimate with dimming green, and close.

A buoy protruded from the tide. Like a parrot, mincing ponder-ously, rocking monotonously, teetering, on stiff, spread legs, on its hidden perch, the buoy heaved unceasingly: and a single, broken note, reiterated, like a leaden cry of wonder, from some body buried, under, *under*, beneath the jellied, carmined surface of the Sound, which the senseless motion could never disturb.

86

Melinda's excitement became oppressive. Was some voice speaking to her from the grave, saying, gone, gone, gone—all gone forever? The past has floated from you like this still horizon. You can never bring it back. Gone is your youth. Gone all your faith in Thomas. While the mists of evening draw on your unnoticed life, and wrap you and your prematurely demised children in a winding sheet.

If Thomas would come to her now, she could love him. She could forgive him 'everything.' Who was she to protest against Fate, or to cry to God who had willed it thus? Oh, penitence and sorrow are a woman's life—indeed, indeed. As the dark, protesting land rolls by upon the dying west, so do a woman's dreams retreat. Anguish, anguish , but beauty still. He came upon her and his lids were touched with sight. He gazed upon his patient helpmeet and was astounded by her beauty. He sought through foreign lands and climes, and here, at home, by his own hearth, found what he quested for. Mimms will be better than California. (Melinda dared not quite believe it. She was feeling ill again.)

She was rudely interrupted. Hearing footsteps, she faced about quickly, and saw Thomas, descending from the bridge, approaching her with set features across the glinting deck.

Obstinately determined, he was hurrying toward her. So was the dream of twilight shattered! Reproachfully, antagonism to what he might say aroused by his very glance, she awaited him. Yet, for the moment, she invited rather than dreaded familiar hostilities. So much Thomas had offered to him that he could not see!

Halting beside her, he addressed her, without preamble, in that tone of reprimand which anticipated a chronic opposition to his authority. He seldom felt it advisable to communicate to her the assemblage of reasons from which his conclusions for action were drawn. With shining, decisive eyes commanding her warily, he laid his bony grip on her well-nourished arm. "You and the children must go below at once. Captain Dugan has sighted what may be a coast patrol, and if we are located and boarded, you must keep out of view. Agnes! Euphemia! Don't let them lie sprawled there in the way of the sailors. Go and wake them up."

Melinda was frightened. Perhaps alarm had filled her eyes with tears. But she gazed on him resentfully. She had never wearied of a satisfaction in his superior energy, in his physical imperiousness.

87

If only there were more—more—and she could 'swoon' upon his bosom, yielding all her female weakness to his 'fiery intellect.' "I don't believe you," she said. "You are trying to shock me, Thomas. I shall ask Captain Dugan if there is any basis for such a panic." She longed to obey him, to be 'overpowered.' But she held back sulkily, her bright blue eyes darting sparks of malice, of disappointment in his behaviour. Oh, how she could revere a husband had he been more dignified!

"Don't be a fool, Melinda," Thomas replied shortly, baffled into merely staring at her, when, embarrassed by a voluptuous quality in her regard, he dashed from her side, and bent himself to rouse his daughters. "Agnes! Euphemia! Ma is calling you. You mustn't go to sleep up here. You must go downstairs." He shook them gently. He did not forgive his wife that she had always made him feel ridiculous in 'the paternal rôle.' Whenever she praised him highly before his children she seemed to speak sarcastically. Why overrate him to 'these helpless creatures' when, at other times, she quibbled so ungenerously about all he did? Melinda. Melinda, if you only knew! Yet, since his resolve to return to the Eastern coast and offer his services to the Confederate cause, he had enjoyed some relief from this perpetual 'sordidness.'

"Melinda!" He returned to her. Sternly he gripped her flesh through the tight, merino sleeve. "You must go below. If we are searched, you must keep hidden. You must keep your mouth shut. Captain Dugan will declare that we are passengers for New Bedford, but I do not trust to your discretion. You are to do as I instruct without wasting words. There is the vessel out there to the left, if you will only look at it."

She had the briefest opportunity to reconnoitre the new sight, for he was 'bundling' her toward the gangway inconsiderately. However, she retarded her progress long enough for a surprised glimpse of a small object, forcefully inert upon the water, which left, as it drew nearer, greater wastes of sea behind. Ah, it was indeed another ship! She was as if suffocating with terror. And Thomas, pushing her down there into the dark, would leave her to endure the children's whimpers, and to suffer unnamed anxieties, while he remained upstairs in relieving cognizance of all that was occurring. In a crisis, man and wife should be together. "Thomas, Thomas, do not leave me! Do not insist that I stick in that cabin alone," she began to beg. "I feel in so much greater danger when I am thrust away all by myself than when I am with you. Suppose you were arrested and I did not know it! Oh, I can't go downstairs where it is so dark and hot!" The mood of alienation had departed. In any instant of stress, the constant criticism in which she expressed her fretting ambition for him abated. Rather would she imagine him all that she had hoped to find him, and lean upon him utterly. "Thomas—if anything happens—and the children with us—I can never forgive myself for encouraging you to take such risks!"

Agnes and Euphemia had risen. "Ma! Ma!" came Agnes's shrill plea and query; and she raced gawkily across the deck, bearing after her, in a banner of piping, Euphemia's treble protest against desertion.

Thomas, become rough in finality, encouraged Melinda forward brutally. Not even with the gory shadow of the war upon the air could he free himself from the curse of 'domestic trivialities'! He had always been 'firm' with his 'spouse,' and had deluded himself into a belief that his nature was 'chivalrous.' Yet a most primitive hatred could be aroused in him by Melinda's most inconsequential word of argument. He did not believe that she loved him less than formerly. She exhibited her jealousy too frequently. Nor had she lost faith in him. Or had she? It was not so much that he could not bear up under her distrust, but that he had a fear, more haunting, more profound, that she would convince others of his 'failure.' Worse—and he did not state this horror—she might persuade *him*, falsely, that his self-esteem was a mere boast.

"Hurry! Hurry! Do not wait a minute," he insisted. "Captain Dugan is already signalling. I can see them running colours up."

Melinda, dragging her shawl in disarray, already had the tip of her shoe on the first rung of the stair. Agnes and Euphemia were clutching her hands and wailing their bewilderment at 'Pa's' excited accents. Melinda felt inclined to cry hysterically. She was afraid of the 'bowels of the ship,' afraid of the stuffy cabin; and she could discern, in the eyes of Thomas, in his 'ranting' manner, something like a note of triumph. *He*, she fancied, seemed to 'court' calamity. Did he take some cruel pleasure in the children's fright?

In the world so muted by the rapid quenching of the sun, the

Federal vessel appeared full-fledged, the black triangle of its bows always more towering. One could hear an anchor chain grinding. Feathery plashes from nowhere disturbed the sleek, iridescent calm of the subsiding world. Gyrating sounds of men calling to each other twirled and sank. The islands stood about in patches of of black wool floating in a glaze so moveless it was as if a vast runnelled shoal lay exposed. The very hiss of sand disturbed on the beaches was audible.

Thomas, with false passports to explain, did not expect the worst. Yet it might be said that he almost hoped for it. His entrance upon a scene of action would not exactly relieve him of family responsibilities, but would, he believed, give 'scope' to his powers. Jealously, he was determined to exclude Melinda from initiation in these happenings. Too long already had he been circumscribed by her interests. He would not allow her to further deplete his 'manhood.' The life lived from this moment should be for his 'country.' And he looked ahead toward all the times and places into which she could not penetrate. War was an 'ennobling enterprise.' It was the salvation of a civilization in which women had assumed a 'disproportionate part.' War, Thomas thought, as he glanced out at the ship, restored the 'moral health' of the race. But he was very uneasy. He wished Melinda would descend the stairs more hurriedly. It was his duty to conceal his trepidation. If he did not 'brace' himself and continue to be emphatic with her, she might delay.

IV

Sometimes Lee Shuck would get up, move stealthily to the flap of the tent, peer out, and draw in a deep breath of the chill spring air. A soldier with a bayonet over his shoulder was walking up and down in front. Farther off were other tents; low stacks of white canvas, breaking the order of the trees, brightening the spare greenness of the fields. Amidst this cloth sea rolling in stiff, pouting waves, men had collected in little groups and were laughing and talking. Some passed briskly on formal errands. The greater number, in noisy idleness, enjoyed the reluctant sun. Lee, in the conviction that he was dreaming, that he was crazy, could not believe that this was his last day alive. True he had witnessed the execution of other military culprits, but *his* could not be the same fate. It was not possible. Lee gazed longingly at the face of his guard. The soldier with the bayonet tramped the fifty feet between this tent and the tent nearest, reversed himself methodically, and came back again. Lee caught his eye. The eye of the sentinel did not disguise embarrassment. In the effort to appear impassive the man looked uncomfortable. Lee saw that the soldier did not like his job, and wished to evade any communication with his prisoner. This gave Lee an irrational hope.

"I say, Mister, maybe it wouldn't be bustin' no rules if you was to gimme a chaw of tobacco," Lee called suddenly in a trembling voice. To speak humiliated him, but he felt that he would soon be frantic if he could draw no admissions from that stolid face.

The soldier stamped by more quickly, his flat tread sounding in the muddy earth. To command a reply Lee had to repeat his petition. "Ain't got no tobacco," the soldier murmured, veering on a line which swerved him nearer the tent. He talked thickly, in a low tone, and kept his gaze averted. He had not halted in his march—only delayed his pace. Now he went on more rapidly, carrying his patrol to a remote point, where he rested an instant on his lowered weapon, his back, full of self-consciousness, squared deliberately to resist Lee's appeal. Lee found it strange that a fellow in such a posture of advantage should be so fearful of the smallest generosity.

Lee glanced up and down. There was no way to get out. If he attempted it he would certainly be shot at. But would not even that be better—to be fired on while running—than to be dragged in front of a line of fellows in the morning and— His imagination failed him. His attention to the future scattered. The ache in his brain convinced him that thought was useless. Nothing could be as it now seemed. A deception of some description or other was being practised on him. But that anybody should *pretend* to kill him and not do it—

Previous to this experience, Lee had fancied himself one with his comrades, with the 'boys,' and the 'old stagers,' too, who composed his regiment. He had been in the war a long time, now—since he had left his home. Home was a long way off. If he could convince these people that he had a home, maybe they wouldn't kill him. He had trusted everybody. It was a fact that he had always been too trusting, and had let Harry Smith borrow a whole month's pay 'off' him. Day before yesterday Lee had cursed. He was giving up cursing. Things happened so 'quick.' His first mood, on finding himself incriminated, had been one of indignation. The court-martialing, the trial had 'gone off' like occurrences he did not understand. He had had no idea what was going on until the sentence had been read out to him. He had 'quit' protesting. He felt humble. He didn't care any longer whether they misinterpreted his conduct or not. They could blame him all they wanted to, could place upon him the moral onus for almost anything. He was used to injustice. But they might give him a longer time to live. Just a day, he told himself, as he stared at the trees floating dazzling mists of green, and at the rainy sky in which the crude sun weltered vacantly. A day was not enough. A week then. A month then. Why not just a month? How was it that it had only taken them an hour or two to make up their minds about him. And before he had gone to sleep that night on sentinel duty he had done his best.

Asleep within gunshot of the enemy! They made a point of how close he had been. They had accused him soberly of criminal negligence. Why, the very fact he *could* sleep with Confederate pickets so near might have showed them the kind of condition he was in after two days' marching. For the thousandth time he reviewed with anguished hope the state of his being which had made him yield to slumber. He remembered that he had been able, once in a while, to hear a voice in the blackness, and had judged it, though the words were uninterpretable, to be that of an enemy. And because his whole body, with every sense dull and alive, had dragged on his spirits like a hunger, he had been grateful whenever the shock of an unanticipated menace revived his terror and his wakefulness.

He recalled sitting down under a vague tree. Such submission to fatigue, he had realized, was risky. He was not supposed to indulge exhaustion. And he had tried—if they only knew how he had tried—to retard the creeping of a lethargy like sickness, beginning, almost at the instant in which he had sunk heavily on the soaked ground, to cloud his mind with indifference. He had been desperate. He hadn't cared. Yes, he had to confess it. He had been aware, perfectly, that to fall asleep on sentinel duty might have consequences very awful. He had struggled to keep security with his alarm. Yet he hadn't cared. Wasn't *that* a proof? If you were so tired that you would go to sleep and run the risk of being shot, wasn't *that* a proof? Oh, God, why hadn't he been able to make them realize that he hadn't been able to help it. If he could have kept his eyes open, didn't they suppose, with the enemy so near, he would have done it? Wasn't the fact that he had 'busted' his 'guts' trying— He recalled rousing just one time, and knowing, in his stupor, that he had been asleep. He remembered his terror. For a second he had really felt it. But the terror, almost immediately, had vanished in that awful ease. It must have rained that night considerably before the stars came out, and, when he had found his elbow in a puddle he had enjoyed an assurance that it didn't matter. In all his life he had never had a sleep he could recall that had seemed as sweet as that.

His pleasure in it must have been the sin. He had been at a post requiring responsible attention, and the security of his company had depended on him. What they didn't seem to take into account was that he had been 'real proud' of the part he took in things. Nobody made Lee Shuck enlist. Well—he guessed that he was patriotic. His mother hadn't wanted it. Why didn't they understand that? It was too late. In the trial he hadn't said enough about his mother—though he recollected that his counsel had just mentioned it. The trial had seemed bad. But if they would only let him have the trial over again! It had happened so 'quick.' How could anybody in his 'sane mind' condemn a fellow because he went to sleep? They were a gang of bastards. They were a gang of murderers, the sons of guns. The matter with him was that he had trusted people. He had believed—a little, anyhow—of what they said about loving Christ and loving your neighbour.

Lee moved away from the tent flap. Through a crack, he could still see the soldier passing and repassing, and the men in uniform, farther off, who were undisturbed by the information of approaching execution. The guard just 'dodged letting on' there was a man in the tent at all. Sometimes he took 'shifty' looks at the tent, but he did so furtively, and always as if he hoped that Lee, inside, would not notice him. Lee's gaze burned with an animosity wilder than his insistence on 'understanding.' The —— —— bastard. The dirty —— —— bastard. I hope you go to hell and rot.

There was a cot in the tent. Lee sat down on it, on the single, fuzzy blanket, that was damp, that smelled of wet cotton. He leaned and buried his face in the gross cloth. He could stifle breathing, but not meditation. When he shut out every impression of the place of his confinement, he tried to make his mind as blank as unreflecting water. And he was indeed slowly conscious of a calming incredulity. He was disgraced—maybe. But he didn't 'give a dern.' That he would actually be led out in the morning, blindfolded, with the braid ripped from his uniform, and fired at by a squad of fellows just like himself—who were in the army— Say, he was getting funny in his head all right. He began to laugh— 'cackle.' Yep, it sounded to him just like a cackle.

Abruptly, he restrained himself. He was feeling ill. Had anybody heard him make a sound like that? He got up and began to 'move around.'

The tent roof was so low that his feverish forehead sometimes butted the moist canvas that the sun was stiffening. Once he struck himself painfully on the tent pole in the middle of the grassy floor. He had an idea. There were two men talking not a yard away from him, back of the tent. Why hadn't he heard them before? They must have been there all along. Why, if they were going to shoot him, hadn't they shot him today? Why had they given him another twenty-four hours of desperation in which to torture himself? Why the hell can't they kill me quick, he said to himself. He thought he'd better crawl outside, at the rear, and run, and let them kill him whether they wanted to or not. If they didn't want to give a fellow a chance, they had no right to keep him 'hanging on.' I didn't know anything alive was as mean as these skunks, Lee said. What he could do to them! But he never would be able to.

No, it wasn't a joke. It wasn't a kind of trick they were playing on him. He was still. He was quiet. He kept twisting his neck around in the open collar of his undershirt. It was his mind. Something—like it had nothing to do with him—kept working around in his head, *making* him think. Why, all the fights he had been in! Why, all he had done that they asked him to! If he had known this was going to happen to him, he would have taken more chances—on purpose. He could have gotten killed 'easy,' and then where would these fellows be? He had seen a lot of dead men recently. There must be thousands of fellows who were dead or wounded in the last two years. How could anybody tell you how

94

you had to die? There was a fellow Lee had seen had a hole in his chest like a cup. The blood didn't even run. It just stayed in there and you wondered how he was dead. Some were worse. They'd stink when you'd leave 'em out a day or two and didn't bury 'em. 'Ma' would say they were all in heaven. Was there any heaven? Lee was disturbed by the inward question. He put off consideration of an answer. It wasn't time for that—not yet.

It sure is a certainty, he decided suddenly, alarmed by the fresh fecundity of his ever busy fancy, I'm goin' crazy. He didn't *feel* crazy. He felt —*nothing*. That was the 'funny part.' The eaves of the tent sloped, bald and watery with light, around him. They shut him in more completely than any man had ever been enclosed before. On the inclining, shelving walls, translucent images of leafing trees would burst instantly into being, rock there tautly for a space, and, with gliding motions, withdraw, leaving only fringes and disjointed blots and stripes of shadows at rest.

Lee stupidly resumed his consideration of the incidents which had led up to his failure. Just before 'it' happened, the boys had secured some good Kentucky whisky. He had drunk a little—not enough to get him drunk—but a little. The officers drank when they felt like it, so why shouldn't he drink! Perhaps—and the new thought, coming sharply, seemed profound because unexpected— the whisky, being rebel whisky, had been 'charged' with something! Why had it not occurred to him at his trial to explain that the whisky had been 'charged' with something? The conjecture, in this present instant, appeared an inspired truth. The boys, three days before the tragedy, had come upon an abandoned still. Why should anybody go away and leave good whisky in invaded country? Usually, whisky helped you get through the hard places. Lee could not get over a feeling that a remembered sensation of calm carelessness represented the best moment of his life. But that was a day before. The effects must have lingered.

Lee felt queer. To those others, outside confinement, he must seem *different*. Maybe the whisky had *made* him different. He guessed they already considered him a different kind of critter from themselves. But if you would die a thousand times—no, not die—but stand any kind of punishment worse than hell, just to take it all back, just to get another chance! I went to sleep. Yes, that was it. I went to sleep. It wasn't whisky that night anyhow.

95

This was almost the first time Lee had thought about whisky. He had never drunk 'much.' Now he 'wished to hell' he had drunk more. Gosh, if I had a drink! Caught in the mechanism of his torment, his helplessly active mind again reviewing stale happenings, the involuntary effort of his reason brought him only nausea. His gorge rose. "Shoot me! Kill me! For Christ's sake kill me!" he cried out hoarsely, springing from a moment's respite on the cot, and able, here in the seclusion of the tent, to cry out so they would be obliged to hear him. "Kill me! Fer God's sake come and put a bullet through me, you old putty-face. I ain't gonta stand no more of this." Then he moaned, and hid his brow in his crooked arm, and muttered, "I *can't* stand no more."

He was shivering, sweating. In his underwear and trousers that were held up by suspenders, he felt his appearance vividly as the stigma of some confirmed inferiority to other people. He began to tear at his shirt and to open it desperately over his panting chest. Nobody had listened. If they heard, they 'let on' not to. He was ashamed. If they caught him 'yelling around' this way, they *would* think he was 'funny.' Now the situation appeared to him to demand craft. He was queer all right, but they mustn't find it out. Something had to be done. He couldn't go on like this until tomorrow morning. He couldn't keep recounting to himself over and over again how it had been that night—how he had dropped asleep— how his mind had just 'gone out.' Just gone out, fellows, he wanted to call to them, the way you squench a light. Yes, that whisky was charged. Or if it wasn't charged, the fellow that dished out the pork and beans that night put somethin' funny in 'em.

He walked to the flap. His fingers twitched at it. He was heady with the noon sun, strong and iridescent in the tent. He wanted to hide himself in some cool place where it was shady. God, why hadn't he considered that the whisky was charged before he had given his defence? His thin mouth opened. In a sudden paroxysm of renewed, unendurable doubt, his pupils contracted in glassy irises. The way he looked was 'wrong,' he knew. But it didn't matter what he said to them. They wouldn't believe that the whisky did it.

There was the sentinel. The soldier was at last walking more slowly. His bayonet point glistered and little trickles of reflections ran up and down the barrel. The glare was full upon him, but he

96

did not seem to mind, though his brow was speckled with sweat. The sun gliding up the bayonet, as the soldier stopped under a tree, and faced the tent, reminded Lee of the way a spider crawls up and down on a thread it has spun. How long the day was going to be! And not long enough. They'll get you no matter how you act. Though it was warm, everything smelled cold and quiet. Grass was coming up through the mouldy scurf of dead leaves on the edge of the wood. A blue jay fluttered over a bush, alighted on a twig, and teetered there. A catbird buzzed overhead like a saw.

Again Lee was aware of a harsh shout rising in his throat, stifling him with a precipitate utterance that did not come from his will. Not intending it, he must have made a sound. The sentry was annoyed, looked attentive, but did not see him in the slit. Quickly, quivering as from some new mutilation of his pride, Lee sprang back out of sight. As he did so, he stumbled, inclined to his knees, relaxed his weight blindly, and lay sprawled on his face, pressing his lids shut, obliterating the suggestion of shame in all his surroundings. It was the whisky did it! My God, it must 'a' been the whisky. They're all crazy or I'm crazy. *The world's not hell!*

If he could only go to sleep again! If he could only sleep a little longer! He clutched at matted roots, exposed in the soil under him. He laid his cheek on the cold of the ground. But it was *impossible* to sleep. Woo as he might the state that had made his undoing, the dull wakefulness of his intelligence persisted. He began to beat his forehead gently, lifting his head up and bringing it down, each time more forcibly, on the too-soft floor. It must 'a' been the whisky. If they'd only give him some! If they'd just leave him alone here inside the tent forever! If they wouldn't look at him! If they'd just give him anything, *anything* that would stop him thinking. God, that whisky ud feel good inside his guts! And he kept on beating his head, but he couldn't stop thinking.

IV

MR. SAMUEL WHARTON, one of the leading bankers of Sterling, Vermont, walked home with a tired and thoughtful tread, down a street so rich in shadows of giant elm trees that, even in the fragile leafage of the springtime, his way, between white-painted houses, seemed to lead into a cavern between mammoth pillars. The sidewalks were of damp gravel, neatly raked, and almost every picket fence glared with a stark limey coat of white-washing.

Bushes of lilac and snowball flanked doorways as reserved as tombs. There was bleakness in the outlook, yet a kind of homeliness. Mr. Wharton knew every citizen of importance in the town. He knew, and venerated, through association with his forbears, every foot of ground he trod. And he had a feeling that, because the Southern states were in rebellious turmoil, he should enjoy more frugally the security for which his hardy ancestors had once fought and bled. The Providence which had permitted him to escape a general disaster required gratitude of him. He had a smooth upper lip, but there was a stout greying growth of hair under his chin. He stroked this meditatively. It was too bad that he was too old to volunteer in the battle for the right, he ruminated, but he could do his part, while the war continued, in financial matters. The disastrous effect of the Forced Loan Bill was a weight on his mind. First the banks of New York had suspended specie payments, then, last December, had come that bill from the House providing for the issue of a hundred and fifty million dollars in treasury notes. Of course it was strictly a war measure that gave Congress the power to issue such notes, and Mr. Wharton realized the dire national emergency. The Constitution provided that no state should emit bills of credit or make anything but gold and silver coin a tender in payment of debts, the prohibition upon the states by intendment reserving this power to the National Government.

98

But I would have supported the Government in any event, Mr. Wharton reflected aggrievedly, and if there had been more like me, no stringent measures would have been required. The bills have realized money, and if the Government uses them to pay for munitions of war, they *are* money. Perhaps, in the long run, it will prove a feasible scheme. The crisis has been one that would not have occurred to the wildest imagination, I must confess, so it is hard to say how it could have been better met.

He was constantly divided between natural caution, and a yearning, born of the current fever for a noble gesture, to be patriotic, altruistic—not too expensively. He felt that he had to consider himself and Sadie first. They were growing old. Ten years had passed since the death of their little son, Thaddeus, and they had aged mightily. It was the sad reward of their tardy marriage to lose their only child ere he had reached gracious maturity.

Mr. Wharton, with his conscientious, doubtful eyes, behind whitish lashes, gazed, with heavy sentiment, at a clump of glossy, dark green lilacs that were just unfurling. He was poignantly aware of the early spring this year, and of its incongruousness. The suspension of specie payments by the banks had made it impossible to procure sufficient coin for current disbursements. Mr. Lincoln acknowledged to the world that he was pressed. The greenbacks were away below par now. It sometimes seemed that Southern greed, and Southern ambition to extend slavery northward, would have to be paid for by all the innocent. Sadie called the battle the struggle of 'the armies of the Lord' against the numerically superior hosts of 'the King of Darkness.' Mr. Wharton, more reserved in language, half admitted it. The attempt to nip in the bud the valid ambition of the East to be a manufacturing centre would be put a stop to anyhow. And that was worth some sacrifice. The future was at stake. Sadie, in her simplicity, often used expressions on the situation which appealed to him. She had touched him when she had asserted yesterday that Thaddeus, had he lived, would have been among the first young men enlisted.

Mr. Wharton coughed into his beard, took off his 'stove-pipe' hat, and stroked his longish, thinnish hair over his dry crown. It stirred him strangely, in connection with this war, to think of Thaddeus.

Musing vaguely, he had come to his own gate, which was of iron.

99

He had lately felt some pangs of conscience for the money he had spent on it. He had a brick house, with a porch, and it seemed that he had been too lavish in his expenditures. He and Sadie were tired and elderly. It was the *Lord's* harvest they must sow and reap. He wanted to be generous in connection with the war, but he could not bear to see money 'wasted.' If people would only realize that his aversion to heedless charity was not stinginess!

Sadie had brought a rocker out of doors. He was glad to find her there, for a moment at least impervious to the demands of housekeeping. Since the papers had been filled with 'sensations,' almost daily, he was a little anxious for her peace of mind. He wanted to see her idle now and then, and had at first encouraged her to read the news. But women lacked the sense of proportion that kept men calm. Her female soul was too easily affected. For a woman who was a good churchgoer, and a paragon in domestic tasks, she was much more excitable than he would have anticipated.

"Mr. Wharton," Sadie exclaimed, as she saw him, "I've been waiting for you this half-hour. There was nothing for us at the post office today and I can't rest for thinking of our poor boys. Have any victories been reported that I haven't heard about?" She had been a very pretty girl, small and 'elegantly formed,' as Mr. Wharton remembered her. She often told him now that she had become indifferent to worldly affairs, and it was true that the only present characteristic which recalled frivolity was a floridness in her caps. She had certainly been a 'stay-at-home' body for years, and the tendencies of a recluse more pronounced since the loss of Thaddeus. Mr. Wharton 'fretted' about her, wondered at the zeal with which still, ignoring the 'hired girl' he provided, she swept and dusted, 'cleaned house,' or made apple butter, continually.

"Well, Mrs. Wharton, how does your garden grow this evening?" Advancing up the path with its little fringe of hesitant grass, he caught the nervous, vigorous turn of her head towards his approaching figure, and the sombre, almost vacant animation of her glance. He knew that she would scarcely allow him to seat himself before she would begin on 'war talk.' She was on the *Ladies' Committee,* which had set itself to provide equipment, and even luxuries, for war troops, and to that he could not object. He liked to see her at work with Mrs. Elijah Varney, wife of a man who had long been his own rival and opponent in the banking business. It 'got Sadie out.' Anything to take her mind off the spots the sun had made on the Brussels in the parlour. When some trifle was to be bought for the house, he helped her select it. Not a penny was spent, between them, on these personal acquisitions, but with his consultation. Not that he demanded an accounting from her. Simply, he felt a genuine interest in all she did, and recognized that, enjoying late prosperity, he owed Sadie something for her careful contribution to it. Just the same, there *was* a world, however limited for womankind, beyond their own front door. He wished to give Sadie new aims in life, broader aims in life; but he wished even more to contribute to her 'sanity.'

"How can you expect our troops to make you a present of a victory *every* day?" he asked, mounting the few stairs cumbrously, and halting before her spread-out crinolines, while he stared downward below the frills of the cap, into a narrow, harshly vivacious face, and into eyes which, though she might smile, were never lighted by a trace of humour.

"I don't believe you. You're keeping something from me. Hand me that paper you have in your coat pocket." She spoke in a small, brisk, peremptory voice, with a stiff, nasal intonation.

Mr. Wharton felt a jealous desire to resist her demand. It was true that, since Pittsburg Landing, the news had been disappointing. There was really nothing to show her. Yet he would have preferred to hold the journal back. He handed it to her helplessly, and her knitting fell into her lap, while her scrutinizing gaze, in frantic earnestness, moved up and down the lines of wet, fresh print. He had always believed newspaper items beyond the range of the female mind. Indulging Sadie as he was now doing, he reaffirmed this opinion.

"Is that *all*? You're keeping something from me, Mr. Wharton," she accused. "I was talking to Mrs. Varney today and you wouldn't credit all the things *she's* heard about those Southerners. Mr. Varney takes a journal called *The Clarion*—somewhere in Boston. Why, they've printed the most *frightful* things. I just felt when I was listening to her that the whole future of civilization would be proved by whether we are victorious or not. The abominations that have been practised down there are just more than any decent person can get through without blushing."

She was blushing herself, as she turned upward cheeks stained by the small fever of her discomfort. "I calculate you must have heard it, too, but I just can't talk about it." The paper slipped cracklingly from her knees to the floor of the porch, and Mr. Wharton, with an avid gesture of possession, leaned and recovered it.

His wife, as if to disguise something that brightened her colour and made her eyes burn with nervous tears, was resuming her knitting. Her lips moved. "Cast one stitch, knit alternate plain and purled rows, increase both before and after the middle stitch of the knitted rows, until you have nine stitches on the needle, in the plain rows increase one stitch at the beginning of the row, knit three stitches, turn back and purl the same stitches, turn back again and knit plain up the middle stitch." Her whispered words came scarcely audibly.

Now and then, he felt a positive annoyance at her industry, at the importance she seemed to attach to it. Ah, those woollen flowers for the bazaar, of course. He said: "You've tried most every other kind of garden thing, Sadie. Why don't you undertake to do some cabbages?"

"Sweet peas," she explained, with a briskness that was contemptuous, and went on, covering a pointed weariness.

Mr. Wharton, wondering when she would 'bounce' up and come after him to remind him, perhaps, to wipe his feet, or to rebuke him because it had rained that day and he had not worn his galoshes, passed into the sitting-room. It was a comfortable place, and he could look with some pride on the modern sewing machine in the corner, and on the red plush armchairs, not as good as the horsehair in the parlour, yet quite good enough. But he had no nook of his own. There was a pocket in his long coat into which Sadie, to his relief, had not fumbled, and in that pocket reposed a book called *Facts Behind the Veil*, or *The Depraved South*. Had she spied it he had hoped to explain it as a bound volume of *Arthur's Home Gazette*, advertised on a flyleaf as 'Free from Vulgarity, Low Slang, or Profanity,' for the two books were of the same size and shape.

Mr. Wharton, disposing of his hat on an elk head in the hall, wandered uncertainly toward the kitchen. It also was pre-empted. Dishes clinked, and the voice of the hired girl singing *John Brown's Body* was wafted shrilly to him before he looked around the door lintel. He must seek the parlour or the dining-room, for they were never used.

There was something exacerbating to his sensibility in being obliged, in his own dwelling, to search out furtively some privacy. Charlie Rice had given him the book and had told him that it was a 'duty' to peruse it. It contained information, Charlie Rice had said, for every 'thinking citizen.' The enemy was foul beyond imagination. You should know the worst about him. Sadie was morbid. She was hysterical. He had determined to conceal the volume from her, 'for her own sake.'

The parlour shades were drawn as usual, and, when he had closed the door carefully, the room was almost dark. He was grateful for his familiarity with its contents when he evaded the felt-draped centre table narrowly, and bumped his shins on an edge of the harmonium.

Mr. Wharton moved to a distant window beside the mantel. His bony hand parted the curtains stealthily, and he took the book out of his pocket. He supposed he would have to read at the bank, after all, but he might as well have a peep at it.

The pages, under his fingers, stirred like the sound of breathing. The waning glow of day, spotted, as it came through the blind, conveyed only a grey indefiniteness to the print. And Sadie was likely to call him to supper almost any minute.

His jealous eyes had deciphered, disappointedly, no more than a dozen lines, when the expected interruption came. His interest in the war, always more keen under this kind of stimulation, was just unfolding to the first luxuriously hinted horror, when he heard a step. Angrily, making a soft thud as he did it, he slapped the book shut. It really did seem that, with all the sacrifices he was making for national welfare, he might indulge himself in some acquaintance with the situation. For a long time, the food served at his own table, had been very bad, the most meagre Sadie had ever provided for them in his married life. But had *he* complained at the scantiness of provisions! And she was losing her head, absorbing the general hysteria. The week previous he had missed a dollar from his trousers pocket and said nothing of it. He suspected the servant. A dollar was a dollar, yet he had refrained from reproaching Sadie for her careless supervision of the household, because, lately, with the war contagion, she had been disturbed too much.

Mr. Wharton could not counteract a conviction, unspoken but deep, that certain elements in the national disaster were comprehended by him alone. It was not possible that his wife, with her sheltered outlook, enter into all the profound emotions in defence of decent living which publications like *Facts Behind the Veil* aroused in him. She had condemned in him what she considered 'coldness.' Little did she dream of the harshness stirred in her behalf, which was prompting him, even at this moment, to lavish resolutions. Because she had misjudged him, however, he would write a check for the *Defence Fund* and not tell her a word about it. She was no doubt right in consigning to her own sex 'intuitions, spiritual insight;' yet a man purchased such integrity as he retained in the 'mundane' struggle at a high price. He endured tests of his 'finer feelings' which she need never undergo.

Moving, with resentful stealth, toward the mantelshelf, he was in the hasty act of secreting his book behind a squat, flat-fronted majolica vase, when a gash of daylight was struck diagonally on the gloom, and Sadie was silhouetted, like a black umbrella with a rotund handle from which the frills upon her cap stuck out.

A slight scream accented her appearance. Mr. Wharton denied to himself his own impression of his lack of dignity. They stared at one another in the imperfect gloom.

"Mr. Wharton—Samuel—I—I didn't know." Sadie's voice was thin and high with anxiety, and she tore at her handkerchief. "You're so particular about where every penny goes, and it was just a matter of sentiment with me. I might have guessed that you suspected something when you missed that dollar but you never spoke of it, and it was my natural feelings as a mother. I mean you never have let me put in enough, and it seemed like we could deny ourselves something with victuals so high anyway, and Abbie Varney throwing money right and left. I'm sure if Thaddeus had lived *we* wouldn't have had a thing to say against it—I mean even the greatest sacrifice—and I would have been so proud to see him doing everything he could for his country. I might have expected you'd be slow to open your purse strings, but I said with our darling boy gone where he can never play the hero's part that would suit him, and we two old people not a speck of use to the greatest cause that any man ever fought and died for. I don't guess you recollect how excited our little precious was that time in Boston

104

when we took him with us to hear Mr. Garrison speak, and the blessed mite, so tuckered out afterwards he cried in my lap, and proud of his new Scotch bonnet, and he took the penny you'd given him for the church collection and says to me, 'It's for the poor Black People, Ma,' and when we got home put it right there in that very vase. So that's what put the idea in my head, and I'm not even scared of my own husband when I have right on my side, and I wanted this to be *my* part. So, if you've made up your mind to take it back, I wrote Captain Bailey all about it, and he has already promised he can make good use of it."

Breathlessly, as if in a race with her own volubleness, she harangued; then waited. Mr. Wharton's heart-beats had grown thick with resistant excitement, and he could make no sense of what she said. It seemed to him connected with his last stealthy gesture.

His wife, as if unable to bear the delay of the inevitable reprimand, rustled, in hasty abandon, toward him. The slow realization of his authority finally made him active, and he stepped between her and the mantelpiece. "It's so dark in here I don't know what you are talking about," he muttered vainly.

She seemed frantic for a last exposure, dodged his uncertain, detaining hand, snatched the vase from the shelf, and, turning to the table, ponderous with its weight of Bible and hymnals, tipped her receptacle upside down and poured money out. "It's nigh a hundred dollars, and if you knew half how I've pinched and scraped on my own part to get it!" She stood there, tense, her body vibrant.

Mr. Wharton, dimly shocked by the spectacle of hoardings he had not provided, gave a feeble glance behind him. There, upright against the wall, though a little tilted toward the peacock feathers beside the clock, rested *Facts Behind the Veil*, the title, fortunately, but an indecipherable gilt twinkle, yet exposed to everybody. He coughed. Just as it irritated him to see a woman lift her skirts to expose so much as an ankle, it offended him to find his wife capable of initiating generosity that he had not advised. He said, sternly, though not quite firmly: "So you've saved this money up yourself to give the army fund. I could say a good deal about the deception you've practised, Sadie. I'm pretty disappointed in you. My judgment has meant a good deal to you during all these years." He hesitated, computing silently sums made from the possible sources of this acquisition. His rule as a husband certainly had not been a hard one. Sadie should be ashamed of herself. If Elijah Varney was 'fool' enough to let his wife do just as she liked— His face felt heated.

Sadie, not quite able to distinguish the expression on Mr. Wharton's features, did catch the tentative quality in words taking the place of an expected tirade. Advantage was, for her, self-justification. The weeping she had withheld rose under her lids, and tears took possession of her utterance. "Mr. Wharton—Samuel —I knew you were going to be aggravated with me—but it's *Thaddeus's* war—little Thaddeus's war. 'I'm going to give all my pennies to the poor Black People,' is just what he told me, and I've always called it that."

Mr. Wharton thrilled to some uncontrollable, undevised pain that was in her voice. *Little Thaddeus's war.* So it was. It was ridiculous to anticipate with embarrassment Sadie's discovery of the informing volume which he was obliged to read out of conscientiousness. He might even have to tell her somewhat sternly not to 'worry her head' about it. They were both moved out of themselves by the 'sublime' deeds that were being performed now, every day, on almost every side of them: she in her woman's way, and he, perhaps, more earnestly. He could sometimes wonder at himself when he realized what a change the spectacle of great events had brought about in him. Before, it was business, business, day and night—exemplary business, performed honestly by a conscientious citizen, but not much else to think about. That was selfish. As Sadie had been impelled to pray for the 'boys' down there in that 'pit of hell,' he had been stirred to recognize the existence of all sorts and kinds of things and people hitherto ignored. Why, even that book, *Facts Behind the Veil,* did him good. Disagreeable as was some of the content, there was a 'lesson' for the purer-minded contained in it.

"Little Thaddeus's war." He said it aloud, his voice gently breaking. Sadie was a very 'good, high-principled' woman. In the darkened parlour, he seemed to feel about him the atmosphere of all the love she had spent upon their child, a child whom she would have readily offered up for the benefit of suffering humanity. He knew the samplers she had worked, the hair picture designed as a portrait of their little boy, the many signs and symbols of her vir-

106

tue, setting the moral key for the home. He could not be hard
on her, no matter what she did. It was his privilege to protect
her, and, though he would not permit her to read that narrative of
the 'depraved South,' he almost gloated upon her revealed independence. It was a new idea for women, that they must think and
act for themselves, and he conceded it only 'within bounds.' Yet a
circumscribed 'freedom' they must have, else he could not demand,
'reasonably,' a little more than that for himself. It was indeed a
beautiful fancy she had conceived—'Thaddeus's war,'—he must
see that he lived up to the idea.

II

At two o'clock in the morning the moon rose. The *Itasca* was
ready, and took advantage of the hazy illumination and a southerly
breeze to get ahead. Renfield was glad when all hands were called
on deck and the order gave him a chance to escape from further
depressing conversation with Harry Dewey.

The two had been lying in their adjacent hammocks for an hour,
and Harry, as usual, had allowed nobody rest. By the thin, brown
glitter of a lantern, Harry could always be seen rocking gently,
trying to propel his hammock near enough to Renfield's to excuse
another confidence. Ventilators were few down there, and the night
air, which Renfield had anticipated as refreshingly cool, scarcely
diluted the emanations from confined, sleeping bodies. He had
wished for space in which to calm himself, for, despite all effort to
reject fancies, he had been acutely conscious of the concealed batteries of the rebels on the invisible land they were floating past.

"Derned if I can shut my peepers tonight," Harry had whined
superfluously, for he could not bear a silence, as Renfield knew.

The hammocks had gone on swinging, titillating with motion,
the faint uneasy feeling that *would* come in the pit of even a comparatively accustomed stomach with the smell of bilge and tar, on
a hot spring evening; and with anxiety.

"Has the Old Girl begun to move up the river yet?"

Harry realized as accurately as Renfield did that a faint, trickling sound of water, heard from nowhere, was no sign of a departure. But he would keep starting, lifting himself on a shaky
elbow, and staring with catastrophic premonition at the huddled,
suspended shapes lurching quietly on either side of him.

Harry was 'pretty.' He had beautiful, limpid, blue eyes, a little wild in expression; a fine, thin little nose with wide eager nostrils; and a sweet, drooping, uncertain mouth. It was his chin and the 'bottom' of his face that 'Renny' didn't like. It was too plump, and Harry's throat was white and full, 'like a girl's.' When you saw him in the navy it somehow made you angry and disgusted just to look at him.

Renfield so detested that beautiful, drunken, disturbed gaze of the youth, that he called Harry 'Molly, Mary,' and all kinds of things. Renfield was always on the defensive with Harry, who invited compassion, so it seemed, unknowingly. You could 'spit in his face' and 'the damned fool would always calculate you were being nice to him.' Harry thought 'the world and all' of Gunner Renfield. The admiration was so trustingly bestowed that it made Renfield vicious. It took so very much for granted. And 'Renny,' though he tried, was always being beguiled into the position of an elder brother giving 'little Harry' good advice. Cursing, Renfield often said to himself that he was going to do something some day that would make Harry hate him. He would dream of arousing, upon Harry's helpless, mobile countenance, the stupid, agonizing expression of outraged sensibility. But Renfield had never let himself go *yet*. The desire to hurt Harry, though it grew, did not find expression.

Discourage Harry purposely, Renfield did. "If the raft's not still open the Old Man won't let us leave tonight," Renfield had said, down there in the stink and gloom, where everybody was ready to 'puke' with tension; and when Harry lifted his voice a little louder, the tousled head of some fellow he had disturbed with his questions would rear menacingly from a vacillating heap of blanket, shouting, "If you two ——— ——— blabbers don't shet yer mouths and that god-damned rumpus I'm gonna break your necks."

Renfield realized, however, that the double challenge was not really hurled at him. The men with him were a good deal in awe of him, and it was 'little milk-faced Harry' that they all detested. Renfield never spared a word he could avoid uttering. Harry, 'the white-livered little piece of rotten tripe,' talked 'in season and out.' Renfield believed that it would improve Harry if some hairy-chested sailor would thrash him so thoroughly that he had 'something to go and squeal to his mammy about.' He could not explain his own reluctance to administer direct chastisement. Harry was simply so easily disturbed and so often excited, that it gave you the 'shudders' just to see his face when he had been upset. He had run away from home and first gone to sea in the merchant service, so he said. According to his own account of things, it was a 'dog's life' that he had led. From the instant he had set foot in a galley in the capacity of cabin boy, and general handy-man, it had been 'hell' for him. The funny part of it was that he seemed really to enjoy recounting all the loathsome things that had been done to him. He hadn't a 'stitch' of pride, was the common criticism of him. And it was queer that, with all he had undergone—some of the details Renfield himself didn't care to dwell on—he had kept that girlish, almost 'simpery,' nervous manner and that trusting, childish face.

Lying in the hammock down there below, Harry had 'worked' Renfield up, by mere proximity, to such a pitch, that the older man, even when given some respite from inquiries about the prognosticated fight, had not been able to enjoy the small opportunity allowed for quiet. Renfield, having played 'possum' for a long time, had not been able to endure further the seeking, deferential scrutiny of the—at last—obediently silent Harry, and had himself risen in his swinging berth, to exclaim, in violent annoyance, "What do you lie there starin' at me for, you fool? Are you tryin' to make me think that you ain't lookin' at me any more, you god-damned, yellow belly?"

The two hammocks had vacillated vigorously. On the flowing motion of the ropes suspending them, the two swathed shapes had approached one another until their shoulders had bumped. Renfield, helpless, had cringed rebelliously at the involuntary contact. Being in the 'regular' navy hadn't changed Harry a bit. There was 'no glory-hole big enough to hold him.' He'd be talking, before the night was over, about the way he loved his mother, and how he hoped she'd got his last letter. Renfield had a mother, too, and he revered her dutifully; but he was a *'man,'* somebody with the kind of feelings that were too 'decent and self-respecting to be referred to openly.'

All Harry had said was: "Naw. I knew you wasn't nappin', Renny. I was only wonderin' where you and me would be this time tomorrow—whether we'd be here or on some other ding-busted planet when New Orleans is taken. I didn't go for to upset you, Renny. You can't help wonderin' when you're in a fix like this, but you keep sayin' that it's gonta be all right, so I guess it is."

"I hope *you* get shot anyhow," Renfield had muttered, burying his head vengefully in the suffocating covers. "You're enough to drive the dander out of anybody. You make me *think* too much, damn you."

It was fortunate, Renfield decided, that at this moment a bellow through the hatchway had 'rooted up' the whole lot of them. It was good to be out of doors; good in spite of a physical resistance to activity that made it 'like pullin' teeth,' at this time in the morning, to have to stir about.

The river seemed very quiet. He understood that the *Mississippi*, the *Oneida*, the *Varuna*, the *Katahdin*, the *Kineo* and the *Wissahickon* were to go on; while the *Sciota*, the *Iroquois*, the *Pinola*, the *Winona*, and the *Kennebec* had been instructed to keep with the *Itasca* to the middle of the stream. Aboard his own ship, the atmosphere was one of waiting, yet he felt less strain on his nerves than he had experienced below. The *Itasca's* sister vessels sometimes loomed to the right and left of her in an intimacy that, in a doubtful channel, made him wonder if the navigator's information were sufficient for his task.

At other moments nothing intruded on his sense of the still globe of the moon, rising, bathed in clouds of yellowed chiffon, over a low mute shore, above the auburn ripples of the path she spread. A faint twitter of steam would be audible above the lap of the water. Then, from the deep black night farther away, would reverberate the crash of a mortar; while a burst of fire, revealing Fort Jackson luridly as with paper walls, would swim languidly downward, too remote to carry danger, yet sufficiently near to bestow an unconvincing ruddiness as of sudden daylight on the *Itasca's* funnel.

Every time one of these sonorous explosions charged the moist, torpid air, Renfield, trembling a little, would say to himself, One for you, Mary Anne. I'd like to see your little pippin of a face when you heard *that* one.

The signs of an attack increased. An hour after Renfield had been called from his hammock, every hand on board was hard at work, answering fire with occasional, more guarded fire, and sav-

110

ing wounded men. When the moon was observed at this point, it was only a shadowy clot of milk, dim and silky in bronze vapours. In intervals the least reverberant, there was opportunity to watch the faint shudder of a rocket, withering, in scattered brilliance, on the starkly revealed horizon. But the pounding of the *Itasca's* incessant guns would begin again, and the soggy air, combined with fog over a low river, became so dense, so bitter with smoke, that, but for the glowing signal rafts sent out, haphazard, by the enemy, and now adrift near the land, the firing could not have been directed effectively.

The hesitant ascent of burning objects cast rosy vibrations upon the channel. Spread upon a trembling golden tissue, gloomed pines and live oaks on the shore, jaggedly illumined, were a charred, upright multitude, doused by occasional flames. A shell would burst as in the silent heavens; and the trace it left, dissolving, revived the stars that had appeared extinguished. The booms, shrilling fire, mounted the darkness with fearful velocity. Sparks disappeared from the sky. The night was dulled. The gunners, unsupported by excitement, were dizzied, disconcerted, even sicklied, by that one instant of inanition; and it was more bearable to resume industry.

Renfield, following instructions, tried to lessen the discomfort of concussions, by standing frequently upon his tiptoes with his mouth open. He had entirely forgotten the uneasy venom aroused by 'pretty Harry,' and was indulging a furtively assumed pause to wipe his powder-grimed face on his dingied sleeve, when a new, surprising light, leaping from the outlines of St. Philip, arrested his attention with the vague menace of its novelty. Scarcely had he observed this when a thick noise, close to him, and out of focus with the brief glare, seemed to wake echoes almost underneath his feet. The deck quivered sturdily under an enormous impact. Involuntarily, he sprang back from his gun as though the threat he sensed around him were contained in it. Abruptly, his power of vision seemed swept away in voluminous tides of scent and hearing. Men were shouting. Something peremptory was being said, but he could not understand it. A man who, two minutes before, had been beside him, now called from nowhere. Hurried feet thudded past. A second report came like an ache in his sudden intolerable fatigue. In the void created by his incapacity to realize familiar objects, he felt a cloud of steam rising from the deck about his ankles, enveloping his features in scalding breaths. A torment of hot water flowed across his boots.

Renfield, dumb with panic, tried to run. His intention to escape had no goal. Stumbling, butting callously against blurred, reeling shapes of other people, he seemed but to extend his agonies for a few yards. Somebody, grovelling in the creamy dark, clutched his ankles; and he kicked wildly, his panic tangible, like a livid beckoning against his eyeballs. The *Itasca* must have got a broadside that had almost finished her. The boilers had evidently burst, and the decks were running liquid steam. She had listed, and Renfield, still struggling as against a human deterrent, climbed toward the up side, seeking for the rail.

Day was breaking. When he had crawled to a position in which he could stand, he saw the river, smut-coloured and cold in the shadows, but mild with yellowed rays and sparks where the morning struck on it. The firing from the other boats continued with dull booms. The *Winona*, nearest, a still tower spouting menace, her keel ruffled with a fringe of sudsy white, seemed to be veering off. Drawling embers sank out of the sky, and the feeble daylight seemed scorched and stained by the constant drifts of smoke.

Renfield's feet were like bundles of fever, useless for motion. He looked at the chill, dead flowing of the sallow water, and the water drew him. Deep and cold up to his brain he longed to feel it, and his sensation for water, even before he could plunge, was like a gratitude.

Men, ignoring one another, collected about him. They could not loose their boots on their swollen feet. Some mounted the rail, but demurred, with stark looks of anxiety, conveying their indecision to those who clustered behind. There were shouts. There were curses. One pushed another off.

Renfield stared over the side and below him. Heads were already bobbing there. A strange face peered sightlessly through a drench of spray. Arms in soaked clothing grappled nothing. Wreckage eddied, sizzling with extinguished flames. The smell that pervaded the damaged ship recalled a washhouse on a Monday morning, save that there was mingled, with the reek of the boilers, that other metallic odour of the guns, stale on a new chill. As he was about to yield himself to the headlong gesture which almost rapturously disregarded judgment, Renfield saw Harry, and halted.

Harry was not thirty feet from the *Itasca's* side, and was making weak efforts to swim. But Renfield realized that, with but a short span between the boy and the shore, he was giving up. His slight arm fought at the air, slapped on the current as a baby slaps at the surface of his bath. Then his chin sank. A wave rolled over his brow, and quenched, for a minute, some last reproach in pain-stricken eyes which gazed at nobody.

Still Renfield delayed. The little sniveller was going to drown, sure. Nobody would save him. And a good riddance.

Again Harry rose. This time he was helpless, his clutch at the evading waters almost idle. His head rested backward as upon a pillow, and Renfield noticed what he had not before observed—that the boy's forehead had been gashed, probably in falling, and trickled perpetually refreshed blood—blood washed now by the river but always shed too easily.

Fascinated, Renfield, his terror for himself ignored obsession, watched Harry's limp, indifferent body carried past, downstream, amidst the bolder drift of broken timber. Some impulse he was determined to restrain, made Renfield obstinate even to the saving of his own life. Shouldering off impersonal opponents, frantic for his place by the rail, he refused to jump. Harry was now exactly below the spot on which, diving, Renfield would strike water. Harry opened his eyes, coughed, and, with a feeble spasm which again inundated him for an instant, rose once more, and sank finally.

Renfield, not daring to move, held to the rail with both stiff fists. He had to get out of this and into the current, but he put it off as long as he could. Harry had recognized him. He was certain of it. And that awful, sickly, unreproachful glance lingered and lingered, with the sense of a loathly touch, upon his tormented flesh. Damn the little bastard, damn him, damn him. He got his deserts, Renfield thought. Gasping deeply, he pushed himself to the height from which he could spring unobstructedly. Sun glinted in the smoke, and the day boiled in the brightened water. He jumped heavily, as he did so lurching to blank abandon in that awful pity Harry always forced on him.

Parker idled on Canal Street. The way was lined with trees that cast, however, unimportant shade, and though this was but the first of May, it was '—— hot.' Fifteen thousand cotton bales had burned, before the occupation of the city, ships laden with freight, and the half-built ironclad, *Mississippi*, anchored near the Algiers' shore. Parker had arrived in time to witness the spectacular ending of the plotted demolition, and was even yet excited by the memory. The burning cottonseed, explosive, filling the morning air with smutty tinsel, had made 'a grand sight.' Particularly had he been shocked by the condition of burning steamboats, their blackened, gilt saloons exposed, their cracked, discoloured mirrors catching the sun unbearably. Speak of 'cutting off your nose to spite your face'—the natives of the city of New Orleans had surely done it. Though not himself affected by the loss of property, merely to watch the crazy, intentional disaster confirmed his prejudice against the rebel South.

"You can bet your breeches I'm a Yankee, and a damned good Yankee," Parker would say aloud this morning, whenever he found himself scrutinized by any hostile-looking vagrant; and it seemed as if the benches on the grass were filled with persons who stared askance at his uniform. Hadn't they tried to insult General Butler, too! Parker, among the troops in the escort, when the general arrived, had been obliged to listen to the rebel 'caterwaulings' uncomplainingly. Shouts of 'Bull Run,' and hurrahs for General Beauregard had 'turned' his stomach.

After the 'fool' attempt of that 'scoundrel,' Mumford, to pull down *Old Glory* and run up the *Stars and Bars,* or 'whatever they called their dirty rag,' on the Custom House, almost any kind of spiteful violence could be expected. Everybody said Butler would have the 'bastard' strung up, and a 'damned good thing that would be.'

Christ, what a dirty swamp this place is! Parker, having mopped his steaming forehead, felt consciously at his waxed moustaches. A young lady, passing with a little boy, stared right into his 'gizzard.' He could give her 'as good as she sent.' He adjusted his cap a trifle more jauntily, and gazed, with a faint, belligerent smirk of condescension on his features. It was somehow painful for him to maintain this scrutiny, but his unwilling discomfort made him doubly obstinate. Thinks she's the Queen of Sheba, he meditated. The heated condition arising from his sense of an injustice, combining with the weather, sent a dull redness to his cheeks; but he looked along his nose with all the arrogance that his title among the men as 'cock o' the walk where the ladies are concerned' allowed him.

The girl certainly must have regarded herself as 'one of these here Southern beauties.' She was small, with dark eyes; and wore a full dress of sprigged jaconet and a coquettish leghorn bonnet. Hump, guess it's right they're starvin', Parker derided silently. She's not so gosh-dern pore she can afford to be anything but right in the style, anyhow.

She was crossing the canal, and now quite close to him. The child, in his short velvet jacket and long white trousers, followed her reluctantly, and was attracted by Parker's military appearance and dawdled an instant to expatiate on it. The girl grasped the boy's arm angrily. "Tu es bête," she reprimanded, in swift, suppressed accents. "Vite. Ne touches-pas le vilain!"

Parker did not comprehend the quick, scornful words, but the intonation with which she uttered them expressed enough. The hysterical jerk she gave to the child's sleeve fixed the Union soldier in a bitter sense of protest, half astonishment. I'm dad-blamed if I won't treat one o' these hussies like they deserve, he said to himself.

Again his eyes met the girl's. Christ, ain't she got enough! He had half a mind to tell her 'right out' what he thought of her behaviour. Bold as brass. Jest invitin' you to make eyes at 'em, and then hoity-toity if you do.

The antagonism exchanged in the common glance outraged Parker's feeling of the appropriate. Come on. Give us a kiss and I'll slap your face. He had almost said it aloud.

But she was hastening on, flouncing her skirts. For a 'red cent' he'd tear all those hoops an' ruffles an' things off of her. Leave her in her skin, like she was made, an' no better'n anybody else.

It seemed to Parker that life was 'pretty hard right now anyhow.' He had a 'bellyful' of the army. Victuals you couldn't swallow, risk your life almost every day in the week, and what thanks did you get for it? But when it 'come' to these Southern belles 'puttin' on airs, figurin' they could treat you 'like the dirt under their feet—hell.'

Parker, his jaw hard, but his mouth a little tremulous under his preciously tended moustaches, watched the disdainful young woman's progress all the way across the broad street, where, reaching a corner, she turned.

Rue Royale—that must be where she was going—Rue Roy-i-el. He was learning the names of these 'gosh-dern' thoroughfares. French? Well, we all heard about *you* before. We all knows the French is a race without no sense of religion nor nothin'.

He moved on, detaining himself, making his footsteps laggard, so that she need not imagine that he was following her, 'the stuck-up bitch.' As he wandered, his fancy dwelt vengefully on stories he had heard of the abuses of slavery, of Southern immorality. Wisht we hadn't stopped the hawkin' an' sellin' of niggers 'fore I had a look at it, he mused vexedly. If the old general hadn't stopped the practice I'd be able to see some things ud set the people up home by the ears. Like to show that Judy that just went by what I know about her and her aristocracy. Aristocracy, they call it. ——!

Parker remained so incensed and absorbed in indignation that he lost his way. He had left the canal, but scarcely knew where he was going when a shadowed alley, damp and cool, invited his bewilderment. He traversed it grudgingly, sheltering himself under the blank wall of a house, but soon arrived, to his disgust, in open sun again.

Jackson Square. Yes, this here's the place where they got the statue. He halted, blinking uncomfortably, and attempting to throw off the nettled sensations of affronted dignity which came with every casual contact with the populace of New Orleans. Wisht he had somebody along he could 'shoot craps with for a drink.' There was a 'heap' of 'mighty good liquor' stowed away in this city, if anybody who 'looked like a Federal' could get at it. Trouble was, during the first few days of the occupation, the 'boys' had celebrated victory somewhat too freely. General Butler had placed restrictions on their indulgence. It don't touch these —— Creoles. I'll bet they drink more than they can hold, like a lot o' hogs.

Parker strolled toward the river. He supposed he 'ought to see the sights.' But the stolid glitter of the water palled, and for some

116

reason a glimpse of the bulky hull of one of his own Federal war-ships, anchored farther down the wharf, heightened his uneasiness.

It was certainly a gorgeous day. A moist, blue sky swam indefinitely above the crumpled, fresh leaves of the square. Crêpe myrtles, for him unnamed, flung a withered pink, as of discarded gardens, among the deeper foliage of the larger trees. Under the profound arches of the Cabildo, an old negress, her face stoic beneath the gaudy insolence of a red and orange bandanna, sat, upright, on a stool, before a basket of pralines, and, with a palm-leaf fan, waved ritualistically, somnolently discouraged flies.

Parker liked sweets, and considered buying some, but there might be the usual discussion about Federal money—and was this valid, or was that valid, as an exchange. He had heard enough.

Tramping back and forth in the contracting shade of the Cabildo's façade, a sentry in blue conveyed to Parker a certain comfort in the recognized Federal possession of all state buildings. He glanced at the fellow without speaking; but the intangible reassurance derived from an inspection of a soldier under his own colours, soothed. Parker had never been 'too pious,' but he had been told that the Cathedral of St. Louis was 'worth visiting.' He'd be 'damned' if these '—— damned rebs' could 'keep' him out.

Indeed it was so warm out of doors that the vast, hollow twilight which he glimpsed through the open cathedral entrance drew him irresistibly. The square fumed with cloying sunlight. A little wind blew hot from the alleys on either side of the church, and loosed crêpe myrtle petals fell like a pink, rumpled confetti upon the earth worn bare by children's constant feet. It was true that a stink of sewers did come, with the breeze, and the perfume, and the pale magenta flowers, and he could curse righteously the filth of adjacent streets, paved with boards that made an imperfect enclosure for the stagnant marsh water running sluggishly beneath. And there were the nasal shrieks of little boys in black smocks who broke the quiet with play. And the glare fatigued his hating eyes almost unendurably.

Parker saw two ladies in white, lace shawls draped like mantillas upon their heads, mount the stone stairs and disappear into the church. With irritable bravado, he followed them. Religion, he had always understood, was for 'everybody,' and they might keep their prejudices undiscussed in a sacred place.

The yearning for 'a drink' was strong in his thoughts, as he passed over the threshold; yet, baffled by the impression of a reticent, high-windowed interior, his step, as it sounded on the inner flagstones, became superstitiously diffident. The church, in contrast to the square, seemed cold. For an instant, he had the illusion that it was almost empty. Then he saw the deserted gallery, the pillars lost in oppressive obscurity, and away, in an exalted recess, vast above many stairs, the altar twinkling in its gloomy gilt.

As he halted by a granite holy-water basin, the antiphonal murmurings of many voices became abruptly, alarmingly distinct. "Seigneur, ayez pitié de nous. Jésus-Christ, ayez pitié de nous. Jésus, écoutez-nous. Jesus, exaucez-nous." The faint, almost surreptitious sibilance was like the droning of insects amidst dim flowerings made by the ladies' shawls, though there was predominant, in the colouring, the repelling note of black.

The word 'pitié,' repeated incessantly, did indicate, for Parker, a certain quality of desperation in the words. But he resisted intimations of feelings with which he was not willing to credit 'rebels.' The two women he had followed, had advanced, without noticing him, into a side chapel, and knelt in the flat glitter reflected on burnished saint's robes from candles, drizzling wax over a circular wire frame. And from their lips, too, there soon was audible, "Seigneur, ayez pitié de nous. Jésus, écoutez nous."

A sense of formal calamity seemed to pervade the place. Parker acknowledged to himself 'the creeps.' A context of general melancholy in the undefined mutterings, seemed to him an especial, unmerited rebuke. Gawd, he thought, you'd think they was the only ones the war was hurtin', like as if the occupation of their gosh-damned city didn't cost *us* nothin'.

The same frustrate need for escape from injustice which had urged him to essay this spot blind of all proper daylight, now drove him toward a narrow exit through which sun obtruded baldly from the alleyway. Pursued by a discomforting awareness of the crouched, painted statues, in their perpetual postures indicating suppliance or mercy, he walked hastily, allowing his boots to ring, and gained egress into the foetid usualness of the heavy noon. He thought, Hell, I seen enough dead men in my life to gimme nightmares for a week, but I don't go 'round huggin' the recollection of such things, I ain't got no use for Catholics anyway.

The glare fell, flat and unalterable, on the mouldy plaster walls of the houses. He strolled on more rapidly, glancing to the right and left of him, hoping that, on the next thoroughfare into which he turned, he might discover some establishment in which whisky was sold. I *got* to have a drink, he thought. He threw back his shoulders. The 'boys' had to admit to him that he had a 'good, muscular set' to his figure. Any 'reb' that was 'calculatin' , to overthrow *him* would have 'his work cut out.' Females like a man what can master 'em, too. 'A woman, a dog, and a walnut tree—' That's about the size of it. That Jezebel that wanted to put a gob of spit between my eyes this mornin'—she'd have a surprise fer her, if she knew how used I was to tellin' gals like her what they got to expect.

Parker had, habitually, a great reverence for authority. But this conviction that he 'had to git a drink or bust' was becoming overpowering. Nothin' to do in this blame town either. When you do git some time to yourself, nobody to spend it with. They say these nigger wenches ain't hard to git at. Buy about anything they got for fifteen cents—ef you want it. But I guess I'll leave that sort of carousin' to the Southern *aristocracy*. That gal—guess her pa an' her brothers an' all the rest of 'em have that kind of thing. I certainly did have bad luck that ol' Ike Pryor didn't get his leave when I did. He can raise enough rumpus to wake the dead. Bet he wouldn't let none of the *real* sights of New Orleans git away from him. He'd show these here cussed heathen what was worth somethin'. 'Member how that rebel gal leaned off to smack him and he popped her a kiss right on the mouth? She liked it, too. See her lickin' her chops an' makin' eyes at him the whole time she was gittin' off that sass. I'd do more'n kiss her ef I was in your shoes, Ike, I says. An' he says, fer a little more jaw I will. An' I believe he done it, too. When we was all off, an' I seen her an' him alone at the gate of that farmhouse. You got to git *some* fun outa the war. Christ, I been wadin' round in muck up to my ears, and so tired I couldn't tell my head from my left toe, and I says to Ike, what we want when we gits to some town where some rebel gals are is a good time. If I wasn't so —— —— particular, I could o' had it more than once. They're just eatin' themselves up with jealousy an' askin' you to make up to 'em. And when you ain't laid eyes on a decent female fer the last fifteen months, you could stand even *their* kind—like that pepper-pot tryin' to git me to insult her a while ago. I wouldn't give her the satisfaction of *sayin'* nothin', but I'm thinkin' a heap, Miss Frenchie. I guess if you had any idea what I think about you, you'd just about drop through the street and right down into the dirty water in that canal. I could handle *you* easy enough. You got the thoroughbred idea of yourself—like the Kentucky colonel—fast women an' fine horses, they says—an' a pretty fancy lot. 'Tain't no different down here, you can be —— sure.

Parker covered up his thoughts. He was before a shop with dirty windows, in which reclined, cobwebbed, and seemingly unsought, three or four wine bottles. He wheeled, heady with abrupt decision, pushed at dirt-clouded door, and stepped inside the place.

It was nearly dark. For an instant, he fancied himself alone. Curiously, on entering the shop, Parker experienced the same chill, and the same hesitation that had come upon him in the cathedral. He was determined not to be a second time vanquished by unreasoned doubt of his right to intrude. He was a free citizen of the Union. Any shop in this —— city, he could 'buy out' if he felt that way.

To the rear of the room in which he stood, another door was ajar. The vividness of green, deep in acid yellow sunlight, revealed a courtyard. He hesitated, confusedly. He was in a place where, behind the shop, people lived. Rapid glimpses of these secretively constructed courts had annoyed him for the length of his walk from the church. He had glanced through massive iron grilles, rapidly closed in his very face, and had observed that stolid house-front after stolid house-front, with its shuttered balconies, walled in some such nook of luxurious verdure. In his antagonism to the city, it had appeared to him that the very architecture, with the habits of life implied, defied the just prerogatives of conquerors, and was designed to keep him on the alien fringe of the native life. So he was pleased that, intending only to demand a purchase, he had strayed into an atmosphere so intimate.

There were several tables in the store. A woman sat in a corner with her knitting, and in the protected garden a little negress and a white baby were romping together. A counter barricaded one side of the room. Parker advanced toward it and brought his fist down peremptorily on the bare boards. The stout woman who was knitting—doing 'crewel work,' maybe it was, Parker decided, after a second brief inspection of her occupation—rose, went out to the edge of the court, and screamed something in French, in a vibrant, alarmed voice. In apparent reply to her words, a small hunch-backed man teetered softly indoors, tiptoeing swiftly, and gazing cautiously, from his child's height, at Parker's pugnacious face.

Stepping diffidently behind his own shelves, the hunchback said, "Que voulez-vous, messieu?" and, staring up with his large, inordinately meditative eyes, his big, narrow head cocked at an inquiring angle between his scooped, pointed shoulders, waited for an answer.

"I want some whisky," Parker retorted, uneasily ready to assert comprehension despite the tongue spoken to him. "Gimme a straight whisky, or if you ain't got any whisky, gimme some gin. I see a gin bottle settin' up on that wall behind you."

The hunchback, with a smile, so sad, so filled with timid apology, his large eyes funereally direct, begging, it appeared, for lenience, twisted his neck slowly, gazed consideringly at the shelf. "C'est dé-fen-du: Eet ees—I am—not—allow—to sell eet. The Fed-er-al a-thor-i-ty prohibit. Zay say no more strong lee-quer to soldier." Still smiling wanly, he waited to be understood, his hands spread out doubtfully. "Ef I sell you strong lee-quer I am ar-res-ted." The last words, haunted by uncertainties, were a lame effort at joviality.

"The hell you ain't allowed to sell liquor. What you got your store open for, if you don't sell anything?"

"I sell you a lee-tle mild wine. I have some very nice—" Interrupting himself, the dwarf moved back, placed a chair to assist him, and, when he had clambered upon it, removed a bottle from an upper shelf, dusting it lovingly with the tail of the short smock he wore. "Eet ees ver-y good vintage."

Parker interrupted him. "Take your slop back. Gimme that bottle of old Jamaica rum up there on the top shelf. That there bottle with the nigger head on it. Give it to me quick and shut your mouth. I got some honest-to-God money to pay for it with, so you better take it and be thankful."

The hunchback, his long slender hands beginning to tremble,

demurred. "You take dees, *Capitaine*. I cannot afford to be fined. I get put in jail. *Générale* Butler he issue an order, no wheesky or strong drink to de soldiers. I have my family. Dees war go good for you, eet go bad for everybody else."

Parker fumbled a bill from his pocket and laid it on the counter. "No. Come on and shut up. I'm usta gittin' what I want. Hustle, now."

The man began to climb, with feeble agility, from the chair, just having replaced the wine bottle, and bringing the gin with him. As he descended, Parker noted that he exchanged a swift glance with his wife.

"Henri—Meester—I deman'—I say my husband shall not sell dat gin." The slow, stout woman was youngish, and not unhandsome. As she rose weightily to her feet and came toward the two, Parker observed her plump, neat features moulded heavily by indignation. She was rosy, and had small pencillings like faint moustaches on her upper lip. "Fermes la porte," she stopped to call, in an angry shrill to the little negress; and herself anticipated obedience by slamming the door which opened on the court.

Parker ignored her, and grasped the bottle from the hunchback's half-withholding hand. "Gimme a corkscrew. I'm gonta have a drink here and now, and she"—nodding to the woman—"aint' gonta interfere with me."

'Henri' rattled objects in a drawer beneath the counter and finally brought the corkscrew forth. The woman, panting, dumb with righteous rage, tried to intercept its presentation. Abusive French flowed querulously and excitably from her lips. Parker fought, obstinately restraining himself from a temptation to do her injury. When he had secured the corkscrew and was inserting it in the cork, she clutched his elbow. The corkscrew, dragged, raspingly, over the neck of the bottle, scratched his sustaining fingers painfully.

"Ain't you got a tumbler?"

The hunchback, as if worried by a blind subservience, evaded his wife mutely, and hastily sought out the glass. Parker took it avidly, and, resting firm against the woman's attempt to intercept the gesture, poured the lucid rum, with its faint tint of yellow, into the glass. "Tais-toi, tais-toi," the hunchback kept murmuring to his wife.

122

Parker held the tumbler up, three-quarters full, and drained it difficultly. He was already in a fever of exasperation. And the rum, washing like a scald down his tight throat, sent a wave of hatred to his brain. "Now look ahere," he announced, setting the glass down on the counter and staring about him, with a feeling that the blurred glitter from the sunny street, bubbled, in the dim room, under his eyelids, "I stood enough from you ruffians. I ain't got no more patience with you. I come here as a honest American puttin' the welfare o' the Union before my own selfish interests, an' I ain't gonta be sassed and talked up to by no son of a gun south of Mason an' Dixon's line. What's more, you ain't *even* Americans. I dunno what you are or how you come here. But I ain't fought and bled in this war for nothin'. I like a good time same as anybody. Your wife, there, she knows what I'm talkin' about. She knowed when I come in here and said I wanted rum— or whisky—that I *wanted* rum. She'd be the last person to deny me. I see through you, old gal—ol' Madame—Madame What-you-call-it. And there's some pretty well set-up boys in the army. Some you'd be glad to have take notice of you. They can manage some o' you thoroughbred customers same as they'd manage a horse. You don't believe me, old gal? You calculate to git around me, eh? Well, you know how I come up to that reb fellow an' stick the whole length of a bayonet right through his derned *en*trails—right through so it come out behind and stuck through on the other side of him. And I can do plenty more'n that. Female folks, too. You ask my partner, Ike. I ain't complain', old woman, 'cause you set out to defend your husband's business and acted hasty with me. The bloom is off the peach this time, an' I don't commit no crimes fer *that* kind. But when Mr. Abe Lincoln took me on fer a fighter, he took me on fer a fighter. A fighter's respected. He's got to do all the damage he can in war time, and he's got to do all the damage he can when he's on his leave—like me. I mean where these hoity-toity females is concerned. Good-bye, weasel-face. Me an' my bottle are goin' out. I wish you joy o' that bitch o' yours, but before I get through with this city I'm gonta find some gal who's good-lookin'. And if I don't beat the rambunctiousness out of her, an' give her more'n them kind of fancy gals deserve, you can eat my hat."

Parker, exhausted by the fluctuating excitement of narration,

123

poured out more gin, drank it, with more pain than enjoyment, plucked the bottle from the counter, and turned toward the street. As he left the shop, the terrified anticipation of becoming sober seemed to follow him. He was only vaguely conscious of what he said—save that he had insulted that woman. But before he finished with the day, he was going to hurt somebody sure enough—physically. Catch him with this liquor on him and the military police would 'land' him in the 'lock-up.' Even that didn't seem to matter much. His reflections were just one dulled vituperative sensation of abuse. He was an abused man. Before evening, he was going to 'raise hell.' He guessed he had 'got used' to seeing folks shot to pieces and bayonetted to pieces so they looked less than anything that had ever been a human being. But if he had to feel like this, he had to. He wanted to do something to somebody—preferably a woman—that would make warfare seem 'next to nothin'.'

As he stepped out of doors, and swayed on the wooden banquette, the sun's glint sinking little nauseating rays into his eyes, he tried bitterly to ignore the loathing, hating glances that were following him.

IV

The night might have been made of grey lead. Then that was the moon, swinging like a prism in the big catalpa tree. The night was something you could stand in secretly, and not a heartbeat overheard. It went by. Three little grey, silver fingers crept over the lawn and fingered the Rose o' Sharon. The night was something big, like a carpet of grey moss, to walk on, over the hedge, over the stone wall that divided the field from the garden; and you tiptoed on the soft boughs. You would walk on with your face bleeding from the silver claws scratching at you, scratching at the foliage.

He could see Callista at the piano, playing eloquently, with wrists arched over the yellowed keyboard. George and Rowena and Robert Ramsay were there beside her, singing *Loreena*. And the room, so enchanted through its veil of lace spread fine like a stiff mist over the window, floated, terrible, definite on the vague face of the out-of-doors. Hallie knew that he was waiting. In a mo-

124

ment she would be beside him. He had sent the message to her before leaving Williamsburg.

> "It *mat*-ters lit-tle *now*, Lo-*reen*-a,
> The *past* is *the* e-*ter*-nal *past*.
> Our *heads* will *soon* lie *low*, Lo-*reen*-a,
> Life's *tide* is *ebb*-ing *out* so *fast*.
>
> But there's a *fu*-ture, oh, thank *God*,
> Of *life* this *is* so *small* a *part*.
> 'Tis *dust* to *dust* be-*neath* the *sod*,
> But *there*, up *there*—'tis *heart* to *heart*."

The voices, in a din of shrill emotion, flew fast through the window, and scattered: Rowena's in thin, youthful soaring, and those of the young men strong and husky with some awkward sentiment. When the tinkling chords crashed emphatically on the last feeble ecstasy, and George laughed hoarsely, the ostentatious clink of spurs and sabres could be heard. A cardboard figure that was Robert Ramsay clasped Callista's waist and lifted her from the piano stool, and a wheel of white muslin revolved unconvincingly in the glow of the astral lamp. Then could be discerned, as in that other world beyond the half-drawn blind, two people embracing, something relentless in their common posture as they crushed each other close.

The young man outside waited. When Hallie came—when they could smell together the odour that crept to him now, of the new garden, of the young nettle that *would* catch her flounces when she was near him, when a damp chill warned her of the brook below, even before she could glimpse its scalded waters rushing with vivid brands of moonlight through the deep bushes—when Hallie came: then he would try to see her eyes. And he was frightened of what he would understand in them.

It wasn't that she didn't love him. She loved him enough—more than enough—and he loved her equally. But he was alarmed.

The night burned now with a *grey* smell, bitter in his nostrils, and like something blown backward to him from the place that he· had come away from—to escape to Hallie. He always escaped to Hallie. When there were ugly things around him, he could 'get through them somehow,' and he would spend hours awake, afterward, staring up from his cot through the tent flap at stars that

125

drilled some wicked insistence into his brain. He wished to ignore this thought, half a thought, and suggested by something permanent, and, so, indifferent, in the aspect of the monotonously studded heavens, and dwell entirely on her familiar gestures: on the turn of her head, her neck that was like a column of milk, a curl dishevelled from her chignon and intimate as a serpent with the white flesh it embraced. And her eyes—there was something almost oppressive in the disarmed gaze that became limpid and eager to shallowness on his mere insistence that she must love him 'completely,' and hold nothing back from him. He was afraid of some as-yet-secret ultimate possession of her, because, when she had really given him all of herself that she had to offer, the gift was one that, in his way of thinking, he could not give back. He dreaded feeling responsible for Hallie. What he wanted most in this life was his 'freedom.' Freedom he did not define, and shame prevented him from calling her attention to this necessity. She would not comprehend what he considered his freedom, nor recognize the importance, for him, of encompassing it. Since the war began, that freedom, which was a sign, a symbol, of the enjoyment of all earthly things, had an added preciousness.

Hallie would look at him. He fancied he could hear her coming now. A moth drifted in a mild spark out of the grass. Rain was gathering. Soon the moon would give way to another urge in the thickening air. Drops, falling, chill and teasing, would mark him all over with faint, insistent touches, like the reach of hands. Hallie approaching over the brook, they would retreat into the summer-house. Then the rain would come down in the dark, and they listen, muted, their bodies still and happy, because thought was not needed, and no more was needed till the world should end.

It was misty already. The people in the parlour were indistinct behind the bright, active yellow blind; and they were farther off. More alive were the spasmodic glitters of the fireflies. One, fallen, glowed numbly in the mat of weeds by the water's edge. Fireflies, bled, twitching, from the overcast sky, dripped in the neglected garden paths, and lay, in iridescent litters, among the rosebushes. Little febrile accents grew, and glowed sharper on the stolid, sultry dark out of which the moon was fading. Then their brittle dancing fever on the sightless calm ended its space of living as if in obedience to the authority of a distant thunder clap.

The lamp in the parlour went out, and left the house, grey as salt, with its wooden pillars in some deep woe under the trees. At last he could see *her*, wavering toward him, undecided, in a pale dress, down the path. Another rain-drop blessed his cold face, fixed in an expression which he knew, somehow, to be very ugly—some expression not intended for Hallie—never, *never* intended for Hallie. He had to live for himself. The war had taught him that much. He could feel something cruel, satisfying at last, coming into his anticipation of her. Some demand had been made of him which he had found at first too hideous to fulfil. Little worms ate, fancifully, in and out of his brain—as the fireflies had scuddered, in their glitter, through the black lawn—Hallie and himself, passive, in the summer-house—and some awful hate, for himself—and for her, too—of George, Callista and Robert Ramsay, singing *Loreena* in the parlour, the flat, tinny notes of the piano arousing in him the conviction that he would go entirely wild—out of his mind—if he could not see Hallie at once. There was absolutely nothing of herself that she had any right to, that he would not demand of her.

The rain was arrested. Stars swam, for a minute, in a green dish of sky. Their wicked spice was in the clouds that were drawing away from some nakedness he could not endure facing. Dead, solid trees rolled from the east. The sucked bushes made death rattles all around him, sending, in the spring wind, paper leaves of last year over the bleared ground. A dog barked, stately, monotonous as a frog. In the lights that crept, slithering, over the sleepy boughs, the house faded. The garden was like crowded water. The gliding pinnacle on the roof of the summer-house shrivelled stilly to a bud of whitewashing. Serpents, tossing on the path, lay inert. Soon, only sky would remain.

Hallie was *here*. Neither of them could speak. Like the answer to some stifling interrogation, their warmed faces touched blindly. The worms crawled over the grass, he imagined, and he thought, miserably: In fifty years from now—in nineteen-twenty—or forty —who cares.

It was only later, when he had drawn her inside the summer-house, and they crouched together in a kind of shame of their own silence, which neither could bear to break, that his relief in being so close again to her warm body which yielded to him before he could desire to hurt her, made him say to himself, painfully, as he crushed her harshly to him, If we weren't going to die anyhow I couldn't stand it. The compassion he had for both of them because they *were* 'going sooner or later to the same place as those other fellows —up at Williamsburg' broke down a fierceness, a hate even of his own infatuation. The gentle-lonely relaxation to the thought of death made him long to cry on her breast. Only one red window on a hill, 'at the Gordon place,' seemed left in the night to signal the blinded. He glanced at it, afraid, like a child, and said, "Hallie, I do love you, and that's the truth—I know it now."

He had never before confessed to her outright that he loved her. Still she felt uncomfortable. She believed that he ought, if he loved her, to tell her that he wanted her to marry him, and he had never mentioned it. It seemed to her that the demoralization of war-time had made them both unclean.

V

ELOISE sat in the upper room and waited. It was after the soup served to the 'pensionnaires,' and Madame Ducros, seeing that the darkies had left everything in order, had gone out. Eloise, listening for the subsiding of her mother's footsteps, heard them depart only to find the silence fill with other noises. Major Stafford, Captain Deering, and Colonel Alcott had not delayed long over the evening meal; so that furtive tread below in the *salle à manger* could but mean that *he*—Lieutenant Fisk—had remained at home again.

Eloise listened to him, trembling. The benign, last daylight, rosy on the high-walled ceiling, was absorbed gradually in a colourless substance that was night. A breeze from Lake Pontchartrain, acrid with the swamps and gutters the winds traversed, flowed in the tall, opened windows that fronted the balcony. The shabby consoles stood with their polished legs in a twilight like water. The shadowy plush-brocade of the curtains formally enclosed the inner dusk, but revealed, through their substantial partings, the more radiant reflections left in the aqueous sky, gorgeous beyond the close roofs of the street.

Lieutenant Fisk's bedroom was in the rear of the house. Eloise, when, later, she tiptoed boldly to her own room, could see, above the well of black-smudged foliage in the damp court, the fleet, soft spire of the candle flame on his writing-table. She hid herself, keeping the cathedral heights of her four-poster bed between her and her own window, and spied on that precise, remote, little profile of the man writing and unaware of her observation.

Lieutenant Fisk was so meticulous as to grooming and deportment that even to surprise him without his sabre—and she had watched him unbuckle its belt and lay the weapon across a chair—was to see him undressed.

Could it be that he was composing for her again one of those correctly apologetic epistles such as he had already sent her by his servant, in which was explained the entire innocence of himself and his friends in the matter of interpreting General Butler's ultimatum to the females of New Orleans? "Methinks he doth protest too much," Eloise had heard Colonel Alcott say. And she burned with futile indignation when she recalled that remark and many another like it: added to the fat colonel's smirking glance that always commended her appearance.

It was the opinion of Eloise that her mother had made an irretrievable error in accepting the billeting on her of Federal officers. Madame Ducros had foolishly consigned the cotton from her own plantation to the fire which had prevented the Union government from making use of the commodity. After that act of heroism, the lady had seemed crushed.

"Why did you do it, Maman? You complain that none of our relatives any longer concern themselves with us. Why sacrifice the pittance we could get from cotton when you receive no thanks?"

Madame Ducros, on her return after witnessing the conflagration on the levee, had succumbed wearily, in an armchair, to her discouragement. She was a small woman, dressed always in a plainly flounced black garment, the upper portion of which flowed loosely, like a *matinée*, over bosom and stomach. Her dry face was firmly peevish, and her eyes, filled with the glitter of a perpetual resentment, somewhat crafty. She used few words.

"What was there to do? A widow—no father to protect my children—what could I do? How did I know that the Union forces were going to occupy the city? If I had tried to save my store from the plantation, it would have been said of me that I had Yankee sympathies. I am not rich enough to ignore the criticisms of my neighbours.'

Eloise, baffled by this final argument, and loath to display weak emotion before a mother so indomitable, had left the room angrily, to fling herself upon this very bed by which she stood and watched the constant enemy, now lodged inexcusably inside her home.

Food was very scarce. Shortages in victuals were actual, and shortages more discomfiting already prophesied. Madame Ducros had deemed it the best solution for her equivocal beggary—for 'beggary' she rightly termed her reduced state—to suppress resentment and apply at Federal headquarters with offers of her own establishment for a Union boarding-house.

"But what will people say, Maman?" Eloise, always fiercely sensitive to the cruelties of public opinion, felt that Maman's reckless decision to court the foe took the family from the frying-pan into the fire. After the scandal of proffered hospitality to Yankees had been spread about, no decent person in New Orleans would ever speak further with one of its members.

Madame Ducros did not pretend to discuss conclusions with her daughter. Tall, pale Eloise, with her white, thin face—'*très distinguée*,' she was called by the generous minority—her grimly pretty mouth, and her brilliant, over-prominent eyes, remained an enigma. Madame Ducros had begun life with theories of filial obedience, but had been obliged to discard them. When in a sentimental mood, the elderly lady was wont to explain, for the benefit of outsiders, that her child had 'suffered.' "*La pauvre! La pauvre!*" Madame Ducros would expatiate. "She is too high-strung, too true and noble in her feelings—has too much sensibility."

Despite these propitiatory tenders, made rather from family pride than from personal sympathy for the girl's ways, the elder lady refused to consult the younger one about anything. "General Butler, he has declared our slaves contraband. Work on the property out in the country is at a standstill. There will be no cane and no sugar this year at all, and we are poor enough. Our overseer, he has been found out to be a Union man. He wants to see the property ruined and us deprived of the barest sustenance. I have three girls here—Angèle, Toinette and Gigi. They are so far satisfied, but if they see the example of other servants abandoning their masters and we have not enough to *feed* them, what will these three girls do? That little slattern, Gigi, is becoming already impudent. She would be glad enough to quit us in her honest position of a slave working for a good mistress who requites her beyond her deserts and pays some attention to her religious needs, and instead of maintaining herself in useful employment accept the shameless advances of some Yankee who would beguile her into thinking an existence passed in concubinage worth the loss of her immortal soul—since Père Favre is generous enough to endow her with one. If I offer pension to five or six Federal officers they will pay me well enough—having taken all our own money from us—and we will not have to face the problem of an empty larder. If there is a food crisis, it will not affect us. That will give us opportunity to look around, and consider what provision we can make for ourselves when this accursed war is finished."

Eloise had been almost maddened by this common sense. Her opinion of men in general was very low, and her fastidiousness was affronted by the injection into her own sphere of men searching for handsome little negresses like Gigi with whom to beguile their leisure hours.

But poverty was a terror which Eloise appreciated. Gazing, through her window, now gratefully dark, at the forwardly inclined profile of Lieutenant Fisk, who was earnestly pushing what must be a pen over some obscure surface that must be paper, she longed for language sufficiently eloquent to express the wrath, the wretched indignations, she had suffered in his enforced society.

Inscrutable as Eloise was to Maman, and as she gloried in being, Maman herself presented aspects of conduct unelucidated to her daughter. Take Maman's attitude toward Colonel Alcott. He was a fat, pursy old man, almost as obnoxious in person as that grotesque mountain of pomposity, General Butler. Colonel Alcott had a very red face, a big nose, like a Guignol, and a wise manner, insufferably familiar. Eloise had attempted to present her view of him in the English language and had not been able to do so. Limited English was beginning to provoke her to mad humiliations. Eloise was 'not' a Creole. Maman had been born near Paris, at Fontainebleau, and Eloise resisted vocal inclination to the Creole 'dis' and 'dat.' But Lieutenant Fisk, beyond a capacity to state 'Bonsoir,' had no aptitude whatever for the French tongue. So, when Eloise, as now, felt most abusive toward him, she was physically half suffocated by a sense of frustrateness.

Colonel Alcott 'loved' his stomach. "He is a gourmand," Eloise would say fiercely, "a peeg, a peeg, he is a peeg," in English. Yet, somehow, he and Maman had already come to a kind of 'understanding.' He joked with her. Maman invited him to the kitchen and showed him how sauces were made. He delighted in gumbo, in crawfish bisque. Maman plied him with all the available luxuries of living, and, in his quietly offensive way, he responded with stodgy appreciation.

"He insults me," Eloise would insist, her flat breast heaving.

"Whenever I come into the *salle à manger* he glances first at me, and then at Lieutenant Fisk. He makes remarks about us, fit only for Gigi to listen to. Have you no pride for your daughter? I will leave you all. I will not bear another moment of his insolence."

Maman responded *so* patiently, her little thin shoulders sagging over the bowl in which she was mixing madeleines. "He is old. He thinks of nothing but what he has to eat. Besides, he is a useful friend. If you will condescend to be more practical—ignore if you must, but do not try to deliberately antagonize him—he will be very good to us."

Eloise made several paces up and down in the dark. The courtyard was so still. Gigi, Toinette, Angèle, Maman, Louis, they had all gone out. She felt herself yielding to some debasing plot. Had Maman gone and taken everybody with her and done it purposely?

There was no answer other than could be vouchsafed in observation of the sleek head of Lieutenant Fisk, dapper with its carefully combed side-whiskers, which Eloise had often, between violence and the conviction that he repelled her, felt that she could 'pull out.'

In the several panes of the window, the candle's reflection bloomed multifariously. At his desk, the young man sat neatly on the background of the obscure room behind him, working, it appeared, with aggravating diligence. Slowly, between her and the abhorred image, the milky thunder of a big moon rolled up from the wall, drew its charnel length on the roofs, and left the courtyard a thicket of silver spars. A hackberry tree, growing there below, reared like a mast with dustied pennants. An oleander spread frowzy peaks of uncoloured flowers to a glow brighter than the daylight, but deadly. Like a vivid disease, every star on the jasmine by the fountain whitened to timid revelation. The world of the courtyard spread through ten thousand miles of languor and the gloomed planets, apparent half an hour before, sifted away in brilliant centuries of denuded calm.

As much as was possible, Eloise resisted the invitation to ecstatic feeling. What was moonlight and the privacy of night to *her*, who hated men and marriage and was done with the folly of yielding anything! At sixteen she had been '*très belle*,' and of the first successfully offered by the mammas of the generation in the marriage market. It was hideous to remember her own cocksure satisfaction with Maman's discovery of a wealthy son-in-law. René Blanchard had been his name. Eloise had only to close her eyes to the present to see that pert, debonair face—then described by Maman as '*si mignon.*' René had ogled Madame Ducros, Eloise had lately decided. Such had been the origin of the whole thing. It was Maman only, not admitting it, who had desired the match.

After the announcement, after the public declaration that they were affianced, he had gone away. In American, when René had discovered that Maman lied and Eloise had no 'dot' worth while, he had 'jilted' her. All that was of ten years before. Some said that René Blanchard had migrated to California in the 'gold fever' and had grown rich out there.

Eloise did not inquire after him or his whereabouts, did not mention his name. When he had left her, and she 'disgraced' by 'as good as marriage' she had suffered intensely—too much to care, in these recent, still more impecunious days, to dwell on recollection. At the mere suggestion of that scoundrel, at the mere hint that he still existed, she would shudder, as she was doing now; because, though she would 'cut out' her tongue before she confessed as much to Maman, she had once believed herself in love with him.

Love? No, she had 'adored' him. With all the devotion she felt for bitter moods, she could lie here on her bed, on her back, under the quilted tester that swung sombrely above her, and—watching Lieutenant Fisk writing, watching the secret rosy streamer of his candle sinking in the obliterating moonlight—augment past miseries with other, present miseries, until very horror became elation. The familiar monotony of these meditations was like the throbbing of a numbed wound. The boldness of the glare, falling directly upon her face, was an appropriate insult to her abandon. She was admired and respected, as she deserved to be, *by nobody.*

At the time when the wound to her *amour-propre* had been freshest, and her indulgence in indiscriminate reproach most hearty, Maman had given it out to their friends and relatives that Eloise revealed a 'vocation' for religious life.

Would that this had indeed been true. Eloise grudged her own ambition for matrimony. She had long been torn between the impossibility of acknowledging permanent failure, and a kind of recklessness very nearly wanton.

But no one should know. No one should *ever* know. Had it not been for the unhappy accident of having an idiot for a brother, she might have resigned herself to the designation of a '*vieille fille*' more becomingly.

Louis was the unbearable thorn in her most tortured flesh. Imagine a man of thirty, very fat—round, indeed—good-looking, with a profile in some way resembling the profile of young Lieutenent Fisk;' but an utter 'innocent.' He had fresh-coloured cheeks, plump short arms and hands, a small, beautiful, little black moustache. Yet his features seemed entirely unimportant; his blue eyes, in particular, retaining no hint of 'mind' or 'character.' He was imitative in a most primitive degree, and liked to consider himself dressed as one of the military; but his mother allowed him only the old clothing of a wealthy nephew very much younger. Louis's pink wrists always protruded from cramped sleeves. His coat would not button across his paunchy chest. His fat buttocks strained his abbreviated trousers to the point of conspicuous absurdity. And he was infatuated with the Federal lodgers.

To be sure, Lieutenant Fisk admired Louis's sister. That had been evident on the first day, when the idiot, with uncanny observation, had presented the almost brusquely bashful officer with a handkerchief that Eloise had dropped unwittingly upon the stairs. This was bad enough. Worse fate had governed the impulse which had brought Louis to the *salle à manger* bearing, like an offering for the disturbed officer, Eloise's soiled stays. The idiot had gone into her room while she was absent, and had picked these up.

What a scene among those at the supper table! Eloise, sent by her mother on a diplomatic errand with a plate of shrimp, entered the room just at the awkward instant which made her the audience of the merry-making. Lieutenant Fisk, obviously, to judge by his tight mouth, and the repressed fire of his eye, had been indignant. He had rejected the stays. Eloise had seen him push them away with the gesture of one avoiding contamination. And the heartiness of the others—Major Stafford and Captain Deering slapping their hips, bending double with mirth, Colonel Alcott laughing so heartily, in his cunning, almost 'gloating' way, that the tears rolled out of his little wicked eyes! Louis, taken with the contagion of the rest, and mightily pleased by his ingenuous endeavour, had also, like a child, in emulation, begun to shout and to rock his body appreciatively.

135

Eloise suspected plots. Maman had argued that, if plots existed, Lieutenant Fisk's spontaneous rejection of the corsets proved his guiltlessness. The young lady did not forgive him on that account. Above certain suspicions he might be, yet the ardent repulsion he had displayed for the admittedly unsightly garment revealed, in her way of thinking, a lack of delicacy. She would not go into the hateful *salle à manger* more though she be annihilated for her obstinacy.

The long days had been terrible. The privacy of her home gone, Eloise had stolen through its corridors like a thief. She had gone to the courtyard for a breath of air only after Gigi, 'the disgraceful, spying, giggling creature,' could assure the youngest mistress of the establishment that the horrid men were out.

"I will not endure it any longer!" Eloise groaned in her bed. Moonlight crashed in the lifted window-panes. The room was as chalky as a tomb, the flowers on the bedspread silvered. Lieutenant Fisk must have snuffed his candle. She could no longer distinguish it.

Eloise had already destroyed the letters he had written but she could remember these offensive lines:

MADEMOISELLE:
My companions in arms, if I may call them so, have led me to suppose that you are under some misapprehension in regard to my conduct toward you in an episode which, though the result of an innocent impulse on the part of your brother, I am obliged to consider most unfortunate. We are in a relation to each other that demands considerable of mutual tolerance from us both, exemplifying as we do, in our opinions, the two parties of dispute whose disagreement, no doubt sincere on both sides, has rent a hitherto united country asunder. I cannot believe you so unjust, mademoiselle, as to suppose that I would, for a moment, take advantage of the privilege I have in being housed under your mother's roof, to show any disrespect for you, or even for your opinions with which I so completely disagree. Your brother's simplicity of mind, far from exciting us to condemnation, is something we can compassionate and even, I may say, envy. He meant no harm in what he did, and, while I must apologize for my brother officers, who did look on the matter in a way that must be highly offensive to your feelings, I have nothing to say for myself but that I was no more to blame than you are for what happened, and am very sorry.

And Eloise had been obliged to accept these excuses and admit Louis's fault. For days, the sight of her brother had filled her with such frenzied annoyance that Maman's emphatic statement that Louis 'spoke with angels' became intolerable. The idiot knew that he had earned his sister's disapproval, and it was evident, by his wondering, questioning manner, that he sought to comprehend his fault—even to make amends for it. His smooth brow dented like a baby's in a simulacrum of a frown. He brought his sister little treasures: scraps of bread that he had picked up in the kitchen, bits of broken crockery. But he was faithful to the soldiers, grinned earnestly and vapidly whenever he saw one of them, and assisted the military servant esconced in the kitchen to black Lieutenant Fisk's boots.

Madame Ducros was irritatingly lenient. "I begin to be sorry for that young man," she had told her daughter. "You are making his stay with us very miserable."

Eloise *would* not go downstairs tonight, since Maman had maliciously abandoned her with the lieutenant to the empty house. The new proclamation made by General Butler rendered any alteration in the present course of conduct impossible. Eloise, just as she could transcribe that hated letter from Lieutenant Fisk, could repeat the more-than-hated proclamation—every word of it.

As the officers and soldiers of the United States have been subject to repeated insults from the women (calling themselves ladies) of New Orleans, in return for the most scrupulous non-interference and courtesy on our part, it is ordered that hereafter, when any female shall, by word, gesture, or movement, insult or show contempt for any officer or soldier of the United States, she shall be regarded and held liable to be treated as a woman of the town plying her avocation.

The significance of each phrase glittered hard in her mind, as with the bitter heat of the moon. He *must* insult her, since this was so—yet how she dreaded it! She was becoming suddenly cold. She rose, craftily, always conscious that, in the puddled, moony window opposite, *he* might be standing, might be looking in. Defying him, she fumbled for the *prie-dieu* in the corner, and with a feeling as intense as illness knelt there. Maman—ah, the shame!—had tempted Eloise, in the beginning, to dress well for these abominable people —to wear her India foulard with the spots on it. Now she was habited like a nun, and had allowed herself no ornament beyond the brooch of Papa's hair. Yet, if she remained forever closeted in her own chamber, how could Lieutenant Fisk be compelled to notice these scornful alterations in costume?

Eloise prayed for what seemed to her a long time. She could see the moonlight shrinking away from the browned ceiling. The out-of-doors, invisible, seemed shrinking with it. She was aware, blindly, of the court below diminishing. The jasmine faded. The oleanders swam down into a stillness more resembling everyday uninterestingness. Shadows played deeper between the windows. The moon plunged solemnly under an opposite roof, and she was once more confronted by that insignificant pane of glass filmed by reflections from a sky traced with but a dimming opulence.

She was suffocating. The scorn of her—a Southern woman—implied in Butler's injunction, seemed to mingle with some previous distrust of her own helpless flesh. She would rather be 'dead' than have *that* man gloat over her, as he must now be doing, without suffering a rebuke which could—but murder, if she were capable of such a thing, would be inadequate.

Eloise rose and tiptoed guiltily to the window, rejecting, however, this sense of guilt. The court was a supine spot which the moon deserted. Green heavens were gloamed as with the emanations from a pyre, but nothing remained to suggest that hideous, too-beautiful exposure of the secret thought which the moon insisted on. It would not be possible to stay in the house. Isolate in her bedroom, Eloise was, she felt, trapped to be the topic of *that* man's impure meditations.

She opened her door. It *cre-eaked*. Panic improved her defiance. She was trembling in every limb, but if she was to be mistaken for one of Butler's immoral women she could, as a Sainte Thérese welcoming seven swords, welcome this indignity.

Lieutenant Fisk had walked up and down his room a dozen times. While the moon was soaring over the roofs, he had turned his shoulders resolutely to the white glare, and had sat himself down to write, dutifully, that letter to his mother that he had so long owed her. His conscientious fulfilment of this task was a source of amusement to his comrades, and he was rather irascible toward them when they presumed to comment, either on his exemplary filial attitude or on his methodicalness. Nevertheless, he

138

preferred to inscribe such epistles when he was not liable to inquisitive interruption. Evidently, he had made the letter longer than usual, for the moon had begun to slide away on some dim background of greenish heavens, when he got up from his table. Perhaps he had made his formal outpourings more lengthy than usual because, engrossed in this familiar occupation, his pulse was steadied, and he was able to leave off worrying about 'that Creole girl.'

The lieutenant detested New Orleans, and if taste, not obligation, were his measure, would never again, so he had told his friends, set foot in it. His whole experience while in this house had partaken of the quality of nightmare. And the women of the city—they were simply devilish—they were all alike. He could not blame the girl for the episode of the stays—though it might be said of her that she could keep them cleaner—but that only went to prove the absurdity of selecting as a boarding-house a place in which a member of the family was an idiot. The colonel had picked on the establishment as his choice in many offered, and Fisk, baffled by a natural inclination to revere authority, was repelled, in a helpless antagonism, by all the colonel did. "If the young lady is half as pliable as Mama, I advice you strongly not to let your opportunities slip," Colonel Alcott had said. Fisk, familiar with the colonel's solemn style in joking, had only made the enigmatic answer, "Yes, sir. You think so, sir?" But his uncertainty of just how far he would be allowed to go in resisting affront, still rankled in him.

Later—there had been the stays. Fisk felt compressed by a restraint that was torment, whenever he recalled Louis's mild gleeful entrance into the dining-room, and then the dim, offended look upon his pink, naturally childish face when the gift that he extended on his spread-out palms was ungraciously returned to him. He had refused to have the stays back, but had laid them, with an obstinate, though mild, belligerence, upon the carpet. And he had shaken and shaken his head in wonder, for, in his wordless fashion, the idiot was very ruminative.

Fisk walked to his window and stared down into the court. The position in which he had been so unfairly placed made his head ache. Morning and night, morning and night, he was compelled to worry about what that girl—with her thin, wide nostrils, and her sharp excited (yes, he *almost* thought it pretty) face—had decided about him. "If I were your age, my boy, I really should feel it a point of pride not to ignore such a brazen challenge from a member of the fair sex," Colonel Alcott had declared.

Fisk, dull to the night wind on his feverish brow, seemed to see the colonel's Punch and Judy countenance in all its ridiculing soberness. To remember a twinkle in the small piglike eye, only made things worse. Fisk, curt and polite, and embarrassed in the colonel's presence, had resolved, with a weak, harsh integrity of purpose, to 'get even' some day.

Discreet, furtive plans for revenge did not, however, solve the present difficulties. Fisk had asked to be allowed to find another boarding-place. The colonel had refused to hear of it. "You must be careful, Fisk. You know these French people have very strange ideas on marriage, and now you tell me you have written a letter of apology about that corset matter, I'm afraid you have laid yourself open to real difficulty. Why, to write a letter like that to an unmarried Creole girl is considered the same as a formal offer to her. I'll bet my hat that you won't get out of it very easily."

Fisk could smell flowers. The silent darkness, the fading moonbeams, and the subtle, mingled odour of the jasmine and the gutters upset his nerves. It was the first time that it had occurred to him that he and that 'rabid Creole woman' might be alone together in this hateful house.

General Butler's proclamation was 'the last straw.' How was he ever to convince these hysterical females that he meant no harm —that, in fact, he really loathed them—when, as Alcott said, Madame Ducros, simply upon reading Butler's orders, had a fainting fit?

He was very tired. The situation actually was obsessing. He did not seem able to dispel it from his mind for an hour together. He felt injured. When a woman insists on taking mean advantage of her weakness, what in the devil is a man who hopes he is a gentleman going to do about her?

He hesitated. The time seemed very long in the stillness, and he was half angry, half abashed, by the growing certainty that Madame Ducros, whom he had observed as she went out early in the evening, had not come home again. Suppose this *was* a plot.

His face turned numb and hot with the sudden rush of blood to his head. If that girl was waiting, with her door unlocked, she could wait all night. These people were disgusting. They were French, too, as well as Southern, and had no inkling of true morality. And there was General Butler's proclamation, and that fainting fit.

This unexpected physical discomfort hardened him. Damn it, *he'd* show them. Show Alcott and Deering, too. If he refrained from acting in the way offered by the Federal ordinance, delicacy need not be construed by anybody as a failure of his masculinity.

The moon was now so nearly disappeared that the courtyard might have been the vague depths of hell. The perfume of the flowers hung flatly, with that sour smell of the streets, in a chill that was like the interruption of midnight. Surely Madame Ducros would not remain away forever.

Fisk jerked at the collar of his uniform and pulled it open. The quiet was terrible. Then he fancied that he heard a slight noise. Somebody was here. Somebody was moving—after all.

That girl! And awake, too. If she were a little younger and better looking, I'd show her what General Butler's proclamation meant, he reflected viciously, warding away that creeping conviction that would come—the conviction that Alcott and Deering had all the time considered him a weakling, almost a 'ninny,' because he could not overcome the restraints of a gentlemanly upbringing. He simply *had* to get out of doors.

He stepped into the hall. His first impulse, when the door *cre-eaked*, was to start. He defied it. His heart beating thickly, he determined to force her attention, to let her know that he was going. He walked heavily. His boots, thudding on the deserted stairway, sounded ominous even to himself. In a panic, because he did not know the house too well, he rushed into the dining-room. A window was open, the heavy outer blinds ajar. He halted—good God, what was the matter with him these days!—in a sudden fright.

But he regained his courage. A sudden wildness seemed to come into his blood. He was a little frightened of himself, but the covert gibes of his sly old colonel seemed to impel him forward.

Eloise was astonished when she glanced up from the flags where she stood, her heart throbbing with a nameless disappointment, and beheld, in the window above her, an elusive silhouette.

Fisk sprang impetuously from the low sill to the court. Eloise parted her lips to scream, but was mute. From eyes that were points of glistening, indecipherable challenge, they gazed at one another.

Fisk said to himself, Butler's right. They are a lot of hussies—all of them. Not a shred of decent modesty in the lot.

This conclusion conveyed to him a violent new emotion, an evaded discovery of happiness. He was not equal to his own elation. Disconcerted by the long pause, and the gelatinous glimmer of eyeballs which appeared to him like a cat's, he said, "Mademoiselle—I don't believe that you really think that I—"

Eloise saw him come nearer, saw some gesture made toward her, and thought: Since he has read the proclamation, he is sure I will not dare to repel his overtures.

She watched him. It was very still yet, here in the pit, with the roofs black iron against the last acid traces of faint green moonlight. Eloise felt that she would surely die if that awful little man laid his hand on her, but she did not move. In an agony intense and welcome, she waited. Maman always declared that Eloise had the spirit of a martyr.

Lieutenant Fisk, though he could not distinguish her figure clearly, was perturbed by her statuesque posture. Beholding her so apparently rigid and impervious to his approach, himself so humiliatingly nervous, he was swept by a wave of anger with her. Damn her, *if* I don't treat her as she deserves—as General Butler would commend me for doing—I do demand her acknowledgment of my generosity.

Hesitatingly, as he stumbled nearer, he touched her. Her hand —for it *was* her hand, and he grasped it convulsively—was as cold as ice, limp, and the fingers quivered. Then—he did not know what he was doing, he said, describing it to himself afterward—he leaned and, to his own surprise, kissed her heavily, hurtfully, full on the mouth.

It was like some satisfaction which exhausted her to feel that a Federal officer was being revealed at last, in all his foulness, undeniably. She struggled conscientiously. Her thin fingers clutched him, held him.

He, encouraged, pressed her more firmly in his arms. Buoyant with what he imagined to be his own brutality, he tried to shut out his sense of the still house and to proceed ruthlessly toward its absent occupants.

As they clung in this embrace which each believed conceded nothing to the other, a timid, cajoling chuckle drove them tensely apart. They glanced about and perceived only a palm frond, dripping and swaying like a grey wing, in the night wind. Stars speckled the mist-dusted sky which, bereft altogether of its earlier light, was become murky, like an infinite dust. The windows were as deep, each in its dense pool of glisten, as mill-waters. Once more they clasped one another. *"J'ai peur,"* Eloise murmured, astonished at herself. "Don't be afraid of *me*," the lieutenant insisted, hoarse and alarmed by the demand for speech; oppressed and a little bewildered by her unexpected yielding; but fighting off the possibility of awakening from his triumph. He dared not allow her to escape him, yet, dreading responsibility for each incident in his behaviour, wished that some wine might flow to his brain and intoxicate him beyond degrading foresight.

The chuckle, as of propitiatory mirth, was heard a second time. The sound was no fancy. To release her now would be too ungallant. He controlled himself, and gripped her hand again. Eloise stared. A podgy form, rising from an iron bench under the palm tree, fluctuatingly approached. Both recognized it instantly, and with a common thrill of chilling premonition. Eloise, regarding the vague shape of her brother, hated, and longed to be buried in the earth. *Blanchard,* she thought. Her nails pressed in the flesh of the lieutenant's palm. Involuntarily she was clinging to him as one near bereavement clings to a lover and demands the last word. She was disgraced. Louis would tell Maman everything. He will marry me, she thought wildly. Maidenly decorum, all traits engendered by her rearing, seemed to have been torn from her by Lieutenant Fisk's impassioned embrace. And some furtive joy she had found in it was already gone. Her great necessity to revenge herself on Blanchard came uppermost in her distressed emotions. For some reason it was like retribution for her suffering to demand, though she scarcely knew what she was wishing, Lieutenant Fisk's unwilling constancy.

The high fatuous chuckle now focused in the spectacle of a bland and trusting face. "Maman, *elle m'a laissé—moi,*" Louis was announcing proudly in his lisped, thick tones.

143

Lieutenant Fisk found his very manhood departing in the nerveless languor of defeat. He would 'brazen it out.' If it had not been for General Butler's proclamation this would never have happened, he excused himself quickly. But added, with fierce, weakening fervour, I *won't* be inveigled into offering her marriage. They're as bold as harlots.

II

FROM THE CINCINNATI BUGLE

While anxious spectators, comprising the loyal population of the city, throng levees by thousands in order to confirm with their own eyes the news of an impending triumph for the cause of justice and liberty to all men, Colonel Ellet's boat, Queen, receives the first shot from the Confederate fleet. Ellet responds by hoisting the signal for action, and the Queen and the Monarch head down the river. The prow of the Queen, aimed to strike the broadside of the leading rebel gunboat, crashes at full speed against the enemy vessel, with such violence that the wrecked ship remains pinned to the bows of her destroyer, and a panic-stricken crew of rebels jumps overboard.

Henry Thomas Buckle, author of "Introduction to the History of Civilization in England," is reported dead at Damascus, where he was sojourning for a time in the course of a tour through the East. He was forty years of age and an historian of note.

Grand Duke Constantine has been appointed Governor of Poland.

Great satisfaction has been expressed in England over the ratification, on the twentieth, of the treaty between her Majesty's Government and that of the United States of America, for the suppression of the African Slave Trade. A copy was laid on the table of the House of Lords the same evening, when Lord Brougham suggested that some arrangement should be made by which the rights of search, now conceded within thirty leagues of the coast of Africa and Cuba, might be further extended to within thirty leagues of the Island of Porto Rico. With successful

144

execution of this pact, the South's play for foreign sympathy and foreign aid in conserving her nefarious interests and giving subrosa support to her illegal institutions becomes a joke.

From the Vicksburgh Chronicle

Yesterday morning at a little after daybreak, the Confederate rams and gunboats protecting Memphis were borne down upon by the Union fleet which has been anchored for some days in the neighborhood of Fort Randolph. The appearance of the Union vessels so early in the morning was a complete surprise to our commanders, but their onslaught on us was met by a speedy and courageous action. Several boats suffered severe injuries in the fight, lasting a little over an hour, and the river was strewn with wreckage; while the gallantry of the resistance offered to the Yankees made an inspiring spectacle for those loyal citizens of Memphis who, undeterred by dangers to life and limb, lined the levees and shores above the city by thousands and heartened our defenders with cheers and prayers.

Henry Thomas Buckle, author of "Introduction to the History of Civilization in England," is reported dead at Damascus, where he was sojourning in the course of a tour of the East. He was forty years of age, and an historian of note.

The Grand Duke Constantine has been appointed Governor of Poland.

Yesterday we reported in these pages confirmation of the ratification of the treaty signed by Queen Victoria and those who are falsely representing themselves as emissaries of all the American states. This treaty is for the suppression of the African Slave Trade, and the signature of the Queen to such a pact is being used by our enemies as further argument for the disgrace of the South in the eyes of the world. Britain has not offended us by taking steps to end the abuse of slave-trading. We are not even offended at beholding Lincolnites as co-signers of the treaty. It is

145

*a treaty we ourselves should have been asked to sign, for we are
the ignored victims of this very abuse. Our many sympathizers in
the British Isles will doubtless agree that, on the instant that the
collapse of this war of oppression gives the South its full rights
as an independent nation, the Confederate States should also draw
up a treaty and present it to her Majesty. As benevolent protectors
of the negroes already in our midst, we resent and shall resist the
thrusting into our civilized areas of further barbarous blacks from
the Congo jungles. We are not for nothing the masters of peaceful,
Christian, contented slaves.*

III

Carrie was 'promenading' along the river, near the Custom
House. Deep, gradual clouds passed over her, carrying the murky
glitter of a rainy evening as from shore to dark shore, across the
broad, soiled glinting of the water. She could still distinguish the
rumpled Yankee flag, dangling from the frail staff on which it had
been run up at the occupation of the city some days before. But
she avoided the groups collected for gossip along the dank
wharves. Her frantically demure scrutiny was, rather, for some
loitering solitary, who would, she hoped, turn out to be an officer
and a gentleman.

Carrie's nerves were upset. Disturbing events had left her uncertain whether to mourn or to rejoice. Miss Tate, with whom she
was temporarily abiding, considered the arrival of the Federals
just in the 'nick of time,' for the Yankee soldiers, unquestionably,
had the most substantial money. Carrie resisted this sordid view.
And her heart would have inclined her to the Confederacy had not
the inexplicable behaviour of Captain Fischer shaken her belief.

For a good slitch of fat, streaked bacon, however, one could be
persuaded to almost anything. It had come to that. Miss Tate, also
undone by hunger, had decided, only that morning, to report her
establishment and its single remaining inmate to the Federal authorities.

Carrie, avoiding the angry puddles stained with sinking sun,
paraded mincingly. She could have cried as she recalled how hard
it had been to convince the last gentleman she had 'entertained' of
her ladylikeness. Her grey silk was the one remaining genteel
souvenir of the days when she had been a governess, and a rowdy

146

caller whom Miss Tate had invited to the house had spilt beer on it.

Carrie was annoyed that Miss Tate attributed to histrionic talents all symptoms of an anguished state of mind. Carrie, while in attendance as a pupil at the *Young Ladies' Academy* in Natchez, had 'acted' the rôle of Desdemona, and was in the habit of recalling that long-past performance with a certain vanity. In those days she had not been driven to consider coffee made from parched cornmeal a luxurious drink.

The evening wind blew along the nearly deserted streets. When a glimpse of the river came, the great clouds hanging above the water had become like islands, and the world, but for the close glimmer of the boats at anchor, seemed turned toward sleep.

Carrie, grown callous to so many terrors, was afraid of the dark. A soldier passed her. She gazed at him sidewise beneath her homemade bonnet—Miss Tate had instructed her in how to weave and dye the straw and press it on a pail—and she was defiant enough to toss her head contemptuously, when, at the little frustrate cough she gave, he did not look up.

Anybody would think that *Miss Tate* was the tragic figure. She never left off telling of how, in her youth, she had loved not wisely, but too well, and had been abandoned by the faithless one. Carrie had surrendered every cent given her by courteous admirers, and Miss Tate—the slut—pretending she was going to buy provisions for them both, got drunk on the money. There was no use listening to her explanations. Carrie had heard *them* often enough. But when Miss Tate was discovered, maudlin, weeping by the kitchen table, only *one* explanation could be relied upon.

"It's Fate, my love. The same Fate has marked us," Miss Tate would insist. She was ready, when her gaze was bleary, to forget all misunderstanding, and, by her own account, she had treated 'poor little Carrie so generously.' When two women, like them, were scorned by a brutal world, they must be 'true' to one another. "For friendship is life's noblest gift," Miss Tate reiterated, lifting streaming eyes to heaven.

Carrie caught up her bedraggled skirts daintily, suspicious that, because she wore no hoops, somebody who was really in the fashion would suspect her, cruelly, of immodesty. It seemed to her that there was no end, in this awful city, to misinterpretation.

147

The night preceding the firing, she had been wakeful the whole while, and Miss Tate, though they were both so weakened by privation, had come into the room, in curl papers, and had insisted on regaling her with woes already known by heart. It had been a relief to be driven from compelled attention by the sudden *brrrr-bring, broom,* of the distant guns. Then Miss Tate and Carrie, alike primed for a calamity, had rushed, in little clothing, into the morning street.

Carrie had that fearful, crafty feeling which was now becoming too familiar. She would experience it when she was roused from a sleep to remain under the strange impression that she and Miss Tate had exchanged places—that she had *become* Miss Tate.

No sense in such a mood. Carrie was a 'lady' and had been educated almost elegantly. Carrie knew that *he* was to blame, for he had sought her 'ruin.' Yet there were times when she could not but argue to herself that her papa and mama were responsible. 'Papa' had behaved like a tyrant and a 'martinet' when he had turned her out.

The summer twilight seemed chilly. She coughed again—not purposely. If it were not for the bread knife she had hidden in her basque when Miss Tate reviled her, she would be driven to returning to the house. Carrie thought that if Miss Tate told her once more she was going 'crazy,' she would use that knife. The fat old hag with her raddled cheeks was growing very jealous. And Carrie, before she had fallen in such low society, had been accustomed to people who were *'comme il faut.'* It was a rebuke to Miss Tate, with her dirty cunning, to hear Carrie's French.

After all, Carrie had not been denied 'bed and board' by an outraged husband, and Miss Tate's real name, though she did not dare to be called by it, was Mrs. Wilkins. Miss Tate could say when she liked that this was 'proper' and that *'not* proper,' but it was she who had lowered the high tone of things. Mr. Wilkins might have 'robbed' her of her 'reputation,' but he had paid for it.

'Miss Ernie' was Miss Tate's bosom friend. Carrie knew, when the simpering female visited them, that intended treachery to a 'younger and more fascinating woman' was in the air. Captain Fischer had seen as much. Carrie was honestly grateful for his 'discrimination' and his words of warning. If he had left more

than a brass locket when he went away she might have remained
faithful to his memory to her 'dying day.'

It was dark. There was a soldier standing on the street corner
under the gas lamp. Carrie, as she approached him, watched him
cautiously, then looked away again.

Rain brooded. If she got wet and was draggled, where was the
'wherewithal' for a new gown to come from? Her Mazarin blue was
already worn out.

> There is no winter in my heart,
> No blighted flowers are there;
> Sweet buds of bright, unchanging hopes
> Are blooming everywhere.

She could go on until she died and nobody would ever get it
out of her that she did have 'aspirations' beyond the bounds of
this world of flesh in which Miss Tate took gin three times a week.
If he says anything to me that sounds presumptuous I will fix him
with my eagle eye of scorn, as Mr. Mallow in St. Louis when I
was governess to his daughters and he took advantage of my
situation.

Carrie had to admit that Miss Tate, in St. Louis, had been 'most
kind, most condescending.' When a lone female creature is hounded
by a brutal male and cannot convince his spitfire wife that she is
innocent—and where was I to go with the worst storm of the
winter and my boxes—no, my box—I had the little tin trunk
then—thrown by the slave domestics of that hateful woman right
out into the street?

But we never should have met afterward. She persuaded me
that I had to look out for myself and said I was not to fancy anybody who was less than a major. Gentlemen in responsible positions feel obliged to be generous, if it's only to protect their own
reputations and save a fuss.

> No damp and chilling winds are there,
> But zephyrs bland and still,
> Play gently o'er Æolian harps,
> (Chords—no, it must be chords—)
> And draw sweet sounds at will.

Carrie stooped to tie the ribbon on her slipper—but it was
string—and Miss Tate had helped to mend the broken slippers

with an old piece of string, so what could you do with darned mitts? The only occupation left would be the vile one of domestic servant in the place of a negress. Or I could keep a boarding-house—but it needs cash to begin with.

The young soldier hesitating by the lamp-post saw Carrie lean to fix her footgear, and cleared his throat. She saw him, upside down through her extended arm. Perhaps if *he* were the one at last—

> The dew-drop glistened in his eye, a shade came o'er his face,
> It recoiled from my eager grasp, it shrank from my embrace;
> Alas, alas, in my hot haste, my sense had failed to see
> The violet was too beautiful, too precious far—*for—me.*

Like an anthem it rang in her *so-oul*. She said 'the proud woman passed with dagger drawn and arms extended,' and felt for the bread knife protruding uncomfortably under the basque. I never meant to frighten her too much. (Miss Tate's screeches of alarm, as Carrie had rushed toward her, *had* conveyed some pleasure.) "You won't spoil everything, and I'm sure you'll be attracted to a nice one tonight," Miss Tate said. "There's plenty and to be had of the common, vulgar woman following after the army, but the next thing you know they'll be offering you marriage. You won't forget your old friend when you have a carriage and all that a fine, lavish husband can tender his bride."

Honi soit qui mal y pense. Not where winds blow shrill on the village hill nor down on the flowery lea but afar o'er the deep there's a quiet sleep and the dead rest well in the *se-ea.*

I never saw more than the Mississippi River.

The young soldier came nearer and said, "Did you lose something, miss?"

Carrie was relieved that he did not call her 'madam.' She never told her age and Miss Tate was sure, anyhow, that at twenty-nine the rose sheds its most *ex*-quisite perfume. "I say it with all modesty, my love, but gentlemen do admire the fulness of form that comes with maturity."

Carrie was thin, unfortunately. She kept fumbling at the bread knife. Miss Tate considered it would be a noble aid to the Union cause— or the Confederate—if they found employment as spies. Carrie, when she took the last cent out of a man's pocket, said,

'It serves him right.' What if she could *use* the bread knife? Heroism on the battle-field is not alone. Only she was so confused as to what was the origin of the war. I am alone, alone on earth, my heart's bright treasure fled.

Carrie's decorous nature persuaded her to put the memory of all unclean details from her. She could forget everything but her intention to prove to *everybody* that the spirit survives the indignities which a possession by the flesh has forced on it. Some of the gentlemen used very foul words—but who can say I am not more chaste than Diana, because I *refused*—I put him right in his place? She had horrible nightmares. It looked as though the more she was determined to rise above adversity the more she thought about fat bacon. So she had prayed God to 'cast off this filthy garment.'

"I think it fell out of my reticule." Carrie gazed at the young soldier too steadily and he did not believe her.

"What was it?"

She didn't remember that part of the lie. Ah, yes. "It was a keepsake. It must have rolled away in the mud and now it's so dark I can't see anything. What *shall* I do?"

She stooped again and was desperately conscious that the coin really was lost. She had really lost a copper in Federal money.

As the young man also was bending their hands touched. Oh, God, how weak she was! It seemed as if a man had only to incline himself toward her and she could feel sick, like this, as if he were going to 'grab' her. She wondered if she really wanted to—and propose marriage afterward.

"Warm evening," the soldier said. Both their hands were tingling, as *she* knew. "Warm evening, ma'm," he said again. He looked amused. All of them did—or she fancied—and she could not decide what it was about her that they found funny—or did they presume that they could treat her any old way just because—

Her fingers, as she rose, clutching the reticule, pressed on the knife handle. They could all be lying in their graves, but her father had owned as many as sixty slaves, and she could just *teach the damn* Yankee—

Carrie was afraid of 'damn.' When she was losing her self-possession, foul adjectives much worse would come into her mind, and it was all she could do to keep them back. Miss Tate said Carrie talked in her sleep 'like a fishwife.'

151

Carrie said, "Oh, what shall I do! Yes, it's warm." (*Cold.*) "I reckon you think you can speak to anybody these days."

"You aren't *really* upset?"

"I suppose you think you have nothing to do but insult us."

"I wouldn't say that. My, you reb girls are pepper-pots."

"I don't feel safe to take the air alone."

"You must feel safer than you did before we took possession. I hear Memphis has needed law and order badly."

Carrie did not know how to continue the conversation. If he went away, there was Miss Tate to answer. Something in the other experience, now she was growing more accustomed to it, she could look forward to as a kind of orgy that kept you from thinking.

"Let me walk home with you if you're scared," *he* joked.

She hesitated. "I could teach you a lot about rebel ladies you don't know," she said peevishly.

"I'm willing to learn. I've been lonesome enough since we got here to learn most anything." He stood quizzing her with his arms folded.

She suspected him. Ridicule from *them* was what she couldn't stomach. Fairer thou art than star of night in the estimation of Captain Fischer who dragged the last fond thought through the mire. "If that was true, you could learn enough."

"Which way do you live?" He took her elbow.

Carrie was trembling all over. They asked for 'a little diversion.' She could predict that from the first—*damn* them. That's war, Captain Fischer had explained. She was so tired, hoped he would not notice the rent in her sleeve, but if he *did*, "I reckon you found it a little peculiar that I let you speak to me."

He didn't seem to think so. She made out his amused profile as they passed together stiffly through the long glow of the lamp that faded away like a stain on the puddly road. He said, "Well, I don't know. I guess I figured you were as lonesome as I was."

She began to fumble at the front of her dress, and he, his attention attracted to the furtive gesture, halted. "What's the matter?"

"Nothing I could tell *you*." She bridled.

"Oh, come along now. I'm not such a bugbear, even if I do wear a blue uniform. What's ailing you?" He stood still and dropped her arm, and they tried to stare through the obscurity.

She couldn't bear to have him move away. Maybe he's going and leave me to God-knows-what the blessed bridegroom hath planned. "Nothing's ailing me. What I want to know is, how—how is it all you—you Yankees—take it as a matter of course—"

He said, "Take what? That you want me to escort you home? There's nothing in that. I like you girls." There was a pause.

"If you knew all I'd been through—all I had to put up with from some in the army that call themselves gentlemen!"

"I figure it they must have been rebs. You ain't being fair with me, my gal. If you're thinkin' of turnin' me off because I'm stingy, you have mistaken your man. Why, I've been scared of havin' leave while I was here, I been so lonesome in your derned unfriendly midst. I'm a fellow that would like to trust everybody. And you're better lookin' than I thought at a first glance, too. I can't stand animosity—not from girls, anyway. Some of you Southern belles are regular fiends the way you treat a man. I've seen you act as though Union bank-notes were less valuable than this Confederate trash. You gals consider us game, don't you, for any little trick you can play on us?"

Carrie knew he would see she had been working and never could keep her hands neat any more. "You have no cause to complain of *me* yet."

Facetiousness maddened her. If she lost her temper she sank, *sank* into that black pit from which Miss Tate with puffy hands folded watched the end of everything.

"Give us a kiss. Let's be reckless."

Carrie tossed her head.

"You're stubborn, ain't you? I'm set on making friends. If we both had a drop of something inside us we could get on better."

She imagined gracious heat in the pit of her stomach, under her wishbone—and so humiliated by the 'grosser' appetites. Better be dead.

He drew her again toward him. "I want to see what you look like. Nobody's spyin'. Come on."

"Not here. You'll get us into trouble. Come on back to the house."

He hugged her. "When we get better acquainted, I'll tell you all about myself. You'll take to me. I ain't got a mean bone in my body."

Carrie swooned in that close, familiar masculine odour of an embrace.

She said, "I ain't used to making free acquaintances. You better be different from the others."

"Well, I *am* different. Besides, you all say that. But the war gets you sick of serious talk, so we'll let what's bygones be bygones. Introduce me to your friends and let me show 'em a Yankee's idea of a spree. It ull be somethin' different from this starvation talk."

Pardonnez-moi, monsieur. Je ne vous connais pas. All was turning cloudy in her mind, with this feeble sense of anger. You have to hear me—you *have* to hear me, she began to tell him, in her thoughts, her words burning and mute. She said, "It's not as if I was *born* to act common. If you listen to what I want to tell you, you'll see how it is that I'm willing to treat you fine and still I'm not like them others."

She was offending him. Miss Tate said that was the reason she hadn't brought a man back to the house all week. "You can't be too finicky when you're not the woman that you used to be," Miss Tate had said, to Carrie Williams, genteel and well brought up but with *'la beauté du diable.'*

Carrie saw she was spoiling her only chance. If she told the same story over and over, they got tired. They wanted amusement.

"Whatever's the matter with you?" said the soldier. "I figured you wanted some sweetheartin'. Don't tell *me* how you got in this fix. I have worries and troubles enough of my own. I'd run faster from a tale of woe than from rebel cannon. I'd pay higher for a laugh than for the grandest play-acting story you could make up." He was uneasy.

"When Papa learned how trusting I was—and Mama said—" Now she realized she was talking 'queer.' She ran on—about her home at Vicksburg, when she stepped proud and downcast from the house that had sheltered her since infancy where darkies heard all her infant prattle.

"No. Stop. Don't say any more. I'll give you a dollar anyhow. What you need is a snack to eat. You sound loony. Get somethin' to put sense in your brain." He began to unroll his bills.

He hadn't done *it* to her, and she would, like they had, hundreds of times, or it seemed so, the stars are fairer when afar, others may

154

proffer louder love but none more strong than mine—how black the street. He *wouldn't* see her. He was counting out money into her shaking palm. The gas lamp trickled its crossed rays long behind them, but he would leave her longing for she-knew-not-what, because there was a perpetual dissatisfaction. I'd soon forget its heartless strife and lose myself in *thee-ee*. He had touched her. She could still think of his hand feeling her arm under her shawl. And what he has felt his eyes shall not behold. It was wrong. Passing through her body, they did not ask am I happy I answer thee by sighs and thank thee for the pitying look that beams in thy soft eyes. Not one of them would ever relieve her of this burden of herself, take it away, and let her lose it forever, because they looked at her pure as the driven snow and willing to be married to the first one that asked her. There are some things you can't ignore—like *they* do.

The bread knife was dull. She jerked it out, and surprised herself, forcing the blade through his coat, so many times—but I'll dig it right through your heart. He never said a word, and she stumbled and fell beside him, crouching by the fence palings.

It seemed to her that somebody was running toward them up the dark road. She wanted to faint. Doff thy dark idolatry and be the Christian's bride. She felt crafty. He was a *Yankee*. She had done it because he was a Yankee. The street was too still. That must have been why she was called to high and noble deeds. But she was unrelieved. Something was unfinished.

IV

Fanny May, after her long illness, had to be lifted into the barouche. She had asked tremulously, and with that distrait eagerness perturbing to those unwilling to disappoint her, to be driven to one of the hills above Richmond from which the manœuvres of the opposing armies could be safely watched. It was a damp afternoon. The wheels of the carriage, grating continually on unoiled axles, sloshed through puddle after puddle. Often, the body of the vehicle swayed so violently that an involuntary expression of suffering would pass over her pretty face.

'Cousin Rachel' held Fanny May's wasted hand, surrendered half-heartedly to the firm pressure meant to comfort. During invalidism, the young woman had acquired the luxurious habit of

155

living completely in herself. Cousin Rachel's constant, fussy solicitude was an intrusion on the inner life hard to bear. Fanny May was then glad when Mr. Small, who was accompanying the two ladies, relieved her of responsibility for answering Cousin Rachel's affable questions.

Mr. Small, in his rhetorical exposition of the situations of the contending forces, demanded their complete attention, and Fanny May, nodding absently, kept her eyes, wearily, almost closed. She knew his every gesture.

He had a wrinkled little pink countenance, earnest, insignificant blue eyes, and wore a white goatee. Awed by Cousin Rachel's wealth and position, he was, while expansive, oppressively polite. Cousin Rachel's chins, framed in the muslin strings of her black bonnet, shook like turkey-wattles whenever she inclined her head in agreement with him. She had a large, bland, sallow face and no eyebrows. She was accustomed to condescending and did all she could to show Mr. Small that his intense delivery of loquaciously offered information was appreciated. He wore his broad felt hat jauntily. Sometimes he became so warmed up, in the importance of his knowledge of strategy, that, shaking back the sleeves of his long black coat and so exposing his immaculate, fine linen, he was impelled to wipe his high forehead with his white silk bandanna handkerchief. In his cuffs were heavy gold chain links. His watch was supported by a cable. When Mordecai, the negro driver, allowed the pair to lag, Mr. Small would take out his timepiece, larger than a muffin, and scrutinize it anxiously.

Cousin Rachel had enjoyed the friendship of Mr. Small for many years, and they never failed in the consideration for one another's comfort which each showed now. Mr. Small asked her if she found it warm. He told her that he would be glad to examine for her one of the horses that jogged along as if ailing. He was full of theories as to how, should the Federal march invade her country property, she might best arrange her belongings so as to circumvent looting or similar devastation.

Then he would revert to his favourite topic, which was politics. He was expressing approval of President Davis's decision to remove General Johnston from command of the Army of Northern Virginia and give full responsibility for the direction of these forces to General Robert Lee. "That's the man—that's the man for us—a Vir-

156

ginian born and bred and a gentleman to his finger-tips, Miss Rachel. His father son of one of George Washington's contemporaries, and his wife the daughter of a grandson of Martha Custis. A lineage to be proud of, I assure you, and the inherited tradition that makes for leadership. Yes, ma'm, the change should have been made long ago."

As he discussed General Lee, Mr. Small's face seemed to grow rosier and more wilted-looking. He was on the front seat with the coachman, and, in order to see Cousin Rachel, which he found necessary when he spoke, had to squeeze himself sidewise, pushing his broad hat still farther toward one ear. Cousin Rachel agreed with everything he said, stared at him almost lovingly, and, to emphasize her conviction of his infallibility, would give little pats to Fanny May's feverish hand. "You ought to be a general yourself, Mr. Small," Miss Rachel said, smiling wisely. Mr. Small's wondering, self-absorbed little eyes twinkled aptly. But, however gallantly he insisted to her that she 'flattered' him, he did not look humorous. Fanny May suspected that to be his own opinion. He was excited and 'jumpy.' "The Yankees are away off from their base of supplies while we can have access to ours at a moment's notice. And that is why, ma'm, Richmond is as secure today as if a Yankee army had never heard of it."

Cousin Rachel always pretended to consider these statements carefully. She was meditative, pursed her mouth, and murmured, "Um—oom" doubtfully. Fanny May realized that the elderly lady was really only delighted by the interest Mr. Small showed in her.

"Are you comfortable, lovey? Are the pillows behind you disposed properly?" Miss Rachel queried, conscientiously bending to examine the pale features of her frail niece. "Mr. Small, Mordecai isn't allowing you half enough room." And consideration for everybody had to be gone through like an elaborate formula.

Fanny May was so wearied with questions about her health that she could have wept in sheer pity for herself. "Yes, thank you," she would reply listlessly; and be glad when the older people, who really had eyes only for each other, were engrossed again in their perpetual, stilted conversation. Dreamily, she was mindful of Mr. Small's statements. More clamorously did she require oblivion in which she might be left to nurse the sweet, unexpected revelation of the early summer day.

Every accent of green, poignant after her dark closeting in a sick-chamber, seemed strangely precious. Though she drooped her lids obstinately, she could not shut away *that* cherry tree, *that* sky, *that* valley, glinting rain-refreshed foliage, that grass by the road, combing the air, sweeping up the ravine. Scenes along the miry turnpike were constantly unanticipated. Spring had come, while she ignored it; but in the opulence of young summer, which she accepted, her weakness, which had previously alarmed her, was become a subtle blessing.

Slowly, luxuriating in the queer rediscovery of familiar spectacles, Fanny May turned a furtive head among the relaxing cushions, and spied obliquely along the passing road. A goat was browsing among rocks. It lifted its horned brow, and, as the carriage rolled heavily by, became stone; save for its quick ears, the absent waggle of its young beard, its flicked tail. It stamped delicately. Its glazed eyes, in their vivid indifference, interrogated its audience.

The barouche was encountering other barouches. Landaus swept past. A sluggish wagon was met and left behind, the crunch on gravel of its recalcitrant wheels audible afterward, like a pursuit through the still air. A trap overtook the barouche. The trap was a high, conspicuous one, and was crowded with ladies, their parasols slanting, in glowing colours, toward the low sun. The trap circled a bend, and the slack legs of the horses spun road and more road from their flashing hoofs. Miss Rachel recognized acquaintances and greeted them affably, waving, as the other carriage exceeded her own. When she signalled to her friends, she crooked her elbow, flexed her wrist, and fluttered her stout fingers mincingly. Children in a ponderous hay-van huddled together and displayed the alert, curiosity-seeking faces of picnickers. Richmond, Mr. Small commented, was on an outing—the whole town driving to its several hilltops to witness the wonder, fortunately removed, of the Federal and Confederate armies, strung out over the June countryside in full sight of peaceful citizens and of one another.

Fanny May wondered what Mordecai was thinking, as he humped in his linen duster, flapped the reins of the off horse, and muttered crabbed 'Yes-suhs' and 'No-suhs' when any word was addressed to him. For forty years he had been Miss Rachel's slave, and before that the body-servant of her brother, Ned. He ignored

158

the uproar being made about him, Miss Rachel had declared—took the war, she said, 'philosophically.'

Fortunate, Fanny May decided, that darkies never reflected very deeply. And she, like Mordecai, was an 'onlooker.'

Too feebly at ease for protest, she felt mildly bitter. Philip had not even been given opportunity to see the baby before its death. She and the baby, who was in its coffin, were both 'onlookers' at his heroic deeds. Recollections of the baby were yet too painful. She had been obliged to doubt that she had really loved it. Had it not been for the baby, she would have followed her husband from camp to camp as other women did.

To enjoy this world, she had to put the baby from her mind. It was over—everything for which she had lived was finished, she thought. The first muffled thuds of distant firing which she had listened to some days ago had failed to stir her. She had not then realized, as she did this afternoon, that Philip might be near.

The idea had come to her in the night. She had aroused, horrified, certain that she had just let slip some unduplicatable opportunity. The armies were but six miles from Richmond. Philip was with them, with his regiment. She was there in bed, inert, calloused by the scars of months of suffering, and Philip was only six miles off.

Fanny May felt broken by compassion for herself. She had risen, for the first time without assistance, and had called Cousin Rachel to bring the candle in. In her hysteria, Fanny May had insisted that she must quit the house that very night. She would go to President Davis, to the military authorities, to everybody who was influential. She had felt so strong, because they would not 'have the heart' to stop her. But Cousin Rachel, fat, kindly and harassed, had offered every obstacle of common sense.

Fanny May, in the carriage, yet found it impossible to comprehend them. She had already made up her mind to die, if she did not see Philip; and these, who adored her, who could not bear to see her exposed to this awful anguish, they had kept her back. Mr. Small was very good about arranging things. Mr. Small, incapable of understanding desperate ardours, had been consulted. This ride to the hilltop, in the cool of fading afternoon, had been offered to her, who was asking bread, as a soothing compromise.

Fanny May, in the pale-blue-solitaire cashmere trimmed with

159

the knots of straw-coloured ribbon that Philip liked, succumbed to the monotonous bounding of the barouche, and reflected that this life was but a murky veil clothing her impatient spirit. The baby, thank God, was in heaven, its little soul among the angels. It had achieved the conquest of sickrooms, medicines and degrading weaknesses. Through the languid screen of her lashes, she examined her consumed young hand, ugly today, with its full, unhealthy veins. *My* hand, she thought—and he had kissed it. Her sorrow for her unique self was so intense that she would have burst into weeping had Cousin Rachel then offered one stolid, kindly phrase of supposed comfort.

Fortunately, the commiserating company beside her was too much occupied. Mr. Small's features appeared to Fanny May to resemble the goat's. To calm himself, he had evaded decorum, and she saw him slip into his mouth a small cud of tobacco plug. He was chewing surreptitiously. Once he forgot himself, and spat openly upon the turning carriage wheel. "Yes, Miss Rachel, in just a second the whole thing will be spread for our inspection—the two great armies that struggle in a conflict that I call the modern Armageddon." In eager apology, he glanced at her face.

"Is this too much exertion for you, my lovey?" Miss Rachel, disapproving of the 'weed,' yet gave him opportunity to dispose of his 'chew,' and regarded her niece.

"Don't turn back. Don't turn back," Fanny May pleaded, instantly afraid of disappointment. Hope was like a guilt. Of course she knew that six whole miles meant a long way off, yet she felt that she was dying in the expectation of some kind of miracle. Squeaking, the barouche dragged up the last length of slope. The rumps of the horses cut off anticipation of the final thing she had come to see. Mr. Small, in his high, confident, little falsetto voice, was explaining to the ladies what terms like 'deploy' and 'redoubt' meant. Then Mordecai startled them all by saying "Whoa," very sharply and importantly, and the carriage halted, giving its occupants a jolt. Mr. Small, his chest heaving under his tight coat, sprang nimbly over the carriage wheel, turned, like a showman, to assist Miss Rachel, and announced, "Here we are, ladies. Here we are. We couldn't have found a better spot to see them. They are all in sight."

Fanny May's eyes were closed in terror. She stood up. She was too weak. Cousin Rachel had to support her, and Mr. Small hesitated, before the spread-out scene, reluctantly.

"There—you see, ma'm. What did I tell you? See those white dots down yonder? They're tents. I told you you could see tents."

Tottering, Fanny May clenched her hands. She must look at last or expire. Everything would be over. Even Cousin Rachel insisted. Swaying on the carriage step, half in and half out, the elder lady, dully rosy, her chins aquiver, cried, "Look, Fanny May. Look, child. Good gracious, who would ever have imagined— You're not going to faint."

One of Miss Rachel's clumsy feet sank on the ground. Her petticoats tilted and showed her stout ankles in elastic-sided boots. Her breathing came in thick gasps. "I am much affected, Mr. Small, much affected." Tears were in her flat, prominent eyes, and she shed them without concealment. Mordecai and Mr. Small, together, had to help her in assisting Fanny May to the road.

Were they all thinking of Philip, Fanny May wondered jealously, warding off Mr. Small's grudging gallantries and doing her best to remain upright. "There, there, Fanny May. Not that way, child. Don't you see those white specks? Why, there's a man on horseback. You can see plainly. Yonder's another—and another. And way off yonder—that must be where the actual fighting is going on."

Mr. Small and Miss Rachel drew together in their awe. Mordecai, shrewdly quiet, was apart. All stared. They *did* seem to perceive, through the vapid haze of sinking sunlight, the growing films of evening, a dim stain of smoke. At the peak of the hill, the heterogeneous persons encountered on the pike were already collected. It was the presence of these others which prevented Fanny May from recognizing anything before her. Miss Rachel again noted old acquaintances, smiled responsibly, and, with the gracious wafting of a podgy mittened hand, did conceal from observation her shaken niece. "Howdy. Howdy, Amaryllis. How d'ye do, Mr. Corley."

Resting horses were everywhere. Some were unharnessed and snuffled calmly in their nosebags. Fanny May, bewildered, observed only the browsing animals near her, or saw the ladies, strolling elegantly to the side of the road, their hoops twirling drolly, their affected gestures indicating appropriate patriotism and astonishment. The quiet air was filled with the clink of bits, the cheery impersonality of floating voices. Fanny May saw, also, the lines of hills, soft and deep on the stone edges of the sky. Her glance roved from the cloying, far-away shadows of the valley, to a man in a straw hat ornamented with a fluttering ribbon band, who carried spyglasses.

Miss Rachel had just discovered marks made upon the landscape by others than the 'boys in grey.' Her cheeks shook with her rigid indignation. "The audacity of it. The brazen audacity of it. Right here on our own front doorsteps," she kept repeating, feeling, Fanny May suspected, that this must be an especial type of resentment treasured for Philip's sake. "All along the Chickahominy," Mr. Small was explaining, elucidating some vague point to which nobody had attended. "Come a little nearer to the edge of that field, Miss Rachel. You can see more advantageously." And, forgetful, once more he expectorated.

Fanny May, relinquishing herself to the guidance of Cousin Rachel's waddle, also beheld the soldiers; the dry scars of entrenchments, the midget men making the green fields move with alien bits of light. Over the tender platitude of the river, the dying sun cast rays scored by soot-wet shadows. The flat waters were a moody jelly. Roads, stony-coloured, their white become lavender, crawled stilly into thick green fields, into dense woods, that looked solid blots of dark, and were surrounded by the deep wavering of the lucid evening sky. The talk of sightseers echoed thin over the somnolence below. The twilight rolled on, crushing even this into whispers and, finally, into silence. All was remote, remote, under the gorgeous smutted heavens, in a minute lifelessness: little people, little spindling legs of toy horses galloping. The doll tents were no larger than pocket-handkerchiefs. The men rode rocking-horses. Good God, could it be true? It was true. Why had she come? There *was* no Philip! Was it to see these puppet riders tumbling through the dusk that she had lived in anguish all these many months?

Abruptly, paddy-raps of sound thumped those lurid, distant shapes of cloud. A boiling up of heavy noise from somewhere seemed to spill over. Raucous exclamations of alarm rose from the groups of observers. Shrills of surprise, uttered by the ladies, were clear in the air like the cheeps of frightened, winging birds after a

162

clap of thunder. Pails emptied by giants clattered their leaden content on the horizon. The sensation-seekers ran hurriedly, furling parasols, gathering up the shawls and mantillas they dropped. Horses were wheeled about rudely and backed into clattering shafts. A few lingered, and, in the blurred twilight, *ohed* and *ahed*, loudly, but there were intonations of hysteria in the excited exclamations.

Mr. Small, triumphant but cautious, gripped Miss Rachel's ponderous flabby arm, and hurried her toward the barouche. He caught Fanny May on the other side and pushed her dragging weight before him. Mordecai was dumb, but his eyes glistened fearfully, and he pulled with superfluous viciousness upon the reins as he turned out the wheel. "But I understood it was safe," Miss Rachel kept protesting. "Didn't you tell me it was safe, Mr. Small?" She was panting, bundling Fanny May to the seat first, and stumbling weightily after.

"Our boys will soon have them on the run," Mr. Small cried, speaking above an unimpeding din. There were detonations suggesting an uninterrupted rainfall of shot pouring down from the clouds. Dull mountains toppled into an unseen pit. The noise spouted.

Carriages reversed, and followed carriages, speeding down the hill. The wagon-load of children passed, and a boy shouted, "Hurrah," jubilantly, but most were dumb. The ladies in the trap floated by to the *clickety-click* of steady hoofs, that struck sparks from the vague ground; and the blown petticoats were like tiny sails.

Mordecai, tense to overtake the others, cracked his whip, and the barouche lumbered on. A rocket was crawling low over the beginning night. Its dry snort was thinly audible, ending in a nasal scream as of derision. Starry tentacles unfurled in long arms which became embers. The barouche rattled and leaned like a caravan. Richmond was nearer. The river was wider here, and a steamboat, like a hollow red-hot needle was moving on the water, stitching through the dark.

On the outskirts of the town, the horses were advancing at a diminished pace, when Fanny May looked out through the curtains and saw, by the roadside, the old, bent figure of a man who was digging. Though the sky was so nearly black, she could make out very plainly the meagre figure leaned on the spade, the spade pushed labouredly into the resisting soil, the arm lifted and the soft bitter shower of the loose clods scattered nearly under the carriage-wheels. Active and alone in the silence, the old man plodded, and a shadow before him deepened, grew, it seemed to Fanny May, to the very length of the man himself. It appeared to her overwrought fancy, that the strange creature dug his own grave.

The barouche pounded on. Reflections shed by no moon sprang in the evening, but died. The sandpaper sneezes of the rockets dwindled until she could hear them no more. The maggot lights that had writhed down the horizon faded away. Still, she could not reject the impression of that lonely man who was digging his grave unknown to others. "Cousin Rachel, I—I think I must be very ill." She fainted gratefully.

VI

THE train had to wait for sixteen minutes in the Mimms depot, and Saunders, wearing civilian clothing, had no difficulty in boarding it casually. One car had been allotted to ordinary passengers, and the other coaches were filled with troops. Saunders purposely entered the wrong car, took a look at the soldiers, and was told, peremptorily, that he had better 'get out.' As he made this excuse of discovering a proper location and was able to traverse almost the whole length of the train, he felt amusement in the possibilities which the situation afforded.

The boys in blue were usually young, and seemed to him a 'well set-up lot.' Lolling jauntily by the windows, they shouted jokes, and were evidently inclined to regard the unfriendly appearance of the citizen loiterers upon the platform as extremely funny.

Saunders reached his own car and found a seat from which he, too, could regard listless idlers who preserved, while they scrutinized the Federals, deliberately immobile faces. Since the capture of Donelson, and of Nashville, this part of the country had been constantly overrun by fresh importations from the North. It was the first time that some of these youthful soldiers, already bearded and showing negligence of toilet encouraged by travel, had ever seen negroes.

You wait, Saunders derided comfortably, crossing his short legs and leaning back as if luxuriating in the hard bench on which he sat. Obliquely, he could still discern peering heads, rakish caps, and the twinkle of brass coat-buttons; while, down the aisle, through the open door of the car in front, steel stalks of rifles were visible to him.

Saunders had always treasured the excitements of gambling, though, in his 'make-up' he acknowledged caution as well. Until the hour of his enlistment in Morgan's Cavalry, perhaps his final care for his own security and boastful reputation had been predominant.

Certainly, his 'poker' face had always been as precious to him as his periodic indulgence in some reckless enterprise. He had once been proprietor of a farm near Lebanon, Kentucky. His grandfather had been what was called 'a mover,' but his parents had 'settled,' and Hezekiah, more successful, had made a little money. He enjoyed the luxury of owning 'niggers' and, without admitting his ambitions to anybody, had already placed himself, in the opinion of his neighbours, in the 'gentleman class.'

Saunders' darkies had all been faithful to him throughout the Yankee invasion, and this despite the Republican bias of Kentucky politics. He was a ruthless master, when it took his fancy, but was prodigally generous at other times; and the negroes overlooked contempt for his 'poor white' origin in admiration of the lavish way in which he spent his money. He talked to them of the war, ironically. 'Old Ed,' a darky who had once petitioned Saunders for freedom, had been invited to depart when he wished. "Maybe the Yankees can make you work, Ed," Saunders had suggested. Ed, grinning, sheepish, and disconcerted, had ignored 'Mas' Hezekiah's' generosity. In view of some spectacular incidents which had occurred since then, the slaves believed unanimously, so Saunders had learned, that he led a 'chawmed' life.

The car in which Saunders sat was low-ceiled, with a double row of grimed, unupholstered benches. The floor was littered with fruit peels, scraps of paper, and little drying hummocks of expectorated tobacco. He felt somehow that he was fortunately placed at the rear of the train. The caboose came next. He stretched his burly legs before him, clasped his knotty, laced fingers over his respectable watch-chain, and threw his chin up, his sardonic gaze resting inscrutably upon the extinguished lamp in the oppressively close roof. After some preliminary jerks and bumps, the bell clanging, the car was in motion, and he was able to follow, nonchalantly, the swerving, then the diminishing of the platform, the retrogression of the dingy depot, and, finally, the abrupt vanishing of the scattered houses marking the confines of Mimms.

Saunders drew in his feet, and assumed uprightness. He rubbed his palms together vivaciously, then passed them meditatively, in a lengthy gesture, along the onion-skin surface which constant sun-

166

burn had given to his ruddy cheeks. He was dressed well enough, though without dandified care, in the long black broadcloth coat of the man of important affairs, topped by a wide felt hat. He wore neither whiskers nor moustaches, and the oddity of being smooth-shaven was a provocatively conspicuous attribute.

Saunders' whole person exuded bluff geniality. He glanced about him. As travelling companions of civilian order, he had only the society of a fat man, a thin man, a boy and an old lady. Resuming his previous semi-recumbent posture, he bared his head, fidgeted, cast speciously benevolent looks on those in his society, and began, as if thoughtlessly, to hum a little. He was humming 'Dixie.' The old lady heard him, stared; and he went on with his *sotto voce* tune, his gaze keen, though so fatuously veiled and kindly. Saunders knew that people said he was a 'shifty customer.' He would chuckle with inordinate appreciation when he was called that. To create bewilderment delighted him. He had discovered long before that men and women stood in horrid awe of anything requiring an original explanation. Sometimes, as at present, he would be surprised by his own daring, and admire himself. What the devil had prompted him to assure Morgan that the train of troopers should not reach Hampton Junction without such delay as would allow the Confederate cavalry contingent to overpower the small, unassisted garrison there? Saunders venerated his commander. He would rather win praise from Morgan than from any other man on earth. Stronger than the desire for laudation, however, was a cold conviction of his own indifferent attitude toward the destruction of human life. He wanted to be known as a 'high liver,' a man who did not care a 'whit' for ladies' company. For the public, he would take care to paint his portrait in colours somewhat bolder and more gay than could represent him in fact. There was malice in his anxiety to astound his contemporaries. He regarded them with unemotional scorn. He was doubtful that, even with the proof of his exploits in this war, he would ever be appreciated.

The train dragged between clay hills, through sparkling, shadowy woods, and emerged among fields so still that, in them, the chugging of the engine resounded labouredly. Before the conductor had asked for Saunders' ticket and his papers, the coaches were jostled to a sudden rest in front of a station as unimposing as a negro cabin. "St. Pancras! St. Pancras!" a distant voice intoned over the corn patch which supplied all the prospect. A fireman, descending from the high steps of the engine, peered at a switch on a curve ahead, among abandoned rails.

Then the train moved on. The corn patch glided stilly backward, and the space it had occupied was usurped by the ruins of a house, a monolith of bricks marking, in a heap of rubble and charred beams, where a chimney had been razed. Saunders, noting, sighed, and felt the imminent demand for action becoming acute discomfort.

It was very hot. The muffled *chug-ga-chug* of the engine enchanted him, made him desire a quiescent lot. A log home was drawn attenuatedly past him. A starved goat browsed in the acute glare of a stony garden. Gourd vines fluttered, luxuriously green, over a deep cool veranda in which a well was set. Trees, seething with bright sun and wind, lashed inaudibly.

Another station—Kildare's Run. The train suspired wheezily, its tortured woodwork screeching and bleating. Soldiers in the coach ahead were bellowing:

> "Yes, we'll rally round the flag, boys,
> We'll rally once again,
> *Shout*-ing the *bat*-tle *cry* of *free-ee-dom!*"

This was followed by three blurred *hurrahs*.

An ox-cart waited by the platform, the ox switching flies and shuddering its dewlaps, its head moving constantly in slow annoyance. Beneath the contracted shade cast by the cart, chickens, tipsy with the heat, squatted, humped, flapped the dust, and crooned gratitude. The voices of those in distant conversation floated to Saunders strangely, and were as if overheard by an absent mind. Kildare's Run wavered, grew small in acres of burned grass and stubble, and the telegraph wires, in clefts and bars, continued musically across the glaring sky.

Saunders could bear most things more meekly than suspense. He watched the elderly conductor in his shabby clothes toppling uncertainly down the swaying aisle. "Well sir, want to see my credentials and I reckon I'll show 'em to you," Saunders said jovially, as the man came up. "I wouldn't like to have you take me for one of the bushwhackers."

"Um," said the conductor, not prepared for such generous loqua-

168

city, and giving Saunders a scrutiny which was returned with disarming good nature. The conductor wore a shaggy, iron-grey moustache, stained with tobacco, and his faded, mournful eyes showed him weary of the stress of the times. "Only politics pays these days is to keep your mouth shet," he asserted, with nervous emphasis. He accepted the papers offered to him and began, grudgingly, to examine them.

"Keep your mouth shut and be loyal to the Union, eh?" Saunders elaborated slyly.

"I should think *so*," retorted the perpetually aggrieved conductor, handing the papers back after no more than a summary glance. And he turned to resume his tour of the car.

"Say, mistah," Saunders insisted, confidentially delaying him, "I want to ask you if it's true what I've heard that those sons of guns from Morgan's Cavalry are gonta make another raid in this neighbourhood? That news almost disinclined me to travel, and I want to know if it's so."

The conductor, furtively worried, scratched his stubbly chin with his thin, broken-nailed fingers. "You heard *that*? Well, all I can say is I hope it ain't so." He took a step, halted, and then said, "I wouldn't believe those stories, mister. We hear 'em all the time. They're circulated a-purpose to keep folks down here uneasy."

But the conductor had only proceeded to the collection of the fat man's ticket when he came back again. "Keep yer mouth shet, mister. That's my advice, and you can't overrate it. Them bastards has set us all by the ears more'n once. I don't believe what I hear till it happens."

Saunders had a perverse impulse to prolong the talk, but the conductor was too preoccupied. He stared, with his credulous, suspicious eyes, at Saunders' flatteringly serious face, then continued up the car. Saunders watched his crestfallen shoulders. He was evidently regaling the fat man with Saunders' doubts.

A third time, and masking some unexplained perturbation, the conductor found excuse to halt by Saunders' seat. "I was talkin' to that gentleman up there in the duster about this Morgan thing, and he said—" The conductor did not finish his sentence. "We got to look spry. If anything goes wrong on the line we're the one gits the hot end of the poker." He paused, embarrassed, and added,

169

"Lemme see them papers of yours ag'in, if you don't mind, mister."

Gladly, his blue eyes sardonic in affected frankness, Saunders complied. The conductor now studied the documents cautiously. "Yes—yes. I know the signature. Lieutenant Colonel Johnson—Lebanon. Don't misconstrue me, mister, but you can't go too carefully about these things. It seems easy to you, but if anything irregular gets through, it's the trainmen who are blamed. That's all right. You see I've had enough nuisance with these gentry of General Morgan's, and I don't want any more."

Saunders felt vain of the prolongation of this encounter. "I should think you *would* need to be on your guard, conductor. I read the account of what Morgan did at Pulaski—took the whole town, they said. And at Cave City he burned up a train with forty-eight cars when nobody thought he could get at it. Same thing at Tompkinsville—took all the wagons and mules and horses the Federals had. Story is his men didn't even have good arms. I don't know what we're gonta do about it. He seems to think he can order the Union around like it belonged to him. They say he got control of the telegraph the other day, and hasn't let any orders through except what suited him—tapped the lines or somethin'. *You* ought to know whether it's true that he has a big influence over the railroad men—bought a lot off, or something. Found more loyal to the South than to the North, I understand. He's pretty lavish with those that side with him."

The conductor seemed to find this banter too nearly earnest. He was quiet, reading Saunders' hearty face, then said, fiercely, "Well, he better not come around where *I* am—'makin' any offers," and teetered on again, evidently even more discomfited.

He abandoned the car completely for several minutes. When he came in again, he ignored Saunders rigorously for some time. Finally, however, he approached the seat. "Look here, mister, I've decided to collect those papers and keep 'em till we git to the junction. I want to show 'em to the station agent, and he'll hand 'em back to you. You say they're all regular and I guess they are, but a man can't take too much precaution nowadays. I'm not makin' any exception of you. I'm gonta take 'em all up and redistribute when the train stops."

Saunders had intended to gain some clearer idea of how brakes were worked, but he could not hesitate more. As far as he could gauge the position of fleeting landmarks, Hampton Junction was but half an hour away. Obligingly, he rose. He was searching his pockets. "I understand, conductor—that story about those Morgan men. I understand all that—but—where *are* those confounded papers? Where's my damned wallet?" He slapped his pockets, fumbled in his coat. "I can't make it out, conductor. I must have lost—"

He had a transient impression that the fat man just ahead had half risen, was listening. There was no time to wait.

"Do you think they might have slipped under the bench, conductor?"

The conductor leaned stiffly and peered. Saunders' heavy hand rested on the cold surface of a pistol in his right hip pocket, and the contact gave him as keen a pleasure as though he had not anticipated finding it. If he delayed much longer in his crazy enterprise, he would be too late. In some manner he must stop the train—and for twenty minutes at the very least. He had promised with a boast.

He made a rapid movement that was instantly ineffectual. The fat man in the duster was on his feet, rushing to intercept the gesture. Saunders was astonished by the fat man's agility and presence of mind. They clinched in a vicious embrace. Before a word had been uttered by either, the fat man had pinioned Saunders' lifting arm. They continued to struggle together.

"Hey! None o' that. None o' that. Well, I *never!* Damn him!" The conductor, flurried, aghast, straightened himself, and sprang to grip Saunders' other wrist. The conductor's soggy cheeks greyed, his eyes roved, his brows twitched. The grave misgivings, which he himself had considered foolish, were now alarmingly fulfilled. Saunders strove. The fat man laboured and panted audibly.

Saunders, acknowledging miscalculation, also acknowledged fright. But only fear could arouse him to this indomitable sense of self-responsibility. In calm moments, Saunders could be secretly self-abashed. Fighting to retain his weapon, seeing the thin man rise, the boy rise, and all prudently approach; while swift glimpses of distant soldiers in the car ahead flashed intermittently across the space afforded by the open doorway, he was impersonally animated by vexation at his own false impulse. Chagrin was courage.

The landscape flashed in a perpetual torrent across the lifted window. His senses were not very keen, and he lost the *chug-chug* of the engine, and the blurred cursing from several throats. His plaid trousers were tucked in riding boots, and with one of these he delivered all his energy upon the conductor's shaky shins. The man, in agony, reeled toward the aisle. The fat man, jolted, lay upon Saunders' shoulder, blew hot breath on his cheek; then, as Saunders swerved, crashed against the window-pane. This impact with shivering glass, weakened the fat man's clutch, and finally transferred his hold on Saunders' arm and shoulder to a feeble wrench at Saunders' fluttering coat.

Through the expanded aperture made by the shattered pane, smoke blew inside. The engine, rounding a curve in the track, shrilled dismally. Saunders forced himself free, placed his frenzied palms, in aching support, on the back of the rear bench, and vaulted over it.

He ran the few steps to the platform. As he hurried across it, the horizontal tide of landscape flooding past him made him feel a little dizzy. The door of the caboose, unlatched, flapped and banged, flapped and banged. Saunders jerked it open, sprang inside, and was shut in, while, with anxious fingers, he blindly sought a bolt. He was able to lock himself in before the first bedlam of pounding for admission announced his pursuers.

The car contained two wooden bunks parallel with its sides, a tool chest, surmounted by a hanging cluster of extinguished lanterns, a sheaf of dry, earth-clotted picks, set upright in a corner, and a heap of brownish oil-soaked rags. He crouched against the door and bent his ear to catch the clamour beyond. Then he glanced around to discover brakes.

It was dim in the compartment. Two small windows, at the end and high in the wall, sent the sky and clouds scudding along after him. The mutter and racket of the wheels and rails prevented him from distinguishing the separate noises that went on without. He was still madly examining the enclosure in his search for some means to halt the train, when the caboose ground, with a roar and ringing clatter, to a precipitate standstill.

Saunders was thrown to his hands and knees, and remained so an instant. He conjectured that the train was among fields. Light-flaming telegraph wires were white threads on the blue sky sunk

172

deep in the little square of window that had no glass in it. The other window was closed, and filmed dingily with a milky residue left by cinders. Two brown butterflies floated irresolutely into his space of gloom, continuing there a timid, monotonous rotating flight. Saunders listened to the crunch of footsteps on the gravel of the roadbed. A braided cap, a head, a face, featureless upon the afternoon, pushed into sight. Saunders abased himself further on the dirty floor and prepared to shoot. As he aimed, the dimness was prodded with a bayonet point on which the greasy sunshine tingled. "We've got him, boys. The loony ain't got no gun."

Saunders fired. The soldier's outline, deep and flat, on the gay aura made by the sky, resolved, for a second, into a bleeding mass of disfigurement. The head, the face, the gun, fell out of sight. The windows emphasized, like targets, could present no menace with which Saunders could not cope. It was the persistent creaking of the belaboured door which made him feel trapped. He expected, in an instant, to hear the sharper resonance of an axe.

The next shot from without was announced invisibly by its report, and there was the *pat* of a bullet in a beam of the car above Saunders' head. In order not to fire obliquely and above him they would need to risk his level aim. "Quit that pepperin' us or we'll git you," was bawled from outside.

Saunders moved, bearwise, against the door, squeezing it with his buttocks. He was shaken by the painful iteration of thwacks delivered on the other side. In predicaments like this, he denied himself thought. He felt, as yet, brutally alive, and equal to the next emergency. A second rifle now lay, its cold snout ruddy with sun, on the window ledge. As it poked in further, aggressively, a clubby fist, calculating the trigger, also appeared. The 'fool' with the gun must be standing on another man's shoulders. Saunders fired once more and had the unexpected pleasure of seeing the weapon tumble into the caboose itself. His mouth twisted as he reached forward and wrenched the gun from the floor in which the stiffly vibrating bayonet was plunged, upright. Another shot here, perhaps, without waiting to load. Jeers from a mysterious audience followed the catastrophe to the volunteer guard. "Hurrah fer Willie. Git that old lady in the back coach to help you, Willie. She says he's crazy." And a voice, happy in excitement, answered,

"Don't waste no more time there. They're gonta smash the door open. It's one of Morgan's gang, er I'm a liar."

Saunders, anxious for his own 'skin,' felt now as when hunting and the witness of the last quiver of a wounded animal. When death ended everything—for others—some brooding distrust in his nature was appeased. The uncertainties of life, which he could not resolve for himself, were mitigated for him by any clean, intentional cruelty. He felt 'better' for a murder. Callous to the details of suffering, he was determined not to anticipate his own miseries. He hoped he was 'ready,' should the time appointed come, to resign himself to the consequences of that brutality which he enjoyed.

The door crackled, flashed into raw, unpainted fragments, strained from its hinges, and fell forward upon him, stunning him momentarily with its inert force. Two infantrymen, in the vanguard of aggression, stumbled to their knees and before Saunders could pull himself out of the ruins, were heavy on his collapsed body. Saunders, shocked to revived keenness, at once discarded active desperation, and became wary.

He was surrounded, lugged to his feet. His legs dragged. His arms were half wrested from their throbbing sockets. Some blunt object battered his aching head and just missed his dazed eyes. It seemed to him that he was being attacked by a dozen persons with a dozen implements.

The soldiers in charge of the essay, lost patience with the informal assistance of the fat man and the thin man, and the peevish scoldings of the conductor. "Look here, think we can't take care of a prisoner that's got no more sense than this one? For Gawd's sake, quit all talkin' at onct. You ain't the public executioners, are you? Let's git this crack-brain outside. Major Perry wants to have a look at him. Anybody round here got a piece of rope?"

Saunders was so nauseated, as the result of blows, that he could scarcely keep his feet. The conductor rummaged in the tool chest and brought forth a few lengths of frayed cord. Saunders submitted to having his hands tied behind him, loosely and very carelessly, as he quickly noted. Poked forward by the butt of a rifle, he was thrust to the platform, his captors attributing his awkward, reluctant progress to guilty cowardice.

As he appeared in the still, sunny air, he found groups of soldiers all along the roadbed, watching for him. Faint *halloos* cheered his defeat. The 'boys,' stretching their legs, or running down the line to 'have a look at him,' were obviously enjoying this unforeseen interruption to an uneventful journey.

Saunders blinked. General Morgan was probably at Hampton Junction already. Whether he would find it convenient to send out riders who would meet the train and rescue the victim of strategy was another matter, more problematical. At the instant, Saunders was ready to say 'To hell' to the cavalry. His interest was in his own security. He fought the torpor of exhaustion. "Want to see officer—officer in command—got information—can explain—trying to save—" He was mumbling, searching for an excuse. He gained no attention.

As he was prodded from the platform, he lurched. "Not a pair of handcuffs in the company," somebody said.

Major Perry, a thin, pompous, consciously erect man, was contemplating him from some distance, up the track-bed. It was apparent that he was upset by the inexplicable commotion, and annoyed by the unruly behaviour of the more youthful of the soldiers, who, forgetting discipline, were greeting the prisoner with the derisive jubilance of boisterous holiday-makers. "Have you sent the wire on to the Junction, conductor?" the major was asking, peremptorily, assuming less curiosity than he revealed.

Saunders came forward in a cowed way, and kept his head bent to hide the purpose which might be displayed in his sharp face. His cumbrous coat had been stripped off, and he was relieved by its disappearance. His face was bleeding slightly.

"Bring that *murderer* here," ordered the major tensely, looking hate and disdain at Saunders. "Is Molloy being looked after?" Somebody said, "Yes, sir." The major turned his back, speaking to the conductor again, and purposely attempting to shame Saunders further by delay. "Looks like you men might have averted the antics of *one* man without all this disturbance," the major called angrily over his shoulder.

Saunders' guards, claiming approbation, were confused by the disdain which the officer showed. People were climbing from the coaches, and other officers approached. Saunders, peeping spitefully through his downcast lashes, was examined curiously as though he had been inanimate.

Only the conductor, defiant of the major's irking criticism, flaunted the worth of a fine indignation. His timidity was at bay, and his small rabid countenance flashed on Saunders the animosity of which the major merited at least a part. "It's an outrage. A robber, you are. A highway robber," the conductor muttered, but restrained himself to reply calmly, but with quivering mouth, to the major's curt inquiries. "We've sent a flagman up the line to Mimms and the other way's clear until the down train at seven. Here's his papers, major, and if he ain't forged the name of Colonel Johnson, I don't know what. He ought to be *hanged*. He's ready to get us *all* in trouble. Hangin's too good for him, is what I can tell you."

Saunders was jostled by the curious. He began to provoke the crowd by stares. He was in the custody of a dull-eyed young man with a brick-red face and straw-coloured hair. While anticipating impatiently the major's bored judgment on the future of the prisoner, the young soldier, fidgeting on the loose earth at the edge of the embankment, stumbled and narrowly saved himself from the indignity of rolling down. Saunders took the cue. Finding an opportunity for accidental awkwardness, he fell against the guard and the two reeled helplessly. Saunders was calculating the fall and thudded, amidst loose earth, into the gully below the track. The soldier sank more heavily and lay, for a moment, as if stunned.

Cursing, he rose, but not before Saunders had anticipated him and was running irregularly, while fighting to free himself from the rope. He had plunged into a field of oats and was tormented by the tide of dusty stems which still more upset the equilibrium disturbed by the position of his hands. As he realized that he was actually some lengths in advance of a tempestuous pursuit, he jerked his shoulders spasmodically, and gave, with the faint hope of drawing some concealed assistance, the hoarse, half-articulate, rebel, "Whoo-oop!"

"Where are your rifles? Shoot, you greenhorns. Don't waste time on that ass's chase!" the angry major called unreasonably. Released from a spell of deference, a dozen men were bounding down the clay bank by the train, offering their nimble aid to the disgruntled guard, who proceeded, limping. Colonel Gooch had alighted from his coach and argued reprimandingly with the major. An informal tyranny was as if wasted on desert air. "Git him, Quarles. Git him, Allen. You'll git your medal ef you keep on goin'. Hey, Beany, did ye ever try to kitch a jack-rabbit! Put salt on his tail!" The bright afternoon rang with halloos, catcalls, whistles and joyful cries.

Where Saunders raced the sunshine twinkled low, and the stalks of the oats were thrashed to brilliance by a million criss-cross shadows. On the other side of the field was some open, weedy ground, and, beyond that a wood from which the dusty blankness of the road to Hampton Junction emerged invitingly. But Saunders was being 'headed off.' Though it was not possible for those in the track to shoot without endangering comrades, the chase seemed foreordained to brevity.

Saunders halted, exhausted. Thirty feet in front of him, a cluster of elated, perspiring faces showed, with broad, military shoulders, above the whiskered riot of the oats. A bullet sang like a bee over his head. The paper cups of the grain tickled his smarting wrists. The glaring country blurred, as sweat oozed in his lashes. He glanced behind, and saw that the bell-shaped funnel of the engine was emitting more languid steam. The lines of coaches, emptied of their occupants, were a low glimmer of sun-crushed windows. Ahead, vacant rails converged in a slick vague-ness that interrogated distance. Where the Hampton Turnpike crossed the track it passed on in the blandness of haze and un-stirred dust.

A crackle—*pi-lick, plick*, briskly—from nowhere, failed to rouse even Saunders from the bitter weariness of defeat, when a faint, accelerating "Whoo-oo-oop!" did turn several doubtful heads. Smoke, in a cloudy forecast, bloomed among the trees of the wood. As it lifted, the road disgorged a helter-skelter of swiftly riding men and horses. Saunders was abandoned. The soldiers on foot zigzagged toward the train. Shouts of instinctive protest echoed through the field. The raiders came from the right. Saun-ders, endangered by the firing, rushed on toward the left. Beside the coaches, there was pandemonium. The raiders galloped, break-neck, around and around the train, crushing down the oats and casting up clots of dry earth along the track-bed. The Federals crowded to shelter and windows soon bristled arms. The sun, setting, reflected crimson on the burnished cars. On the steps of the engine, somebody leaped, threw wild hands into the gilded evening, and fell out of sight into the gully. Saunders, crouching behind a hummock, listened, his heart thumping like a bursting drum, while the train flashed with dim explosions, and the inspired riders sent their *whoo-oops* coarsely over the suddenly enhanced quiet of the ruddied country.

II

Smith turned on his stomach and began to drag himself through the prickly grass. The night had a September fragrance of well-dried hay. He recognized it, and was thrilled to discover that he could still smell things. How precious every such symptom of reassurance had become! He was indifferent to all other matters. What obsessed him was a beginning realization of the poverty of his own strength. While he had been lying there in the weeds by the church, he had not been able to consider any existence beyond pain. Intense pain had left him with a sense of inner light, revealing some self yet under a cloud. For an unreckoned time, he had made every effort to refuse recognition to some experience which, if borne, would end all. Very fierce and apart from the literal dark had been that obliterating feeling of energies loosed only to torture. After that had come passage into another, sicklier gloom. Now he had the night, through which he crept, bearing the burden of his continued life, and even, for self-assurance, hoarding the resuscitating symptoms of his misery.

As he dragged his bleeding length through stones and twigs, each paroxysm that delayed him was suffered with a patience furtively triumphant. He fought against being engulfed in his own always more inexorable longing for submission.

He found that he was becoming able to utilize the increasing impressionableness of his erratic eyes. He wished to see only in one certain way which would mark for him a path from the Antietam toward some lane not yet made unreal by association with scenes of agony. Feeble memory told him that somewhere, at some time, in his disintegrated world, somebody—people—carrying lanterns and a stretcher—had gone mutely by. He could visualize the light that had flashed upon him, hollowing his mind, leaving a great space in his thoughts. Then he had felt unjust the effort that would be demanded of him if he cried for help, and had let the lantern pass. He could recall the wings of steady, pale radiance wedging the solid dark and turning up the richness of the thinning trees and bushes. The light had gone on, and his sense of it, as the timid glitter had relapsed in a density beyond him, had been of some horrible, unnamed loss from which he never could recover.

A gurgle of suffering in his throat left him breathless. He fought with some intimate foe in his own languor, and tried to revive that departed spectacle of gilt fans gliding and deepening the growth of grass, of darkness swaying, of the blenched, rigid trees moving steadily off.

It was the horizontal shapes upon the stretchers which he now remembered, and he was bewildered by a fancy that the self he knew had been carried away, and that he was left alone with something alien and terrifying. What had become of the horse, riderless, dragging a dim bridle through shapes seen earlier in the evening? He had attempted, in a blind impulse of assertion, to secure the animal. Its neigh of fright had been the confirmation of an affront to him as it had galloped on. Wind was curdling the rattling foliage.

Smith summoned all his force, held his consciousness firmly, collecting it avariciously and keeping it close in his mind, like something held preciously in the palm of a shaking hand. There was an object lying near him. He touched it. He could feel a sleeve, a coat. He fumbled, and a stiff face, answering with clamminess, menaced him. Restlessly, he refused the thing recognition.

He writhed further. A hummock rose before him, regal outlines of dark fleshy mass against paler dark shed from the sky. Smith accepted the horse's belly, and even investigated inanely the crusted mats of hair bristly in the shrinking skin over the swollen substance under. The dead horse did not alarm him. He was crazily indifferent. Yet fear was required of him, and he held himself to fear, that stirred him to rebel against the ease of sprawling in helpless sloth by the upturned wheels of a broken ambulance.

He saw a light rising, and hated a coming demand to distinguish whether its source might be benign or threatening. Intermittently, his body jerked in the seizure of agonies perceived mechanically. It was the moon that edged a circle of ice over the last black hill. A suaveness saturated the multifarious forms which he had not comprehended, and all appeared to evolve the lineaments of a smoother, less divided world. As the glow and resultant glitter steadily increased, pain grew steadily. While he watched, he rested. While he rested, he fed pain with his attention, and made it bolder. He began to anticipate the paroxysms, and to measure his hope by the degree with which he could evade their violence. The moon burned unwaveringly upward in a perfect and enormous globe. At its fulness, it seemed to rescue him from the treacherous glamour of indecision. Its quicksilver, fluting the grass, was his fever, brightening the cold, September air. Then the darkness expanded with a radiance too much to bear, and the moon itself turned black.

He had mistaken clouds for a dearth of light that would endure. The moon sparkled, sagging in scuddy lace, long before its setting. There was nothing left, when the moon had vanished, and the intimated secret became some final enigma which he had no courage to probe. Lost between this and some other world, he sought for the one comfort remaining in the bitter perfume of dying weeds and moisture. Thirst began to draw his throat together. Thirst squeezed a mumbled utterance from his thick tongue. The hills were expressionless, their edges sharp on some background submerged and garish. Shreddy noises began in the undergrowth. It was raining a little. He panted. The raindrops blew softly across his crusted lips, and he sucked hoarsely at the illusion that he had refound the river, that he could plunge into a shadow and rise shedding the disturbing water. He foresaw rapture, and was maddened. The rain was grey on the hidden moonlight. The fields smoked brightly, and he was now convinced that the rebels had begun to fire again. The night flowed sharply through his burning nostrils. He flung himself on his side and rolled in the grey wrappings of fog, in the smooth grey sheet that folded him closely. His mind was warp to the woof of strange tender threads. He picked at the rain and would unravel himself from the freezing tentacles.

When he had brushed the web from him, the glare was more brilliant. Of the stuff of the moon, a wall of a ruined house broke the field before him. A block of moonlight, the house stood, its gutted interiors revealed in soft nakedness amidst heaps of stones. The reflection of some miracle seemed to shine in the trees and over the faint, brightening hills. His chin swerved slowly, and he attended, shuddering. But he could not discover the fading reason for that alteration, like a thought, that had passed over the silence. The fields were bled quietly of their rich differences. The livid moon, under her blazing coronet, sprang ruthlessly out of the sinking sky. Instantaneous with the pure intrusion of moonlight, Smith saw a face, lying in the grass before him, then another face. The shapes twisted. There were groans. Somebody called for water. A shriek flew up fatuously from mutilated lips, and he was filled with a sense of loathing and of degradation. All were in torment, but he made it plain to himself, through a vital effort, that he was done. It was ended. He had nothing to do with it. He sprawled, and hid his eyes in the speared, coarse sod. Limp on his bruised brow, the earth he bore upon pressed misery from his mind. He was already dead, as he now perceived, and, vaguely, he was very joyful that he was 'out of it.' He relinquished himself to a torrent of dark.

III

Dawn came and surprised Frazer. The languor in his very bones was a dangerous delight. He raised himself on a stiff elbow, but yearned to go to sleep again. He had, somehow, to climb to his feet. Then the muscles in his legs twitched weakly. He felt drunk; and with the thin pain of the cold on his temples, on his cheeks. There was no sun—not yet, though it was fully daylight. The sky was like a dull steam amidst the oozy boles of the trees. The million twigs of the wood were fattened by the cottony snow. Its shadow was everywhere and bestowed on the commonplace landscape a blankness which it was discomfiting to realize. That look of something untouched combined too well with his own present view of the insignificance of thought. Frazer had always said to himself that the time would have to come when the fight would go out of him, and he would be satisfied to be no more than were the sort of fellows he had always despised, the kind that gave in to hard luck and let it master them.

Christ, just for five minutes more! He squatted. His knees gave way under him. He sat meanly on his heels without the spirit to move. He rolled limply to his side and lay there. At intervals the cold would give him the very ague. His teeth would chatter, and he would almost relish his degradation—lying there as if anybody could kick him and he would not have the spunk to object. Stevens would get a shock if he could see his old friend in *this* state.

Frazer wished Stevens to see him. That boy was responsible for enough. He was responsible for the fact that Frazer had held on through all these months of shortened rations and hard fighting, that he had swallowed abuse from superiors, that he had made almost every sacrifice humanly possible for the Confederate cause, though he had no faith in it.

Well, escape once begun had to be finished. Desertion accomplished, there was no turning back to put another face on the matter. And to think that a dozen happier opportunities had been allowed to slip just because a man as hardened in ill-usage as was Frazer had not been able to stand the disapproval certain to be aroused in Stevens by the behaviour of any son of a gun of a soldier who gave in to a licking and went back on all the oaths he had taken.

Why was Steven's good opinion so precious? Frazer called his erstwhile messmate 'a good deal of a fool,' too young, too inexperienced, too wrapped up in ideas of how the world ought to be run—if run by gentlemen—for his criticism to count very much. Yet there it was. Frazer had been attracted to the boy—well—because the boy, for some fool reason or other—had been attracted to him. How much was an admiration worth that had to be supported by a pack of lies? From their very first encounter, Frazer had been obliged to lie. Stevens assumed so many things that weren't so. And Frazer had distrusted him. What confidence could a poor white feel in the goodwill of one of the quality—the goodwill of somebody who, like Stevens, had enlisted 'on principle'? Stevens had rich friends. He had a second cousin, so the fellows said, in the Richmond cabinet. He could have secured a commission. He hadn't done so because he had felt it better for his soul to get right down on the fighting line with the ordinary run of men. "The Confederacy is going to be licked, Steve," Frazer had said this very winter. "There ain't a hair's breadth of a chance of it turning out any other way. And what's to be gained by what we're doing? You say yourself that you don't believe in slavery—that the old-fashioned South has got to go. If there was a big man at the head of the government, the South would have some chance of making

182

itself into a separate nation. But Davis won't do it, and nobody in Richmond will be big enough to do it, and handle all the problems of international politics that are going to come up. What's the sense of using up all these men and so much money, when at the end of whatever time it will take, everything is going to be just like it was before, except that the Southern states will be heavily in debt, and a good many of the lives lost can't be replaced easily? The Yankees have got all of the resources. If we ever had any, the powers that are running things have made as little use of them as possible, and we are getting starved out. Look at our own company since we have been fighting around Nashville and think if you ever saw a worse looking lot of starved scarecrows than this. Leslie run off, Couts run off. Minnot and Stuart run off. Wells run off and got shot. The boys you know have been deserting like flies. And you can't blame 'em. An army without enough to eat is no better than *no* army, anyhow. A man who is hungry, or a man that knows his wife and children and family are hungry, in want of everything necessary, and nobody to look out for them, cares precious little about his duty to help keep up parties and governments."

The more Frazer had talked about the common sense of deserting, the more obstinate Stevens had become. Stevens looks on me as an educated man like himself, Frazer would think. Otherwise he wouldn't listen to me at all.

Oh, Frazer had fibbed enough, and had spun yarns that nobody but a sucker like Stevens would have believed. And yet he like's me! Or he has figured out that he does. Wonder how he would take it if he found out that I haven't given him one blamed fact the way it really did happen—about Pa, and the money, and the reason I joined. We weren't much better than crackers to start with. Our first acquaintance with the quality was when the judge down in Allatoona sentenced Pa to jail, and Ma tramped all the way to Augusta to raise some money to fetch him back.

Frazer, thinking about 'Ma,' groaned. He was too numb for sentiment, yet, after all these years, and even in this place, she meant more to him than anything else. About the pluckiest gal that I ever struck, he thought. The way she fit for us youngsters when Pa wouldn't stand by her—and the way she raised us to do the best we could for ourselves when she didn't have no help on this earth—Yes, Stevens, you'd be surprised if you knew how my education was picked up—Ma sent me to that abolitionist school-marm that had come out from Augusta to do some charity teachin' to save the poor critters down South from their evil ways and their ignorance, and how I married Hattie when I wasn't more'n eighteen and she thirty-five. One of the chief reasons that I sold my vote to the Davis hangers-on was 'cause I was at the end of my tether as regards influence and this world's goods, and I would join almost any cause on earth that was against Hattie and the abolitionists. Poor whites that we were, and being kicked about from pillar to post by the rich folks and planters that didn't have no use for the small, independent farmer—Ma with her corncob pipes and sunbonnets—and us youngsters not taught so much as how to cipher or sign our names—and every Sunday when we tramped six miles to church in that old log house carryin' our store shoes in our hands to save 'em— I was a slave trader in New Orleans, once, Stevens, my boy. When I got away from Hattie I was ready for anything that come along, and I had picked up a pretty good gift of gab, and I thought I would make money by going against all her particular ideas, and wearing a big hat and a long coat and ruffled shirts, and sleeve links with twenty-dollar gold pieces on each one, and get up by the auction block and sell the dirty niggers to the planters that would underpay me for a slave if they could, but wouldn't soil their clean linen by going into slave-selling as a business. I was in California, too, in between. While I was out there, I tried about everything under the sun. Mostly, I was successful. But I got tired. I was lonesome. I came back here, hoping to look up Ma, or maybe find some good in the folks I had turned up my nose at. But they were dead, or gone, or moved away. Ma was dead two years and I didn't know it. And then this war come along, and somehow I had managed to get rid of almost all I had anyway, and was in pretty desperate straits.

Frazer's meditations had continued like the soft dreams of final inanition, while he was lying on his back, with snow, cold like a burn, on his outstretched fingers as he flung wide his arms. He was just one mess of frost-bites, he reflected. He knew his ears to be swollen and purple and lumpy with glossy blisters. Tennessee might just as well be the coldest state in the land. Let me give up,

184

he thought. Let me give up, and have no more Stevens and no more scheming on my conscience—not because I regret anything I've done, but because it don't matter.

There was a dogged instinct in man, tied in his very bowels, that knotted with cold, and the instinct would not allow him to quit all ambition to live, or see himself out of danger, or make any motion or gesture whatever that required effort. Frazer felt hunger. The fellows in the camp he had left had been hungry enough, and had done almost anything to secure a bite. Still, they did have rations, if short ones. Mush and water now and then were better than nothing. In Frazer's middle was the deep sensation of a scald, and his unappeased lust for food mounted to his brain in a black nausea. The iron demand of his body compelled him to resume a sitting posture, but it was with a brilliance of dizziness, floating in little speckling dots of red in his brain, in contrast to the grey impression of the dingy morning which prolonged itself through his marrow. Frazer, to overawe Stevens, had run the most superfluous risks in the danger of being shot. No bullet had ever touched him. Now was the final defeat of his energy to come through this crazy effort to reach security.

Frazer's will was his pride. It was a pride he kept to himself. No one had ever known or ever would know the tests he had set himself, or, for each, how well he had been acquitted before his own vanity. He stood at last, and rocked on his swollen toes, inanimate clods of flesh broken through his tattered boots. He tried to stare about him accurately.

When the dark dazzle of his inner being left his mind, he saw that the woods were still in early twilight. The sun was hardly bursting through a sky in which the submerged glare gathered as for a grey bleeding.

Intermittently, from the branches overhead, dripped bits of fluff, dislodged from the frozen fringing of the twigs. Even while he reviewed the direction he must take which would lead him farthest from the Nashville Pike, a ray, out of the dusk of morning, sprang in pale mock-fire, on the topmost spire of a pine tree, others were lit more distantly, and the slope became labyrinthine with the glitter from marble orchards. He was so weak and giddy that the spectacle seemed to go to his head. It reminded him of spring. Deep in the unformed world of the sky, a star was yet gloaming angrily.

The torch lit for his escape gave him the greatest despair of all, and he began to run.

Stumbling feebly, he went, helter-skelter, in the dour light, under the pale, flashing ice. His teeth clicked in his tight jaw. His coat was torn, and, in his exposed chest, was a sensation as of the buried claws of some probing enemy, and the claws reached tentatively inward, as if to grip his heart and stop its beats, or to stifle breathing in some tight embrace. He might as well consider himself done for. Pinned in his shred of shirt was the letter from Stevens's old school chum, Horace Kerby—an offer to deserters, the crude map of a meeting point included. Kerby had not allied himself with either army, but he was not Secesh. In some manner he had learned that Stevens's regiment was in this neighbourhood. He had sent the invitation through a darky. If Stevens was 'sick of the Secesh fiasco,' Kerby, for the sake of 'old times,' would secrete him for a day or two, lend him horses. Stevens's name was on the envelope. Kerby's was not signed. Frazer had stolen the message from Stevens just when Stevens was about to tear it up.

Frazer reached the bottom of the hill, and halted. Something fine and brazen, like the faded echo of a bugle, smote upon his ear. Was he then but rushing to another camp, when he had trudged half of the night? The shock of disappointment held him abruptly motionless. He was too *tired* for flight. What infatuation for torture could send men to pursue men such as he, who had no fight left in them? But of course that was foolish. He was not pursued. Desertions had now become too ordinary. Stevens had no doubt, by this time, rigorously excluded him from memory. Frazer's stiff mouth grinned in mirthless self-derision. He clenched his unshapely fingers, steadied himself adamantly upon his tense and throbbing leg-muscles, and made his pace more careful, beginning again to walk.

Here, in a field, the snow-patched earth was littered with caps, crushed boots, fragments of shattered wagons harbouring coves of snow, the twinkling, rimy bits of broken bayonets. He loved life. If you're not afraid of dying, little Stevens, you're an idiot, he thought anguishedly. I knew exactly how I prized my life when that mob in Kansas slung a rope around my neck!

What hurt Frazer most was that flight, with pursuit, in its very nature, robbed him of all dignity. His belly was his master. Every ounce of challenge had departed from him. The glare smote on the vague intoxication of his mind, and he began to retch, and to look about him avidly, feeling that pretty soon he would have to chew on bark. Hunger made him angry. Anger, a second strength, like a 'second wind,' was his salvation. The sun, hairy like a young, cold monster, bored, with its unfelt talons, through the ice-fluted branches. Ripe, and slowly eager, the bloody ball wallowed flatly in the mat of dazzling twigs. Frazer, in an ecstasy of feebleness acknowledged, shook his fist at it. His breath came whitely, like a fever. His universe, mildly glorious with daylight, partook of the fever. It tingled with animosities which he was helpless to contradict. *You see me*, he thought. Well, I've been through all the things you read about and never have to know by heart. I've been kicked around like a yaller dog—treated worse than the niggers themselves. Going hungry in your army while your politicians in Richmond go on living on the fat of the land is the *least* I've been through. People have been treacherous to me. I would have begun by believing in your ideas if I'd been given half a chance. But I was a poor white. I was *trash*, I tell you. What I thought, and the likes of me thought, didn't count—not with people of the kidney of those that mollycoddled *you all!* You all don't know *what* I'm like. You don't *want* to know. I'm a mush of hide and bones and insides that you can *hurt*. That's all you realize. But you'll hurt me no more after this time. I'm licked. I'm licked. Stevens, why didn't you ever try to find out what kind of a fellow I really was? Why didn't you ever try to find out?

Frazer had come up abruptly to a fence and a road. Along the top of the fence the snow grew a little white hedge which he would need to rest his palm on in order to vault over. He did put his hand there and could feel the particles melting on the agony of his naked hand. The bushes growing on the other side were delicate furry animals. He became afraid of them, of all things, because all things were alive, yet so huddled, so impassive. He became afraid of the length of the road which so few feet had marked. Transparent knives whittled his stubbled cheeks. The mossy, sugary thoroughfare gave up eddies of crystal dust. The trees creaked. There was the papery, shuffling sound of some one walking. Some one was coming toward him. The group of men looked large and apart walking on the fresh, immaculate gloss of the snow. Because the snow was so blank, so untrampled, the men were larger than they ought to be. He stared at them, and shuddered. Leaning his whole weight on the burdened fence, he was inclined toward the approaching men; and the fact that they were soldiers, that they wore the uniform of his own army, did not seem to interest him very much. He thought maybe they would give him something to eat. Like an animal—a dog—looking at a man, he looked at the men coming, and wondered if they had something for him, something that would still his uncertainty, that would put peace into his bowels, that would stop his guts constricting, and give him a feeling that he could look any man in the face, as he always had done.

"Hello! What ails you?" one soldier said. They had come up even with the fence, and were examining Frazer, who was half lounging there. Frazer's frost-bites always seemed to pain him more when he was being watched, though, actually, he knew that every susceptibility of feeling had gone out of him. He felt stupid, almost dreamy again—like when he had waked up in the morning and seen the trees all covered with white and gold flowers. But he was cunning, as well. He saw that the soldiers, for all their aggressive, cocksure fashion of address, were pinched with cold, and were ragged like himself. He saw that, really, they were afraid of him, because he had deserted, and they wanted to desert, too, and they were afraid he might persuade them to desert.

"What you got in them pockets?" the first soldier said. Something else—some other words—had passed between the three men. But Frazer had not cared to hear, had not cared to listen. This soldier was small, thin, with a drawn, crafty, white little face, and a long bluish nose. He looked bullying and officious. "Where'd you come from?" he said. "What's your company? What's your regiment? Whose command are you under?" And he added, "You look like one o' that ornery gang we been chasin' all night. Gawd knows why you all fellows keep desertin' on a empty stomach. You all make yo'selves a nuisance to the patrol, and what you all get faw it is to get shot. Look like you might have better sense."

Frazer saw they never would find the paper in his shirt. He despised them. He hated them. But he wanted to help them. They told him to get over the fence. He obeyed, and almost fell upon his head. "Drunk, you act," the little soldier said. "Well, march

188

then, damn you! You kin explain yo'self afterward. March—aw you all git a boot in yo' behin'!"

They began marching up the long road that nobody had ever walked upon. The snow was soft, dry and slick as starch. Frazer thought the world looked as though something had blasted it, destroyed everything. It looked as if it all began over again with the white fur on the fences, and the rocks sticking up like big clots of white moss. A bush with branches more limber, drooping, rocked and lashed out with its pure fleshly arms. Stevens had white skin, just like a woman's! Frazer, surprised that he remembered that, thought fretfully about his own body, senseless as a lump of dough. Because it had hurt, till it couldn't hurt any more. The soldiers were talking about snuff. One said snuff killed his appetite. "Want a pinch, you? Seein' what's ahead of you all, it might do you good," the big, burly soldier said jovially to Frazer. Frazer glanced into scared eyes, and saw the burly soldier also afraid, thinking Frazer would find out that he, too, didn't like the army. That was why the burly soldier giggled so much, sending his breath out in little evil-smelling puffs of warm white on the blue air.

Frazer lurched and fell on his knees. He gazed up at them as they gathered around him. It must be true that they had been walking in the snow since early morning. The folds of their coats were crusted with glassy particles. On the cap of each of them was a dusty, brilliant coronet. Frazer wondered that they were not afraid of the snow. It sent the numbing thought straight through to the brain, he decided. Nothing worked. He seemed to be gazing up at them a long way through the morning. The snow warmed him to a kind of stillness. "I'm doggone tired," he said, looking bleary at them, through a kind of skim of light. It was a film like cataract settling down over his eyes. When they shook him, he retched viciously. And he was maddened that he had nothing but spit to puke up. It surprised him that there was any wet in his mouth. One kicked him, but the other said, "What he needs is a square meal. Give him a piece o' biscuit."

"Biscuit?" said the other. "I ain't got no biscuit. Leave him alone. What's the use of roundin' up men that ain't fit to carry a stick, let alone a rifle. Seems like since Franklin the fight's gone out of everybody. Naw, I'm through with this. Bailey's got five or six more, an' he can carry them back. Most likely this one's a goner anyway. Leave him rest."

"They won't pick on us faw contrivin' to help nobody get off?"

"Where's he gonta get to?"

"You can shoot him now. Nobody won't mind."

"Aw, hell! He ain't a dog. What for?"

"To take him outa his misery."

"Well, I ain't in this war faw charity. Leave him alone. Come on. We ain't got the strength to tote him, and I ain't gonta try."

They were moving away. Frazer, with a leaden effort, sat up, gurgled in his throat, and made a word, "Hold on!"

"Look—there," he said thickly. "Inside—pins on the damn shirt." He fumbled, tore his coat apart. The ice of the morning pressed in the wind upon his bared, scrawny chest. "Paper—note —plan help 'serters. Stevens, Company ——, received plan—he helps getaway. Traitor!" His last phrase came out clear and strong. Then he plopped backward and once more took his sickly ease in the snow. Oh, what delirious comfort! He snuggled in the drift, and was impervious, he felt, to any effort that ever would be made upon him by this stinking gang. Little dartles of pain sprang sharp in his temple where it pressed the icy particles. Ought he to get up and call? They were going away. No. He had given them that note. He wanted to see Stevens's eyes when Stevens knew that, not only had he deserted, but he had, after stealing the note which it was a risk to preserve, relinquished it to authority needlessly, out of wilful perfidy. I loved that boy, Frazer thought stupidly. And, fiercely wakeful through his somnolence, hung his longing for revenge, itself a yearning. Damn you, Stevens, you never knew me. You never wanted to know me. *See me. See* me. I'm a damned sight better than the fellow you invented.

Would they stand Stevens up before a firing squad? Would they — Perverse in his delirium, Frazer insisted that the bandage be removed from Stevens's eyes that had gazed so often, so superciliously on men they did not approve. (And now he will behold *me!*)

Through his crusted lashes, Frazer, opening his lids again, stared overhead, fancying himself strangely near the barren blue of the wintry sky. The sun was warming him to undesired strength. The

190

soldiers and the note were gone. Though an inclination persisted to continue to wallow here in the snow, his own will, with which he was at war, told him to rise and run, now that the coast was clear. He would never again behold Stevens, hoped never to behold him. But the hatred of him remained, vivid as hunger of the belly. And the look—like a touch, *intimate as a kiss*—the look that was bound to come on Stevens's face with every future thought of his treacherous comrade—that also remained. Frazer exulted in its conception, a triumph. Stevens put on airs, but power was a fact. He'll never be able to forget me to his dying day—if they let him live, Frazer thought. He groaned. He was tired of Stevens. Christ, he was tired of Stevens—and of all this—Southern quality for which his skin was risked!

IV

Miss Araminta rose cautiously, fearful of arousing Sister Maude Mary, who was asleep in the gloom, in a rosewood bedstead. After two years of war and poverty, this room was the only one in the house that retained its handsome furnishings.

Miss Araminta had never been very bold as a bargainer, and for the objects she had been compelled to dispose of, she had received very little. A few things of value were stored downstairs in a pantry cupboard. She had tried to sell them only recently, but the ladies of Richmond felt that, with strict economy the mode for everybody, an acquisition of Dresden and Sèvres vases would be in 'bad taste.' She sighed, and even failed to guard them under lock and key. Food was more precious. Had she not learned that Uncle Peter Paul Garnett's collection of porcelains brought from China had become quite valueless? The willow ware, the junk in ivory, that he had kept so long among his 'curios,' she had almost 'given away.' Sixteen dollars had been the Jewish dealer's highest price for the wine and liquor sets in old Bohemian glass. The Sheffield she herself proudly donated 'to the Confederacy.' The gentlemen in the Richmond cabinet did not appear to recall even *that* generosity. There was no symptom, among their wives, of a further desire to employ her for their 'plain' sewing. With flour leaping as high as two hundred dollars a barrel, the pittance she had earned last month did not buy enough to shield Maude Mary from the miseries of poverty.

Miss Araminta snatched up her patched stays, her long chemise, and her several dingied petticoats, and stole into the hall. As she passed the bed, she glanced, with a wretched anticipation of the approaching moment of awakening, at Maude Mary's fine, pale worried brow, at her high nose, meagre in its twitching breathing, and at her lids, calm in a deathly stillness upon the hollowed cheeks from which, in recent months of hardship, all colour had faded.

Miss Araminta was guilty in this dread of the inevitable: dread of the cold, accusing eyes opening; dread of the querulous lips, that had been so pretty, always parting now to utter accusation. Sister Maude Mary's voice was flat, these days, with an intentional weariness. She despised comfort. She despised Miss Araminta for wanting comfort; despised, and considered hypocritical, Araminta's 'cheeriness.'

But Miss Araminta, in order to endure, had to speak with more hope than she felt. In her worst moods, she believed, like Sister Maude Mary, once a 'Richmond belle and beauty,' that they were both old, they were both neglected, that they were both 'fairly on the road to die,' and would be mourned by nobody.

Whenever Miss Araminta wished very much something for herself, she immediately transferred expression of this longing to a wish for some benefit to Maude Mary. Thus, she did not 'mind *small* deprivations' for herself, but it was a 'sin, a crime, a wicked outrage' that Sister Maude Mary, who had been the 'most courted' of young women in Richmond, 'in her day,' should lack 'necessities.' Miss Araminta had always flaunted her own 'plain tastes.' When, in her youth, she had been sought after, she had carefully attributed what might have been regarded as a testimony to her attractions, to 'reflected glory,' shed on her from Maude Mary.

Miss Araminta called herself 'a homely body.' She had always been vigorous in declaring that her sister was the one who, by her 'rare gifts of person,' was adapted to 'society.' Miss Araminta was sixty-four, had eyes that had once been considered 'fine,' and were full of honesty. Her nose and brow were insignificant. Her mouth, in its thick, unconsciously rebellious lines, was really ugly. Always the 'tiny' member of her family, while Maude Mary remained the 'statuesque,' Miss Araminta's little body had been so affected by privation that she appeared shrunken. As she clambered hastily into her coarse underclothing, her neck shook slightly in a palsied way. Her clumsy hands, in contradiction to Maude Mary's softly withered snow, were calloused and knotted. Though the big, dim house was by now as bare as an empty barn, there was plenty of work to be done.

Miss Araminta pattered, flat-footed and stealthy, down a creaking spiral. She intended to make the parched corn coffee in the library, where Uncle Peter Paul Garnett's Latin books still reared neglectedly against the brown-gold walls. The kitchen was in an outbuilding, and, since the slaves had run away, she could not bring herself to deal with its rusty stove, its spiderwebs and its unfriendliness. The library was smaller, and seemed happier. It was better than the dining-room, because it had a better grate.

Out of doors, the sun was long up. Reflections bright as crocuses dartled in the slats of the long blinds. This strained warmth, like a cloudy, moted amber, in the leanly furnished interior, seemed to her too bright. Maude Mary never wanted the shutters open, and Araminta had grown accustomed to the furtive atmosphere of constant privacy. Since financial affairs had gone from bad to worse, old Aunt Lindy, the negress who had once been Maude Mary's maid, was the only soul from the forgetful world who intruded on the sisters' poverty.

Araminta, searching out a paper sack hidden behind *Apuleius*, took it with shaking hands. She had tried to ignore how small the quantity of meal left yesterday. Her wizened little brow ached terribly. The sense of a constriction, an oppression, like a dank cloud lying on her mind, was growing daily worse. In the beginning she had tried to make so very light of patriotic sacrifice. It's not for myself, she decided. I was a tomboy when I was a small girl and liked to pitch a ball with Bruce Ray that afterwards wrote the verses likening Helen's cheeks unto lilies. Well, poor Jasper was killed in the Black Hawk uprising, and a nobler Southern gentleman never lived. And Bruce's son married Jennie Gill. Washington Lee Custis, Frank Littleton—every one of them worshipping at Maude Mary's shrine. And what would *they* think to see her now—hardly a shadow of herself? Even after she surprised us by refusing them all—I *was* so grateful that Maude Mary, with all her belledom, never married— And not a family in Richmond that wouldn't have been overcome by her condescension if her health had allowed her to attend *every* function they gave. 'Quite the *grande dame,*' your sister is, Mrs. Johnson said to me. That was after Maude Mary's hair turned white as snow like it is now. A genteel, *regal* appearance such as hers is not to be aped by the first little upstart. I could have swooned with admiration when she played the harp at Mrs. Byrd's. And she was at every rout and picnic in the land.

This chirping inner talk did not silence some unmentionable despair about the long day just beginning. Maude Mary drifted about the house like a ghost. Or she would feel too weak to rise and lie in bed, exclaiming dully, time after time, "They have hearts of *stone,* Araminta. They may *fight* their wars, and they may *try* to keep the country from a revolution, but what of us?"

Maude Mary was unreasonable. When she was most peevish, she described Araminta as 'a hen.' And Araminta, brisk, tired, trying to be patient with her 'poor dear sister,' would usually manage to answer these gibes quite gallantly.

Hunger gripped like a tight fist in the pit of the stomach. Miss Araminta often ignored it as long as she could, and then would rush out, with that 'scarecrow of an old bonnet on anyhow,' and make another essay at selling something. It was difficult to keep Maude Mary alive. Old Aunt Lindy had brought six eggs only the week before, and that had helped a bit.

Miss Araminta was stooping over the split remains of a chair, laying in the grate sticks and twigs from the yard. Paper was scarce. It was rarely now, when you made a purchase, that it was wrapped in anything. Aunt Lindy *deserves* her freedom. The conviction came abruptly, with a kind of vicious earnestness, as Miss Araminta laid a bit of chair-rung across her huddled knee and tried to bend it. The dear familiarity of Lindy's dusky, wizened, sympathetic face drew tears to the harassed eyes. It was *such* a relief to see her when she made her periodic visit. She 'did' Maude Mary 'worlds of good.' And Aunt Lindy had troubles of her own. Her son, who was a preacher, had gone up North, and she had no use, she said, 'faw dem treach'rous abolitionists.'

The war had spared none. I reckon it's all in the design of Providence, Miss Araminta insisted, always schooling herself to the proper meekness which became a lady. But she was growing 'frantic.' *On Maude Mary's account entirely,* she was growing

194

frantic. She was going to tramp to town that day and make a last appeal for work.

When the meal coffee was concocted, it occurred to Miss Araminta to 'get right out of the house,' without even delaying as usual for Maude Mary's awakening. Anticipation of those blue eyes greyed by a constant veil of apathy, and of that voice, once so 'dulcet,' wasting itself in futile sarcasms in that empty, perpetually twilight house, made Miss Araminta a trifle grim. She 'reckoned' that her temper might be 'altering.'

Taking her shawl and bonnet from behind the door, she quickened her movements and gained the veranda so hurriedly that, with the daze of sun, and the lawn, among its old leaves, startling yellow with the jonquils, she had to halt to catch her breath. Maude Mary would whimper, and drone, "You *can't* beg, Araminta. We can't be brought so low as that—to accepting charity. I'd prefer death first."

Miss Araminta's steadfast, usually so kindly eyes, glittered abstractedly. The firmness of one near defeat showed itself in the straightening of her small, stooped shoulders. She did not say to herself that Maude Mary's despair drove her to begging, but, resolving to beg, should it come to that, she felt instantly fiery with abuse, haughty, and covertly revengeful—*not,* she insisted, toward Maude Mary.

The Richmond cabinet certainly ought to be reminded that the Decatur family had a 'history,' and that the last surviving daughters of its house could not live 'like niggers.'

Her home was on Church Hill. She had already, only two days before, walked all the way to the Park, and then out Main Street, Grace Street, and Cary Street, canvassing the possibilities for securing more employment in doing 'plain' sewing. Families who had known her family, and ladies in families with which she had no more than a hearsay acquaintance: all had been approached. As Maude Mary had abjured her so violently *not* to show humility, she had received nothing.

Today, in the event Richmond proved no more fertile, she was resolved that she would go across the river to Manchester, and see Uncle Peter Paul's old friend, Colonel Carver, who was eighty-eight.

As she could never resist the Park, she walked there first, her knees already aching from her trudging. The place appeared to her, as she approached the gate in her new defiance, full of interlopers. Her passion for trees in the early morning was not often shared, and when she saw 'common men and women loitering,' she could not but regard them as interlopers. Poor women in 'wrappers' and sunbonnets disturbed her strangely, though her aversion for them did not at once exceed her sense of obligation toward the lowly, and at the first one she encountered she squinted graciously.

The woman looked sullen. Red with quick antipathy, Miss Araminta strode more briskly. Had these people, then, nowhere else to go? Was it some new consequence of Yankee malice that drove them into the Park in the early morning?

Yet she was certain that something should be done about it. Idle gatherings of persons with disgruntled-looking faces suggested to her some improbable danger. She was always very kindly with the humbler orders, but that was due to her sense of *noblesse oblige*, and displayed no real liking.

Soothing 'Nature' overcame her, however. She dreaded her pretended undertaking, and moved more slowly. Sister Maude Mary would look her regal best, beneath trees like this. "Nothing she ever does or seems but smacks of something greater than herself," Miss Araminta quoted.

A little insect was drilling up and down, up and down, through the quiet over the wet paths. The spraddled grass blades had been crushed by careless feet, but were not yet dried of their perfect weight of dew. The sun, in early clouds, above the looming foliage, looked snug in pinkish drifts of cotton. A cat, on densely clothed feet, sought, without a sound, without a quiver to deflect motion, for some precious living object minute by the flower beds. A single tree might have been a whole forest, and the boughs, dark and damp, twined like rooted serpents among the new, pert green.

Miss Araminta enjoyed these things, today, inadequately. She felt she should go on. Then compassion overcame her, with the sickly consciousness of her own evaded hunger, and she went up to a 'nice, sweet, respectable-looking young woman' who was bareheaded, carried a baby, and seemed ill, and said, "My dear, won't you be good enough to tell me what all these rough people are doing in the park this morning? I never saw such a crowd here before, and I don't feel quite comfortable about it."

The young woman, though she looked so frail, did not have such a gentle eye as one might expect. She said, with a sort of acid patience, "I reckon this is the first time any of us ever had the grit to git up a real protest about things, ma'm. It's somethin' to eat we're after. I used to make plenty myself, and Ma could turn her hand to almost anything, but I was took sick and she followed, and my husband in the army, and the babies on my hands, so there's not much left of either one of us." She shook back her sleeve and nodded toward a wrist which Miss Araminta felt it indelicate to expose. "See *that*, if you please," the young woman challenged unnecessarily. "I thought I didn't have hardly the strength to complain, but when I heard that a whole crowd was expected and we were gonta tell folks what we thought about it, I came along. I can't keep nothin' we can git on the baby's stomach. Ain't he a bag o' bones!"

Miss Araminta, the victim of that hard gaze, felt her sense of persecution driving her to tears. She said, "Well, if *I* were you I'd just go home peaceably. You look like too nice a girl to be in a crowd like this." Half murmuring her last words, she moved on, in panicky diffidence.

"Yah—en ef they don't do nothin' to help us, we're gonta git rocks and smash the 'White House' windows," the young woman shouted, in a cold, derisive tone, speaking to Miss Araminta's humiliated back.

Miss Araminta realized that she must quit this hallowed spot instantly. The day yet seemed graciously small, and made for the faint bird sounds from which she was distracted by the angry muttered talk. But the sun, lappy and shapeless, was oozing a stronger fire where foliage broke on clouds. God made the world for the pleasure of all, Miss Araminta meditated. She conscientiously considered that the poor people *did* have a right to heed all the inspiring sights of Creation. But she wished the tender spectacle might lull them to gentleness.

It's the fault of the Yankees. I never saw more peaceable or law-abiding people than the humblest kind right here in Richmond, she argued feverishly. And fixed her mind on a flashing wing and a faint chirp lost in the etiolated sky.

"You better come along with us, ma'm," a giber invited. "You don't look too fat and rosy yourself. If they ain't gonta ration us nothin', we're gonta *take* it. There's plenty of groceries and bakeries wants us to pay gold for what they got, and they may have to give it to us for nothin'.'"

Miss Araminta disregarded the voice, yet some sense of the words arrested her to sharp, unwilling attention. "The government ain't starvin'," another woman called. "Slaughterin' the pas of the chillun to save the niggers may suit *some* people, but it don't suit us. We been patient. We been *too* patient. The more load they think you can carry, the more they'll pile on. Ain't nobody so low down they ain't the right to some say-so about what ull keep their brats alive. A woman's got a right to live and raise up her young uns, no matter *what's* takin' place."

If Maude Mary should ever hear of *this!* The impulse of panic again extreme, Miss Araminta wheeled and returned toward Church Hill. She could feel wary eyes scrutinizing her as she walked. Bitterly resentful of their suspicions, the doubts she imagined they treasured toward her were compensated for, in her own mind, by *certain* doubt of them. A female, even in war time, could know little enough about what was going on in the world. Richmond was disorganized. It might be full of 'cutthroats' and 'murderers' for all she guessed. And there was never a sufficient number of police or military around the city nowadays. All males who were able were in the fighting lines.

As she escaped the confines of the Park—escaping the cat, still picking its way with sleeping feet in the wet grass in which all that the night winds and dews had beaten down, remained beaten down; escaping the solid white gauze of sunny haze embedding the smears of trees, and the grating bluejays, the sparrows sailing like fish in a pond—she found herself uncomfortably in advance of the very people she was trying to avoid. Her conspicuous departure seemed to have confirmed in others some reluctant impulse. She could hear accumulating footsteps, *halloos*, urging exclamations of "It's now or never, folks"; and the crowd, agglomerating all its components, came trailing on behind her, under some overtaking leadership.

Miss Araminta's always self-abasing spirit desired immolation. She could not bear to be in the front of stragglers whose accelerating cheers, though half-hearted, suggested the more robust antics of circus paraders. She heard rapid breathing, the *pit-pat* echoes from the feet of barefoot runners, the flapping of slippers, the dragging of tattered shoes. The marchers were quickening to reach her. "Follow yer leader. Let the old gal lead us," she heard; but she could not take that to herself. Several stern-looking women encouraging their following children, passed on. A baby wailed transiently in her ear. Despite occasional ribald threats, many of those overtaking her moved on silently, dogged, and too engrossed to notice her.

She was shamed. She longed to turn aside. But the flood of figures accumulated, and she was hemmed in by lines of the passive and excited. Women predominated. A few old men, and an occasional ragged negro varied the aspect of this progress which disgraced her sex. Miss Araminta had for a long time denied sensations of madness. Maude Mary always seemed to her, in that important matter of a ladylike example, a paragon. It was impossible to conceive of Maude Mary in such a situation as this. And if she had been trapped momentarily, she would have evaded association with this perverse group. Not a person here would have dared to 'hustle and bustle' *her* along, and to bear her forward as Miss Araminta was being borne, in sheer helplessness. Shaky, and vanquished almost beyond reflection, she doubled her small knotty fists, and the tears of exhaustion rose beneath her lids.

She longed to run. She stumbled. She went on interminably, and reached Main Street. "Don't get in our way, old lady. We mean to get to business," somebody yelled to her. And again, from somewhere, in explanation, "We won't get riled and start to doin' damage to their dirty stores unless they force us to."

It was all so undirected. "Good as a picnic, ain't it, honey?" a hysterical voice pleaded. "We got to git hold of the mayor."

The more boisterous, who were in the lead, brought those behind to a sudden halt. Miss Araminta believed that her opportunity to wriggle from her predicament had come at last. As, trembling, she pushed carefully, trying to find egress toward a sidewalk, there was a thrilling sound of breaking glass. Immature *hurrahs* greeted the noise.

"What's that?" Miss Araminta stared about into faces fervently dumb and expectant. "It's the bakery. We might as well start in now," a woman announced.

The mass stirred. Miss Araminta was so short that she could but peer among reddened necks, shoulders, bare female arms—brutal or leanly vicious—and see, through ramparts of impetuously lifted fists, to the chatter of scolding from dozens of throats, a turgid wavering ahead. She despaired, and felt that she never more would have any faith in President Davis. How would decent people ever be able to do their duty when the government afforded no protection to their endeavours! Poor Maude Mary must be really weak of hunger, and with things like *this* in Richmond there would be no work. Even if you could *buy* bread, after this mob of women had wreaked its havoc on the bakeries, there would be no bread to eat. She had 'half a mind' to tell her companions what she 'thought' of them. "Bread,. Give us some bread. We ain't kept our men out of the army, have we? We won't stand bein' put off with promises." The call grew stronger, harsher.

Now and then Miss Araminta was able to see the front of a store, and some perturbed clerk locking the doors or pulling the blinds, while querying faces peeped, careful and silent, through the darkening windows. That man *there*, he could see *her*. Why should he stare out at her as if he expected her to formidably break his glass! Oh, it was well enough for *them*—those who had a business and could *live*. But a decent, respectable lady from as aristocratic a family as any in Richmond had to submit to *any* hazard the war could bring.

The throng became impatient. "Order. Remember, you got to keep order. Go inside and take what you want quietly."

But the small multitude was no longer quiet or composed. Men and women quarrelled with each other, and an increasing expression of blind determination grew on each tense countenance. I don't blame 'em if they *do* take bread, Miss Araminta decided suddenly, realizing that she was to be compelled, whether or no, to go where the rest urged her.

When she had reached the bakery, she saw people pushing one another, disputing, and forcing their way inside. The shattered glass was visible, sparkling like stalactites. Maude Mary needs bread and decent food as much as anybody, Miss Araminta declared to herself. She was dizzy and weak. Her temples throbbed, and she was recklessly aware that her bonnet leaned to one ear, while her shawl was being drawn from her back. If they were going to behave madly, they need not suppose that she would permit hoodlums like these to take *all* the bread.

Released from the wearing obligation to remain superior to her surroundings, she drew on her jaded strength. There was a flutter of elation in her breast as she found herself able to insist on her admittance into the jam at the door. She squeezed inside.

There was pandemonium. A frightened man in his undershirt and a floury apron, was just retreating through some passage beyond the counters. Miss Araminta's cheek was scratched by an elated 'virago.' She defended herself admirably.

The place smelled so warmly of fresh bread that she sickened, and her eyes trickled tears. There was a nauseous ardour through her whole being, and she felt that she would be struck down like 'one of God's martyrs' before she would leave the store without securing just one, out of that tumbling heap of coarse and crusty loaves, for dear Maude Mary. Bread was the very perfume of mild passion. She hunched her little rickety body bravely along, and arrived at baskets, on the floor by the counter. Bread tumbled to the ground. People stooped and argued for the fallen burden, scattering its fresh dust of white pollen over their ragged clothing.

Miss Araminta snatched a loaf rudely, covetously; and desired, once she held the sweet, tepid thing in her arms, to break crumbs from it. But she did not dare. It was hers. She was alone against these other unruly longings, hatefully opposing her own. She drew her torn shawl over her precious, sinful acquisition; and there was the second struggle of flight, out of the hurly-burly made by the disappointed, and toward the bright, no-more-familiar street.

The bakery was tumescent with some ogrish menace. Its narrow walls and counters were barriers against her instinctive 'right.' She had never considered herself more degraded, more abused; and she disapproved even more aggressively of the treacherous spirit of her companions. "You should be ashamed of yourselves to behave like this," she reprimanded, to a burly figure of a washerwoman who tried, densely, to knock the bread from her grasp.

Miss Araminta, awkward in her long skirts, kicked. She gained out of doors, but her egress was undignified. Her stiff petticoats tripped her. Far from freedom, she saw the sun only from the depths of a further extended gathering. Main Street was like a market. A carriage had in some manner driven through the press and was drawn up at the corner. She could just glimpse the horses' satin backs. On the carriage steps, a flushed man, in the broadcloth of an important functionary, was declaiming, "Fellow citizens and townspeople of Richmond—" She saw his arms waved in a very anguish of insistence on calm. He was calling on them to remember what the Confederacy expected of them in its time of stress. She joined the intermittently sensed phrases in a vague jumble of meaning.

"Talk on. It does yawl good. You think you kin give us a lot of fine language in the place of bread fer our sick stomachs."

Miss Araminta, baffled by her position, grew red, and felt ill. But her conviction of some outrage, impersonally perpetuated upon herself, was curiously revealed by the false measure of consoling oratory. She had endured all she could. Even Maude Mary, when she saw the good loaf, would not demand consistent modesty before the continued rudeness of Fate. And men, men, men— They ought to have *women* in the city government, Miss Araminta decided, a little wild, but abruptly swerved by an involuntary loyalty. Hugging her bread more rapturously, but still secretively, she glanced at her comrades. The obligation to condemn faded, in a furtive conviction of her own triumph. Let him *go* on with his flowery speeches. What did *he* know about the miseries women had to undergo! Two fellows on horseback, who had followed the carriage, now rode slowly along, in defiance of the inconvenience of the loiterers, who would only step back when actually threatened by the screened hoofs. Faintingly, Miss Araminta recovered from a last reluctance. "You're brutes!" she yelled, in her fierce cracked little tones. "You have no right to interfere with these women—with *any* of us. You don't know what you are talking about."

Though she was unalterably resolved against apology, it was relief to be conscious of the so-much-louder cries, drowning her own. *She* had experienced this thing. Nobody could tell *her* that this riot—if it could be called a riot—had no excuses.

There were other horsemen. Another carriage dragged, impeded, among the excited. Glinting ominously, it drew up, protected by the outriders, who sent the resistant marchers backward over the curbs, and made them fall against one another. *President Davis!*

Miss Araminta recognized him at once, before the few, faint

202

contradicting cheers informed her. She had revered every lineament of that neat, harsh face. She knew that cold, small erectness of deportment. That 'eagle,' slightly miscast eye. She could not hear what he said, as he stood in the landau and pleaded, nervously but haughtily.

And she had no explanation of herself. Maude Mary had 'met' President Davis, years before. Miss Araminta's pugnacity withered, in tiny, submissive resentment to Maude Mary's opinion, Maude Mary's will and comment.

Then the crowd lurched. President Davis had opened his wallet —she only realized it tardily—and was throwing pennies, with a free, chill hand, to the prideless populace who forgot him, who reached, who grovelled, who fought in the gutters with the shrill, pleased children.

She could endure no more. Determined as ever to keep her bread, but so spiritually driven that she could use its mass as a bludgeon, she fought her way on and on, gaining remoteness from the horrid scene of indiscriminate gratitude. By great endurance, she really could continue until she was among thinking groups and out of earshot of the cries of unreflecting jubilance. Giving us *money*, she thought. The idea! Does he consider us *beggars!*

She corrected herself. Why, these poor women don't want *money*, she complained weakly.

Then it came over her that she *had* to face the world alone. Nobody understood her. Nobody knew what she had undergone, or ever would. Poor as she was, she had been born a lady. And she wanted pity from no one. Maude Mary need not pity her, or criticize her. What she had done, and was going to do, would 'stand,' by her own conscience. People were starving hungry when they behaved that way, and President Davis ought to know it. He ought not to tempt them. They were not responsible. Well, she never would trust or believe in anybody again.

Somehow, the resolve edified. She seemed to have saved her life with it. But she remained uneasy, dreading the vanishing of this mood. Something passionately necessary to her self-respect still eluded her.

VII

DIS March. Dis mos' nigh April. Dis spring a-comin' tickles de
roots o' mah toes. When dis pickaxe go up, she come down
blam. She bustin' her way to somepin, nobody don' know what.
Dat Williams Channel nevah took no 'count uv Gen'al Grant. De
ol' Mississippi, she nevah took no 'count of Gen'al Grant. *She* ain'
mindin' no dams. *She* ain' carin' ef all de Linculm sojers in Chris-
tendom wants to git across dat tongue uv lan'. Vicksburg's safe,
far as dat Ol' Lady Water is concerned. 'Less she make up her *own*
mind faw to drown de Confederates, Vicksburg kin set dere high
an' dry, and nobody won' git ovah frum dis side to her.

Was Chester 'glad' that the Yankees had so far failed in
their effort to approach the city by unguarded routes? Did he
resent his conscription in the Federal army to do manual work
for it?

How come Ah know? Long as Ah stuck by Miss Lady, dere wuz
somepin to worry 'bout. Since hit become understood dat Ah had
to leave her, an' Ah tries mah han' at dis Yankee freedom, hit don'
seem to mattah. Ah stan's here on de sho', an' Ah takes dis fool
Yankee's o'dahs, an' hit don' seem to mattah. Ah's makin' roads
frough de swamp faw de Yankees to find deir ways on, an' *dat*
don' seem to mattah neithah. Ah's like Pontius Pilate, lookin' out
his window an' seein' dat *nothin'* don' mattah—nothin' nothin',
nothin', since Ah ain' got mah Miss Lady on mah han's faw to
trouble 'bout.

> *Pi*-lot's *wife* she *hed* a *dream,*
> *Pi*-lot's *wife* she *hed* a *dream,*
> *Oh, Pi*-lot's *wife* she *hed* a *dream*—
>
> *Git* some *watah* an' *towels!*

Chester called out deeply over the muddy landscape. The picks
struck *Pi*-lot into life, and the reiteration of his *wife* and *dream*

204

was solemnly emphasized by the simultaneous heavy *lam* of metal striking slime and rocks.

Chester glanced up and down the line of bending labourers, then, at the two white soldier 'guards' who were idly leaning on their rifle butts. Above the softly watered countryside, the still tents of the encampment rested like pale arks upon the only high ground.

Ol' Noah, he was fooled. Dat dove fool Noah. Miss Lady, she believe in dat dove an' she got fooled, too. Dere was times las' wintah, way 'fo' Chrismus, when Miss Lady was so distracted in her mind, seemed like she didn' have no mo' religion faw to faw-tify herse'f wid. Dat when she come to me an say, We-all's in trouble, Chestah. We's in de wuss fix well-to-do people evah was in. Ef Ah didn' have y'all heah faw to depen' on, Chestah, Ah sho' would give up strugglin'. Ef Majah Massa don' come back *dis* time faw a furlough, den we-all's gonta die uv starvation sho'. Y'all loves mah lil boys, Chestah. Y'all *knows* Ah done mah bes' faw 'em. An' it ain' cause Ah was de onliest one uv Mas' Will's niggahs can read an' write dat Miss Lady frink so high uv me. Hit's 'cause she reckon ol' Chestah got a good heart. Ol' Chestah's thirty-eight years old, an' he nevah done nothin' but work faw Miss Lady since she got married an' befo' dat.

> *Ches*-ter *Jack*-son *hed* a *dream*,
> *Ches*-ter *Jack*-son *hed* a *dream*,
> *Ches*-ter *Jack*-son *hed* a *dream*,
>
> But he *done* woke *up!*
>
> *Wake* up *in* de *mawnin'*
> An' it *won'* be *ve*-ry *long*,
> Thinkin' *bout* yo' *honey*
> An' *he's* done *daid* an' *gone*—

Well, Miss Lady ain' thinkin' 'bout *me*. Her min' too sot on Mas' Will. Ef Ah hedn't been so respectable in all mah conditions, Miss Lady, y'all mought hev hed mo' reason faw to quarrel wid me an' sen' me off like you done. You broke ol' Chestah's heart same as you could break a bowl made out uv gold pieces when y'all done dat, Miss Lady.

He rested, spat in his palms, and again the pick lurched into
the air.

> Us *nig*-gahs *onct* we *hed* a *dream,*
> Us *nig*-gahs *onct* we *hed* a *dream,*
> Us *nig*-gahs *onct* we *hed* a *dream,*
>
> When *am* dat *springtime comin'?*

He sighed, falling silent, and the others, following, silent also,
the picks flashing in a gesture like a battle-cry, the thud of the
implements steady like drumbeats, steady and harsh like the
pounding of blood in black, swollen temples.

Was it Chester's fault that Miss Lady had been unable to conceal from him the humiliating state of her health, and the fact
that Major Massa had gone to war and left her just at the time
when there was another baby coming? For a long while, he had
pretended not to notice.

Georgie run off. Wash run off. Neddie an' Lou run off. When
Miss Lady an' me was by ou'se'fs out dere in de country in dat
big house, an' dere wasn't no use pretendin' no longah, da's when
she looked me in de eye, and she say, Chestah, yawl took mah
message to mah sistah-in-law et Lowestoff, an' you say she ain'
dere, an' you run ovah to Miss Lily Farmer's et Grimesville, an'
she ain' dere, an' you says de Yankees ain' ten miles way frum
heah, en de neares' neighbahs is dem ig'rant Evanses down de
road, an' *dey* don' know nothin' 'bout doctorin', now y'all got to
do somepin faw me. So da's how Ah come to walk all de way to
Prizeacres, where de Tylers was an' left Millie in charge. Miss
Lady say she be grateful ef Ah fotch back anybody black aw white
det knows 'bout doctorin'. Well—da's long ago. De ol' Mississippi
done po'ed a heap uv watah pas' Vicksburg since den. Da's las'
wintah—mos' a yeah ago—*an' Ah ain' fawgotten hit.*

Chester rested, and the soldier on duty, passing, halted.
"It's gitten late, you chocolate-face. Beats me how you expect
to be free an' be fed, too, 'thout doin' nothin'. Act a little
spryer."

Chester, his eyes twinkling maliciously, kept a wooden countenance, while he stared, with purposed insolence, at the blustering
features of the young man in the uniform. "Ah don' *know*, Mistah
Sergeant, an' Ah's jest axin' you, but how many hours to a stretch

206

has you *worked* on dis kind uv road in yo' life?" Chester scratched his big, bare head.

"Don't git too forward now," the soldier admonished, sharp, because uncertain, and moving on.

Chester, purposing irritation, continued to mumble humorously, presumptuously. "Dis heah's freedom, boys. Ah means, de mo' us niggahs work—'cause we's compelled to—faw Gen'al Grant—de freer we is. An' da's how come we give de boss de goodest day's worth uv work he evah got faw his money."

It was growing late. The budding trees, reflected in the wide, irregular mirrors of flood water, were catching, the last light. If the clatter of picks ceased, the silence of evening became instantly audible, broken only by the glassy lisp of constant runnels.

"That ull do for today. Carry your picks back to the quarter-master's shed and be on hand here at sunup tomorrow." The fussy, white adviser stalked uneasily by them, and marshalled the group in order to march them back to the encampment. Chester realized his time was free until morning. "Ginger, ef dat man take his eyes offen you an' me a minute, you take mah pick along wid you an' lemme slip off down de bypath. Dem two gemmen wants to quit work same as we does, an' dey nevah even call de roll call when we come in las' night. Dey leave hit to us to show up faw de mess— what's lef' frum dey own mess—an' Ah ain' gwina show up. Ah got somepin to do dis night."

Ginger chuckled uncomfortably, longing to evade the performance of a favour, but fearing more Chester's important scrutiny and the bravado that few among the labourers had ever dared to challenge. The soldiers were already wandering, in confidence, along the path toward the tents, and had left the unsupervised negroes to return at will.

"Bout free as de chain gang, we is," Chester remarked acidly.

Ginger was timid of agreement. After all, they were nobody's slaves. He said, 'You ain't arrangin' faw to meet Dicey tonight, is you, Chester? She was axin' faw y'all dis noontime."

"What she doin' at de camp?"

"She come dere 'gin faw to sell yams an' goobers."

"Is anybody pesterin' dat gal any mo' 'cause she got her hair ropped?"

"Naw, Chester, dey ain' pesterin' her. Dat uz jes' pokin' fun, when dem fellahs say she got pawcupine quills on her haid. Dey too 'fraid you mought lambast 'em, Chester, faw to pester Dicey."

Ginger could not bear the grim interrogation of Chester's muddy eyes. He was glad to accept the pick and hasten to overtake those already on the path.

Chester waited. He wanted to see the last group well in advance of him, when he would sneak away down the swampy lane he preferred. It did lead to Dicey's remnant of a cabin, but he did not intend to go to see her. Her buxom unattractiveness was a provocation to his senses, and a barrier to unrestrained expression of the compassion she aroused in him. Sad-eyed, apologetic as she was, with her foolish, anxiously grinning face, the hare-lip that turned her smile into an idiotic agony, he had said, in defence of her, "How come all dese sojers makes fun uv yo' roppin's, Dicey? How come dey frinks yo' gaudy calicos is any mo' funny dan de clothes dey wears? Ev'y kind uv clothes is scandalous 'cordin' to de preachahs an' yo's no mo' den de res'. Come to me ef dey nags you any mo'. *Ah* ain' shamed uv y'all."

Too gladly would she obey. Chester saw that now, as, breathing in some wistful sweetness of the evening air, he waited his opportunity to steal below the elevation of the roadbed, and seek that other lane.

If he succumbed, if he went to her and her clean bed in that tumble-down shack, something ended, and a new life of despair would begin for him. How could he actually *want* her, he wondered. Back on the plantation—before he went away (or, to refer more accurately to his humiliation, before Major Massa sent him off)—he had rejected every 'likely' woman in the neighbourhood.

Dey ain' mah kind. Ah don' want none 'at ain't mah kind, he had said. His pulse *thrub-thrubbed* in his wrist and brow. Ever since he could remember, an inclination toward the need of a woman had seemed to him sinful. Hit ain' sinful faw de res', but it's sinful faw me—'cause I don't like it, he explained, evading it.

But why? Evah since Miss Lady call Millie an' angel, mah distastes faw dese goin's-ons wid females has got worse an' worse. Dey's too wise. Dey's full uv de serpent sho'. Ah nevah wanted Millie on dem grounds wid mah Miss Lady, but when Ah seed dat lil face gittin' so peaked an' she was hol'in' in her pains so she

208

couldn't hardly speak, an' Ah recomlected how Millie done acted faw plenty folks 'at was too po' an' too disgraced to git a doctah, Ah fotched her ovah. Seemed like Millie *knowed* somepin soon as she set eyes on me. Y'all ain' *made* to be lonesome, Chestah, Millie says. Y'all's too pow'ful. Lawd, man, what muscles y'all got; Lemme *feel* dem muscles. Don' tell me, she says, dat a man wid *dem* humps in his arms an' back, an' shouldahs, kin git frough de world widout any lovin', an' a pow'ful heap uv it. What *y'all* needs, dat 'oman says, is some gal jes' as pow'ful as y'all is to do de lovin' back.

Dat gal tempt me like de Devil tempt folks in de Bible. Ef Ah hadn't wrestled wid her hard, Ah would 'a' fallen sho'. Dat how hit come on me fust dat what Ah needed faw to solve mah diffi-culties was dat sugah juice. Reckon Mas' Will figurin' yit where-'bouts Ah got dat jug, an' hit was hidden all de time under a pile uv rubbish in his smokehouse. Well, Ah ain' tellin' an' Millie ain' tellin'. She knowed mah stomach wasn't fixed faw none *uv her* anyhow.

Stumbling down the loose earth of the road, Chester hesitated again. In the flood waters surrounding, swam the shallow blueness of the fading sky. Toward the river, there were half-submerged trees, and these, against the sinking sun, were in a light visible like dust. The whitish sun seemed to shed a pollen over everything. A chill soundless breeze ran over the obscure, rosied landscape, wrinkling the tinted blots of muddy water. Every little inundated bush smouldered. Every hairy protrusion of young grass was bla-zoned. A thistle-pale mist was beginning to rise, and to grow, enveloping, indefinitely, the implied dark.

Between Dicey and himself, lay another opportunity. He fum-bled deep in his loose, ancient 'sojer's' trousers that he had bought at the commissariat. Most of what he had earned that week had gone into the surreptitious purchase of a bottle with a pint of rum in it. Slowly, conclusively, he took the bottle out, and held up its transparent contents, warming them in the last rays of day. Better let Dicey come to him, anyhow— And then—if he *still* had a 'hanker' for her— But she could wait.

Mas Will say I's no-'count. Chester's plump mouth twisted sar-donically. Well, ef Ah's no-'count, da's it. Seven months, Ah tended Miss Lady when dey wasn' a white soul on de place. On

Christmas Eve, Ah shot dat rabbit faw de chillun, an' wid dem apples Ah stole off Jedge Bass's place, an' dem popcorns Ah saved up, dem po' lil critters could mos' preten' hit was like de ol' times agin. But Ah's no-'count. De Lawd put de first faw dis stuff in mah belly, an' Miss Lady don' fawgive me. She say she 'fraid uv me. Ah was sleepin' out in de wood lot to sleep hit off, an' nevah come nigh to her once, an' *still* when Mas' Will come she has to tell him she's afraid of me. Dat's women. Da's ladies, like mah white Miss Lady, same as every one else. Dicey, hit seem funny dat a fine, strappin' man like what Ah is, kin take up wid a footloose ijit like y'all—an' Ah don' say Ah's gonta. But like Ah says to Millie, don' be 'fraid dat when Ah wants a gal Ah don' git her. Ef Ah takes a notion to y'all, y'all's done faw.

Chester glanced about carefully. Secure in isolation, he uncorked his bottle preciously, and turned it slowly upward to his mouth. The drink was 'good.' But he must 'save' it. How often might he need this solace? He could recall 'yaller Millie's' luminous, provoking eyes. He hated her. "Ah, ain' none uv yo' fickle, high-handed niggahs pretendin' to freedom, Millie," he had told her. That was the truth. Miss Lady, she nevah let on to show her real feelin' an' Ah don' neithah.

Is Ah a wuss sinnah dan dese othahs, dat Ah feels like dis? He surveyed, with a more comforting doubt, now that he had drunk a little, the two skies between which he stood: the sky above becoming duller, colder; the sky that lay in the water in grass blades and bushes, always deeper, always more radiant. "Da's *good*," he said aloud, emphatically, rubbing his lips with the back of a heavy hand. "Da's bettah an' bettah."

He meditated uncertainly. It was a fact that, as his companions had accused, he did not appreciate his freedom. As far as that went, he had been free long before leaving 'home.' Y'all's a free man, Chester, Miss Lady had said, an' dat ain' only cause yo' Major Massa an' me wants to set you free, but because Mistah Linculm took dat priv'lege from us.

Ah guess hit's de mattah wid *me*. When de Lawd made niggahs wid mashed noses an' black faces like a tar barril, he sho' done some foolishness. Ah says it to *y'all*, Mistah Sunset, 'cause y'all keeps on gogglin' at me frough dat willow swamp. Dis sugah juice is somepin, but hit ain' sufficient. An' Mistah Linculm may be de

bigges' man in Washi'ton, an' *yit* he ain' done de trick he set
out to.

The bottle tilted and remained, for several seconds, obliquely
upright in the forcibly steady fingers. Fierily, it darted last splinters of clear red into Chester's stubbornly closing eyes.

> *Mis*-tah *Lin*-culm *hed* a *dream,*
> *Mis*-tah *Lin*-culm *hed* a *dream,*
> *Mis*-tah *Lin*-culm *hed* a *dream,*
>
> But *he* ain't *woke* up *yit!*

He staggered on into the dusk. The atmosphere was chalky. The
sun flopped from the sky, and a mass of murk and crimson remained to welter in puddles amidst black spears of grasses. Ah's
sorry faw y'all, Dicey, but Ah's sorry faw me mos'. Ah reckon
y'all's *good* enough faw me. Ah ain' ugly as y'all is, but Ah's ugly
'nough, Gawd knows. An' what lil edication Ah picked up from de
newspapahs, hit ain' wuth much. Dis heah *is* freedom. Dese new
swamps round de rivah is free as de cemetaries. Dis heah feelin'
Ah got in mah stomach, don' *nobody* own. An' da's 'bout all. Ol'
man Sun, he got his work cut out, too, an' *he* gone. Mistah Linculm, he got his work cut out, an' dat's carryin' de wah on. Mah
work, now Ah knows Ah won' see Miss Lady no' mo', maybe even
if Ah die, mah work is *me*. An' Ah reckon Ah's de lonesomest man
dat evah lived. Y'all can't save me, Dicey, but Ah reckon y'all kin
hev me. Dey ain' much else 'at Ah is good faw, an' if y'all gits any
pleasure from dis corruptin' body, y'all might as well hev it.

II

"Anenu adono, anenu b'yom zom taanisenu, ki b'zoroh g'doloh
anachnu" (Answer us, O Lord, answer us on this day of the fast
of our humiliation, for we are in great trouble)."

Solomon, droning on, and with slight rocking motions, knelt
alone in the denuded parlour. The tallow dip in the neck of the
bottle was sucked by the drafts, and, flickering, tilted to a further
incline its oozy stalk, the flame gushing like a mild elixir. Solomon's stubby hands, clenched tightly in suppliance, rested on the
edge of the table, and he did not heed the hot grease falling upon
them, leaving its cold blisters on his reddened skin. In his worn
talith, the dirty white fringe also receiving the sizzling baptisms

of the dip, his yarmelke somewhat rakish on his grizzled hair, he was the mean picture that he thought himself, shrunken with misery, bereft of any present capacity to challenge or wrest a living from an unyielding world.

The door opening on the hall was a little ajar. In the crack made, Rose and Esther, their pinched faces awed, watched 'Vater' excitedly. When Jacob, woolly-headed but golden, like a gilt, negroid cherub, his blunt, bony nose too pronounced for his child's face, tiptoed from the chilly kitchen and stood behind them, they moved aside deferentially. Rose and Esther, twins, were ten. Jacob was eight. But the girls realized that 'Vater' toiled and 'Mütterchen' wrecked herself with economies more for the boy's sake than for their own.

It was for Jacob to wear the fine clothes Mütterchen had purchased in Vicksburg: the short jacket with the brass buttons, the frilled shirt, the round collar, the flowing tie, the roistering cap with the handsome, dangling 'streamer.' When he was dressed for Shabbas, not even Sally, the caustic, furtive-mannered slave girl, self-appointed arbiter of 'white folks'' fashions, could take exception to his appearance.

"Heve no ko-rov l'shavosenu. Y'hi no chasd'cho l'nachamenu," murmured the voice of sodden anguish, chanting on in the parlour.

"She's gone," Jacob was whispering, using the Yiddish despised of the very servant of whom he spoke. Since Sally's hostile advent in the family, Yiddish had become uncomfortable on the children's lips. Yet they turned it against her, to speak their fear of her and to betray her secrets.

Rose, with gentle cowardice, preferred English. Sally, she believed, had fearsome powers, acquired through the assistance of a hoodoo man. Besides, Rose could never refer vindictively to anybody and find it a relief. "Mütterchen never seen her go?" Rose asserted, half questioning, her heart colder than ever with this new chill that had fallen over the house.

"No," admitted Jacob, "but she says the Yankees have set her free, and we can't keep her any longer."

"Is that what's the matter with Pa?" Esther demanded nervously. She, too, was ready to consider the evil Sally author of some unnamed power which was devastating all of them.

Jacob was as doubtful as his sisters of the real cause of the symptoms of disaster, but he had a cocksure reputation to maintain. "Pa ain't stronger than the conjure man," he said. He was shivering, not so much downcast, as too alive with presentiments that were vague enough to be half enjoyed. The hall was dark, though a light shone out from the open kitchen. But for the prayerful iterations from his father, the house was still.

Cousin Abe had been conscripted. Jacob knew that. He now wondered if, through the malicious efforts of the conjure man, Vater, as well, was about to be led off to the war, never to come back. Just a fortnight had elapsed since a group of mourners had 'sat shiva' for Cousin Abe. Jacob recalled, with dim, terrified resentment, that oppressive epoch. Rose, with less defiance to the ritual of sorrow, remembered equally. When she had seen the cracked mirror in the bedroom unwound from its wrappings, she had expected to find, in its emerging twinkle, the assurance of a renewed happiness. Today, and particularly this evening, the atmosphere had been as contradictory of the usual as was the silence in which huddled relatives sat in a continual abasement with their shoes removed. Rose and Esther had not liked Abe, and had been muted by the obligation to a public hypocrisy which demanded they lament loss. Tonight, the menace to which they bowed had approached nearer. Judging by the violent interchanges, unendurable to hear, which had passed between Mütterchen and her one black chattel, the children were sure that Sally's threats to her proprietors were being fulfilled.

Jacob was the boldest. He had called Sally "Schweine!" that very afternoon, and had spat contemptuously into her face. Not long after, Mütterchen, calling him cautiously to the bedroom, had reprimanded him tremulously. Even Mütterchen, always so valiant to defend her own, was afraid of Sally. Jacob, realizing it for the first time, had started at his mother curiously and had felt a qualm. The absence of her familiar support to his defiance had humiliated him.

Ever since Sally had been purchased she had been slyly vituperative, and, more than once, in their parents' absence, she had slapped the girls. She had never dared to lay her hands on Jacob. Jacob was perfectly aware that, as often as he gibed at the servant, his sisters paid for his presumption. Vater had forbidden

Sally to chastise Jacob. He would 'kill' her if she did, he said.

Listening to the omen of Vater's prayer, Rose recalled the painful and exasperated phrases of his conversation with Mütterchen. "Yes, Rachel, I got it here, all printed out. And besides, dot man, he come today to de General Store. You got your warnin', Mr. Rosenbaum, he says to me, and ve can't extend dot leetle permission any longer. General Grant he ees a man nobody kin trifle wit'. We'll gif you all fellahs chust twelve hours longer to close dees beesiness." Rose remembered without understanding, and a hand pressed heaviy upon her heart. Vater had never allowed her intimacies with him, but she had revered him from a distance, warmly and contentedly. When he was gay, he was lenient. Then her spirits rose to his cheerfulness as to the impersonal benefits of clement weather. So much, so irritably ignored by him, her self-importance gained from his mere shadow. And it was in a religious pitch of thankfulness that she would see him lay aside the long coat of his Shabbas broadcloth suit to pour the festal wine for them on Friday night. She depended, somehow, on the happier aspects of his ceremoniousness.

Almost all the nice furniture had been taken out of the house. Mütterchen had explained, bitterly, why all valuable belongings were being sent for indefinite storage with their benefactress, Mrs. Davidson. The Jews must leave the state of Mississippi by tomorrow. She and Vater and the children were compelled, by the new enforcement of a military law, to abandon the very house. Why Jews? Why us? Why Jews? Why Jews? Rose, in the dimness of an almost sensual fear, kept asking it. Jacob, shrewder than the girls, though not better informed, had heightened, with his boastful guesses, their sickly curiosity. Esther was less patient. She did not want to know the reason why, but felt indignant. It was as if an indignation like her mother's explained it all. Rage against an act was sign enough of its injustice. Indignation was sufficient. Esther was the vainest of the three. It was she who stole oftenest away from home to play with gentile children disobediently. It was she who had always baited Sally with pertest questions, and had refused to believe herself, as Sally said, the lowest of the very lowest race.

"Sally told me Pa ain't gonta be allowed to keep the store any

214

more, or anything," Esther expounded in sibilant tirade. Rose, wrestling with a mystery, shuddered. Jacob, afraid that Vater might overhear them and descend on them like vengeance, stepped back from the crack. Vater might be most abused of men among the gentiles, but the belief in his omnipotence in family life could not be thus wiped out.

It was raining. Mütterchen, with stony face, her tears exhausted, had left them all an hour before, to go, with some final desperate petition for aid, to Mrs. Davidson. The children wondered if, when Mütterchen returned, this dread, this doubt, would pass away. They wished that she had not allowed the men to take off the furniture. It was the emptiness of the cottage that they could not bear, the fact of the removal which had made disaster final. Disloyally, between hope that was torment, and incapacity for more discouragement, they were ready to allow it that Mütterchen must remain, on her mission, a long time. Mütterchen, formerly to be relied on, had this day undermined their faith in her.

A flat tread sounded for them on the small veranda. Yes, it was she! After all, the signal of the wanderer's reappearance lightened a burden. Vater was aloof, a god before God. Mütterchen was sometimes stern with them, but she was stern with love. They were glad, they were glad—she was coming back! Perhaps they were glad, though secretly, that Sally had already fled. With Mütterchen's restrained hatred of Sally they had sympathized; but the ire that had burned between the two that afternoon had been a spectacle which crushed. It was odd that, just the year before the war began, Sally had been Vater's thoughtful, long-anticipated present to his overworked wife. The children knew he had picked her 'cheap'—her low price due to a squint, a limp, and a sulky nature—in a slave market down in New Orleans. In the era when Sally was a novelty, they had shared his pride that Mütterchen now owned a slave, such as the gentiles kept, who could do the heavy work. Mütterchen, when Sally was first given to her, had seemed bewildered. Yet, with the same zeal which hoarded to buy horsehair and a Turkey carpet for the parlour, she had set her heart on just this last possession. The children did not recall very distinctly the pack days, the days when, freshly immigrated, they had lived uncomfortably with some cousins in Cincinnati, while Vater, with his trunk of pins and mitts and brass brooches, made endless country pilgrimages. But they were aware that Mütterchen had drudged very hard. Perhaps the trouble was, as Mütterchen insisted, that Sally, with her slattern temper, did not wish to work. At all events, after the horse and wagon and the constant years of moving, Sally, brought to crown the comfort of the cottage and its permanence, had proved a curse. So they were not regretful that she had fled the house.

To leave Vater the ease of privacy, they did not rush straight to the door as they felt inclined to do, but were quiet in their expectancy, while Mütterchen, still on the hidden veranda, must be furling her umbrella. Then the noisy door swung back.

Rose, unable to repress herself more, moved swiftly toward the joyful encounter. The night sky, deep as a forest, sprang before her, and the quills of rain beating gently on the doorsill in the wary luminance of oblique candlelight. If Mütterchen should be as upset as ever, Rose wanted to die.

She was. Anguish was contagious. Before she spoke, before she said anything at all, before her mechanically devout lips pressed the mezuzah on the table by the door, before she could hide away the downpour of rain and fumble with her soggy shawl, they knew that the visit to Mrs. Davidson had but affirmed the worst. Stolid woman of staid gestures that Mütterchen was, she came toward the children almost fiercely. "He is *there* yet?" she asked; and it was as though she reproached their blamelessness for something Vater had not done. The children huddled about her and nodded.

Jacob was jealous of her self-absorption. She dropped the fach-ayleh from her head, but let it drip on her shoulders. Her plain black sheitel made a harsh outline of artificiality about her haggard face. Jacob was accustomed to her constant flattering distress on his behalf—her 'spoiled child,' as she would fondly boast. Even in a crisis, he would not leave her to herself. "I'm hungry," he whined, with a hidden delight in that quick fixing of her wild attention on him. "I ain't had nothin' to eat all day, Mütterchen. I'm so hungry I can't stand no more. What for do you go off an' leave us all so hungry?"

There was, at best, a little stale bread in the house. Mütterchen, hesitating, watched him with that resentment which we feel toward those whom we love, but whom we cannot succour. Had she not heard that cry every day for weeks, and from the girls

216

as well! Jacob pressed against her wide, bedraggled skirts, and clung, with his two meagre, grovelling hands, to her one large wet hand. It was callous, inert. My God, what should she do! "Where's Sally?" she demanded. But this was less from anxiety concerning Sally, than from conscience-stricken fear of Sally's spying. In a cupboard, hidden, Mütterchen still guarded the remnant of a ham bone, a gift from Mrs. Davidson. With eggs and milk beyond bargaining, with flour at fabulous prices, with no kosher meat available, such gifts were not refused. Solomon alone was unaware of the sins against the laws of diet which his wife committed. When Rachel had first fed ham to whimpering Jacob she had expected him to die of it; but her love was weak. She did not know that Jacob had grown so used to a lean stomach that he made a pleasure of it; that it was voluptuously, in a longing which enjoyed misdemeanour, that he pleaded for the ham. She would bear the burden on her single conscience, if only Sally, outrager, from the beginning, of all Jewish law, did not witness virtue's frightening defeat. "Ham too good faw y'all," Sally had told the children. "An' what faw y'all so finicky, changin' yo' plates an' knives faw vegetables an' meat, when yo' ma don' own no decent tablecloths, when y'all ain't got enough to eat!" The children had repeated it. Jacob despised the black slut in the kitchen, yet she, and the exigencies of war, had poisoned his faith in parental infallibility. He took his vengeance on his parents now in vicious selfishness. "Sally's gone," he told his mother, ruthless toward her chagrin. "She says the Yankees set her free. She don't belong to us."

"Ach! That woman!" Mütterchen, speaking in whispers, trembled before added calamity. She would rejoice, in her soul, to be rid of Sally, but not without a toll of voluntary dismissal. Then, too, every new incident on this day of slanders increased Mrs. Rosenbaum's sense of stored defeat. She clenched her hands. She stole toward the kitchen. She would find Sally. She would berate Sally, once, at last, and for all time, saying what she thought. Had not Sally told the children that all Jews possessed the evil eye!

As Mütterchen, hurrying, dominant even when at loss, passed the parlour door, Solomon came out.

She was an obedient wife, but she could scarcely endure the sight of him. "Bo-ruch da-yan ho-emes. (Blessed is the Judge of Truth)," she said quickly, anxious to slay his hope before it em-

217

barrassed her. Solomon, standing before her like a man convicted, bent his head. Jacob, too, eyes sly with the malice borne of privation, saw, and did not revere, the squat figure clumsy in its frayed shawl, the broad head, tight and doubly ugly in the close yarmelke, the beard of grizzled silk, the fat, patient, sardonically protruding underlip with which Solomon's gross hand toyed. Jacob felt everything unpredictable. He was unhappy because his stomach hurt, and he blamed *them*.

Solomon's mouth was loose with weeping. He took a bandanna from his vast pocket, slung it on the air, and, when it was unfolded, wiped his forehead. "No hope?" he muttered. "Then thou hast not brought me any hope, Rachel." He sighed. His chin wallowed on his breast. He had expected it.

"No!" snapped Rachel aspirately. "*You* should begin to make plans to stay after you allowed the furniture to be moved away!" Then her defiance broke. She wheeled from him, and hid her face in her sturdy palms.

Solomon ignored her. He saw his wretchedness, and that was all. He had forgotten even his children. He beat his clenched right fist upon his cupped left hand. He had never known how terrible that humble woman's gaze could be! With the strength, he would be cruel to her. She insulted his trust in her devotion. Years he had devoted to the frail security enjoyed by his family, and it was destroyed in a day. He reached again inside his coat and brought forth a handbill, the flimsy paper on which it was printed already macerated by repeated perusals. His mind was bruised on this monotony of print which he had conned by heart. Fumbling his slack mouth as before, he read again: "*The Jews as a class, violating every regulation of trade established by the Treasury Department, and also department orders, are hereby expelled from the department within twenty-four hours of the receipt of this order.*"

It seemed to Solomon impossible that General Grant, issuing this order, realized its import. Could a man see the docile, faithful wife, the children innocent of wrong, even the slave— How could it be that this was his last night in a home made his own by such decades of toil that the memory of each was blood, and a curse to the tyrant! True, Solomon had already acquiesced. True, he had consented that Mrs. Davidson should store his furniture. True,

218

that the goods in *Rosenbaum's Emporium* had been already confiscated—and they were few enough. But the problem of moving remained, the problem of means. Should they try to pass through the hostile war zone to reach Cincinnati where they had relations, or should they attempt to get to New Orleans—and beggary?

He brushed his pain-angered wife aside, and began to stumble up and down the hall. The children shrank from him silently. Jacob stole into the kitchen to peep, and Esther watched, like a little girl, with her finger lolling in her open mouth. Rose, entering the bedroom, threw herself face downward on the dusty floor and tried to hide till it should be over—tried to have no thought.

Solomon had acquiesced, but he *could* not acquiesce. Solomon was one who, out of necessity, had eased hate of the gentiles to tolerance. Now every lenient view seemed punished by God. Rachel was almost illiterate, but Solomon had a fair education. He could compose protests. Ever since the morning he had been composing protests, sending them to the newspapers, imaginary diatribes, confused with prayer, to be delivered publicly against General Grant. There was a cry in his throat, but it found no utterance. The energy of his hatred consumed his intelligence. He devised plans and lost them, his heart too occupied by its sense of one wronged to hold the slyness, the craft to which it was used. Strange ideas peered, leered, performed antics of treachery in his mind. Not once in his life had Solomon been care-free. From childhood poverty had always been with him, obliging him to confront, without surmise, things that no man confronts willingly. He had a peculiar pride in seeing what is called 'sordid fact.' His pride allowed him to glorify that conscience which egged him on to lie, to cheat, to commit all offences to free will, and for the sake of his own, that those who were dependent upon him might profit by his abasement before the gentile, by his soul's undoing.

"Jacob! Come thou to me." With a glare of a drunkard, Solomon, halting, beckoned his son. Solomon felt profane. Religious utterances came into his head, but with lewd implications of self-derision. He wanted to say kaddish for the dead. He thought of telling his boy to utter his own funeral prayer. The impulse waned, however, before any blasphemies were spoken, and Solomon, once he had his son beside him, only stroked the blond head absently. Vengeance was the Lord's, and the Lord's only. He sternly kept himself to that. Jacob was thrust aside. Solomon began to stagger up and down the hall again.

He chewed his nails. Such a *little* contraband, Solomon thought; and that was choking irony, not apology for the crime. When a man who lives by trade is paid for all his stock in Confederate bills, and the Yankees infest the country, and Confederate bills are rendered worthless, that man, if he would support a demanding family, must use desperate measures, take desperate risks. Pins, needles, stockings—he had smuggled, too, a few barrels of flour. No more. And he was ruined.

"Who reported me to dem doity Federals first?" Solomon asked his wife. He had already asked that of her twenty times. There were few Jews in the town of Bailey and Solomon recognized no active enemies. The authorities might easily have passed him by, but that some malcontent and busybody had been at work.

Jacob leaned against the wall and watched, thinking how many times he had heard Sally say, "Yo' pa ain' nuffin but a ol' Jew ragman, anyway." Jacob shivered. Recalling Sally's words, and oppressed by them, he felt a new awe, and a horror in his father's grief. Maybe Sally had told the soldiers about Vater. Maybe Sally had reported. Again he was enveloped in that furtive, abashing dread of Sally. Sally was the one being in the Rosenbaum household who had ever given insolence to Mr. Rosenbaum. Jacob had never known any one like her, so wicked, so irrepressibly shameless. He was almost envious of Sally.

"Thou hast earned this!" Mütterchen said with biting calm. She had found another dip and was moving from kitchen to hall, hall to kitchen, hall to bedroom, making bundles of the remaining trifles they could take away, stowing the little remnant of their clothing in a carpet-bag. She had spread pallets for the children on the floor, but she knew that they would never go to sleep. Usually so kind, she wanted them to suffer with her, wanted all to suffer.

"That demon of wickedness is not here." Mütterchen had peered into every corner, in the pantry, even behind the stove where Sally's bedding sometimes lay. She had found, it is true, a precious and forgotten parcel: Sally's comb, some rags, a charm she had, a 'lucky' bone, a fragment of flawed looking-glass. She hid them, hostages for Sally. If Sally had left this hoarded trash behind her, she could not be far off. Yet Mütterchen was timorous as well as desiring of the return: Sally, lean, slovenly, in her one dress, Sally's loose mouth slobbering snuff; Sally, with her covert sneers at true religion, with her superstitious talk of charms and rabbit's feet—it was a presence that drew evil with it. Mütterchen believed that it was Sally's company which had drawn the anger of the Lord upon the house. Slavery was 'wrong,' *not* because negroes were unfit for freedom, but because, in slavery, the negro brought an unclean presence to a decent family. Mütterchen thought of that evil chattel now discarded, and feared even sleep. She would not have dared to sleep with Sally near, even if fatigue did not keep them all too tense for sleep. And as one dread must succeed another, she must wait tomorrow. Rose and Esther were at last worn out, and did breathe heavily upon the floor. Jacob, fretting, teasing his mother wearily, was still awake.

Twice Mütterchen, imagining odd noises, went back to the kitchen door and opened it. Oh, God, the ache of her bones! She was a woman who lived for her kin and for nothing else. What had she to do with war, and the making of war? What had her Jacob done and her little girls that they should be its sacrifice?

The rain was lessening, and the moon, appearing, was like ashy flesh. Its light showed a pen where geese had been kept, and a damp path leading to abandoned cotton fields. The soaked leaves blew and beat at the candle as she thrust it forth, and the puddles near her turned to gloomy sunsets in the dark. The world seemed old. How old she felt!

Vater, always grimly reasonable about such things, might prefer that Sally be recovered. He had paid for Sally, he always insisted, and he meant to have her work. He would not allow it that the Yankees could deprive him of Sally's labours until they reimbursed him for his purchase loss. A husband was both a protection and an affliction. Mütterchen, preparing to close the door a second time upon an empty night, resigned herself relievedly.

What was that? Just under the dripping eaves of the house, an angular figure stood in silhouette. Perhaps the figure had intended flight when Mütterchen spoke sharply to it. At the "You!" of scorn, the wraith moved, raised a skulking head, and marched defiantly into the light. They looked at one another. "You doity runaway!" cried Mütterchen. "Ah come to git what's mine," said

221

Sally savagely, and, passing nimbly by her startled mistress, ran into the house. They were close together in the kitchen.

Mütterchen was so shaken that she was dumb. Her wide bosom heaved with repressed contempt, but what she felt was beyond articulation.

Sally raced like a wild thing to the stove and began to prod and poke behind it. Mütterchen, abashed by the petty form revenge had taken, said not a word. Sally's belongings were reposing in the cupboard. But let her search!

"Y'all dirty Jew folks ain' stole mah bundle, too, is y'all?" Sally asked. She had a whining voice, sycophantic when she wished, but now shrill with bravado. " 'Cause ef y'all takes what rightly belongs to me Ah's gwineta set de Fed'ral law on y'all!" She stood there, with her arms akimbo, breathing cautious hate.

Mütterchen felt restraint useless. It no more served to defend her dignity. She felt a nakedness before this creature such as had shamed her in no other relation. The world was represented by its mean connivance with this less-than-human one, this erstwhile slave. Mütterchen said, "Oh—oh," gasping, not quite knowing what she meant to do, and ran heavily forward, her fist lifted. Sally, mute, malicious, though a little frightened, dodged, crouched beneath a table, and stayed there, gibing, out of reach.

Jacob was the first to overhear. "Dot slut! Dot hussy!" Mütterchen was calling brokenly, arrested in her self-exposure and now ready to cry.

"Debbil 'oman, debbil folks, dat's what y'all is," Sally was muttering. She was so excited that her words were hissed, and she made little sputters of saliva when she talked. Her ragged dress, not wider than a shift, half fell, in its low neck, from her shoulders, and the bones that thrust up, hunched, under her brown varnished flesh, were like chicken wings. She was thin to reproach, to emaciation; and was very ugly.

Jacob's sense of this war was of constant, horrid changes. He associated an increasingly familiar feebleness of ill-nourished nerves with constant untoward happenings. When he was hungry, he was wiry, keen, on edge. When he was on edge, in his dumb, desperate pugnacity, he was gratified if he saw, on the faces of those around him, expressions which represented for him his own unrest. He called to his father, "Ach, Vater! Vater!" He screamed.

He rushed to his mother and tugged her sleeve. He ran to the outer door and, for some reason—he did not know why—he fastened it.

The altercation between the two women grew loud. Mütterchen sobbed in Yiddish what Sally said more coarsely, as she squatted, hugging her knees, under the table, and prepared to dodge blows from whatever quarter they might fall.

No one perceived Solomon's entrance—or none but Jacob, who, when he saw the livid rage upon his father's face, regretted the temerity that had made him shout. "Ees *dot* how you come back here after you run off! You sneak!" Solomon said, fiercely, shakily. And the wranglers started. His voice, vibrant with all the pent miseries of the last hours, made his wife close her eyes. "Ach, mine Gott! Mine Gott!" she murmured. "Vat vill he do!"

At least his business was not with her. He strode by her.

Rachel pulled herself together. "Let her go, Solomon," she said, in a suddenly calm voice, tidying her clothes, fixing the brooch at her neck, and not daring to catch the negress's eye lest victory, flaunted, challenge quieter resolution.

Sally was distrustful of an alliance offered by a foe. Creeping hastily from her barricade, she made a step toward the door; then halted. Solomon, also, had stopped. Jacob barred the way out of doors.

Sally was as lean as a rail, and leaner. In her single skimpy calico garment, with her unropped wool in a bushy, unconfined aura about her crafty face, her small, miscast eyes squinting dull recrimination, she inspired Jacob, as ever, with the loathly attraction which he sometimes felt for things inhuman and bizarre. She was barefoot—Solomon had never brought himself to buy her any shoes. He was kind to people who were kind to him, but toward those who opposed him and were in his power he showed no pity. Pity had too often betrayed him. He felt, indeed, too weak for pity. It was the nauseating false emotion of those who were in affluence.

"Come here!" Solomon ordered, pointing one quivering finger at the floor before him, where, so his wife suspected, he intended to make Sally kneel.

Squinting covertly, testing him with a terror-stricken glance that was almost a smirk, Sally refused to budge. "What faw Ah got to come dere to you?" she said at last. Her flat chest rose and fell, rose and fell, so that Jacob noticed the breathing which betrayed too much.

"I say dot you come *here!*" Still Solomon's rigid, shaking finger pointed, without dexterity, at the selected spot. His voice gained an enraged volume.

Sally, cowed, tried subterfuge. She moved, then veered, then darted, with accelerated pace, toward Jacob. The boy could not brave her. He left the exit he had closed unguarded.

Sally must have determined violently on this escape, yet she did not seem able to resist a last retaliation. She delayed herself to make a wide pass with a black hand at the dodging boy. "Heathen Jew!" she yelled. The blow was inaccurately aimed and missed its mark.

Solomon, seeing his child threatened, rushed upon her. His suspicion of the extent of her treachery was suddenly confirmed and fury convulsed him with all the tensity of strangulation. He kept her from the door, but could not reach her. She was again in the middle of the floor. Mütterchen withdrew from the two, and leaned on the wall, trembling, casting down her eyes, and saying prayers.

Sally, for all her hideous mien, had the agility and swiftness of a deer. "Ah don' belong to y'all!" she yelled hysterically, "An' Ah ain' goin' to. De Linculm men dey gonta tel y'all straight out dat Ah don' belong to nobody."

Mütterchen was a dreamer in a nightmare. She put out her hand sleep-walkingly. "Let dot mean gal go. I don't vant her, Solomon. I vill not haf her more to make nasty dees hones' house." She spoke in English, awkwardly, a little gutturally.

Solomon was absurd in a moment when he could least endure absurdity. Yet this abandonment by his wife made his misery towering.

"Ah's goin', Mis' *Jew* woman!" Sally screamed, half sobbing her derision. "Ef y'all talk 'bout nasty, Ah ain' nevah seen mo' dirt—greasy, goose-grease-eatin' Jews. Ah's lived mah life wid a Christian mastah, 'fo' Ah's took away by you. Ah's used to decent, Christian ways, Ah is!"

"Take dot word back!" Solomon, evading his wife's discouraged effort to restrain him, bore on like a judge. "Do you mean to insult me—dot dirty slave you are, dot low, ignorant nigger!"

224

Sally galloped toward the hall. The twins had been roused and were there, aghast. When they saw her coming, they retreated, dumbly, uncomprehendingly. With her dense halo of wool about her face and her recalcitrance before hitherto unquestioned law, she appeared to the little girls a devil.

Sally, though frantic, showed a giddy confidence in herself. "*Ahs's* hones'," she screeched. "*Ah'* ain' been tol' Ah gotta leave dis town. Ah ain' no tacky ol' Jew pedlar dealin' in contraban' stuff!"

Solomon gained his end. He had her gripped well in his clawing fingers. He pressed her to the wall. He slapped her face repeatedly. But, as she turned her head from side to side to elude the blows, she still yelled at him. "Jew! Ol' Jew pedlar! 'Tain't mah talk. Hit's white folks' talk. Come on, you ol' Shylock—da's what dey call y'all! Crucified Jesus! Crucified Jesus. Ah ain' nevah hung mah Christ to no Judas tree like what y'all is! Hit me. Hit me, you mean ol' man. Ah got mah Jesus on mah side. Ah's tol' de neigh-bahs what y'all is. You's goin' to hell, y'all an' dem measly chillun an yo' goose-greasy wife! No Jew don' own *me!* Yo' ol' 'oman bal'-haided, da's why she wear a wig. Won' eat pig cause hit ain' good 'nough! Won' eat pig: Won' eat meat an' milk. Won' eat meat widout de blood drawn out. De pigs an' de chickens, dey's too good faw y'all. Ah ain' nevah fawgot to cross mah fingahs when y'all looks at me, you ol' Jew debbil wid yo' evil eye! Ev'ybody know what a Jew is like! When mah ol' missis down in Florida sees a man like y'all, she set de dawgs on him!"

Solomon's intoxication equalled her own. As the administrator of Divine Justice, he felt agonized, but he also felt colossal. Never in his life before had he allowed himself a recklessness which conscience did not curb. For the first time in his whole existence, his God was his utter ally. He pushed Sally to her knees. The thud of his fist played on her shrinking arms, her breasts. He could notice the yielding quality of dark, soft, quivering body, and could glory in its helpless sentience. "Devil!" he exclaimed once; then finished with speech. It had become needless. If he could kill her, if he could kill her, if he could *only* kill her. What he did to her, he spent upon the whole world.

Her moans had begun dramatically, while her gaze kept its taunting, upraised malignance. Now her shrill voice had the pure note of pain, and she was like a wild thing tortured in a cage. Cries were unvolitional. Solomon had broken the strength which supplied vanity. She hated him yet, but for a reason that dignified her. She had flung herself wildly about. Now she was prone, and gave no more than what was wrung out of her. Solomon panted, and felt vaguely the loss of Jehovah's presence. He must leave her to the Lord, leave all to the Lord. 'Thou, even Thou, art to be feared, and who may stand in Thy sight when once Thou art angry?' Resignation is an iron to the soul, but it makes the strength of the godly.

"Stop, Solomon! Stop! For the love of your family, stop!" Rachel pleaded. "Remember the neighbours and that they are all against us, that we have no friends." Rachel was like a woman who abandons principle to save a life.

Solomon, revolted by contact with the negress, took her under the arm-pits, and lifted her slack body. He dragged her to the door, opened it, and almost slung her out. "Go!" he said. "Go! And may no honest people ever set eyes on you again." Rachel waddled thankfully to the cupboard, removed the ragged bundle from it, and threw the thing after its owner into the lagging rain.

Her limp body lay in the weeds and young grass. Solomon longed to flee the sight. In abusing that woman, he had robbed himself. He stood before his family in unaccustomed exposure. The midgy moon, darkened with crusts like old silver, still shone through the trees, and he shrank from its revelations. There was no peace for the strong. With precarious gestures, shamed, in anxiety for his dignity, he swung the door shut and turned the key in the lock.

Rachel had collapsed hopelessly on a rush-bottomed chair, the single one left in the room. Her apron was over her face. She could not, *could* not look at that victim of everything, her husband. Woe, woe, woe. And she rocked herself silently. Dawn was approaching. The endless pilgrimage which she had made so often through a forgotten world would be resumed.

Esther, weeping in confusion, in anger against being made to weep, stole from the kitchen, leaving them. Jacob, in the security he had sought from enlarging strife, squatted stupidly in a corner. Rose remained.

She, too, had cried. Now she was tearless, preferring not to see her parents, but so baffled that she did not withdraw. Her heart beat terribly. Watching Mütterchen, a stout, disconsolate old woman, crushed in spirit, Rose thought of this same figure, altogether different, as it appeared at the hour of 'licht benschen,' eyes closed, hands in their humble gesture of blessing, on the face an eloquent remoteness which conveyed to the children, solemnly, something inward they could draw on from her that no outsider could touch. At that hour, a gentle excitement pervaded all of them. Vater, after the transient piousness of saying kaddish, would be almost jovial. And all the nice food that they ate together—the noodle soup, gefilte fish, chrain, boiled chicken. Would they ever have such things again—when they were people so genteel, so respectable, so much to be depended upon?

Wearily, Mütterchen rose. "You'll have to see about dose permits an' dem steamboat tickets, Solomon. It's nearly five o'clock."

She tied her tuch on her head. Though she was long accustomed to America, she would not wear a hat.

Rose glanced doubtfully at the window. Morning was coming, sure enough, but the moon still swung there like a glassy apple. Greying clouds swam by, carrying the bright circle in their drear islands. Outside, unexplained to her, an evil bundle lay. Rose was afraid. She was afraid, afraid.

She *knew* something. Something had changed, something had altered. She *knew* something. Even Jacob, who would soon be ready for his bar-mitzvah, and would be a man, did not seem to know it. But Sally had known it. Sally, because she was very, very wicked and was acquainted with the Devil, had found it out.

"Bo-ruch a-toh a-do-noi elo-he-nu me-lech ho-olom, ha-ma-avir she-no me-enoi u-s' nu-moh me-af-apoi," Rose recited, timorously, twisting her apron. (Blessed art Thou, O Lord our God, King of the Universe, who removest sleep from mine eyes, and slumber from my eyelids.) "Bo-ruch a-toh a-do-noi elo-he-nu me-lech ho-olom, asher no-san lo-nu to-ras e-mes, v'cha-ye o-lom no-ta b'so-che-nu. Blessed art Thou, O Lord our God, King of the Universe, who hast given us the law of truth, and hast planted everlasting life in our midst. Moses commanded us the law as an inheritance of the congregation of Jacob . . . And thou shalt love the Lord thy God with all thine heart and with all thy soul, and with all thy might. . . . And these words which I command thee this day

227

shall be upon thine heart. And thou shalt teach them diligently unto thy children . . . And thou shalt bind them for a sign upon thine hand, and they shall be for frontlets between thine eyes. And thou shalt write them upon the doorposts of thy house and upon thy gates. . . ."

But the Jews must have done something wicked. Mütterchen was not to blame, and Rose did not think that Vater was to blame. Yet God only punished his own people when they were wicked. If she *had* to be a Jew, and Vater and Mütterchen and Jacob and Esther had to go on being Jews *forever*, and being punished, she must find out the reason. And if all the mitzvahs a good little girl could perform would not help to stop the punishment, she must still find out. Mutely, she wrung her hands. O Lord our God, King of the Universe, help me to find out why I'm bad, she said. And she went on crying softly, while Mütterchen, not noticing, collected the things; and the house seemed to grow emptier and emptier with daylight, as at the time when they began to live in it. All felt guilty. All knew themselves just. Why was it?

III

The swamp began suddenly, out of clear sky and water. Cecile hesitated as on the brink of some doom, and gathered her petticoats in her fastidious hands. Her present repugnance for herself and her state seemed to find its tangible expression outside her, as she gazed through the leaning woods, over the tattered, bristling palmettos. The moss drooped from the live oaks and cypresses in garlands of mourning. Reflections like ashy clouds stood in the brackish water, that was the colour of rust. Whenever she observed a log, inert in a puddle, she sought for eyes, and a snout.

"Virginie vini ave vous. Li pas peur," Virginie had said. But Cecile had sent the cadaverous nigger girl on ahead of her to Tante Marie's cabin.

What if Uncle Césare should know? Cecile had spent all her girlhood with Uncle Césare and Tante Julie. Tante Julie guessed nothing at all. The war had left her as unmoved and as unimaginative as she had always been. Poor as they all were, Tante Julie could not realize it; and considered that her hauteur had completely subdued the Yankee soldiers who had come to search the house. Clos St. Antonin was in the hands of Federals now. The

228

family no longer appeared to have the right of exclusive ownership in the property. Cecile had been very formally polite to Captain Anderson when he had come to visit them, and to apologize, in a sort of way, for the selection of some land enclosed by the plantation as a spot on which to pitch a camp. Uncle Césare, who had once been a beau, a rake, a spendthrift, had received the captain warmly, inviting him, with fatuous generosity, to share a meagre dinner. Uncle Césare had a fat, drooping face, bloated, and of a despairing expression. Though his manners remained as elaborate as ever, he appeared, in some subtle way, to feel relieved, and secretly astonished, whenever anybody condescended to pay a little attention to him. It was Uncle Césare's reputation for dishonesty that had been the first torment to Cecile's self-respect. She was proud. Long before meeting Janot, she had determined that never, never would she make for others any explanation of herself.

As she hurried along the slimy path, she pressed her knuckles to her lips to keep her teeth from chattering. When the swamp thinned, she was grateful; and she could walk along the gulf's edge, her slippers sinking clumsily in the leaden softness of the beach, where the fiddler crabs, emerging from their hiding to confront the evening, made little black embroideries of twinkling, moving legs. Where she was, in the open, she was somehow less dispossessed of that privacy she had always worshipped. Here, she could almost imagine that she had nothing to conceal. Conchs propelled themselves by some invisible means along the salt-smelling, iridescent expanse. The strand bubbled continually with the swift punctures left by minute, crawling creatures, who dug their ready burrows as she approached. The horizon of the water wavered in a drunken line beyond. A pelican, flying low, seemed to creep toward her, on wide white wings, over the sea that was blue as a stone, but already withered by the mists preceding sunset. The clouds were pearl, becalmed in hyacinth pools of sky. All the edges of the world, withdrawing from the pine trees, shone. A slow waning seemed to sap each grass blade of motion. The earth was bitter-still.

Cecile had rejected sin, yet terror itself had the guise of sin. If she refused confession, if she would not share Tante Julie's luxury of false humility, which was a price paid to God and the Saints to purchase the damnation of the Yankees: Cecile's condition was the same. Janot was more than vain of his good reputation. Uncle Césare, Cecile's guardian, had furtively wasted his niece's money to pay his gambling debts. He had been evicted from his club where his evil repute had grown. Now he sat at home all day and played bezique or patience, while Cecile had to ask for Janot's help in making disposition of the sugar crop.

From the instant of Janot's enlistment in the Confederate army, the ruin of Cecile's plantation had been imminent. She understood his need to join the fighting forces. Janot's father, once so wealthy, had died a bankrupt and a suicide. At that hour of general disgrace, his mother had temporarily lost her mind. Janot wished to be re-established, and defy his father's critics. Even after loving Cecile, he thought first of that.

She agreed with his ambition. They had been affianced promptly, but had resolved that they would not marry for at least five years. They would retrieve the property. Cecile was, above all, considered 'sensible.' She had that repugnance for confusion and half-way measures which was the result of contemplating Uncle Césare's doddering. Tante Julie was pious. Tante Julie was bitter. She was sanctimonious. And Cecile feared for herself and loathed the petty scandal that Tante Julie talked. Not even tragedy could convey to Tante Julie any earnestness. Cecile had made up her mind, very long ago, to rise above all this. She was as clever as a man, Janot had often said. For herself, she believed that her temper was 'cold.' But she would not attempt to behave toward her lover any differently. He must accept her just as she was. She had sometimes been ashamed, when in his company, to feel relief in the certainty that their marriage would have to be postponed again.

Burning-hot as the roof of some aquatic conservatory, was the water she was obliged to leave behind her, as she demanded of herself more calm with which to plunge again into a reach of swamp. The landscape today had for her some new, terrible aliveness. Her own emotions had become too wakeful, and that was why she could no longer think composedly.

Cecile hurried on. The thoughtful paths were empty. Between the floating patches of moss, the sky leered, with a green-blue acid as a poison.

It seemed to her strange that, when she should next pass through here, she would be already committed to an act with consequences that would be irrevocable—that would affect her in the flesh. That she could endure contemplation of her resolution, was due to the persistent fact of her incredulity. She would not yet believe that folly as yet merely imagined could have results beyond a revocation by her will.

Janot's secret visit had been an error. When she had first received his message, she had refused to connive at a meeting. She and he both hated recklessness and taking foolish risks. But, in the end, she had not been able to resist him. And it was because she was weak, and could not make up a successful plot, that she had taken Virginie into her confidence.

Janot had traversed the Federal lines at night. It was not until she had walked up through the canebrake with him that she had observed his limp, and he confessed his wounded leg. She had been so sure, before she met him, that she could retain her self-control: but when he was in her room, and she had seen his haggard face, she had begun to weep. Janot never admitted failure. He resisted sorrowful abandon. He had pleaded with her to make this assignation happy. Cecile knew that the awful, crafty feeling which had come upon her was sheer wickedness. Uncle Césare did not guess the arrival. Tante Julie, with her senseless flutterings of excitement, might have revealed it all. Janot had dared one night at Clos St. Antonin, but he had trusted nobody.

Cecile saw a toad, and halted. As a habit, she despised the tremors of the female. Now she was timid, because, in this awful, strangely moving world, she seemed to have brought herself too close to these alien things. The toad, also, was alarmed. Sidling, hopping lumberingly toward a stump, it reached upward and grappled at the bark with its ineffectual little hands. Virginie would scream, and snatch a broom, in panic, if a toad came in the house. And Cecile, ridiculing her absurdity, could not escape the spell already laid upon her by her superstitious confidante.

How did Virginie know? She had known long before Cecile had told her. She had known on the very evening Janot had departed, before Cecile had herself suspected her own dilemma. Virginie was quiet, usually silent, usually grinning: yet given to occasional startling volubility. She sat perpetually on the floor in a corner of the kitchen, and rocked herself. A free negress for a long while, though none were certain of the way she had come to freedom, she was called a little mad. She was dirty, she was shiftless: yet she gave advice. She was a beggar, and she called herself a prophet. She lived as she might, with no possessions but the ragged clothes she wore; and she could run like a deer, Cecile had discovered, when sent on messages. Virginie had large eyes humid with perpetual apology. Her head was covered with little dusty knots of wool. She had the distrustful gestures of something wild. She crouched, with her thin, limp arms about her lifted, bony knees, and stared, and observed the family, and scratched herself.

To a girl of refinement, communion of any sort with Virginie must be odious. Yet Virginie anticipated what she was not told, and, in the end, Cecile had accepted this shame, which was like the living garment of her being, and had kept nothing back.

The toad in the path reared on its bowed legs and looked at her, its black-stone, red-rimmed eyes silly with fright. Its pimply bronze skin fitted it loosely like a pair of drawers, and was of the mottled tint of a slightly rotten leaf. Because Cecile was obsessed by a horror of sensuous contacts, she imagined its touch. This tree-flesh heaved, throbbed deep heart-throbs hidden in the fat body. She heard its gentle, steaming hiss, that was like a meek, venomous defiance, though its beetle gaze showed only melancholy. She took a step. It flopped to the ground and rustled to seclusion under a bush. Cecile, conscious that she could not leave her oppression here, clenched her small fists and again hastened, denying a compulsion to scream. Janot had revered her. He had arrived at nausea of women who were less than ladies, and she had come to *this*.

Little ice flecks of spilt sun dissolved in the dulness of the trees and the somnolence of the puddles. The sun itself was like a lurid lamp in the blackening boughs. Pale bergs of cloud, scudding in the zenith, carried their chagrined light onward to the sea. Soon that, too, in darkness, would wash the long coasts. Was the soul an illusion? When Virginie whispered her thick sibilant words, Cecile, who could comprehend so little of the patois, felt her mind bruised on the substance of a world which, in her own tongue, had no articulation. If Janot *knew*, he would loathe her. Yet it was dread of Janot's reserve, of the contempt she could anticipate, which sent her now to Tante Marie's cabin and its voodoo rites.

Late as it was, Cecile found the swamp warm, and took off her bonnet. The arid vapours of twilight fused in an insidious heat. She believed that she wished to die. Yet her jealousy of Janot's life, which would then go on without her, restrained her from too morbid ease. And this was she, who had kept no single thought from him. In a manner, it was her new awareness of people dying that had degraded her. Until the war had come, and Charles had died, and Eugene had died, she had not credited death's actuality. She rebelled against indecent self-exposures; but could any outrage be worse than that stripping away, even of all that clothed Janot with recognizable features? A corpse in a salon outdid any other impropriety. The war had made her gentility trivial. She could not define the source of a falseness that was in all she did.

If Janot died, she would relinquish every effort to understand and acquit herself. With a child— She would not call that a child which lived under her tight gown in continual denial of her determination to bring her world once more under her control. Or, if she was guilty and condemned to purgatory, tortures could only keep vivid her exultance in sacrificing her self-respect to save her lover from the sharing of humiliation.

Cecile, I have been a scoundrel. She could hear him say it now, condemning himself, because a broken man had, of all persons, the least right to a self-indulgence which entailed responsibilities. All she had been able to think of then had been his white hair, and an austerity that rebuked her. She had longed to compel him to confess to a helplessness when without her, which equalled her own despair in a contemplated loss of him. But it was recently that she had recalled, in the harshness of his unhappy face, his eyes that suspected her, seeing that her love, and her demand upon *his* love, would purposely destroy all the hardness he was able to keep. If the baby was born, and Janot came back, he and she would spend the remainder of their lives together: yet, if Janot championed her, under such conditions, it would not be because of his affection for her. His loyalty to her, should she add another burden to what he bore, would be a veil for hate.

Tig, tig, malaboin La Chelma che tango Redjoum. Tante Marie was already as old as the deceased. She did not ask questions of the white people. She was never critical. She would know that what was happening had to happen, and that the squeamishness of the white ladies was only vanity. Uncle Césare, with his foppish waistcoats, and his soiled linen, he knew, too, with his flat, dull stare, and his pouched, opaque eyes, that pride was senseless. There were only the very old left in this existence, and they were never surprised. Tante Julie would not be surprised, though the facts were such that she would doubtless prim her lips and refuse to mention them, for when she regaled her niece with scandal, she never spoke outright. It was Cecile's spirit which defied contempt. Yet, with hunger, with her body distorted by a new demand, there could be no defiance, because there could be no liberty. Crimes committed in the appetite for food, the old forgave. Or was this a hunger, to be condoned like the other, that had forced her to ignore her modesty? God created the world. God revenged himself on his creations. Tante Julie and Uncle Césare, with Père Martin, were in league with God. (Uncle Césare would like his carpet slippers, Tante Julie would remark. Permit me, Cecile, won't you have another cup?)

Then Cecile saw her repulsion for this rejected life lying there before her. A log moved in the twilight. A log floated in a puddle. She dropped her bonnet and caught with both hands at her choking throat. Rosy evening dingied every twig and root. The pyre leaped, in blushing alabaster, through the last loopholes in the boughs, but the radiant orgy in the sky left the swamp cold. The log, for an instant, thrashed phlegmatically with its stuffed, dead arms; the log, with its dead eyes painted high above its shoulders, stared at her, stared from the distance of an incalculable inertia, and sent to her rapid heart, in the silence, a loathsome thought that was not a thought. Again, feebly, the fat dead hands paddled. The leather bolster of a shape heaved idly through the mud. She saw the chubby legs of segmented iron; the webbed feet, and stout, yellowed nails; the befouled armour of a dragon tail. The alligator's thick neck bulged and sank, bulged and sank, with the motion of a bellows encased in shell. It sprawled and hissed. Beneath a brow, like the crushed brow of a stallion, the jaw opened, and teeth hung there, under the horny folds and prickles, in the semblance of a smile. Ridged like a harp, it swam on, sank deeper and deeper in the slime: and she ran, holding her crinolines high above her frail ankles, wondering, and somehow disappointed, that she escaped so easily.

Between sorrow and morning the world seemed to stand. She

was on firmer earth, and near the edge of a clearing. A dog's bark came to her and was as hoarse as a remote whisper. The trees, under their last crimson, rested their branches, quieted every leaf. Every bird was secret. The unmindful voices of picaninnies called through the thin dark. Trembling, uncertain whether to go on or not, it seemed to her that she felt the night growing for all.

Negroes were singing, far off. She caught a greeting: "Mapè dinin." Virginie was waiting for her. And a negro man. Cecile glimpsed his slouched, doubtful form. A drum was beating in the distance. That flat iteration, suggesting the Congo, dinned the final protest from her mind. "Toi malade!" Virginie caught her, supported her: and for Cecile the musty odour of a negro body mingled with the smell of pines. But she did not regret her flight. That she should not have the baby was something that Tante Marie would comprehend. Negroes did not make a pious war for 'freedom.' Negroes did not try to kill Janot. And they did not condemn. Blankly, Cecile allowed Virginie to lead her on. Denying her own distaste for her surroundings, she found a link here with that mood, so unaccustomed, which had produced her state. The bush by Tante Marie's log doorstep was hung with flowers, had come fully into evening wakefulness, and was all alive with little white corpses. A few tumbledown shanties huddled in the dusk in a New Eden; with the night creeping in on her sorrows. And if cataclysmic events had defeated her every effort to resist, she discovered, even against her will, sin the same, but horror less. It was as though the negroes were about to show her something she had foolishly refused to know.

VIII

From the Richmond Appeal

*W*HILE *the plans of General Lee are wisely locked in his own breast, and details of strategy revealed only to those in a position to co-operate with him, Southern people must content themselves with assurances, ever trusted, from those who know, and with President Davis's assertion that never before have the troops under the direction of our Commander and Chief been in a stronger position.*

Owing to General Lee's wish to make doubly sure that the Yankee gain no advantage by anticipating the steps to be taken toward a triumphant culmination of the Maryland campaign, the usual sources of news fail to yield knowledge of the exact position of either army. We know that on the twenty-second of this month Ewell crossed the Potomac and took Chambersburg. Since General Imboden destroyed the lines of the Baltimore and Ohio, his activities seem veiled under a hopeful air of mystery. Sedgwick's retreat, compelled by the performances of Ewell when he quitted Winchester, allowed General Hill to cross into the Shenandoah Valley, and since then the Yankees have given no indication that they will be able to retrieve lost ground.

While it is hard for the people of the South to labour under their present anxieties, they must admit that the old adage which says that no news is good news was never more apt. Stringent draft measures adopted by the North, and to go into effect next month, on or about the thirteenth, are receiving that unfriendly criticism which betrays which way the wind blows. New York City is said to be in the throes of a protest . . .

When General Jenkins returned to Virgina a fortnight ago, he brought with him requisitions of horses, herds of cattle, and a large quantity of victuals. This attempt to reprovision us was an

236

*accomplishment without violence, and all the supplies requisitioned
have been paid for fairly in Confederate money. The conduct of
our own troops when on soil that, if not, strictly speaking, Yankee,
is neutral, contrasts with the unjust, outrageous, even blasphemous descent of Yankee marauders upon peaceful Virginians,
women and children and tillers of the soil, alike.*

FROM THE LONDON GUARDIAN

*War news from the United States of America is infrequent and
independable, and, owing to constant censorship, such information as we receive is of doubtful authenticity. Officers of the American mail steamer, "Persia," which docked in Liverpool yesterday,
reaffirm a previous intelligence to the effect that General Lee, of
the Confederate Armies, continues the offensive, and that the
Army of the Rappahannock is meeting with little success in its
invasion of Northern territory. This may be good news or bad
news to those who, watching the struggle from afar, and disinter-
estedly, begin to feel that anything short of catastrophe which will
bring this long war of brother against brother, and friend against
friend, to an end will be a relief. The North considers Lee's offensive a move of desperation and sure to end disastrously. Whatever
the result, however, this year will produce no further cotton crop
for the Manchester market. The innocent suffer with the convicted,
and mill owners, employers and operators, alike, are faced with a
state of affairs that, though we cannot question the Will of the
Almighty, is distributing broadcast the miseries resulting from
financial ruin. As charity begins at home, so does the obligation,
shared by all British statesmen and every loyal subject of Our
Gracious Queen, to protect British trade and British interests, take
precedence over any other duty. British interests once safeguarded,
Britain is ready, as ever, to complement, with third-party counsel,
any move, made by either party in the conflict, that will initiate
the re-establishment of an equilibrium. . . .*

*It is gratifying that the Society for Prevention of Cruelty to
Animals obtained a conviction before a bench of magistrates at
Loughborough, against the Marquis of Hastings, for cock-fighting*

237

at Donnington Hall. The Marquis was adjudged to pay the full penalty of five pounds, and the three gamekeepers concerned, twenty-one shillings each. The Guardian has ever been a supporter of this humane organization which strives to protect the dumb and faithful friends of man, unable to plead their own cause, against those owners to whom possession means, not benevolent exercise of responsibility, but tyranny. We hope that this decision indicates that cock-fighting, as a fashionable pastime, is waning in popularity. . . .

Yesterday the discussion in the House of Lords on the case of Mary Anne Walker, who was said to have died from overwork, and from sleeping in a badly ventilated room at a fashionable milliner's establishment in Regent Street, was continued. . . .

The Guards gave a grand ball to the Prince and Princess of Wales in the picture-galleries of the International Exhibition Building. The decorations were of surpassing splendour, and it is calculated that the gold and silver plate used represent a gross value of two millions sterling. The guests invited were limited to 1,400. . . .

II

Mrs. Drew had just said to her daughter, Sally, "My, what heat we are having! Seems as if you couldn't breathe in it," and had retired into the back parlour to take off her corsets, because it was 'so hot you almost forgot decency,' when Sally, very pale, her eyes wide with trepidation, pulled aside the brown wool portières, and, ignoring her mother's "Whatever—Sally!" cried, in the peculiar tone of voice that Mrs. Drew never afterward forgot, "It's *them*, Ma. Oh, Lawsy, Lawsy, it's *them!* You know Mr. Hach had a notion they would come through here."

Mrs. Drew's gouty fingers trembled so that she could scarcely get her clothes together; and she decided to leave the corsets off, anyway. But there were so many strings. She was perspiring 'in rivers.' "Is it the Yankee boys or the rebels?" The sense of an event unprecedented, coming upon her suddenly, made her as dazed, in her own house, as though she had been in some unfa-

238

miliar place. Her basque hooked up the back, and she wished herself a man, to be able to swear a little. "Sally, for gracious sakes! No! Well, what do you think I *am*, anyhow! Now it's *all* crooked." She gasped, and her chins wabbled, as she ducked and tried to snatch her stockings off the floor. As leave be in a lunatic asylum as in a house where you get to strewing things about. She said, "You say they *have* come? But where are they? I don't hear a sound in the road. And you might know that if anything is on hand *Mrs. Harris* will be at the gate. Any bit of news or anything that happens never escapes *her* notice. She's got eyes in the back of her head, *I* always tell her."

Sally was pressing her hands together, squeezing the palms against each other, and she wished 'Ma' was not so stout that it always took her an age to move anywhere. "Well, they *are* here, too. I can hear the racket in the street now. It ain't rebels, or there'd be shooting. Mr. Hach and Tim Allen both said that nobody was going to stand using *this* town for a short cut."

Mrs. Drew waddled forward quickly, her skirt half on, and her petticoats dragging. "Must be the ones Tim saw in Middletown yesterday. And on the way back here he run on to some other soldiers that he took to be Confederates."

Her most precious possession was her 'White' sewing-machine—'one of the first that ever come to this place'—and she thought that a Confederate army, if it came to town and began to loot, would select that to make away with. The dresser, as well, holding 'real nice china,' invited to profligate theft. And, though the furniture was heavy, there was an easier lure in the tatted 'tidies' with which each chair was hung.

"Ma! Quick. There's a whole line of them crossing at the corner. It's Union men, Ma. They're all in blue, thank heaven, so we needn't be upset."

Mrs. Drew, with her face of an oyster, rushed to the window beside her daughter; then hesitated miserably. What if they *should* turn out to be the others—and the way people behaved nowadays —well, *anything* could happen. She arranged herself behind the curtain. "What if anybody sees me, and the pesky hooks and eyes!" And she clutched firmly and defensively at the bosom of her dishevelled dress.

But there was no time to consider. The opportunity was too

239

engrossing to permit one to wait on caution. "Sally—you open those shutters and you'll spoil the dog on the carpet right off. And don't lean so far out. Those soldiers will think you want to show yourself. If it's *our* boys, why don't somebody cheer? Why there ain't any cheering? They'd never let *our* boys go by this way. You'd think we were at a funeral."

"Why, I hear a lot of cheering, Ma. The biggest crowd's down by the post office. There's Mrs. Harris. How she can ever worm herself along and nobody stop her!"

"I knew it. Well, she'll know all there is to know, and tell us whether there's any need to get out of the house, or whether there's going to be a battle or anything."

With the animation of worry, Mrs. Harris, bareheaded, in a clean grey calico, entered through the gate and crossed the parched grass of the small yard. She observed Sally, and came under the window so that they could talk more comfortably. "Sally Drew—where's your ma?" Mrs. Harris shaded her eyes with one thin, freckled hand, and stared up, evidently too annoyed for geniality.

Sally said, "Ma's in her bare legs and curlers and won't show herself, but for heaven sakes tell us what's happening! Mr. Hach told us something about Tim Allen seeing soldiers, but I was so surprised I pretty nearly dropped."

Mrs. Harris slapped her own flat bosom, indicating exhaustion and despair. "*Speak* of surprise! You could have knocked me down with a feather. And what I can't understand is that I sent special word to Maria Smith—she lives right on the road toward Middletown—and I said if there was any sign that there was gonta be any trouble down that way she'd send Johnnie to let me know. These *are* our boys for certain, ain't they?"

Mrs. Drew, unable to restrain herself longer, opened *her* blinds a crack and called, "I never was so taken aback in my life, Mrs. Harris. I'm sure as long as it's *our* boys it's all right, but who would have expected the war would get as close as this."

Mrs. Harris leaned with dramatic limpness against the wall of the house, and smiled grimly. "Nobody can say now that we ain't seen the war. Sounds like about a million. Look at that fellow on horseback, Sally. Some of these gentlemen in regimentals have a up-handed way of admiring you girls. Looks like he might run off with you."

"Don't put notions in her head, Mrs. Harris. She's flighty enough already."

"I ain't, Ma. But there's the flag. There's the *flag,* Ma. Look at it. Ma, I want to cheer! We ought to be cheerin' like the folks down yonder at the post office."

Mrs. Harris tapped one small, flat foot on the grass. "Tumpety-tump, tump, tump. A day for Gettysburg sure enough. But there's no band. I love a real good band, and plenty of players and instruments. There's times when I can't keep my feet from jiggling."

Sally looked disappointed. "I guess this is the end. Wasn't so much excitement after all."

Men and women who had been standing at their fences began to go indoors. Mrs. Harris glanced up and down the sun-stilled street in its quiet lengths of dust. "There's Mr. Hach. You always say I'm ready with the latest reports, Mrs. Drew, but Mr. Hach gets things before I'm out of bed of a morning. He can't be delivering his milk at *this* time of day—so it must be us. Pity that man limps so. He'd make a fine soldier. How d'ye do, Mr. Hach. How's your liver today? I knew when I saw them men marching along you wouldn't be far behind."

The square-faced, frowning man with the wooden leg, came hastily into the yard and approached Mrs. Harris without even having returned her greeting. He was in his shirt-sleeves, but wore a brown plush waistcoat and a wide felt hat. Very fiercely and officiously, he said, "I want you ladies to git right indoors. No time for talk or anything. There's gonta be trouble as sure as I'm alive, and if you stand around out here, you're gonta regret it. Git down in the cellar. And if I was you, Mrs. Drew, I wouldn't stop for to collect none of my family heirlooms." He spoke in thick, stifled tones, and his rapid glance, under grizzled eyebrows, was needlessly rebuking.

Mrs. Harris started, then delayed herself. "Look here, don't you scare us out of our wits for nothing, mister. Why, Maggie's down to the post office this minute, and if anything should happen— But what *can* happen?"

"That's all right, ma'm, what can happen. I'm not prepared to say. All I know is that Jeb Turnley and Tim Allen seen the Confederates comin' into town at the other end—out there by Blitz's store—and rode ahead just as fast as they could gallop. Now you mind *me,* Miss Sally. Don't let yer ma fool you into thinkin' there's time to pick up no bric-à-brac. Git down in the cellar and *stay* there."

He wished them to realize that he had no moment to spare, so turned away instantly he had delivered his information, and set off at a great pace through the gate and up the street.

Mrs. Harris watched him bewildered. "Is there gonta be a *fight?* a battle? a *real* battle?" she shrilled anxiously. But he did not turn his head, or heed her.

"Well, this is ahead of anything. Now he's going into Judge Webb's. Now he's up to the Hendersons. Mag-*geee!*" she shouted loudly. "Look at that girl——just as if nothing was the matter. I left Sam's dinner boiling on the stove, too. You better take his advice, Mrs. Drew. I don't know what he means, but I see everybody going indoors." Mrs. Harris's last words were spoken over her shoulder, as, choking with abrupt alarm, her realization of her peril tardy, she hurried away, no longer curious as to the decision of her neighbours.

There was left the road, given over to sun, to the last bluecoat vanishing in the distance, to maple trees spouting shadows. A kind of guilt seemed in the air. Final loiterers hurried up the steps of houses. There were faint reverberations of banging doors. In the Pffening cottage, across the street, somebody began to pull down blinds.

Sally, ignoring her mother's smothered, tearful protests, was consumed by an expectation careless of dangers. Not satisfied with her view from the window, she opened the front door and ran to a corner of the fence from which she could see the way as it led from town. All seemed crushed by sun, and even bushes lifeless. There was still one person existing with her in this strange vacuum of arrested habits. Amelia Grant was taking clothes off the line. She was working with that swift collectedness that women show when a rain is due. "A-*mee*-li-a!" Sally wailed, to the stiff, busy shoulders. The woman gave no sign that she had heard. Sally saw the washing, crisp in a frowzy heap in a big basket, lifted awkwardly and bundled up the back porch.

Amelia Grant disappeared. A little dry wind swept giddily over the glaring platitude of road. A few shirts, yet remaining on the extended rope, were stuffed instantly with the parched air, and, hanging upside down, dragged what seemed inflated arms across a rosebush near. One sleeve caught, and flapped. The rest, in final lassitude, swept to rest above the worn lawn.

"Come in this instant, Sally, if you don't want to be the death of me." Mrs. Drew had pursued her daughter, and was now blinking in the sun, tears of excitement blotting her cheeks. Into this incongruity of preparation as for inclement weather, a sound burst, like a torrent of stone. Heedful at last, Sally fled toward the house, carrying with her through the brilliant nightmare of fifty paces from fence to doorstep, an impression of Seminary Ridge toward which, instinctively, she had turned and glanced. The ridge was a bulk of high earth, fallen upon the peaceful silence of the sky. There trees hung. Pines leaped solemnly upon the blue stillness. But it was from somewhere in that inviolate spot that incredible, swift blows were being flatly dealt to reprimand surrounding emptiness. *Shot!*

Sally followed Mrs. Drew into the hall, where both, temporarily, collapsed. "My God, my God, what *shall* we do! Why, it sounded as near as anything, Sally—right up by the old seminary. If I'd only had a chance to get Mr. Hach to move the machine. And it's *so* hot. And where *did* I put my corsets? I can't find a thing. Your blue mantle, and the plated teapot, and if we hide them in the cellar they'll find them anyway." Mrs. Drew shook her hands wildly, her fat, creased wrists aquiver.

Sally, as frightened, was also elated; but was held passive, suffering a kind of pleasure of wild unbelief. She and her mother might as well be dead and buried in their graves. It was almost more than she could bear—and in Gettysburg, too, where nothing ever *did* happen.

. . . .

Murray could hear, in the night pouring by him, only the heavy, torn breaths of the horse. He knew the route, on paper, but, as he could make out almost nothing of the scene around him, his sensation was of giving himself to speed and to the darkness in utter recklessness. Confederates repulsed in their attempt to enter gettysburg have withdrawn to cavetown leaving pickets as close as four miles from gettysburg i have taken up a position in seminary ridge a mile west of town reynolds already informed of expected concentration of lee's forces here i will do my best but hope you agree that haste is imperative haste is imperative—*haste—is—imperative!* He had rehearsed it until the words had become as stupid as a nightmare, and he knew that in the event of losing the message he carried, he would be able to repeat them endlessly. Haste is—haste is—haste *is imperative!* The horse's feet flogged the dim road with the words haste is imperative—haste, haste, *has-ta-has-ta-haste, haste, haste, haste, haste—IS—im-per-a-tive.*

Murray knew that Buford had only two brigades, and that, with these, he must attempt to hold off Lee's army until reinforced. Haste is imperative the repulse of an advance contingent in the streets of gettysburg has given buford a little time in which to select his *haste* is imperative his present situation but its advantages has-*ta,* has-*ta, haste, haste, haste,* its advantages will not compensate for heavy odds odd it is generally suspected that this encounter has been as little anticipated by gen-er-al *haste* is imperative, *haste* is, *hás-ta, hás-ta, hás-ta, hás-tá, háste, háste, háste,* by general lee as by ourselves by ourselves young lochinvar by ourselves *hás-ta, hás-ta, hás-ta.*

Murray could endure any strain other than that resulting from inaction. There was no moon—no moon now at least could he remember if there would be he had tried to find out if there would be he had forgotten to ask what time haste, *hás-ta, háste-a, háste-a.*

The shapes of the evening were mere intimations. He entered a cave of shadows, and the long boughs of the wood tumbled creakingly upon his shoulders as he *háste-a, háste-a, háste, háste, haste.* A body in black—no that was a shadow—but when young lochinvar no that was a shadow, *háste-a, háste-a, háste, háste, haste.* When he emerged from the wood the sky was spread before him like a field, and he rode there. His horse's galloping feet strewed the night with sound—no other but the tinkling crusts of cinders, the stars haste-a, haste-a. No stopping. No stopping anybody, good lord if I'm late.

Murray leaned down his face in the coarse, dry tangle of the horse's mane, come on, prancer, come on, prancer, come on *háste-a, háste-a, hást-a,* and Murray experienced a kind of rapture in the sense of new power over this sweating, lunging flesh. The night streamed on like a grey banner. It blew all thought clean from his perspiring brow. The saddle girths creaked monotonously, *haste-a, haste-a-haste, haste, haste,* o god i am so tired of that word die—run. There was in him a strange conviction, and it was as if riding were flying, and flying, sleep. He thirsted for the moon. His anxiety for the moon was to clear away all the density of this matter that frightened. Though it would be danger, too, to be seen by any. His wrists were soothed by the hot, stirred air flung reassuringly from the horse's nostrils; but he could not exist in that alone. He was not secure enough. It was impossible to delay, to halt, to draw himself up against the wild exhilaration of *háste-a, háste-a, háste-a,* nowhere nowhere, as if general lee's eye might open in the night over there where he looked for a milky rupture in what must be clouds, and he must fly down swifter in the dark like an arrow, he plunged into the dark, the road went down, general meade's headquarters and taneytown must be down, down down in dixie hate that rebel *háste-a, háste-a.* Disappointment would, after all, be divorcement from this headlong motion which must never end, suppose he turned at the wrong fork; but he halted before turning.

He spurred the animal sharply, and halted. The landmarks must be accurate and could you tell a house, a barn, a tree, a house, a barn, a tree. Murray's horse snuffled painfully and began to back. The horseshoes clicked in a pile of loose stones, o god, if they should *háste-a, háste-a,* i said i'd do it, I'D do it. last chance. The sky leaned a little nearer. The flash of the stars showed quieter. Prancer stumbled. Murray felt the road drawing them both, the ponderous heaving of the animal giving way to the road, sinking. He flung his feet out and back on Prancer's flanks, and his heels clung there like burrs. Prancer leaped, and Murray swerved sidewise nearer *god-knows-what-danger.*

They were on again. Fear grew up stilly in the ironweed by the edge of the field and the smell of ironweed because *lurks, lurks, lurks* fear lurks, *haste-a, haste-a.* He remembered leaves growing like vines over the dead moon's face. Moon that did not come now because he forgot, forgot, forgot— The stars dazzled him. Night was retreating, in his own defiance, his bravado, flying away backward in the silence from which he who so much longed because if i should never see the old people again refused to hide. A stone wall rippled away. Like dead water it ran past him, dimmer and dimmer, in this no-light. Even in the horse's neck there was a heart.

Murray's palm felt it and his own, swelling, bursting with air, like fish hauled up from the old swimming hole, flapping, there was a terrible pulse beating on the dead air and in Murray's temple, why should he pick out an animal that had been ridden all day because i am used to him don't go back on us prancer. There were torrential gasps from the animal's nostrils. Its teeth *clickety-clicked* on the bit. If the horse lagged again, if this pace died, Murray died, because I *can* not. But he refused to be tired. He resented that tired animal breeding mental contagions. When the body and back and strong haunches and flanks went under, all went under, buford too. The rocking legs seemed to sag, and Murray was without, only on his own useless legs leaning.

The hoof-beats dropped sound that was dead, nerveless, falling into the pit where no one mattered if or not general lee—

A spark glittered. It was near—not swift and far away like the stars. Other sparks flew out and hung their webs in Murray's wind-battered pupils, flat and blank and unwilling to see. The lights drew together in a finished accent, as though saying there is no other road, this is the end. Longer and longer rays fell from the clustered centres of lamps. Then strange miracle of windows associating themselves in bulky houses. *Taneytown!* Murray was getting into Taneytown. For the first time, since leaving Gettysburg an hour before, he realized that this was a hot, still night.

. . . .

Wadsworth's Division was nearing Gettysburg. It was dawn. The hills, in the iridescent morning, exhaled faint light. Johnny Perkins had been in the war since the start. You hate it when you are in it, and you feel like a yaller dog if you ain't, he had explained. During the time he had spent in the hospital he had thought of nothing but returning to the fighting line. He and Madge were 'keepin' comp'ny,' and intended to be married when the war was over; but even that distant expectation didn't seem to 'matter' much. Johnny had a perpetual inclination for ridicule. His 'sense of humour' was 'jest bigger'n' he was. He had been impressed by an incident that had occurred while he was 'helpin'' in the ambulance corps. He had been authorized to examine the contents of many pockets in the coats of corpses. In the breast of one dead man Johnny had found certain documents which he had been obliged to read. One of these was a letter to a 'gal, no better than she should have been,' whom the author of the epistle had known and flirted with while in New Orleans. The other letter, folded with a memorandum listing the addresses of 'fancy houses,' in Nashville and Memphis, was a 'flowery' outpouring written to the dead man's wife. The way some people had of taking the war as an excuse for any kind of 'triflin',' almost made him 'sick.' Madge was 'pure gold,' and had 'looked' at nobody else since he had begun to court her. She was not too 'strait-laced,' either. He didn't like 'strait-laced' women, or 'blue-stockings.' He had never seen the 'female critter' yet who could 'make a fool' of *him!* Humility was Johnny's fetish. To a man who would 'brag,' he felt no loyalty. People in Plainsville could see him 'dead,' before he would send the message back to them of the medal for bravery that he had lately received. He was not to be 'taken in' by the kind of praise they would exaggeratedly give him. He was not 'a gaping sucker' any longer. Life was not as pleasant and as easy-going as people liked to have you think it was. He was 'hard as nails'—or he hoped he was. And would never again be 'fooled' by anybody. Once, he had been 'fairly truthful' with Madge; but that could be dispensed with, also. A female was a 'pesky' thing to 'handle' if she thought she 'knew too much.'

His absent eyes followed lines of tilting boots ahead. This was going to be a 'big day,' he had heard. The rebellion might collapse altogether if General Lee could be routed. And those before him, Runt Beers, Fish Keezee, Hen Sifton—what were *they* thinking? Feeling the moist sun already too hot on the nape of his own neck, Johnny wondered how *they* bore it. Any one of them might be dead by night. He shivered. That hay might have been rained on, it seemed so wet—but it hadn't rained last night.

What was that noise! Every head swerved, involuntarily, toward the sound. Then the men resumed, as with an effort, disinterested obedience.

Johnny could feel his own face purpled. *Halt!* The bugle, brazen and clear, plunged its notes into the quiet, defiantly. It was evident that the companies here were to leave the road and take a shorter way across country.

Shadowy, like a wind, shadowy, like the spouting of a veiled volcano, came the reverberations. The west was yet sodden and delicate, blue-white as an eye with cataract. (Johnny felt blind.) No sun ever was there. But in the east, transparent fires played; shafts sent from a welter that the human gaze could still bear.

A leaden bubble broke, and there was an uninterrupted rainfall. Johnny's chest swelled tightly under his thick, dusty uniform. He supposed that going back to Plainsville would just about kill him. There was, in anticipating it, a sense of inevitable loss. The hardware business of his father did not interest him. Madge would be all right 'for a while.' But here—but here— He never would be the same kind of a 'hypocrite' again. So help him God, if he'd 'sowed a few wild oats' during the last few years, that was the due of somebody who had risked his life so often. None of these fellows were any better than he was, either. He believed in *some* things, more than they did—wasn't too stuck-up about himself—even if he didn't go to church. Old Jones, of course, was regularly 'crazy,' praying all the time. He wanted to turn the mess into a campmeeting. But that was because he was 'scared.' Any fool could see it. Johnny didn't criticize. He was too 'philosophical.'

The boys ahead were beginning to lift down the top fence rail in order to get over. Solid ripples floated invisibly toward a dark strand in heaven. Then little short, lathery noises, scudded toward the clouds.

Johnny clambered above the fallen rail and his ankles sank in weeds, in dew. *Get it over with. Get it over with.* This was the feeling that justified his desire to keep Madge from finding out 'all' about him. Situations had betrayed him into recognizing much he would have otherwise avoided. *Get it over with. Get it over with. Get it over with. Get it over with.* He began to run, doublequick, after scattered lines of comrades, treading the meadow into a sudden holocaust of dew-oozing stems. Where they were 'bound' for, nobody knew. But there was nothing deceiving about *this* experience. From now until nightfall, he would feel scarcely anything at all, reflect on nothing. And afterward, it would come back —this anxiety for 'the worst,' like the hunger of a disease. He simply couldn't live without it. Maybe he'd join the regular army 'for good' and leave off thinking altogether. The place a man 'fitted into' was the best place for him. *Get it over with. Get it over with.* The shots whipped an iron wall. They were like a thick,

248

molten batter drummed into bursts of noise. *Blub-blub-blub-blub-blub. Bloo-oom,* softly. With the rearing sun in his face, he hurried on.

. . . .

A small piece of timber cut the Federal front in two, strengthening the centre; and the extremity of the wood was thought to be the key to the position. The protection of this copse permitted the Union men to turn an enfilading fire on the Confederate columns as the lines advanced. The Confederates were running. General Acre, riding along, was dangerously near being engulfed in the action. He was impatient of the discretion obliged by the responsibility he bore. *Crick. Clume-clume-clu-oom.* A steel fist smack-smacked gigantically upon the surface of a muddy lake. General Acre was deep in this quagmire of impressions represented by the shooting. It was so recently that the doctors had given up hope for him. He had been told that he would never see a battle front again, would not regain his health. The pampering attentions of his wife and daughters had cast a blight upon his confidence. Ida was a devoted helpmeet. The 'girls,' as adoring children, could not be criticized. Yet as he was certain that complete yielding to their suggestion that he was very ill had almost laid him with his fathers in the family cemetery.

He was not afraid of death. It was not that, but he would rather, he believed, die a thousand times, than be considered weak.

He admitted to himself that the heat of the day placed an unwonted strain upon his physical resources. His organism was in such a state that it could not bear very much. Just the same, action was tonic.

There was a cessation in the roaring of the morning. The bleared vapours scudded slowly from the trees. And he could see, as he drew his horse up, not only the dwarfed, hastening figures of the rebels, but Gettysburg itself, its white houses singularly irrelevant to the other scene. On the opposite side of the valley, bone-pale stems of forest climbed a hill more distant, on which, as his maps had designated, spread a burying-ground. He stared, felt a tremor like remembered guilt, and, in vague humiliation, looked away again. He was an old soldier. In Mexico, and in the Black Hawk days, he had been through much of this. It was all familiar to him,

249

all obvious. There was nothing in the sight of war that could surprise him; and in this he found his comfort. His horse, now—what did Pompey think about the eternities beyond the grave? Why, it was 'wicked,' it would have been a crime against 'manhood' to dwell too seriously on Ida's 'maunderings.' Piety had its admirable side, displayed in its moral effects; but a mummery propitiation of the Angel of Darkness was not a virtue. General Acre could congratulate himself on being 'sane and sensible,' and on having led—'Thank God,' and he admitted it—a 'worldly' life.

With a click of his tongue, he urged Pompey on, and cantered up his lines. Occasionally the sides of his mount shuddered under his legs. The animal flicked a furry ear. Beyond this, it was stolid. Deliberately the general accommodated his own impulsiveness to that lack of urgency in the horse's body. "What time have you, Major?" Major Chambers had just ridden up, and General Acre, unconsciously showing annoyance, held back an important discussion, in order to ask trivial questions which would inevitably convince the major that he alone was flurried. Chambers disapproves of my levity in exposing myself, the general meditated.

But he was obstinate. Let Chambers fume and fret, and anticipate defeat. Chambers could afford, perhaps, that kind of playing with the devil.

Acre had a brown, thin hand, through which full, delicate veins wandered purply. His clutch on his bridle seemed to grow firmer, as Chambers's deferential voice rose more querulously. Well, Wadsworth's Division has been brought into play just in time—but now it *is* there—

Anybody who has been as near his end as I have doesn't go into a cold sweat over nothing at all, Acre said to himself. He was glad of it when Chambers left him. Damn the man! And Chambers and Ida, together, seemed to stir the general's blood. Imagine yourself fond of a man, and torment him with caution! It was as if they were 'driving' him. He was determined to get as near the focus of the mêlée as he could. Why, ten years ago, he reflected, I was nearer to giving in than I am at present. It was something that could not be explained.

The blubbering torment of quick noises would soon take him completely out of himself, completely away from that confession of age which his world, lately, seemed to demand of him. He *liked* the bedlam. The smoke, irritating one surface in his eyes and nose, he blinked on and breathed in gratefully.

Dear Papa—if we should lose you—Acre pressed away out of his brain, all those degrading memories of pity. A last company, sweeping on to fill gaps in the wood's edge, trotted close to him. Pompey started. Disproportionately angered, Acre, with a jerk, quieted the horse, patted its lathered neck, and was unwillingly aware of sweat trickling from beneath his own hat brim. "We're giving them their deserts, boys. Congratulations to you and to myself for having such men in my command," he called out, addressing the furtively interested faces of strangers.

The soldiers, hastening, left him in the sudden isolation of authority. Bewildered by his own mood, he felt jealous of their herded courage. All of these young people going on, leaving him behind. Yet all were *not* young, and that spectacle of the old fellow with grey whiskers only made things worse. Even the aliveness of horses disturbed. There was a *po-loom,* an extra density of dirty vapour, and Acre saw a pair plunging, tossing their heads in a kind of frantic petulance, their strong muscular flanks shaking, heaving. Then they were down in the grass, straining, half overturning the ambulance carriage. Their plushy nostrils sneered agonizingly, and weed-stained teeth were bared in last plaintive snarls of menace, while he seemed to hear their treble whinnying above all the ponderous perpetual other racket. He could not sustain more of this. Ida with her medicine bottles, Dr. Custer, and the minister—they were bad enough. But he would *not* see himself in the wretched, accepted decline of his hardihood.

His senses felt as thick as wine. There was a risk now, he realized, but compared to a peril he already knew, it was insignificant. He shouted. "Come on, boys. I'm with you. Pour it into them." Ignoring Chambers, Acre pricked his spurs lightly into Pompey's shaking sides. The horse sprang forward, and nicked tufts of sod, sending a helter-skelter of earth from its hoofs. Sixty-nine, Acre was. He hoped Chambers appreciated being outranked by a young fellow of sixty-nine. Chambers had never been offered the 'bitter cup' to drink, had never been taught the value and the luxury of a little careless peril.

The rebels were wavering. To Acre, outdistancing his own men, the hesitation of the enemy contradicted all the nagging doubts of the cautious. If he took time to consider possibilities as Chambers did, he'd be dead already.

Smoke blew long up the hillside. For a minute, all was turgid nothing. Acre could distinguish the advance he had initiated, but he was becoming confused. He halted the horse. The sun really was volcanic. He had never known such a very hot day. Undecided, he looked about him, feeling somewhat the fool, but clinging to the conviction that he who escapes senility and poisonous drugging leads a charmèd life.

Plick! Pompey raised up his heavy forefeet. General Acre leaned back woodenly, and seemed to be resting the whole burden of his flesh on the fierce sun streaming on his back. Something had happened. Little nagging, viper pulses crawled in his thick mind. There was a sticky sensation in his shoulder. He was not afraid of *this;* and his eager hearing tried to catch, through some wide, enfeebling emotion, the bray and turmoil which were the symptom of a vivid world. He reeled in the saddle, but he had not fallen. Not yet. Though dust smelled sweetly in his nostrils, and thick threads of saliva, blown in froth, from the horse's distended muzzle, clung coolly on his quivering wrists. Chambers had no courage. It was the 'good' fight that they were fighting, and Chambers, though so inexperienced, had abandoned the struggle.

Trees, sun wheeled, in a great arc over him. Still he resisted, knowing that, ultimately, he was going to fall, but not yet ready to yield up this ardour of the senses that he loved to bitterness. All was a blurred storm, in which he discriminated; even through pain selecting these trifles which Ida never *had* been able to take away, for, though she could talk to him of heaven and hell and of repentance, he was *not* indifferent. It was *good,* good. There was even odour to the clouds, swimming close, in the aching pools of blue, down on his heavy eyes. This was being alive—something heaven could not exceed. There could be nothing better.

. . . .

Jerry ran, stumbled, stumbled, ran; running down a field below Seminary Ridge. When he glanced behind him, the windows of the Seminary were a vapid multitude, flashing upon him through the funereal plumes of trees. He could thank God that the place and the morning of arrival there were both a long way off. The last he had seen of the rebels, they were in a railway cut, and fighting hard. He was grateful that flight was now the accepted thing among his comrades. Impetuous resistance had passed its culminating point hours previously. That had come after the loss of all the horses, when Confederate skirmishers had attacked his section. He and his companions had worked like mules, pulling off the gun carriages. Jerry felt as when at work at home after a 'spell' of cutting corn.

The air was full of churned dust. The fields, from which the heat of day retreated, were profoundly somnolent.

Jerry was obeying a general order for a withdrawal to the other heights of Gettysburg, to the old cemetery. This might even mean that his own side had won. Who cared? Down there in the valley it looked cooler, cooler. Sun just sinking. Sun just getting cooler, cooler; settling in the west. He looked obliquely, cautiously, at those who were taking the same course he kept. Some said Doubleday's lot was keeping the rebs engaged. What did it matter? Retreat, retreat, to the old cemetery. His knees sagged, his knees jerked, his arms dangled drearily in his sweaty sleeves; and he thought vaguely of 'Ma.' *Retreat, retreat to the old cemetery.*

The sun was more than ever downward, yet its glare struck him broadside. Strong waves of light rolled molten, and with downy edges, out of the dry weeds. They bore him lower, his spirits lower, bore him down to rest, labour passed and Jordan ended, *at the camp-meeting.* This labour passed and Jordan ended filled him, exulting, sullen, full of bitterness. There was no name to Jerry for this kind of bitterness. It was in his bones, it was in his aching body. It meant, simply, time for rest. No more time and no more liking to enjoy the things he used to do. He was not afraid of being dead. He was not glad he was not afraid of being dead. The taste in his mind was just—more like—nothing. Just the taste of dust.

Suddenly he knew he had to plank himself down right here where he was. *Got* to rest. (Goad him, beat him if you want to, but he's *got* to rest.) Fatigue became dimly triumphant. It was now a blessedness. He sank down. He smelled hay. Hay had the odour of weakness itself. He drank it in. No more, no more, no more Jerry he can't go no quicker.

He was near a brook. Maybe he was alone. Maybe he was alone here till the day of judgment. Maybe the others who had been excited with him went on hurrying by.

The brook fluttered its wings of water deep in the thin grass. The brook turned, with its darkling currents, glassy whirligigs. The currents were choked with rapid bubbles, sometimes iridescent, sometimes colourless. Jerry leaned upon the bubbling water and gave his hot face to a chill as virulent as acid. It bit to his heart. Lie down, lie down, don't care anything about those others. What's orders, what's Gettysburg, what's the war to you? He seemed, somehow, to have *earned* the right. Despair was the reward he had been searching for. Despair was final. Despair was not like quitting. It was whole, complete. There was not much left that anyone could say to it. And no man owes his haggling neighbours another cent when he's through with life. They're in it. They've got to pay somehow for being in it. He's paid. He *has* paid. But the cemetery seems a long way off. To have a coffin there would be superfluous.

He rolled to his back. Strong, immeasurable indifference allowed him to observe the sky, purged, at last, quietly, of all but stains of sun. The long day and the long hours were at last over. Wiped out, he thought. And he, too, wiped out, wiped out, almost—at twenty-one. Enough left, maybe, to begin again if he wanted to, but the body, with its throbbing muscles, was itself a stupor, a ponderous mass of inanition. It did not want to rise and wake. Sluggishly, it overpowered him. It overpowered him almost graciously. It left no protest in him against aching, blistered flesh. Retreat to the cemetery. Sleep, sleep, sleep, at last—Jordan passed. He lay there staring at the pending sky indifferently. The twinkling granules of the stars came out. Don't care, don't care, don't care. Thank God for this rest at last. Don't care, don't care. I've *got* to rest till I can care about somethin'.

. . . .

There was no cellar in the house. Betsy did not know where to hide the children. Running from one room to another, trying to keep her mind clear of the confusion implied in that pandemonium which shocked her self-control and undermined faith in the permanence of anything existent, she at last succumbed to their

254

screams, their whimpers, their pleas: "Ma, Ma, where shall we go? Ma, where shall we hide? Ma, Ma, is Pa there with them? Will we all get shot?"

The fleeing Federals were pouring through the town. Would dark stop them? Then the firing exploded near at hand, and she could not but conjecture that the rebels had followed the retreating forces and the two were met. She peered through the closed blinds and could see men running, men all headless or cut in two by slats, running zigzag down the street. Her horror would not permit her to sort her impressions and reconstruct their distorted lineaments. The rebels were fiends, the rebels were fiends; and she prayed for night—that it would come quickly like a blindness on the madmen, like a final vengeance.

"Everett, Martha, Matthew, come here. Come here, Everett." To stare out of doors deprived her of the little courage remaining to her. Yet sounds must have shapes, reasons. *Broom, plick-plick-plick-plick, broom.* The fist beat on her dizzied brain, yet she could not find unconsciousness.

Martha *knew*. She stood there in the middle of the dim room, and Betsy could imagine the look in her eyes. "What *is* it, Ma?" Martha screamed out suddenly. And she caught up her apron in a fierce clutch and waved it, crying, "I can't stand it, I can't stand it, Ma. You must make it stop."

Betsy made herself rise from the floor where she was crouched, go over to Martha, and take her arm firmly. "Martha! Stop that. Stop these tantrums. Shut your mouth, this minute."

So they all knelt together again, in a heap. Betsy wanted to be where she could see out, if necessary, and sidled over the rug and fixed herself by the window again; but she drew Matthew and Everett to her and kept a tight hold on Martha. When Martha knew that she was being forced to a position which made the street visible, she leaned on her mother's shoulder and clung there. "I don't *want* to see out, Ma," Martha wailed, and she hid her face.

Matthew was as mute as a ghost. Betsy was frightened by his silence. He remained standing, very stiff and upright in her embrace, and she could only judge of his sensibiltiy by the feel of his heart, beating through his jacket so forcibly that it was as if a frantic little wing battered her own breast where they touched each other.

Everett was unlike the others. He wanted to behold all. He was not content with his mother's occasional swift glance, and would not heed her warning to keep his curly head below the sill. She could detect his aversion for the common passive attitude in the enclosure of walls so vague that they scarcely existed save through the twinkle of gilt on the picture frames. There was a clock on the mantel, but Betsy had lost record of its tickings long before.

Once, after a *pi-ling, pi-ling,* which seemed to come from some spot almost in the yard, Martha whispered, "I know what it is now, Ma. It's the worst time in the world. But didn't you know it was coming?"

Betsy wanted to shake her.

All at once Everett began to jump up and down. "There's a man in the yard, Ma. A man ran through the gate. There's another man after him. I *guess* he's after him"—more doubtfully.

Betsy, in a kind of brutal anguish, jerked at his trousers and tried to pull him down beside her. But he struggled. She could hate Everett sometimes—and when he teased Matthew, particularly. Was she making a mistake to remain here? The house was all windows, however, and where else could they go?

"Ma—let Matthew look?" Though the room was so increasingly in twilight, Betsy realized that Everett, moving away from the shutters, was very tense, and that his voice had a strange, painfully exultant sound.

She said, "No. I won't let Matthew look. He's too small. And besides, he has more sense. You get away from there yourself."

Pling, pling, pling, Bloom. Echoes scudded all through the darkened rooms. The window panes rattled heavily as if a cart were passing by. Betsy, in despair and hateful terror, sensed her own ardour as some molten loss of courage. She would never be able to stir again, never be able to do anything. Martha was sobbing softly, monotonously, trying to make her own small, iterant grief louder than the foreign turmoil which besieged her.

But Everett caught Matthew's arm. "Look, Matthew, you *must* look. 'Fraid cat. Ma don't mind, and you've *got* to look."

Reluctantly, Matthew resisted his mother's restraint. He struggled free of her flaccid embrace. Everett dragged him to the blinds.

Matthew gazed, peered, stood on tiptoe; and turned away slowly. Panicky, he huddled to Betsy again. She said, "What is it, Matthew?" He did not answer. She shook him. "What is it?" And she said to Everett, "What have you done to Matthew, you bad boy?" Inwardly, she was wretched. She had to strain her voice to make them hear her, and the weight and silence of an empty house behind the rattle in the street seemed to drive her to a lunacy which would soon leave her indifferent to her love of the children.

Matthew lifted himself stubbornly from her shoulder and ran into the back room, where it was as dark as pitch.

Betsy had to go after him. She stumbled, caught her petticoats on a chair, and found herself weeping fretfully because she could not put her hands on him, though she could hear sounds he made.

"Matthew!"

"Go 'way," he called frantically, and it was the first word he had spoken since she had hushed them to cautious quiet.

Betsy was now as stubborn to discover him as he to evade her. She put her fear for them all aside, and searched until she could see better and was accustomed to the dinginess.

"Matthew! You are sick! Why didn't you tell me? You were sick on the *carpet!*" Her exasperation was petty, but she could not restrain it. Let worlds roll down and torrents of lead submerge her. She was unable to feel anything more. The clatter of shaking window frames was becoming merely an irritant to some violence living in herself. It was as if these sensations in her mind could go on forever, though the noise might cease.

Matthew's retchings demanded solicitude. She controlled herself and felt his clammy hands, allowing her touch, but not answering its fever. She said, "What on earth *did* happen?"

"I don't know. He's—funny."

"Everett! What *did* you do to Matthew?"

But Everett was beside them. He had crept in, following her excitement, following her unawareness of him; and she was shocked to find him at her elbow, where she could just make him out.

"I didn't mean to scare him, Ma. There's a dead man in the yard. He fell on his face, and he looked so funny."

She was dumb. "Everett!" She was weak. Her flesh was wax. A dead man—in their *own* yard.

Everett had rushed upon her, gripping her about the throat,

pressing his mouth on her cheek, wooing her with some repentance as desperate as her own alarm.

"Martha!" Betsy called. And the little girl came headlong, sure through the dark, and finding her refuge with a lack of hesitation bewildering to Betsy's less keen senses.

Betsy did not push Everett away. She permitted his enfolding of her waist, and drew Matthew against her, too. There she rested, waiting. Now all were one, and her whole being focused in the fleshly conviction of all these little rapid-beating hearts held in tight suspense upon her own supporting body.

The noises of the fight grew thinner, vaguer. She could not move. The dark was still and solid in the room. Now and then a fire burst in the far-off out-of-doors, and an evanescent rose fluttered on the watery ceiling. Dimmer and dimmer sound. She waited for it. She pursued the sound, greedy of its diminishing. At last, and unexpectedly, like a new alarm, she began to hear the clock. Then she groaned.

Resisting her imaginings, she felt the dead man in the yard, lying there like a burden upon her freedom.

"They're gone," Martha whispered, stirring all with her daring commonplace. Betsy clasped her hands together. That horrible tangible oppression remained with her, defeating all her passion for disbelief. Now she was again angry with Everett. If it were not for the presence of the dead man, life might begin again.

Jay Smith, in Birney's Division of Sickles's line, was in the peach orchard at a crossway on the Emmitsburg Road. To a taciturn man, such as he was, action was a relief because, in this terrific blending of sound and movement, he could somehow lose self-consciousness. He hated the part he had to take, yet could find no better outlet for his harassed feelings than was to be experienced when he was obeying orders blindly, unreflectingly.

Back home, they used to talk to him about the war. He had never seemed to know just what he thought; but, when he was bewildered, he was embarrassed, and, to avoid the suspicion that he was without opinions, he had volunteered for the Union recklessly.

At this moment, which was three o'clock of the second day, the blundering of Hazlett's Battery, turned on Hood's Second Division, then assailing the Federal position on Little Round Top, boomed louder than the infantry firing in which Jay was involved. Instinctively, seeking a dependence for his senses, his submerged hearing attended that distant, supporting rhythm which invigorated him.

A line ran out of the orchard into the wheat field. Jay, in the midst of comrades, was dumbly willing to follow. But, when he realized that his haste had thrown him, also, face to face with rebels, he fell waveringly back.

The wheat smoked. Over the swinging tops, strange men, strangest in the grey of alien uniforms, sprang up before him like a dangerous, sudden growth. Bayonets tingled light through the vague gold water of the wheat stems. The field grew florid and alive with an animal vitality. He was afraid, now that the fight had lost its buoying largeness, and he could see men's ruddied features separately.

The sky rocked. *Bloom. Bloom, bloom, bloom.* The sky broke apart and poured only noise—beyond trees, beyond hills. Miles and miles of quickening, violent sound flowed from a distance over the wheat field and the peach orchard. Jay was baffled. The repetition of grand echoes from invisible sources was a thing his dull and cautious mind responded to. But the direct approach to a fellow being made him long to retreat. He put his bayonet to his shoulder, ahead of him. Somehow the long spike of metal pricking space was to stand between him and some inevitable sensation that he would resent. He squinted, ran—forward, and centred all his ardour on the cloudy rumble from the hilltop opposite. As he pushed through wheat, he grudged each needful gesture that demanded definite thought. The length of his bayonet shrank, left him unprepared for the tangible obstacle to the required evasion. Men came on, pell-mell, and one, that he hated, because so heedlessly determined, was not five feet off.

Jay controlled himself, and prodded stolidly, with a wild anger against the fellow who disregarded his own inarticulate fastidiousness. The sharp steel came in contact with a glittering button, slipped downward, slightly, and Jay was annoyed, was even mildly, feebly nauseated, by his delayed awareness of the yielding ponderousness of struggling flesh.

Just as he was wrenching at his rifle butt, trying to **untangle**

259

himself from confusion, from dazzle, and demanding, brutally, avoidance of contamination by another's blood, a sharp pain pierced his side, and he relinquished his effort to keep his mind at bay. A man's face had shrivelled before him, as if withered in one ghastly look. Jay lurched to the ground. He lay helplessly, deep buried in the constantly bruised thicket of grain. Pain called ceaselessly, with a ruthless demand, to absorb all his understanding. Around him floated hurricane cries. The long *whoo-oop* of his adversaries grew intense in the hot air, receded, grew strong again; and there was a shudder—through all the underpart of the field. Jay was glad to abandon himself to recognition of the uselessness of further effort. But, even in suffering, a phlegmatic interrogation heckled him—scarcely a thought at all. Clumsily stanching the sticky exudation from his own wound, he lay and wondered. He was always wondering about something. Excitedly, feebly, as, through the accident of some mad progress in the fight, he found himself deserted, he wished, foolishly, that he would get a medal. That seemed to explain something.

It was five o'clock. Mary Murdock tiptoed to the back door of the house and looked out. Shameful of fear, but shameful, too, of the elating curiosity that had caused her to sneak from the parlour where 'Ma' and 'Pa' were praying, she passed to the open secrecy of the fenced back yard. Hay's brigade of 'Louisiana Tigers' was assembling in a rear street, and, through the interstices in the limp palings, she could just make out bits of men's faces, portions of the gaudy Zouave uniforms. She was drawn, helplessly, nearer the goal of her inquisitiveness. She gripped the points of the scaling fence, and drew herself up. With her chin resting on top, she could see the soldiers uninterruptedly. Three or four of them were very close to her. She was conscious of swarthy skins, beards with the very hairs distinct, and the sweaty napes of turning necks on which the setting sun bore down. There was nothing very wrong in stealing here to look, but she felt embarrassed. Her thin fingers clutching at the palings were not very steady. She realized that she was blushing, but she would not glance away, though they counted every freckle on her sunburned face. These were '*the enemy.*' Her heart beat too strongly. She did not know what she ought to think about these men. In consequence, her mind was uncomfortably aware of its simplicity. She could distinguish eyeballs glinting, and the separate expressions of varying pairs of eyes, all fixed on her direct. When she was stared at by strange men whose bodies were so close, she could not withhold nervous tears. Her lids winked. The sun hurt. And, her heart also tightening queerly, she wanted to cry.

Try as she might, Mary Murdock could not overcome the sense of something oddly festal in this occasion. The profiles spreading in a line far across the road were, in numbers, rigidly averted. They suggested the highly coloured faces on her wayward brother's playing cards. An unstated conviction that to gaze on this was wicked, added tremulousness to faint, anxious delight. It was the first time in her life she had ever seen so many men together. She felt them as in a different category from herself and Ma, and resembling her brother whom she did not wholly like. One cautious chin had swerved; then another. The regard of whole furtive rows of eyes played slantingly upon her. It was as if they showed her something of herself that she would rather ignore. They were 'rebels,' she was reminded, and she did not think them quite polite. She would not let them stare her 'down.' Limpidly she gazed back at them straight over the fence, while her heart stayed itself on one painfully triumphant beat, and the blood ran hotly up her throat. Although she was only fifteen years old, she was as good a patriot as any. She tried not to realize so plainly how they looked at her, but she could not shut it out. Her small breasts, squeezed against the palings, ached. Then the wretchedness of believing that they considered her immodest left her in the glow of an excitement unobtrusively resembling happiness. Because of her obstinately blank attitude toward them, those fountains of scrutiny playing upon her searchingly, with a wistful yet insolent demandingness, seemed to disturb her less.

One man was so near that she might have reached forth her doubtful fingers to lay them on his burly arm. He kept on watching her, she watching him, and she observed his long, handsomely curled moustaches, his unshaven cheeks, with their mist of stubble, as through a magnifying glass.

Her tangible sense of his presence grew, momently, uncomfortably. It was late, and the gnats were already humming in the dampening grass, but she felt too warm.

Commands were shouted, curt, staccato. A bugle burst in her ear. The bayonets spangled all the road with steel, then shot to rest. An officer, on a big bay horse, came riding by. He wheeled and drew up by the fence. The dusty buttocks of the animal flashed ponderous satin. A sweep of dry tail, flaunted from a great root, switched its coarse hairs stingingly across Mary's wrists and fingers; and she retreated, rebuked. Feet were shuffling. The massive haunches of the horse swung aside. Its horny hoofs struck the fence boards. The boards rattled. The horse clattered on bits of rock in the road, and they threw out sparks. Horse cantering on, and men moving, were a part of something too actual, something Mary found too much for her. The gaudy, dingied shoulders huddled by. Mary felt, dimly, a heaviness passing. When they were gone completely, she could breathe again.

She rushed to the vantage point and peered once more—reluctant. Why? She would be glad when these horrid people left the town. Pressing on the fence, she was again conscious, faintly, of her slight breasts, which the palings bruised, and she was more than ever modest. It seemed to her that the exit of Confederates from the streets of Gettysburg could not be quick enough. She dared not forget to be afraid.

The glitter of tarnished braid was a bright sullen current in the dense onward passage of the throng, as the men marched forward docilely, 'like sheep,' Mary thought. And her little, timid contempt for them was now permitted ardour. Then the tall man with the blond moustaches and the haggard cheeks glanced behind him, glanced aside and at the fence palings where Mary's fragile, rosy face was set.

This time she had an almost certain sense that they recognized each other. Where had she seen that man? He stared at her, backwardly, until he stumbled—then passed out of sight. A peculiar fear—and exultance—went with him. Mary really hated these exciting times to end.

"Mary!" Ma's voice, brusque with alarm, rang across the grass out of which the last light seeped. Her daughter felt a silly, overpowering guiltiness. It was as if Ma had surprised a secret. Mary could not have said what it was. She wanted to hide.

Up on the hills, where it was still smoky, and little feathers of smoke crawled in flat scales and dove's plumage across the dying brightness, a wind, unfelt in the valley, in the hot evening, seemed to rock the trees about. Little men climbed there among the shadowy trees. A firefly blew like a speck of tinsel over the murky yard. The last regiment had jostled by. The road was smooth and empty in a calm and radiant haze of settling dust. The windows of the shut-up houses burned with heated blobs, like melting iron— iron that was the colour of fiery tea-roses. A memory of the tall man's eyes, softly examining her, stayed in Mary's mind, like a touch she refused but could not quite shake off.

"And I looked, and lo, a Lamb stood on the mount Sion, and with him an hundred forty and four thousand, having his Father's name written in their foreheads." The Second Coming! It was of that Pa and Ma had been reading, in the parlour, when Mary had left them.

Po-lon-ga! Plonga! Pliiiing! The bubbling, popping sounds of mystery had begun again, though it was almost dark. Swift on her long legs hampered by the calico flounces of her dress, Mary ran across the dimming grass. At the door, her mother was craning, looking for her. Mary bounced against her, jerked the door-knob from her, and shut them both inside; and the two, pressing their hands to their disturbed bosoms, regarded one another inscrutably. "What on earth have you been up to, Mary? Did you forget Pa told you not to step outdoors? You'll be gettin' shot."

"No'm," Mary said vaguely, leaning against the pale wall and seeing indistinctly her mother's worried face which seemed, always, to exclude others from a fair share in its troubles. *Plonga!* Remote as all sounds in the night, the noise came again as from afar off. Both shivered. Mary said, "O!" agonizedly. But she didn't *want* the Second Coming—never, never, never—when *He* would appear. It was foolish, when that was something in the Bible, but she was afraid of *Him*. What *was* the Second Coming?

· · · ·

It was the third day: one o'clock, midday. For a long time it had been so quiet—so unbelievably quiet—that men's voices, as they conversed, casually, were beginning to grow in volume, and to be overheard for the sun-flashing fields had been as abruptly becalmed as a sailing vessel on a windless ocean.

Even the smoke had cleared. Gauze filaments lifted, sailed, and the banners shrank and shrivelled as the clouds departed. The sky, from glaring in sulphuric green, emerged, as from a gradual baptism, serenely blue and pure. Yet the whole countryside, from Gettysburg to the abutting ridges, had the dishevelled, trampled-upon appearance of a landscape abused by the feet of men and horses at a county fair. Lieutenant Northcliffe, in Pickett's division, was ill at ease, alike with his surroundings and his occupation. He made few friends, and the fact that his only comrade, René Blanchard, was a private, left him isolated. Besides this, Northcliffe was in the doubly depressing position of a British subject in a foreign regiment. "You got de commission, and I mus' take my orders t'rough you. Well, dat relieve me of considerable responsibility," Blanchard had joked. "My family ignore me. Since my mother die, they look on me as de thorn in de flesh. Eef I want to reinstate myself with my wealt'y sister, it mus' be in de rôle of de hero of de rebellion. You and I have done pretty well in California, but we ain't possessed of dat fabulous wealth we intended to get hold of. Dis is de best moment for de prodigal son to convince his relations dat dey have misjudged him."

Northcliffe, with nothing to do at the instant, longed for action to release him from the perpetual discomfort of association with his fellow officers. He was very correct in his demeanour, too correct in his dress, and had earned for himself the nickname of 'Dandy Northcliffe.' He was aware of it. And he was constantly ashamed. Ever since he had first encountered Blanchard—and many years had passed since then—Blanchard had appeared the gallant, reckless partner in their enterprises; Northcliffe, the cautious, the reluctant one.

The locusts sawed monotonously in the rumpled, sunny trees. Captain Kelly liked to expatiate upon the inferiority of Federal leaders, and to enlarge admiringly on Lee's recent strategies. Yet Northcliffe's fine eyes, around which doubt had drawn harsh little exquisite lines of unhappiness, avoided the affable gaze of his friendly superior. The Englishman disliked, even resented, each approach to amiability.

"Good time for a siesta," Captain Kelly said.

Northcliffe said, "Yes." When he found the opportunity, he walked away and sat down on a stump. He could see Blanchard. The men, in the grass, were resting, and were at ease. Some of

264

the very exhausted had gone to sleep, handkerchiefs spread on their faces, while flies crawled on their sprawled arms and sweaty hands. A few, who were nervous, gazed suspiciously across a declivity toward the place where the Yankees were located. Blanchard was behaving like a minstrel. He had squatted on the ground, his knees hunched, and was strumming an imaginary guitar, while he sang, "Mo con-nin, zinz, zinz, ma mour-ri, oui, 'nocent." He liked to bewilder the other soldiers with his Creole songs, though he had cautiously refrained from any attempt to join a Louisiana regiment.

Northcliffe knew Blanchard was aware of him, though ignoring. It was always like that. Realizing Northcliffe's reserve, his painful terror of self-revelation, Blanchard, in the presence of outsiders, was invariably determined, when Northcliffe was the audience, to act the monkey.

And why? Blanchard was accustomed to excuse their companionship by saying, "I learn all dey is to know about de females when I am in de cradle, Northcliffe, so I put up wit' you rather dan risk one of dem." Yet on many occasions, during their career as prospectors, as 'business men,' as gamblers, the little Creole had shown real devotion, real gratitude. Northcliffe recalled such episodes, and repressed the resentment that the ostentatious, silly singing always aroused in him.

It was Blanchard's feigned indifference, Blanchard's insistent pose of nonchalance with which Northcliffe could not cope. And it was always Blanchard's callous disregard of consequences that presented, for Northcliffe, a fascination he could not resist.

Bi-onga! It was a thick, startling, finished ejaculation. It had the effect of instantly arousing from relaxing postures all who had heard. Northcliffe rose quickly and hurried to regain the small group of officers. He realized that Blanchard had left off his song, but there was no opportunity to scrutinize him further.

Horses were stamping, fidgeting. An odour of manure, dust, human beings, made the field heavy. The ticking of the grasshoppers, the strong twang of the unceasing locusts, filled the world with a minute murmuring yielding nothing to the single, distant explosion. The sky, bald as turquoise granite, the woods, refulgent in shade, the lisping, gilded wind: all were a part of the mystery of an involuntary anticipation.

Northcliffe was so excited he could scarcely speak. The strain of the two preceding days had almost made him regret his need to force Blanchard to some renewed recognition of his existence; a demand of the emotions which had driven Northcliffe to the re-establishing of old ties in Trinidad, to the exertion of rejected 'influence'; all to the end that he might procure a commission in the Confederate army. Loathing extremism as Northcliffe did, his intentions, when under the compulsion of an unadmitted mood, were very violent. He had owned a gold mine. He had sold the mine. He had invested money for a woman Blanchard liked, and she had kept a boarding-house. Northcliffe detested America. His repugnance to the new thing had not been diminished a jot by his ten years' experience in California. It was for this that he dared everything but rudeness to his equals in command. He disliked America, and he disliked the South. Blanchard pretended not to see any of this. When Northcliffe had demurred, and had withheld enthusiasm for the rebel cause, Blanchard, who, as Northcliffe knew, believed in nothing, had teased the Englishman with the inept description of him as a 'Black Republican.'

Northcliffe had used to sit opposite Blanchard at table, over a glass of whisky, and stare, with large, morbid eyes, at the pert audacious face of the little Creole, who confronted his companion jovially, gibingly, with a contempt of pity. And Northcliffe had wanted to kill him.

If Northcliffe had been less wretchedly self-conscious, less on the watch for ridicule, he might long ago have made some defensive gesture expressive of his misery. When they had won at faro, Northcliffe had done so fairly. Blanchard had used his friend's disarmingly naïve appearance as a cloak to his own unscrupulousness.

Bonga, bonga, bonga! A circle of echoes widened, widened, became endless. The mind followed helplessly that recession inaudible of what continued to be felt after the nothingness of full trees blossoming sunshine had rolled back on itself. There was a seething of foliage, like a preparation. *Bonga!* In a dry whisper, the parched earth spent itself. The plaster earth was abandoned by all sound, all motion. *Bonga!* General Lee's signal. Each pulse leaped beyond the moment. *Bonga!* The quick, empty thud of this one last cannon had only declined to half the length of a stone hurtled down a hill, when its reverberation became insignificant. The heaving of simultaneous thunders quenched the light utterly. Northcliffe ran for his horse. The ground shook. The hundred and thirty cannon planted by the Confederates had opened upon Meade's front. Fire was rosy under a shrunken, brown-rimmed disk of sun. Smoke lagged in the tree tops, laved the grass with dimness. Smoke crushed the greyed leaves. It sank in the rotten foliage underfoot, and each twig and bush, unblazing, smouldered in a radiant fog. The tree trunks flattened. An apple tree, loitering in a meadow, stood uprooted, flashing darkness from its waxed leaves. There was no earth. The tree vanished. Trees vanished. *Broom! Broom, broom. Broom, broom, broom, broom! Bonga!* Smoke, smells, brightness lingered. A cloudy, towering indefiniteness lingered. These, destroying even anxiety, filled the heart, the mind, the hearing. Nothing existed that could resist that sound, and it was as if, by those beings who controlled it, the battle was already won.

Northcliffe saw a white butterfly, wavering, doomed, lap through the haze, spurt upward, and fall. He felt for his horse, and put his foot in the stirrup. Lines were already forming, and the density of groups of massed men humped and blotted the more ethereal volume of haze. Blanchard was somewhere in the half-visible current of marchers. The danger was undeniable. Blanchard, the indifferent, the debonair, the ruthless teller of truths which, shocking Northcliffe, bound him, in habitual loyalty, to passive connivance in plans he resented; Blanchard might be rollicking on to his own death. Northcliffe controlled himself, held himself in. It was the sense of Blanchard which distracted him from meditation on his own peril. All at once, Northcliffe's desire to *seem* fearless became fearlessness. He swung himself heavily over the saddle. In his youth, in Trinidad—some unwholesome contempt for himself that had urged him, though he had not the courage, to put an end to his own life— Why was it? He, the adored, the son of wealthy parents who had made him the very fetish of their devoted natures. It was his hatred of feeling too much. *That* had humiliated him. That had conveyed mutilated contours to his whole existence. The companionship of Blanchard, Blanchard's wilful coarseness, had not put an end to it.

Northcliffe spurred the horse and rode on through the stinging drench of vapours that still sent their lean filaments upward from the recurring earth. Damn Blanchard. Damn Blanchard.

Longstreet was sitting on a rail fence, whittling a twig. Trying to keep his mind steady, he fixed his attention on his own large hand, moving vigorously, with fingers that looked oddly independent of him, rasping the jack-knife down *again*, down *again* on the knotty stick. Smoke still crushed the vegetation and seared, as with brands of pallor, a universe to which clean sunshine was being once more slowly born. For an hour the artillery battle had gone on without cessation: a hundred and thirty Southern guns, and perhaps a hundred answering from the Union side. Now, unexpectedly, the Union cannon had refused reply.

There was something vacuous in these instants of recovered quiet. Longstreet felt afraid of them. General Lee believed the Union batteries vanquished, yet, if an order were given for Pickett's men to charge, it would be on Longstreet's own responsibility. He and Pickett had demurred for ten minutes already, and both were unreasonably exasperated.

"According to instructions, you *ought* to go," Longstreet said again. If his instinct protested, there were Lee's suggestions, countermanding caution. Thank Heaven, there was *some* advantage to be had from military discipline.

"But *shall* I? Do you agree that I shall go forward *now?*" Pickett was obstinate. Though he was not aware of it, his eyes, fixed on his superior, were glinting, fervid with a kind of animosity. Yet he himself longed for the affirmative decision. Fatigue and delays had put him in a mood in which he was ready to cast all temporizing aside. Only he would be damned if he would allow the general to thrust the burden of conclusion on other shoulders. That unpredictable silence of the Federal artillery left Pickett with the sense of hesitation on the edge of an abyss. He would rather 'go over' than totter here any longer. His men were in close quarters. Blame in these affairs was indiscriminate. If the day was a failure, he would be blamed anyhow. And what was an army for, if not for fight? To the devil with consideration for the men, when any ground was to be lost by it.

Very deliberately, Longstreet slipped from the fence, tossed his stick aside, and began to shut his jack-knife up. The odour

268

of the smoke was choking him, and he was obliged to cough before he could speak. But this could not continue. His gaze met that of Pickett. Why don't he say he can't do it, Longstreet wondered irritably. Slowly, he nodded his head; and it was as if, in doing so, he pronounced some awful doom on himself. "Yes."

"Very well. I shall go forward," Pickett answered quickly, repeating the phrase triumphantly.

Longstreet's eyes fell, a flush came in his cheeks, and he turned abruptly on his heel.

Pickett went away feeling angry, but the more determined to see the thing to the end. He was excited, and doubted anybody would ever come through the charge alive, yet his tormented nerves were soothed by a conviction that Longstreet, in his vacillation, would be taught a lesson, 'once and for all.'

Across the valley, all was a flood of trees tossing in lowering sun, but Longstreet had an oppressive and intimate sense of the smoke-screened enemy just opposite. He thought, What's the matter with Pickett! I never discourage advice when it's sensible, and if he had any comment to offer he was certainly free to make it. Pickett's behaviour seemed most unjustified.

"Morton!" Longstreet called, speaking to an orderly. "Take this note over to Major Gregory, and tell him I wish him luck."

Longstreet felt obliged to make some considerate gesture toward *somebody*—because, he reflected, why should Pickett blame *me*, anyhow! And his heart contracted painfully.

Pickett's men emerged from the wood with their guns at right shoulder, as on parade. It was a peculiar sensation to realize the protection of the trees, like an outworn garment, cast behind them suddenly. All dis is funny, Blanchard thought. Poor ol' Oliver! Blanchard's resistance to tender feelings was such that he had a way of crediting Northcliffe with such of his own emotions as his pride denied. Poor ol' Oliver must be in a state. He ain't de bravest man in de world even if he want you to believe he is.

Blanchard's face was very pale, and a pulse in his jaw fluttered tensely, but whenever he imagined himself regarded by a comrade, he smiled ostentatiously. Northcliffe says I am de mos' selfish man he ever met. Well, den, I am living up to dat opinion of me now. All dis we are goin' t'rough just in order dat de fatted calf be killed.

A man stumbled on Blanchard's feet. "Hel-lo, Todd. Give me warnin' when you are ready to make dose Yankees run. I hear las' time dey just had one sight of you, and turn in de opposite direction. It is a gif' of de gods to be as ugly as you are."

This was his gibe to a burly mountaineer with whom he had never been able to converse amicably. Todd, clumsily lurching beside him, did not deign to reply. Blanchard's shallow eyes glinted. No use to try to snub me now, because you are jealous dat I am a beauty. We are in de same boat now, my boy, he thought.

It was difficult to keep a quick step over this cloddy earth. The sun's lengthening rays struck the grass tops diagonally, and all the feathers sprang forth in gauzy clouds of revelation, confusing vision. Feet beat in muffled measure. The sounds of the artillery fire had so retreated that the muteness of their surroundings was oppressive. *Plick-plicks* sputtered in the distance, and now and then a *boo-oom* rolled fresher tides of bitterness along the white-shadowed air, but it was impossible for them to see what they approached.

Blanchard was disconcerted by the loud thumping of his heart, and attempted to whistle. Such vainglorious bravery was folly. He was ashamed of the sound that no one heard. Besides, he was out of breath. He had to hurry. Ahead of him, the glare, too steady on his face, and diffused through the white gleam that pervaded everything, showed him rows of bowed heads, necks, florid, brick-red, spotted with freckles, or swarthy like his own. An ugly lot, 'dese soliders' were, too. Trembling, determined not to lose his 'courage,' he allowed himself to find some satisfaction in his own good looks. Even dat girl, Eloise—whom he had so nearly married— But he was out of that. Oliver love me like a brother. Oliver's affection, so unacknowledged, Blanchard, despite himself, found very precious. He could not understand it. Well, frien' Oliver, you know I am a scoundrel, and still you consider de sun rise and sets by me. Den you are de worst fool I ever knew—but all right in your way. Mon métier et mon art, c'est vivre. You don' realize dat.

The low glare raced like a mild lightning up and down the rifle barrels. Blanchard's heart felt cramped. His nostrils distended avidly and the atmosphere seemed to refuse him breath. The Union line must be a mile away. Here we are, so safe an' far from trouble, yet we walk right into it. It was not that he was afraid of being shot. For ten years he had carried a bullet in his body, and he was used to it. De souvenir of dat ol' codger Grainer. You t'ink I cheated you, did you, an' da's why you shoot me. And you imagine dat I make trouble for you wit' dat ugly wife of yours. It was worth dat little exper'ence wit' dat bullet, Mr. Grainer, to see anybody so bad-humoured as yourse'f so very much upset.

Left-right. *Left*-right. Bump-*bump*. Bump-*bump*. Blanchard could hear a little tune going through his head. To, to, *to!* Ça qui *là?* The tune annoyed him. Oliver don' like dat. I won't sing dat, Oliver. Here we go marchin', marchin'— Blanchard, taking a running step to catch up with his column, glanced anxiously aside. What were these fellows thinking? He could discern the gleam of eyeballs in impassive profiles. Images! No more dan a lot of wooden images. No heart. No feelin's at all.

Yet Busted was crying. Blanchard had only one glimpse of a lean, distorted jaw, and blank humiliated eyes. What a fool dat man is!

> Jeune j'étais trop sage,
> Et voulais trop savoir;
> Je n'ai plus en partage
> Que badinage,
> Et touche au dernier âge
> Sans rien prévoir.

A knot swelled in Blanchard's own throat. But what de hell's de difference, he insisted.

They had come to an obstacle in the advance. They were at the edge of a ravine. Blanchard, following the others, used the butt of his gun as a staff to support his descent. Crouched just below the brink, he abandoned more careful means, and allowed himself to slide on his buttocks over the last incline. The rifle, almost dragged from his clasp, battered on the rocks. His knuckles were rasped until blood was drawn, but he was not aware of it. In the gully, the shadows were so deep that night seemed to be already approaching. Tangles of grape-vine threw their stems, like ravelled strips of hide, from bough to bough in the bent trees. Old pools of rain water stood between the boulders, and there was a whining sound of gnats. Looking up over the other slope, one saw the white glitter of the retiring afternoon lustrous on the tips of the higher bushes. Blanchard slipped in the springy pads of moss, virulently green in the half-night of thick, dingy foliage. The men were loath to emerge from their retreat. Blanchard saw some purposely contrive to linger, then clamber hastily on. *Bluuuum.* The sound was woolly, strained into the depths. Fils Redempteur du monde, qui êtes Dieu, ayez pitié de nous. Damned if I am as superstitious as Northcliffe wit' his Trinidad blacks. The roots of the trees, clutching at the green-furred rocks, exhibited a kind of paralytic torment. Even the mould here retained, like a vivid secret, the lost sun. Damp rust-flakes of last year's foliage lay all about. A bird flirted a ghost wing above, and sped on, higher, farther, to a place more steeped in ardour where the light penetrated more brilliantly, and the quiet, imagined, as one gazed upward, became more oppressive.

There was no bugling. Orders were conveyed from lip to lip, quietly. The columns reformed awkwardly, as the men arrived on the upper slope. In the way they had come, every sound of battle had ceased. The soldiers—many realizing that the Confederate artillery was muted to protect them—glanced at one another questioningly. There was a sudden, general sense of loss. Unsupported by that fine echo, which, however remote, had encouraged, they must hasten forward. They began to run.

Blanchard felt cold. He had given up his jovial meditations, and his whole consciousness was fixed on a kind of sensual desperation. Shapes exceeded him. He hurried blindly, and would avoid any interchange of looks reminding him, queerly, as though to say he had forgotten it, of his trepidation.

Pling, pling, pling, plink, plinga! Zoom! There were rapid explosions, then a humming, like bees, out of the drowsy air. An umbrella-shaped clump of trees sprang ominously forward toward them through the wraithy wall which the Union canister, fired now from so very near, reared a little higher. Todd sank on his knees, and Blanchard, irritated, stumbling unmindfully on this impediment of huddled body, leaped nimbly back. Busted threw his arms up. His rifle flamed on the faint sun, then rattled beside him to the earth, As though attack were pursuit, and his leaders vic-

272

tims, Blanchard dodged and recovered his unsteady column. When he believed that he was being deserted, it aroused in him a kind of plaintive viciousness. The lines, depleted by these constant abrupt vacancies, drew constantly together, and the men were as if hurled onward upon one another by the growing spaces left behind.

Plinka, plinka, plink-plink-plinka. A dozen runners, hurtled to the ground simultaneously, extended the common impression of isolation. The soldiers who were in the rear of the advance were in a fever, and would almost turn to fight their comrades who would keep them from the front.

Several horsemen galloped, with danger to the infantry, and kept a pace beyond the running men. Blanchard caught the hoarse voice of encouragement. A flag, borne ahead, was riddled, and tatters continued to flutter drearily on a miraculously upright pole which, in the hands of an invisible bearer, appeared to float. The sun all at once burst into view and Blanchard saw it, implacable as red iron, pressing its mute glory full on the aching brows of those who involuntarily, with halting tread, hesitated foolishly while they stared at it.

Blanchard's mouth, under his trim moustache, was fixed in a kind of savage sneer, his jaw stony, tears of weakness on his lashes. Dese fellows wallowin' like a lot of cattle—dere *dead*—dead as de butcher's meat on Saturday, went through his mind. This chill flash of a thought forgotten relieved him. The *blitter, blit-blit-blitter* of shot came as from all directions. Over the heads and bumping shoulders of his own contingent, he could now make out, like another deadness through the vapour, the rock-walled line of the approaching Yankee barricades. His heart laboured brokenly. His exultance ebbed. Yet he had no course but to proceed. Then, unexpectedly, he was *there!* A mere handful beside him, and in an ecstasy of astonishment, he plunged into the deeper, nearer smoke. *Plink. Pling, pling, pling.* Successive brambles snapped, and little rosettes of fire ornamented the haze. Blanchard was on the wall. His hand, steady now with an alien exultance, dragged on the rope of the inclining pole where the trivial Yankee flag depended.

No use, damn them. Dis ambition—it was the devil! God, dem bastards, dey got me. But, as he rolled to his side, and fell heavily into the grass below, his habitual declaration of a failure was again rejected. His bowels were in torture. His whole being shrank, and reflection dissipated to make way for pain. The tramped grass scratched, through sharp sticks and stones, at his insensitive face. He grappled with his agony, found its focus and tried to press endurance to him, his palms tight on some sticky exposure of defeat. Then he rebelled, and, while the white darkness of the smoke found out his squeezed eyelids and insinuated a way to his pupils, he said, dumbly, *I* did it. *I* did it. Damn de lot of dem, de ——, dey'll never believe it. O Sainte Marie, Sainte Vierge des vierges, let me leave dis sufferin' quick.

.　　.　　.　　.　　.　　.　　.

Inadvertently, Myers had entangled himself with the retreat. Walking along the railroad track which, even now, after the passage of so many hours, was dust-churned and bore, in the beaten-down weeds, all the marks of feet, he decided that the best part of valour, for a newspaper correspondent, would be discretion. He was trying to find a cross-country path which would take him to the other side of Gettysburg, where he hoped to join the Union forces.

Myers was a New Yorker, and accustomed to heat in summer; yet it did seem to him that he had never felt anything as oppressive as the muggy atmosphere of the last few days. He was worn out, and tense, and that might account for it; but he thought the fact that there had been several cases of sunstroke in the armies excused him of weakness. The clouded sun, as he glanced toward it, gave him a premonition of worse to happen—though, as he was rather proudly convinced, it would be difficult to conceive of horrors in the way of bloodshed which could exceed those he had already witnessed.

Myers was engaged in writing, for the *New York Banner*, a series of articles on the comparative strategy and tactics of Northern and Southern generals. Impolitically, he had been championing Lee's methods as contrasted with those of Halleck; so the Gettysburg defeat would be an embarrassment to his theories and might demand that he completely readjust the point of view he had adopted.

This annoyed him. The discrediting of his own public statements was, however, to his intense, almost abstract egoism, insignificant when compared to the gratification of his avid curiosity,

274

and he had just had the good fortune to behold an 'unforgettable' battle.

He stumbled along briskly. Dapper in dress as he always was, it did occur to him to throw off his coat and carry it upon his arm; and he finally so far abandoned himself to his discomfort as to undo his high-pointed collar. Lord, he was thinking, look at Pickett's charge—what a story that will make! His sense of a triumph over his competitors put him in such good humour that he could almost ignore the rage of prickly heat in his unaccustomed flesh. His back was blistered, and he expected that he would take off a piece of his skin when he removed his shirt. But he would have endured 'a good deal' in order to profit by this opportunity.

Myers was an 'attractive-looking' young man, with a keen, high-bridged, Semitic nose, a feeble mouth, and a round, obstinate chin. His brow was high, and was called 'meditative.' He was so distrait that he stepped over the edge of the rail bed, and only saved himself from falling; but the mishap did not dim the glow of ardour in his handsome, friendless eyes. He took off his flat little bowler hat, and rubbed his short, unformed fingers in his thin, brittle hair. He was sweating profusely. His clothes—he hoped that nobody would take him for a newspaper man. He was glad, suddenly, since his appearance might suggest a tramp, of the isolation he pursued. Just the same—the hills around here looked as high as mountains—and what might occur should he fall into the company of fleeing Confederates, he could not guess.

Despite his name and his physiognomy, Myers was a Christian, the child of a woman who, before her marriage, had been a Miss Worthington of Lowell, Massachusetts. His father, dead six months at young Myers's birth, had been a mill-owner, and only remotely suspected of a Jewish ancestry. Or, if the elder Myers had actually confessed an oriental strain, his wife, after his decease, did not refer to it.

Young Myers was not the man to probe personal histories so near him. His inquisitiveness was devouring, but it was a nervous interest expressed for abstract problems, or for those who were public figures, and, whose lives might be considered, in their detail, public property. He was a hero-worshipper, though not humble. Shy in manner, his persistence in gaining any end he had deter-

mined had earned him an inappropriate reputation for 'bumptious-
ness.' He and his mother were no longer possessed of wealth, and
such means as they had inherited from the elder Myers had been,
in a large measure, already absorbed by young Myers's education.
He felt not the slightest hesitation in accepting his mother's sacrifices made in his behalf. He was certain, dumbly, with a will almost
despairingly firm, that a time would come when his natural merits
would be recognized, and he would be able to repay her over and
over again. It would be straining at the gnat and swallowing the
camel if he refused her assistance now, with the result to be anticipated that, later, when she really needed him, he would not be
able to offer her the protection that a great man could.

Known in college as a youth resentful of the slightest, even the
most amiable, criticism, he had defended his timidity belligerently.
He had not altered in manner. He professed to be shocked by his
mother's diffidently patriotic attitude when she discussed the
South. The truth was that the stand taken by the mob—by people
in general—was never valid. The mob was an instrument, and
throughout all the aeons since Creation, it was left to the genius of
affairs, the leader, to set the tune. He was working out a 'sound,
philosophical background' for his opinions, and would expound
them in the book he was elaborating—he had already taken notes
—*The Man or the Party, Which Rules the State.*

Myers hugged his hat, took a large silk handkerchief from his
pocket, and wiped his throat. Its contours were plump, and, despite
his three-days beard, were faintly womanish. Once more his foot
slipped. He descended to his knees, and scrambled up again, his
bowler rolling away. When he had recovered the hat, his tender
palms were scratched, and he was obliged to beat the plastery dust
from his checked trousers.

Slavery was a relic of barbarism. It was not for ethical reasons
that he disapproved of it, but it was 'out of fashion.' Why, in this
day and age of steam-machinery and new invention, live anachron-
istically? He hadn't shown the manuscript of his essay to anybody
yet, because that would not be 'safe.' But wait until things had
settled down to their usual pace. Then he was going to tell these
insane idiots a thing or two—North and South, both—not a 'lick'
of clear thinking or philosophical outlook at the command of
either. The real leader of America had not appeared—was no

276

more a 'cautious, sentimental Lincoln' than a 'grandiose Davis.' When the war was over, and the issues were reviewed in retrospect, the condemnation those two would receive was going to 'serve them right.'

A jumpy, excitable argument went on eagerly, perpetually, in Myers's active mind, while he slid, on dust-fogged shoes, down the embankment, and clambered through a cut. The great lesson of the wasted heroism of the last few days was an added inspiration to his 'common sense.' The man of destiny would always be there to instruct the mass, but the time was coming when he would not be able to stir them with 'mere humbug eloquence.' Ethics will some day cease to represent mystical systems of values, Myers said to himself. The duty of man toward his neighbour and toward the state will soon be explained, reasonably, as sane selfishness.

Myers's mother felt that he should be a lawyer, and he often agreed with her reasons. There were moments when he could beguile himself with the illusion that he addressed an audience. He walked swiftly over a field, in which corn was parching, fled the rattling stalks, the aborted ears, the clammy silk, in tufts, tickling his chin; and began to climb up a rocky hillside toward a higher field. The heat—Lord God, damn the heat! Though it was a relief to be at last separated from a press of people, all alarmed, all 'looking at the old world upside down,' and with a blindness of panic that soon grew contagious. The advantage of the spectator to these conditions was that he was able to keep his 'sense of proportion' and to judge events 'more scientifically.'

Everything was quiet. In the whole landscape was a kind of languid expectancy. The grass was deliriously still. The boulders glittered as if filled with mica. Science—yes, science. The scientific age that was evolving would soon alter the entire conception of the universe—but it was too warm to think.

Myers was uncomfortably convinced—and the conviction had been with him for the length of his memory—that facts, numerous and general facts about 'things,' about 'matter,' as objects for reflection, made 'human nature' unimportant. He was engrossed in accumulating information as to what the war itself had added to discovery. He had recently examined the new American target rifle, with its 'telescopic sight,' 'false muzzle,' and 'starter,' and had found it worthy of note that this weapon was impracticable for military purposes, 'while all the improvements in the rifles made during the past ten years have been confined to the breech-loading type.' There are three models of repeating arms that have gained a reputation: Colt's revolving rifles, and the Henry and Spencer repeating rifles. Or look at the progress we have made in medicine.

The air was suddenly lifted. A chill breeze began to blow across the weeds. Myers felt it on his ankles, while his face was untouched. What a fuss his mother always made about his 'taking cold'! The rain, if it came, would bring salvation. Rain would discourage a fervour for battle. Corpus domat aqua. It was *good*. Perhaps in the future there would be a chemistry of human feelings. He could imagine the conduct of some unborn general who would comprehend such affairs. With a pleasant sense of defying the solicitude he had to bear at home, he struck through the wood.

In the thick, inert leaves, that were being oscillated, so gently, began a padding hiss. The sun had drifted away to nowhere. A green glare radiated from the tossed foliage. As the sky was more shrouded, the stealthy glow grew more intense. Really, you know, if he could complete his book—Lincoln was no more fitted to control an army—though, in the matter of emancipation he had proceeded shrewdly. What did Lincoln care about the niggers—and he had made a public reputation with his 'Union talk.'

Myers's very anxiety regarding the 'ducking' he seemed about to receive was effective as a stimulus to further and further fancy. He ran a little, slackened his steps, and repressed a tendency to pant. Gettysburg, he was certain, marked the end of the South's military ascendancy. Only the young and the very old had the courage for prophecy. People would see, when the war was over, what a myth they had made of that old politician, Lincoln, with his orang-outang face.

A rain-drop fell upon him, unseen. Its chill was a caress, and ardent. Nature, apostrophized, had always annoyed him. He was done with 'poets.' Byron, he decided, would never have been the man he was without that deformed foot. The true conquest of the elements would not be initiated by the dreamer, but by the 'practical' man. What was needed was the control of sensation and 'sentiment' by 'pure intelligence.'

It was raining hard. Myers stayed an impulse to flee, purposelessly, and gazed around him, worried. Better to walk on calmly, get out of the country, where the lightnings played, and return to Gettysburg. The average human would always demand superstitions with which to nourish his cowardice. That would not deprive the freethinker, the fellow who could see the world just as it was, from receiving the laurel wreath 'of adulation.' Lee was superstitious. Stonewall Jackson had been superstitious—and Lincoln, altogether undistinguished by his 'backwoods' humour, showed superstitiousness. He bore the war upon his shoulders, and now he was trying to propitiate his moral critics with 'this emancipation step.' People were 'not at all different from animalculae.' Clarity, hardness—what the Greeks had, if you like—was beauty; though they had exerted a bad influence through their 'confounded mythology.' If a man has grit, and refuses to pamper his lower self, he prefers his reason undiluted. We *ought* to be humble, Myers was deciding excitedly, not as an acknowledgment of false inferiority before our erring fellowmen—but before logic, before 'universal law.'

Puddles were accumulating in the path, under the dripping boughs, and the puddles were scummed with empty lights, reproducing the vacancy of the intermittently revealed sky. Myers's coat was soggy. His shirt was sticky on his shoulders. The raindrops pitted the cupped water rapidly. There was a constant *clitter-clatter* in the leaves, rain ticking, ticking. It had left off blowing, but the suspended air was alive with rushing sounds. Myers, shivering, deflected from rapt self-argument, traversed a brief clearing above which the dazed heavens yielded at intervals a spotty glare; which indicated, 'Thank goodness,' he said, that the sun was still up. He was now faintly regretful that his fear of the rebels had taken him so far from the road.

He was on the farther rim of the hill. He stared beyond him and saw the whole valley glistening under the advance of the storm. It was as though, over the entire landscape, a thin sheet of transparent silk had been stealthily drawn. The grass on the flats flamed green. Far below him wandered a weed-grown road, intermittent in the precipitations of the shower. Myers, halting, sneezed. He said to himself that to be caught in a summer flurry like this would be sufficient to drive a Keats to his pen. Like an animal seeking cover the young man glanced this way and that. Flashes of rain, giddy, perpendicular, beat without cessation on all that distant vapidness. Myers tried to feel encouragement in the benefit this would bring to the crops. There was a sort of utter passivity in the countryside which even he appreciated. For a fortnight this downpour had been awaited with prayers. Good Lord, it was awful! His teeth chattered. In the seething path, the ropy waters boiled. Twigs and foliage rushed by his feet. The trees ahead, motionless, unrolled a glassy seepage. He walked on. *Trip-ip, tri-ip, trip-trip*. The green tongues of the leaves stirred at last and lapped thickly at the steady drizzle. Worse havoc was gathering. The leaves rolled. Across the valley toward Gettysburg, wiry, spinning lightnings twirled, unannounced. A moment, and, like an after-thought to vision, the flutter of thunder beat woodenly.

The muffled reverberations recalled to Myers a half-dreamed echo of yesterday's firing. The thunder rumbled, vacuous and guttural, died, and the sound was rediscovered in echoes. He contrasted the lavial dampness of his surroundings with his memory of this same world, spent with sun, and above it, faintly greened and like flowing dust, the smoke, surging, travelling, without wind, away, away. He feared the lightning, and, also, suddenly, this terrible quiescence where, so recently, there had been a multitudinous agitation of human beings in a flight for life, in agony. He longed to escape his recollections. His initiate's privileges, as a correspondent of the *Banner*, seemed to weigh on him. Since childhood, he had detested pain and all its impressions. Sometimes, furtively, he acknowledged to himself a certain 'sensitiveness.'

A white blow was delivered on a tree trunk which, falling with a muffled crash, emitted a damp vapour. Indiscriminately, he fled the open, hurried, and, half-running, went deeper into the wood. When the lightning gyrated in swift colourlessness, there followed torrents of a ghostly bombardment shaking all the bushes. The thickening forest revealed caves made by laced boughs, and from these grottoes, emerald-pale, and as if enchanted, issued greasy murmurings.

Myers, replacing his hat on the back of his head, gave way to impetuosity, and crawled into a stony gully, where he hoped to find shelter in some crevice or beneath an overhanging ledge. He fronted a low gash in the hill, in which a helter-skelter of shattered granite did make a kind of barricade before an aperture. Snakes there, probably, and other slimy life. Yet he made an effort, abasing himself, feeling his way on his hands and knees, to push into the cavity. A dank smell flowed out. He shook the vine-hung undergrowth, and his cheek, and his bent neck, felt splashes colder than the falling rain. The earth on which he placed his palms bloomed with an indefinite stain of minute moss.

Despite repugnance, Myers was obliged to consider all the dead, lying in the wake of battle, who had not been buried. This chill submission to the elements did violence to an impression of the exposed, wanton bodies he had left behind. He stooped, hid his face, and was annoyed by a perpetuated sense of glazed eyeballs, glinting baldly on the clouds, and stiff lids that remained unblinking to the forceful pat of water.

Excluding the lightnings, he retained an awareness of some disquieting presence. There was a snuffling near him. He could no longer disregard it. He sprang to his feet, crushed the crown of his hat, butted his forehead stunningly on the depending boulders, and stared—his eyes, for a moment, bright with fright and incredulity.

The bear swayed its sagging head restlessly. Its wet snout uttered snorts. Its coarse tongue, too cleanly red, lolled on its breast. It raised itself, reared humanly, upon its squatting haunches, and stood like a vast, shaggy doll, its fat arms stiffly apart, its clawed hands waving inertly, almost helplessly. In its upright position, it expanded its fluffy belly, the rain crystals clinging perfectly in its dry, glossed fur. Myers could distinguish the yellowed teeth in the black lips, the snarl, like a foolish smile, which exposed the fangs in either jaw. He made a hasty gesture, seeking blind escape. With a kind of dull peevishness, the bear plumped heavily upon its all-fours. Its body careening a little, it advanced, with pigeon-toed thuds of its spongy, flattened paws. With resilient indolence, it came on. Its small, steady passionless eyes blinked.

Myers could not decide whether or not he had been observed. His forethought was blind, but he remained self-conscious of grotesqueness. Stumbling quickly from the hollow, he grasped at the root of a tree, fumbled for a branch, and, in the discovery of a strength that made him exultant, swung himself up. Exacerbation to his flesh did not hinder him. He dropped his coat, and it descended limply. His fingers were scraped and bloody. He braced himself, climbed again, held to weeds that threatened to discard his weight. When he was free of the pit, he ran on, imagining in his ears and nostrils a hot, fetid exhalation of pursuit. But he did not look around. Regaining the path, he hurried until he gasped, and his heart was like an enormous hammer, while there was a giddy flow of blood under his pupils. When he was once more in the open, he urged himself to a renewal of his spent energy, and rushed, headlong, down the hill, to the deserted road beneath.

The storm was quieting. The washed countryside seemed emptier than before, but more placid. He ignored the refreshment of the bitter, lucid air. No matter how he got there, he was determined to arrive at Gettysburg before the night set in. He had escaped a possible calamity. Now his urge was to escape an unexpected, awful loneliness. He had been through 'a real experience,' he assured himself—an insufficient solace. His nerves remained aquiver and he was ready to leap aside at the least sound. Over the purged greenery of the valley, and the unused road with its beaten weeds, the filmy parasols of elder flowers, the ivory cushions of Queen Anne's lace, the dim sky exuded, as from a bruise, a twilight emanating from excoriated, wind-swollen clouds. Feverishly attempting to turn to account the acute depression he felt, Myers said, They aren't afraid enough. That's what's the matter with these crazy militarists and fire-eaters. They're too dull to understand fear.

And this seemed to him, peculiarly, a last wisdom. It was almost as if he had been vouchsafed a revelation.

IX

EXTRY edition! Extry edition! All about Lee's retreat from Gettysburg. All about great Union victory at Gettysburg, Pennsylvania. Vicksburg surrendered to General Grant. Whole Mississippi in hands o' the Union. Gettysburg an' Vicksburg! All about panic in Richmond. Lee turns an' runs from Gettysburg battle-field. Vicksburg siege is over with. Vicksburg is surrendered. Special edition! Special edition!"

A leaping curtain of gauze, the rain fell. Little puffs of chiffon beat up in silvered tatters from the roofs and doorsteps. Then the darkness drew slowly on the echoing voice of the runner. Rain dripped, flickered. Trees along the street, pulled apart by the wind, revealed, in the soft glare from lighted, runneled windows, threads of burning drops. Lamps blotted the square. Wet paper, speared on a bush, flapped. Now and then, a watery thrill of lightning gave blanched being to houses, to trees, to dense, unformed sky. The rain buzzed like gravel falling. The small, disembodied voice passed on.

"Extry edition! Special edition. Times! Times! Lee and rebels on the run!" Ginny, intoxicated by his lonely challenge to the storm, hurried with bare feet patting noiselessly on slippery pavements. A doorway opened gustily, pouring its secret of a glowing interior carelessly upon the night. A man, rapid, cautious, descended trickling steps. With his wet hand, the papers pressed under a naked arm in a torn sleeve, Ginny fumbled for a sheet. "Tscht! Tscht!" Ginny could hear the gentleman cluck, either in surprise or in exultance, as, a wavering shape, he returned, inward, peering, trying to read, even before he could see the print.

Ginny clutched pennies in his chilled fingers, pushed them, all icy and comfortingly metallic, into a soggy pocket. "Extry edition. Special edition!" A window sash squeaked. "Little boy! Little boy! I want a paper." He could not distinguish the woman's face, but, as she threw four pennies from her window, he had to crouch an instant in a reeking grass-plot and search out his reward. "Hester, is thee in bed yet?" she called, aside.

Ginny escaped the lost answer. A drunken man, reeling, halted him, and demanded thickly to know what had occurred. Ginny left him. Blackness had triumphed. Now and again lightning split the darkness and displayed grey motion. The thunder boomed, burred, and diminished—like a top dying. The gas jets, in bracts of luminosity, flashed on dripped pools of golden glass. The heavens were a forest, the lightning behind them as behind a dense screen. Steel rods on the roofs spindled the brief glare. Wet leaves treasured glitteringly uncoloured crystals, glimpsed only for a minute. Red and gilt bottles in a drug store glowed as stilly as unshed blood. In front of a bright shop with a barber's pole, somebody was whistling. The whistle wandered swiftly. Neutral beads of moisture spread on the lamp-blooming glass behind the whistling figure.

"Special edition!" Ginny shrilled. His tiptoes covered, with all the sensations of his young and eager flesh, further miles of streets, streets where the inmates of houses, behind their drawn blinds, would answer, with a querulous reluctance, the adamant cries with which he called them out. "Come on an' git yer special extry!" he yelled. Chestnut Street, Jayne Street, Warren Street—he meant to cover all the city. He rushed into thoroughfares where, at this time in the evening, he found everything deserted. It did not matter. He danced on the cobbles. He cavorted. He butted the wind, ran backward, and waved at the unseen sky, at the drizzling shadows, his rattling bundle. HE knew them. HE knew that they could not resist him, the people in their shrouded parlours so enwrapped in comfort. His lungs expanded in his thin, tight chest. He leaped goatwise. With the vim of a small hurricane, he sowed his yells, his vindication. "Extry edition. Special edition. Special, special, special, special!" Jesus, he'd be sorry when the war was over—but he'd be rich by then.

II

Stuart's cavalry was acting as escort to the wounded. Now and then Wilbur sensed horsemen rubbing close to the wheels of the

284

ambulance wagon. A horse whinnied. Harness tinkled. The rain dripped, and seethed, and trickled. The night, trickling and roaring, swept along beside the closed wagon.

"Give me somepin' to drink. For Christ's sake, give me somepin' to drink." Mumbling, the same voice went on, begging, at last, indifferently, for a boon no longer wanted. Wilbur tried to close his hearing.

There were two tiers of stretchers suspended in the vehicle. Wilbur lay on the bottom tier, and was suffocated by his awareness of the man above, turning, moving, groaning. His own leg was in a cradle, and he was gripped, helplessly, in this wood and canvas vise. Feet stumped on with him in the dark, as he was borne horizontally forward, feeling paralyzed. Twinges of lightning unravelled, zig-zagged, made an instantaneous dazzle that was shed through the curtains. The remembered odour of chloroform yet seemed to invade the thick quiet, and now and again blankness crept over his hot flesh. He could hear a driver swearing, but the sound had no place in a space which had disappeared. The sound was idle, out of no form. More profound than the outer dark, another density pressed on him, floated in his brain. Under its red edges, capping his thoughts, he did continue to detect that constant mutter, "Gimme a drink, gimme a drink." Mercurially the fever seemed to run over his body. Its little thrills were like a laughter all through him. Of the heartier pain of his crushed thigh, he had no further consciousness.

Angelina was not in the room—not in the night, where the moon, if it was a moon—gleamed like moat water. She bent above him, and he said, "damnation, Angelina," and something sprightly in him leaped up and took a tight hold of her throat. Then they were both *here* together.

Angelina, not quiet embodied, bowed and swayed. To the grip on her throat she dissolved blandly. Just because he had hurt his thigh, she told him.

Somebody vomited. Wilbur was annoyed by the deep retching, which insisted on recalling him, on collecting his awareness, diverting him from the rush of shapes—animals, people—pressing the downpour—in his imagination. "Why the —— —— couldn't they leave us behind?"

Wilbur started, tried to move. Wiry, boring, the long pain ran

285

through him from his hip and seemed to drive itself into his heart. "Gimme a drink. Gimme a drink."

Somebody moaned, sobbed. Wilbur lay back, holding still, furtive, tempting the pain to quit him. Icy as glass, he lay, and that febrile winter swept his whole length and body, so that he began to shiver. Angelina was placed in his mind with one word. He did not seem able to keep her there. Hating her fresh cheeks that mocked his useless mass, his lame desires were like a violence. He could not endure her. Why had he ever emerged from the bath in nothing, which had been the chloroform.

The wagon jolted. "Hell!" An enraged voice—that of some one fighting agony—groaned its vituperation. The curtains flapped. One, unloosed, swept over Wilbur's forehead. Leaves by the road exhaled faint light. The trees, burnished by the illumined rain, grew into quiet grass.

The smell of vomit was sharp, like a sour bite in the nostrils. It contended thinly with the cloying fumes from the bandages. Occasionally, the spiral rain, hissing stonily, and like a blue, phosphorescent dust, scattered its frigid scalds on cheeks, on brows, on mouldy blankets. What more could be endured? With the crushing of his leg, had come some exposure of his mind. His pride had been stripped from him. Let the blazing moon pass with its fatigued glare, or the shower bristle crystal from the sodden heavens to enrich the dark; he could not cover the naked thought of his dependence. Thunder wavered voluminously. Squelching boots *plop-plopped* beside the cart. Angela's fancied presence was a bruise on his thoughts. For her he had dared everything. To consider consequences, even for her sake, had always seemed to him to insult, with limitations, needs as endless as the spirit.

There was something rotten in the green night. He rose to his elbow, defiant, pushing aside coverlids, and brutal to the pressure of his forehead on the stretcher above him. He considered a bound to the road below. The wagon wheels *crea-eaked*. "*Gimme a drink. Gimme a drink. Why the ——, don't you listen?*"

Wilbur's hip dragged. The deadness below it was a stiffer pain. It commanded him—and he gave a cry so hoarsely impetuous that it anticipated any preparation for its utterance. It was not fear, but humiliation that laid him low in an inertia which, he felt, would be until he died. With all the coarse weight of his rigid thigh, he hated Angelina, because he could not love her, because it would be useless, it would be degrading, it would be horrible, ever to love again. *"Gimme a drink. Gimme a drink. Gimme a drink."* The wheeled hollow bored on. Wilbur *saw* it an ambulance, with its canvas sides shielding him from a too terrible knowledge of anything lovelier than these smells, sighs, groans, and imprecations. More profound than the outer dark, another density crowded. Under its red edges, an irritating light grew stronger, like the lustre of a dumbness that tantalized. *Gimme-a-drink-gimme-a-drink-gimme-a-drink-thousands-ofus-thousands-ofus-thousands-ofus.* He rested on his wide mind—*thou-a-sands*—thousands resting on his wide, dead mind.

III

In the Rua Aurea, Dom Manoel, who had just strolled from the mass said in the church of são Julião, stepped into his carriage Fernando, the coachman, regal, even in the summer, while wearing his heavy, snuff-coloured coat, with its three authentic tiers of cape, and its large fox collar, cracked his whip resoundingly. On rolled the somewhat antiquated landau, on the doors of which the Soares coat of arms were embossed conspicuously.

The pair were not a match, for one was a horse, and the other, supplanting a bay that had lately died, was a mule of more longevity.

Blumping steadily over the cobbles, the magnificent progress of the vehicle sent fluttering upward on steady wings all the dozens of pink and brown pigeons, flown down from the mossy eaves of the blue and white tiled dwellings and the ornate towers of the plaster churches.

Manoel's erect spine soon became numbed by thud after thud against the jolting, stuffed cushions from which the hair was spilling. Yet he was in a sufficiently hopeful humour, as he pressed his lilac gloves on the handle of his Malacca cane, to regard 'as mulhers do povo,' amicably, while they scurried, in their round little hard black hats, set on their flowing veils of green and yellow handkerchiefs, out of his way. He could even, in his genial admiration of their regal deportment, ignore the broad, bare feet on which they trod, excuse the 'fleas and dirt,' which he sus-

pected; and he finally grew so warm in tolerance as to offer, to a young girl staggering valiantly under a basket burdened with opalescent fish, a deliberate, confidential wink.

Manoel had a fattish face, a liquid eye, and his full, sallow cheeks, with their black, curly 'Piccadilly weepers' marked him as a fashion-plate. Not for an audience with Luiz I, and his new bride, Pia, was Manoel bound for Cintra, but on a personal mission the result of which, though it would not disturb court circles, might be announced in print. He was presenting his addresses to Senhora Doña Viuva Pacheco, a lady of sufficient wealth; and this though his account in the Bank of Portugal indicated such prosperity as might relieve many another of the burden of ambition. Just at the beginning of the war, which continued to rend North America, he had bought up cotton. The 'luck' which had resulted from this accident had almost awed him. He was becoming pious. He was considering some sugar trading with the Brazils, and in order to arrange his affairs with perfect confidence in Deity, he had gone to church.

He was cautious. If the war would but continue, if the war would but continue—yet, though he addressed all his most respected saints, he dared not be too sanguine. Laura Lopez, the Spanish actress, whom he despised as something paid for, cost a lot of money. And ever since he had quitted the university and laid aside his student's cloak, he had treasured the reputation of a reckless dandy. Patriotic as he was, and ready to extol, before his mother, the virtuous loveliness of the ladies of Portugal, he found them 'leite muito fraco,' and yearned perpetually for something foreign, something 'diabolical'—at times, since tradition and Catherina de Bragança had set a lasting mode—for something 'English.'

The sails of a squat windmill, shaped like a tankard, whirled slow petals of canvas upon the sky. Pena, the new palace, resting high above the cloudy park and the eucalyptus trees, on the outcrops of jagged granite, thrust up its fretted tower. Under the dank grandeur of the royal enclosure, lay Cintra, pink-and-blue villas, in the waning orange light. Virgem Maria, Virgem Maria— not to find it necessary to wed Viuva Pacheco after all—but to save one's affections for a youthful dancer who would do one credit. Why, if the war would but persist for another year, Dom Manoel and his mother could afford to angle for a presentation.

288

Like a blast, the chalk void descended. Giles left Jennie and the children in shelter under a doorway, and hurried off. Jennie would stand there for hours, waiting for him, and never a reproach. He could think of her red hands fumbling dumbly in the knots of her shawl's fringe. Jennie had tramped with him all the way from Manchester, and he had thought of no excuse for leaving her behind.

Who could say for him what comes into a man's mind with a woman so devoted that, when he says, "Jen, I 'aven't the 'eart for it any more; since the mills closed down, there is no way for us to turn, and I 'ave been thinking I would go down to London where there is more to be 'ad in the way of work and try my luck without you"—when he says that and she stands staring, not shedding a tear, until, finally, she is on her knees (where no woman ought to be even before her husband) and she has clasped hold of his legs and will not let him move? "Unless we can come with you, Giles. The boys will not be able to bear it without you, Giles," she says. "They've trudged enough before this, so I don't see why they cannot come with you, for it's no help to us to stay here without a roof to cover us—or it will soon be that—and the girls and women turned off, too. As long as the war in America goes on, Giles, there's no luck for anybody. I cannot pinch and scrape no more than I've done already, and I would rather try my 'and at something in London, too," she says.

The fog bore a faint, ocreish dye, but it did not conceal the river, and, when he turned toward the embankment, he could see the water plainly. The proud husk of a barge, travelling slowly, left pearly scales. Each barge, with its scald of lamplight, beat a silk glow through the ripe dusk. The hull of a boat, fanged with light, bit the crepuscular Thames. There were the alive flakes of gulls' wings.

He could not face her again. Though a man has thought of a woman he used to know, and how much easier it is with the light ones who will appear to have nothing sorrowful to remember— yes, he thought of that, even before they came, before they had walked so far this afternoon how it would be to have no worries. There is precious little reward for a man with a woman like Jennie and a family. God knows, he did not reproach her. If the mill had not closed down, things might have been different.

No number of parsons would ever find excuse for the hate he felt, nor he himself know why he had to behave as he did. It was the sight of her misery, her perpetual misery.

Should it be the water? If a pub had been there— And why should a man who is loved by his family long, above all things to hurt them, to threaten them, to make them hate him?

.   .   .

Like a carving in stone, its bluntly rounded bill, with the neat black tip, resting pensively on its smooth, pouting bosom, the swan floated, paddled backward with its leafy feet, and sped forward, forward, on a current it had made itself, without a ripple. It was a double bird, repeating, in its reflection, the slow, impassive curve of its down-bent neck. The ruffles of its wings were flutings in a shell of alabaster. Scarcely did the horny stems of its short legs seem to move, dragging after them languid, powerful toes. On across the black pond swept the boat of its body, in immaculate sculpture, and stirred the fish, the flakes of bitter scarlet, like dropped autumn leaves, in the world of inverted trees and sunny caverns made by the drownèd boughs.

Elizabeth, in her muslin dress, with the two tight pigtails laid carefully and consciously forward on her shoulders, looked at the swan; then, with a furtive vanity, beheld herself, also still and white. In her soft, plump fingers, she was breaking bits of bread. Gentle, but eager as a serpent, the swan thrust out its long neck and gobbled deftly, soundlessly; little bubbles gurgling in the holes that were its nostrils by its feathered brow. When the bread was all gone, it swam 'round and 'round, again nestling its throat upon its own breast, so like in brilliance to an untouched mountain peak. But, every now and then, gaping its hunger, it uttered, raucously, a plaintive whimper.

"Wie kann man so dumm sein?" reprimanded Elizabeth, lifting her ruffled petticoats in both her hands and making a rebukeful motion. Yet she was flattered into tolerance by the swan's evident attachment for her, provoked by the bread. "So ist das Leben!" she complained aloud, gently arranging her corn-yellow hair once more. And her large brown eyes, regarding themselves in the shaking mirror, held a soft unhappiness. Yet it was a comfort to know that Cousin August, at least, admired her: and, now that the war in America had done such damage to the tobacco trade,

290

Adolphe might come back. She had been but a child when he went away, and she was trying not to hope too much. But— Ach, mein Gott! How she had wept! Day and night, day and night, almost spoiling that complexion of which 'Mütterchen' always made her take great care.

Elizabeth's slight chest, under the tight fabric of her dress, heaved rapturously. Thank God for that war. She was trying not to think too much of Adolphe—too much for a nice German girl who is not yet betrothed, and is of excellent family. But summer was too beautiful. She could almost pity sweet little Ida who had not yet loved. Being the eldest, sometimes an affliction, Elizabeth now accepted with exquisite complacency. Under her breath she began to sing, hummingly, "Mein Schatz ist ein Ritter!" ending guiltily with a "Tra-la-la-la-lá!" that drew the swan, in its dumb anxiety, closer to the water's edge. Suddenly, even its abstract observation was embarrassment. "Fettkopf!" she called; and realized that her tone, helplessly, thrilled a caress. She was the nicest person in the world. The nicest sister, the best, the most obedient little daughter that ever lived. She would make a superior wife. Let Mina look down her nose. Elizabeth was not a prude. It was just that—Oh, the pretty morning! "Der Krieg! Der Krieg!" she carolled. Could it possibly be wicked to be so very happy? No, no, no, she thought. It is only when I am very good that I love myself so much!

. . . .

The horses moved with slow haunches. Straining tendons bulged and crawled in their flanks. Hoofs grappled flatly on the creaking wood of the pontoon. A horse slipped, half lost its footing. Hoarse voices called together, "Whoa—whoa there, you —— ——," and whip cracks exploded. Animals lunged in the mud. A mule, fallen, reposed with that absolute abandon to fatigue, which, when expressed by animals, looks like resignation. The mule's forelegs were flexed. Its muzzle was so lowered as to rest in a puddle, while it snuffled dirty water mixed with blood. The two soldiers in ragged coats tried to push the grudging creature to its feet. Its eyes were indifferent. They leaned on its heaving side. They shouted. Realizing they had stopped the march of wagons, they stared about them doubtfully. "Give him a kick. Knock the guts out of his damned belly."

One of the soldiers had a bandaged head. An eye was concealed by the stained lint, and the other, bleared and swollen, regarded, with that ruthless antipathy which is exhaustion, the dying mule.

Its inertia seemed incalculable. One of its ears flickered in a waning attention. Its earth-crusted, powerful shoulder was offered to them as for support. Then its neck relaxed. Over its whole body, and along its legs swept an immense, ruthless tremor. The muck clotting its nostrils bubbled to its thick, quiet respiration. Invincible at last, it lay as if offering itself.

"Damned lucky you are, too, confound you!" said the second soldier; and stolidly gave his strength to forcing the living corpse back toward the water's edge.

The air smelled of weedy, rain-bruised foliage, of the cold, sweet river, of manure and the urine of animals. When the caravans moved again, the two soldiers stood aside, by the broken wagon. Under tarpaulins, crushed shapes jolted by. It was difficult to distinguish carts for stores from those used as ambulances. All were filled with men. Some sat behind, dangling their legs. All were dishevelled. Through the icy envelope of mist, so strange in summer, the bulky heaps of men and objects glided waveringly. Stale gaze encountered gaze, in the pervasive dumbness. "Damn the———!" The soldier with the bandage swore profusely, cursing everybody, cursing nobody.

X

"FAITH, 'tis the worst injustice the workin' man has had to suffer!" exclaimed the harsh-featured man on the curbing. He had already attracted Effie's notice, and she was regarding him belligerently, for some reason or other assuming that she could not possibly find a champion for her beliefs in the person of *this* graceless individual. It embarrassed her to hear him the spokesman for her own views. She was obliged to readjust her opinion of him, and to find his face, if not prepossessing, at least 'honest.'

He had declared himself boldly, and now his vague, chill eyes, circled with whitish lashes, stared about, demanding appreciation. Effie gave it dutifully, primming her small mouth and nodding her head emphatically; while a frowzy woman nearer, loudly and slyly approving his words, called "Indaid it's the Lord's truth ye're tellin', an' the pity 'tis that there are not more of thim with the courage to stand up fer thimselves."

Effie was blushing violently, because the man, having detected her agreement with him, stared her almost out of countenance, a wily expression of approbation twisting his thin, bitter lips into a half-smile. She was repelled by his every feature, his long, sharp, inquisitive-looking nose, his coarse complexion, his air of defiance that did not cover any of the appearance of a calculating nature. He had a wooden leg, and Effie was astonished that he should find it necessary to protest so ardently against the draft, when his infirmity would indicate that he must be exempt from it. There seemed no honest, simple reason for his resentment—unless, of course, he was one of those creatures whose pleasure it was to stir up trouble for others. And he had ignored the ardent encouragement of the slattern who had voiced her complaisance, and was riveting his whole attention on the meek Effie. "It's the *respectable* workers that the government has got to listen to," he said.

Effie's presence here, in the crowd that had assembled before the conscription office, was a matter of conscience. Yet she had to struggle against a regret that she had not accepted 'Brother James's' advice to her to remain modestly within doors, and, above all things, not to be inveigled into sympathetic conversations with strangers. The wholesale application of a conscription act made protest from the workers a duty, but objections should be stated quietly and with dignity. The 'ideal atmosphere' in which she had grown up, since her childhood passed as a doffer in the Lowell Mills, had taught her self-respect in her position of a working-woman. Pity that all these in humble stations had not had her advantages. Even the little 'taste of fame' which had come to her as a contributor to the *Lowell Offering* had helped to inspire her with the conviction that all effort having a noble intention was worth while. She did not blame the Irish labourer for being what he was, but the Catholic Church.

"A disgrace to the counthry," the Irishman declared ornately. " 'Tis the workin' people of this blessed nation Misther Lincoln ought to liberate!" Again his eyes discovered hers, and commanded of her craftily her endorsement.

It was very hot in the street. The July sun turned brows waxen, or made them glow with the ardour of sweating brick. The people had filled the street to overflowing. Carts with horses, attempting to enter at the corner, were halted by the press, and policemen, clustered about the conscription bureau, above the door of which the Stars and Stripes hung limp and bleaching, waved the drivers back. "The trruth if it was iver told ye," murmured a fat woman in a red skirt, and nudged Effie for agreement.

The woman had a hard jaw, under which was knotted a spotted handkerchief that protected her head from the glare. Her thick red hands, as she rearranged her bandanna, were viciously tremulous. Waddling a pace or two toward the short flight of stone steps descending from the entrance to the bureau, she set her arms akimbo and flaunted her hatred to the policemen. "Have ye no love in yer hearths fer your brother workers? 'Tis not so long since ye came over frim the ould counthry. Have ye left yer Irish hearts behind?" she gibed loudly, in a raucous voice.

The policemen ignored her guardedly. "Shtep back," they said, to the jostling, too-eager, who craned, and threatened, in their curiosity, to behold what was occurring in the interior of that building where all fates must then be under decision, to invade the stairs and the hall. "Shtep back, or ye'll be gittin' a good clubbin' on the head."

But the policemen, also, had their adherents. "Keep your pigs and praties at home if you do not like the land!" a small, fierce, clerical-appearing man was shouting, shaking at the knot of Irish his clenched fist which held a walking-stick. "Go back where you came from, if you do not want to fight! There's plenty of boys here whose grandpas sent the English packing in the Revolution, and they can put the rebels in their place down South without the help of none of *your* kidney!"

The fat woman cast toward him a scornful scrutiny. "Then I hope the first number called is yer own, ye crowin' cock," she bawled. " 'Tis fine to make the long voyage overseas to save the childrun from the plague of starvin' an' then be killed fer the likes of niggers, as me son might be! Bad cess to ye!" She shuffled indignantly.

"If you come to this country you should abide by its laws," argued the irate clerk, involuntarily meeting the fat woman as an equal, and led, now, to discuss the issue with her personally.

"And who made the laws? If ye was to be hanged at sunrise, Misther Blusterer, wouldn't ye be tryin' to escape the rope, and wouldn't ye be thinkin' in doin' so that yer cause was right?" she demanded of him, her little eyes snapping. "May the divil fly away wid you!"

The policemen shook her. The crowd jeered. She stuck out her tongue and spat over her shoulder laboriously.

Persons excited by a disturbance and, seemingly, avid to create another, ran this way and that. Little boys, with animal hoots, egging on first one faction, then the other, danced on the edge of the huddled gathering. Young men, ready to be 'called out,' hung about the cavelike shadow of the open hall, and, one after another, as numbers were announced, responded to the disturbing invitation to satisfy their curiosity by going lightly up the steps and entering the hallowed precincts. Every time the impersonal mentor boomed a number, from a window, or from the door, the police on guard on the sidewalk repeated to the onlookers "Twenty-nine! Twenty-eight," or whatever the decisive numeral intoned might be. Then there were groans from all sides. The mob moaned voluptuously, an immense wave of commiserating sound echoing the length of the block, the intonation of misery only less impressive because it was well along toward noontime and a cheerful sun was pouring down its beams.

Effie, carried hither and yon, by the fluctuating intensity which drove people together toward the steps, or pushed them back, was now very near a young officer who was regarding her compassionately, regretfully, and seemed on the verge of offering her some advice.

She had a virtuous terror of police, and when she noticed that he had picked her out for observation, as she lurched immodestly toward him from the forefront of the crowd, she was immediately placed in the position of the guilty ones. How did he dare to stare at her so, when she had done nothing at all that could merit censure, when she was as honest and true an American as he was, and knew full well that she had the right of every law-abiding citizen to an independent opinion as to what was going on? She supposed that he must be shocked because she was a woman, and, she admitted, in comparison to some of the rest, so ladylike.

Effie's glimpse of the two was suddenly intercepted, and she did not see them for a minute, when they were before her again, and she realized that the hasty fat woman was slapping the clerk's hateful face.

"None o' that! None o' that!" The clerk returned the blow, prodding at her and awkwardly attempting to use his cane. Two policemen intervened. "This country and its laws are for decent people!" the clerk was yelling. "Then 'tis not for the likes of you becase ye're not dacent. He lays on to a respectable woman and the mither of four sons thet could aisy make mush of the miserable little squirt he is, and he calls it dacent. Oh, but childrun air the livin' heartscalds!" the woman shouted, her handkerchief on her neck, her grey hair tousled, locks hanging against her crimsoned, sweating cheeks. And she beat at her attacker and at the policemen, unselectively.

Effie was trembling. Violence, no matter what the provocation, always drew her abhorrence. Heaven only knew what courage had been demanded of her childish soul on the day, in Lowell, when she had walked out with the older operatives on their first strike against a reduction of wages. Yet what a difference between that scene and this! Then, the girls so neat, so cleanly dressed, so orderly, and the song:

> Oh, isn't it a pity, such a pretty girl as I
> Should be sent to a factory to pine away and die?

The threat to quit the mills forever had somehow created a mood no more disturbing than a holiday. But *this*—oh, this!

"To hell with the government! It's run by a lot of slave drivers!" called another voice, from some source unobserved.

The police were dragging the Irishwoman away. As she stumbled along with them, against her will, her head turned, she surveyed the specious triumph of the unmolested clerk, and screamed, " 'Tis you that's to make this counthry the home fer freedom an' the workin' folk, is it? A murrain on yer laws. Ye cannot desthroy the Irishman's habit of bein' free wid his tongue no matter what ye do. And 'tis not a sin fer the mither of a family to try to save her sons from dyin'! "

And why should she not be ladylike, Effie demanded of him silently. Had he so little knowledge of the working people that he did not think a simple air of breeding and refinement appropriate to them? Summoning all her will, she gave glance for glance, in what she insisted to herself to be the unashamed look of a pure heart. The policeman, removing himself from his position by the doorway, made a step toward her. She was rosy with anguish, but she was not the timid young thing of her days at Lowell, and she would dare even *his* corrupting reprimand. Her head went up, and instantly, because she felt herself so *right*, and him, in his affiliation with oppression, *wrong*, she was threatened with the loss of her self-control, with the possibility of doing her cause injustice since she could not hold herself in. Oh, she was thinking, as his hated bulk loomed nearer, oh, if he ever *dared* to lay his hands on me! Oh, oh, what a horrid man he is! If he comes one step nearer —if he tries to stop me—and I have a right to be here—I shall slap his face!

The policeman halted. "If I were you, ma'm," he began protectingly, "I would get out of this crowd of hoodlums. If these grumblers keep on airing themselves there may be trouble. If you come right along with me, I'll help you find a way out."

Effie's lips quivered in a smile, while her eyes remained vacant, screening helplessly her foolish indecision. She was relieved, of course. After all, the poor man did but do his duty.

Then anger swept her. But he behaved like this because he saw in her only a meek woman, of pacifist views, or of no views at all. She would not be diverted by his boast of politeness. Compressing her mouth firmly, so that minute wrinkles were indented about it, she drooped her lids and shook her head. No, she thanked him, she would stand where she was. He continued to argue with her, but less patiently, and more suspiciously. Oh, she could see in his horrid eyes the suspicion of her, growing, as if, because she was a working-woman, and was here firmly present to espouse the issues affecting her humbler class, he doubted even her respectability. "Surely we are doing no harm," she said. "It cannot be against the regulations to assemble on the streets for a peaceable purpose."

"But can you be so sure it's peaceable, ma'am? I'm after thinkin' this looks more like sedition than peace."

Listen, listen! Effie no longer hears what he says. A female voice in the distance is singing. Something familiar in the melody, in the words that grow distinct and become plainer every moment as the new element which will add to the excitement of the crowd approaches. Effie can make out a woman's voice leading, the men's voices echoing, augmenting the tune, and she also, elated now, and very desperate, makes a feeble claim to sing.

> The overlooker met her
>   As to her frame she crept;
> And with his thong he beat her,
>   And cursed her when she wept.
> It seemed as she grew weaker,
>   The threads the oftener broke.
> The rapid wheels ran quicker
>   And heavier fell the stroke!

"Get back there! Stand back there! None o' that, or you'll all finish the day in the lock-up!"

A heavy, ambiguous air of determination was on the policeman's face. His tenders of courtesy discarded, his recognition of Effie in her distinction from the mass was abandoned. He ignored her being with a completeness which offended her more profoundly than could have any onslaught. Bewildered, she bridled toward him. Her piping accents, lifted, at first, timorously, grew into shrill certainty. She even fought for his attention, elbowing herself in front of others, and forcing herself toward him, while he, with his mates, all using their billies, probed the heaving agglomeration of persons bent vaguely on defiance.

> That night a chariot passed her,
>   While on the ground she lay;
> The daughters of her master
>   An evening visit pay.
> Their tender hearts were sighing,
>   As negroes' wrongs were told,
> While the white slave was dying
>   Who gained her father's gold!

The old song had gained the day for the oppressed. Effie, wild-eyed, enjoying tears which, as she felt them course down her cheeks, were to her the symbol of a purification of purpose, glanced headily aside, and beheld a unanimous rapture. Mouths opened and emitted such vociferous singing as must have made even the stoic policemen quail. People who did not know the tune, yelled as loudly as the others. There was a stamping of feet, there were ya-yaing, yodelling sounds from the elated who recognized no music. The more intense the senseless joy of the populace who celebrated a triumph before any fact of victory, the angrier became the policemen. Making themselves a moving buttress of half-crooked, extended arms, they would first climb the stairs before the conscription office, then descend together, all of a rush, and fall with their combined weight against the press of aggressors, at the same time belabouring all those who could be reached.

Effie's bonnet was torn from her head. Her face was scratched. The very fellow who had offered kindly to lead her from the mêlée delivered a blow at random that bruised her shoulder and gave such outrage to her pride that nothing less than to see him trampled on the ground before her would have eased her. Since she could not fight, she continued to sing. The oftener the heavy hand of abuse fell on her and bore her back, the louder she screamed. And she began the song again:

> 'Twas on a winter morning,
> The weather wet and wild,
> Two hours before the dawning,
> The father roused his child.

In the highest focus of her excitement, when to be a woman, and to passively suffer all the abominations of tyranny was to be exalted among the elect and the martyrs of the earth, she heard a shot. The explosion, like a low-pitched, irrelevant ejaculation, was ignored heedlessly, though every ear detected it. But the realization that something untoward had occurred did slowly invade the dazed sense of the mob. There was a pause in the confusion. "Man shot! Man shot!" somebody was yelling, boastful in the announcement of that which might astonish everyone.

Effie's meaningless progress was halted and she was in a becalming pause. Necks were craned. The policemen, more aggressive, yet too alarmed to pursue instant revenge, turned away from their opponents, and Effie could see them all, crouched or bending in attitudes of indignant wonder, about the fallen shape of some comrade lying stretched out on the pavement just beyond the steps.

The crowd hallooed. Effie saw the man's legs in the blue of his uniform stretched stiff before his screened body, while a fellow running out of the building was bringing a can of water, either for the wounded man to drink or to bathe his face.

Curiosity overcame diffidence before a catastrophe. "Who did it? Where did the shot come from? Did they knock him down, or was he shot? Who fired the shot? Didn't you hear a shot?" people were asking. And they drew nearer.

"If anybody comes a step closer to this here man, or to the door of that office, they get shot!" a policeman called. He had risen from a kneeling posture beside his hurt companion, and now turned, at his full height, exaggerated by his mood of threat, to confront those who presumed on further interference with the law's function. At his words, pistols were whipped out of hip-pockets, and the crowd, that had been disconcerted by its unpremeditated association with murder, and inclined, therefore, to more humility, was instantly aggrieved and sure of itself in the discovery of what it might have before assumed—that the police were armed. "Get any closer than twenty-five feet from this office door, and you'll get a stream of lead into you that you won't never wake up from!" the policeman yelled again. He was very pale, and the implacable nature of his fright showed in the hardness and brilliance of his unwinking eyes. A bevy of followers, all in the same mood, congregated beside him; others lifted the wounded man and carried him into the house, from the windows of which protruded the heads of anxious clerks; while from one window in particular, on the second floor, leaned a moustached man in military clothes, who shouted, "Keep that carrion out of here, officer. Don't hesitate to make any arrests that need be. Shut up the front of the house, and keep these people out. The business of conscription has got to be gone through peaceably and without any interference from the riff-raff."

Effie did not consider herself of the 'riff-raff.' With her hands squeezed to her oppressed bosom, and her challenging and tearful eyes fixed hatefully on the vituperative person in the second story, who was now beginning to curse and to use the foulest language, because the policemen had not yet succeeded in closing the front door, she felt more than ever the villainy of injustice which had permitted President Lincoln, himself born of humble people, to favour and finally sign and make legal an act to conscript all the young men of New York, sound in wind and limb, and, regardless of their personal decisions, problems, or predilections, send them down South, into the jungles and fever, for the rescuing from a lesser persecution of so many insensate blacks. She was distracted by her untenable alliance with an act of crime, but she would not 'climb down and lick the dust'! Not for anybody.

It was, therefore, as if for the express replacement of her own self-esteem that a younger woman, bare-headed, with her black eyes glowing, her glossy hair dishevelled and gleaming upon her shoulders, and two red spots vivid in her cheeks, emerged, half dragged, yet half through her own determination, from the concealment of numbers, and, being so revealed, in the nudity of a conspicuous position, exposed frankly the very weapon from which the bullet must have been fired not ten minutes previous.

"There she is! There she is!" the crowd exclaimed. Several cried, "Set the coppers on her! Hold her! Don't let her get away!"

But there were more who, murmuring defensively, said, "Give her a chance! Tell her to run for it! It's only one of them dirty policemen in Lincoln's pay and it served him right!"

Effie, for the moment horrified, allowed her hatred of the police to outweigh niceties. Besides, this was a woman, who, if she had erred in having sought revenge through violence, had but assumed the privilege men called their right.

"Come on! Arrest me! Take me to jail! Show them how you can treat a woman that works for her living! What right has *she* got compared to you rotten paid oppressors!" The girl had mounted the first of the flight of stairs, and thus elevated herself a little above her admirers. "What's the matter with you?" she yelled, as police caught at her uplifted arms, and wrested the pistol from her. "Not one of you has it in you to make a fuss about this! I'm the only one with the spunk to show the stinkin' coppers what they oughta get!"

Effie, in a jealous rapture, endeavoured to reach the side of the shrieking orator, and '*show*' them,' too; and once more the song rose hysterically:

> Their tender hearts were sighing,
> As negroes' wrongs were told,
> While the white slave was dying,
> Who gained her father's gold!

Lucy felt the vise that was the policeman's grip closing on her wrist, twisting it, the grip pulling on all her weight. The pain was excruciating, but her eyes opened brightly and stared straightly and vindictively into the policeman's eyes, which were blue—just as if he had put up a blue china wall between her and him. He must know that, while she kept on struggling, and he did not desist, he would wrench her arm clean from the socket. But pain was not to hold her. She had nothing to lose. Did he understand that? And this sense of her utter, utter nothingness was her greatest pride. Her chest swelled, and the pride she had in being nothing, with nothing to lose, choked her, stifled her. As soon as she could free one hand a little, she struck back at him. She had been a fool, when she had stolen money from the till when her kid was sick, but she would not be a fool again. She was not going to eat dirt now for any rotten magistrate. Mat was willing to be conscripted. He hadn't had the grit to come. He had been ashamed of her when, at the meeting the other night, she had spoken out. He was afraid that, if he made a row about the draft, he wouldn't hold his job. "If you can scrape and pinch till you get together three hundred dollars, they'll let you off," she yelled, "but if you're too poor to rake and scrape enough to bribe 'em they'll herd you up in their stinkin' army! Stinkin' army! Stinkin' army!" She kept on saying it.

"Shame!" derided a loud, stranger voice; but it could not be told whether the contempt expressed was for the brutal officers or for her martyrdom. She did not reject any opportunity to feel herself attacked. "The shame's for you, you spineless sot," she cried. "Damn the lot of you!" Coarse language had not come naturally to her at first, but she had schooled herself to it. Everything that seemed to strike them, injured her as well. But when you have been hurt and hurt, and will to go on living, you can thrive on injury. For the loss of half a dollar, the deposit she had made upon a locker key, the dirty miser of a factory overseer had hustled her to court. But she was through with him, and with all cringing to his like. She did not want any cheers from the onlookers. She could stand alone until she was dead. The others were not good enough.

A cold, bony knuckle smashed on her face. Her eye went black and the violence of this unexpected pain was a new alarm. The eye was swelling. Let 'em *ruin* her looks, that Mat did not think worth the price of his job. Let them beat her to a pulp. Still they would not crush her spirit! And if they had never done her the rotten way they had, she might never have known that she had a spirit. That she would stand here yelling at the dirty blackguards till the Resurrection Day. What irked her was the closing in of the circle of obscurity. Closer and closer it drew upon her as they dragged her down. When they had bundled her away in the Black Maria, would any one remember the blow she had struck for the freedom of these snivelling working people? Would Mat hear of it?

The sun on the housetops across the street began to dance and shoot sparks, send out rays of burning black, but still she fought. They could wear her out, they could bear her down. Her shoulders were bumping. They could drag her mercilessly the whole length of the steps, but they could not kill the hate that she was nourish-

303

ing because it gave her life. "You whine about bein' Christians," she was shrieking. "You got no right to talk about lovin' these here skunks that take your men and homes away from you! If you got any sand at all or any self-respect, you got to hate. Bribe 'em! Bribe 'em! Give 'em dirty bribes. They can all be bought!" They had torn her clothes, and her breast was bare. She felt the sun's heat, and their 'nasty eyes,' she thought. The rich fellows would wink and grin and make their dirty propositions, but they'd never marry you. And now, no more, since the way Mat done about the baby, would she marry him. Let them tear her dress, let them drag her naked. "We gonta *all* be naked, folks!" she screamed, with scorn, "before we reach the Judgment Seat!" She'd help them. She'd show them all she thought about them. She'd wrench the last hook and button off. What they said was decent was just a sham. She was god-damn tired of their 'decentness.'

Lucy, weakening, everything blurred in the sparkling dance before her, heard women cry, "Fie! let her alone!" But Lucy would do without their —— mercy! She had had enough of it.

She jerked at her clothes, and she would as soon be before them without a rag. It was as if her very coverings were humiliation. They had said enough about her moral character. Let them have a look. If she didn't care what they had said about her what satisfaction were they going to get from her? What could they do about it?

"Now shut up and come along. Don't do that again. Pick up her legs!" she heard the murmurs. The policemen lifted her. She beat at them and at herself. She despised this body which she could not keep from them. And she tried not to know what they were doing to her. Her eyes closed willingly. Worsted, she was weak willingly. She shuddered, and wanted to die. But she could not die. They were keeping her alive. Her own aliveness filled her with a kind of loathing. It was her aliveness that she hated. She writhed in their steeled arms, in the boisterousness of the crowd, as in a lewd darkness. And she prayed, vituperatively, that they would hurt her more. She longed for them to torture her until her very breath fled out.

There was a thing in front of her which she was forced to recognize. She accepted dimly its definitions—the patrol wagon. Its security she dreaded. One last look at the blank sky—at nothing—

and the desire for freedom, for being nothing at all—just like she said she was—was stifled by undignified peace—peace that was a horror—peace from which you never got away.

"Poor lamb! The saints be wid her!" Lijah's anger was slow to gather, but when he heard this exclamation from a stranger, it expressed for him the pity that, until this moment, he had refused to yield. The girl had been a fool to fire a shot and kill a copper, but that was to be expected since no woman ever had good sense. If the folks were going to bust the conscription bureau up, he would not stand back.

He made a rush with them up the stairs, past the spot on which the girl had fallen (and he had not seen since, for the jostling mob, what the police were doing). She had been bundled off.

The doors were locked. Lijah ran against them with all the strength he had, and there were enough beside him, so that the panels shook a little. He was glad that the door was solid, only made of wood, so that he, who was squeamish about shedding blood, could expend, unhampered, all his rage on it.

In her speech what had hit him hardest was that those who had three hundred dollars for the government need not go to war. He had three hundred dollars in the savings bank, but was *that* a reason, just the government's whim, that he should give it up!

Laughing, crying out, those who had mounted the stairs, pell-mell, and then half tumbled down, hurried against the door excitedly. Lijah, power growing as his ratiocination dimmed, hurled himself, with his shoulder pointed against the door, and heard the panels creak. Like rats that were trapped, the working people were being hunted. It was them that made an army. Mr. Lincoln, Secretary Stanton, did not go to war. Lijah had little use for the Republicans—still less for Democrats—but his stoic nature was very grim, and he interfered with nobody. Let them, the goddamn scoundrels, leave his life alone. He was not going to war. That was settled. But why should he give up all the money he had laid aside because the niggers wanted liberty? Niggers and liberty! He had seen the niggers. They already had too much. Liberty was not for everybody anyway. If a man had saved, and stuck to his job, and never broken law or commandment, he deserved his liberty. Had Mr. Lincoln and old hard-tack Stanton ever worked for it!

He ran up the steps. He attacked the door. He was silent. People beside him, who cursed and yelled, aroused all his contempt. *He* was a fellow could do all that he set out to, without making any fuss. He was going to get inside that government office and tear up all their dirty documents. He fought when he had a mind to— when there was something that concerned his own business that he ought to fight about.

"She'd put the come-hither on a lad. She'd such a way wid her she could make the birds sing!" the old woman had said. Lijah had no use for women at any time, and he had no use for the Irish and their flowery talk. But he'd three hundred dollars that he would not waste, and the girl was right!

Gus had seen very plainly the spot from which the shot had been fired, and he had enjoyed knowing, when none of the others knew, that the girl had done it. It had disappointed him just a little when she had shown herself. Then he had realized that the big excitement was only about to come, and had begun to dance around the outskirts of the crowd elatedly. By the time that she was dragged away, and a wavering line of people butting at the bureau doors, he was past all self-containment and could but squeal and chuckle his delight. Oh, that sight of a policeman, reeling, bleeding, then stretched prone upon the pavement, what a joy it had been! Gus was still too much in awe of all officials not to fear this last delight. As a child, in order to annoy his mother, he had pretended 'fits.' He had been so admired for the exhibitions of voluntary twitching he could give that he had been tempted, on the advice of onlookers, to utilize his talents in making a living as a beggar. But he was much too timid to deceive the law—at least so openly—and he had a presentiment that, if he cultivated his ability to twitch too freely, he might find himself unable to control it.

But dis here was a racket! Dis here was a sure 'nough racket! Sweating, his little, 'peaked' face showing, through its girlish colour of excitement, all his small blond freckles, he raced madly up and down, approaching the steps, allowing himself to be bumped along with the mounting crowd, then wriggling out of it again to

306

find space for the utterance of the cheers he offered it. A riot call surely had been turned in from somewhere, but, in the meanwhile, the chaos which was his element was his to appreciate.

What if dey caught me! He shivered, half in delight and half in accurate misery. He had served his time for having stabbed that nigger with a razor, yet had never been truly able to convince himself that this debt to the mysterious State was cancelled. The State was something that could always get him—like a bogy man.

What he dreaded most to repeat was the *monotony* of prison. Hardships had not troubled him. Lice, filth, meals of thin, greasy soup, or of bread and water, had not troubled him. Often without any means of sustenance other than he gleaned in a search through refuse pails, he was accustomed to the fact of a gnawing belly. But his freedom and activity were very precious. Work in the prison yard or on a road gang did not move fast enough. To Gus, it was torment to be thrown inward upon his own vacant resources. For the first time, in that 'jail house,' he had thought of dying, had observed to himself that he had no friend, no wife, no mother, no sweetheart, sister, or brother, who would care for him. His mind, when he was idle, always seemed to hurt him. And he would prefer even to toil than to be left alone. It was because, when he had to, he could labour like a mad thing, that his good conduct before the warden had allowed him to get out.

Memory, however, was no restraint to his gestures, when the mood of those around him gave such provocation to his spirit. When the doors crashed in, on the dingy hall littered with crumpled papers, Gus was one of the first to take advantage of his chance and rush inside the place. Men who had been in the vanguard were already rummaging in the drawers of massive tables, and Gus, drunk with the spectacle, and catching the hint from the voice of somebody else, did not hesitate to lead the shouting clamour made by late arrivals: "Let's burn it up! Let's burn up the whole dirty place! Burn down the whole damn shack!"

At the rear of the passage a stairway vaulted emptily to the floor above. Gus, always tempted to explore that most beyond him, darted past cursing laggards and jubilantly mounted it. He could look below him into dirty offices.

The steps were gritty with dust, slimy with the moisture of expectoration. Over a landing, a cobwebbed window, without a

307

shade, allowed the noon glare to enter starkly, without mellowing the grime. As Gus's light feet bounded to the summit, two men, stupid with trepidation, emerging in flight from some room above, met him face to face, ignored him wildly, brushed by him, and hurried the descent which would permit them to mingle, unnoticed, with their attackers. Very vividly he caught an image of their mute, alarmed eyes; and he was happy, and chuckled, and uttered a shrill ejaculation, half tremor, half merriment, while he had an intuition of the reason for their wish to reach the entering throng. They were *afraid*, afraid of *him*. His heart leaped in a thrill of malice. He could have shouted.

Yet the spacious quiet of the upper story made him, also, eager to become silent, and to tread more stealthily. He was *here!* He was *alone*. The whole dern place, it belonged to him. And his chest swelled out.

Disappointment followed. Too soon he had praised his luck. Other hasty feet were plodding on the same way. Those who had seen him run up the stairs were overtaking him. His sensations now became more familiar, for the echoes that grew behind him were like an old pursuit. After all, he was pleased to pretend to himself that the chase was hostile. The idea that he was to circumvent everybody else added savour to uncertain resolution.

There were no carpets anywhere. On tiptoe, he slipped into the first office, and found a chair overturned, ink spilled and trickling, grape-blue and mercurial, from a table with a green baize cover on which lay some open ledger books. A cold stove, with a tilted, rust-flaked pipe, sagged bulbously from a chimney-piece. On the wall hung a framed document, unintelligible, and, beside it, in ornate wood and red plush, a lithograph picture of President Lincoln, with two flags draped, cross-stick, underneath. A man's hat and coat had been left hanging on a peg.

Gus's curiosity was ripe, and sobered. How had these fellows left the building? Had they clambered down by the lightning rods on the roof next door, or was there a hidden corridor for their escape? It occurred to him that they might be secreted in some cupboard, and he glanced about him very warily. Sunshine lay on the planks of the floor, and in its gauzy bars, suspended, motes hung in still dust. Somebody that was 'gonta git' him was concealed in here. But he was crafty, he was treacherous. He would

do what those fellows downstairs had told him. He would *burn*
them out! There was a gas chandelier thrust from the peeling ceiling, yet he hoped that he could find some lamps and matches.
Somebody was coming. Somebody sensed that he was already in
the room. He was sightless, all at once, with intense happiness,
with his voluptuous recognition of some outraged privacy. He hesitated only long enough to realize himself acclaimed with shouts
of discovery, and glimpse a man's tousled head, thrust in from the
hall; then galloped on soundlessly to an adjoining room.

Through empty apartment after empty apartment, his brisk,
nervous little legs carried him in coltish delight. As one races, in
sensual wickedness, across the immaculacy of never-trodden snow,
Gus tiptoed, cantering, through all the office suites. In one, a cupboard, full-length, compelled his inquisitiveness, and he peered,
and found a scared boy secreted, militant, ready to emerge precipitately and fight.

In this encounter, Gus suffered something like disillusion. The
boy growled and moaned; but Gus, mute in deference, drew away
with speed, and darted on avoidingly, depressed that this realm
which had appeared untenanted was no more inviolate.

Perhaps a dozen, whom he called 'hoodlums,' were, by now, in
the first chamber, where, the circuit of the house made, he found
himself returned. He shouted his agreement to their yells, but for
their company he could not delay. Kerosene, kerosene! There must
be kerosene in some cranny or other, or his grand morning was
lost! Just a week before he had been hilariously present at a fire
on the Bowery, and he felt an avid hunger to reproduce the sensations then conveyed to him.

Dis is de right t'ing, too, he thought. Dey ain't got de right to
compel a lot of hard-workin' men an' women to sen' deir sons off
to war. For his own part, he might have welcomed the variety of
a soldier's lot, had the cause to be supported been any but that
of the nigger lover. He hated niggers. It was to revenge a nigger
that he had been sent to jail. Oh, Gawd, dis crowd! It was gonta
git him yet.

Gus had a hard, tight-muscled little body. Every nerve and fibre
of him seemed continually tense-screwed, like the strings of a vio-
lin about to break. He was now shaking with a kind of fevered
chill in every part of him. His throat contracted dryly. Then he

309

felt weak, and suddenly, again, saliva flowed freely in his mouth, and he spat copiously, indulging himself in the nastiness he added to the floor. But he'd burn it up, burn it up sure, now that the crowd had come, and the specious pleasures of isolation were no longer his. I'll git de coppers next time, he decided vauntingly, as he fled to a dark recess behind the stairway and crawled further, beneath protecting rafters, inside its shadow.

To his elation, he found here a rag, a heap of rags, a jug with a pungent stink that pleased him—and, in his flimsy pocket, until now forgotten, three detached matches, a trifle damp. Matches! Oh, Jesus Christ, and he'd been prayin' for matches. To burn up the conscription bureau now seemed to him requisite to ensure his own survival. Screened as he was from all observation, the clamour and clatter of the mob in which, a quarter of an hour previous, he had been a unit, took on all the character of externality which made it enemy. He was losing his head. The tales he had heard about the war down South filled his mind voluminously. He drew a match softly across a rafter, and the sulphur, sputtering peevishly, instantly went out.

He remembered. His teeth fixed on the cork of the jug. A greasy, mineral flavour was on his lips and in his nostrils. He had the jug open, satisfying him with its further amplitude of fragrance. He tilted it boldly, and could hear the *lip-lip* leakage as the oily wetness trickled soakingly. His last match! He had stolen it from a man's pocket at a saloon counter. Dis place ull go to blazes. Dat's what de government gets when it don't do right, he thought. A flame floated abruptly from beneath his hand, sprang like a gas and caught the rafter in a scorching breath. He jumped back. His heart was in his neck. Nothing could stop it. Nothing could stop it. He'd show dem dirty people down in Washington. The cranny was brilliant, and the glow embarrassed him, as he felt himself revealed to the *nothing*—his ragged overalls, his smutted face, his bare ankles, in their nudity of hair, his cracked shoes. And it was growing very hot. Sun, falling dead through a tiny gable orifice, sent a flat ray down to struggle passively with this other brightness which shimmered more livingly, more intermittently. Gawd! It was so hot in here he could hardly stand it. Pretty soon the whole house would be shot through with this glory that melted flesh and boards alike. Gus, noticing the insignificant window, wondered how the burning house would look in the noonday sun; and felt another thrill, the premonition of something rare. Then the stairs would crash, the windows crack and splinter, and the toppling walls dissolve! The stairs! With a stifled, horrible feeling that changed his mood, he realized that, cops or no cops, he must run for it. The flames were approaching him stilly, their light vapours beating now and then against the sloping roof from the shadow of which he had removed himself. No, he had to do it. He must run. He must run.

He waited no more. In the hallway, the crowd babbled. Gus edged a progress between gesticulating men. When his eyes, that were shining with triumph and a bewildered fear, met theirs, he started, and hurried.

But when he was actually on the stair, on the landing, he could contain himself no more, and shouted, "De house is on fire, folks! De house is on fire, folks!" And once more joy overweighed disaster.

There was a buzzing of blood in his ears. He knew it was necessary that he move in advance of the excitement which his deed would provoke, for he was the easy prey of numbers. Where numbers controlled him, as they were always sure to, his leadership would be taken from him, and himself reduced to something infantile which he hated, which shamed him. Packed amidst the swelling mass of persons in the lower passage, he was insanely the victim, not of the fire he had ignited, not even potentially—but of *them*, the world. He was urged by a wildness, only partially due to the odour of the burning timber, to fight them desperately. After his one cry, and the faint stir, lapsing in incredulity, which his announcement of a fire had provoked in the crowd, he was determined on gaining the street and air before he said anything further. He could not keep to his resolution. People, with their shouts of "Down with the Lincoln Government! To hell with the war!" shoved him, pressed him, squeezed him, choked him, hit each other, took the very breath from his body, would not let him out. His animal hate of them, of their power, their strength, their literal oppression, forced his discretion from him. "Fire! Fire! De house is on fire! De depot's on fire!" he screamed. To his ecstasy, he affected them. They leaned, they moved. There were people from above already howling, clumping down the stairs. Biting, wriggling, bruised but persistent, Gus, with an instinct the most invincible there, made a foot, a yard, two yards nearer to the door, the street. He felt the air—the fresh hot air—warm with sunshine, oh, so different from another heat! And he had done it. In the helter-skelter pandemonium of flight, he was the first to gain egress from that trap for the emotions. His wit was as quick as ever. With the first respiration, he recuperated. He must excuse himself, he must have a reason, he must divert all heed to such conspicuousness as he had invited.

"Fire!" he shrilled bravely. "Fire! De Conscription Depot's on fire!" To his surprise, his brazen calls left him a path which the astonishment of others cleared. Boys, men, women, in the street, began to run after him. Giddied by his obligation to provide a fresh diversion, his explanation of his conduct altered. "Burn out de niggers!" he was declaiming, his gaze madly elate, his face glorified by his painful, yet precious awareness of his revived conspicuousness. "Burn out de blacks! Burn out de blacks! De niggers tryin' to make you go to war for dem! It ain't right, folks! Teach de goverment a lesson! Burn out de niggers!" Gawd, this was killin' him, he thought, but it was worth it. "Burn up de niggers. Don't have no pity on dem niggers! Haul 'em out! Dey deserve it! Burn dem niggers up."

The crowd hooted and followed and agreed in impersonal passion.

. . . .

Kalicz worked quickly in the dusk. It was dusk outside. Here it was always dusk. The moulders were putting oil on the moulds over the moulding sand that was burnt black as a charcoaled face. Kalicz took the bellows from them and blew off the loose sand so that the casting would be perfect. But he was not one of those who made the parts, who cast the parts, who riveted the parts. He was a labourer only. His mother, when he and she had come here, on the long way, on the ship, on the waters that wash all countries, had scolded him to learn a trade; but he had never cared to learn a trade or to do any work but such as could please God and the little Christ Child Himself.

In Poland, on November 29, 1860, on the anniversary of the great revolution of thirty years back, there were political outbreaks in the churches and streets, in Warsaw and in all the principal cities of Poland, and the family of the count, the family for

312

whom Marja, the mother of Kalicz, (because he had no other name, because at about the time he was born Marja went to live at Kalicz) because the family of the count, suspected by those who made the government of the Czar and were the Czar's rulers in Poland, because the Pan and Pani were abroad to escape the trouble; and Marja went to Kalicz to live, and there had a child, born to her maybe as the son of the coachman, or maybe the child of a man in the weis who was known for his strange behaviour, and known never to have done a day's work in his life, and to be wild in his ways with women, Marja had borne a child, and, because the child had no father, had christened him Kalicz. That was what Kalicz knew. And when the Pan and Pani had left Poland forever, he and his mother had left Poland forever, but in a different ship. And this was because people who were like the count and like his mother who served the count and his family and had served them for generations, and Marja, the mother of Kalicz, worked in the folwark and did the churning and made the butter, because people who knew the count and knew Marja and Kalicz and had travelled over the greater part of the world, these people said that America was a place for people who had always been the friends of Poland, and where the count and his friends had themselves come to raise money for Poland to pay the soldiers to fight the Russians and to fight all heretics, for these reasons when the count left the majatek and the folwark and all he had, and believed he would never see Poland more, he gave Marja the money to live on there under the Russian landlords for her whole life. But she liked to wander. And when the new people had come and she did not like the new people, she told Kalicz to come with her, and she and Kalicz walked for maybe a whole year, and came to the shores of what maybe was called the Black Sea, and took a boat.

Now Kalicz walked up and down in the dark. The belts ran in the ceiling over his head, and they ran from the engine, and there were many belts turning wheels, and these wheels turned belts that turned other wheels, and this was the existence of Kalicz, the son of Marja, in the foundry, on the East River, in America where they made the war. For the war that destroyed Poland, and destroyed the folwark, and turned the property over into the hands of a Russian landlord, that war had also come to America, to Kalicz in the foundry where they were making the castings for

313

the cannon and the castings for the ships. For Marja said that
Kalicz would never be a good workman and never learn to speak
English well, and the foreman of the foundry said that Kalicz
would never learn to speak English well.

He walked along slowly. The floor was of earth, and when he
walked on it slowly nobody heard him, and nobody knew that he
was coming. He did not walk that way for any reason, but because
he had walked a great deal in churches—in the grand church at
Warsaw where he had followed the count, and in the little wooden
kosciol at the town of Kalicz from which he got his name. In that
place he had been accustomed to sit in the church door and take
alms, because the priest had given his permission, because Kalicz
was a man who thought of God and did not work. Some said that
he was crazy, or an idiot; others, that he was a wiseacre. But
Kalicz corrected them in either case. He was humble, as he told
them, and (as he did not tell them) very vain of his humility.
When the other workmen gibed at him here, he did not take
offence.

Kalicz had a white, meek face, not at all ugly. His mother, indeed, when she looked at him, called him her 'pretty boy.' He was
thirty-six years old. He always kept his eyes downcast, when he
was among strangers—and all those in this world are strangers. It
was only, as in the old days, when he had roamed the country in
search of an understanding of the ways of God, that he had looked
at the sky. He was meek, and he was lowly, but his body was very
strong; one needed it in these times of antichrist. Killing and burning, killing and burning. On the last day when the angels struggle
with the hosts of Evil it will be like that! Already, coming back
to his work at noon, Kalicz had observed the darkness on the sunshine, and his mother had said that the negro quarter of New
York was burning, that a mob of the Evil had set fire to a negro
orphanage which had two hundred little negro girls in it. Kalicz
was like the Lord God Himself. He had no name. He had no
father. And when he saw the works of destruction all around him,
he had to bear it patiently.

Kalicz walked by the core-makers, and saw the hollow cores of
baked sand mixed with oil. He walked by the bench-moulders and
saw all the dies that were used for the things that were not all
created for the devastation of the world, but were some of them

314

for ornament. He walked until he came to smoking moulds. And then he had to take up, in his soft, shapeless hands, the spread, thin handles of the ladle, and support his burden. But when the ladle was empty, as it was this moment, it had little weight.

Kalicz walked behind the man ahead who was helping him to carry the ladle to the cupola. And when he reached the cupola, and set the ladle lined with clay upon the floor, the flames from the cupola were already bursting out. Under the spout of the cupola the big ladle was set upon wooden horses. The ladle was cold now, since the last pouring, and was lined with a silver, warty skin. But the cupola was charged. When the man who had stopped the spout with the bob-stick, jumped back, pure, fiery water bubbled forth and fell whole, flickering, into the pail. The iron spattered, and the red embers, cooling—but not before they had shrivelled the leather—fell on the men's shoes, and some of the men stepped back, frowning and blaspheming; but others did not appear to notice it. Kalicz stepped back a little, because the air that came out of the cupola was glowing hot; and he saw it shining rosy on the faces of all the men, as though it came, not out of the furnace, but out of the mouth of the Devil. For the Devil, in this time of evil, was all-powerful, more powerful, until his day should come, than the Almighty.

The embers that lay on the floor were like glass fruit fallen, ripe and hot. And the iron that brimmed the pail was whole and like glass. It shone with a great light, as if the Spirit of All Things swelled, alive, in the pail. Jets came up from it, clean spray came from it, and the jets were like bloody dew. The jets were as the dew of blood that spouted from the seven wounds of Jesus Christ Our Lord, on Crucifixion Day. And the iron, like a pot of lurid, sparkling jelly, held in its flesh the radiance of the Holy Ghost. There were a hundred and fifty pounds of iron in the ladle, and the iron looked like nothing at all, just as if it were nothing at all, and no more to be caught and kept in the pail, than was the sun without. Sometimes the iron was too heavy for a man to carry; then the ladle was not a hand ladle, but a crane ladle, and the crane, that was a great thing with iron claws, came down, with a grinding sound, all the chains and ropes that worked the crane making a grinding sound. And the iron that came out of the cupola and poured into the ladle was a thousand tons. And it, too, might

315

have been as nothing. But the light that sprang from it was as if the sun lay in a casket in the middle of the foundry, and basked itself, and the men basked together, in the light of the sun, and it was as in the beginning when the sun was near and there was neither day nor night.

Kalicz seized again his end of the forked handle of the ladle, and raised it up, and staggered, though it was not so much heavy, this ladleful, as awkward to carry. And the man ahead, who had spat upon his own hands and cursed a little for comfort, also had picked up his end of the ladle, and the two walked together through the dusty gloom, Kalicz and the man, carefully, because the iron in the ladle bulged, and flickered. And the light that was to light the world lay like the heart of all things, bulging over the pail and often dripping down the pail's sides, but not so much dripping as burning over, like burning water, that spouted, that sparkled, and then grew cold. And Kalicz had the idea that fire was not so much to blame, but that fire was a material thing and had no soul until it was heated and was hot in the cupola, like the pigs of iron that were piled in the shed outside the foundry, and that fire had its good uses and its evil uses, that fire was of God, originally, and that fire here, put to these uses, was of man and of the Devil, of the Evil One, who used fire for the torment of the wicked, but that might be because fire was of God and became, when the Evil were immersed in it, painful to them.

There was a heavy, dinning sound, like wind blowing, and it never stopped, in the place where Kalicz and the man walked with the iron that was red-hot like the heart of God, so that no man could approach it or look on it unless he blinked and his eyes watered. But the heart of God was a cold thing, even to sinners it was a cold thing. And the liquid bubbling, sparkling in the pot, was like boiling ice that had caught the sun. Never had Kalicz heard of ice that was hot, or seen ice boil, but the iron in the ladle, and the iron in the reservoir, and the iron that coursed down the conduit into the mould for the casting of the cylinder, when Kalicz and the man with him emptied the ladle into the reservoir and the iron ran down into the mould for the casting of a cylinder, *that* glowed like ice, but ice in which the sun is caught, and the sun melted, and fire and ice blended, as if the sun melted all the polar regions. And perhaps it was like that in the beginning of the world the priest had talked about.

Little burning streams, that were like the coiling of serpents, that were like the rotting and decaying of the spirit into the cold death of flesh into cold iron, like bodies rotting and decaying when the souls have left them, these ran bright and dying, over the floor. And when the iron gushed down into the cold mould and seeped through it, there was the loud pop of an explosion, and the men stepped back. But the iron always made a heavy sound when it ran into the mould. Once had Kalicz seen a man killed by an explosion, and the mould burst with the gases and the man did not step back in time, and was horribly burned, and was dead, because he, Kalicz guessed, was a soul God wished to save here and now, before it was too late, and the man would not descend from earth to purgatory, and would not go straight to hell, but would ascend to God, whose heart is tender for all sinners, and sit in heaven with Him. Why did God allow the fire and the iron to be used to make cannon? Kalicz was troubled, worried. There was a reason for this and there must be a reason for all things on earth, but what? He wondered sometimes if God had sent him here, in this place, to save the soul from sin and turn the iron to some good use. Because Poland and America were all one to God, and God's children did not fight, and it was said that in America brother fought with brother. Kalicz believed that all negroes were descended from Ham, not through Abel, but through Cain, and it was because Cain had killed his brother that God had punished them. But Kalicz believed that they had suffered enough. Maybe when the war was over the negroes would come again into white faces, and the faces of those who burned the negroes and tormented all the negroes would be black as coal. For I have sinned, Kalicz said to himself, yet God tells me if I carry my sin for a thousand years, I shall be forgiven in the end. He wanted to tell all the workmen that carried all the ladies that they would be forgiven. The priest at Cracow—yes, Kalicz had been to Cracow, too —he and Marja had been everywhere , to Cracow, too, because they had often been, after the count's trouble, like the Son of Man, who had nowhere to lay his head—the priest at Cracow declared that not even the nobles would go to heaven because they gave the church so little money. But Kalicz did not believe that. He did not believe that the priest had told the truth, or was a true man of God. The priest was, maybe, a false priest, and like these here in America who had no God; and here there were always the grimy men carrying the ladles, the floor where the earth was black with the dust of the iron, the moulds smoking, the castings in the moulds smoking and covered all over with the blue flames of the gases that sprang from the crevices in the moulds, and the moulds with the castings were covered all over with blue fire like the fire of the Devil, for the fire out of the Devil's mouth is always evil and is made with phosphorus. The iron, when it came from the cupola, would be pure and glow with a white light like the light of the sun, and the sparks that jetted from the cupola would be like the rain of the stars themselves on the last day, and the lightnings that sprang from the cupola would be bright as the candles on the altars of the churches. But when the fire was poured into the castings that made the guns and the boilers and the engines of the ships to carry guns, it was turned to evil and burned blue, and there were *pop-pop* sounds all through the shed and through the foundry like the sounds the guns make, and the men's faces as they stared downward on the small moulds and upward on the big moulds were like the faces of Satan's foul imps, and the moulds and the castings burning with little flames of blue were like the devil's altars, not the altars in a church. Because all was given over to the devil. The Corliss engine that turned the wheel that turned the belts that turned the other wheels—it was fed with the fire, and the steam, and had a flaming breath, but it ran by itself. Day and night, day and night it ran and was hungry, and was always red-hot. And the air in the foundry with the castings was white with steam. The men were sometimes hidden from each other in the steam.

Kalicz's punishment was to work here where Evil reigned, for God had told Kalicz not to be a man, and never to look on woman as Adam in his original sin looked on Eve, and Kalicz was thought generally never to have come to manhood because he had no beard, and people who had known him said this, his mother, Marja, was the man, and Kalicz, her son, was not a man. And there had been a time when Kalicz had been troubled because no hair grew on his face or anywhere on his body, and he knew none of the pleasures of being a man. Marja had three hairs in three moles on her

318

chin, and she was not a man. But the priest told Kalicz he must be content as God had made him and must do God's work. But the Jewish girl had come to Cracow from Warsaw, because in Warsaw, or some other place, there was a pogrom. The people of Christ had risen up to destroy the Jews and the homes of the Jews, and the family of the Jewish girl had fled to Cracow where there was no pogrom—at least in that year there was no pogrom. And Kalicz had pitied the Jewish girl because she and her family had suffered the wrath of God, but not the compassion and forgiveness of the Son of God who forgives all who confess the True Church. But there are no Jews in the True Church. Kalicz pitied the Jewish girl, and he used to follow her. And he followed her until, one day, she was frightened. And he saw that she had not understood what he wanted, which was to tell her that in all things we are brothers, and that even among the Jews there may be Brothers in Christ. But Kalicz had an infirmity in his speech, and when he tried to talk he became confused. And when he could not tell the Jewish girl what it was necessary to tell her to bring her comfort, he ran after her, and he followed her into the Jewish quarter of the city, among the evil of her own race, and he caught at her shawl. But she believed that he had intended something different. And she cried out, and the people of her own race came and thought that Kalicz was attacking her. And he had to slink away. But he continued to want to save her. But when Kalicz told the priest, the priest thought the same as the girl, that Kalicz had seen a woman who was a Jewess and had followed her, not for the sake of her soul, but for the satisfaction of a base desire. And Kalicz was shamed, because what the priest said had seemed at the time to be true, and because Kalicz was not a man, and did not even know how to behave himself properly in the company of women. Yes, his desire for the Jewish girl, after the talk with the priest, had grown and grown, though the priest said that no Jews could be saved. For the Jews, like the Russians, who are worse than the Jews, belong to the damned who have no true religion. And Kalicz had scourged himself. But he had never forgotten the Jewish girl. And he had never quite given up the idea that even the Jewish women who, like the Russians, are often beautiful, may be saved for God and the Church. Marja could shed tears over her son, who would never grow to manhood, and Kalicz was patient with her. In America, Kalicz and Marja lived in a loft not far from the foundry, and Marja, who was small, so short that she was no taller than a child of twelve, worked in a factory for making pants. And Marja sang in America just had she had always sung in Poland. She was a little brisk woman, with a cheery face, who wore a black handkerchief, and moved about all the time and could never sit still and was always busy. Marja had the soul of a cricket that will chirp no matter where. In New York she had bought a hen and a cock, and the hen laid an egg now and then, and the cock lived in the loft, and the cock went to rest on the rafters, and the cock crowed every morning and waked up Marja and Kalicz and was better than a clock and was not a machine and cost less and was more company. Marja called the cock 'Kochanek' (dearest), and Kalicz she called 'Kochanek,' also, for she loved both. In America there were few Poles, but Marja was very gay, even when sad. In Cracow where Marja had lived a long time she had learned to dance the Krakowiak, and she could dance very spryly for an old woman. Marja knew all the dances of all the towns and the countries she had lived in, and she could dance obertases, and Cracoviennes, and the mazurka, and the hop-sa-sa, and even dance the polka like a lady. In Cracow, she had worn two earrings, one in each ear, but on the ship coming to America she had lost an earring, and now she wore only one. But she was saving to buy herself another earring. Kallicz often wondered how it was that Marja, who was never troubled by the decrees of God, and who had lived a sinful life and committed the sin of her sex long after the time of life when it is common, still seemed to be a good woman, and was never troubled by her conscience. Kalicz loved his mother and she loved him.

"Nech będzie póchwalony," Marja used to say in Poland when she met a man or a woman on the street. And the man or the woman would answer, "Na wieki wickow," which was the pious way to greet people and not as it is done in America. Marja was a woman who greeted everybody piously, but she was not pious, and did not love churches, though she was proud of her son. Kalicz could not understand, but he knew the Lord forgave her. Kalicz knew that his mother had one day been drawing water from the studnia and had met a stranger there and they had spoken to one another, and the next thing the gossips said was that Marja, besides entertaining the stranger in her own cottage on boiled potatoes, had been free with him in other ways, and the next day he had left the town. And Marja never answered anybody's questions. When they tried to question her or abuse her, she began to sing and to praise God. Kalicz could not understand how his old mother, who was grey-haired, and must be well on to fifty, had this attraction for men who were always younger, and boys like himself. Marja was not lazy. She could carry big sacks of flour, almost as heavy as the iron, and could work like a man. Maybe God then forgave her for other things, because in this world, whether it appears so or not, all is arranged justly.

Kalicz saw the last pail of swollen, glowing iron run out from the cupola, and the men were swearing and were much excited, because they said New York was burning. New York was burning up and there was rioting in the streets not six blocks away, and they told the boss they wanted to quit work. And the boss was scared. And Kalicz, who had only been two years in America and only understood a little English, knew that the boss was scared and would let the men quit work earlier than usual. And the men were saying that the rioting was about the draft, but they had nothing to do with the draft, because they were engaged in what was known as 'vital labour,' and they could not be called on the draft, because they were especially excused, because they made the guns. But Kalicz was an ordinary labourer and might be called upon the draft because he could be replaced.

Kalicz listened, but he did not say anything. He listened and trembled a little, because he was not a man to fight, and he feared death as much as the others did; even after the promises of God he feared death. The men did not wash their hands that were greasy and smelled of oil and dust, and he did not wash his hands. The belts were still running and some of the castings were still hot in the moulds, but many men, excited like children, were leaving the foundry to go home, and some were alarmed and wondered if their homes were burning, but if their homes were burning they only cursed.

Kalicz saw the last spill of myriad coals scattered on the ground when the cupola was emptied and left to cool, and he picked up his hat that was battered and put it on and he picked up his coat and hung it on his arm and he walked on with his eyes bent down on the ground as if he were looking for something. Nobody noticed him. The workmen were running to get their hats and coats and shouting to each other, and the boss said he would have to close the foundry for a few days if the rioting kept up, and he was afraid, and the foundry had to be locked up carefully, and the boss was especially afraid of fire which was already only three blocks off, and the fire engines could be heard, but the foundry was on the river and by the water and if the fire came they could put it out, and the boss was going to leave a special watchman to watch the foundry. But he did not want Kalicz to help. Kalicz was in the way.

He went out of the dim, smoking air of the foundry and it was already dark, and the fire that was burning up some negro houses was much farther off than he had imagined, but there was a glow in the sky. It was quiet around the water. There were some people in the streets and they were going home. They all seemed afraid of each other. A man passed Kalicz and looked at him, and Kalicz, shuffling along slowly, glanced up sidewise and looked at the man. And Kalicz thought both he and the man must look as if they were afraid of each other. And Kalicz was troubled. Why had man turned against man, and why had people who were brothers in the eyes of Christ begun suddenly to rob and burn and to murder?

Some workmen from his own foundry passed him in the dim street. One of them was running. The others began to run, too. And one who had reached a corner and was waiting there called, "I got to go down there where the trouble is anyhow and see what it's all about." And the others seemed to want to see, too.

Kalicz was frightened. He had to follow them, because the way they were going was the way home. He hesitated. Just beside him, only a little ahead, nearer where the men were, was a big wall like a box going up into the sky. And the big wall, that was not half finished, was flanked by lumber and a little scaffolding. Kalicz knew that this was the big grain elevator that was being built and would be like the Tower of Babel, and would go right up into the sky. They were building more and more things that would go right up into the sky and would affront God. Son, the fine women were never meant for you, Kalicz could hear his mother saying. Rolling her sleeves up, when she was at work, she would go on talking in her little raucous voice, or she would sing shrilly. But Kalicz knew that even Marja was not so happy in America as she once had been. None of them were happy in America. He was oppressed by a great sorrow for the world. Marja always told him that she was never tired, that she could do the work of ten men at least. But he had caught her crying. And he had been a bad son to her, because he had never grown to proper manhood, nor here in America had he ever done God's work properly. The work done for money and for hunger is never done for the love of Christ. Kalicz believed as long as the Powers of Evil were reigning in America he must work in the foundry. In Poland he had received alms and praised God.

The flood of light on the dusky sky stirred him. He was certain that he owed some duty to this burning world. What could it be? When he had reached New York, he had meant to do as before, and had made inquiry if there were any churches. But the people had shown him no churches, and the churches they had were not the True Church, and here all that was preached and was called the Word of God was intermingled with a foreign tongue.

Kalicz, standing by the water, hearing the water lap under the wharves, and seeing the faint huge shape of the grain elevator high above him like some heathen effigy, was troubled because already God had begun to destroy this world of Evil, and to destroy it with fire. He longed to ask God to desist. But who was Kalicz to question God? Two hundred little negro girls had been burned. Two hundred little negro virgins had been claimed by God's Word and had gone to Him in Heaven. But the foundry would be destroyed. Would the belts running and the engines turning the great wheel be destroyed, and would the cupola itself be melted, and would the steam machines that bound the souls of men be melted? Kalicz could not hate anybody. The greatest hate he felt now for the factory and the foundry was more like a thorn pricking his heart than a hate that could consume or seek revenge. Yet he was not sorry. The men who were enslaved by the engines would be freed. The men who had cursed Kalicz and had abused Kalicz and had called Kalicz a dirty Polack would be freed and they would forget how to curse. The boss would be freed. But only if the foundries that made the ammunitions and the factories that enslaved and destroyed the souls of men were destroyed.

Kalicz took off his small, round hat and turned it and turned it in his formless little hands. There was a great responsibility upon him to do something at the end of the world before it was too late. There was no joy in America. He gazed up and down the dingy street of warehouses and by the new elevator that he could just make out in the dark, and thought there was no joy in America. Men were enslaved and did not know the joy there is in believing on Jesus Christ Our Lord, and not in machinery. But the fire that was destroying the world of evil had begun in the wrong place. It should have begun here first.

There were a few dim steps leading down to the yard of the new elevator. Sidling carefully, because it was too gloomy, and too near night for him to see very well, Kalicz went down to the yard. He laid his hat on the ground—no, he picked it up and replaced it on his soft, fine black hair. He went on, walking like a blind man, and he found an armful of excelsior, some scattered wood. He took the wood and the excelsior and laid them up against the wall of the new elevator. There were two elevators, this one and one a little beyond. They had cost three hundred thousand dollars. Kalicz went on piling up planks and kindling. When he had made three nice heaps against the new wall, he took some matches from his pocket and lighted the heaps. He was cold, he was shivering. Yet he thought that was what ought to be done. If God was destroying the world and was destroying the houses and the homes of people, it was not that which should be destroyed first, but the factories and the engines, and the foundries where the engines lived and were making armament. Kalicz hoped that he would not attract God's anger, yet if he had done so, so be it. God had once been angry with His only Son, and Him had He crucified.

Kalicz was not angry with anybody. It was very quiet. The water plashed on the posts of the wharf. There were night sounds, some cries very distant; but all the workmen had gone home from the factories and nobody passed. Kalicz watched the fire burn. It crackled in the kindling, spread more lushly up the planks, and soon was towering farther, sending a reflection like a curtain of gold over the whole face of the night, so that Kalicz could not see anything at all but the fire burning. With the back of his hand he wiped his bland brow. Maybe the people to whom he tried to do good would punish him, would be angered with him for making way with that which cost so much money, which had taken so long to make, and would not understand that their real interest did not lie in pleasing those who employed them, but in pleasing Jesus Christ.

He blinked dazedly. The fire was growing bigger than he had expected. He was uneasy before it. He hoped that it would consume only that which had to be consumed, the demons and pestilential spirits—even the big wheel, that turned in the shed, half in the ceiling, and half under the earth. It never tired. Or, if it hesitated for an instant, the piston, which was as bright as a steel bone, and indicated that the wheel lived without eating, would thrust at it suddenly, and the wheel, that was as big as the sun seen when it sinks in the ocean, would begin to move again. Kalicz crossed himself. Unlike the fire that shines from heaven, and that shines fine in the cupola before the soul mixes with matter, is steam, which some say issues from mountains. All that belongs in the sky is of God, while all those forces active in the bowels of the earth are given over to the Devil. Before man learned to imprison steam he depended for everything on God's bounty and the work of his own hands. Kalicz had failed to please the Jewess, but he had never since been able to reconcile himself to God's will. He had asked for a wife. A wife, Marja said, was not to be had for the asking. Kalicz saw plainly that one thing he had sold his birthright to the factory for had been for an answer to his prayer for a wife. He had deceived God and sometimes he had deceived himself. But that was the truth. The love of Christ, so all-sufficing, had not appeared to him enough. O God, humble me, God forgive me, Kalicz thought, crossing himself. Eleven thousand black virgins have been sacrificed to the lust of the wheel and the engines. Save us from further sin and the penalties of sin.

Far out on the river a steamship moved. He saw its hollow lights and heard the shuffling whistle, while the hulk passed mysteriously. That also is of the monster. Naked like a bone of the unburied dead, a steel arm pushes, and the wheel, glad to obey, revolves its glittering eye in a halo sacrilegiously borrowed from the saints.

Hearing the steamboat, and realizing how numerous were the wheel's progeny, Kalicz panted, sweated, resumed a more diligent

325

labour to pile the wood higher, until the monolith of Babel should be lit like marble.

There was a moon rising. With its rosy hair spread out, it showed like a sign above the roofs of the warehouses. There were angels in the dark clouds rushing from upper New York over the moon's face. They spread themselves over the moon of blood, over the moon of iron. They covered the lamps in the houses of Brooklyn. The moon hung like beaten iron in the sky. The wheel turned. The wheel turned and the spokes that were fashioned of the bones of the workers turned in the wheel and flashed over New York. The moon was cold and the earth was cold.

Kalicz threw more wood on the blaze. The whited sepulchre was igniting. Flames ran along up the new boards in the scorching walls. Exorcised demons flitted high in the clouds of smoke. With the stare of a blind man, Kalicz lifted his head and gazed at the high, infinitesimal windows of the elevators, and saw the demons quaking, the demons howling, the glass shattered. The silver glass burst asunder. The eye of fire looked out from the window. Fire was purified of all its dross, and there was only water and light, where the flames shone molten and the East River was enmeshed in blood, where the East River was like brass, where the East River flowed out to the Harbour that was blood. Kalicz was a very, very humble man of God. He was scarcely mindful of the hoodlums that were collecting and were prancing about him, or of the frightened people who were pointing at him, saying, "This is the man! This is he who called himself King of the Jews!"

XI

SO they would meet at last! Edwin George, waiting in the hotel parlours, found it impossible to remain stoically seated. After all these years, and in the light of the sentimentality of their last encounter, what would the woman think of him? He restrained his emotions cautiously, and glanced about. She had always exercised on him the devilish power of making him uncertain of himself. He had to keep in mind the really cold-blooded motive which had brought him here to Cincinnati in answer to her unexpected letter to him. She had professed herself—how recklessly!—as in sympathy with the Southern cause, or at least had intimated it; and he was still puzzled as to how she had managed to get her letter to him uncensored. With the uncertain state of Tennessee, mail was often liable to surveillance from both sides. And how in the deuce had she contrived to come from Richmond to Ohio! He must find out. In the meanwhile, be wary! He did not trust her. He admitted to himself that her expressed desire to see him had flattered him. Human nature was susceptible to such suggestions. With the conceit of a 'Brother Thomas,' he might have gobbled the suggestion up. Yet look at his own existence. Edwin was fond of saying that he could not trust himself, and that made a whole-hearted credulity toward another person folly. Ironically, he meditated, his own doubtful position in the war was the result of what is called a 'noble' determination. In a belief that charity begins at home, he would stick to it. If he emerged from the war the same beggar Fredonia had married, the chances he had seized would never come again. She and her children would be reduced to penury. (He thought of them, obstinately, as 'her' children, since she had been the one most to feel the desire for parenthood. With what he had learned of the bitter hardness of existence, he could have done without.)

Pacing the Brussels carpet, Edwin strode finally to the open window, and stared. Cincinnati was very familiar to him—Fourth Street, Vine Street, Race Street; he had come here often in his tobacco dealings and knew every inch of it. But he was excited that this should be the site reserved for his encounter with Eugenia Gilbert—after eleven whole years—or more. This would be something that he never could forget. He could think of it when, obliged to swallow the critical hints of the neighbours at home who contrasted his circumspect behaviour with the headlong patriotism of his brother, he remembered this fleeting mission he had accepted from the Yankees to act as spy for them. If he succeeded in securing all the information that they wanted, Fredonia and the children would not starve to death. In the meantime, he would, while hearing Thomas boasted, be allowed the pleasure of supporting the caustic and disgruntled Melinda and all the family. Edwin threw back his curly, greying head, made a wry mouth; and sat down. The Southern people loved a ranter. He was not a ranter. Nor was he any more at one with Yankee moral piousness. He was alone, and he wanted to be alone. If charges that might be some day brought against him should exclude his virtues, he would be satisfied just the same. "But he, poor fellow, had a wife and children, two things for dying people quite bewildering." Edwin did not consider himself a Byron, but he believed, with envy, that the fellow knew a lot.

Of course 'Donie' would be the first to condemn my wildcat plans, Edwin said to himself. That, too, pleased him. Her perpetual scrupulous, petty virtuousness was a thing for which, he had decided, he always paid. "If this be true indeed, some Christians have a comfortable creed." He wished her joy of it—honestly and simply, he wished her joy of it. No, Donie could not say that he had once, ever, failed to design his affairs first of all to provide her comfort. He had not a single fault to find with her. She was a perfect wife. And, by Jove, as there was not a flaw to find in his conduct toward her, he was a perfect husband. Let those who would accuse him of contemplated dalliance with Mrs. Eugenia DeNegre Gilbert remember that. Though what an idea to imagine that this dashing woman of the world had really any notion of permitting such a contretemps! He had progressed from a drug store to the wholesale tobacco trade, no further. He was still of that world of the insignificant town of Mimms which she despised.

328

And he doubted he would ever hold any larger citizenship. He had married 'for love.' He loved Fredonia. And that, maybe, was what was slowly killing him. Donie was so trusting, so pretty (yet), so utterly worshipping of her lord and master, that who could resist? There were times when her utter reverence for his opinion, when her uninquisitive confidence in all he did, got too much for him. He could not protect her enough. She was open to the wounds of gossip, to the wounds inflicted by all the quibblers. Through her tenderness to criticism, she left him exposed. Even the fact that her parents had been Irish farmer immigrants was a ticklish topic. The Irish were under a cloud just now. But Donie should ride in the finest carriage in Mimms, and should own the finest house there. He had set his heart on it. That was what gave him the courage to 'brave' the dashing Mrs. Gilbert. He would sacrifice the lady for Fredonia any day. "Pleasure's a sin, and sin's sometimes a pleasure." It was cruel, but he could not help wishing that he, the acknowledged self-despised, and the haughty-humble Mrs. Gilbert sink in the same boat. Perhaps his lack of faith in any man had been born as the result of his observation that the Georges of Virginia were simply nobodies after they had lost their money. Then there was 'Brother Thomas'— Thomas's brag, his adventure West, his failure to live up to it.

It was a late afternoon in early autumn, and the spicy chill of the air suited Edwin's mood, as did that vista of withering leaves, up and down the street, raining their pale yellow in the fading light. There was a close quiet increasing in the room. Soon the blue ineffable would grow upon the window pane, the nigger would come with a lamp to throw its lustre there, and night would begin, a night, even in Cincinnati, such as the poets wrote about. Edwin had a dislike of those very poets, though he read them constantly. All save himself could evade the humdrum side of things. Mrs. Gilbert, no doubt, underrated him—hadn't half a notion of his 'wickedness.' That was his revenge. She had parted from him formally, politely. She was 'grateful,' because, so long ago, he had hidden her from the anti-abolition mob that wanted Gilbert and his 'nigger' wife. He ought to have looked down on her properly. Her respectability was a rag. She should have remained 'placée' in New Orleans. Gilbert had certainly been a martyr to his creed of abolition when he married such a woman. But she had wealth. Damn it, yes, she still had wealth, no doubt. Though he had heard Butler had confiscated much Louisiana property. And there was Gilbert on the Yankee side. If she had been staying in Richmond through the war, they must have broken. Treachery was the half-caste's habit. The doubt applied to her letter as well. Suppose she had brought him here on a wild-goose chase.

Here was the soft-footed nigger with the lamp—*her race!* The clock under the bell of glass, the pampas grass in the majolica vases, the red plush sofas and the tidies, the marble-topped tables and the consoles bloomed in their colours and stood in relief. He watched the nigger go with a kind of horror. *That* should keep him cool. To Edwin the hotel was almost elegant, but he doubted she would find it so. Her dissatisfaction with all that had pleased him back there in her home in Mimms had disturbed his vanity. He remembered the fashionable look of her attire. That brown brocade, that grey dress, that plaid silk in *bouton d'or,* her leghorn hat —Eugenia in an India muslin, all white—cherry-coloured slippers —the rosy light her sunshade cast upon her pale, suave face. But he was damned if he had not seen to it that Donie looked as stylish. He would go to Shillito's tomorrow and buy a length of silk for her, if his plans went right. 'Donie's' jealousy of that old memory of Mrs. Gilbert should be compensated for. Lord, to think that Donie could ever be jealous for *him!* His gratitude for her meek jealousy constituted a bitter, humble bondage. (Edwin regarded himself as a kind of yokel. That this view of him was not shared by the townspeople—apparently—was only another excuse to sneer at them—at the narrow circle which was his in Mimms— at his own life.)

If Mrs. Gilbert should try to flatter him into unwariness, she had found her match. He had refused to be victimized by the hocus-pocus of war talk. He was neutral, indifferent—and would remain indifferent. He had been born like that. And here he was on this secret service. The point of danger he would risk for the sake of Donie and the sake of further wealth for her, astonished him. It was his only assurance, so he told himself, that he was not, after all, entirely commonplace. No, his was more than ordinary villainy —if Donie, darling Donie, Donie with her damnable, canting Methodism only guessed! It was this thought which was to keep him from the clutches of 'the siren,' to *remember* that he was a villain. "They smile so when one's right, and when one's wrong they smile still more." His clenched fist beat impatiently on the arm of the sofa. Let her do her worst. His effort to be kind to her in the past had resulted in the jealous misery of an innocent person. So much for 'honourable' behaviour. She certainly would not have forgotten that he had shown a weakness for her—but let her beware.

> An *ev'y little nig* she had
> Was the *ver-y image* of *its dad,*
> Dey *heels* stuck *out fo' feet behin'*
> Like *Dan-*dy *Jim* o' *Car-o-line.*

The woman was a *nigger.* Never stop thinking of that—the woman was a nigger, servile breed even when 'educated,' and not to be trusted—not to be reckoned with as a man reckons with a person of his own race. It relieved Edwin to despise her. Impure product of the worst institution of our century, she is, and myself the renegade to the cause my Brother Thomas is blithely offering to die for, Edwin thought, trying, deliberately, to work himself up.

So they would meet at last! Eugenia had arranged every detail of the meeting according to her own plans and desires; still found the encounter hard to face. It was on this account that she delayed so long with her toilette. It was as if everything she tried to do for Geoffrey, her husband, acquired some incalculable quality that made it false. He would never be able to appreciate that it was for *him,* and not for any principle at stake that she had assumed work as an abolition spy. She was no more in love with freedom for the black race than she had been at first. If Geoffrey could only ever grasp this from her—that she did this *not* in admiration of his nigger freedom talk, but while she hated it. In the beginning of the war, he had accused her of mean self-seeking. She had been loath to lose her property in New Orleans, he had said. Actually, it was through her acceptance of his Yankee views that she was now in a position where it seemed likely she would get all her money back. What she was really willing to do for Geoffrey did not cease to her to appear as something base—not simply because the work was spying, but because the ends she sought to gain were in contradiction of her own leanings, her own heart. But there was a 'morbidness,' which she acknowledged, acquired perhaps in early

331

years, during her convent education, that made her long for sacrifice. Any man who had ever shown that he admired her, she felt free to use. And her deceit toward these was meant, also, to be a kind of offering to Geoffrey. *He* loved 'morally,' on a fine basis. His very offer to marry her, to ignore her *sang-mêlé,* the scandal of her past with Count Wittorski, had been a gesture made like that. She was now able to endure no more of obligation. What she was ready to offer in return to Geoffrey was the whole of her sense of decency toward others. *She* had no *'principles'* she would not lay aside for *him!* "Man's love is of man's life a thing apart, 'Tis woman's whole existence." Well, it was a lesson he should learn; and if cruelty lurked in her determination that he should learn it—God, God in heaven, she might be excused! She, too, was suffering, with every day of this. Her hope that she could make the 'sentimental Mr. Edwin George' her tool was' her own secret. She would keep it until she had found out whether or not her wish to maintain her former influence over him was utterly ridiculous. So far, he had more than fulfilled her anticipations. He must have run some risk to reach this side from Louisville, and for a gentleman to çome this far, after eleven years, might mean very much.

Still she delayed before the glass—though it was too dark, at last, for her to see herself properly, and she had to light a candle. She dreaded the stronger glare in the parlours. It was for the impression made upon him eleven years before that he had come. Had he realized that, all the time, she had been growing older? How she despised her position as a woman! In the most selfless step a woman took, her appearance counted; and if she had determined on the Way of the Cross she would arrive there only by her coquetry. Even by this glisten on the dresser mirror you could tell her hair was greying. She settled her hoops, picked up her handkerchief. Then she bethought herself of a little scent. Mr. George had always a vulgar liking for perfumery. If only what she had set her mind on doing did not make her in the end *hate* Geoffrey—just because she *had* to do it! Mr. George had once saved her life. She could not look too contemptibly on him. Yet, if his eyes followed her with that sensual, almost sycophantic gaze that she recalled, she knew her heart would harden. She would create an atmosphere for him deliberately; but, if he accepted her at her own face value, it would be a torture to her that she would not forgive. That was her security against pollution from her own conduct. Perhaps the saints have endured as much, she sometimes thought. She was 'branded,' at best. A woman suspected of a negress grandmother, had been born branded.

Eugenia, stepping from her room into the hall, felt slightly ill. But even the physical nausea of this retrieved contact held some horrible consolation. It was a pleasure to her to know that she did not care what happened to her, that she could be hurt, and hurt, and that Geoffrey, narrowed by fanatical beliefs, would never grasp what it was that had been done to her. She would *'die'* before she exonerated herself at Geoffrey's expense. Nothing she ever did could make him love her as she wanted to be loved. Or she did not believe in any lasting love but her own. That was why she resented her humankind so much. It was not any specific thing that she regretted—but that she had been robbed of her trust in anybody. That seemed to her to convey some right to be unscrupulous.

Edwin George sat back almost *too* easily upon the sofa, fearing that, after his first, meticulous, and gallant greeting, he might reveal something. There were very few people resident in the hotel. A man in a captain's uniform came to the door of the parlour, looked in hurriedly upon the two who were there, and withdrew casually. Edwin had been shocked to observe, on her appearance, how old *she* was. She was handsome yet, but she was haggard. It was not the face that he had come to see, was scarcely one he recognized. Still, in the old manner he remembered, she retained her elegance. If she did not look a European—and he was not quite certain what that would be—she was from the East at least. She ought to have lived in New York City, with its buses, its activity, its foreign population. He—he, as usual, was out of things. He was not like his neighbours. He wished he could tell her that. He did not feel self-complacent in merely being the big frog in the little puddle. If this woman had only known it, it was she who had first confirmed for him his suspicion that the so-called aristocracy whence he was sprung knew but a meagre part of life. Maybe it was a conviction that the party squabbles at Washington would seem grotesque to citizens of the world that had, in the beginning, prevented his enthusiasm for the war. Yet, after the shedding of so much blood by North and South, he was envious of the leaders of the rebellion. Lee had become an international figure, discussed in the newspapers in Paris and London where this Mrs. Gilbert had resided. Well—Edwin was a modest man. Though he had allowed himself some self-deception, he could not have lived up to the requirements of a popular hero. Nothing that he had done or that he would ever do would accomplish much.

"I am astonished by my own temerity, Mr. George," Mrs. Gilbert was saying. "But as much as my letter to you, after all this time, requires apology, it is such a relief to see an old friend, and to feel that our regard for one another has remained the same, despite all the changes made by the war, I can't very well regret that I wrote. I know you will want to know what I am doing here"— she lowered her voice—"and I am going to explain everything. But—that you are here—actually in Cincinnati—I suppose it is the pleasurable emotions that upset us most." She used her handkerchief.

"I think it is," said Edwin gravely. "So how do you imagine I am feeling! When I heard from you—at least I was certain you had forgiven me for saying what I did that night. As I had not risked my life for my country, I thought it was a good chance to risk the worthless thing for you. The look you gave me when you came in just now was a good deal more rewarding than official acknowledgments of bravery." He kept the bantering tone because—because he did not know what he could say to her. There would not be time this evening to interrogate her about the Richmond plans. And as shrewd as he had often called himself, how had he ever preserved such faith in his own cuteness? Lord, Lord, he had only to see her as she sat before him to realize plainly that he had no cunning! What shocked him was her worn-out look. Had he the stuff in him to make him cruel to her? Could he use this acquaintance with her ruthlessly? Or was he such a fool, such an utter, doddering fool that, as in those other days, she could make wax of him?

As Edwin gazed, and thought all this, a little harshness came into his eyes, just warmed voluptuously to the unpredicted actuality of her presence. He was beginning to pick out again that something subtle, indefinite—which he supposed he should describe

334

as 'nigger'—varying her face so that it resembled no other face—certainly no face of any woman he had ever known. Her gentle stare was as unreserved as ever, or at least, lacking in the quality of female modesty he was accustomed to. Yet he was certain that Eugenia Gilbert was not a 'frank' woman. He had never for an instant believed that she told the truth to him. He hoped, honestly, that she never would. He had enough of truth-telling, as he understood it, from Donie. Maybe he was looking for a woman with something of the 'devil' in her. He had tried hard enough to convict himself of that tantalizing devilishness.

"When you hear what I am going to ask you," Eugenia said, "perhaps you will consider the goodwill, the gratitude I always shall feel for the past"—her voice was unsteady—"a cheapened exchange." She was smiling slightly, smoothing the folds of her dress in her lap. When she glanced up, her large, dark, distrustful gaze seemed to mean something more than what she said. She was going to appeal to him in some especial way. He was sure of it. Perhaps the fact that she had pleaded—almost pleaded—for the meeting here, had some connection with a low financial state.

Edwin himself recognized his own attitude in regard to money as peculiar. Here they were together. Here was a woman who had excited his senses, and had led *him*, the most careful man in Mimms, to a gesture of sympathy, eleven years ago, which had endangered his position in the public confidence and his whole business life. He had been suspected of an alliance with the Underground Railway because of it. And he had never regretted. Not even when abuse of the story had brought it, garbled, to Donie's ears, had he regretted. But he would not lend Eugenia Gilbert one cent of his money. He would be damned if he did. Every cent that he had, every cent that he made, by fair means or foul, he dedicated to his wife. If Eugenia was decoying him because she had been pauperized by the loss of her property, his heart would grow hard. Her clothes contradicted such a supposition, however, and, as he noted them, it was as if he had escaped a menace. He would have a rich wife, but a poor mistress. Though that, too, must be regarded as a self-derisive observation, since Eugenia Gilbert had never shown any inclination to be his mistress. It showed, he thought (punishing himself) that he was Thomas's brother.

Edwin wished he could reject his intense consciousness of her, as of himself; of this still, yet public room, filled, like a shell with its enchanted sound, by reflected murmurs from the busy street. Through the open window he could see the quiet, laddered lights in mounting windows opposite. The reflection of the lamp beside them, shining in the clear blue dusk of the window pane, made a moon-shaped blot that was faintly pink. Against this deep wavering of rose, empurpled blue and silver, he could discern, in the console mirror beyond Eugenia's outline, the marble mantelshelf, the opalescent bubble that enclosed the clock, the grey, spouting mist of the pampas grass, the bulky red of chairs and carpet, the hospital white of the lace-trimmed antimacassars. Though he had often been in this room, in this unlivable hotel before, the place took on exciting unfamiliarness.

Without means by which he could deceive himself with the idea he became a different being, intrigue grew grotesque.

Edwin straightened himself, abandoning his ostentatious, ill-bred lolling, leaned forward, and touched her arm. "Look here Mrs. Gilbert—Eugenia—I called you that once, and I don't believe that it is taking advantage of you that I want to do it again—I believe we have earned the privilege, in each other's company, and in circumstances entirely apart, to a little frank speaking—to some plainer talk somewhere else. Don't go into any details here—please. I am prepared to stay in Cincinnati several days—I have arranged for that. Will you meet me tomorrow somewhere else? Will you trust me to make some arrangement whereby we can see each other and talk more unrestrainedly, more comfortably—say at some private house? I have been in the state when I would do anything for you. Maybe I am not far from that now. But to repay me for the capacity you have to make me lose my head— don't let's try to go into anything too deeply in a hotel parlour— don't let's try tonight."

Edwin knew that his suggestion had two motives: one was to assure a further and more private interview with her; the other was to delay decisions. He had not half surmised, before she stood, in the flesh, before him, what this was going to be worth to him. There was satisfaction in self-discovery. If he embroiled her in his plans—yes, she aroused in him an unexpected brutality. He could envisage—or was this lurid melodrama?—*both* in betrayal of their country, *both* detected, *both* being hauled before a tri-

336

bunal, *both* being shot. (Of course he was 'absurd,' as usual. Why should it ever come to that?)

Eugenia lifted eyes tearful to affect him—but with tears of pity for herself. "Why—why, I think it would be a relief to me too," she said, "if we could talk more privately."

A moment previous, she had 'writhed' in anticipation of what she had to do. Now she caught his look with its full import: that coarse, handsome, incipiently distinguished face flushed with ardour in observing her; those grey eyes moistened by an admiration they could not conceal, an admiration which she strove to find repellent. Her heart was a painful ice, and she felt herself the stone woman in whom she liked to believe.

Not to prolong this evening—since there would be tomorrow— she rose, impetuous, but concealing her tremors, and held out her hand. No, if it must be that she would have a tête-à-tête with him again (and what had she expected), she was obliged, in order to preserve her self-control, to leave him now.

Edwin, astonished by the brevity of the visit, accepted this intimation of dismissal disappointedly. He, too, rising quickly, con-fronted her with hurt self-love. Calculation revived. It could be the more guileful since, if she was callous to hurting him, he would not have any scruples in appealing to every weakness he thought her to possess. There was too much of shock and readjustment in these few minutes. But of tomorrow, of the interview which he could foresee, and for which he would have the whole night, in his new knowledge of her, to prepare—let her beware.

She held out her hand. "I should have explained to you—there are other matters—when I have a chance to talk more openly you will understand my behaviour this evening. I am so dreadfully up-set about something. But you are quite right that we can discuss nothing here." She was very quick to catch the chill in his glance, and, with an instinct to defend herself against it, she laid her free hand where he kept the one he had politely captured. But she had no sooner offered this encouragement than, as she perceived hastily, he melted. Her distaste for him was so strong that it was a voluptuousness. He had now accepted eagerly all her cold, limp fingers in the clinging, hardy pressure of his own. Reckless, he forgave her.

Hours before, Kildare had been able to make out Moccasin
Bend, its curve sewn with a thread of glass over the plain that
seemed such miles below. That was when, wriggling through brush
and cedar and mountain laurel, he had arrived with his comrades
at the edge of the shelf on which the Craven house was set. When
Geary had been ordered across the creek beneath the bluffs, the
move had been executed in this same white darkness, that had
lifted later, for an hour only, when the sun came out. Forty or
fifty of the Confederate pickets had been captured instantly. Kildare continued to have the sensation of dreaming, as he recalled
the moment in which, out of the moist, grassy silence, he and a
picket had come face to face, startled out of all warlike impulses
into a common friendly astonishment. Kildare's temper was, naturally, so very mild, that the discovery that he could behave ruthlessly under vital circumstances inspired in him a modest conceit.

If the straight advance of the right up the mountain had not
been interrupted, the attack might have been nearly bloodless and
the captures wholesale. But a few scattered pickets must have
glimpsed Cruft and his men prematurely. Unexpected firing had
halted Cruft's attempt to get over the water. The Confederates,
though they were evidently half blinded by the fog, had been
forewarned, and had descended and taken possession of the rifle-
pits and breastworks about the bridge. Kildare conjectured that
they had hidden, also, along the railway embankment, for the
Cruft contingent had certainly had a hard time. The artillery fire,
which Kildare yet seemed to hear, as it had boomed soddenly
against the damp mountain, surely had cut the rebs off from retreat. Yet, if Geary had not shown the wits to swing a new bridge
higher up, the 'rumpus' might still be going on.

This obliging absence of a sun was giving the boys a chance
to get ahead again, though the sparkling wilderness was somewhat
frightening now that through the confusion of the mist so many
companies had become separated. Kildare was the kind of man who
had no courage behind his own initiative. But he was obstinately
willing to go a long way in support of some one in authority.
In years of peace, his habit was to make, constantly, ambitious

338

plans for his own future. When the hour came to execute a positive gesture, however, an unspoken conviction as to his own incompetence compelled him to delay, with some self-sacrificing excuse, the fulfilment of his aggressive plotting. He had renounced his early sweetheart, because, in order to marry her, he would have been obliged to connive with her family to shield from justice her younger brother, then involved with rustlers in extensive cattle-thieving. That he had been the victim of his own scrupulous caution, confirmed his opinion that his motives were superior to those of other men. He did not condemn and did not betray. All he asked for himself was the privacy in which to do as he thought 'right.' It was the same in the army. He had wriggled, 'belly-buster,' into the tall grass, had risen almost in the enclosure from which the Confederate fire had proceeded. Who would ever be the wiser for it? He had a frank loathing, almost a terror, of those more eloquent about their exploits, who 'talked too much.' He was not going to be 'slapped on the back' by the others who had taken no risk whatever. Only when, by accident, the eye of some commander caught his own, Kildare, feeling emotional, would think, *He's* not a man for bragging, either. Maybe he noticed me.

The whole plateau was cleared. Walthall's men had been mostly taken. It was deadly still. Kildare, pleasantly aggrieved by his obligations as a sharpshooter, hesitated, for an instant, on his hands and knees, and tried to reconnoitre. It was growing cold enough to 'freeze your gizzard,' but nobody would ever get a word from *him* about what he was going through.

A rock fell with a deep silk *pa-lash,* below him. He had lost the footsteps of companions. This loneliness of the rain, stinging him with its white nettles, harmoniously conveyed to him a pathetic sense of the isolated part he was playing—had played, all his life. Nobody had any idea of what he was 'like.' It was certainly true that the men who 'shouldered the load' most uncomplainingly were unappreciated. If it could ever be 'dragged' from him—the horror, the 'plain creeps' that possessed him when—but he would not dwell on *that* on this 'Godforsaken evening'—he was obliged to remember the dead, the wounded he had seen, the 'boys' afflicted with ineradicable injuries, the lacerated and misshapen. I suppose some have the idea that I've been through nothing worth talking about, he mused nervously, uneasy, as he crawled on, trembling a

339

little. Autumn had come here sure enough. This was no 'sunny South,' in these —— blank mountains. He resented the erroneous information he had had of them. Thank God, he was not superstitious like the rebs and darkies. Occasionally, the cumulus summit of a tree sprang, with branches unfurled, out of the fog below him. He was a 'reasonable' man. It was with a view to physical security only that he prayed for delay in the bitter advance of that unseen night.

Now he had to lay his fumbling palm flat on the stones, squat, and feel his path stealthily, gauging, with a pendent leg and tensely pointing boot, the distance he would be obliged to drop to find another footing. It might be four o'clock in the afternoon. It might be after five. The vaporous filaments, skimming tree and bush, had the appearance of a white tide rolling steadily and obliteratingly upon such world as was left him. It was growing dusk already. A trunk of some kind stemmed from space, and he sensed the corrosions of bark lovingly. A flapping drizzle spattered his cheek and wrist. A neutral glow, that must proceed from sky, was fading. His eyelashes freckled, with the drops they shed, even this last dim vision. He longed to hear firing: the moist *pffle* of close shot; the lava flood of cannonading—if that could but flow like a firm river under this creeping, lightless universe. Jesus, who could ever believe that Chattanooga *was* somewhere yonder, and that the river, in its dark glass, crawled on through the nothing making Moccasin Loop!

Kildare, his prominent eyes bulging palely to the flitter of invisible dews, longed to shout. Such cries seeking recognition were foolhardy and had been forbidden. He had been the last to leave Geary's ledge. His memory of it was of a space warmed by human invaders. His companions might have gone to Jericho for all he could discern as he teetered above a conjectural declivity.

Something rattled. Something stirred. The twilight was ochreish, brown, soiled. It absorbed the last faint intimations of the chill and torpid vegetation. Green was sucked away. Kildare moved his stiff, inquiring fingers anxiously through the bruised grass, and realized that he had just saved himself from annihilation. Shaken a little, he stretched at length, resting hip and elbow in a hollow of the precious earth. Sidewise, he could dangle his ankle brokenly. What was under?

340

He was beginning to *feel* the night. Helpless to resist its encroachments, his gaze widened coldly, opening to admit its sightlessness. His pupils distended, and were wells of vacancy expanded to a brain in which meditation was featureless. The icy air swept stilly his revealed eyeballs. He could look and look, but as if into his own mind, where there was, annoyingly, nothing at all. He pressed on his fist and pushed himself to a sitting posture. If he turned this way—if he leaned. He could be certain only of the absence of any underneathness. He rolled to his reverse side. He waved his arm. The damp came downily between his stretched, disappointed fingers. Once more he gave himself the comfort of confined abandon, and 'belly-stretched.' On the contracted remainder of a once substantial land, his grip fierce among the slithering twigs of a too pliant bush, he was as if about to dive into the foreverdark of mists that he only knew were floating there because he remembered them.

Doubling, and half rising to his knees, he drew back. Then he collected himself and crouched, waiting. He had arrived here, headlong. The shelf on which he lay was against such a height of straight rock wall that he believed, in this obscurity, he could never remount. Self-righteousness was, in Kildare, as strong as reserve. This was a rational moment for exceeding orders. Let them courtmartial him if they liked. And he could see himself in the situation of a man unjustly persecuted. A shuddering indignation lent him defiance. His chest rattled with a quick, choked breath. Then he called, boldly, "Hal-loo-oo! Ow-oo! Hallo!" the last shortly. "Gimme a shout so I can git your situation."

Supposing a shot should answer. But on a night like this, in a 'fix' like this, companionship was worth any price. The aloofness which Kildare had achieved, suddenly became the supreme penance which his sterling character had paid for virtue. He had always distrusted friendliness, anyway. Ned Macey had been 'making up' to Kildare lately, and then had revealed an assumption that a reciprocation of expansiveness included loans of 'pay.' Kildare didn't owe a cent of money and never had. Most of what he got, he sent home to his parents. They had always been 'pretty good' to him, and he supposed that he owed them something for having 'brought' him 'up.' Then, they would leave him the farm and the general store. Anybody who was willing to endure self-denial, as

341

Kildare did—sometimes not even allowing himself a 'chaw' of tobacco—could keep out of debt. Some men were 'easy come and easy go.' They were generous enough with what they didn't own, but if a fellow was in real difficulties he would find that the only thing he could depend on was his own resourcefulness. Kildare hoped that folks would keep their blabbing tongues out of his affairs, and he would do the same for them. He 'kept the law.' Nobody 'up home' could ever say a thing against him. For that, he could do his 'duty.' He was harsh, in satisfied disgruntlement, with those who in any manner affronted accepted standards. If nobody came to his rescue now, it was what you could expect.

"*Hal-lo-oh!*" he shouted once more, in a hoarse, passionate voice, that had all at once swelled large and loud in his stringy throat: and he followed, with foreordained depression, the thick vibrations of the silence, the sounds wandering, abruptly non-existent while there was a *throt-throt* trickle of slow-dripping water in some spot concealed.

"*Hal-lo-oh!*" A quick reply, in a tone Kildare had never before heard, was as if ejected from the night, and on the very ledge beside him. He had torturingly demanded this word, but when it came he felt as if the black, rapid fog retaliated upon him for his weakness. His pulse beat like a flame in his neck. His blood pounded his insensate eyeballs. There was an instant of rapture, after which his whole being contracted to defy the snares of the attraction. By his call, he had revealed nakedly a necessity which he could never admit. He waited, stealthy as a hunter.

"Hal-loo?" sang the voice again, tentative, yet hearty. Kildare could no longer repress temptation. "Hal-low," he yelled, casting habits aside. And added, to prevent reflection, "Where are you? Who's there? Give us a hand down here. I'm under this derned rock."

Twigs snapped, and he imagined some one furtive like an Indian crawling toward him in the blotted grass. No hand was laid on his.

"I've got a hurt leg," the man above explained, after the pause of hesitation. "I'm on top of your place, I guess, but I can swing over a little ways and maybe manage to give you a pull up if you can reach me."

Kildare did not enquire further who the man might be, did not wish to know. He simply renounced his struggle against accepting the comfort of assistance. If he did not move soon, the intangible evening would shrivel away altogether, and leave him a mote in a universe the largeness of which killed him. He crept carefully toward the face of the rock and turned his blank stare overhead. His hand, ardent to discern substantiality, found the stony surface and examined it, entreating it. He sought for the encouragement of even one small crevice. "Can you reach me?" his friend questioned, making a superfluous effort to be heard. To Kildare the voice was as if in his ear.

Some warm, refuted feeling roused in his aching body. A desire for reassuring contact compelled him sensually toward the required exertion. Not able to ignore the wet snoring of the wind, the far-off noises, of trees, or water, or either—faint sounds that grew, with their indecipherable components, and died away again —he yearned embarrassedly toward the voice, loved it. He caught at a jut of rock, but his clutch nipped it free, and, for a second, he reeled toward those impressions that giddied him—the plains below Lookout, the imperceptible pace of waters deeper, in the darkness, than any current.

"No good," Kildare said, after a moment. Tears of disappointment were tepid on his freezing cheek. "I don't know how I ever got down here. There's not a blamed thing sticking out."

The man was shuffling about in the obscurity, making clumsy movements which Kildare could not distinguish. He said, "Well, we gotta do better'n this. I'm in bad shape, too, and I need your company like hell."

Something tinkled against the boulder. "Can you git a holt on the tail o' this rifle?"

The massive rippling of the wind seemed to grow heavier, sweeping an increasing vacuity. The two crags, one over the other, were a pinnacle, not to the Tennessee valley, but to spaces and oceans across which Kildare had never travelled, of which he had never dreamed. The fluting in his ears was like the shudder he had been told of, felt by a sailor on a masthead. He lay on the wind. The rifle, tap-tapping on the wall, was like a blind man's stick, and came lower. "I got a hell of a hold up here. You can try it once. Just make a jump at that."

Kildare heeded. He was vain of physical prowess, and a sense of the 'silliness' of his position remained with his trepidation. He had the rifle butt. He sprang like a cat—or a man on a gallows. His lean arms leaped, wooden, from the sockets of his shoulders. For an instant, he was a limp pendulum, stupidly rhythmic, lashing the night with slow strokes. The veins in his neck crowded and he could feel them bulge. Though his eyes had been blank from the beginning, he was now conscious of an added defeat to perception, and all will to see was pressed from his pupils by the labour of his blood. Plunging along the slimed stone, he at last held it with his clattering, shod feet, and his hands were able to mount ponderously along the rain-greased barrel. Kildare anticipated, though hope held him, the unannounced slackening which would tell him that he and the rifle and the stranger on the upper ledge were to descend altogether in one helter-skelter to that ravine conceived of as bottomless. What a muscle sustained him! His own hanging weight must be less than supported by the unknown who had not uttered so much as a grunt.

Kildare's breast was sawed by the grating edges of the stone. He clasped some object—an arm—and could feel the yielding throb of life in it. His collar was seized. He embraced his formless captor. The rifle bumped away—nowhere—and the two men rested, dishevelled, breathing in each other's faces, among the broken bushes. Neither could talk. A second time, Kildare, out of sheer weakness, had the impulse to cry 'like a brat.' The night seemed gentler. It was as if they left the wind behind. Feebly, almost adoringly, Kildare investigated the spent body relaxed against his own. "Well? We done it." "Yes, sir—we did. You done me a good turn, sure enough. Must have taken it out of you. I ain't light." Kildare, recovering somewhat, said this pridefully. "Well, you ain't no three-hundred pounder, or you wouldn't be here." "No. I got more muscle than fat, thank Gawd." "It took some husky tuggin', partner, and now you're up here, maybe you can help *me*. The Yanks done somepin' to my leg would 'a' pleased 'em if they knowed it." Kildare's sumptuously relaxed mind awoke, with a start, to craft. There were pistols in his belt. It seemed providential. Dumbly protesting his unconcern, he shifted his position. He could sit up. He judged that the stranger, also, had resumed a sitting posture.

"What regiment did you git lost from?" Kildare demanded at

last. The silence had been tormentingly lengthy. He dared not let himself credit the other with too perfect innocence.

" 'Pears like I don't belong to nobody any more," the man answered. "I was under Walthall once upon a time up yonder at Craven's house. Who turned *you* out in the cold?"

The jovial intonation disgusted Kildare. He felt ill. Why did the fellow try to save him if he was a rebel! Kildare could not discount the subtle hint of betrayal within betrayal. He did me a good turn. That's why he's careless. He thinks, because he yanked me up here off that shelf, he's got the best of me. Letting your feelings have the 'upper hand' was just 'plain, chicken-livered,' a means of evading the painful things duty bade you do.

The fog was lifting. The wind tore by stiffly with a thinner sound. Kildare dreaded the moment when he must see plainly the burly huddle, now scarcely an apparition, before him. A dim glamour, as of a conflagration, scored, with black, crystalline marks, the peaks of the hills against a vaguely reappearing sky. Faint flickers dappled Kildare's pistol. The suffering he was enduring , in indecision, appeared to him totally unjust. All his life he had been placed 'in the wrong.' He never seemed able to do anything which would make his merit recognized. He tried to be angry. He *must* be angry. He must think of himself. That it *was* himself, if it was not the other fellow, Kildare had not a doubt. Desperately, watching eyes where he felt there must be eyes, yet discerning as yet no more than the form of a bared head, he sprang to his feet. "You're my prisoner. Don't budge. I saw you first. It's a pity, but you can't help it." Deliberately, he thrust forward his weapon so it stood its measure between him and the man's chest.

"What the devil!" The stranger climbed to his feet. Kildare, anticipating a dangerous quarrel, was yet relieved that his own foresight had not yielded humiliatingly to sentiment. "No, you don't. You don't touch me and you don't come a step nearer." But the man had sunk again to the ground. "Jesus! Ouch! Don't git excited. You beat heck. God, that gimme a twinge. Well, you know your business best, but I can't run away from you—that's certain."

Kildare *hated* the man. You don't suppose it's easy for *me*, he reflected belligerently. But he would not say it. "Git up then—if

345

you can walk. I think I can find the way back from here," he made himself announce gruffly. He was so 'shaky' that he was terrified of possible observation.

The stranger groaned a little. "I'm doin' my best, but you gotta gimme a hand. I must 'a' been here an hour before you chanced along."

Was this, too, to be suspected as treachery? Kildare's head ached. He began to doubt his boast. Could he really retrace the path?

A warm, calloused paw rested on his sleeve. He bore the burden, but kept his pistol cocked and ready. They stumbled together for a little distance. Again the wind and cold and the blurred damp spread over their faces. If we can't git nowhere, we got to spend the night out here together, Kildare thought. And you'd be 'scared' to rest a minute with a fellow who knew you for his enemy. Why did he tell me? Why the hell did he ever tell me? Why didn't he keep his damned mouth shut? Aware of some grotesqueness which eluded his enunciation, Kildare resented it that he had to 'hold on' to the 'bully,' and that he weighed so much.

III

"Yes, suh, when Cunnel Shaw come marchin' ahaid uv us down de broades' way uv Noo Yawk City, dem white hoodlums dey set up sech a racket 'at we couldn' pass. Dere was our white officeh at de front uv de procession an' us behin', an' we hed to be turned back from doin' our duty 'cause we was niggahs. So we come all de way to Chawlston by boat."

"Tell us again, Silas, about your attempt to take Fort Wagner and how Colonel Shaw was thrown, dead, into the ditch behind that parapet."

Silas had spoken loudly, unctuously, like an orator. He would be tempted to do so when *they* were listening, but he always suspected them of furtive laughter; and, in a quiet such as this, since he could not see their faces, he would be beside himself. He was stupid. He knew it. For ten years, he had striven to live in some manner that would impress them, would compel them to recognize what he had always felt, his equality with them. Enlisted in the first regiment of negro volunteers sent to action, he had 'fooled'

346

himself for a little while as to his accomplishment. Runaway that he was, he had thought, he was going 'home' again. Oddly, though he sailed for Charleston in the Federal army, his first elation when arrived on shipboard had come from the sense he had of returning, after long sojourning in a foreign country, to his own land. "How Ah look?" he would ask companions. The query expressed both doubt and hope. Could Mr. Barks, the overseer who had once lashed him, regard contemptuously a man in uniform?

Before quitting New York, Silas had heard, with stolid rapture, stories of the complete disorganization of the Confederate soldiery. He had heard that the rebs were growing tired of war, that they could not be made to fight. He prayed, wordlessly, for the courage that he boasted. When Mr. Barks had whipped him, in the tobacco field, ten years before, Silas with a rage and a jealousy against his own wife consuming him, had found himself unable to strike, in return, one relieving blow. Why didn' Ah hit dat white man, he would wonder. Why didn' Ah has de speerit to kill dat fellow? He took mah peace, like he took mah 'oman. He made mah cabin dirty an' uncomfawtable wid dat yallah baby in it.

And this was the end. Silas realized that no simple interest in his narratives prompted his bored and wretched fellow prisoners to interrogate him. Lewd in their curiosity—though he did not call it so—they gibed, they encouraged, but to listen to his 'bragging,' and make game of him.

Ah los' mah eyes. Fumbling about in his perpetual dark, he pondered his situation incredulously, especially after they had baited him, had tempted him to take some step that he could not control, had laid traps for him, had placed a bucket of filth in his path for the sport of seeing him upset.

The invitation to discourse was a lure against which he struggled vainly. "What did you do when the bomb exploded, Silas?" they would demand of him. He tried to explain things tritely, but, sensing by their intonations a familiar note of ridicule, he would elaborate. Dey don' think nothin' uv me, he mused hotly. Dey reckons dat 'cause Ah come down heah an' got caught by dese rebels, dat's de end uv me.

He *had* to convince them. He *had* to tell them the whole story backward, of how he had *almost* killed that overseer, Mr. Barks, and of how he had been educated—'edicated right, too, 'cause she

347

think a heap uv me'—by that Boston lady.

Certain incidents, he suppressed. Yet the darkness was so impenetrable and his will to resist their contempt so strong, that, at times, he could believe entirely his own invention—'hit mus' be like dat.'

"Where'bouts is we now?" For long he had wished to ask it. When he was in torment, anticipating some exposure of absurdity, he kept a heavy silence. Then, he could smell, mingled with the filthy odours of the unwashed humans, the scent that was like a pang of past humiliation. The prisoners were herded together in a tobacco barn. He was sure of it.

"You're not really blind, Silas. The idea you've got that you are going blind is the result of voodoo worship. You don't pray enough."

He heeded the voice, close to him, out of nowhere, and his lips grew tight. There was a white taint in the very air, mingling with the snuffy exhalations from the old tobacco. Ah gone round an' round de mulberry bush, he meditated, an' come back to dis.

Mr. Barks, so many years gone, had imprisoned Silas in a drying-shed.

"Look here, nigger, don't you sit there sulkin' when I tell you to move. If it wasn't for the mess we all got in through niggers I'd be home tonight."

So it *was* night. Timidly, with this awful hatred like a load on his chest, Silas desired such knowledge. It was night. It was night. They were all in night. When would morning dawn?

"Did you ever figure it out that we could 'a' been exchanged long ago, if it wasn't for you? The government up home offered to exchange us fair, but the folks down here say they won't exchange no niggers. It's raised the question up at Washin'ton. That's why we don't get out."

"Well, leave him alone, Harry. He's got punished enough for bein' a nigger anyhow. Why they ever enlisted 'em in the army I can't make out."

Silas attended in a torment. His mind would go out, searching, just to find one sense. None of the other prisoners wanted him to touch them. They kept away from him. Once or twice he had made a violent gesture, hurled a shoe, a stick, a battered frying-pan at somebody. Pity was as unwelcome to him as chagrin. "Don't play

348

tricks on the poor devil," an unknown would admonish. He despised their pity.

He feared them. He could never find the proper hours for sleep. Now and then he dozed, and their chatter teased him. Or he woke in some silent hour and caught their breathing, the oppressive respirations of the drowsing, when he could not rest.

> Run, nigger, run, de patter-roller ull git you,
> Run, nigger, run, an' hit's *a'most day!*

His anguished concern for the approach of day would widen his still eyes for hours. Then he would hump in his corner, secretive, hoping they might never discover what it was he awaited. At times he seemed to feel a chill, a glister on his lashes. His dense pupils seemed to him to widen; and encompassed, finally, to his horror, only more extended dark.

Silas would get up and walk slowly around the board walls. The place was rotting. He found an empty knot-hole in an upright plank, and poked his finger out. His finger, it appeared to him, witnessed the wind, passing chillily out of doors.

"What are you doin', you dad-blamed fool? Quit walkin' into us!"

Silas was humiliated, like a little boy, because, inadvertently, he had trodden ponderously upon an outstretched foot. He was not modest, but now, embarrassed when he was obliged to ease himself, he wanted privacy. The prisoners said the barn was like a privy, and it smelled like that.

Silas scratched fleas and vermin. In the beginning, the necessity to scratch annoyed him. Often when his mind ached with its no-thought, and he tired of his two imaginings, of hatred and light, he could absorb himself, with turgid sense-abandon, in a 'scratchin' fit.' His wit became sly. Where he had once overturned another mug of soup by accident, he began to do so purposely.

Melancholy was a cloud more dissoluble than dark. I run up Nawth. Dat Boston 'oman done her bes' faw me. Ah got my free-dom. What had happened afterward? What had been the failure of his courage? Why had his determination to become a Federal soldier brought derision on him?

In his most lucid intervals, when he accepted his sightless lot as a temporary state, the veil between himself and his unsympathetic comrades fell gratefully. Don' *nothin'* mattah. On the filthy floor, he lay on his back, flaunting to all his carelessness toward nauseating substances. It had been 'wrong' to join the regiment. Fighting was 'wrong.' White folks same as black folks, he would argue. All is sinnahs. None uv dis is right.

He did not recall his dead mammy, but his deserted wife's addiction to piety was impressively remembered. Fanny she got lots outen Bible talk, he meditated. It was not the injunctions to follow Jesus that affected him, but a memory of the history of the devil's power, which he enlarged. His energy wasted by the calm, hallucinatory violence of his fancy, he would groan, twitch, forget that there were strangers in the prison with him, and shift his posture like a labouring dreamer. When de wicked is wasted, an' de debbil git dem folks up in Noo Yawk dat stop to mock at me, hit gwinta be all right.

The arrival of food compelled him from his slumbers. "These ain't victuals. It's all I can do to get this slop down, Harry." "Yeh, Jeb, but this —— is hot. It suits me better than that there cornpone like a hunk of mouldy rock with all them weevils in it."

Silas would take anything that was given him. He ate in enormous mouthfuls, and the mercy of taste moved him to softness, nearly to tears. He resented the men who derided the condition of the food. Food was equivalent, in its effects, to the accretion of a great faith. He could go on. He was stolid. He sat there comfortably.

Once he overheard a discussion between a prisoner and a guard: "Look here, Mr. Soldier, you Confederates ain't treating your prisoners right. How long you gonta keep us penned up like sheep in this rotten old barn? The walls are so shaky and the timbers so creaky, it's only a kindness to you that we don't get out." "I wouldn't advise you to try." "Well, we ain't likely to. But tell us the truth now, how long do you expect to keep us penned up in here? Seems to me, if your government's workin' an' ours is workin',' we ought to 'a' been exchanged long ago. If you don't hurry up and send us where they got food to eat, we're gonta starve to death. Then, you'll have all your trouble for nothin'. Is it a fact that it's because you fellows won't exchange niggers that we're held back? And why do you pack us in here with niggers anyhow? That ain't white man's treatment of a white man. That ain't gentlemanly." "Don't see why *you* should complain," said the guard.

There was one other negro in the room, somebody named 'Chancey Harris.' Silas was secretly glad of Chancey Harris's presence, but despised him for a truckler, and they seldom spoke.

"Why y'all reckon dey's all set ag'inst us?" Chancey had whispered. " 'Cause dey hearts is black like mah skin is black," Silas had replied.

Did he believe it? There was some riddle. He was in a Confederate camp, but with Yankee prisoners. His very soul hurt him. He was ashamed of an aspiration that had undone him. *Hits because Ah nevah killed dat white man, Barks, dat laid his hand on me.*

Silas was slow, yet his intelligence was too vivid for endurance. Chancey liked to please. When the men were cold, shivering, he would rise, with guileless bravado, clap his hands, and sing. Silas refused to admire. Only, later, when all was hushed, and the sleepers, in the cold wide air, under the rotting roof, dreamed faintly aloud, familiar words revived in his mind with some meaning which he had never before gauged, could not now gauge articulately, but which tormented him with longings and with indications of mysterious things.

> If y'all gits dere befo' Ah do,
> Mos' done lingerin' heah,
> Look out faw me, Ah's comin', too,
> Mos' done lingerin' heah.

The sound of a song grew thin and fine with anxiety. He was mos' done lingerin'. He could bear no more. Then he had to tame himself to patience. For-what, for-what, for-what, *what-faw, what-faw, what-faw,* beat his accelerated pulse. He *could* not end it. There was no way. And he feared.

The prisoners shot 'craps.' Silas, unable to join them, heard the dice rattle, heard the minute thuds of dice on the floor, heard fingers popped softly. Lucky, lucky, lucky. Some folks were lucky. Some won money. Silas attended and thought of wild times. *Ah ain' no sheep an' cow faw to be herded in heah. Ah ain' no fat-stomached preachah faw to lie heah gittin' mah muscles sof'. Ah ain' no mammy's baby.*

351

Recollections came of women who had admired him. Aftah Fanny, an' all her good-faw-nothin'ness, Ah' ain' givin' 'omans no qua'tah, he meditated, largely urging himself to be brutal, but with tremors like the ague going over his body. (What was he to a woman!)

Finally he had to burst forth. He had found his way to the centre of the barn where an upright supported old rafters. He liked to go there, mute and certain, stumbling on obstructions, and, cursing as he went, shake the wooden post under the long beam. One day he gripped it and shouted, "*Ah* ain' no weaklin'! Next time one uv y'all gits too free, tellin' me what Ah should an' should not do, Ah shake de barn on you!"

"What's the matter with that crazy nigger? Look here, Jeb, give him a kick in the shins. I'll be dad-blamed if I'm gonta be shut up in this place with a lunatic. Them men outside have got to take him out."

Afterward, Chancey crept to Silas and pleaded: "What faw does y'all go on like dat faw, Silas? Dey ain' much exaggerationin' when dat may say y'all shake de barn on us. Dey git mad at y'all in heah, an' dey put y'all back to work—breakin' roads faw de sojers aw breakin' stones aw somepin. Be quiet, now, an' let us fellahs alone. Dis is de wah, an' y'all *cain't* change it. Dey's wuss things 'an bein' a prisonah. Soonah aw latah dey gwinta has us changed back up Nawth. Keep yo' gumption 'bout y'all, man."

By the querulous anxiety in Chancey's voice, it was to be known that he was dubious for himself and feared Silas.

Grimly, Silas sulked. Chancey had no eternity to live through.

Silas, as well, was furtively timid of the consequences he invited. Chancey whispered, "Don' y'all go swingin' onto dat upright, Silas. Ah ain' lyin' an' Ah sho' kin tell you dat beam ovah top is rotten to bustin'. *Don'* y'all go an' ac' like no crazy man. Don' pull de roof on us."

Silas bided hours. When he dared, he stumbled over to the beam, maliciously.

It was deep-rooted in the floor of packed earth, and only vibrated slightly to the sudden wrench he gave it. But he would 'scare 'em.'

Then he decided that people were 'mumblin' about him. Enemies with voices lived in the offal, the broken bones, the drying excrement in the barn's corners.

Occasionally Silas was allowed out of doors. Strong as he was, cold withered his courage. During the whole time 'up Nawth' he he had felt an animistic awe for the cold. He was in a drafty shed. Winter was approaching. He recognized it by something metallic in the wind, by the dry leaves that rattled when he was in the yard. The prisoners talked of eating rats. Silas thought about eating the warm meat of a rat, and was savage, because outdone by even these invisibles. When he reclined, and supposed night in the added torpor, the added unfriendliness of dark so little relieved by sound, he caught the grating of a rat in the planks behind his head.

His lids pressed tensely on his misery and tried to make a moon without. The grass looked old, with the whitened grey of a willow clump he had somewhere seen. A shadow had dived and flung itself, in a black stupor, with face sunk forward in the water—no, in the weeds, the grass. The sky was dim like an old platter on 'Ol' Mistis' table. In this tarnish, stars, smoky and pointed, burst, like the gold thorns hammered in a brassy crown. Like pebbles of blood, the stars rolled in the dingied heavens. A lamp, broad in the boughs of a tree, stared with a blazing face, as from a blackened window. The meadow was alive with livid 'ha'nts,' with light.

White folks' ways, Silas thought inertly. He rolled, shifted his position, and covered his head with the old sacking that lay on him, his legs and body bare.

Down in the 'bottom' land, the frogs were croaking. It was after rain. Drearily the frogs, with their *knee-deep, knee-deep,* scraped the quiet—bleating in a void. The great torn wings of the trees brushed over some river. He *knew* that river. It was at that place he had run away from Fanny, had last heard her voice. The twisting, dappled shadows were tormenting him.

Out of his dream Silas sat up. Clumsily subdued, he rose to his feet, feeling against the wall.

Somebody coughed. He hesitated. Did they sleep? Was it night? Was he free—free as night?

There was a groan. "Harry, you got the itch, too?"

Silas moved forward, in his brain, a point of attention guiding him.

"Where in tarnation you goin', you fool?" Then sharply, with a frightened intonation, "Who's *that!*"

Silas said nothing at all.

"Who's that stirrin' about? Wisht we had somethin' to light a dip with. What's that? Who's that stirrin' around again?"

Silas, staggering fiercely upon humped bodies of men drawn together for warmth, felt his ankle, in its bursting shoe, grasped and held. He freed himself wildly.

"It's that blind nigger. I don't trust that nigger. What the hell's *he* prowlin' 'round for!"

Silas stood free among them and felt the upright. His wide hands clasped it boldly, solid in the vagueness. Praying for stealth, he leaned on the post. Fiercely he remembered what Chancey had told him of the rotten beams above. The rotten rafters creaked. High in the air, in the dark, a looseness responded to his sound-less shaking. Silas laid his arms around the post. He laid himself on it, and his muscles swelled his arms. Mas' Edwin says y'all de pow'fulest niggah he evah knowed. Mas' Edwin say y'all kin lift whole hogshaid an' tote hit on yo' back. Silas leaned and swayed and could feel the dimness shuddering.

The post was like a root that had stabbed him. It was the spear of temptation in his bowels.

"Make a snatch at it, Tim. See what it is. Feel around for my shoes an' give 'em to me. We got to find out what this is. There's somethin' walkin' round."

Silas, hearing a stirring and a scrambling, exulted. But he waited for the widening of pain brought by a lantern. That would bereave him of obscurity, his natural medium.

He had arrived at this, vague. Still refusing thought, his desire grew strong and almost definite. What would these folks try to do to him if he let hell loose? He pushed. The upright yet resisted, but it had moved decoyingly, loose in its socket. The desire was very powerful now. It was a lust for hell, but a lust, too, to defeat the stinging glitter of the lantern, and to bring the *furthest* night. A gilt barb from an exquisite wasp had stung his murky eye. He leaned, with all his soul upon the movement, pushed again.

"What the hell, Harry! What's that —— —— nigger doin'!"

Exclamations clamoured in his ears, but he refused the sounds, since they belonged to light. His mischievousness was desperate. It was very sweet. The timber lurched.

Out of the nowhere from whence came all provocation, fell a

354

smacking blow on Silas's shoulder. He had the courage to ignore it. The timber, reeling, like a loosed tooth in its socket, but mammoth, swung him, since he would not let it go, obliquely on with it. There was a crackling, tattered noise. The small deluge came first: sticks, twigs, hay and dried tobacco, bits of shingle from the roof. The dribble of débris scattered on his brow. Then, falling as though he fell a thousand miles in blackness, the beam heaved slumbrously and he went down with it. There was a bashing clatter of tumbling boards. "Fire! Run for it, damn you. He's smashed the lantern."

There were screeches, scuffling, shot. Raucously, somebody, hurt, howled. Men swore loudly. There were groans again. The dark was a litter of pandemonium. There were screams, excitement, bustle of a fight, a searing odor as if planks were scorched. Silas, pinioned, let the noises pass above him. He heard them ebbing from the remote acres of the day. Revenge in him was not replete, but it was *night,* and this satisfied him most. The white men, too, seemed in a kind of night. He reared, as his back bowed faintly under the rigid weight. Then he was satisfied to sink again. The stink of rapid burning and the tingling echoes of the shot seemed a part of night.

XII

*B*RUMPETY-*brump-brump-brump;* the wheels of the train were clicking a blurred cannonade. The car rushed over a trestle-work where the track was rough. In the special coach, some of the benches had been removed to give space to a table. It was filled with flowers. On Grant's brain, the hurrahs which had dinned his ears at the last station continued to impress themselves in memory with a bruising vehemence. Lieutenant General of all the Union forces and Commander of the Army of the Potomac! Secretly, he was astonished by the degree of the enthusiasm shown for him. The terrible responsibility to appear as befitted a public character seemed to increase. His clenched fist, resting on the arm of the seat, squeezed itself tighter, as he spoke casually to his attendants. Out of shyness, his eyes pale in an abstruse expression due to helpless inward concentration, he was a little arrogant.

Blump-a, Blump-a, thudded the carriage, like a rocking horse. Excitement had flushed his cheeks and forehead, and, though the month was March, and the train none too warm, he furtively mopped from his brow growing beads of sweat.

The clouds, watery with an amber evening, rolled on the low sky to which the windows beside him approached steadily without any diminishing of distance Fruit bloom in a meadow cast a snowy explosion after the clotting smoke of the engine. A hill sagged forever on a bleak horizon. In soggy pastures, a cow turned her head and gave a look that was never finished.

Grant was determined to permit nobody to believe him humble. They'll find that I am as firm as steel, he told himself. America is the one country in the world in which a man is rewarded without relation to his antecedents. Yet he would not be overgrateful to the public, either. I guess I owe as little to influence as a man ever did.

Of course there was Lincoln's support to acknowledge—in a

way. (And 'Julia' was already insisting that 'Ulysses' would step, some day, into Mr. Lincoln's shoes.) Grant was fearful of such premature consideration and glanced about him reconnoitringly. Uneasily, he recalled 'friends.' I'm standing alone, as I always have, he thought, but it wouldn't do me any credit to ignore their loyalty.

What he insisted to himself constantly was that nobody could 'shake' him. A certain blandness recent in the attitude of his associates he distrusted heartily. Still—it was a fine thing, the way officers and men alike had 'stood up' for him. He could not tolerate 'sentimental talk.' The results of the war would be 'good' for everybody. The country, and particularly the 'hidebound South,' needed a 'shaking up.' People were as 'obstinate as mules' in resenting the consequences of a situation their own folly had precipitated. In these days, you could feel real hatred only for the 'grumblers,' who insisted on 'rubbing everybody's nose' in their own squalid view of life. But the old Puritans did not live in vain. They left a 'mighty fine stock.'

Another fruit-tree hurled, from its black-wet boughs, a stiff projection of rain-crushed, white rosettes. Grant tried to listen to the conversation beside him, but watched after the passing tree abstractedly, with a certain longing. He required some 'freedom,' something of what he had enjoyed as a 'romantic' boy. When he 'came to think of it,' he had kept his 'nose to the grindstone' ever since he and Julia were married. And if it had not been for this public crisis, he'd be 'drudging' yet. Say the Southerners don't like me, he reflected, laboriously bitter; but I'll show those F.F.V.'s down in Virginia what mother wit can do.

The sky dusked sombrely. Little glintings of the evening sheared over the fields after the progressing train. Grant was restive under melancholy. There was a slithering and a squeaking under the body of the car. Ominously, it seemed, the engine was slowing down. A few houses reared themselves in a clearing, and a mild dazzle shot from naked lamps in uncurtained rooms. There was a garden by the roadbed. In it, cabbages were vast ruffles of coarse foliage, swelled with white, hard arteries. And there were crushed little moss-green heaps of lettuce leaf.

Grant could observe some commonplace detail out of doors, and feel, all at once, giddy in the contrast between it and the expen-

357

sive artificiality of his surroundings. It irked him to restrain himself from taking another toddy. He would have moods in which his conviction that the public could not do without him urged him to boldness, even to superfluous rudenesses. Again it was as though he had been trapped. The hint of a divergence between some one's opinion of him and his own idea of himself was enough to throw him into a panic. He wondered what this cost, what that cost. And I don't give a damn, he would think. If he could keep people comfortably to what they termed 'the military jargon,' he was 'on safe ground,' at ease. The mystery of what was expected of him unnerved him. He was smoking cigars wastefully. The taste of a good cigar reassured of something, some simple, pleasurable thing common to all minds, 'even through this hocus-pocus.'

"Well, General," his aide remarked soothingly, "I suppose you must prepare yourself to encounter the usual reception committee."

"Huh? Yes? Well, it's nice of them. Satisfies me that there is the same sound Americanism all over the country."

He stood up clumsily. The train slurred its motion past a platform. Already he could glimpse craning faces, interjected in staccato sequence just beyond the glass. An enormous banner flooded its ripples over the staid crowd. In the fumes from cigars, in the bunched brightness from the bouquets of hothouse roses, the hyacinths, satiny and violet-pink, on the table, the sprays of dogwood from the South, the car rolled its treasure to rest. The gentlemen accompanying Grant all looked heated, amiably stirred, and peeped discreetly over his shoulders for glimpses of the exterior scene.

Grant, too, hearing their chuckles of good-humour, feeling his aide martialing them all for appearance, and as if he were a diva in an opera, a prima donna, could not withstand the contagion of a great event. I'll surprise my critics by showing them what a sound conservative I am, he thought, arguing against some intimation in his own state which might indicate that he could yield to luxury.

For a moment, as the train became emptily quiet, and the party inside listened to its own voices, the blather of conversation on the platform had no definite words. But there was cheering. A band began to play. Waves of brassy sound eddied through the door. Colonel Jay had gone out in advance and came hurrying back. The stop here was very brief. General Grant must appear at once. The reception committee had begun to board the coach. He could not keep them out.

Grant hastened stiffly and was met by a trainman, also concerned, but elated by his immediate association with greatness. "This way, General. Hurry up, General. At the back platform, General." The trainman could not repeat with sufficient frequency the word of flattering address.

Grant arrived just in time, and Colonel Jay was obliged to request the descent to the station of strangers who, with the growing boldness of approbation, tried to push themselves into the carriage. The night was now complete. Jets of illumination sprang from lanterns on the station front. Amidst the crowd were torchbearers, with ruddy, fuming brands. "HURRAH FOR VICKSBURG," read a white cloth banner marked with straggling letters.

Grant watched. For an instant, he felt more the night and the woods behind the depot, than the jostling, pushing press of humans in the lurid, unreal light. "Ladies and gentlemen—my patriotic friends." Without preamble, he began to speak. The band, in its glimmer of horns and trombones, heard him, and sawed off its tune. "On behalf of myself and my fine men—on behalf of the Army of the Potomac which I have the honour to command, I thank you, and on behalf of all the forces for which I am responsible, I thank you for your hearty greeting tonight."

His throat constricted. Tears came to his lids, and he fought against an oppressive sense of solemnity which he attributed to his 'sacred' regard for duty.

Below him was a girl in a brown plush mantle and a bonnet with yellow feathers. She carried in her arms other sprays of the dogwood which bloomed behind him in the car. The glow from the torches gave her fresh face an added rosy colour, and she was gazing upward with lips parted and with eyes innocently avid for his notice. Grant saw the flowers brush her mouth. Simultaneously, he was conscious of the perfumed, crowded interior he had just quitted, of the flavour of the cigar he had cast aside, still lingering on his tongue, of the redolence of something easeful which he could not name, which emanated, it seemed, from the girl's fine clothing, the jumble of the massed humans, the recklessness of the luxury in which he had made this journey.

359

"Ladies and gentlemen, I am not a sentimentalist. Our finest ideals are involved in the decisions of our statesmen in the matters which led to this war. But once a war is a fact, it is a practical thing to deal with. The soldier who enlists for his country must shoulder his burden in the fighting in the same way that a man, if he is a farmer, or a saddler, or a storekeeper, takes up his obligation to complete the day's work. He must give the best that is in him, and all that is in him, every day and all day, and every minute and hour of the time—and without letting his imagination run too freely on the reward he is to earn. Our soldiers fight in this fashion, like plain men who must do their duty in a crisis to the best of their ability. We would like to stop the war if we could. We *will* stop the war, but only by a final victory. For this purpose we need more and more men. In six months, God willing, the country will be restored to peace, and brothers, sons, husbands and sweethearts returned to their loved ones. But this somewhat optimistic prognostication of the time limit required of us in thinking of the welfare of the country first, and our own pleasure afterward, is based on my belief and hope that we have by no means come to the end of our enthusiasm for doing right. There are thousands of young men all up and down the route this journey to Washington has taken me who, for some personal reason or another, or through inexact information as to the needs of our forces in the field, have not yet offered themselves to their country. I will consider that this trip has assumed the nature of a real pilgrimage if I can feel the few words I am able to speak in passing have encouraged more and more of our young men to take the step that will never be regretted. Americans are fighters. They have spent their energies and shed their blood in the cause of common welfare more generously than have the people of any other nation. Because of my providential success at Vicksburg, and the *fine* achievements of our forces at Gettysburg, some folks assume that there are plenty of soldiers for the Union forces already. With the stuff that is in us, and the spirit I am proud to say my men and every man fighting under Union colours has shown, I dare to say we will win the war no matter what happens, and if we don't have another bit of help. But the larger our reserves, the greater our resources in both trained men, armament

360

and money and other supplies at our command, the more quickly our victory will come, and in the end it will be a victory bought at a cheaper price than if we were obliged to continue with inadequate support from our friends at home. I appreciate with humility, realizing that hardly any man could be entirely worthy of so great a trust, the sacred responsibility Mr. Lincoln has lately laid on my shoulders. That I am not cast down by feeling myself under the weight of duties difficult for any man to execute successfully. is because I *know* that I can perform them with the loyal assistance of every American whose heart responds to the nation's needs. This does not seem to me the time to speak about our enemies. They are misguided, as will be seen later even by them. Their day of reckoning is in Other Hands than ours. Enough, before I leave you, that I give you President Lincoln's message, which, in nobler words than I can form, expresses my own sentiments—as gallant as our boys have shown themselves, their fine behaviour would not have given us our present advantage over our disorganized enemy, if the people at home were not equally full of American *pluck*, equally full of that fervour for right and of that tireless industry which forced American civilization to grow like a flower from the Red Man's wilderness. Mr. Lincoln depends on you, and on all of us, to justify before the world the American idea of doing everything thoroughly, without disgruntled comment, and, in the case of every individual, to the best of his ability. When the victory is claimed, I am certain that not a leaf of our laurels but will bloom the greener as the result of the endeavours of some of you here tonight. I am not an orator. I—I— Ladies and gentlemen, I thank you."

The train was crawling softly. Grant's last words dimmed amidst the smatter of applauding palms. *Huzzas* broke above the grinding of the carriage. All of the faces, radiant, unanimously, with a single excitement, began, abruptly, to drop away. Petals of dogwood whirled in his face, and one bloom hung, like an immaculate butterfly, upon his chest. The band was a stream of discordance poured after him from the squat, retreating station. Streets sailed in broken curves. Some farmers' wagons rested, by one lantern's glow, under a gloomy courthouse porch. First the houses stalked by in lines, one after another, wedges with brilliantly orificed fronts. The last, with stunned light diminishing in one isolated window, dwindled on darkness, and the fresh odour of a field just ploughed, but invisible.

"Better come inside and draw your breath before the next one, General."

Grant hesitated, for some reason weakly timid of reabsorption in the comfort and brilliance of the car. Dense space pressed coldly on his brow. He could see no more than the bulk of indecipherable woods, and a thinner nothing on which beads of stars flashed occasionally.

An immense silence, felt, in the long waves of invisible earth, above the full intonations of the train, gave him respite from a futile social harassment; but did not invite him. When a man has struggled with the elemental once, and knows what the struggle costs, he's in no hurry—unless he's 'crazy'—to renew the effort.

He pushed on the glassed door. It yielded snugly. The flowers, the respectful faces, the thick, imprisoned heat, beat away the tide of vacant air and chill blackness. Grant, unwillingly aware that the night *did* linger, beyond the riding glow that held him, sighed relievedly and thought, Yes. I know what the security of a nation's worth.

II

For a long time, there had been only noises. All the marching feet beat the road with such vivid monotony that wakefulness became itself like some awful prolongation of sleep. When sun, invisible, burst on the grey inertia of dawn, the bayonets sprang first to life. Earl felt a superstitious shock in recognizing again the backs, heads and shoulders of the companions he knew so well. The unaltering character of that which sight revived frightened him. The bayonets were like steely brambles. They were a strange, leafless growth of the morning. When the Rapidan could be distinguished, an abandoned house, in which Grant had his headquarters, looked 'lost,' and seemed to retain, behind the fragile tinsel of the lantern burning in the window, some clumsy secret. Earl could not express it.

Earl Mabray, in one of Burnside's corps, was marching to join forces with the Army of the Potomac, to assist in resisting an attack which, it was anticipated, would be made by Lee, in the

362

'Wilderness.' Earl was short, bow-legged, anaemic, with a putty, pimply face, and dull, alarmed, always protruding eyes. He was a Southerner 'bawn an' raised.' He knew this neighbourhood all too thoroughly. He had once camped near here for several weeks, while on a hunting and fishing expedition. Disaster had impressed the details of that time upon his memory. As he tramped on heavily, he inclined his head secretively, spat sidewise, for a sign of 'luck,' and tried to forget.

Oblivion was not easy. Here might be the place where he and Frank Turnley had made a bonfire. Here—just a little farther on —where they had been 'shooting craps' that night.

Clouds were a ghastly blue chalk, roving quietly, in towers, above a world like evening. The thudding boots slowed from the quick time they had kept up, intermittently, all through the night. Earl succumbed, as to an omen, to the slackened pace. He was obliged to walk along this road so slowly there was opportunity to 'think.'

(*The jury at the Orange Court House said it happened accidentally. The jury at the Orange Court House said it happened accidentally.*) A contracting line of men, lengthening as it shrank in breadth, began, in the sultriness of intimated light, to descend to the river. All the morning smelled of water. It was here—or near here— that Earl and Frank Turnley had begun that fight.

An oily iridescence was shaken from the trees, the weeds, the grasses by the path, with the still notes of black foliage twittering. The weeds, rushing, massed, sprang up with the protesting white of flowers. Greenness shone in the black enamel of the oaks. Voices eddied, with shrill motions, over the remaining dark. The sky broke open redly.

Several horses had been halted by the infantry and were standing deep in the river, drinking. Earl, as he plodded docilely, observed with satisfaction their inundated muzzles, seeping bubbles, their steeped ankles. He wished that he was in the cavalry. He had joined the army to escape perpetual uneasiness, terror of isolation. He was not much happier now than he had been in the days when he had 'hoed' corn for his 'pappy' and his 'ma' had nagged at him. He tried to refute this admission of failure by reminding himself that he had, at last, 'plenty to eat.' He was fond of eating; fond also, but a little wary, of 'gettin' drunk.' Sensations of immediate, bodily comfort were alone dependable. Earl had worshipped Chance since the 'accident' which had caused him to lose his head, in a fit of craven anger, and shoot Frank Turnley. If 'luck' would hold, Earl, before the war was over, was going to make some money, with a turn of the dice. He had never been able to 'git hold of money no other way.' Certainly, he had never felt that an increase of riches was the fruit of labour. It shamed him to be told that he was superstitious, 'like the niggers.' He 'went by signs.' They were many and mysterious, but he kept them to himself. The 'trouble' with the fellows in the army was that they thought they 'knowed too much.'

When a group sat around the camp fire 'yarnin',' Earl would listen silently, and with obscure attention, to the *words* they said. Chewing a straw reflectively, he always answered firmly, either 'Yes' or 'No' to any question asked him. The 'sense' of the conversation, through his furtive wonder at the 'edjewcated' phrase, always evaded him. And when the soldiers were through with 'jawin',' his mind was exhausted. He was respectful of their travels, their information, their sophistication, but his true preoccupations were in himself. Shrugging humbly, he threw off awesome impressions. His intelligence resumed its stealthy function. If y'all was to put on yo' lef' shoe fust, all you has to do is to take it off, walk round a tree three times, an' begin on yo' right foot ag'in, jes' like nothin' happened. You kin even git round seein' the moon th'ough a tree branch, ef you know the right chawm. Was this correct? He longed to consult the opinions of another mind, but did not dare. He was accustomed to spitting carefully, at various intervals along his route, directing his saliva toward some erratically selected bush or plant. If I kin plug that burdock in that fence, he'd think, I won't git hurt tonight.

If any one spied him in the exercise of these peculiar rites, he would set up, at once, an elaborate whistle, push his cap askew, arrange his stride more jauntily, or stare up grimly at the sky as though he saw a bird in it.

"Gimme a chaw o' terbacker, Earl? Why, certainly, I thought you chawed terbacker all the time, you got to spit so much."

Earl had ignored this covert gibe. Yes, suh, edjewcation is a fine thing, Earl would remark to himself, as, recognizing the apparent eccentricity of his behaviour, he became suddenly inwardly

364

embarrassed. I got through a heap of learnin' myself, his medita-tion would continue, as before an audience. Nothin' like reasonin', neither—an' when y'all know how to read an' write an' figure—it ull do anything faw you.

Earl pursued his comrades through some underbrush, and found himself again near the river, and on a level with the horses. He caught the warm stable smell of their bodies. The sun was rising higher. It was growing hot. Earl was always noting odours. Some-times his comparative perceptions were very acute and surprising. When he realized that his 'nose' for scents astonished others, he kept his observations to himself. He had stepped on something—some kind of root. He and Frank—such years before—had trodden on that very sort of root—that berry—had wondered why it smelled like that. Earl's heart leaped, now, in his chest. *Wilder-ness.* When Lee fit Hooker down here months ago they called it 'Wilderness.' Sounds jes' like somethin' in the Bible. Earl glanced ostentatiously behind him. When we all took that fork out yondah, did we take the left aw right? If y'all take the lef' fawk when you oughta take the right, it ull bring bad luck. He hummed. His voice caught in his throat. That was a horseshoe down there on the bank. If you saw a horseshoe and didn't hang it up something would happen. If you hit a man—not exactly on purpose—but you want to hit him, and you 'lay' him out, is that your fault or not? Can you hold yourself responsible for that man's death when the jury at Orange Court House discharges you— *accidentally?*

There are places in the *wilderness* where oaks and scrubs grow so close together you can't see a yard before you. It's not like ordinary fightin' in the army where you don't hate anybody in particular. (There was a reb gimme a swig of water one day when mah ol' water bottle ran dry.)

Earl stumbled on in the strange chill rising from the river's brink; while the sun beat, with the heat of different zones, upon his neck. He felt fretful. His mind *would* go on ferreting out old associations. Seemed he could 'tell' a path 'jes' like an Injun,' when there was nothing to mark it. (Frank Turnley could bully the devil.)

I'm gonta die today, Earl said to himself unexpectedly. He was as cold as if he were frozen. The weather made no difference at all. Excitedly, he turned about, zigzagged a little, abstractedly, and the man behind him told him to 'hustle.' You can finish all the rebs you want to when it's orders, Earl reflected, but it 'tain't alike. They don't call it *that* then. Oh, Christ, why did I have to come back here! I never could 'a' done it if I'd meant to, Frank. Honest, I couldn't.

The corporal yelled, and Earl ran on swiftly, obediently, his pale, prominent eyes timidly attentive, timidly searching this significant earth that was cluttered with last year's leaves. A knot tightened in his chest. If he was going to be killed he didn't seem to care any more. Only he wished *they* would hurry. Evasion scarcely occurred to him. In the army it was 'like everywhere else.' Things happened to you and 'no sense' in them at all. And that word—*wilderness*—always seemed to him to *mean* something. He had the same feeling about words of which he didn't know the use, words that 'edjewcated' people talked. It's a sign—aw somethin'—faw Frank an' me. He was held, in this wretched, fatal curiosity about himself, as in a spell. *Wilderness*. Words. All different. All seeming to be 'concerned' with something or other. And no 'sense' to anything. This tortured him, voluptuously—*wil-der-ness*.

III

There was Meade at last. Grant jerked briskly on the bit of his horse and the animal became, instantly, restlessly still. His staff waiting with him, the quiet was broken by the icy jingle of harness, a sound agreeable in the warm May dawn. A rasp of impatient hoofs was to be heard, a cough, the murmur of low conversation; and faint shouts and the concerted thud of descending arms echoed from company after company as these came to a halt along the woods behind.

Impatiently, Grant accepted Meade's stiff, neat salute. "Meade, I'm glad you're on hand again. I understand Lee's troops are already on the plank road from Orange."

"I believe we are ready for any contingency, General, but it would be of great advantage to us if we could find any point for observation that would give us even a bare idea of the lay of the land in this immediate neighbourhood—especially in the direction from which attack is anticipated." Meade spoke very precisely.

With his meticulous demeanour, his slightly frowning, near-sighted gaze, and a 'womanishness,' uncontradicted by his full brown beard, his appearance had its invariable effect in making Grant feel heady, perversely 'rough-and-ready,' the crude man of battle. Grant knew well, however, that Meade's good sense was not to be 'sneezed at.' It had required some time for the self-conscious commander-in-chief to realize that Meade's exaggerated formality—his attitude of extreme respect—concealed no satire or covert derision. Behind that ladylike front, Meade was colder and not more timid than Grant himself. Yet Grant would have been happier with a little rudeness to be bluffly snubbed. Meade could be stern. In dealing with offensive subordinates, his rather light-timbered voice could vibrate adamantness. Then his whole body, slight and tall, with its 'stoop of learning,' gained an added suggestion of the uncompromising. He was menacing in a way that Grant recognized and could not hope to equal. When Grant wished to discomfort an 'upstart,' he would, coarsely humorous, 'sick' Meade on the fellow, as you 'sick a pup.' The 'lady' kept an iron hand in the velvet gauntlet, Grant was musing, and was pleased to observe that the gauntlet, literally a very worn one, was not so clean today.

With the masklike countenances of men utterly incomprehensible to one another, they rode on a few paces. "We are going to walk up in those pines where the land is higher and see if we can place the details indicated on our map," Grant announced suddenly; stopped his mount, and, throwing a clumsy leg over the horse's side, descended to the ground. Meade, more agilely, and in good form, also dismounted. Two soldiers who were standing near rushed sycophantically to secure the bridles. "We'll rejoin you gentlemen in a minute," Grant called back to his attendant party; and he and Meade strode off.

Meade, though thin, was the taller; his gestures wooden, his neck, viewed from the rear, lean, the polished leather of his unworn boots immaculate. Grant was brisk, rakish, his way of speech composed, laconic; but, beneath the bravado of a superior, he displayed, subtly and involuntarily, the constant symptoms of one ill at ease. His resistance to all heat and excitement was too obviously pronounced. The crudity of his vigour admitted, now and then, even to Meade's unfanciful observation, the intermittent doubt of self which will must contradict.

They had vanished only briefly into the forest when walking became difficult. The luminous sunshine was sucked away in the dry shade cast by interlacing boughs wrapped together in the horny knots of 'bamboo vine.' Virginia creeper raddled with its colour the paddy foliage of long ago with which the earth was littered. Grape roots hung in thick, shredding loops, dead as rope, thrown in rich entanglement from bush to branch, and to last clutches higher up where heaven was indicated by a cracked opening in the close leaves, and a whitish twinkle. It was by the occasional intervention of the pines that the two officers were permitted to stand upright. Then the gloom became more severe, the darker green more funereal, but they could see the clouds again.

Grant, stumbling, lost his dignity a little, and swore good-naturedly. Meade, with less visual assurance, picked a guarded route, extricated himself from briars, hesitated to kick a small log out of the path, and did not smile at all. Grant, growing impatient, took a clasp-knife from his pocket, and began to hack about him recklessly.

They were emerging from the worst confinement. Tree trunks, inclining at gnarled angles, sank below them. They could see a bit of country: the tops of more and more woods like this, and a ravine, parting the slope toward a little valley, casting further riddles of interlaced shadow. Roads opened, for a moment, signs that could be read. But the dustied, empty thoroughfares, perused at this distance, would vanish, after a yard or so, in the stealthy, rigid, encroaching oaks and pines. For *their* purposes, the lanes, wandering into view suddenly, and with the look of leading to other worlds, went nowhere, and were the thresholds to solitudes disturbed only by jack-rabbits. A turkey buzzard, just above them, was beating broad revolutions of its wings, and was intent on some object beside them which they did not notice. Its vast pinions dingied as it wheeled, its deliberate flight followed, on the sun-stripped open, by one small, languid clot of shade, wavering with its waverings, and gliding, at last, transparently, through the enchanted, glistered oak branches. The pines wheezed faintly, but there was no wind. And that opposing armies were hidden here and and soon to meet did not seem credible.

Meade was fiddling harassedly with the riding whip that he had brought with him. He was squinting, and minute, painful wrinkles

368

gathered, in worried pleating, the flesh between his eyebrows. Grant was flushed, his blue eyes introspectively brilliant. A quick impetuousness had come into his manner. He, too, was uneasy, but with an uneasiness which stimulated him. "Lee ought to be out there somewhere, but he might as well be buried," Grant remarked; and a tone of confidence obscured the pessimism of his comment. "Sedgwick and Warren have their troops in position already. As they are on the pike and Lee is advancing on the plank road from Orange, I've ordered Hancock to hurry forward his troops and place them on the left of Getty. Warren can engage the enemy as soon as he meets it. I believe that is clear to you already—or the most of it—but I want to know what your suggestions are."

"Then you are forcing the fighting?" Meade continued, defensively, to examine the landscape. But his voice sounded absent, bemused, strained; and Grant, obstinately provoking disagreement, sensed the objection which Meade would not state.

"That's always been my policy, and I've never had any particular reason for going back on it." Grant was curt, watched his alarmed subordinate almost elatedly. If Meade should become argumentative, Grant would 'take him down a peg.' But 'the devil' of these situations was Meade's capacity for interminable reserves. Did Meade think Grant was going to sacrifice to 'petty' caution what he had gained *now*, after the ovation tendered him in Washington! A man would be a poor defender of his country who 'pulled out of close quarters' merely because they *were* 'close quarters.' Yet Grant had experienced these same emotions previously— back in St. Louis, when he was so in debt, and the real estate firm just about to go to pieces. He would prefer it that the war should go on forever, if he had to choose between the present and repetition of that 'hell' long past. Almost—

He fidgeted stoutly. The vapid sunlight spread undeviatingly about them on a world too vague, too bright, and too passive to invite man's invasion. For an instant, the clear, grey dreamed-of shadow of the turkey buzzard, as it swung by, sank into their eyes, and it was as if they were gazing at one another through the dim uncertainty of the mind itself.

"*Wilderness,*" Meade enunciated slowly, constraining himself as he started to the rustle of some twisting, obscure leaf.

Grant glanced at him cautiously, but made no echo of the ejaculation. In the glare overhead, trees swished softly. Then the delicate tapping of breeze-stirred vegetation again subsided. All the life which remained, after the uncertain passage of a wave of heated and laconic air, might have been focused in the searing vapour that was sun. "Yes," Grant admitted doubtfully, an edge of hostility in his voice, "they've given it a good name. About the worst place to engage cavalry that I ever saw." He turned hastily, not relinquishing his determination to make Meade speak, but anxious to escape this perfect privacy. Damn the place! But a hundred and sixty thousand against—at the most—eighty thousand could not be called a risk. Of course, when things were in motion, Meade would take as many chances as anybody—if you wanted to call intelligently calculated opposition 'chance.'

The sunny silence moved again, though with a motion not visible, and the long, eddying sounds, beginning in the ticking scrub oaks, flowed, with the roar of dry seas, through the mildly agitated pines, whispering, as with the muted voice which Grant rejected, in his hardy unimaginativeness—*wil-der-ness.*

IV

There was a plunging of sound as of the lunging of some heavy object into space. Wild, like a wild mare plunging in the roof of bright clouds, was the *plonk-a, plonk-a, plonk-a* of thick, released noise. Returning like a tide, its echoes breaking on a distant strand, the *roo-oo-roo-roomble* re-exploded itself more faintly. A travelling gloom of smoke hazed, as with tissuey verdigris, the unpenetrated scrub oaks. The smoke was an ever more translucent flood, until—*broom, broom, roomble*—and again the world was dyed with the whited dark. In the darker growth, the smoke foamed milkily, and cast upward more and more islands, curdling the blue sky.

Men running, how many men running. The horses, with fearful looks, snorted, wheeled. Beverly, dreading that Cannonball would lag, pressed in the spurs with agonizing viciousness. But the great weight was subsiding beneath him. Despairingly, Beverly inclined from the saddle, and rolled off skilfully, yet in abject terror. His impulse was to hesitate, to find out what had happened to the

370

wounded stallion: but he dared not wait. The retreat was as of the horses only, as though the men who were riding and the men on foot had nothing to do with it.

Smoke was like the breath of the ground. The trees steamed whitely. The vegetation whirled in the wispy rotations of opaque blots of vapour. Beverly had just seen General Jones fall with leaden ease and his mare run on beyond him. Jones had always been a brute with horses and it served him right. Even to know the commander's bloodied face exposed to pounding hoofs was a gratification. Yet Beverly could not remain equally indifferent toward his own fate. He tried a decisive clutch at a trailing halter, missed it, and gave up the attempt to impose himself between the galloping animals. Over his shoulder, into his neck and collar, flowed the hot sighs from dilated nostrils. A rider shouted. Beverly sprang sidewise and saw a seeming drunkard swaying over a powerful, vanishing rump. As the man's lolling shoulders shrank away in the folds of acrid vapour, it was apparent that his grip on a mane tossed by a frenzied horse was growing very feeble. Soon he, too, would recline in the dust. Another rider passed. And he was gone, with purple countenance, his left leg kicked over the horse's back, his head and body depending, like a performer in some equestrian exhibition, doing an expert's feat.

Broo-oom, broo-oom, plick, plick, plick. A horse cavorted, waltzed. Its tail flashed, scourged Beverly's forehead. He grovelled blindly toward a ditch. If he could make them strike the trees, like a flash of lightning, he could halt their panic. A cavalryman gurgled an exclamation of choked pain. Beverly saw the man, wounded, hurtle soddenly over the rearing horse's head. There he lay, prone to the implacable hoofs, that flashed on by him monotonously, insistently. A mare, unmounted, balked precipitately, stopping short in the middle of the lane and desperately impervious to her overtaking fellow runners. She whinnied shrilly, craned her slow bloodied neck, rolled her glazed eyes anxiously. A headlong charge against her turned her. Her hoofs flirted awkwardly, and her haunches rose in feebly kicking protest. Then her forefeet clattered against some stones, and she sank down oppressively on vast, relaxed buttocks. Even before she had relapsed her length in death, the animals, pursuing one another, sprang above her anguish as above a hurdle.

371

Beverly longed to avoid the dangerous impeding bulk of twitch-ing flanks, the snorts of the bloodied muzzles, the patient snarls. He sought to escape altogether the channel of flight. But when he had almost reached the close trees, his movements excited a detour on the part of the animals, and once more the heaving rocking of enormous bodies bore down upon him.

He did his best to think collectively. The disorganized cavalry which he could glimpse ahead seemed now to be abruptly reversing its course. He knew that Ewell had received instructions to fall away slowly if his troops were pressed. Was the flight then to be so suddenly contradicted? If the horses, in this panic, were streaming back, it must be that Ewell had perceived the desperate situation and was reinforcing, somewhere at the rear, for a renewed attack.

Hatless, his uniform torn, his brain clouded by the heat of his exertions, Beverly urged himself to the most daring course. If he could regain a saddle, these shameless tremors, which he felt those of a coward, would be defied. He dodged into the mêlée. The stampede that, a few moments before, had been behind him, was at once in his face. With a power almost mechanical, like liberated machines, the animals were driving against him. The impact with the arriving support, he conjectured, had maddened them to a renewed effort, to a more headlong uneasiness.

In the middle of the road, where he arrived without intention, he gave up hope. Then he was obliged to flee in the advance. In a blindness, in a perturbation which was like exultance, he evaded, he avoided, he willed an achievement which became the more impossible the more he set his heart on it.

The hoofs dinned, dinned in the puffing dust, and one flash of metalled feet or another was the same to him. Lather-soaked breasts, reddened with strange painted gore, loomed to his cheeks. He crouched. He sprang. He leaped insanely, and hurried onward. A leaning rider, sweeping by, looked down with dazed eyes, help-lessly, and without a word. Beverly gave a wild glance after him. Somewhere behind were those who pressed the terror-swift for-ward, a fresh cavalcade, whose bright, undimmed accoutrements conveyed a sudden shining. Beverly made a frustrate sign to speak, he waved his exhausted arms in signal, he tried, for a moment, to stay this menace of arriving friends.

372

None attended. Among the heaving, tilting rumps, the violent manes, he remained submerged. Dew blown from lolling tongues drizzled on his brow. Sweat-matted bellies pressed upon him. He began to shout and to run together. *"The horses have revolted! The horses have revolted!"* A change came in his frenzied mind and soul, and he uttered his conviction hoarsely to the dull unhearing. Belief was upon him like a revelation, and, on cramped legs, he hurried with the animals, not seeing further, having, at last, in the misery of an attitude which he still realized as strange, no further desire to see.

He shouted to them crazily. Stretched necks were taut in pace with him. He ordered them wildly. He was panting. He was gasping with a respiration like a fever. His heart was as steady in his breast as were the pounding hoofs upon the stony dust. It was as if he must go on until he fell down dead. There was no turning back. Here and there an ear, inclining swiftly with a flicker, seemed, as it exceeded him, to become attentive. An animal, impatient, lunging, with the halt of a fraction of a second, bared greenish teeth. A horse ruffled the lips of its grimed plush muzzle, and threatened his flung-out arm. He fled on ahead of it yet more impetuously. A horse swerved from him, its sides moist bellows, its tense bulk quivering with animosity. Soft, quick eyes, pitiless with fear, cast their unobservant glance, as a flattened throat extended beyond him; then a hind hoof, rapping, like a methodic hammer, the unfurling road, caught his bending knee.

With a stunning pain in the crushed joint, Beverly half fell. He could not linger to recover. Suffering was intense, as he revived, but the impulse to flight was whole. Another muscular breast, roan-coloured, satiny over its strained tendons, bulged, with its heated odour stifling him, just above his forehead. The mare took him like a fence in hunting, her speed only the passing of a heavy shadow, while the twinkling half-moons of her feet seemed to strike their sparks out of his harshened brain.

His thought-silencing effort to save his life was already carrying him deep into the seeping smoke of the enemy battalions. When crimson splashes guttered through the morbid daylight, the rumbles that succeeded them were not from the firing of Grant's regiments, but continued the dense *ke-platter, ke-platter* of unceasing galloping. Horse cries echoed all around him. He who had loved

373

his horses so, saw a fine gelding career, slip, descend to the earth on brittle, broken ankles; and hated the sight triumphantly, ecstatically.

The red flares through the creamy sunshine now approached the runner virulently. His neighing pursuers scattered. Shapes of spectral Yankees glided cloudily out of the bright fog. A greyed flag drooped, with uncoloured stripes, from a swimming, upright staff. The horses, entangled in their dangling reins, crashed into the pines and oaks. Beverly was left naked of their company in a momentary liberation. He yelled, he commanded like an officer. With the rank, steely grass of its drawn blades shaking light as in an iridescent wind, his own reinforcements descended upon him steadily. "The horses have revolted. The horses have revolted," he kept insisting, calling behind to them. He was confirmed as unbroken lines, which should have been of comrades, did not deviate. Revenge knew no reason. Since the last time he had seen a horse, with viscous entrails trailing, sink between the shafts of a ponderous ambulance, he had expected this. Stupidly, as a man in the track of a railway engine may wait, without the will to move, before it, Beverly hesitated. His indecision was final. Thinner, finer, more restless ankles pawed the raw-burning mists. Stronger and less used bodies stirred it. Glossy breasts bore on him proudly towering unbent throats. Nostrils were steaming fragrantly. Still animal eyes, yet confident in their obedience, glistened mercilessly. Beverly was struck, first in the chest, then in the shoulder. He reeled, drenched in the puffs of dust that rose even before the onslaught of the riders. His wit was hammered to delirious dulness. He lurched to his face.

The ton-weights flew above him. Before his brain was pulped to quietness, he attempted to inform the men of what had happened. "The—the—the horses—have—" His swollen tongue was unequal to the words. But he was satisfied by his own comprehension. He had anticipated this since the beginning of the war. He hated them, but they were justified. He felt it gratefully.

．　．　．　．　．

At first, the heat was no more than is blown out by an oven, warming the face. Then it began to penetrate the clothing most uncomfortably. Mingled with the ache in his slightly wounded leg,

374

Bob felt the scorched sensation which made retreat involuntary. In the glassy wall of the flames, he could see men running. Then, like creatures imprisoned in some ruddy amber, they were trying vainly to get out. He could see them wriggling on charred stumps of ankles, waving shrivelled arms at him. Their blistered faces seemed to melt, and their twisted mouths were mobile scars, uttering soundless words of agony. Fortunately for Bob's self-control, the rushing, crackling noises of the fire consumed, as in a great wind, all those other noises. He clung to the colours, and still, when he was abandoned, would not let them go. They seemed to him, in some vague way, to supply his sanity. If he cast them aside, upon the sizzling earth, it would be because he hoped no longer. It was as if the dingy flag itself opposed this wilderness. As long as his physical sensations remained quite clear, he could at least imagine himself avoiding a death so obscure and hideous that it would leave, for another's reading, no indication of his 'fine' last thoughts. It was not death that he seemed to be afraid of, but the way he had to die. It was a cruel circumstance which could demand of him a thing like this, with no recompense. When a shout for assistance did, finally, reach him, through the *blat-blat* of the fire, beating like flapping blankets, he hurried on to offer succour relievedly.

He had just opportunity to reach, again, the smutty edges of the conflagration, when the cries were exhausted. All he could discern in the smoke was a body inert as an old sack—the face was hidden—and a limp arm, fire running in the sleeve, eating the flesh under it, the sooted cloth all edged with the aliveness seen in embers, as though embroidered with rosy threads. The dying man was not precisely in the centre of the blaze, but as if surrounded by it. The sappy burble in the fuming twigs did not menace him directly. Rather, the haste of the flames ignored him purposely, protected him from any other approach. The seething flicker, leaping from one suddenly ignited object to another, left the huddled shape undisturbed, intact, in a mirror of heat.

Bewildered, Bob ran backward for twenty yards or more, but halted again. He was trapped here, in an inner acre, where the sun, only slightly shadowed by the dusk of the fire, continued to dazzle freshly the untouched earth. But he could not get out.

Twice, he gestured to toss away his flag. But, if he lost his flag, if he was here 'for nothing,' the whole stunning predicament would seem 'like foolishness.'

He retreated carefully toward the middle of the encircled plot. Fallen horses hummocked the grass. The dead here had not yet been made hideous, and he was not afraid of them. Indeed he considered their postures those of people in mysterious security. But the fire was encroaching. It would torture even that drab, stolid countenance which he noted enviously. *He*, Bob, was yet aware and on his guard. The dead were listless. The dead stared mindlessly at the down-pouring sun. They had no sense of the hell in store. Bob, because he had a conviction that suffering would surprise those fellows, feared death, and felt his own advantage.

A big grey, on its side, was a swollen mountain. Not an insect crawled upon its crusted nostrils. There was a pit gouged in that horse's breast, and the blood stood there, unflowing, thickening, as in a brimming cup.

All at once Bob understood the absence of insect life for what it meant. A dead sparrow, lying in the twigs, was so doubly dead. How instantly it would shrink to the weight of its draggled, lime-soiled feathers, when the breath went out of it. The air was full of hot currents, flooding from the burning trees. Bob felt a hectic chill, and drew the jacket of his uniform tight across his chest. The rain of sparks was perpetual. Now and then, a brand, spouted from the furnace, twirled rottenly to earth near him. He had already been over the whole free space, but he began to run about in circles, and to call out desperately for some answering voice.

It was the monotonous character of sound which he found hardest to endure—that, and the fact that the prostrate forms against which he stumbled, over which he had to hurdle, would not run with him. The wall of vapours was rising higher. Through the aqueous appearing curtain, drifting upward, he could discover no stirring animal. The woods were given over to the constant motions of strange lifelessness.

A tree, on the outskirts of purgatory, after waving its branches for a moment, wanly, toppled, with a thwack; and, where new showers of cinders scattered, other wildfire started.

Bob was choking. His chest strained with a breath he could not utter. He had come to the end of his rope. This was more than any man could stand. Then fear revived him. This is how you feel when you suffocate, he said to himself quickly. Again he ran. Again he was searching, going nowhere. Again he clung the tighter to the colours which explained his sanity.

Oh, he was *really* choking! Not merely to *think* of being dead— but to *be* dead. He had always welcomed suffering a little morbidly, but only because he so much dreaded it.

If he could make up his mind to run right into the fire, all would be over. Or would it? If you held back, if you held back till the final instant—there was still a hope. You couldn't see yourself as you had seen those grovelling men. *They* had not been forewarned as you were. But it was crazy to stand here passively waiting on disaster. The way to evade it—it *must* be evaded—was to be doing something.

Bob's lungs swelled achingly. He opened his mouth and tried to draw into him that clean breath that was above the trees. The air that he panted after would not come, and all that he was obliged to breathe made his wretchedness more ponderous.

It was hot everywhere now. If only in the beginning he had been more desperate. If he had ignored pride and had tried to flee. His feeling for the state of mind that had made his bravery was turned to useless hate.

The very ground was warming. The change in temperature penetrated his boots. Even the growth concealed under the dead leaves was smouldering furtively. From where a horse was spraddled, oozed the stink of singeing mane and hair. Sunshine was failing in haze. The flames, seen clearly while the fire was distant, were only purling intermittently. A pine toward the centre of the clearing had become alight. It bounded in branches that were sizzling torches. The needles evaporated, leaving limber bone exposed. Everything was catching. The whole forest was catching. Yet how could woods burn in a circle? When people quenched prairie fires, they laid the trails in opposition till the two fires met. Bob suspected some aberration of the usual. This gave importance to his danger, and was passing comfort. Then he grew exasperated with the fact that contradicted theory. He was vexed, he was rebellious, as a child is vexed when its will is thwarted. It was all the while as though he were gazing through a defective window pane of rutilant glass. Out of the aspirant fragrance of the smoke, slowly tormenting his sense of smell to dulness, darted a stiff ripple

377

like thin blood. It attacked him. It pursued him. He escaped it frenziedly. All at once the zooming of the conflagration became a terror to the ears. Spirals, swift as lightning, but more suave, began to edge the dry vines and creepers looping the forest. Green foliage, fresh with May, wrinkled, shed cracked edges, and tightened, until each stem glowed with a tip of bud like a minute coal, all raging-hot.

Another dead bird tumbled from a fork. The straw nest from which it reeled vanished utterly, leaving a little mat of hairs of an ashless red. A hurled twig caught Bob on the cheek, and branded him to a more tremulous indignation. He wanted to exclaim with some awful cry. That it was not possible for him to do so, was due to the conviction he would not yield—that he could be seen, could be heard, that it would not be possible for him to die alone, and without a trace, folk forgetting him utterly.

The charred sticks of the farther wood now stood in the deep, vibrating atmosphere as in a pool. He searched for the corpses he had before evaded. He could not endure an acceptance of their eternal inattentiveness. O God, hear me. O God, all you people hear me, know I done my best this afternoon. O God, *damn* the heat!

A branch close over him crackled. Flaunting fire, it swung and danced as though a sudden wind had been aroused for it. The spread flame, in its lambency, encased the whole bough. From it, thinned a gauze of radiations. Miraculously, twigs yards higher, aud out of contact, spurted an iteration of the blaze. On and on hurried the fire, lapping, with its suspended tide of glare, at a sustained distance above the woods, all the air at which it snapped. Bob, still eluding its enchanted rush, was moving dazedly.

There was no time to lose. He felt faint, depressed with a misery which effort could not surmount. His drunken feet caught in the folds of his smoky banner, and he flung it down viciously, with a despairing heedlessness. But he had no more than done so, when he felt its loss superstitiously, sank on his hands and knees, tore the silk from the staff, and hastened on with it. That was what they *had* to know—he had kept the flag. But you couldn't climb a pine and reach the outer, clearer atmosphere encumbered with three yards of stick.

He had decided to try a tree. Beneath one, he could yet gaze into the blue sky as into a garden. It was a pine with low projections. If he could once climb through it and suck in one untainted breath, he would believe that he defied the fate which drew so ruthlessly upon him. The knot tightening in his chest cramped his very bowels. The glow around him made his face tingle rawly, and, for some reason, he was already certain that his features were turning black. He threw the flag across his shoulders, and sprang for an armhold, determined to ignore his flabby wrists that, in the first instant, scarcely supported him. His physical self, as it betrayed his pride, was what he loathed. But he was secret about it, even in his mind. *They* would never find it out. He had never hinted an alarm to anybody.

As he clambered, his fierce hands teased by the scratching bark, the boles around him seemed to float by in the haze. Droves of trees, wriggling stiffly in methodic outline, each an exact distance from its fellow, pushed by him. The smoke was heavy, low and arrested. The oaks and pines cavorted, in their rooted gliding, while he struggled with his dizziness. Rankly, they escaped the holocaust, and rose up as though to smite him from the branch. He hung, teetered in a higher space, and crawled on, upward. Flat on his face, watching, with blood-congested brow, he joyed soddenly in some triumph over the treacherous soil, while twigs pressed stubbornly into his belly. The drifting earth rolled on beneath him, so close, so close, and yet, already, like some danger passed—earth that was guttered with little winding, spiral fires, and could offer pain, but no substantiality.

Bob's lungs remained locked. Effortlessness was itself causing added torture. He was no more afraid of torment, but afraid of effortlessness, afraid of an insidious indifference to his victory. Keep alive, keep alive, it don't matter how, but you must keep alive, he felt. There was no particular person whom he was longing to impress; yet there was something he must 'prove.' He was here, not because he was a fool, he kept insisting, but for some good reason, though he couldn't remember.

Then he stood, bold at last, and, with his hands against the upright trunk, steadied himself. There was a strange undulance in every contour on which his vision fell; and in his seared eyes the trees were yet advancing as monotonously as boats in the pale current of the smoke. He looked down on their constant passage almost resentfully. The pine swayed, as it spindled, and his weight seemed all that it could bear. His thoughts, also, were swaying slightly, in peculiar dreaminess. It was as though he were climbing on a mast to a lookout over strange, bright waters. He had gone as far as he was able. Clasping a pricking spout of clean, damp needles, he gaped his mouth for the hardest trial of his endurance, and drew a breath of choked eagerness.

The wind was of piercing clarity. At the first giddying inhalation, he nearly succumbed to pain. Relief was so complete that it was like debauchery, inviting him to utter heedlessness. With reviving staunchness, he had to fight the peculiar temptation to let himself go, and drop forever and forever, out of peace too perfect. He choked with the lovely attempt at breathing, and was inclined to vomit. Then his mind was stirred with quick intelligence, and he began to fear again.

The May afternoon was bitter. The pure intolerable atmosphere seemed to stretch his every thought wide. His body lived even beyond his mind. The pinnacle of the pine had only a young, tufty growth to bear him, and, as he moved, rotated supply. It smelled with its rusty bloom, so he was vaguely conscious, as did no tree on earth. The sky astonished him. It was valid blue and cloud. A faint sun, coiled in a smoke-dappled horizon, had just begun to sink. There was the world, spread out, real and usual, beyond the insignificant smudges of the fire. There were miles of forest, quiet and green, and farther, somewhere, there were soldiers marching. A tenuous, glinting line of agitation broke the happy stillness—artillery, or infantry, or, maybe, cavalry, he could not make it out. They were men—they were 'Uncle Robert's' men—if they could only see him. He *had* to feel that they would see him. On death that was being merely dead, he now refused to dwell, but he could not allow it, in contradiction of some awful hope, that the whole universe of beings he had tried to please refused him final notice.

Hysterically, he tried to shred a strip from the flag that he might knot his banner to the pine, for he was unreasonably convinced that, doing this, when he should fall, there would remain a mark to show to others what he had attempted. Doubt overcame him. The doubt was in his arms and legs and body, in his feebleness; and was like the doubt of some one very old. He swayed, his feet slipped, he clattered to a lower bough; then retrieved himself.

He tried to wave. His fatigued signal fluttered for a second's space above all the acres of sun-rosied and unobservant solitudes on which the tree, as it was islanded above the fire, could yet give his eye egress.

He was slipping toward the smoke which was like a mildew in the leaves below him. He was slipping toward the resignation of that other singeing flesh. His youth rejected this abdication.

But when protest came, it was more the irritation of accumulating pain than any confirmed thought: Why did they make me do it? Why did they make me do it? But I done it, damn it— Oh, I love them boys—O, God damn these people. Oh, they've *got* to look!

v

"Well, I'm afraid we are properly lost, general." In the complete midnight obscurity, the cavalcade drew up, and, for an instant, nothing but the breathing of the horses could be heard.

"Where do you figure Lee's lines are?" Grant repressed his usual profanity. He was 'past swearing.' It had been bad enough two days before when his officers had been obliged to direct movements through this 'God-forsaken' country by the use of compasses. There was something alarming in a different way in the prospect of a sudden, inadvertent intrusion into Lee's very camp.

Somebody elevated a lantern; and a map, its surface dimmed under the gloss of reflections, was unrolled in a stubby fist, and held at such an angle that all could simultaneously observe its tracings.

"Todd's Tavern—that's the place. If we can locate it, we'll get the road to Piney Branch Church." Grant laid a blunt forefinger on a minute mark. He certainly believed that he had done well in sending the trains in such direction as might give Lee the impression that the Federals, emerging from the Wilderness, intended to reach Fredericksburg. If the ruse carried, with evasion of an encounter, the first to arrive at Spotsylvania would find the way to Richmond comparatively easy.

"There's a lane back a hundred yards or so that might lead to the fork we should have taken."

Grant, squinting, ruminated on the map. "Try it anyhow," he decided tersely.

The fluttering paper rustled out of sight. The lantern was darkened; and the faces, that had been warmly ruddied by its focused glow, disappeared from one another. Solid contours of animals and riders did, however, persist, outlined against an atmosphere which remained oddly lucid. The small assembly turned, and, once more, little was audible beyond the squeak of saddle girths and the thumping of hoofs. Night wind lapped the cheeks, muffled damply the strained hearing. Its choking *thrush-thrush* eddied from the trees; or it hackled weeds and bushes beside a half-traced fence. Further, the night decayed slowly, toward the horizon, in a vast blanketing of dreariness, over the no-coloured vegetation.

Once, there was the burble of rocketing water, churning a stony creek-bed. Then irregular canters diminished. The riders leaned backward slightly, reclining against the heightened rumps of the stumbling horses. The feet of the animals slithered. Somebody observed that this was no spot to select for a 'swimming hole,' and that the water seemed 'derned cold.' There were faint, soggy plashes. The night grew brighter where the shrinking stream meandered amidst 'saplin's.' And the centaurs were again visible, each to each, as they reared in dusky silhouette procession on dry ground ahead.

Grant was thinking of Lee. A desire to encounter Lee in person was one to which Grant never gave utterance. Yet he confessed it often to himself, as he might confess to his wife some of his social shortcomings. At times—and he felt that way now—it would appear to him that the whole war, as a contention between parties, was a myth. In his heart, the struggle would more and more present itself as a contest, unadmitted, between two men. When Grant executed a strategy, as at present, he was wondering all the while how Lee, when he detected it, would regard the matter. If the James is crossed—if a surrender comes this summer—at least this autumn—by God, if Lee hasn't acknowledged me his equal yet, he'll have a bitter pill to swallow!

When Grant heard others speak enthusiasm for the Confederate commander, he always joined them with temperate, cautious praise. It was more 'credit' to defeat a fine adversary than an ignoble one. Actually, he was saying to himself at this moment, Hell, he's a wonder! Of course he's a wonder. Then, his pulse rapid with an emotion which he could well attribute to the excitement of this expedition, he added, caught in a wave of sentiment which disconcerted him, Why, I could *love* that man—if he wasn't so damned hidebound, so damned chock-full of piousness and prejudices!

"Here we are, General. If this doesn't end in a bog, we'll find Todd's Tavern not far beyond that rise."

Grant, startled out of himself to embarrassment, retorted quickly, with the instinct which contradicts all argument, "And from there we go to Richmond. We've given our adversary a tough nut to crack, and we'll damned well see that he breaks his jaws on it." Lee *owed* him something. Why, confound the obstinate old fellow, I *admire* him, Grant thought resentfully.

XIII

"I'VE never seen such tactics approved since I went into the army!" General Meade, impatient as a fidgety old lady, rose desperately and slapped his tightened knuckles on the table sharply. When he was as irritated as now, he could put squeamishness aside and look 'that old outlaw of a Sheridan' straight in the face. Meade, in a rage, coloured only slightly; but even that faint signal might be taken as a dangerous warning. Sheridan's flat-footed way of putting things was a manner that Meade could not, and never would, tolerate. There was a 'good deal of the brute' about Sheridan, anyhow.

"If you want my opinion," Meade went on, "you are responsible for the fact that Fitz-Lee worried us. If you had stayed where your instructions placed you and not kept the road blocked the infantry might have been made of some use." His rather high-pitched voice became tinny with menace. Longstreet's corps were in Spotsylvania Court House already, and but for this insufferable 'hard-head' of an Irishman—

"Who prevented Merritt guarding the bridge?" Sheridan thundered his interrogation with as much disregard of official etiquette as though Meade were a culprit and himself the examiner. Sheridan had made up his mind that the best way to 'handle' Meade was to give him no quarter at all—'never acknowledge a mistake to a fellow of his kidney, anyhow.' Sheridan's bulky, slightly hooked nose widened its nostrils, and he hunched pugnaciously on his stool, his shrewd eyes gathering about them all the little wrinkles of suspicion.

Meade's eyes, pin-pointed with distrust, with antipathy, turned their answering gaze stonily upon the red, withered countenance to which excitement now seemed to give a kind of hilarity. It was only the observation of symptoms which indicated Sheridan's

384

notable lack of self-control that brought some reassurance to Meade's shaken nerves. "If you are trying to make this argument the means of placing official responsibility, I refuse to enter into it," Meade continued, with brittle fury, but with articulation again regulated to hostile niceness.

"Look here, General Meade, you know what General Grant wanted, and I know what General Grant wanted. My men were already in the lead, and would be holding the place now if Merritt hadn't been removed." Sheridan's ponderous hand toyed with his viny, yellowed moustache. He had had enough of all this 'educated' opposition. In his thick, flaccid throat, in the low collar of his uniform, his pulse trembled with a thready rapidity imperilling health. Yet he was growing colder, more dogged. Meade had tried to 'stir' him up before.

"Does this mean that you are questioning orders?" Meade was always self-conscious before the accidental audience, and the sight of loiterers on the sunny grass just beyond the open tent flap robbed him of any further capacity for abandon to his ire. In being obliged to bandy words with a subordinate, Meade felt not alone the injustice of Sheridan's shifting of the blame for failures, but a downright offence to self-respect.

"No, sir, this doesn't mean that I am questioning orders. I have done as much to uphold discipline as anybody, and I don't expect to make an exception in behalf of myself," Sheridan replied, stubbornly; but with just that tentativeness, that wary return to half-admitted deference, which showed him alternating between the reckless egoistic assertion that, somehow, in Grant's service, 'paid,' and a subtler doubt of the value, at a critical juncture, of forcing the issue in a personal dispute. Sheridan held in secret contempt Meade's constant necessity to 'dress-up' a fact—give it a well-bred' appearance. Grant will be on my side, no matter what I do, Sheridan thought. Thank the Lord, *he* doesn't have to pretend that war is a little affair between gentlemen.

But did he? Sheridan knew that Grant was always partisan in his behalf; regrettably, not quite openly enough. Sheridan and Grant could 'get on together.' Covertly, Sheridan was determined not to 'play too high' himself. The instinctive harmony of viewpoint was preserved on that basis. Grant is glad to find out that there's one person in our organization who won't try any political tricks on him, Sheridan had said. He couldn't 'fool away' time on a commander who 'beat about the bush.'

Sheridan was, frequently, purposely overbearing. He could depend on Grant's favouritism 'within limits.' But they would have to serve. Meade and the first cadet sergeant who had provoked the young Irishman to mutiny at West Point might be one and the same. Sheridan did his best according to his 'lights.' He was a 'good eater, a good liver, and a good fighter.' He never pretended to be 'squeamish' and never would. The world wasn't run like that.

"What I maintain, and have from the first, is that cavalry exists for the purpose of taking care of enemy cavalry. If the cavalry is going to be an ornament to the service and nothing more, then, damn it, Meade, I've got the wrong job and I don't want it." He knobbed his fist, struck it soundly in his palm, and, cocking his wise head, with its backward shock of greying hair, sidewise, rose stoutly from his camp stool. This, he felt, triumphantly, should indicate to the punctilious that the argument was ended.

Meade woodenly resisted taking the cue offered. "Well, it's my opinion you *have* got the wrong job. Division commanders who refuse to co-operate under the instructions of the commander-in-chief never do much to advance strategy and never offer any profitable tactics." Meade was the more disturbed because his instinct perfectly informed him of the reasons for Sheridan's presumptuousness. But the idea of an official break, while it tempted Meade to a precipitate point, also represented for him the invitation to a kind of disgrace—or, at any rate, to a deluge of public criticism which he could not bring himself to face. It was repellent enough to be 'forced' into this 'row.' Worse to concede that Grant could not get on without Sheridan to do the 'dirty work' for him. Meade felt Sheridan's utter lack of fastidiousness contemptible. He had seen the big Irishman jovially acting the bluff soldier full of rude camaraderie, and had been 'thoroughly nauseated.' Yet it was wiser to refrain from condemning the man who had the brutality now and then required to replace courage when the ruthless nature of the task strained the capabilities of the more scrupulous. The damned scrub! Or am I too violently prejudiced, Meade wondered.

Sheridan, even at his apparent headiest, allowed little to escape him. He sensed that coldness was becoming modified to scepticism and, then, again, unwilling tolerance. Looking boldly into the severe, finely edged features that confronted him, his blue eyes twinkled with a humour and a malice that were frankly coarse, "You complain because Stuart beat us to Spotsylvania. Well, by God, with the kind of approval I demand as my right in a situation like this, I can pitch in and lick Stuart so he won't have a leg to stand on—and that by tomorrow."

"I won't suggest that you go ahead and do it, because, as far as I can see, your idea of the way to conduct warfare is entirely personal, and your own business." But when Meade became sarcastic it was always a grudging sign of yielding gracelessly.

"All right—so it is. There's the chance—my chance—your chance—everybody's. I can guarantee to you that Phil Sheridan can make an end, once and for all, of Stuart's nasty habit of riding round the Federal army. When you and General Grant have decided whether I am going to be of any value to you or not, I'll know whether it's time for me to send in my resignation. That's plain enough, I hope."

"Nothing could be plainer."

Sheridan smiled viciously, and sucked in his moustaches against his somewhat unlovely teeth. He was thinking, If this breed of hen figures he has shoved me to the wall, he's welcome. If Grant don't know yet which way the wind blows, it's time he found out, and I wash my hands. I never made my way in the world by standing still, and I'm going to get through this my own way if it kills me. I gave up drudgery as a way of earning a living when I left father's farm and had enough of store clerking! And I was snubbed enough by this gentry when I had to find my own appointments down in that left-over piece of the universe, Texas. If I don't brag any more than I do, it's because I don't have to. Let 'em see for themselves. I've accomplished more than the whole caboodle. I can help 'em round up what's left of the rebel army, and do it well. If I didn't have a fancy to be on hand when old Lee hands over his sword I wouldn't take the trouble. Not that I oughtn't to be in at the death. It's due me, if anything is. To the devil with Meade! In a case of sheer individual courage he wouldn't show up any too bright.

Trip-trip-trip, went the pulse, like the drip of tiny silken waters

387

in Sheridan's short, flabby throat. He wished 'to the Lord' that Meade would go before his own indignation broke in fatigue. He could 'stand up to any of these —— —— sons of ——' if he was 'mad' enough.

"Your point of view is a trifle beyond me, General Sheridan. I was never under the impression that a few brigades of cavalry counted more in deciding our tactics than the manoeuvres of a hundred thousand or so infantry and artillery. The theory interests me so much that I think I will go over and ask General Grant's opinion on it." Testily, aware of something childish, and so degrading, in the whole episode, yet self-righteously certain of its serious ingredients, Meade bowed hotly and took his departure.

Sheridan, without stirring, watched him go out and mount his horse. Strangely, his exasperation grew the warmer as its cause retreated. *Tell* Grant, ye blabber. Ye tattle-taler, you! To the divil an' Tom Walker with ye! He felt at his suffocating collar. The blasted Southerners were 'giving out.' Follow the chase just to lose the spoils, not much, ye idiot. He would *not* be beat!

II

SELECTION FROM A LETTER WRITTEN BY GRANT TO HALLECK AS GRANT TURNED FROM THE NORTH ANNA IN MAY, 1864

Lee's army is really whipped. The prisoners we now take show it and the action of his army shows it unmistakably. A battle with them outside entrenchments cannot be had. Our men feel that they have gained the morale over the enemy, and attack with confidence. I may be mistaken, but I feel that our success over Lee's army is already insured.

III

The Fredricksburg railway and the Virginia Central crossed at Hanover Junction, which was inside Lee's lines. Grant, intruding between Lee and Richmond, intended to leave a gap in both communications and so cut off all supplies to the Confederates. Hez thought that 'old Ulysses' was 'pretty cute' to make such a thorough job of this railroad destruction. A brigade of men extended down each side of the rail bed. At an initial point, the track had been cut, and when a long, "Whoo-oop, up with her!" ran through the crowd, the first ties were lifted with a creaking wrench. Hez

388

and Gus Miller were among those who, using as crowbars the first dislodged rails, continued their prying on the compact sequence not yet loosened. Gus worked silently, but Hez was 'sociable,' and kept up a ruminative chat about their occupation.

" 'Tain't been so many years since this here track was laid. 'Member when the first train come along to Harmony Junction, up home. The railroad business has growed quicker'n any industry in this country. It ull take a nation longer to remake this than what it takes to yank it up. I can tell you that."

It was hot. "Jest a little too much like the Sunny South," Hez insisted. There was a sow, its guttural grumbles never ceasing, standing, four-square, on its stiff, pronged hoofs, just below the embankment, "Where'd *you* come from?" Hez asked. "Gus, there's a live sow belongin' to the enemy that General Grant forgot. We ain't tasted fresh spareribs for a long time, pig. You better watch out."

The purple heat stood deep in the woods on a rise of ground. At some distance from the labourers, the brusque shade ended. It was very quiet in the country around, and the heavy, boisterous interchanges of the soldiers echoed millennially. Weeds in a gully waved quietly. Hez said, "Seems like you was talkin' to yerself, or makin' some comments on the weather to the Almighty." The pig, in stolid inquiry, was approaching closely, its snout churning dust.

"Hey, you pig—and there's a sheep. Fer Christ's sake, what we all been goin' hungry for! The folks have moved out of this God-fer-saken neighbourhood, and the sheeps and sows come take possession of it."

The rails were 'sizzlin' ' hot. Hez touched one and swore. Then he turned his uneasy attention on the pig again. "Beeg, beeg, beeg, beeg," he invited. The sow shook her fleshy jowls, and moved a step nearer. Her rubber-limp ears, which Hez poetically compared to arum lilies, flapped idly. Her flat-tipped, grass-stained snout, pink, and flexible as vegetation, nosed sunshine eagerly.

Hez, sensing that he was momentarily unobserved, clambered toward the gully that protected her, and, reaching forth a free hand, scrubbed his nails deep in the dried mud caked on her cushion of a body, sagging like a barrel and sprouting, from its slick hide, salt and pepper quills. At his touch, her half-naked tail made, nervously, an involuntary curl. Her short, spraddled legs, with their knock-knees, gave way slightly as though she contemplated the more voluptuous submission of lying down.

"Good girl. Great girl. Fine old girl, she is."

He essayed the friendship of the sheep, standing there like a bundle of brown wool supported on its tiny ankles that seemed encased in delicate black stockings. Its flexible, rubbery lips moving incessantly in untiring nibblings, it evaded him, awaiting his approach, but leaping, with a squat start, out of his way. Only the sow, snuffling, stuttering, delaying now and then to wallow unctuously, heaved, like a ship of fat, after the bestower of unsolicited rewards. Her horny teats dangling under her wide-breathing belly, her ears lopping her near-sighted brows, she pursued Hez almost up the slope. There she stumbled, lunged, caught her toes, and was frightened back.

Hez abandoned her reluctantly. The ties were on fire. Stooping enthusiasts, piling them crisscross, struggled with old leaves, twigs, and bits of paper. A blaze, beginning to lick up briskly, discharged, upon the waver of the gaudy daylight, suffocating smoke. Fanning the fire with their caps, the soldiers soon found it impossible to remain within the range of the waves of burning that undulated invisibly even far from the crackling mass. The rails bent and were heated red.

Hez contemplated it all. "That sheep looks at you like a piece of machinery." He met its tarnished amber gaze, which seemed to see, without conclusion and without meditation, as a glass reflects. "Your hindquarters gonta taste good yet, partner. And this here place—most like it looked when the Injuns come here for a little scalpin'. It's funny, sure. But I ain't quarrelin' with nothin'. I hope I got as much sense as you have, sow. It's all the same to me."

IV

Molly ran across the field dragging Ted by the hand. She had the best spoons wrapped in a paper inside the pocket of her petticoat. Ted had clung so persistently to his rag doll, Lettie, that he had been of no assistance to his mother. When she had seen the rebel soldiers arriving, she had been shocked enough; but when Mrs. Webb had told her of their general's proposition, it had seemed a laughing matter. The rebels had wished to levy on the pockets of the citizens of Chambersburg. Five thousand dollars in cash had been demanded, with a threat to burn the town at once if the sum asked was not produced. And now the worst had come. It was worse to be put out of your house by force, and then allowed to stand about and watch it consumed in ashes, than to suffer the same loss by accident.

Mrs. Webb was standing in the field, too. Molly reached her, and said, breathlessly, "I'm not a mean woman, Mrs. Webb, but I vow and declare that no kind of torture would be punishment enough for this kind of thing. How the men let them do it, I don't know. I'm not speaking of *your* husband—because he's not so very well—but if Joe had been here—*oh*, I say, if *Joe* had been here, he'd have done his best to put a stop to it. They set fire to McNeil's barn with a lot of straw: I saw it myself—Mrs. McNeil coming out and almost on her knees—she *did* go on her knees—and told them Mr. McNeil was away in the war and if she got burned out she and Mehitabel would never be able to face him. And about Perry's cows—and the pony—and all the poor babies and the women and the children in the world without milk to drink. Well, I know I rattle on like a crazy woman—but who wouldn't? Ted, don't you cry, birdie, and that old rag doll—I didn't know you loved her so until this minute. No, stop that! If I slap the child, Mrs. Webb, I'm not responsible. They say spare the rod and spoil the child, but he's the only comfort I *have* had in these awful days—as long as the war kept where it belonged it was bad enough, but now they send raiders up here—and General Grant— well, he *will* take it out of them—that's one comfort. I wouldn't let a nigger on the place, much less keep them. When the fire first began to pour out of Landry's front door, I asked Mr. Gracie if the men couldn't get the old fire engine out and try to stop it, but as well try to stop wild horses as when things like this get started. Mrs. Gill and Jess out in the yard screaming and the nasty brutes told her to shut her mouth. They *did!* The government simply *has* to do something for us, Mrs. Webb. If ever there were martyrs to their country's cause we are. I didn't want Joe to enlist in the beginning, and now we've gone through so much —not as much, they say, as the others, but why should we? Sit down here, Ted—here, Mrs. Webb, we might as well watch it— all my poor little things piled up in the Frys' onion patch, and

Mamie said she'd have Douglas keep an eye on them, such thieves. Just like them to take everything that's left. Dear Mrs. Webb! Now don't you go on, too. The grass is so nice and cool. It's wet, but I guess you won't take cold. Well, this is what you call hysterics. I could cry and laugh at once. Now I've frightened the child, too. But didn't you suppose when Early failed to get to Washington that we were through with the whole mess, Mrs. Webb? I believe Grant is our saviour."

"So much smoke. Almost puts out the sun. And it's all we've got, Molly." Mrs. Webb sat down, 'plump,' beside the mother and the child and threw her apron over her head.

Molly looked dazed. "My God, it's true!" Just as if she hadn't known it before. "Well, I don't go to prayer-meeting much, Mrs. Webb, but I won't be convinced that Jesus came on earth to save us just to let a lot of bloodthirsty murderers be victorious. Our homes may be ruined, but we'll fight for our lives and our children. If I'd had Joe's old musket used to stand around in the kitchen I'd have turned it loose in that miserable officer's face. Anything you have to do to save those who are near and dear to you is justified. Oh, Mrs. Webb, now don't! No, Ted, don't be scared, she's only worried 'cause her house is burning. I'd like to see anybody explain to me *now* that the war ain't entirely the fault of these Southerners. If anything makes me sick, it's trying to dress up the devil to look like a saint."

XIV

MARTIN felt the water rising, like a stillness, over his ankles; while the hot sounds of the guns continued intermittently. The condition of the vessel had driven him backward from his own post, and he now hesitated uncertainly. Up to the present, Captain Semmes had kept everything in perfect order. Confusion was imminent. Boats from the *Kearsage* were approaching, but Martin had a feeling that the command for surrender would be complied with imperfectly. His own impulse at the moment was to jump into the sea. There had been nothing for it but submission to approaching disaster, yet it aroused rebelliousness to realize that all were giving up. Larry Todd was waiting with him, and Martin was exasperated as he realized that his companion was furtively watching him for some clue as to behaviour. An instant later, when no sound was left but the murmur of voices, and an odd vacancy which was created in minds liberated from the concussion of firing, it was possible to distinguish the name of the yacht, *Deerhound,* from which the other boats were being lowered.

The excitements of the *Alabama's* career had long helped to distract Martin's thoughts from more personal troubles. He had been in her crew when she set sail, out of Laird's yard, under the name of *The 290.* And he had witnessed her friendly pursuit by the British vessel that, docking with her in the Azores, had transferred to her her permanent skipper and officers. Life in this way had perhaps cured him of that 'dry-rot of the intelligence,' as he was fond of calling it, which had been responsible for his condition when Roddie, his old chum in Richmond, had taken a bottle of laudanum away from him. Anyhow, disregard of safety during these last few years had performed, he felt, a kind of miracle of restoration for his 'amour propre.'

The brevity of naval warfare, as evidenced this morning, made his grandiloquent escapade something of a fiasco.

The deck certainly was settling. Though the enemy rescue was now close enough to show blobby faces of men at the oars, some fellows were running up the sloshing incline of the *Alabama* shouting, "Every man fer himself. Every man fer himself. Git yer life belts and jump!"

"What do you think we'd better do, Martin?"

Everything was awash, and when Todd saw Martin lingering by the rail, undecided, he called to him that he had better hurry and make up his mind, and ran on aft.

Martin was astonished to sense his own, slightly pleasurable alarm. A gun, loosed from its moorings, came careening along the slope, splintered a hatch; and there was a panicky helter-skelter as crew and gunners scattered out of its way. Ed Bates said, "Good luck, Mat!" and prepared himself to climb the rail and dive over. But it was always possible to be sucked under by the eddy of a sinking ship. Martin ranged himself with a knot of the white-faced who had decided it was more sensible to wait until the boats were something nearer alongside before taking the plunge. "The boats won't get here," conjectured a grumbler. Martin glanced at him angrily.

What was the matter with these fools! Several officers were on the bridge and one of them was yelling to the demoralized group of sailors below, demanding to know why in —— —— —— it was taking so much time to get the *Alabama's* own boats lowered. Martin stumbled up through the water and inconsistently offered to 'lend a hand,' but was sworn at for intruding on an undertaking in which he had no concern. The damned thing upset before it could be launched. Three fellows were floundering in the sea. One had his head butted on a piece of broken timber and went under. Martin could imagine his body beaten against the *Alabama's* side. The davitt halyards were becoming as much entangled as the yarn in an old lady's mending basket after the kitten has been playing with it. You felt as if hours had been wasted. The first boat to keep upright had to make off quickly to escape the pounding of the water that drove it against the settling hulk. When Martin realized the tension, amounting to suppressed rage, with which the men were struggling for a decision as to their allotted places, he felt callously reckless. Rather than to 'hang about' admitting fear, he chose immediate escape.

394

Nobody noticed him. He removed his coat slowly, being very deliberate. He was getting wet to the knees. He had to clamber through a mess of all sorts—rope and broken wood and stuff that had floated up from below—before he could reach an angle from which he could get off into the water. Then he kicked his boots away, saw them drenched, and felt the wet in his socks. As he prepared to jump, he was frankly 'scared.' But, going down, down, with an obliteration of vision that put all reflection from his mind, he came to the surface, relieved. It was not so bad after all.

There was an undoubted pull toward the wreck, and that frightened him again, for a second. But he was a strong swimmer. The spectacle of several unfortunates bobbing about distractedly and in obvious danger of drowning, depressed him, but stimulated him more to bravado than to despair. He took some frantic strokes; afterwards, a couple of dozen more leisurely; when he had to observe that he had given himself this opportunity by selecting his escape on the side farther from the *Kearsage,* and hence less accessible to her life-saving party. His exhaustion had, all at once, accumulated in complete disproportion to the distance he had covered. There was nothing for him to do, but to turn, for an instant, upon his back, and refresh himself with inertia. Panic gave him a wild, erroneous impression that spaces had become augmented. The sea, with its evidences of comparative calm, appeared to have deceived him. Or else it was being freshened by a sudden wind.

This breeze came crisscross, against the general direction of the troughs, and the spray broke repeatedly upon his face, drenching him in blinding, stinging, crystal flurries.

If he should be done for here, he wondered, when and how would his sister and his mother hear of it? Theatrically remote, the suggestion of a possibility served only to remind him that his armpits ached. Unexpectedly, he swallowed an abrupt mouthful of salt water and began to cough. Hell of an end, drowning. He recovered himself anguishedly. His chest ached. There were the *Kearsage* boats, sure enough, but like 'pea shells.' On the deck of that yacht, a man seemed to be uncoiling a line of some kind—spinning it gently overboard, though the purpose of his gesture could not be discerned. Among machines, little black people moved nimbly in jets of steam—or was it lingering smoke?

Martin concluded that he would need to detour the wreck elaborately. It astonished him to behold, vaguely, the rapidity with which the *Alabama* was disappearing. Or had he merely gone so far away from her? In an increasingly icy languor, he rested as long as he dared. When he became awed by his own nauseous submission to the undulations of the troughs, he struck out more determinedly. His sense of direction was distorted by the great height of the approaching waves. Every time he lost his head and neglected to swim, a sea caught him sidewise, and he would feel himself descending into such blackness as that from which one never rises. His longing for inactivity, growing stealthily, so alarmed him, that he resumed his strokes impetuously, ignoring the preciousness of guarded energy. Speed seemed requisite as in some race with time. The boats were all, equally, nowhere; and he began, with feigned calm, to consider the stretch between him and the French shore.

Trying to maintain clear calculation, he stood in the airy water. Treading it, he kicked and fumbled for his trousers, and dragged from his shoulders his loggy shirt that tore in its seams. That he had jumped in fully clothed seemed incomprehensible, disturbed his faith in himself.

So disgusted was he with effort, that some sickly impulse was gratified when a half-inundation reached his chin. *Why move, why move?* His lungs were choked. Again he wheeled himself and lay upon his spine. Reclining so, he had a sense of himself on the verge of some vague discovery of what rolled underneath, a discovery that he both craved and dreaded.

The atmosphere, under the close, blue sky, bristled with sound. He heard sizzlings; and small *tick-ticks* of spray grew louder in his muffled ears. He must fight clear of something. He nerved himself, made spanking strokes, allowed his face to go in, himself lost in the green, swollen vagueness, and was intent only on swimming, on getting nearer somewhere, something—on getting cn. When his chin lifted, and his eyes saw level once more, thousands of hills, walking swiftly down upon him, were his only company. The constant, light-smeared tents of water were erected in their hundreds, and cast down to his advance as before a hurricane. He reversed himself, attempted to place this flashing band behind him. His tipped feet were lifted, weightlessly, up above his head. He acknowledged defeat. A quiet avalanche was flattening to descend to him its long auburn slope. His lungs were as tight as gourds. They refused him the most necessary breath. Grains of glass continued to drip-drip inside his brain. He was stupid to any impression beyond that one, granular, wiry sound in the dense skull of which he was conscious. The thousand, the trillion little iron hills merged, dimpled bleakly in a mountain scalded with brownish sunshine. Bursts as from pearly volcanoes dazzled all the crystal acres. On the horizon, spurted haze curled in a sinister fin, lacy and gigantic. The water, rubbing his ears gently, made a plushy noise. Once more he exerted himself furiously. A vividness coiled in his thoughts. Some fresh sense of life—of a life lived happily long before the beginning of the war—expanded in his tortured chest, was almost rending him. He had a feeling that he had done something silly, recently. He could not remember what it was— *back home—Davis—mother—Richmond—all that.* Hope seemed something bigger than he could handle—too much for his years and strength. He was glad when it subsided. The tiny, boiling trickle followed his thoughts, the awful, endless and unwearying sea pursuing him.

II

"Fuse has stopped, Roy." Carl lowered his voice ineffectually, for the veriest whisper in the gallery seemed to rebound upon the speaker, menacing him. The proximity, in each lateral, of three hundred and fifty kegs, each keg containing twenty-five pounds of gunpowder, awed the nerves of the two volunteers. At three-fifteen that morning the fuse had been ignited, but, after nearly an hour of waiting, no explosion had resulted. The men, excited by their own daring, moved in the subterranean excavation as in some holy place.

Before the opening of the war, Carl had been a printer. For six years, he had been affianced to a widow, whom he had saved from drowning at their first meeting, when a pleasure boat upon the Hudson River had capsized. He was too cautious to marry before he had amassed some capital, but he wrote to his future wife, when his military duties did not interfere, at least twice a week. The letters he inscribed to her were always filled with 'information,' and were couched in a very 'literary' manner. Just recently, since he had been encamped near Petersburg, he had entered a riffed dwelling and had taken from the wall, under a roof gaping with shell holes, a chromo picture of a young girl looking pensively at pansies; had removed it from its carved, acorn frame, had rolled the paper neatly, and had put it in his haversack. He believed that the maiden of the artist's fancy resembled 'Amy,' with the single difference that 'Amy' was a little stouter.

As Carl squatted to examine the dead fuse, his flat features, in the weak reflections from a shrouded lantern, were a mask to the romantic elation revealed very slightly in his glistening and bloodshot eyes. "Don't bring that light any nearer, or you may regret it," he advised Roy peremptorily. Carl, usually timid, was tyrannical whenever invested with responsibility. Roy, who was younger, was more impetuous, and his sense of self-importance less pronounced. Carl took no interest in the peculiar, literal atmosphere of their surroundings; but Roy noted every detail avidly. For weeks, the weather up above had been scorching hot. Down here in the tunnel, though this was the thirtieth of July, the impression might have been of January. The damp odour of a burial ground pervaded everything.

"Hey, Roy! Can you set that lantern aside awhile and give me your help a minute? No, not like that!"

Carl was absorbed in the intricacies of what was really a small repair. Roy could scarcely bring himself to attend with sufficient concentration to be of aid. He felt an excitement almost jovial as he realized, for the hundredth time, that he was deep here, hidden beneath the Confederate works. The glow of the lantern sank from the close roof to the packed dirt of the corridor. There, in the frayed circle of radiance, such a minute thing as a beetle was exposed. Minutely ponderous, struggling to free the glossy fringes of its legs from a loose clod in which it was entangled, the beetle, in its feeble frenzy, rolled to its back. Its harsh, tiny, elbowed ankles pawed subtly, despairingly, the moist grains of soil. Roy, conscious, in awe, of the dense weight of passive earth, on which grass grew, trees leaned, and people slept—a sentry tramping at his post, perhaps; a bugle sounding a reveille to the weary— considered the impenetrable bulk he was releasing, which would so soon descend on folk and beetles indiscriminately.

He roused from the torpid grandiloquence of his dream, and two pairs of deft, unflinching hands combined in their effort to leave the fuse intact. The repeated ignition consumed no more than a fraction of a second. When it was accomplished, Carl rose and ran on, brutally heedless of his companion whom he had ordered to follow. The main gallery was five hundred and ten feet long. As Roy hastened, he seemed to feel that length accumulate. The shadow-fuzzied glisten from the light was soaked away, and a chill dark closed in. Roy, though he was shivering with anxiety, experienced an insane desire to lag, to delay. A moment before, he and Carl had been as powerful as God. Now Roy was vaguely conscious of his circumstantial exclusion from the planned triumph. He did not pity the rebels, on that land of sky become, for the time, almost mythically remote. But he wished that he might have put off the explosion just a little longer. He was as if pursued by some danger to which he became a party, which he could not keep in bounds. He was confused, running, not able to comprehend how he had been suddenly robbed of the fruits of his voluptuous anticipation.

Thankfully, he sensed the icy freshness of unheralded dawn. The greying of the sides and ceiling of the passage announced palely an imminent liberation from the stifle of the profound mould. A bat scuttered past his shoulder, and he exulted in its betrayal, as it swooped behind him down the tunnel. It was seeking privacy but courting death. Yet his blank thoughts were drawn backward after it with a kind of shuddering envy.

A dingy arc of daylight opened. Dark boughs speared the fleshy indefiniteness of rain clouds. Wind, with its metallic freshness, touched panting mouths and shrinking nostrils. Carl, satisfied with his work, crawled gloatingly through the hole to the out-of-doors. A brief shower was tapping the dusty shelf of earth left by the labourers, marking it with sticky thumb-prints and polka dots. On the rim of this new world the rising sun weltered. The eyes of the two men grudged each the other his poise, yet their glances met complacently. Only Roy remained dissatisfied, his curiosity unappeased, intense, and with a precious sense of sin.

.   .   .   .

The growl was deep down, as if under the rearing sun. When Uncle Mose, stumping through a corn-field, heard the sound, and looked back toward Petersburg, his knees began to tremble. A feebleness of wonder was added to the feebleness of age, and he sank helplessly in a praying posture. His ash stick flopped from his bent, grasping fingers, and he forgot it. For an instant, he was proud in the privilege which, he felt, was accorded to him alone, of witnessing some especial catastrophe. His daughter, Jane, had gibed at his ardent conceptions of a millennium. What would she think of *that!*

The whole surface of the world seemed to be rising slowly. The fields themselves were smoke, falling apart indolently, and covering the sky with their deliberate vapours. After the first, immense foggy turmoil had subsided, the eddies of stone descending with unreal languor, came other and other spurts of noise, and lesser belchings of dust. *Boo-loom. Boom. Boo-oom.*

The trees rocked harshly from their indifferent roots. Roads and fences seemed to move. *Bonga!* There was a quick, defiant explosion. Then, slower, more massive, the dreary expansion of reverberations, leaving room for no other life. Contracting like a whirlwind, the mist of erupted landscape revolved on itself, sagging like a rain cloud.

As the choked poundings at last faded, and the dwindled sunshine reasserted, against floating whorls of dark, the immediately surrounding universe, the guns burst forth. *Broom-broom-broombroom, broom, broom, broom, bonga, broom broom.*

Under the thinning vestige of surging, powder-black dirt, the glare in the distance tingling with the vestigial scintillance of sprayed stones, the artillery fire purged, with echoes, the impure stillness following on the first rending shock.

Oh, dem po' fellahs, Uncle Mose thought, suddenly realizing that even the great disaster which had happened for his revelation had a target, dem po' daid fellahs!

Flopping decrepitly in the weeds among the stalks, his bony old hands fervent as they resought his stick, he accepted disappointment. "Dis yo' day, Debil," he murmured aloud. "An hell hit's a grand sight. De Lawd he got to git pow'ful busy to beat you. But Ah's prayin' faw Y'all, Lawd. Ah knows dis ol' niggah ain' much account but he's prayin' faw Y'all."

"Have they burned the corn, too?"

"Yessum, Ma. It's all down."

"Is the wheat finished with—not a bit left?"

"Yessum, Ma. It was all beautiful—brown as toast on top an' ready faw the threshin'."

Mrs. Stoner, in bed, but not 'sick enough—O, Lord why can't I be sick enough so I don't care about anything'—had imagined, all through the night, that she listened to the scraping of scythes. Ellen Ophelia ' 'lowed' that it must have been Mr. Humphreys on the hill, trying to get his crops down before the Yankees reached them. "They say, up Mr. Humphreys's way, where some Yankee soldier was killed—and serve him right—the Yanks has already started burnin' houses up."

Mrs. Stoner sat straight against the pine-cone pillow and stared at her children as if she were going to leap to the floor and rush at them. And Ellen Ophelia, who was ashamed that her mother behaved so badly, looked at her maliciously. "They burned the barn, too, Ma. Everything's black an' smokin' between us and them." But when the new baby began to fret, Ellen Ophelia was useful as well as important in her manner, and came and took it up. Under her breath, she sang to it, *"Scotland's burnin'."*

Her thin voice must have been soothing, since the baby's whimpers were immediately stilled to hiccups of fretful content. Mrs. Stoner could not be pleased. Again she lifted herself up, leaning on an elbow, and cried, hoarsely, "You'll knock all the chance faw sense outa that chil's head ef y'all don't quit shakin' it!"

So Ellen Ophelia, embarrassed, swayed her burden more gently. She was glad when she could put it aside in the basket. "Pete Snell begged 'em not to cut the grapes, Ma, an' he was right funny, beggin' as ef the grapes was somethin'. General Sheridan ain't gonta leave a single thing that kin grow in the valley—houses or nothin'," Ellen Ophelia half wanted *not* to tell the worst news. That rasping quality of the tone in which her mother spoke made little shivers of anxious expectation go up and down your spine.

You wondered what she was going to do next, and, though so frightened, you longed to invite her to behave 'that way' again to show you what you had never before suspected—what she was 'like.' But Mrs. Stoner had left off speaking, and was groaning. She was lying, in her soiled, ruffled nightdress, like a dead person. 'Ma's' face was 'scary' these days, even when she slept. It was marked all over with funny little lines, as though the 'foxes scratched at it.' Ellen Ophelia felt that she and her brother Rob were much better off since 'Pa' had gone away to war, and the farmhouse no more disturbed by his perpetual grumbling. But Ma was 'changed.' She had turned 'mean,' and cross, and 'diffrunt.' For even if you *have* fallen sick yourself, it's nobody's fault. Even last winter with the pox, Ellen Ophelia had not acted as Ma was acting.

Rob's snub profile pressed against the cloudy, sunny, broken window pane. When he was interested in something for himself, he 'minded' nobody. Ellen Ophelia supposed that Rob was timid of the Yankees because of Pete. Pete was Rob's own possession. He was the best sheep in the neighbourhood. Mr. Snell was always joking, saying that the Yankees, when they saw how big and fat Pete was, were going to eat him. But Pete was hidden safely in the springhouse. Yankees hadn't gone there yet.

There was a clatter in the road. "What's that, Robbie?" She did not wait to hear his answer, but began to 'shove' him. The window was so dirty, so unwashed, since Ma was 'took,' it was difficult for either one of them to peer through it.

Rob held his place stubbornly. There were the cows from Mr. Humphreys's farm. The road by the fence was all twinkling horns, and here, indoors, the sound of lowing could be heard. Ellen Ophelia was excited. Did they dare go out? "Shucks! These ain't nothin' to what I seen while y'all was he'pin' Ma," Rob said. "A heap of wild ones come by here, an' the sojers frowed a clothes-line ovah Colter's steer—hit was kickin' up so much."

Ellen Ophelia wondered resentfully if it were really true that she had missed a better sight. "Mah Lawsy, Rob, I'm glad Ma ain't awake. Y'all gonta scare her to death ef y'all tell tales like that. Oo! But you reckon that ol' spotty's gonta git inside our fence! Jes' see her butt our gate! What ef they gits mixed up in that bob wire yondah—I couldn't stand to look at it!"

402

Rob, with his back resisting her intrusion, was quite adamant. "Well, that ain't nothin' to the rumpus they was makin' 'fo' y'all came to look. They's about a thousan' cows gittin' driv' along the stone wall by the Meachems' place, an' when they gits down to the rivah, they git driv' in by the cavalry an' has to swim across."

She was convinced. "Rob, what y'all reckon we-all bettah do ef they git hold of Pete?" Her sly, open gaze examined nervously his half-averted face. Rob, sometimes, could 'git as mad as Ma.' There was a continual wonder and a longing in her. Why should he 'git so mad,' even with the Yankees? It was a temptation to her, in her own uneasiness, just to 'draw him out.'

She smoothed her braids smugly, and, with more propriety, drew down the folds of her ragged, dirty little apron. Rob would not bestow upon her the satisfaction of one glance. He said, keeping his face flattened to the window, and mumbling, "They ain't gonta git him."

"But what ef they *did?* Mr. Snell allus tol' us all that the Yankees was gonta *eat* Pete, Rob—an' now they's burnin' houses up."

Impulsively, he sidled away from her, away from the view of the lowing, passing cattle. All at once, however, he turned upon her, his round cheeks red, his blue eyes wide with a dazzling hostility. His fists shot out in a succession of vicious blows, and he was upon Ellen Ophelia, pommelling her in the stomach. "Oh, Rob, ouch! I'll pay you back faw that! Ef Ma was awake—but—Ma, *Ma!* I'm gonta tell her anyway!"

"Tattle-tale-tit! Tattle-tale-tit! You *ain't* gonta eat mah sheep! You *ain't!* You *ain't!*"

"Well, y'all ain't gonta hit me when I ain't done nothin' to you an' git off so easy. I'm not the biggest like y'all's allus sayin'— or if I am, I ain't a *boy.* Y'all's the worst brothah anybody evah had. Ma, Ma! Now, see y'all's gone an' done it! See, y'all waked Ma up!"

"Rob! Ellen Ophelia!" Mrs. Stoner had made a desperate movement to spring out of bed. She threw away the tumbled patchwork, rose, swaying on her feet an instant; then sat down weakly in the covers. Her elderly youthful features glistened with sudden sweat. Her gaze, in its tortured concentration, rested wildly on the children, yet not seeing them. "You nasty bad chillun!" she ac-

cused, abruptly. "You *fools!* You *fools!* Don't y'all see *nothin'!*
Oh, mah Gawd, delivah me, don't y'all *see* I'm sick?"

Pity for herself streamed from beneath her gently closing lids,
and she reclined in unpremeditated abandon, with her scrawny
arms flung wide, and her glance shut away from them. Ellen
Ophelia was trembling with that awful shame again. She went to
the baby and 'shooed' a fly that, chilled by the autumn morning,
was droning purposelessly above the infant's forehead.

Rob was taking the opportunity to escape. His bare feet pattered
over the dirt floor. He opened the back door of the house, and
darted swiftly out.

Mrs. Stoner said: "Don't y'all know how to take holt of a baby
so you won't break its neck? Mah Gawd, she's clumsy! The gal's
clumsy. There's pains all ovah me. It must be 'cause I ate them
greens y'all cooked me, Ellen Ophelia. I got no milk to feed that
chil'—that's why he frets so much."

Ma complained in this way, but she did not really seem to
care. Ellen Ophelia was often sorry for the baby because Ma did
not love it. It was better to evade like Rob. Ma was groaning
again. "Oh, the pains! Them pains in mah legs an' all through
me—oh, they're killin' me!"

Ellen Ophelia just stole forth quietly after Rob, closing the
door behind her, and shutting in with her mother the "La-a, la-a",
of the disturbed baby. If only Miss Jessie Snell would come to
take charge as upon the day before—"an' there ain't nothin' to
eat." Ellen Ophelia was a little disappointed that the Yankees had
ridden by. I reckon there ain't nothin' that they kin take from us,
she thought.

The springhouse was distant. Ellen Ophelia, secretively pursuing Rob, followed a path deeply threaded through a rusty fluff
of goldenrod. The leaves were falling—not all together, but one
at a time, in dry raining, tapping her hair occasionally. There
were balls hanging on the oaks. Nothing interrupted the sunshine
drenching all the half-bare branches. The smell and the haze
from the far-off charring crops was not unpleasant.

Rob was annoyed when his sister stole upon him, and pretended
obliviousness to her. He opened the padlock on the springhouse
door, and entered its gloom, not glancing back.

Pete was engaged with a little heap of grass. From his broad

404

shape, heavy as a mattress, rose a musty, greasy odour. Just once he lifted up his head and butted Rob out of the way. Pete's eyes, sending forth the sunshine that flowed in from without, did not so much as wink to indicate he heeded. His loose clump of tail twitched methodically, and he spilled, as if absently, his neat, perpetual droppings.

Rob made the pretence of tightening the sheep's halter. Ellen Ophelia interrupted. She could never bear to be excluded when Rob was doing anything. "Oh, Rob, please, Rob, the Yankees is sho' to find him here. Please let's take him out."

Rob, vulnerable to her suggestion, still refused to speak. "I was gonta do that anyhow," he said. And, nervously, he began to unfasten the knot he had but then made too secure. To show his sister what he thought of tenderness, he 'yanked' at Pete.

The sheep whirled, retreated, and softly presented dangerous horns. Ellen Ophelia, with more persuasiveness, tried to throw her arms about the animal. Rob defended possession. Pete was pushed from the springhouse, and, as Rob flapped the rope encouragingly, abruptly altered an attitude of obstinacy, and sprang toward the incline of the gully in which the springhouse rested. Rob's small arms were tautened in their sockets, while he climbed, at a run, the slope attempted by the stubborn sheep. Ellen Ophelia, avid to assist, rushed nimbly on ahead, and interfered with Pete's intimation of direction by stopping short and tossing up her ragged apron just in front of him.

When the three arrived at the back door of the house, they found it locked. The baby, as they listened for its whimpers, must have left off its complaint. Ellen Ophelia knocked several times, politely, then began to shout. "Ma! Ma! It's me an' Robbie, Ma!" When there was no reply, the children, hesitating, gazed at one another.

Rob said, "Oh, Sis, please hurry. I can see Mr. Snell comin' down the road an' he might tell somebody 'fo' we let Pete in." Rob's cheeks were violently red, his hard eyes indicated perturbation.

Ellen Ophelia covered uncertainty with reprimand. "Hit's y'all she's mad at. No wondah she don't wanta let us in when y'all kin ac' so ugly."

Rob, frowning, was unrelentingly reserved. "Maybe she's been

405

took sick ag'in," he suggested, reluctantly, in an involuntary tone of worry. "She couldn' git anothah baby quick as all this, could she, Sis?"

Ellen Ophelia, colouring disdainfully, would not meet his scrutiny. "Ain't y'all shamed to talk about sech things, an' y'all most growed up?"

"Quick. Y'all hol' Pete. I'm gonta go to the othah do', an' ef that's shet, too, I'm gonta climb up in the window an' git it open."

"Oh, Rob, don't leave me. Oh, Rob, I'm scared! What y'all reckon's the mattah, Rob? Wait till Mistah Snell is here. He's done seen us a'ready, anyhow. Ma mus' be awful mad at us to keep us out like this."

"He's a ol' story-teller. He's sho' to let them Yankees know 'at Pete is in the house. I ain't a-gonta wait."

"Well, I think we all oughtn'ta go in. Ef y'all's gonta look in the window, I'm comin', too. What y'all reckon made her have a baby, Rob? Y'all tell me, 'cause I think I know a'ready, an' it's awful funny."

Rob, tugging at Pete's rope, was a deep purple-crimson. "Y'all seen it when ol' Mistah Humphreys's Spotty had her calf," he said antagonistically. "Besides, it's bein' scared of these damn Yankees makes her sick so much. When I git big I'm gonta git Pa's shotgun an' kill 'em all."

He dropped Pete's halter, and the sheep immediately began to nibble. Rob, his haste soundless, darted past the corner of the house. Ellen Ophelia, ignoring her responsibility, imitated him at once. The front of the log dwelling was as impenetrable as the rear. As uneasiness increased commonly, Rob, with his pose of stolidness, became imperious. Ellen Ophelia, as though grateful for his domineering, turned inscrutably docile.

The window was small, and elevated from the ground. Rob pressed his straining fingers on the crooked sill, and, feeling, with his toes, the plane of wall beneath, elevated his slight weight. Ellen Ophelia, uninvited, supported his meagre, sagging buttocks. When he slid upon her to the earth, his glance was strange; but he made no remark, beyond, "I kin see the baby lyin' in the basket, but I can't see Ma nowhere. She must have took a notion to go out."

Ellen Ophelia wrung frail, limp hands, and danced up and down.

"Oh, Ma's took bad! Oh, I know she is. She must 'a' fainted. No, y'all got to he'p me. No, I *got* to look."

She clambered toward the window, constantly advising Rob, who, with imperfect effort, pushed her behind. Finally, she hung teetering. "Hold me, Rob. Hold me! Oh, I'm slippin'. Oh, I'm scared! Run git Mistah Snell. Oh, I'm so scared! I don't wanta look no mo'. Oh, let me down frum here quick." Releasing herself with a clatter, Rob springing aside, she fell on her crooked elbow, in the worn grass. "Mistah Snell! Mistah Snell!" she began to shriek.

An oldish, bareheaded man was entering the picket gate. Ellen Ophelia, her face wizened with emotion, sprang up crazily. Her braids bumping, her linsey-woolsey dress wrapping her naked small ankles, she fled toward him, panting, and, throwing herself upon him, clinging to him, her arms twining his neck braced to resist her, cried, agonizingly, "It's Ma! It's Ma! Ma's took the bedclothes! She's tied the bedclothes to rafters! Take her down, Mistah Snell! Take her down quick. Ma's—Ma's—oh she's trying to hang herse'f!"

Rob was upon them, his doubled knuckles frantic on his sister. His features blurred with panic. "She's a liar! She's a liar! I don't wanta hear her, Mistah Snell! Don't y'all let her talk like that!"

As, weakened, bewildered by his steady attack, she continued to insist, Rob darted backward from Mr. Snell's arresting arm, and retreated toward the road, toward the smouldering meadow opposite. "It ain't true," he was screaming. "It ain't true an' ol' sis knows it. I ain't comin' back."

Ellen Ophelia in a peculiar, sudden silence, as she half leaned in Mr. Snell's embrace, slipped to the earth. Stodgily confused, the old man stared helplessly at the child's huddled figure, abandoned before him. Slowly, he reassembled his shocked wits. Then he raised his fists in the hazy sunlight and shook them violently at nobody. He did not comprehend fully what had occurred, but his hate was ready. The Yankees! General Sheridan with his vile excuse of the one murdered Lieutenant Meigs! "Lawd, ef I could git a chanct at jest one mo' of them vermin wouldn't I pick him off!"

XV

AUNT NANCY GREEN, standing in the low doorway of her cabin, watched, with rheumy eyes of wonder, streams of Federal soldiers passing. Some one had told her that General Hood had been defeated at Allatoona, and, since then, it seemed that the 'end uv de world' was not far off. Aunt Nancy Green's 'white folks,' in the years that had passed since the beginning of the war, had all died or gone away. Since the fading of gradual, Southern autumn, with the vague approach of an indefinite winter, Aunt Nancy had sustained herself with a diet of 'yarbs,' a few grown in the poor soil of her own garden, but others sought for as they sprang, withered by the November chill, in the abandoned fields and pastures near her collapsing dwelling.

This was a day 'like rain.' Aunt Nancy, from the moment she had opened her eyes, while she yet lay on her straw pallet on the earthen floor, had 'knowed faw sho'' that 'dis heah somepin'' everybody was expecting was now ripe to happen. Yet the spectacle of Union infantry was a disappointment. "How many Ah seen come down dis road!" she mumbled. "How many Ah seen!" A naked, shrivelled old arm protruded its shrunken, browned bone from the torn sleeve of her chemiselike dress of unbleached cotton. She leaned her palsied weight on a tall stick. Aunt Nancy's wool grew in white, ravelled knots, with glinting spacings of bald, revealed skull. Her features were disguised in bunched wrinkles. Her toothless mouth had a sagging, gathered underlip, sulky with a sardonic droop. Her gaze, beady and still, as from behind a mist, was like that of a dead bird. Age, in her, was the indifference born of meagre strength. Yet there were sudden avid flashes of expression that displayed the crafty longings of her ancient discontent. "Dem's Yankees. Dem's sho'ly Yankees," she mused; and laid her own deep conjectures as to why they were so numerous. The preachers, for many years, had warned her to guard her patience. It was wearing out. An urge for flight would often come upon her, as it comes, unadvised by reason, on some migratory animal. It had been the urge to quit the place in which her loved ones, black and white, were buried, that had sent her wandering half across the state to select, finally, for her habitation, this derelict cabin by the highway that belonged to nobody.

Not dat Ah's lonesome, Aunt Nancy thought. Not dat Ah's lonesome. Ah min's mah peace an' de othah folks bettah min' deirs.

And it was true that, while she counselled the social and the love-lorn of the neighbourhood, she defied them with her solitariness.

Wagons rumbled by under loads covered by tarpaulins. Some of the soldiers plodded past with the dull, laboured tread of duty to which she was used. She saw them but indefinitely. She had keen ears for noises, though she was deaf to words, and she heard the squeaking of the repetitious wheels, the even thudding of the thousand feet. That mere boys were among these legion, she had known before. She tottered closer to the filing companies and watched them absently. Dey's young, she reflected, suddenly. Dey enjoys it. "Mawnin', gemman. Mawnin', young white man," she muttered, fancying or sensing greetings. Then, "Hello, old lady! Don't you want to come along and join Pap Sherman's army?" some one shouted. "What are you makin' such a sour face for? If times is hard, you better come and join the army. You kin bet on us to git enough to eat. It's Christmas almost every day with us."

What were they saying? Dimly comprehending the invitation, she caught, in the voices, an odd note of cheer. It disturbed her. She was not prepared for merriment.

"Mawnin', suh. Mawnin', mistah." Her claw hand, free of the stick, fumbled her sunken bosom. On her shrivelled neck, folded in its loose, brown flesh, her head wagged perpetually. The most she could do, as she listened to the unceasing marching, was to attempt to remember something she had thought of years ago. Ah knows 'em. Ah seems to know 'em. Mo'n y'all kin count. Dey went by heah on dis very road when de wah begun. An' dey wuz all happy. Long ago, back in de beginnin', all de folks wuz happy. Maybe dat was whin Ah seen Mistah Andrew Jackson ridin' by on his hoss. Yes, Ah wuz youngah den. An' who'd 'a' reckoned aftah all dis time, dey'd be comin' back?

The ranks, bawling to her, tramped on. She peered. She craned. Her worried eyes, in their bagging, shrivelled lids, drew to glittering slits. There was a dimness upon her, and she could not look beyond it. The world of so many, many noises, sank in rainy light.

A band passed. She was aware of it as a sharp, unrhymed discordance in an inner harmony. Hit ain' de right tune dose folks is playin', she thought aggrievedly; yet her heartbeats warmed out of their gradual slowness. Irritably, struggling to remember other days and other tunes, she cupped her dry, sharp palm behind her ear, and tried to coax her sense of music back.

But the rapid sounds, the stamping, a burst of sudden singing, forced her out of long, unwilling languor. The mists shrank from her dizzy gaze. Reluctantly she seemed to see again.

'Sho' 'nough,' there was a young 'gemman' marching with two hams slung across his shoulders. A soldier pushed a baby's carriage filled with apples. He invited her to laugh with him, but she blinked, bewildered, confined in her aged doubt, in her incredulity. A cow, dragged on a rope behind one of the throng, abased her head and mooed despairingly. At her deep, broken low of alarm, a soldier, in hilarious imitation, took up the plaint. There came a cart in which three bumping sheep were crowded, while the young man who was driving wore a coachman's hat.

Two boys, hatless, bestrode one balky donkey. A youth, in the muddied petticoats of a lady, flaunted imposing hoops and a feathered bonnet. He carried a clock, and a gilt-framed mirror. Aunt Nancy detected an incongruous quality in his appearance, and began feebly to chuckle. She disbelieved, yet she was soothed by 'all dis foolishness.'

The chuckle came out of a throat and mind to which chuckles represented delirium. Cautiously, she hushed herself. There was nothing which she could tear from the scene to answer her own want. Wagons of munitions began to succeed the vans, the haycarts filled with edibles and poultry. Threading joyfully the crowds of military followed negro boys and women, adding their hurrahs to the intermittent singing of the others. "Git along dere. Move along. Git outen mah way. Hi, Pershy, come along down front." The women rustled hastily in bedraggled calicoes that swept the ground. Now and then they broke into awkward running, shepherding ahead of them half-naked piccaninnies, who carried importantly protruding bellies under tattered shifts exposing twinkling, naked legs. "Jubilee's a-comin', Mammy," a girl yelled to Aunt Nancy. And, "Praise de Lawd, we gonta flee ou' troubles," cried an older voice excitedly. Solitary in an interval of rush, a young man with a banjo sauntered slowly, strumming:

> "Voyez *ce mulet-là*,
> Miché *Bain-jo*,
> Comme *il est insolent!*"

The *tick-tick* of the banjo strings trembled minutely in Aunt Nancy's mind when the young man had been succeeded by many: by one who, balancing upon his head a silver platter, pilfered somewhere, represented himself as vending fish, and called:

> "Pawgy walk an' Pawgy talk,
> An' Pawgy eat wif knife an' fawk!
> Git a nice Pawgy!"

Some dem's Chawlston niggahs, Aunt Nancy determined heedful of the chatter of a patois she had once better comprehended.

"De patter-roller ull git y'all, Aunt Nancy." The taunt came from a worthless boy of her own vicinity. Aunt Nancy was shaken by more intimate doubts. "Where'bouts y'all goin', Felix Henry?" she quavered. "How come y'all out here paradin' wid dese city folks?"

"Savannah, Aunt Nancy. Y'all bettah come 'long," he told her, grinning and speeding provocatively down the road, dodging horses' feet.

The gaiety dwindled. Dingier ranks of silent troops overflowed the edges of the fields, and some circled Aunt Nancy, who, in a mute, attentive attitude, stood in their way. Now there was only the tingle of harness, the rattle of the bolts and screws of vehicles, the snuffles of the labouring mules, and the ringing made by jolted cannon. Militantly uttered commands did not stir her. Still the echoes of the voices of the jumbled merrymakers, remote in the rainy distance of the country, were wafted, like a brightness, toward her, on the sagging, moist autumn day.

The daze of regret held. For an hour, she contemplated numbers, dreary and seemingly infinite. And she was bound there, to the roadside, by a growing burden of defeat. "Dey gone," she mumbled at last, in an awful voice; and her withered features, in this abrupt, undetailed, tardy realization, contracted in a grotesque grimace of self-commiseration. "Ah's waited ninety-five yeahs faw dis," she said, "an' dey pass me by. How come dey do it? How come dey pass me by wid all dem victuals an' things! Dey ain' got no pity."

Famished as was her body, her weak fancy grasped, orgiastically, an impression of all the hams and 'middlin'' she had seen that morning. But her greed was base, so she told herself. On'y dem 'at has got a mighty heap uv patience evah gits to Paradise!

She doddered. There was a peace and a satisfaction imminent, her very frailty informed her. Her gaunt, erect form drooped a little. She leaned more helplessly her pendent breasts against her creaking stick.

The final, straggling soldiers were beyond her, leaving the country wide and solemn for their passing, when her lean energy was roused. Knees bending stiffly, she climbed, with a feverish resolution, from her vantage point on the rising ground before the cabin, and began to exhort: "Wait faw me, brothahs! Wait faw me, brothahs an' sistahs! Ah ain't skeered faw to follow! Ah ain't one uv dem dat denies de Lawd an' all His promises. Ah ain't holdin' back!"

With her rent garments flowing behind her in the small wind that had risen and lisped the weeds and grasses, she rushed excitedly down the abandoned pike. Her face, in its peering anxiety, on her palsied neck, was thrust in advance of her rigid, padding staff. Her naked feet, the flat soles horny with many pilgrimages, flapped heavily through dust in which a trivial rain-drop sometimes left· a pursuing print. And she gave forth gladly, with a faith released and become defiant, strength that she felt would surely be her last. "Heab'n nigh," she kept on saying, as she stumbled blindly. "Yes, brothahs, Ah got de news, an' Ah'm gonta tell y'all whin Ah kotch up wid y'all. Jesus Christ is sendin' me to tell y'all—Heab'n· sho'ly nigh." She panted, she wept—but *with joy, with joy*. She would march to Savannah, with the others. "Jesus Christ tell me. Jesus Christ tell me go an' seek mah peace!

Jesus Christ tell me to go on to Savannah wid de army an fin' mah happiness."

. . . .

"Frien's, Ah sees 'em comin'!" Cicero Stout, his congregation assembled in a ruined cotton gin, waved toward the road, which was visible before them, a fat hand of prophecy. "Didn' Ah tell y'all faith gwineta move mountains? See 'em. Dere dey is. Let dat put a end to yo' doubt."

Dilsy, Cora, Phoebe, and Uncle Tinker Mosley, rising from their knees, followed their adviser's gesture and stared over the dreaming fields. From the distance shouts and strains of band music floated unbelievably.

"Dat ain' de army uv de Lawd," Dilsy objected after a moment. "Dat's some uv dem Yankee sojers dat been stealin' stuff frum ev'ybody."

Cicero, in his grease-seamed, long-tailed, 'preacher's' coat, cast at her a glance of pompous reprimand in which might have been detected a strain of downright malice. Dilsy, in fact, felt her backbone stiffen as against his unjust contempt. Yet the wafted tune was already exciting her irresistibly.

Uncle Tinker, very black and wiry, grinned fatuously, and began, in rhythmic approbation, to wag his head a little. "What do hit mattah ef dey's on'y Yankees?" he objected, shamed as he became aware of Dilsy's stubborn sceptic scrutiny. "Ef de Lawd sen' Yankees faw to lead we-all to ou' salvation, dat's 'nough faw us."

"Milk an' honey," insisted the orator. "Milk an' honey. Da's what dey got. All has to jine an' march to Savannah as mah vision says to me."

"What we all gwineta do when we gits dere, Brothah Cic'ro?" Cora objected, resentful of Dilsy, yet restrained from too precipitate enthusiasm by the recollection of the stockingful of pennies she had been obliged to dole to the preacher in order to enjoy the comfort of his words.

"Did Moses, when he led de chillun to de Promised Land, ax de Lawd about tomorrow and what he gwineta do faw him?"

Phoebe fidgeted. With five small piccaninnies to feed and her husband run away from her, she felt that a reckless departure with the approaching army could present no risks more harassing

413

than those she was already taking daily. "Ah don' keer what de chances is, Ah'm gonta jine," she said.

"Thanky, Sistah Phoebe. Ah specs de Lawd ull be a little kinder to y'all dan to dese doutin' othahs."

He was filled with disdain of them. Ah'm goin', he had decided. Ah got 'nough uv slave-holdahs. Dey ain' no powah in dis world no mo 'kin keep me frum goin' free. But dese blacks ain' sensible. Ah got de knack uv speakin' so dey has to listen, but Ah can' even fool 'em so dey sees things straight.

The tide of blue-coat humans grew. The specks became faces. There was the band, and a 'high-steppin' hoss' waltzed under an officer who rode along in front.

Lige Bean's boy was running in advance of all the crowd. Dilsy recognized him and was humiliated. Ef Lige Bean 'low his chil' in dis procession dey mus' be somepin' in dis talk. Cicero say dat de Yankees takin' frum de rich folks an' de quality so ev'y-thing kin be divided an' 'nough faw ev'ybody.

She moved nearer the road, but still resisted, and tried to conceal, under a guise of casualness, her wavering attitude. "Wha'-bouts y'all off to, Sassy? Is y'all got crazy like dese othah nig-gahs?" she called out to him.

Sassy showed brilliant teeth in a face careless with laughter, and cried, "No mo' pint o' salt, no' whup lash faw me, Aunt Phoebe. Ah got 'nough uv dat!"

Cicero, impeded by his massive stoutness, sidled into the gully below them, then climbed up on the road. He had influenced his adherents all he could ever hope to influence them. He would have preferred to arrive in Savannah with a following—and yet— with their inconvenient knowledge of his history, it might be better to 'shake 'em off' now. There could be no turning back.

So he rushed heavily to join the ragged fringe of those whose enthusiasm led them ahead of the army itself. Cora, her reluctance broken, shouted, "Ah'm goin' along wid y'all, Brothah Cic'ro. Can' y'all wait a mite?" She was fat, she was anxious, but she pursued him with agility, darting past the horses.

In silence, Uncle Mose laboured feebly to reach the others. Phoebe giggled delightedly. "Come on, Dilsy! Don' y'all be so cross wid Cic'ro. Ain' de fac' de army come dis very mawnin' proof he tell de truf to us?"

Her voluble consideration for a friend delayed her, and by the time she had made her quick decision to desert recalcitrant Dilsy, Cicero, Lige Bean's boy, Cora and Uncle Mose were all out of sight. So Phoebe found herself walking with the band, and was disconcerted by her unpremeditated conspicuousness only because the 'chune' had ceased. She glanced about her wonderingly. Yet this was good, no matter what might come. The instant in which she had stepped into the road, she had thrown off the burdens of the past few months and assumed, with an ecstasy she could not curb, an existence of chance, of opportunities unnamed, of irresponsibility. Seem like Dilsy turn up her nose at luck when hit come her way, Phoebe thought. Ef de Lawd sen' trouble, he can' mean it to las' faw evah. When he give folks happy feelin' like Ah got dis mawnin' he want you to enjoy yo'se'f. Cicero say de misery jes' de preparin' faw de good time comin'.

Dilsy had seen soldiers before. She had no faith in them. She remained obstinately by the roadside, compelling herself, against her instincts, to keep her emotions within the proper bounds for a spectator. 'Sides, Ah got chillun, she meditated. How kin Ah go off like dat prancin' Phoebe an' fawgit dose dat belongs to me. Ah can' do it. No, suh, 'fo' Gawd, not faw to please dat low-down preachah. Ah, can' do it. But the next instant, she was weakening. Ah wondah kin Ah pick up Ben an' Pomp an' Susan 'fo' dey all git past. Oh, Gawd, tell me is Ah doin' right! But dey ain' no mo'n a few sticks lef' in mah cabin dat's wuth anything.

Now the riotous began to appear. To the *trep-trep* of a single monotonous drum, the motley, interspersed among hilarious soldiery, were exposed for her review. When she saw the three sheep, their muzzles bumping stolidly against the sides of the cart driven by the ornate coachman, she broke into a grudging laugh.

The trouble, to her mind, was that she recognized exposed belongings. Da's Jedge Bass's roan dat man is ridin', aw Ah's a liar. An' look at dem folks totin' all dat pawlah furniture. What dey gwineta do wid it!

"Wha'bouts y'all goin', Chawlie Pearce?" she shouted deridingly, to an acquaintance. "Dat mule you leadin' 'longs to ol' Mas' Sampson. Y'all bettah watch out dat he don' lock y'all up faw stealin'."

Charlie Pearce, if disconcerted, concealed it amiably. "De time hes pas' whin dis belong an' dat belong, Sis' Dilsy. Gen'al Sherman ain' gwineta lock me up 'cause Ah got dis mule. De things wuth havin' in dis mournin' world belongs to ev'ybody!"

"What got in *yo'* haid, Sistah Price? Is y'all takin' Jake an' Reube an' Marigold an' Molly to Savannah, too? Ah usta think y'all thought mo' yo' chillun."

"Ah thinks too much to stay behin' whin de chanct come. De Lawd ain' botherin' *His* haid 'bout doubtahs an' quittahs."

"Willie Smith, is y'all been riflin' de country, too? Is y'all gonta Savannah wid all dis truck dat don' belong to y'all?"

"Ah ain' keepin' y'all frum goin', is Ah?" Willie demanded, with unheralded belligerence.

"Come along, gals," a humorous white soldier invited. "When we're all as happy as we are today, we love both black and white."

Yet Dilsy lingered. Oh, Gawd, Ah *has* wuked hard in mah life, she acknowledged wearily.

Perpetual worry was like a tautness in her brain. She yearned to break it. Slavin', slavin', slavin' faw de men-folks, slavin' faw de white folks, das de 'oman's lot.

Then august in tottering earnestness amidst the frivolous, walked Aunt Nancy Green. Why, *dat* ol' 'oman sayed to have de second sight! How come *she* go along!

Dilsy, in her common sense, despaired. What de use mah stayin' heah? Dey won't be nobody lef'. Oh, Gawd, has Ah got to take de road wid all dese critters? Oh, Gawd, he'p me. Gawd, faw mah ownest part, hit don' seem to mattah no' mo' what happen. Dem chillun, allus hongry like dey is, take de heart outen me. Ah almos' los' mah gumption. But do Ah know hit's right?

Then, with a swift, grim stride, she turned, and began to run across the fields toward her house. She had not gone fifty paces when Ben and Pomp rushed from the distant cabin to meet her. "Mammy, Mammy, we-all been lookin' faw y'all, Mammy! Ain't we all goin' to Savannah, Mammy, where dey got so much to eat?"

Dilsy halted, panting, eyeing them with a pain like anger. "Yes, we goin' now. Y'all ain't got mo'n dem shirts y'all's wearin', an' you' paw kin look aftah hisse'f, Ah reckon. He kin git as much comfawt frum a jug uv whisky as frum a 'oman anyway."

She gripped their excited wrists. "Susan—where's Susan? Dere y'all is. Now don' y'all cry an' don' you whimper. Y'all wanta go to Savannah an' y'all's goin', but y'all ain' goin' back to de house to look faw nothin'. Ef yo' paw was to learn dat we was runnin' off he'd take it outen us."

.   .   .   .

The two girls waited in the edge of the woods: Anna bold, risking discovery by anybody, and not a whit more timid for the baby in her arms; Lou, with her ladylike mien, still in the grip of the proprieties, and by no means without some pangs of conscience due to 'runnin' off.' The cold, bright wind of fading afternoon ruffled the pine-feathers. There was a scurf of needles on the ground. It was growing late and was very silent. Lou, in her demureness, with that air of decorum peculiar to slave girls who are lady's maids and seamstresses, was perhaps the more excited of the two. Anna was a field hand. She could 'swing a hoe jes' like a man,' and so was accustomed to a life of independence. Her courage, in the eyes of Lou, was further explained by the boast she often made of having 'Injun' blood. It was the attitude of 'Injun blood' toward an unfathered baby that made it seem possible that Anna's vow had been more than careless words when she had declared that Joe Tucker, renegade parent of her child, had 'bettah watch out!' Joe Tucker had run away to Savannah, gossip said, and Anna, deep-bosomed, strong, with her bold, moist eye, her wild, uncombed 'straight' hair, was bent on following him. "Joe he gwineta wish't he nevah had been bawn!" so Anna said. Anna had slung her baby in her shawl. Sometimes, when she remembered, she jogged it carelessly.

But there was no more time to talk, or to discuss repentance. The army was already audible. The two girls, listening, Lou covert and Anna insolent, began to hear the crowd's shouts. Lou was pretty, a small girl of the tint of milk and coffee, with a consumptive chest. When she realized that now indeed there could be no turning back, she began to shiver. 'Miss Dosia,' her mistress, a solitary spinster, had always been 'mighty good.' She had often given praise, before the neighbours, to Lou's needlework. Under 'Miss Dosia's' supervision there was no play, no open interest in men, not even giggling permitted. 'Miss Dosia' had done her best to have Lou 'converted.' Lou could not explain herself, and felt very apologetic that she had been so dissatisfied.

As the first soldiers grew into normal shapes, filling the highway, Anna discarded caution. "Dey's some fine set-up gemmen in dese companies, Lou," she said admiringly; and she stepped forth recklessly. Anna had a shrill soprano voice, incongruous with her shape and her importance, and she talked loudly. Lou, wretched to know such compliments were overheard, shrank timidly. The friendliness with which white marchers stared at Anna struck Lou as shameless. She had a longing to draw away. Somehow she had not conceived of the army as composed exclusively of men. She was humiliated by her indecision. She envied Anna. Lou always wanted to behave herself 'de way de nicest white folks did.' Anna, ostensibly, was 'goin' aftah Joe,' but it was plain that she would not be adverse to picking up some other fellow on the journey. Lou, catching sight of the following peaceful marauders with their pigs and sheep and chickens, laughed hysterically.

Anna wanted to fall in with the first negro stragglers, but Lou demurred. "Wait a minute, Anna. Wait a minute, Anna. Dey's on'y sojers in dis part. Dis ain't gonta be our place." Anna smirked, tossed up her head impatiently, and muttered contemptuously, in her shrill, whining voice, "What y'all scared of, Lou?" Lou shrank self-consciously into her shawl. Anna's brazenness, though it should not have been new, was a revelation. Lou wondered she had ever dared to leave her home with an 'Injun' girl. Where two companies divided, a hundred negroes tramped compactly, announced by their singing. Anna, as though she cast aside the last triviality of discretion, also opened wide her mouth.

> Oh, mah lil soul gwineta shine like a star,
> Oh, mah lil soul gwineta shine like a star,
> Oh, mah lil soul gwineta shine like a star,
> *Good Lawd, Ah's bound to heav'n at res'!*

"Da's right, Perk an' Mamie, be 'fectionate. Love gwineta take y'all to heav'n anyhow!" rang out a woman's voice, in the pause between choruses.

With heavy nimbleness, Anna ran to enter the mêlée. The baby, jolted, screamed and clutched at her bandanna. She ignored it.

418

The coarse hair, that was a confusion to the less fortunate, slipped from its pins, and sprang, stiff, in a wild array, about a face forgetful in delight. "Hurry up, Lou," she called, exultance counting as indifference to her friend; and slipped, at ease, as usual, into the ranks that opened for her. I ain't gonta waste *mah* life doin' chores faw ol' maids: went through her mind, that half needed, yet resented, an excuse for its determination. Grinning, with the eager look of a child, she hastened proudly. Dey ain' no end to what Ah kin do ef Ah gits a notion! she thought.

Lou had hesitated, as before a leap to disaster. Flinging loyalties off, she accepted this freedom; but at so great a price that the hope she would be justified almost broke her heart. She *had* to believe that the road to Savannah was the way to heaven. Tripping, slight, she gained Anna's side; but not reassurance. The big girl, with her swimming looks flung like an indecency on her companions, made Lou quail, feel insignificant. He'p me, Lawd. He'p me, he'p me, Lou prayed, and clenched her feeble little yellow fingers. Anna, striding, with her ignored baby, with her full throat high, with her shrill chant, seemed to be the possessor of something that a girl *must* have if she would save her sanity. Oh, dis is de craziest t'ing to do, thought Lou. Dis is de craziest t'ing to do! The feeling in her was like a sob. She ran on with this sense of wailing, with this hateful, bitter hungriness.

> Rocks an' de mountains gwineta all flee away,
> Y'all shell hev' a new hidin'-place dat day,
> When dem rocks an' dem mountains all flee away,
> *All flee away!*

But where? *Where?* The damp, fragrant air passed over their heads, passed over fields, flats, a last leaf blowing; over something distant, gaudied by the slight sun. The trees rocked slowly from their indifferent roots. Even the stinging freshness of the pine smell added wideness to the world. Their brushing carried recognition of a farther and yet farther enormousness, going on faintly, from this world to another. There was no place to hide.

Anna was 'stuck up,' too proud. She gave Lou the impression of something giddy—'drunk an' don'-care.' She would rush on a few paces, halt, wait for Lou, and tumble on again. Her wild hair glittered with a faint, rusty copper in the low light. Her swollen

419

mouth laughed. She glanced about her in a kind of impudent absence. Lou was excluded from the sharing of this pleasure, this solemnity. People jostled, bumped along past them, screamed at one another. Oh, Gawd, what has Ah done! Lou grieved. But grief had wider wings than joy. One rich branch swaying on the sky was a whole bridge to bear the world from life to death. Lou never expected to see 'Miss Dosia' again. She went on, singing with a shrill sound. None of her 'nice mannahs' covered her. Her clean-starched calico dress no longer covered her. Anna's very presence left her naked to the raw bravado of the men. She tried not to consider anything—anything.

.   .   .

Tabby, gripping the lax wrists of her trudging children, marched with her chin high, and in a kind of wilful blindness. She was leaving Remus. Jay had beat her because of Remus, and when she had gone to Remus for protection, he had denied her. "Go 'long way frum me, 'oman," Remus had said. "Ah tol' mah Hattie how y'all try to tempt me an' she gwineta teach y'all lesson, she say, ef y'all pesters me ag'in. An' what mo', if yo' ol' man sen' y'all heah 'cause he wanta saddle *me* wid all his troubles, why Ah sen's y'all back. Ah ain' de fust man y'all's tried to lead to de debbil. Y'all don' respec' yo'se'f nohow, aw y'all wouldn' come aftah me so shameless. An' dat baby dat y'all says y'all's carryin', why dat's yo' husban's chil'—aw leastways hit don' belong to me. Don' try to take 'vantage uv *me* wid dat."

Tabby had passed Remus at the crossing. He was there in a new checked suit and a red necktie, with a 'stand-up' collar. And when he had seen her he had greeted her jauntily. "Y'all hit de road, too, is you, ol' gal?" he had asked. And he had fallen brazenly into the ranks behind. She would not look at him.

> Oh, by an' by,
> By an' by,
> Ah's gwineta lay down mah heavy load.
> Ah knows mah robe gwineta fit me well,
> Ah's gwineta lay down mah heavy load.
> Ah tried hit on at de gates uv hell.
> Ah's gwineta lay down mah heavy load.
> Oh,—by, an' by,
> *By an' by!*

There was a pressure on her brain where the weight of calamity still rested. Even here she did not escape it. Da's on mah heart. Dat go faw evah, she thought. She stumbled. With gentle chill, the rain dappled her hot forehead. The road went on. Savannah was *'by an' by, by an' by.'* Dat end it. Ah see de chillun fixed somehow, an' den Ah's done. Dat gambler destroy me.

.   .   .   .

At Swamp Pike Turning, an old woman some knew by the name of Aunt Nancy Green succumbed eternally to a trial of endurance which was beyond the strength of her years. Her ever more dragging footsteps suddenly lagged, and she made a thickly muttered plea for support. Thence, for two hours or more, she resigned herself to the guidance of Tabby Merriweather, a stranger.

Aunt Nancy's fleshless clutch on the strong arm offered her became ever more frantic. Her staff ceased to be of use to her, and she cast it wearily aside. Her white head, without a bandanna, and with its contours of a man's head, rocked limply downward on her contorted neck. Many of the darkies watched her, and with a stealthy, superstitious interest. That Aunt Nancy's patriarchal presence carried omen, they could not doubt. In the corners of her puffed, nervously chewing lips, froth began to gather. Her bleared eyes appeared to look out on her companions from a focus of self-engrossment always more remote. She hiccuped, sputtered. Her body was aquiver like a grass blade in the wind. Then, abruptly, in the midst of her mumbled "Praise Gawd, praise Gawd," her gaunt weight sagged. Tabby, arrested by the old woman's twitchings, halted, but was not deft enough to save her. Aunt Nancy, senselessly resisting support, sank as if boneless to the earth, falling clumsily, so that her jawbone thwacked, with a brutal impact, among loose stones.

Instantly she huddled there, impeded groups collected about her, until, pressed on by the succeeding soldiers, they were rudely hastened and obliged to run. Yet there was a space preserved around her, and a few, defying approaching authority, continued to offer her their assistance. To the point of lifting herself on one sharp elbow, she contrived to respond. But the paroxysms that shook her began again. She offered her stiffening face to the observers. Out of her dry brown features, shrivelled with pain, her eyes were little specks of roving brightness. "Jawdon," she enunciated harshly, with a violence of meaning which the word did not contain. "On to Jawdon!"

One arm thrust forth from her dangling sleeve and pointed waveringly ahead. But her speech terminated in further bubblings of saliva from her dry mouth, and in strange gurgles in her throat. She tried to push her audience aside, struggled to her knees, fumbled aimlessly for the stick which she had discarded, and her awkward palms flapped petulantly in the dust of the road. At last she gave up, rolled to her side again, and stretched herself at length amidst manure and stones. For several seconds she gaped, her nostrils expanding to seek a last breath, and oozing sticky moisture. Her dim eyes were still open—'like a fire in a bush,' they looked, Tabby thought. Finally their unwinkingness was marked. A film as of resignation spread over the dull, brilliant pupils.

A group of cavalry, trotting past, was obliged to contract to a single file. "Why the hell don't you clear those niggers out of the road," a man shouted. And steamy mists from the snorting animals blew upon the hesitant darkies who massed themselves deferentially about the corpse. Some wanted to bury the old woman at once. Others, with a terror of being left behind, advised carrying her body with them until all should arrive at the spot at which camp would be pitched. The arguments of those opposed to delay triumphed. A litter of pine boughs was constructed, and Aunt Nancy, already cold, was laid on it.

Her bearers set off at a running walk, which the children accompanied, while older men, women who were ill, or exhausted, or were carrying babies, followed more sedately. Fresh arrivals of infantry intercepted the funeral cortège, and it was no longer continuous. Yet the song begun by the women was echoed to each party of mourners and by them repeated:

> Round about de mountain,
> Oh, round about dese valleys,
> Oh, round about de mountain
> An' she'll rise in His arms.

The autumn sun swam from clouds and was a tepid gold. Dregs of leaves, with their gala artificiality, littered the ground on which the marchers hurried under old oaks.

De Lawd love a sinnah,
De Lawd love a sinnah,
De Lawd love a sinnah,
An' she'll rise up in His arms!

The ornamental litter, shed like flowers before a procession, turned papery and colourless with evening. A fan of radiance opened on the horizon, and pearled rays spread gigantically moted shafts half blinding all the ardent eyes that looked into them. The cold sounds of twilight grew fainter. Even the singing seemed hushed, while, into the cool blaze of the west, the beetles floated steadily on drowsing wings. Then the stars began to scatter their silver cinders. The fiery pines blackened. The live oaks rose like darker clouds in their veils of moss. Dem folks dat kill Aunt Nancy—dey on'y send her on ahead uv 'em, Tabby thought. De Fed'rals aw de Confed'rates, whoevah dey is, dey sent Aunt Nancy on ahead uv us. Dey's gropin', but *she* knows. Oh, Gawd, gimme strength ag'inst dat po' man, Remus.

. . . . .

As the day evaporated, like some rare dew vanished, a full orange moon swelled upon the clouds, only to be drawn away again in added tides of dark. Rain came bitter through the night, and firebrands, ignited, were at once extinguished. People kept close to one another by the comforting signals of running feet. The negroes, worn out, trudged on doggedly, but in silence; and it was to fight the depression of quieted rowdiness and stilled emotion that the soldiers themselves initiated their own vocal music. They sang *John Brown's Body*, and when the refrain was completed with the line, *"But his soul goes marching on!"* huzzas that were a defiance to wind, to cheerless drizzle and discomfort rang in the sightless world in which companionship alone represented a rescue from oblivion.

. . . . .

Luther Peabody, under the trees shedding ghost moonlight through the wafts of rain, circled the camps stealthily. The pallid slopes of soldiers' tents, he avoided; though the mess tents attracted him, and he did hesitate to watch, for an instant, white troops gathered about a seething camp-fire and eating avidly.

Spitefully, he listened to gruff, jovial chatter. The soldiers were emptying a cider jug. One, somewhat drunk, rose and began to deliver a mock oration, while he beat, for attention, a tin spoon on a plate. "——the women, anyhow." The soldier was advising thickly. "You, gentlemen ud be—should be happiest in the world with no ladies livin'. Damn thesh Southern wenches runs away frum ush—'cause they got no more to offer ush 'an th' othahs got."

"I seen you makin' eyes at that black gal, Henry. You may not think so much o' the white ones, but you won't waste your time down South. You need some new experience."

Luther spat contemptuously and hurried on. *Dey* time comin'. Dey time comin'. Ah serve y'all faithful an' Ah serve y'all offen, Mistah Debbil, ef y'all ull git *dem* fust.

Luther had considered the advisability of demanding scraps from one of the negro cooks. But he decided against it. There were too many 'niggers' in the camp already, and the recent order of authority was to deny them charity.

That didn't matter. Luther believed in the devil, and the devil was very strong. He had decided to go on to Savannah with the others, and to make it 'pay.' Debbil, y'all's gonta he'p me, Debbil. Dere's 'nough sorghum an' flour an' meal an' middlin' done been levied by dese Yankees to serve ev'ybody. But what Luther needed, as he always did when in difficulties, was a woman's loyalty. Effen Ah kin git some gal to look aftah me ag'in, Ah won' starve to deaf.

He was not the only scavenger of the gathering. As he dodged, peered, shrank behind trees, essaying to steal forward and snatch from the wet ground the scraps of refuse that servants were throwing out, he encountered shapes moving with a circumspection equal to his own. Frequently, he had a glimpse of hostile eyes rolling perturbed whites; and the slinking darkies, bumping into one another, met revelation with curses.

Despite the weather, there was a barbecue in progress. In shallow trenches, reddened by the sputtering charcoal sticks on which the rain-drops boiled, whole pigs were roasting. The headless bodies, spitted on long wooden prongs, reared stiff, fragmentary legs from parching buttocks. Luther, inhaling greedily the odours of succulent flesh, was maddened to more open boldness.

424

But when he approached, in the rosy, violent reflections from the fire, a soldier threw a rock at him.

So he was obliged to retreat, and to crouch beside the golden looming of another lighted plane of tent.

Five men were within. All, by the uniforms they wore, were officers. Luther, grudging them the warmth and comfort they enjoyed, listened to their conversation vindictively. The one who wore a full brown beard was seated on the edge of a camp-bed, smoking. Three others were idling about a table on which a lantern had been placed. A fifth had just removed from a carpet-bag a bottle which he said contained the best Kentucky rye. He was a young and self-secure person, with sleek hair and full-drooping blond moustaches. There was a quality in his manner so debonair that Luther felt for him especial hate. "I don't want to tempt any of you gentlemen to take the name of the Lord in vain, but no polite words will express the appreciation you are going to feel when you sample the contents of that bottle," he was saying.

Grumbling satirically, the man with the beard rose, and, discovering a teacup on the floor beside him, stooped to reach it and to hold it out. The whisky *throt-throtted*, softly, from the bottle to the cup, and the man with the beard, before tilting the liquid to his ruddy lips, made the sign of the cross. "Pure extract of hell-fire," he commented, after the silence absorbed by his draining of it. "I approve. If the rebels expect to live on that, it won't take long to lick them."

"I thought you opinioned they were licked already, Major. But there's nothing so touching as an empty flask. Have another drop?"

The major demurred in favour of his friends, until all were refreshed. "Geddes," cautioned some one, "look at the shadow you are throwing on that canvas. What kind of an example do you want to set for your subordinates? And there's many a nigger out there who would cheerfully cut your throat with a razor for a drop of this."

"No, no. I won't take any more. Those who have been burned fear the fire—and as for those who have digested half a pint of it—"

Luther stirred, fidgeted, made a resolution to avoid further encounter with the whites; and set off toward that portion of the camp where negroes, resting among their scattered household goods, were waiting through the night. White folks don' know de powah uv evil, Luther was thinking. *He* knew, because, in all this laughter and singing and carelessness, Piety and Georgie and Mary would seem to rise up from the graves where he had buried them, just to haunt his steps. Da's y'all, ol' 'oman, he considered, addressing as Piety some far-off wraith skirting the campfires as he was doing. De p'ison y'all eat—pi'son dat Ah give you, ain' destroyed y'all yit. Y'all wuz too mean to kill, allus preachin', allus lettin' off yo' jaw at me, allus actin' sanctimon'ous. Y'all allus preten'ed y'all wuz gal wid spirit, but y'all was skeered to deat' uv me, ol' 'oman. Ah sho' seen to dat. Is dat y'all, Georgie? Y'all put me up to gittin rid uv Piety, but Debbil he don' let nobody do his wuk faw nothin'. He ax a price whin he see dat Ah got y'all faw mah woman, an' Ah finishes y'all, too. Tas' dis stuff, Ah says. Hit's sass'fras tea, Ah says. An' whin y'all drunk h'it up, Ah says dat's de same stuff Ah give to Piety. Y'all was bellowin' an' howlin', axin' faw de doctah, sayin' y'all's conjured, but Ah hel' y'all back. De Debbil want y'all. Whin de Debbil set his mind on y'all, dere ain' no denyin' him.

Mary was, perhaps, the only one that he regretted. The recollection of her made him fretful. She was de younges'. She pine, she pine. Ah ain' made up mah min' faw to do away wid her yit, Debbil, whin y'all take her off. Y'all is sayed to hev hoodooed two wives, Luther, she was allus saying; what y'all gwineta do to me? An' frum de veriest minute 'at she come to live in mah cabin, Ah sees dat Mistah Debbil gwineta grab her jes' to punish me. Ah got to give her up. De black cat sot on me whin Ah was sleepin', Luther, Mary says; Ah waked up suddent, an' Ah seen his eyes. Den Ah knows, Mas' Debbil, dat Ah had to keep dat pact, an' Mary died in anothah week frum dat. Debbil, Debbil, won' y'all look aftah Mary? Ah ain' so skeered uv dem othah two, but ef y'all let Mary ha'nt me now, I won' be no use.

Luther, happy with that terror of 'ghostes' which he liked to invite, directed himself toward a group crowded about a waning bonfire, and singing drearily. An old man intoned verses recitatively, and at the initiation of a chorus, other voices soared with his. By the lap of the flames, which runnelled glassily the shredding smoke, Luther beheld stoic countenances, bland to the day's exhaustions and glistening expressionlessly. Wondah dese woods don' ketch on fiah, he observed, noting the carelessness with which the moony circle had been cleared of boughs. Ef Ah could fotch one brand outen dat heap Ah could make 'nough trouble wid it to stir dese folks up.

The strange temptation made him 'shake.' He had seen pillage and conflagration. He had seen his 'white-folks' world denuded by the soldiers. But too much peace remained. He could not endure this calm appearance of the docile not of his company.

> Ah's boun' to take a journey, *way by an' by,*
> On de othah side uv Jawdon, *way by an' by,*
> Ah'll fix mah feet faw travellin', *way by an' by,*
> Gwineta drink dat healin' watah, *way by an' by,*
> We gonta drink dat healin' watah dat nevah run dry,
> *Way by an' by, way by an' by!*

Resentfully, Luther listened to the dirge of aspiration. The shrill female singing carried high above the richer, blurred singing of the men. The people swayed their bodies as in a slight, monotonous drunkenness.

When there was a lull in song, the elder who led rose to pray. "Gawd, we has to go fawward on de new road. We has to discovah Yo' wuks in distant places. Jesus Christ teach us to be kin' to ev'ybody. He speak in de year uv Mistah Lincolm an' tell him time come to sen' de sojers uv de Union faw to lead all uv us into de land uv Canaan where milk an' honey flow. Dat lan' may not be Savannah, Lawd, but anyhow time come whin us 'flicted has to put ou'se'fs in Yo' han's. We trus' in de sojers Y'all sen' wid Gen'al Sherman, an' we's gonta follow dem at Yo' disposition. Save us frum drunkenness, an' lyin', an' stealin', an' all weaknesses. He'p us to git to Savannah wid clean han's an' clean consciences. An' ef times is bettah dere an' new life begin, he'p us to recomlect all Y'all done faw us, showin' us po' sinnahs de way to heav'n on earth. Amen, Gawd."

He sat down, but his very wistfulness of doubt seemed to provoke in his audience the need for a more passionate expression of a certainty.

427

Oh, who's dat a-comin' ovah yondah?
   Hallelujah! Hallelujah!
Oh, don' dat look like mah sistah?
   Hallelujah! Hallelujah!
Oh, don' dat look like mah brothah?
   Hallelujah! Hallelujah!

The wild cries, as for confirmation, rang strongly through the wet forest, and obliterated the fainter sounds of casual merriment that floated from the hidden soldiers' camp. Luther was so excited that his teeth chattered. Debbil ain' gwineta hear *dat* 'thout doin' nothin', he thought. He git riled. And, jerking purposefully, deliberately succumbing to an old nervous habit, cultivated since his childhood, he leaped into the shouting, rocking gathering. "He'p me, y'all folks," he pleaded loudly. "He got me. He got me. Debbil got me an' Ah can' git loost. Take me to Savannah wid y'all. *Please* take me to Savannah wid y'all. Ah can' git way frum him. He been chasin' me all night."

Moaning, Luther tossed himself on the ground before the little yellow girl he had selected. He could detect her alarm, and he enjoyed it mightily. The music was silenced in ejaculations of awe, but Luther continued in his trembling fit. "Ah's hoodooed," he explained, turning about the group his wretched, crafty, glazing eyes, but allowing his final glance to rest upon the victim he elected. "Debbil 'fraid uv y'all good folks, but he ain' skeered uv me. Dey wuz white 'oman say Ah steal her cow dis mawnin' an' she put hoodoo on me. She say 'twill Ah fin' some nice young gal dat don' be 'fraid uv a ugly, cripple niggah she won' take it off."

Fascinated, shuddering, Lou watched him. Dat man suspec' mah sins, an' dat why he come aftah me, she thought.

Luther noted her downcast gaze, her trepidation, the ashy tint of her complexion. Da's mah nex' gal, he resolved with satisfaction. Effen she kin resist me, she gwineta save me. De Ol' Nick want his strength broke. She ain' usta men neithah. Debbil, ef Y'all wants to take dis honey-baby frum me 'fo' she git ol' an' measly-lookin' y'all got yo' wuk cut out.

. . . . .

Oh, wrastlin' Jacob, day's a-breakin',
  An' Ah won' let y'all go.
Oh, wrastlin' Jacob, day's a-breakin',
  An' Ah won' let y'all go.
Oh, Ah' hol's mah brothah wid a tremblin' han',
  An' Ah won' let him go!

Divinity held Rowan and Peter 'wid a tremblin' han'. She held them so close, so tightly. The night was still there, like a stale death. Divinity had carried all the load of darkness on her heart. Singing loudly, she tried to breathe more deeply, as if to force from her lungs the cloying air under the trees beneath boughs only a little burnished by the dying camp-fires. The bugle blowing seemed to announce that one rift in the low sky, as when 'de stone rolled back.' Dawn was something to foretell, some mystery, wordless, of which she could not unburden herself.

The children, only just fallen asleep, had to be roused again. They rubbed their eyes. The baby complained monotonously. There was the hamper to be packed once more, the rocking-chair to be carried. The valuables in the possession of the family were strewn about preciously for their watching eyes.

For a year, Divinity's pulse had beat, beat against troubles. Somepin allus troublin' me, she would think. Yankees come. Dey ax me to go away. De Culonel die. Miss Laura die. Cap'n Moses die. De house sacked. Miss Prissy and Miss Maudie lef' off speakin' to one annudah. Miss Maudie say because her brothah sick she got to take de Union oaf. Divinity was one of the negroes who had been left behind to guard the property. De place git wuss an' wuss. Hit almos' tumblin' down. Miss Prissy git so funny-like widout 'nough to eat.

But yesterday, yesterday—day before yesterday—Divinity had found her reason. De Lawd preparin' all dese years befo'. De Lawd come tell me by dese Yankee sojers dat Ah got to leave mah folks.

There were the Jones darkies, the Wilton darkies, Captain Morgan's darkies. Divinity inspected the familiar figures. All were preparing, as she prepared, to 'be movin' on.' All, like herself, made gestures which showed them to be consumed by the same excited restlessness.

Divinity knelt in obscure pine needles to fix the baby in her shawl. She was the man of the group. Rowan, big and awkward, watched her, his dazed eyeballs shining, his big mouth innocently agape. Peter, more impetuous, was more alert. He grudged his patience as he waited for her, longed to take the road.

Yesterday, a woman had died. They had carried a corpse, for hours, in the procession. It would bring more trouble. Buried crosswise of the world, Aunt Nancy Green lay down beside them, ruled above this spot. Peter complained that a man named Luther had wrapped this 'graveyard dirt' in a red flannel bag and was taking it along with him upon the journey to 'do conjure wuk.'

Now the grey light was withdrawing. All the transparent filaments of shadow were being shed by the living objects walking here. The sun was a looming, rather than a presence. It was cold. It was morning. But, the storm not over, it would rain again. Divinity remembered how 'Mistah Richard's houn'' had lain with his head inside the hallway and his body stretched on the veranda, and so had prophesied Aunt Nancy's end. This world of 'signs' was too unbearably filled with evil omen. Divinity would go on to a farther point than Savannah in a search for confidence and quiet. Jesus tell us not to set a-thinkin' uv tomorrow—dat we got to trus'.

The everydayness of this life was doubt. Peter had the hamper. Rowan took the rocker. Hunger was a doubt. The lines, trailing by through the emptying woodland, in the spouting sunshine, sang defiantly.

" 'Oman's wuk in dis world is de hardes', Sistah Tolah. Truf mah thirteen chillun is all daid an' laid in dey lil graves; dey ain' much to delay *me* gittin' to Heaben."

Divinity heard this from an acquaintance passing, and thought, Savannah ain' heaben. Suddenly, came a wild fear of Savannah, since, perhaps—*was* it heaven? The giddiness of no food led directly to this answer. Heaben! Yes, mah people, dis is heaben we all goin' to.

It hadn't taken the Yankees long to get the tents up. The negroes, hurrying, hurrying—because it *may* be heaven, who knows, who knows where any of us are going in this vale of tears— the negroes, hurrying, saw the woods being quickly abandoned, the cleared spaces, where tents had been, now all littered with scraps of refuse, with bits of paper, like a picnic ground, like a camp-

430

meeting. Divinity's children ran aside, while she stopped with them, and Rowan, guiltily, Peter, unwillingly, searched along the greasy gullies of the barbecue for just one bite to eat.

The morsels, already gnawed by dogs, were a disappointment. Not here is heaven. Hurry on, hurry on. And, finally, probably, no more than road travelled so often before—leading nowhere.

> God give Noah de Rainbow sign, *don' y'all see?*
> God give Noah de Rainbow sign, *don' y'all see?*
> No mo' watah but fiah nex' time,
> Bettah git a home in dat Rock, *don' y'all see!*

"Da's why Ah's a Baptis', Sis Peale!"

They could discern a shining over the road. It must be the creek. And beyond, in that quiet sky of morning, flooding the fields with grey, the prismatic wraith of a rainbow hung. It was there only an instant when the bar of its rose-pink-blue-green-orange dew evaporated; and a pyre of opal light burned alone in a low blot over an oak tree.

Instantly, a crippled woman, swinging herself on a strong unbent body, began turning and turning, giving herself, in all her motions, to the sharp, naked wind that was twirling the grass blades. A little soft snow fell in the occasional spurts of rain. The woman, spreading her frenzied arms, uttered strange shrieks of happiness. The soldiers were halted, were crowding the river's bank; and she led her fellows on to it.

The water, visible at intervals, through the mass of men, of rickety, clattering wagons, looked drenched with smut, ruffled with a fine spray of silver. The pontoons were oscillating slightly, and the stamp of feet was hollow, dull and loud above storm and voices. On the other side, the swampy land, covered with arriving troops, seemed to sink away in a vapid midday twilight.

> Ah wan-ta *cross* o-vah in-to *camp ground, Lawd!*
> Ah wan-ta *cross* o-vah in-to *camp ground, Lawd!*
> O-oh, chillun, don' y'all wan' *to go*
> To dat *gos-pel feast*
> Where *all is peace?*

The crippled woman's eyes brightened as with the quick notation of something satisfying which brought to her aroused, stoic features the expression of a purer rage. Her bold, erratic voice quavered richly. Hundreds came to her, and the volume of her hope was submerged in cries, in song as elated as her own.

"Is we gotta cross a swamp, Brer Abel?"

"Well, de chillun uv Israel cross mo' swamps dan us."

"Dey's lots uv rice fields down yondah undah watah."

"Didn' de Lawd say go frough fiah *an'* watah?"

"Don' y'all delay no mo', Jupe. Can' y'all tote lil sistah whin she tiahed, Nellie?"

> Roll de chariot along,
> Roll de ol' chariot along,
> Roll de ol' chariot along,
> *Ef you don' hang on behin'!*

Divinity ran. The baby screamed in the shawl on her shoulders. Peter and Rowan ran. Cicero Stout ran softly, on the fat feet of a well-fed panther. Luther Peabody ran nimbly, secret in the crowd, his 'conjure' bag safe in his pocket, his toes tripping. Lou and Anna—Anna mad, like a hurricane—ran, ran. *Oh, hurry, no more time to wait!*

Francy Dortch, handling her petticoats very genteelly, had sat down on a stone to 'ease' herself. She carried a 'hand,' stolen from her husband, and containing a sand burr, 'seed uv de eerf,' and a piece of 'Sampson's snakerott,' which was wet in whisky. For months she had dreamed of nothing but death, and the charm which she was wearing was propitiatory. Now she got up guardedly, her body sedate in corsets given to her by her mistress. *No more time to wait, no more time.* Fumbling to secure her bandanna properly, she trembled, waited—*no more time to wait.*

The soldiers—the soldiers! They were taking the pontoons up!

· · · ·

Ray Faulkner was in a panic. All the morning he had been trying to discard a superstitious impression that the pursuit of the army by the negroes was a pursuit of him, particularly. When Larry Smith, always facetious, had taken so much trouble to explain to that old man at Milledgeville that Mr. Lincon's whole army was come 'down South' to lead the darkies into Canaan, Ray had listened disapprovingly. "Go 'long, Mistah Sojer," the old man had derided, "Ah knows y'all's funnin'. Ah's black but Ah ain'

432

fulish." But Larry, with portentous earnestness, had persisted, until at length he had overridden incredulity. Winking while he disputed, he had described the North as an Elysium. Then Ray, dumbfounded, yet disarmed, had yielded the smiles he would have preferred to withhold. "Don't say any more about it, Larry. Leave the old nigger alone. He's well enough where he is," Ray had mumbled, rallying to conscientiousness.

"Ah's weil 'nough, is Ah! Y'all don' know much 'bout dis ol' niggah's tribilations, gemmen. Ah's bawn contented, Ah reckon, but whin Ah's twelve yeahs ol' Ah's sold to a mean piece uv trash name' Hoopah, an' he wuk me so hard dat Ah run away frum him. Den Ah's brought back an' whupped so hard 'at Ah's sick faw a week. En hed to git out in de cotton 'fo' Ah could stan' on mah laigs. Den Ah's sold up in St. Louis to a pow'ful boastful gemman dat like to play cards. Den he play en he lose me. Ah's lef' in a backwoods' place to pay de bill he owe in dat saloon gamblin'-room. Den a pedlah man buy me to he'p haul his goods faw him. Dey waz time when he was 'sleep en somebody come steal all he got en he say Ah done it an' mos' kill me. Ah run away ag'in. So Ah come down heah to Gawga en dey puts irons on me. So don' nobody know who Ah belongs to, so Jedge Simpson tuk me. Ah been his niggah evah since. Now de Jedge move off 'count uv de wah an' Ah don' belong to nobody. When de wah frough, he got to sell me, 'cause he ain' got 'nough money lef' to take care his niggahs."

"Well, you've read your Bible, Uncle Vic, and you know it says there that the end of things will be bloody, and after the bloodshed a new time starts. That's what we are workin' for—to bring a new era to you."

Uncle Vic had scratched his head doubtfully. "De sign's blood," he had admitted. "Ah ain't spelt hit out in de book yit, but Ah knows de Lawd deman' a heap uv sacrifices to change de times. Even de white folks—dem as lives easy—dey's brought low dese days, en Gawd He doan' turn de world upside down 'thout *some* sense to his actions. Othahwise de onliest thing to do would be to jump in de creek." And he had been persuaded, and had come on with the army. Now, as Ray was considering, if they would but all turn back!

Dim in the thin, lingering deluges of the rain, the negroes, in

433

accumulating numbers, were mottling the far, opposite shore of the river Ray had crossed already. Vacillating figures, shouting, moaning distantly, were moving steadily downward upon the pontoons.

Roll, *Jaw-don, roll,*
Roll, ol' *Jaw-don, roll,*
Ah *wants* to *go* to *heaben,*
When *Ah di-ie,*
To *heah ol' Jaw-don roll!*

A few of the darkies had already set willful feet upon the first planks, and were exhorting, with their musical cheers, the straggling Federals still proceeding across the bridge. Ray was abruptly surprised by the bugle blowing almost at his elbow, and by the appearance, at his side, of Lieutenant Girdwood, who, dismounted, hurried to return to ranks not his own. "Get that bridge up before those niggers get across," Girdwood shouted; and the order was corroborated by the blaring signal of the bugler.

There was instantaneous confusion. Captain Logan, also retracing his way to the river, rode, red-faced, along the edge, and intruded excited commands for haste. Where Corporal Hadley was directing his men to go out and push the rafts off from their connecting links with the road traversed, a knot of officers congregated informally. That it was imperative to lose no moment of time was apparent as the soldiers first in obedience were suddenly seen to encounter the forerunners of the host of pilgrims. The negroes were startled; then appeared refractory. Ray saw threatening gestures made by the whites. The darkies, struggling against detainment, at first resisted passively. Men tearing up the new-laid planks had already left swirling spacings in the length of the bridge. Shrieks, frayed by the moist wind, carried faintly. Then a pilgrim leaped. The body of a woman lurched toward the water and sank, to rise, nearer, and with stronger cries. Girdwood, calmer as he felt success, walked to the extremity of such platform as was yet intact, and yelled repeatedly, "No violence. No violence. Keep your heads, men. Get them back peaceably."

But discipline was relaxed in the general agitation. The soldiers who had crossed, finding the march interrupted by some unexplained commotion, broke ranks stealthily, and, like schoolboys, sought the shore. A kind of exultant alarm possessed those who

434

beheld the scene on the river. "Gawd, you gotta shoot 'em to stop 'em," an elated man remarked wonderingly. That unasked bodyguard of faithful had amused, then irked those it accompanied. There was a common vague conviction that the security of people 'in their senses' was menaced by such incomprehensible feeling as was being evidenced upon the other bank.

"Gertie! O Lawd, Gertie she's drownin'!" Distinct words of terror flew clearly from waterside to waterside, and with piercing intonations of despair. To complete the methodical destruction intended, a patrol of soldiers on the last floating remnants of the pontoon crouched at one end and pommelled with fists or rifle butts each negro attempting to ignore the interpolated current, and spring aboard. Many were already in the river. Soaked arms floundered, waved in the pitting rain, that touched, as with icy sores, each lifted brow. "Jubal! Zaney!" Names were called frenziedly, as for a reckoning.

There was a larger gathering too late to gain the bridge, or to attempt it; and from this individuals obtruded. A contagious impulsiveness seemed to drive men, women, children, embracing destruction, down the descent to the shallows. A woman waded knee-deep, then leaped, with her baby, and a second after was turning helplessly in awkward, nerveless swimming, while the child was lost. Its woolly head, spangled with shed drops, floated roundly for an instant; then disappeared again.

"Jesus, mercy. O Gawd, mercy. Jesus, mah Gawd, come he'p me!" Prayers culminated in screeches that were wordless. Those foremost in the water beat its surface with their hopeless, outspread palms. The face of a youth already lifeless rose and offered closed eyes to the spectators. As if catastrophe were Fate, fresh arrivals sought inundation. Baptismal voices invoked a Creator. *Hallelujahs* were unceasing, until deeps lapped gasping mouths and choked, with gurgles of suffocation, all grateful utterances. Half a dozen were at home in the new element. These swam in silence, and with wide nostrils, their shoulders up, their heads held high, and were like horses swimming. But the direction they elected was not toward the security of another shore, but toward the raft.

There, uncertainty expressed itself as violence. The Federal defenders, with hunted looks of animosity, did not desist from forcing all the clinging throng, clutching, fumbling, gripping as it

435

did the one stability of plank, back to its own peril. Black fingers, brown fingers twisted like vines, groped like dull roots. Wild eyes were alive in the ripples. The defeated refused to admit to defeat. Hope itself was a threat. The parasitic faithful swooned, died, and rejected every consequence of their impetuosity.

Where Ray, shaken, observed, in the white flakes cast by the shower upon the water, the bobbing heads and the faces inexpressibly longing, mumblings of astonishment passed from lip to lip. Some of the Federals fumbled pistols in their belts, or felt of the triggers of their rifles. The débâcle discomfited all so intensely that it sickened many to a ruthless antipathy. Pity, too keen, made inflexible decisions. Scarcely a man would have required long urging to extinguish movement among the darkies. It was as if the alien negroes, striving with the river, and with opposition, drew from all hearts a sympathy to which they had no right. Ray found himself convinced that a command to fire would be a kindness. And it was with a physical repulsion equal to hatred that he watched the first negro escaping detainment clamber to this shore, gain the bank staggeringly, and assume bewildered uprightness; as he did so, gazing on the hostile features and the hundred, hardening, covert eyes that were fixed on him.

By this time the bridge was discarded lumber. Girdwood had abandoned further attempt to stay aggression. Balanced on the crosspieces of a boat, the lieutenant teetered, feigning obliviousness to chins that bumped the hull, to chattering teeth and enpurpled mouths, gulping, crying, "He'p us, Massa! O Jesus, Massa, he'p us git up, Massa," until constant waves blotted utterance and made it nothing.

As many as could be accommodated, swung themselves up beside him. Those who remained afloat, half wallowing, but without the mind to emerge from the stream, brought from some of the angered officials who had before refrained from interference, instructions for rescue.

Labouredly, Ray took off his boots, unburdened himself of his damp jacket, and stalked into a quiet that girdled him with chill, that hung its floating mantle on his shoulders, and, at last, immersed him to his bearded cheeks. The mud was voluminous, yet he could hear pebbles faintly rattling. He began to swim. The feeling of the water was like a blow. He rocked inertly against the

436

lax body of an old negro man, and took disgusted hold of it. When Ray had dragged the sufferer to security, and could again stand, the dense river was shed from him like a garment, while awakening knives carved little channels of torture through his sudden nakedness.

Mah *home* is *o-vah Jaw-don,* still droned, in fading excitement, from the bank which was mercifully divided from him.

Ray felt drunken with perplexity. He saw Larry, beckoned him nearer, and said, "Get me a drink, for God's sake. I can't stand this kind of things." If we could only let 'em drown, he thought. Damn 'em, they get over their Jordan, but we have to carry 'em. We look facts in the eye and fight out this damn war, and they have all the fun. If I owned any niggers, I'd make 'em work, you bet, just to shut up their God-damned singing. Life ain't a bed of roses for the rest of us!

XVI

TIC-tic-tic. Tickety-tic, tic-tic-tic-tic-tic. Dale rose from his stool in the telegraph office and said, "Here, Lyttle, you gotta relieve me for a few shakes," and hurried to the door. The room was warm, and when Dale let in the freezing night, Lyttle called, "Hey, quit that. Git either in or out. I can't stand it." Dale paid no attention to him. On the platform, everything was as black as pitch. The last accommodation train of the evening was just pulling out.

After a second of hesitation, as his eyes became adjusted to the obscurity slashed intermittently by the glow from the windows of the last retreating car, he discerned Mike Porter, in his greasy overalls, with a wool muffler half strangling him, and his fur cap pulled so low, the ear tips down, that you could scarcely see his face. The light from the train went gliding horizontally upon the glitter of melting snow about the depot, and you could notice, ahead, the stiff trees springing out of the dark and glistening all along the line, to where, at a bend, the headlamp on the engine charged in front of everything and seemed to bore white holes in a black wall about nine miles deep. Then the train, and even its noise, was gone. You lost your bearings, and could be certain only by the shine from the office that the snow was still there. Mike might have been a ghost, it was so quiet, and the rear lanterns, red and green, were specks like 'jack-o'-lanterns,' getting farther off.

Dale had come out of warm, fœtid air where the wood stove was always kept as red itself as a hot coal, and was in his shirt sleeves. As he hastened to meet Mike, Dale slapped his long arms around his frail body, and embraced himself over and over, shivering, so chilled that, when he tried to speak, his tongue, between his numbed lips on which his steamed moustache drizzled, felt like a piece of paper.

438

"Hey, Mike," Dale shouted, when the two men were only a few paces apart, "had to run out and tell you even if I lost my job for it. Our old friend, Abe Lincoln, is re-elected. McClellan only got a majority in three states. Just got the news on the inside wire and wanted you to be the first to know about it.

"Well, now, tarnation, if I ain't glad!" Mike Porter answered heartily. "You an' me weren't born to turn the world upside down, but Abe Lincoln was always the kind of fellow nobody could keep under. 'Member when he used to be stump-speakin' around here? He was pretty slick, the way he could make a p'int before anybody saw what he was after. It took a fellow with some sense about speakin' to make Douglas look as cheap as he done. Douglas was too hot-headed. Will that news be on the boards by now? You know that son of a gun, McClellan, he's too dern easy on those Southerners. Abe knows we got to lick them rebels and lick 'em good."

"Just sendin' the news through. Guess they'll empty a jug of cider an' maybe somethin' stronger at Gooch's tonight."

"Well, we don't have a presidential election every day. Wouldn't mind drinkin' old Abe's health myself. Back last summer seemed like Grant's reverses at Cold Harbour and so on might do for him."

"Aw, Grant's all right. He can stick at his job. Lee won't hold out through the winter. Some folks think that McClellan's idea of grantin' separation would end the war sooner, but that only means that the money we've spent and the men we've lost goes for nothin'. Long as we got this far, we'd look like fools if we gave in too easy."

"Well, McClellan's an army man playin' politics. No good in it. Lincoln's platform is on the basis of straight-out abolition and unionism and no compromise. That suits me."

"Suits me, too—I guess—I can't get so excited about what's happenin' to these darkies. They ain't hardly worth what freein' 'em costs—but still— Anyhow, Abe's a plain man with common sense. He don't forget the stock he came from. I went to Springfield with Rachel over last Sunday and they're all braggin' about him there. Shows you what a self-educated fellow can make of himself. No tellin' but your boy Sam might be a future president, eh, Mike?"

"His pa won't promise to vote for him if he is. You oughta see

439

that little limb of Satan tryin' to lay down the law to his ma and me."

"Got to leave you, Mike. Somebody might send a wire through to tell Gus Brandau that his gal was expectin' him up at Gooch's and he'd leave me in the lurch. When a man's keepin' company with a gal he ain't to be depended on for anything."

"Heard Hester was rakin' him over the coals 'cause he didn't enlist."

"I don't believe that's so, Mike. Gus stayed at home to take care of the old mother. There's plenty of us would like to be on the scene of action and can't afford to. Too many people at home that need us."

"True enough, Dale. Well, you better be gettin' in. Next thing you know you'll be laid up with the rheumatism. Gosh walligins, it's cold. Six inches of snow at Terry Hut and more fallin'."

"Well, see you again, Mike. Army fightin' down South don't have to put up with anything that can beat this."

"Nope. Worst this year. Is that right that Number Nine from Springfield is fifteen minutes late?"

"Yes, that's right. Likely to lose some more before she gets here." Dale's answering cry was blurred by his retreat, the sound of his voice cut off by the thudding bang of the office door, which, open for an instant, permitted a gush of warmth and light to flicker forth, stunning Mike Porter to a new and more depressing sense of the weather.

EXTRACT FROM THE ELLENSVILLE (OHIO), EXAMINER OF NOVEMBER 12, 1864

A sad item for our personal column this week is the death today, from pneumonia, of Mr. Dale Hollis Preston, who has worked in the telegraph office here ever since the railroad was started. Mr. Preston, whose decease while he was yet a young man is mourned by a widow, formerly Miss Rachel Heighter of Cornelia, Indiana, and by four children, Mary Anna, Rachel, Nettie, and Ulysses S., was only thirty-six years of age, was born on his father's farm near Springfield, and was for a long period a faithful employé of Obadiah Murray, General Merchandise, before he learned telegraphy and started on a career with the railroad. It is believed that

Mr. Preston's illness was caused by a cold he contracted on election night when his generous enthusiasm for Mr. Lincoln's triumph led him to go out of doors in a bitter wind in his shirt sleeves to announce the news to some friends. The cold settled on his chest and it was not long before pneumonia set in. Mrs. Preston and her little family have our heartfelt sympathy.

II

From the New York Banner of December 22, 1864

IMPORTANT VICTORY. Triumphant Success of General Sherman. Savannah Ours. *Two weeks ago Sherman stormed and took Fort McAllister. Yesterday, after overcoming the rebels who made only a half-hearted defense, the long period of waiting since the city was invested by our troops ended, and a Union flag is now floating there.* Our Troops Received with Enthusiasm. Hardee Has Withdrawn to Charleston. The Women and Children Have Remained. There Is No Disturbance.

The following Message Sent by General Sherman to the President Was Received at the White House Yesterday:

"Savannah, Georgia, December 22, 1864.
"To his Excellency, President Lincoln, Washington, D. C.
"I beg to present you as a Christmas gift the City of Savannah, with one hundred and fifty heavy guns and plenty of ammunition; also about twenty-five thousand bales of cotton.

"W. T. Sherman, Major-General."

Special Christmas Services in All Churches.
No pimples, no darkness under the eyes after using a few bottles of concentrated EXTRACT SARSAPARILLA.

III

"It was in the autumn of eighteen-sixty-four that the Honourable Mitchel Stout Burnham, of Winfield, Alabama, who, before the war, had been one of the Congressional representatives from his district, disputed the program of the Davis Cabinet, and made various public utterances which the Confederate citizens of Winfield found seditious. About the time that Sherman was seizing Atlanta, Mr. Burnham was awakened one night by the clamours of a masked gathering in his front yard. When he courageously appeared on his veranda and demanded to know why he was being disturbed by a group of people who, though not soldiers, looked militant—all carrying rifles—he was taken by force and dragged the length of Main Street to Fountain Square (so named after Miss Begby had made the erection of a stone fountain there, her gift to the horses) had his clothes stripped off—all but a pair of cotton pants, left on him, it is supposed, for decency—was obliged to submit while the contents of a barrel of tar was poured over him, together with a hamper-full of turkey feathers, and was actually ridden on a rail—a piece of thin plank stolen out of Hope Brothers' Wood Yard. Unfortunately, his orphaned niece, Miss Amy Orm, happened to be paying a visit to her uncle, and was the accidental witness of his misfortunes. The shock of this experience is said by some to have deranged her mind, though others attribute her long mental illness to a quarrel with the young man who was then paying her court. I have no opinion one way or the other, dear Meg, but I am glad that the heat of the conflict is over, and such things not likely to occur again, especially among persons who are naturally law-abiding. You and Beulah know that—"

(*This document, which is the fragment of a letter, was found in the effects of Miss Texas Heart, late of Brighton, Georgia, and given me by her great-niece, Mrs. Tyler Shepherd of the same city, who, knowing that I would find the contents interesting, now gives her consent to its publication in this volume. Miss Heart, when she died, was an old lady of eighty-four, and at the time of the war must have been about thirty-two years old.*)

.   .   .   .

Amy felt that it must be true that she had done something wicked, else why had Lea, when she loved him most, deserted her in her misfortune?

"If you blame Lea," Amy said to her Aunt Lily Orm, "I'll despise you till I die."

Amy couldn't explain why it hurt her, insulted her, that the family should think her obliged to blame Lea. When Aunt Lily said, "Lea Hill is an unscrupulous man playing with a young girl's affections," Amy stared wildly, red in each cheek, and as if about to slap her aunt. "Do you believe I could be loyal to a man who wasn't—wasn't the finest gentleman on earth? Do you believe I'm as cheap as that?"

But how to defend Lea when every one found out! It wasn't a fact that a young girl was supposed to know about. And with a vision crystal-clear he looks out of me upon himself yet knows that he is near. They *can't* blame him.

Aunt Lily left the room and Amy, glad, locked the door softly. But I'm not alone. There was snow on the window glass. It had even snowed in Memphis and was snowing here. Amy was grateful for the candle. At night everything grew small and she could keep the world out. In the deep, purple pane of the window, the candle flame looked rosy, like a stalk of gladiolus. A spark of silver burned on the glass—another and another. Where were the armies now? Who was fighting Lee near Richmond—her Lea, not the same. Prison camps were so bad on both sides, and Courtney even admitted that in the prison camps on his own side some of the prisoners had lain for six months in the open. The doctors gave them pitch pine pills for almost everything.

The snow-flakes clotted the night with silver. Sparkling shadows kept going by, always going by. The window pane was downy with mist. Ophelia couldn't put flowers in her hair—not in December. Eyes that were warm when they loved me, eyes that do not see, now the warmth is iron-cold against me, resisting *me!* Exclamation point.

Theo must be in England. He preferred the navy. Dear Brother Theo, would you feel just the same as the others? The same, the same, the same—I remember when you went away. The sea, the spume, the blanched bitter reflection that flickers for an instant—like snow—and returns sombrely to the steady depths. Well, then, the minute I sit down to think about it I become sane.

Aunt Lily never slept well. There she was back again and trying the door. Amy opened it suddenly as if to surprise an enemy. The old lady, with curl papers showing under the edge of her cap, wore a flannel night-dress covered by a shawl of pink crocheting. Amy began to laugh, "Oh, you look so funny, Aunt Lily—so funny, funny—I can't help it!"

"It's a fine time to laugh. Why aren't you in bed?"

Amy grew serious, compressed her lips, and could feel them twitching. Well, the old devil *is* funny!

Her meditations astonished her. It was an 'outlandish idea' to call kind old Aunt Lily an old devil. But the desire to shock her was almost irresistible—to shock everybody, ever since Uncle Mitchel was ridden on a rail. It's as if they wouldn't believe you. *I'll* show 'em, Amy thought savagely. Then, Maybe Aunt Lily *is* crazy. They're *all* crazy.

Miss Orm shook Amy's arm. "Pull yourself together, child. Don't pretend to me you're not worried to death about that Lea Hill leaving us, because you are. As if any man that ever lived was worth as much as this! You are a girl brought up like a lady to have some self-respect. People don't cry their eyes out about a man that has deserted them. When I was young I would rather have died than confess myself foolish about a man who didn't care two cents for me. He tried to escape the draft last year and that wasn't nice. It wasn't honourable."

"Did they pay you in Confederate money, Aunt Lily?"

Miss Orm was really provoked to an extremity by the spectacle of that silly girl smiling. Amy said, "And I am a poor girl buried nine feet deep in snow."

Frightened, Miss Orm glanced at her. "Don't try to play tricks on me. You're as sane as I am. You've just got to pull yourself together and brace up." But she spoke very softly, later, and led Amy to the bed. "Now get in, cover up, lie down, and I'll blow out the candle for you." Aunt Lily's tone was flat commonplace. "My teeth are chattering." she said. "You'll take your death of cold." Then she blew out the candle and went out.

Alone in the dark, Amy wanted to shriek. She got up, like a thief—they make me feel like a thief in everything I'm doing—and lit the candle again. Oh, my God, I'm ill! If I could make them feel like I do—but they don't hesitate to pity the poor girl served her right. Fat hands all over you nose holes purse in lap full of blubber, like a kangaroo. I'll *kill* Aunt Lily if she comes back here again. What Miss Orm *had* said was that she thought Amy would rather have her tongue cut out than have people know she cared for Lea Hill anyhow. Miss Orm had said that a gentlman precedes his avowal of admiration with an offer of marriage. *I* didn't go about meeting young men in negro cabins, Miss Orm had said. Then Amy had said, Leave me. I'm dangerous. What if I snatched

444

up the water jug? You know Dr. Stubbs told you that I wasn't to be trusted to control myself, that I'm hysterical.

In bed, Amy was beginning to shiver. Are you a hypocrite, Aunt Lily, that's what she asked. And, I *won't* be driven out of my senses by your fancifulness, Aunt Lily had almost shrieked. Then she had gone out. I've lost all the sleep I can. At my age I can't afford tantrums. So Lea evaded the draft, and then when he heard about Uncle Mitchel he was afraid and left me. He said I was persuading him to do something that wasn't right.

Amy was alone with the cold. Aunt Lily's footsteps had died away long ago. She got up. Through cracks in the floor, icy air came up from downstairs and sheathed her bare legs under her nightdress. She enjoyed the misery. She walked to the window. The sash was difficult to move. Then it yielded. The wind slipped its liquid wedge through the opening and flowed all over her like a new, painful being. The sill she was looking at was padded as with white moss. Without, no more was visible than a slow, shapeless motion of white. And from this, now and again, a small grudging star flowered for an instant. If we *knew* the secret, would any one care about President Lincoln or President Davis?

That, she could not answer. If all the mirrors were broken, if there was a fat baby in heaven saying how sorry we are and couldn't touch them if fifty cannon went off. Hearts like a stone furnace. Maybe it's not true. Then I have to lie here for the next eight months wondering if it *is* true and damn those eye-sockets. Why should I have to die when nobody else does—but if they do they have their own reasons—voluntarily. Wish I could go away like Theo. The sun streaked on the smoking rags of current, the livid rags of vapour. Bigger than Memphis or down home in Winfield. Its flying talons sunk as it rides on fierce blazing pinions over the Atlantic—not the Mississippi. In a vastness without motion the tamed hawk rises, quits the untouched, the heavy leisure of an ocean less impetuous. (That's *me.*) Even the coarse, emboweled braying of a steamer cannot awaken. This is to be. Deathdewed the evening. The emerald lamps fleck the harbour, the hills. A chalky lace traces moon, unseen, over the dark.

She drew the sash down gently on its white, crisp cushion, and was relieved by the vivid twinkle of rime on the glass, screening her from something gentler and more awful.

Returned to the bed, she pulled the blankets up to her chin. Better let the candle gutter. Warmth here, oh, thank God, and she was afraid of the new thing that she did not understand, and it was like peace coming into her bones. I'm dust, because we all are, she thought, but it would be better to die in bed if she had to than by taking cold. If they believe I lack pride, I'll strangle 'em, by God. I'll stick my claws so deep in their rotten necks the blood won't come out. I suppose I oughtn't to have tried to keep Lea from going to war. But the baby will have to forgive me for bringing him into a bad world. I hope he never thinks at all. Amy closed her eyes and realized that she was smiling, being *comfortable.* (*That's* crazy.) She was smiling under, *under,* wishing they would leave her lying here for ever, gazing upward at her happy self. Morning stood a long way in the distance. She must ignore it, ignore it, ignore it—if she could. She was growing alarmed again.

. . . .

Lea was in Hood's centre, which was holding its line as best it could. The defence had been weakened by the withdrawal of the men sent to retain Overton's Hill against an assault. In the icy wind, with the smoke blazing everywhere as from a hundred camp-fires, over the slopes silvered with sleet, the hammered *thump, thump* of the rifles kept terminating in a metal drenching, like a steel drizzle, poured from the bleary, hidden cavern of the sun. Gravelly echoes jerked, like whips cracked over miles of country, shedding a trillion pebbles. With each fresh deluge of shot, came a mute thinning of the defence, and Lea was perturbed, almost exalted, by this growing sense of nakedness.

In his breast-pocket was a letter from Miss Texas Heart, an old friend of his sister; and a paragraph in it, referring to Amy Orm, added to the feeling of despair which he no longer combated or tried to justify. "Amy Orm is in a serious state of health, and as you and she used to be such friends, I thought that you might like to know about it. Her aunt is very secretive, and, though I see Dr. Stubbs so frequently, he never allows me to discuss his other patients with him; but people say that ever since she was a spectator at her uncle's disgrace her mind has been affected. I hope you have not added to her difficulties, Lea, and I do not think you have. There is insanity in her family anyway, and for your own sake I am glad that the interest you used to show in her never

446

came to anything. No doubt she is young enough to rally from the blow that has fallen upon her, whatever appears to be its nature, and by the time you get this letter there will be nothing but good to report. I am frank with you, and maybe you will say presuming, but it is on account of my old friendship with Sally, so please don't take it ill of me. If you have any lingering sentiment about Amy Orm, put her out of your thoughts once and for all. The doctors tell us nowadays those things can be inherited."

Lea, dazed as he was by cold, felt the words of the letter the ominous background of some new horror which he could not divine in all its contours, though it approached him. The rocky slaps of the firing had become mercifully incessant. The afternoon was so grey that the fat, feathery tufts of the smoke shone silver against the December sky. There was still a vagueness and a strangeness about this life of purposeless hardships, though he had become so accustomed to monotonous misery that he depended on the habits of the camp for a plan to support his uncertainties. Amy was wretched. He had left her. Well, *he* was wretched. It seemed to him, when he had the time for reasoning, that she, in the sheltered dependence that allowed her opportunity for grieving, had a luxury.

Bouquets of sound spread in the clouds. Lea had a respite from activity. He could smell the sleety woods around him, in the bitter silence of the winter which the fight could not molest. Now and then a reverberation from Overton's Hill was like the slashing of thick glass. He heard, yet he was numbed to inattentiveness. The letter he had read had aroused him from engrossment in his aching flesh. He resisted an injustice in its call on his compassion. He was tired, he was hungry. He had been on these hills surrounding Nashville for so many weeks. Even Amy's face, as he recalled it, made him brutal toward what he had once considered lovely. It was Amy who, the year before, had quibbled with his patriotism. It was she who had confused him by her specious statements of his 'duty.' And now that he was here, in the hell she would never be obliged to suffer, she yet demanded 'sentiment' and pity. She, of course, would never understand how, since he had been fighting, he had become, not less, but more indifferent to the issues of the war. What is a matter of this —— damned politics to a man without enough to eat!

447

The remote noises from Overton's Hill suggested that, beyond the dun heavens, an enormous carpet, hung on the horizon, was being beaten ceaselessly. Lea listened, glanced at the tense, huddled men about him, and wondered if they, also, were listening. Each looked secret in his necessary stolidness. Each was for himself alone. Hood's men had been warned to guard their ammunition. There could scarcely be a doubt as to how the afternoon would end. Each man, nursing knowledge of this disadvantage, defended himself against his fellow who might guess his hopelessness.

There was a charge coming. Major Brownell, who was in a position conspicuous to the enemy, was losing control of his horse. Lea, distracted by a sudden order, was but half aware of the leap of the frightened animal across the barricades, until the gesture which carried the wounded officer among approaching Federals, bore its abrupt fruit of panic.

There was alarm, there was hesitance. Some had broken through the company. A man near Lea threw down his gun. Others set off across the country, to evade diagonally the advancing attackers who were drawing close. Lea saw the men in the light-splintered smoke. There were shouts around him. He, too, longed for this immediate escape. He was afraid of impulse. (He had given up Amy and he was *here*.) The last thing that he would dare to put aside, was this desperate obstinacy. He had thought too long before he came into the thing. What did it matter whether they were killed now or later? What was it worth if they got away? If he went back home, if he deserted, and escaped, there would always be the same old question of what was wrong and right. Quit feeling, quit feeling, he kept saying to himself. And then, when he began to tremble in his isolation, Run, you fool. The only thing you've learned in this is that you love yourself too much.

He leaped aside through the growing haze. He began to run as the rest were doing. His shoes were ragged. He stumbled swiftly on frostbitten toes. The vividness of literal action brought quick blood into his cheeks. People were yelling, instinctively, challenging interference with their flight. He also yelled, half-heartedly. Then yelled again, to convince himself of satisfaction. He was exact. He had always known that he would some day do this, that he was 'cowardly.' This ought to prove to Amy that she was fortunate. In love with a coward—why, she couldn't be. And why should it be considered fine to build a life upon illusion! He was through. He was finished. He knew more of himself than others knew. He liked the taste of bitterness.

The eructations of firing persisted, sometimes very close. Seeing figures running like himself, he skirted friends as well as foes. He trusted nobody. When he had pursued this course over country for half a mile, he realized suddenly, emerging from the dream of action, that he was alone at last. Senselessly he had climbed stone walls and zigzag fences; and he arrived, going nowhere, in this bit of woodland meadow. He had forgotten the firing He no longer heard it. There was a wet log bared of the sleet, and he sank down on it. All was deep with winter stillness, as with the resignation that he hated. A marbled shadow hung on the sky. The warmth resulting from exertion was relieving, like being drunk, but he retained a blind fear of the snow which would soon fall again. Thank God for the silence. It was perfectly his own. That was all he wanted. Something hard, that was his own, that nobody could touch. *She* would never understand.

It took a long time to regain breath. His chest heaved desperately. By and by he grew calmer; but his mind remained excited. Love was a delusion. That was what he thought. It would be a crime to impose on Amy this gorgeous, warming indifference; for indifferent to her he had certainly become, as to the aches of frostbites, to the pains of swollen feet. To speak to her, he would need another language. His exhaustion, which was now a chronic state, like a mood, *had* no language. There was pride in his conviction of unique inarticulateness. No two people could be more unlike than he and she, thank Heaven. Amy depended on man-made judgments as to right and wrong. If he believed in anything at all, it was in himself—just that—in his 'glorious, infernal selfishness.' A rotten, yellow-bellied deserter he'd be when he got through. And he'd be damned if he would ever be ashamed of it. He had never taken stock in her high-flown explanations of his conduct, anyway. Maybe he was his own law. Well, he was glad. He'd *be* his own law. Murder was nothing to him. (Why should it be, after the army!) He had a feeling—a feeling— He wasn't quite sure how much he *had* hurt Amy. On a full stomach, with a fire to cheer him, he might, if he decided to waste time on such things, go into

449

that. He wasn't going to pretend any longer—not after hell—not after this—that he aspired to be anything but a brute—an honest brute. That was about the only virtue of the brutes, poor fools. They were —— honest. Refinements were wasted. Any woman would do. *Any* woman. Lord, how he had once deceived himself! Trusted in anything as fatuous as the code of a gentleman! He looked like a gentleman, he hoped, *of course,* a dirty bag of rags and fleas and lice. If Davis couldn't equip his army any better, let it go to pieces. Lea swore aloud. He sought for some viler expletive than he already knew. He cast about for a more powerful word of violence. Not one was adequate. This 'false' purity of gentle breeding he rejected as a taint.

The sun was disappearing altogether. The ground lay about him in shadowless light. He was spent as on nothing. His teeth began to click together nervously. Drops, very large, mild, like a very pure ash, fell on his hands. The air was a blear. A blank sky exhaled the flowery clots of moisture. The smell of the snow was an ache and like icy soot. Trees stood about him, bouquets of smoke. Little crusted cedars with their tiers of rigid frills, became iron covered with whitewash. The earth, the white world, was doused in bluing. As the afternoon was drained, it gave out vapid azure. He felt he ought to get up and hurry on. It was the stupidity of his refugee's position that made him fretful. Christ, I don't wanta be a man, he thought. I wanta be an ass, a donkey—some other kind of —— damn son of a bitch.

But there was no place for *them,* either. (The Son of Man had nowhere to lay his head.) You could 'cuss' it, but was there any place to go, to stop, to get out of things? He rose, and paused, irresolute. In the dusk, in the snow, in the country, a kind of enormous insignificance seemed to be settling over the world. Every stolid twig on the trees could still be divined. Everything, bare, seemed to lose its meaning. In colossal, stainless ruin, the world, in the snow, was burnt out, only sooty outlines left, like a kind of silly handwriting.

Driven by a panic he could not despise enough, Lea darted on. It disturbed him that he could not hear himself running. No, it was like the end of everything. It was what he wanted, and, because 'true,' unreal. The refulgence in the sky, like wings, behind the milky air all alive with its curdle of white specks, faded, folded

450

away. The impression of the wildness of a ruined springtime became more vivid as the night drew in.

There was a bruise, there was a pressure on his mind. His emotion passed, against his will, into that old wretchedness that was not freedom after all. He had never been wittingly cruel to any one, had he? So why, then, should Amy forgive him! If Amy would acknowledge—if she could *acknowledge*—what he *knew*—what he had found out—about himself, about others—chiefly about himself. Before Amy he *must* be, never *could* be, all her fine thoughts and feelings about him meant, when he could shriek to heaven men *are* these —— damn sons of bitches, bastards, brutes, because, oh, I don't know, something in myself, and if you'd acknowledge it, beat down something— But she never would acknowledge it. There would always be that 'niceness' in her that offended him, that was in the 'ladies,' made him go, maybe, to any whore first, not to be insulted. It was better for her to pity him, loathe him, just as he was, if he ever saw her, if 'twas not too late!

He melted. Christ, he was tired! He wanted the protection of an ugly feeling toward her. Wanted to recapture it. The snow drowsed about him dimly. There was a house, abrupt; a light, a window, across it the moth flakes gyrating with barren glitter. He couldn't stay out here in the night without anything to warm him. He must think of the usual lie he would have to tell. Then it came upon him that he would like to beat Amy, to torture Amy, to speak indecently to Amy.

·   ·   ·   ·

It was on New Year's morning that Miss Lily Orm was reading, out of a 'worthless, Yankee newspaper,' which she had secured the story of how General Sherman had given President Lincoln the city of Savannah as a Christmas gift. She believed that Amy should be told things that would distract her, so commented, with a cheer she did not feel, upon the various items of report.

Coal was not to be had, nor was decent wood; but Mammy Florence had been out 'picking chips,' and had filled the grate. All the while Miss Lily was reading and remarking on events, Amy sang to herself. This annoyed the old lady greatly. She pushed her silver-rimmed glasses to the end of her nose and stared over them worriedly. "What are you making, Amy? It's too late to be plaiting evergreens for decorations. Christmas is already

451

past." The poor, wretched creature *would* wander out on the lawn, and expose herself to the scrutiny of neighbours. I must bear up under the burden the Lord has imposed on me, Miss Lily thought, sighing. But, oh, what to do when the child was born! There were so many months still ahead that Miss Lily often wondered how she would ever get over them. Yet it was best, in a way, like this— nobody could blame the girl.

Amy was obstinate. Miss Lily often felt that she heard, but she was slow to answer, and had to be asked the same question several times before turning her head, in that absent fashion, to reply to it. Amy was smiling. Again Miss Lily asked, "What are you making that for?"

"It's something to make the world better," Amy said, very knowing and amused and continuing to hum. Where the girl had ever picked up that song about the Yankee and the nigger wench, nobody could guess. Miss Lily had been obliged to take note of the words. Abnormal people couldn't be treated as usual, Miss Lily realized. She had gone through enough with 'poor, sick, feeble Lally' before she died. But it *was* provoking to have to listen to rhymes that would make Mammy Florence blush.

Amy held up a kind of clumsy-made basket. She was smiling, with that clear, deliberate look which gave Miss Lily the impression that her niece was removed in spirit from all things dear and familiar to both of them. "It's a cradle," Amy said. "*You* wouldn't understand."

Miss Lily was offended. I can't say whether she's making fun of me and just pretending, or *what's* happened. Tears came to the old lady's eyes. She was angry—angry with Amy and with herself. "You won't need that, dear."

"But I *will!*" Amy said. "Or won't I——I must have *something!*" Amy's face was like a baby's when it is surprised or injured. She did not cry at once. It seemed to take her a long time to decide what it was she didn't like. Now she wailed softly. "I *must* have the baby, Aunt Lily. Why, there's nothing else left! They've taken everything else away from me."

Miss Lily took a handkerchief from her petticoat pocket, settled her skirts over her hoops, and patted her face all over. She felt warm and miserable and could not see why a good church member like herself had been so afflicted. Dr. Stubbs wanted Amy

452

to be 'drawn out.' There was no *means* of getting her mind off awful subjects! "Yes, you must think about something else, Amy. A dear little baby is a beautiful thing to think about and God sends it into our midst straight from heaven—but the baby's not here yet. We must be patient."

Amy did not like patience. When Aunt Lily corrected her, she grew sly. It appeared that she delighted in being wicked, in being tormenting. Amy said, "I'm not afraid of any of them, now, Aunt Lily. I'm not afraid of you, either. You see there's not anything left you can teach me."

"Oh, yes, there is, Amy," Miss Lily answered positively, her hands trembling, fumbling her starched collar, fixing her brooch in place, and retying the strings of her cap. "There is a great deal you have to learn. You mustn't, for instance, get the idea that the world is an awful place and everybody in it unkind. A great many people are very kind to you—very. And you know your body is a temple and God has given it to you that His Holy Spirit may inhabit therein. You mustn't insult God's trust in you by singing that—that— Yes, nasty is a nasty word, but that is a very nasty song you have been singing. Your poor Aunt Lily is very grieved that you ever picked it up."

Amy looked long and troubled at her aunt. Amy grew vaguely angry. Miss Lily was thinking that the girl was no longer pretty, seemed, at these instants, to have lost her youth, though she would grow so young again that the very spectacle of her radiant, vapid childlikeness was more unpleasant yet. She had lost her conscience, her aunt would think. She had lost all sense or decency, morality.

Amy sprang to her feet. "Don't tell me I shan't sing it," she said. "You're an old harridan, an old jade, an old slut, an old bitch! That's what you are. They taught it to me. That's the song I like. And I'm going to sing it. I don't care when they come or what they do. I know all about it. They think I'm afraid, but I've found out about the whole thing. One soldier is just as good as another. You go out in the moon and I eat my hat and it's all silly. I'd be as happy as a jay bird if I'd only found out sooner how many clothes they wore. Take 'em all off and there's nothing to keep back. So I throw it right in their faces. If I'd wanted anything else I could get that, too. Cold won't hurt you and nothing else. I keep turning around and when you're out I'll unlock the

453

door because you're an old prig. You tried to make me think it's safer in the cellar. I'd spit on anything. He knows it. You needn't keep fooling me that *you're* different." She was panting so that she could scarcely speak. Then she wheeled about suddenly and threw herself, face downward, on the hair sofa, sobbing as if her heart would break.

Miss Lily recovered herself as from the stupor into which the torrent of speech had forced her. Very gentle and subdued, she rustled across the room, and laid her withered hands gently on the tossed head, the writhing body. "You must be calm, my dear. Here's your cradle again, if you want it. You can go on making that."

Amy moaned, "But they might put it in the coffin."

"No, they won't," said Miss Lily.

While she was talking, her eyes strayed toward the hallway disclosed to her through the open door. My heavens, *who* was there! Miss Lily wished for the luxury of fainting, but did not dare to yield. She was even so far able to control herself that she could place her finger on her lips and motion to him. How on earth had he come! Amy must not have a shock. If she realized his presence too abruptly it might kill her. (Why not, my God! Everybody's suffering nowadays—and dying, too.) Miss Lily, in her astonishment, could only wish that he and Amy *had* died—but for their country—*what everybody admires.* No more miserable than other people are these days, but with them, for the bereaved families of the nobly fallen, there is recompense. There could be no honourable end for a man in *his* position—and Amy, too. Of course I don't wish the poor girl any further suffering or I couldn't think like that. How she and Lea used to sing *Dye My Petticoats* and *Forty Thousand Chinese,* while Amy played accompaniments on her guitar. And now this disgraceful ditty about the soldier.

"Aunt Lily, why have you such a vile mind?" Amy was asking. Miss Lily had no strength to reply. He looks like a tramp, Miss Lily was meditating, hating the control she was obliged to assume. (No torture would be severe enough to punish such a villain.) Her mouth drew to a knot, a mute pucker, her eyes squinted in tears. Amy must have felt the silence. She sat up, turned, followed her aunt's glance. Miss Lily could not defend them from each other longer. How had he ever dared enter the house? Deserter,

454

of course. He was *always* a coward. But she could not give him up. They must be married first. (Take the spectacle of this suffering off my hands!)

The pause lasted for ever. Lea came forward to the doorway doubtfully. He must have studied Amy well before he entered, for, now that he was drawing near the sofa, he ignored her. His eyes pleaded, gazed at Miss Lily only, and in unconcealed confession of his wretchedness.

"Lea Hill! Where'd you come from? How did you get in here? How'd you dare come in—" Oh, she could not afford the rage with him that was her due. It was wrong, it was wretched. And look at Amy! Certainly it would kill her! Had the man no *sense?*

Amy sprang up. Her hair was all falling out of the net and hung in confusion on her shoulders. She was not neat and dainty any more. "Lea!" She cried out and made a step toward him. Miss Lily caught her. It seemed just that he should have to see her at her worst, and if she swooned, so much the better. He stood very erect, but as though he were receiving blows. But when Amy tottered, he came over and helped Miss Lily take her back to the sofa. Amy kept her eyes closed, her hands twisting about each other, and she said, "No, no, no, no, no," again and again, her voice rising higher and higher in a protest against something neither Lea nor Miss Lily understood. Then she was perfectly silent, with her face buried in her palms. Lea and Miss Lily stood confronting one another.

"I hope you see what you've done," Miss Lily said, whispering loudly and viciously over the bowed head. Lea just looked at her. He was so ragged and haggard that she wondered if she ought to marry Amy to a man like that. It was too late to consider anything different, however. He wouldn't have come back if he had not intended to make reparation and she must accept. Oh, we poor women, we poor women!

"Does she want to marry me, Miss Orm?"

Lea was certain that he was insulting Amy, but there was nothing else for it. The Beards had helped to hide him, and they had told him what a state Amy was in, how every one said that she would have a baby and that he was said to be the father of it. He felt that it was wrong to come to her feeling as he did feel, that it was a species of suicide, a kind of sacrifice. If he was caught, he might be shot. Or it might be merely, now that men were scarce, he would be made to fight again. At best he had given up trying to think out things for himself, since he had been so tired, so cold and hungry, and obliged to hide, most of this week, in the woods at night. He must have been all wrong while he had kept the idea of being free. He had not anticipated, before his arrival here, the effect that the sight of Amy, in her peculiar state, would have on him. Just now, when compelled to touch her, he felt revolted.

"I think we could get a preacher—if you'd hide me for a while, Miss Orm. If you'd find somebody that we could trust who wouldn't give me up yet."

God's ways were strange. Miss Lily wanted to collapse. She had rather see Amy dead than married to a deserter—Amy and her Uncle Mitchel—the family seemed cursed in its men, and only the women who were really left to be patriotic. Miss Lily had stood so much alone. Lea must have *some* chivalry left, and it was certainly her due, she felt, to lean on *somebody*. Amy had now opened her eyes and was watching them. Miss Lily stepped between the girl and Lea. He oughtn't to see what she's come to— something he can *gloat* over. Oh, I know *men!* But he can relieve us of our disgrace. We have no responsibility for his behaviour otherwise.

"Go upstairs and stay until I can warn Mammy Florence that you're in the house. She might find you suddenly and I don't know what kind of a fuss she'd make. Then I'll come up there and talk to you and we'll decide what can be done."

As he moved to obey, glad to go, and feverish to be certain that he was not to be here long—that he and Amy could be married and be able to leave (not obliged to think about it)—Amy rose, unexpectedlly, and put her hand out. He flinched when she laid her hand on his chest. He had to glance directly at her. She was regarding him so wonderingly—not crazy after all, he felt, and he was tricked. It was only the story of her utter helplessness that had driven him to return. He had understood it that she was beyond reproaching him. If her judgment was sane, and he forced to bear her condemnation, he would prefer to be branded as a scoundrel. What a hellish weakness was regret!

"Lea, don't listen to her. Aunt Lily is mad. The war has brought

456

so much trouble on her that she's not responsible. She thinks you and I have been wicked and that's what I can't endure. I've told her that when you came back I'd explain it to you. I went out yesterday to see the other soldiers and they're all so friendly. That's where I learned the song about the Yankee and his nigger wife."

Abruptly, Miss Orm sat down. Humiliations would never end. She had always fancied that the girl might just be pretending.

"My poor Amy!" Lea, caught, made himself caress with his hand her tilted head laid on his breast. Her smiling face did not seem to him 'natural.' He was afraid of her, he admitted to himself, and so unable to feel as she unconsciously demanded. If he were willing to give her everything else, she could not still ask love. That was too much. Something not to be dictated belonged to himself.

"Now I'll sing for you." Amy laid herself more closely upon his bosom, her cheek pressing confidently upon his coat.

> "The Yankee soldier
> And the nigger wench
> Were settin' together
> On the garden bench—"

Her frail voice, in all its tones of nicety, quavered flatly on a high note a little off the key. Lea, agonized, had to stop her. He laid his hand quickly on her mouth. Then he could see her eyes turn to hate, as he pressed her hastily toward the sofa, bent her toward the sofa, and he was glad of the pain, which came instantly where her teeth sank viciously against his palm. This was *not* Amy, but a vixen, to whom he could condescend, but without responsibility. He exulted as he struggled with her in recapitulation of his conviction that brutality was just. She fought, he held her. While Miss Orm made a *tsch, tsch* sound of disapproval, and fanned herself with her handkerchief distractedly. With wonder, Lea subdued, in his false delicacy before her aunt, the new Amy. With an excuse for cruelty, repulsion diminished. When she was weak with sobbing that did not ask for pity, he hated her less.

Far away, the front door rolled shut. Miss Lily, shamed by what she was obliged to witness, feared, though she noted footsteps and anticipated interruption gratefully. "Quick! Hide!"

457

Lea Hill, too, heard. There was treachery, after all, in his predicament. He had been beguiled into the luxury of forgetting that he was hunted. He owed less to Amy than to himself, and he had forgotten that. "Where must I go, Miss Orm? Upstairs? Is there another way up through the kitchen?"

Who could be coming? Miss Orm, with the recollection of his face as he had looked at Amy, wished that she could give him up. "Yes," she whispered, "go out through the kitchen." And she tried to speak composedly.

It was tardy advice. She had walked to the door, spread her crinolines about her to obliterate a view of all behind her, and was trying to gauge the extent of the danger. Three men in uniform were in the hallway. She was so nearly bereft of sense by her anxiety she could scarcely make them out. They seemed to her to grin. When one saluted and spoke politely, his gesture appeared to her merely derisive. Her throat grew dry and her tongue thick, while she waited for him to speak. "I'm not accustomed—" she said.

"Beg your pardon, ma'm. We knocked and nobody answered. We are looking for somebody that you may know and the neighbours told us that he just came in your house."

A sensation of suspense lay blank in her mind. There were a thousand things it seemed to her that she should say. She was silent, not able to realize her silence, Lea Hill there in the room behind her, and she, because she *did* admit to Amy that he was a handsome fellow, debating her 'loathing' of him. How much could it be worth to Amy to save such a man!

The first soldier in uniform advanced, suavely, persistently. Miss Lily fluttered, found her tongue. "I am justly indignant," she began in a high voice.

> "The — Yankee man
> And the fat nigger wench
> Sittin' so lovin'
> On the garden bench—"

Thin, hysterical singing floated, with laughter, over Miss Lily's shoulder. The soldiers, astonished, smiled broadly, looked at her queerly. And Miss Lily's shrivelled flesh rosied softly while her eyes dimmed behind her spectacles.

458

"Havin' a party in there?"

She scorned the rude interrogation. The men tried to brush past her, and, in her helplessness, exposed again by this new attack, she felt frenzy. Her small fists doubled and she beat them off. "Hold her, Jim. Let's see who she's got in here. Mighty funny goin's on, that's what it looks like to me."

Miss Lily, defeated, drew regally from their unnecessary grasp, and displayed to them her agony, rebuked them with it. She had forgotten Lea. There he was.

> "The Yankee says
> For a fightin' man's treat
> You can pick 'em black as hell
> And the —— is jest as sweet—"

Amy cried, "They rode him on a tar barrel! Cock's feathers so they heard the rooster crow, Lea!"

The first soldier brazened the situation. "I'm sorry, ma'm. The girl seems to be in an awful state. But we can't wait on that." He was blushing furiously. "Is your name Hill?"

Lea said, "Yes, it is." He thought himself resigned—*anything to get away*. When the hands of two soldiers moved toward their belts, a rush of despair in his thoughts made him heady, quicker than they, more anxious to escape in action this life which he did not understand. He shot before they could anticipate him. (What for? I don't know. Because of the vanity of trying to think things out at all. I want to quit.)

Miss Orm screamed. Amy laughed shrilly. There was a retort in another shot. Lea, shocked, realized everything darkening. He moved, stumbled, pushed Miss Orm away. She was kneeling over him—every one kneeling over him. Giddy with pain, he pushed them all away, wanting to be left, resenting that, even now, they did not leave him beyond the need for decisions, recognizing, under his feeble, naked hand, the Brussels carpet as *good*, since he could lie there forgetting he and Amy ever argued, forgetting that he ever went to war, forgetting the Confederacy.

459

XVII

JAMIE and Ted ran up and down the street behind the depot, crying, "Right! Left! Right! Left! Company, *halt!* At-ten-*tion!* Ready! Take aim! *Fire!*" Or, again, "Charge those Yankees, blame you, Bill! Charge those Yankees *quick!*"

It was a warming morning, with wind. For hours the children had been prancing up and down the alley back of Leighter Brothers, Cotton Agents, and exciting themselves with the spectacle of the holocaust there. General Hardee, when withdrawing from the blockaded port, had ordered all the cotton sheds in Charleston burned. The military police, left to guard the blaze, were too much occupied in the protection of the menaced neighbouring buildings to keep the children distant.

Jamie was in rare spirits. He had long felt irritation in being relegated to the fringes of the war, and now, in defiance of his mournful, careful mother, was elatedly convinced that he had found the thick of it.

When the delicate bolls, with their explosive seed, spurted from the dingy smoke, and sailed away in blackening embers, the glitter waning in the sunlight, he clapped his hands, shouted madly, and jumped up and down. Jamie was the kind of boy who if really disturbed by anything never admitted it. "Come on, Ted. The Yankees are tryin' to storm the town again. We gotta be busy. Don't stand round lookin'. Come do somethin' *quick.*"

Jamie, who was nine, was the eldest in a family of seven. He was proud of his mother's appearance, and of the fact that she had been a Miss Carter of Virginia. But she had always annoyed him by her compliance to his wishes. She would say, "Won't you *please* do it, Jamie? I think if you knew how much Mother needed your help, you would do it, Jamie." And Jamie, just about to yield, would all at once sense guile, and become obdurate.

If she petted and cajoled, he would use his fists against her; but tantrums did not make him happy. So irked had he been by the atmosphere between them that he had accepted with alacrity a proposition for spending the year, after his father's death at Cold Harbour, with his 'Auntie Cora' in Charleston. Jamie's 'Uncle Maurice' was a paroled prisoner and was very stern and had threatened to chastise Jamie with a walking-stick. Jamie was in terror of his uncle's big beard and hoarse voice. Yet the very anguish which the walking-stick could bring held a fascination. Sometimes, lately, Jamie stole it just to give Ted Ross a 'taste.' When Jamie himself was punished, he cried loudly and unrestrainedly. But if Uncle Maurice was too soon affected by the signals of grief, Jamie was inwardly contemptuous of him. True, there were occasions when Major Lawson was bereft of patience, and Jamie's laboured shrieks became spontaneous. Then he would be 'a nice boy' for a long while. That was boring. Uncle Maurice had locked Jamie in a dark closet. Jamie had decided, if it happened again, to run away and join the army. There in the dark he had sobbed for hours, and blamed his mother for his dilemma. If her conduct in propitiating him so humiliatingly had not been so exasperating, he might have gone to her again. He did not particularly enjoy his 'contrariness.' It was as if some demon had possessed him with it.

Uncle Maurice had forbidden Jamie the vicinity of the fires. Bound as his nature was to disobedience, he became always more reckless as he anticipated retribution. He could not make clear to others his wretched state, and tried to avoid meditation. To soothe his pride, he insisted that Ted take the part of a Yankee, a rôle envied by nobody.

The alley back of the Leighter sheds was one little frequented, and was filled with rubble. The two children were between board fences and blind walls, and only if there had been spies in the black, twinkling windows of the warehouses with their charred sashes, would the game of Yankee attack and Confederate defence have been noted.

A chain, stretched between two posts, was a rusty interference to their nearer approach to the shattered, smouldering ruins. Once, they saw a fireman in a helmet staring at them from the guarded distance. Under his observation, Ted had become cautious and diffident. Jamie, on the other hand, had been pugnaciously alert, had urged his companion to more reckless daring.

Jamie teetered, with shrill exclamations, upon a board laid on a barrel. Determinedly, while his heart fluttered in his throat, he drew attention to himself. When the fireman, too far away to make a speech which they could understand, peered from the smoky welter beyond the fire line, and waved them off, Jamie ignored him, withdrew a trifle as if by accident, and returned at once.

There were Federal gunboats in the harbour mouth. Jamie had watched them, had tried to detect, in their squat commonplace, the source of that peril of which the grown-ups gossiped frightenedly. The boats stood there on the water where he could not glimpse them, beyond familiar sights around him, beyond the sunshine, beyond the morning, beyond the fire that he was looking at. He longed for the awful moment of the Yankee's landing. He could scarcely wait for it. In a week, so his Uncle Maurice said, Jamie was going home. "You are going home a changed boy, Jamie," Uncle Maurice said. "Your ma will be very much astonished at what a little disipline can do for you." Jamie did not believe it. He knew that, when he saw his mother's pretty, anxious face, all would begin as before. For 'a change' he must have some new experience, see something different. He adored the fire; but it was not enough. He'd like to show his mama and his 'Uncle Maurice' how to make a real fire, a fire such as Yankees had made in the Shenandoah valley. He'd like to burn real people up.

Oscillating on the tilted plank, Jamie, in his ineffectual position, became impatient. Dumbly he yearned for a more critical entice-ment to take his thoughts from his wounded vanity, to make the inevitable punishment for his presence here seem more remote.

> Ol' Abe Lincoln keeps kickin' up a fuss,
> I think he betta stop it or he'll on'y make it wuss.
> We'll have our independence, an' I can tell y'all why,
> Jeff Davis gonta make 'em sing, *root,* hog, or *die!*

So Jamie, in frantic treble, challenged the fireman or who might hear. The flames, in limpid gilding, crawled through ruins to the blenching sun. But the vision of them was growing, wrongly, calming, had a sort of usualness.

462

Oh, I'm a ravin' *reb-el,*
An' that's just what I *am!*
For this fair land of *free*-dom,
I do not give a *damn!*
I hate the blamed old eagle
With all his noise an' *squall!*
But the lyin', thievin' *Yan-kee,*
I hate the worst of *all!*

There was an impossible fatuousness in *all* defiance. Jamie sprang from the plank, leaving it bouncing, and ran on, calling over his shoulder, "Come on, Ted. 'Tain't any fun here. Let's go back to the depot."

Ted, reluctant but pliant, followed. Almost together they emerged from the débris, and hesitated at the edge of the railway yards.

Disappointing was the sun-tingling net of tracks on which no 'rains were shuffling, flashing bright, pugilistic arms, belching sooty dreariness on the blue sky. Jamie's curls were dishevelled, his hat lost, his velveteens spoiled. No more had he accomplished. A switch-engine, with a dead, shining, unignited headlight, stood on a siding, and gathered to itself the windy heat of the March glare. Jamie considered climbing to the empty tender. He considered an investigation of the gaping stack, an experiment with the sand box and the whistle. Then he delayed for a more overpowering plan of action. "I'm gonta see what's in that freight shed," he declared at last. And he was off, desperate in chagrin, rejecting memories of his mother's comforting presence while he wished for it. With measured velocity, he jumped rails, waved his arms, and, to disguise his emotions, yelled.

Disapproving temptation, Ted pursued. Actually, Jamie did not once lose his presentiment of a workman doing something under a car.

In the depot, as they passed, were railway employees, telegraphers, idlers, all kinds of persons habituated to interference. Jamie raced down the platform by the stale, known signs: *Waiting Room, Ladies' Waiting Room, Gents' Waiting Room.* Then a vast, open door invited him. The freight station was abandoned, exposed for research, offering a gloomy twilight filled with kegs and crates.

463

Jamie demurred, stared inside. He was restless. He leaned through the unattended entrance and called, "Whoo-oop!" emphatically, and the retort was echo with an equal vehemence. Invigourated by his sense of stealth, Jamie marched on, strutted. "Let's go back. They won't like it," Ted said. And, "Oh, Jamie, don't y'all touch that keg. This is where they got the powder stored. There's somebody comin' down the track right now. He's gonta run us out."

Jamie was as agitated as a monkey. He did not believe in the powder. Then he looked at the rows of kegs and tried to spell out slowly. Ted, as a reader, was more proficient. " 'Explosive! Keep dry!' " he enunciated loudly. "Now you just better mind what you're doin', Jamie. Now Jamie don't y'all go an' fool with it!"

"This is what they kill people with," Jamie said. His incredulity, always strong against Ted's declarations, was yielding to sudden, mounting dreams of violence. He climbed on a keg. He sprang from one keg to another. He leaped from keg to keg. He clutched a crate and shook it fiercely. He *believed*, weakly. Yet, as belief grew warm, it but increased his sickly realization of his impotence.

There was a crack in one of the kegs. Jamie abased himself before it, squatted, tried to rake through it with his finger nail, and so enlarge the crack. "Hi! Yes! It's powder. It's split, Ted. It's leakin'! It's leakin'! Lemme get some out. I'm gonta get some out and make a fire with it."

Ted *hated* Jamie, raking, poking at the crevice. Jamie, dumbly, struggled with the prospect of defeat. Uncle Maurice says I'm a ninny, Jamie thought. I would have gone into the army a long time ago if I'd had a chance.

And *this* was the stuff that had made the war. He felt it voluptuously upon his finger. *This* was the magic that had killed his father. Happy, fearful in his self-engagement, he glanced doubtfully at it.

Ted was won by a thrill exceeding wisdom, and their meagre, contending fingers pried competitively between the creaking staves. Abruptly, in the triumph of his guilt, Jamie was aware that the shed was dim, and was musty-smelling, while a noon sun, crashing on the open doorway, sent a faltering blare of radiance through it. A man, tramping along the depot platform, called out greet-

464

ings to another man unseen. His heed to these details of rejected, everyday existence made Jamie vaguely 'sick.' He had a sudden desire to reject the powder, a terror of its unleashed spell.

The men's conversational utterances sailed off gruffly with the audible wind. The noon was left, baldly encroaching on the boys' secret gestures. Cinders, in a field of black diamonds, were railed as with steely waters. Jamie must decide, or succumb to one of those inexplicable panics which left his boastings incomplete. "Quick, Ted. I'm gonta make a trail of this to where that cotton's burnin'. Come on. Get a handful. I bet when those Yankee gunboats hear the rumpus we can make, they'll go steamin'."

Awkward with haste, Jamie took, not a handful, but a double handful. Doubt was a quantity of his nature, and impelled his greediness. Ted gave a random assistance. He was obediently obsessed by the importance of the moment, and he could not calculate. Jamie had wrenched away a stave. He luxuriated for an instant in the mere mass at his disposal. Then he ran to the door and peeped beyond. He began to strew his wealth. Nobody was in sight. Nobody, besides themselves, was in the freight depot. It would be annoying to the grown people, but there would result no serious consequence for any one if the shed blew up.

Jamie dripped a dash of powder on the doorsill. The wind, which had set his mute nerves on edge this day, wrought instantaneous eddies with the flecks. He feared its destroying influence. "Now that ull all get blown away, Ted. Hurry. Let's get a double handful more. Let's get lots and lots."

They dashed to the keg. They clawed its contents. They threw out powder and danced about. Jamie, rushing on the open, allowed the fluid grit to escape his fingers, sifted its chill around him, as he crossed the track. The trail dissipated mistily, and he returned for more. Ted, with open mouth and solemn eyes, aided. "It's gettin' blown every which way, Jamie. If it gets all over everywhere they'll all be mad at us."

Jamie didn't reflect, would not reflect. Powder, powder, more and more powder. It would be like Gettysburg, he thought. He had heard his uncle, Major Lawson, extol that battle. Or, We'll make more noise than the Confederate army at Manassas did!

As guilt became always less remediable, Jamie needed further the consolation of that fine climax his fancy conjectured. If Uncle

465

Maurice wants to whip me now, he thought, there'll be somethin' sure enough to get mad about.

There was a hunger in him to *be* something, to *do* something. Grown-ups had all the fun in the war. If they expected him not to care what happened, they shouldn't talk so much. Ted said, "What if a lot of people got hurt, Jamie?" and considered himself, abashedly. Jamie answered, his eyes growing large and hard with wonder, "Y'all oughta be a Yankee, Ted. If you do your duty and have sho' *'nough* spunk you don't need to think. I wouldn't be in any old army if I couldn't be the biggest general."

Again and again the precious, seeping burdens were dripped over the track. Again and again the stolid enthusiasts approached the burning cotton in the Leighter alley. Jamie, noticing that a man at the window of the telegraph office was staring at him, felt a delighted misery. He held realization back. Yet he was aware, gradually, and against his will, that it was something horrible that he was doing—or the man in the telegraph office might call it that. There are no limits to recklessness. Jamie, so glad, so dependent on the lurid, gave himself to an unlimited future. No awe could stem this tide in which his gestures hurled him. Sufferings of conscience were insignificant. Hell might await him, but could not delay him. He was stronger than hell. He was stronger than Uncle Maurice, whose walking-stick, applied, would be no more than a futile comment on the already perpetrated.

The last passage was a delirium. The Leighter sheds were now wrecked under towers of sooty vapour, but the cotton was still spouting toward the untouched sky, and was whirling softly downward, burning lightly in street and yard. Wads of scorched cotton were scattered, sizzling, between the alley fences. As a sower of terrible seeds, Jamie, with a dead, triumphant mind, strewed his disaster. There was a drizzling sound. Up the length of the lane, fire ran, in a ready iridescence that escaped time. Ted and Jamie shrank close to the toppling palings that confined them mercilessly with danger. Sunshine, so infallibly the same, depressed them. Despite the spurt, like a faint lightning, vanishing in sucked-up dust, Jamie weakened to the premonition of failure. But, even as his degradation before Ted made his victory sag, there was a *bang-bang, bang-bang—bang-bloo-oo-oo-oom,* from the direction of the freight depot.

466

The reverberations, coming so instantly upon a flat submission to disappointment, left both boys densely uncomprehending. Jamie, pressed flat to a fence, sensed himself rigid against inanimate tremblings. His blue eyes, stern, as he received a blow, filled quickly with excited tears. His heart leaped like a mad thing springing from his chest. He was 'scared to death.' Then, under a flood of rapid feeling, he felt his accomplishment. "We did it. We did it. I did the most, Ted. Goody, goody! I'll bet the depot's burnin', too."

Nothing comparable had ever occurred before. It was an exhausting ecstasy. Mystically, the glory drew him. Bruising himself on the walls, he ran swiftly, to be nearer, *nearer*. He did not quite dare reach *the* place. No, he would rather go the other way. He wanted to flee to a remoteness from all the dull sounds, where nobody would ever find him. After this, life would hardly be worth living. He could think of almost nothing more to do with it. Everything in the world seemed to have happened in a minute.

II

Major Willard was at first surprised and then seriously disturbed when he realized that the moment detailed for the advance of the company of Captain Percius Berkeley would be left to his discretion. Since a promotion in October of the year before, Willard had outranked Berkeley, and to find himself responsible for Berkeley's actions awakened memories which it might have been more profitable to ignore. General Gordon had instructed that the attack on Fort Steadman begin with daylight. It was possible that, surprising the Federals, one of those victories for the Confederacy which were so rare nowadays might again result.

Lord, if only Emily Meeks had not selected just this day before an encounter to make her disturbing visit!

When Willard, who was living temporarily in the old Peabody farmhouse, asked to have the name of the woman who wished to speak to him, he was told by the man who brought the message that the lady who petitioned for an interview was 'Mrs. Berkeley.'

She was waiting for him in the hall. Willard, praying that nobody had observed his start, rose from a chair beside the table in the dining-room, and walked quickly out. He had always been noted for his 'pretty' manners, and, to cover his confusion, when he saw her face, he bent and brushed his beard upon her outstretched hand. The hand was cold, and was very thin. In spite of all his agitation, he took note of it.

Emily had changed. "It is an ill wind that blows nobody good, Mrs. Berkeley. I suppose it was anxiety about your husband that brought you here and I am mean enough to profit by it. How you ever got through to me, I can't imagine. Such visits, even from the fairest of the fair like yourself, are at present strictly forbidden."

Emily, in her black—and he supposed she wore it for her two dead brothers—was too much excited to rise to the occasion of his gallantries as she had used to do. He was erect now, and had to meet her eyes. If she recalled what had passed between them so long ago, her momentary obsession was such that she gave no importance to the recollection. Her bonnet was very old-fashioned, he saw, and she looked very limp and ill in her dyed cotton dress. Never was such an interruption to the business of the hour. "Won't you come into my office—at least I call it that," he said. "We'll waste a rare moment—or at least *I* will—here, in the light of so much impersonal observation." He did not know just how to treat her, and spoke satirically; but he did not feel like that.

"Oh, Mr.—Major Willard—perhaps I owe you an apology— but when I learned that you were here—I mean I thought— Percius is in your command, isn't he?—and that old negro, Samson—maybe you remember Samson—he told me he had carried messages for you—and he brought me over. You know I was with the Garfields. Imogene suspected that you were one of the officers here, and I came over. I never expected to see—to meet you here, anyway—but I believed—*is* Percius here, Major Willard? If it was possible—I hardly dared to hope—that you could help me to locate him. Twice, lately, his communications to me seem to have gone astray—but, as I say, I know how kind you always were—and I scarcely dared to hope."

She talked so rapidly and confusedly that Willard could gather the facts of her situation only by an implication. He had never dreamed that he would see her in the neighbourhood, yet he remembered that her cousins, the Garfields, had always lived near. He had thought of that only yesterday. As for Percius—*Emily Meeks,*

Percius' wife—of course—that is, though she had no right to be inside the lines, the interview with Percius, if permitted, could be arranged very easily.

"Yes. Well, you know I cannot treat you harshly, Miss Emily. If I stretch a point to let you see him, it will be sub rosa. I am as helpless as all my sex in the hands of yours, or I would send you back."

He stepped aside and waved her on before him to the dining-room. He was anxious to close himself in there with her beyond all other scrutiny. The room was very bare and very ugly. He felt, somehow, degraded by its barren aspect. Emily, of course, since he had married Martha, must always think of him as indulging those luxurious tastes which it had once been prophesied would be the 'ruin' of him. He 'posed' before Emily. To himself, he admitted it. And he would have preferred to force himself upon her as the kind of 'Don Juan' she had always professed to consider him. Emily's sudden presence here disturbed him. He confessed to himself that he would not have been loath to make her envious.

An old table, three rush-bottom chairs, a harmonium: those were the only objects in the room. The place seemed staler for the brilliant, shrinking sun that poured into it. Willard gave her a seat facing the ruthless glory straining the uncurtained windows. He turned his own back to the glare. His greying hair was something that he could not hide.

She was restless, nervous. For an instant, disconcerted by her success in penetrating to him, she could not talk.

Willard, smiling almost *too* politely—so he felt—watched her a little cruelly. He was feeling very grave.

"I can't thank you enough," she said, after the pause, twisting the wedding-ring on her finger, "but *is* he here— is he *really* here? Can I see him *at once?* You won't disappoint me, Major Willard? It's six months since he had a leave, and every time I think it may be our last meeting." She was pleading. She controlled herself with difficulty. Self-consciously, she tried to assume a propitiating air of patience, of agreeableness. "Perhaps I should have gone to somebody else— You realize I wouldn't trouble you or think of intruding on such weighty responsibilities—and of course with the welfare of all the South—it seems terrible—the selfishness we all

469

show, thinking only of our own griefs and anxieties—" Her voice broke. She gazed downward at her shaking hands, which she was blind to, and played with her ring.

Major Willard examined her. Hating himself, he luxuriated in this delay which he could not resist. Her amiable niceties hurt him most. Once she had been able to command him to commit any folly. He had never concealed *that* from her. Where *she* had been concerned, he had been as weak as water—and had earned her contempt.

He tried to enjoy being old, feeling fatherly. Then he saw the tight lines about her mouth, the brown darkness under her eyes, dull on that brunette skin. She had aged, had brought closer the difference in their ages. Perhaps she now knew something of what he had experienced. He perceived that he was bitter toward her. That she was less desirable than she had once appeared was a reproach. Youth, even for her, had been fleeting. He had lost all opportunity for the pleasure her youth might once have given. It was *she* who had addressed him as a 'cynic,' as a '*cold* man.' That he had married, 'for money,' half fulfilled her gibes. She did not know that he was trapped in ennui, in an alliance so fatiguing to him, that he had welcomed the war as a diversion. Emily, no doubt, could 'suffer.' She had robbed *him* of further opportunity for suffering. He had become an 'ironist.'

"Miss Emily—" He leaned toward a bell on his table, but hesitated, his hand held over it. "I'll call somebody. One of the men can take you to find Captain Berkeley. But wait just a moment. He can't be located for half an hour yet, and it's such a long time since I talked to you—so long since we have seen each other—well, I hardly like to dwell on the lapse of years." Willard determined not to hurry himself. She and Berkeley probably had a lifetime for their reconciliations, 'damn 'em.' This occasion had a flavour which should be deliberated.

Emily fidgeted agonizingly. Doubtless she was thinking hard things of her 'host.' "It would certainly not be worthy of your reputation for gallantry," she said.

Willard crossed his legs, stretched them. "I don't know how frank your husband intends to be with you, Miss Emily, but—for the sake of auld lang syne—I am tempted, before I let you go to him, to be a trifle indiscreet. It is strictly against recognized principles to do so—but— well, if I were you— Your children are still in Richmond with your mother, aren't they?"

"Yes. And you are going to tell me they ought not to be there." Those large, 'calm, oriental' eyes accused him of dealing yet another blow. No, her greying hair became her excellently. Age— and it was a wonder how these women lasted—had by no means destroyed her old attractiveness.

"They ought not to remain there, Miss Emily—not any longer than you can conveniently help. We hope much from the fact that General Lee now has full command. But—if the Yankees are able to enter Richmond—to their own destruction, be it granted—you will not be safe. I am no prophet, and I am not overpessimistic. But not even the heartiest can perform miracles of courage on cornmeal and water. I tell you this in confidence. Sentiment has such a strong place in my unfortunate make-up. I must ask you not to repeat my discouragement even to Berkeley."

Willard insisted on her gaze. He held it and obliged her, he imagined, to confront that nakedness of spirit which she could not possibly find any more repulsive than he himself thought it. Life is this way and no other, madam, he reflected, his lips bent sardonically, while tears came to his steady eyes most unreasoningly.

If Emily knew that her advent, on the eve of a practical crisis, was as upsetting to him as could have been any calculated revenge, she did not show it. It was plain that he represented to her a certain power over her happiness, and that she was trying to suppress her emotions for fear she might put him out of humour if she showed too openly that he was to her only Berkeley's superior. Willard fancied that she was very delicately exerting her will to conceal the fact that as a human being he no more existed for her. Should he pass on the rumour that Lee was in favour of conscripting 'niggers?' Should he risk his reputation as 'close-mouthed' for the sake of giving her another shock? "What is to become of President Davis and the Cabinet if the Yankees enter Richmond?" she asked bewilderedly. "And my little girls— Is this possibility—is the source exact? Percius has never given me a hint that such a calamity could really come to pass."

Willard cleared his throat. *Like* a woman to take her husband's word as infallible. Why had he told her: 'Morbid and unnatural' as she had always described him, she would, of course, resist his anticipation of a débâcle. It was more than premonition. He was annoyed by her trust in that other. He must overcome this nonsensicalness.

"Unless this is a fact that you can conscientiously verify, you must not discourage us," she said. "I certainly would not tell Percius—I mean, without good reason. It is all such a strain upon his fortitude. You have no babies—no responsibilities. You don't know what it's like."

Willard stood suddenly, and tapped his bell. It was a mistake to drag out the interview. He could not waste his time on her. Emily should somehow be compelled to realize that Martha was a most exemplary wife and that he held her in great respect. If his marriage lacked the ardours Emily doubtless still demanded from a husband, there were ingredients in the situation which compensated. I have not once taken the confusion of my present existence as the excuse for a trivial flirtation, Willard meditated sourly. I have too much sensibility and too much intelligence to enjoy that kind of thing when there is nothing but vanity and a passing whim of sensuality on either side.

The door opened and a diffident orderly came in. Emily, rising eagerly, might be supposed to have forgotten already the fate that menaced Richmond and her family. Her features were transformed, and her eyes glowing with self-absorbed expectation.

"Finley, take this lady to Captain Berkeley. When she has interviewed her husband, see that she gets through the lines unmolested. You can ask Major Childers to write her a pass."

"Oh, thank you—thank you, Henry—Major Willard. I can't thank you sufficiently." Her impatience to be off could not be disguised, but she hesitated as she turned and offered her nervous fingers to him.

Willard scarcely touched them. "It's a great pleasure to come in contact with Berkeley again. I appreciate all the virtues with which you heralded him before I knew him. He is a fine soldier, Miss Emily."

Her smile, her looks seemed to remark that it could not be otherwise. She drew her shabby mantle around her, and hurried, blushing, into the hall. Willard, convinced that she was relieved to quit his presence, did not follow. Instead, he remained as he

472

was, standing motionless, quizzically and hatefully regarding the door that had shut upon her exit. She had not even reproached him for a needless procrastination in detaining her. This was the old Emily—a 'handsome girl, regal, with a presence.'

In the empty 'office,' the sun was turning red on the glass. He sat down. The moted afternoon was a rosy fog pouring on the littered table. He picked up some papers and laid them back again. Honestly, he was growing apoplectic—the smallest diversion from routine, the smallest disturbance unconnected with the army life, and he would be like this. It was really horrifying to consider that, in the event of the South's failure, he and Martha might be thrown once more into one another's company, and without any of those distractions of wealth that relieve boredom. It was a circumstance he was unable to face.

One of the flashing windows was lifted. The air that came in was cold with a spring subtle as a fragrance. Already the sky was fuddled with the shadows of the sun's descent. Midges speckled everything, between him and that cloudy alabaster. In March, as in autumn, the wind seemed heavy with the constant flight of withered leaves, dry rain after rain ceases. Pink reflections were over the red-grey horizon. In fountains like money, the small, yellow, last-year's foliage drooped and swam.

"Damn!" Willard brought his fist down violently on the improvised desk. And I can't help it, he said to himself. By this time tomorrow, Emily will be a widow. There's no use trying to juggle manoeuvres so as to keep Berkeley from the front. I've been dodging a practical issue.

He buried his face in his palms and rested so an instant. When he looked up, he was flushed, recognized it. The constant awareness of his own appearance plagued him. Not that murder would be too much for my conscience, he thought. Gordon can lose a Captain Berkeley easier than he can lose me. But it's too late. I don't want her.

Tilting his chair, he remained meditative. He seemed to sacrifice, in his casual engrossment, the sense of everything concrete around him. He was certainly upset—would feel this almost as much as she would. But that taste of ashes—he supposed she would never have it. If Fort Steadham isn't ours tomorrow I'm willing to see us all hanged, he told himself. I may be sending Berkeley on a

473

risky errand, but the Lord knows *I've* nothing to lose. I don't ask you to mourn *me*, Miss Emily. We have a little more than our private interests to take account of anyhow, and it's a good thing we have. If I had to exist on that woman's petty plane I'd go crazy.

He rang the bell for Smith. Smith ought to be through with his errand. Or he would go and search for Childers. There was more, just now, than an ancient love affair, to fret about.

III

Mr. Quimby had scoured the neighbourhood for news, and came home on the evening of the twenty-ninth just as the rain was beginning to fall. Out of doors, it was not yet completely dark, when the lightning flashes, starting upon the window panes, made such a violent dazzle that, an instant after they had ceased, Mr. Quimby's wife, old 'Miss Irene,' was under the impression that the dips had gone out.

Mr. Quimby, himself nearly eighty, was strongly affected by the general atmosphere of excitement and anticipation of calamity. He had heard that Fort Steadham, taken for a few hours, had been lost again almost immediately. General Sheridan, who must have pretended to march into Carolina, had turned back to rejoin Grant, and Mr. Quimby conjectured that it was that high-water condition of the James that retarded the Federal plan. Everybody knew that Grant had something like one hundred and fifty thousand men to oppose to not more than twenty thousand under General Lee.

Mr. Quimby tried not to think of his son, Allan, but the effort to prevent that association from affecting his own loyalty to the Confederate cause, made the father, in his intensifying fright, more obstinate. The thunderstorm took complete possession of his mind. He ordered his wife to call their grandchild, Alec, and the negroes, to come into the dining-room and kneel and pray with him.

Jane and Ella, the two slave women, who had not forsaken their master and mistress, were gossiping perturbedly in the outbuilding which contained the kitchen, when they received, through Alec, the command to join old Mr. Quimby in religious services. Feeling

474

that some very grievous crisis indeed was pending, they obeyed with alacrity, each throwing her apron over her bandanna, and both rushing with Alec, unprotected, through the back yard in the rain.

All day the weather had been in uncertain preparation for the downpour. The negresses, oppressed, had suspected portent in the lowering sky. It relieved them to receive the hasty decision to pray and to dash, without delay, toward the house and the dining-room.

Alec came in behind them. Mr. Quimby was already kneeling. It was very still. Miss Irene greeted them with a discreet look, warningly. She had the impulse to get up and place a fresh log on the fire, as the last she had laid on the andirons was already crumbling; but she knew that her husband would be offended with her if his discourse should be interrupted by her solicitousness in matters of material comfort. Since Allan had 'disgraced' them with his 'Black Republicanism,' Mr. Quimby had become very 'odd.' Miss Irene suspected that the very fact that the darkies persisted in faithlessness but emphasized for him the bitterness of Allan's 'renegade' behaviour.

"God, Whose Spirit moves the face of the waters, and Whose just rage is mighty, gaze upon us, counsel us, guide us, for there are many today who have offended much against Thy Holy Majesty, and have forgotten that Thou, Who art so merciful to miserable human beings, art also just. Hear us, God. Give us understanding, God. As the lands and waters are bent to the tempest by Thy Will, so also move in us. Let us heed well Thy message. Let us heed the import of Thy wisdom, however terrible. We have lost much, but we are prepared to lose more. We ask, O God, to be ripened for the sacrifices Thou demandest of us."

Mr. Quimby required it of his family and dependents that they assume humble attitudes while he prayed. Yet as he himself became more stirred by his vision of humility, the need for an assertive gesture carried him away, and he stood boldly up.

His eyes were closed tightly. His long white beard was agitated by his breathing. His face worked, as his wife described it to herself, 'very pitifully,' As she would not allow herself to criticize his narrow pride, she excused her resentment with compassion. 'Daniel' had the 'strength' to be firm in condemnation of his own,

475

while she, a woman, born to endure in silence, resigned herself, in her weakness, to his 'intellectual guidance.'

She had never been more affected by the spectacle of him than now. She had observed the course of the ardour with which he had followed the Southern cause. By neither of them could the name of General Lee be mentioned without a catch in the throat. Lincoln, she hated. He and Stanton, so it seemed to her, had deprived her of all contact with her only son. All politicians she somehow distrusted. Indiscriminately, she convicted them of callousness. Daniel restrained the language with which he condemned. Privately, since she was unable to supply reasons commensurate with her animosities, she exulted in shameless vindictiveness. Land, money, investments, everything but his own life which he was past yielding, Mr. Quimby had given to ruin, in the hope that, with the assistance of others like him, the government in Richmond might be supported. Then what of Alec, who has nothing left, Miss Irene would think. If Alec is ever able to assume his proper station in the world, he will need the help of everybody. Miss Irene was the more considerate of Alec's future because, in a sense, with his mother dead, and after the stand Allan had taken, Alec might be regarded as orphaned but for his grandparents.

Miss Irene loved him. She loved his fresh, mischievously cheerful, solemn, almost girlish face. She loved his gawky and impetuous manner, his remarks that appeared to her compounded of profound wisdom and 'holy innocence.' However much she was herself invited to give to the cause she could be thankful that Alec, who was just sixteen, was too young to fight. Slyly, she disparaged his romantic worship of the military.

As his grandfather prayed loudly, with an earnestness exceeding even his usual sincerity, she trembled a little inwardly. Without relaxing the attention she was giving to the storm, driving its pebbly runnels against the window, she watched Alec's peeping features, the doubtful and wondering inspection that he gave, between his spread-out fingers, to Mr. Quimby. Alec was uneasy. She could see that in the glances he would cast upward sidewise, while he huddled, in perfunctory obedience, before the chair on which his elbows rested. Alec occasionally pained her by ridiculing his grandfather. As she gazed at the boy, her determination to rebuke him became a plea. Both were men—or Alec had almost

476

grown to be a man. Both must be 'humoured.' When her husband prayed, she could not dedicate her mind to God as she did in church.

"Father Almighty, Who knowest the ways of men, yea and of *beasts*, and of the least creatures of Thy creation, so that not a sparrow falleth unless Thou willest it, Thou knowest that our beloved commander, General Lee, who has for four years fought the good fight in Thy Name, is being pressed on by his enemies in excessive numbers. Thou knowest that our supplies are diminished, both of food and clothing and of ammunition, and that if Richmond is taken in the next few days even the person of our temporal leader, President Davis, may be threatened. Thou knowest all this, O God, and didst know from the beginning of Thy Divine Plan. Yet we have faith in Thee unshaken and believe firmly that if Thou willest it all the trials which now beset us máy but prepare us humbly for victory. We have abased ourselves, as each should before Him Who made us. We have asked ourselves every question we can ask of our own heart. Give us strength to understand, God. Are our hearts not yet purged of vanities, O God? Is there something lacking, some fault among our many faults that we have not perceived? Hear us, Lord! Save us, Lord. In what manner have we failed Thee? How have we shown ourselves unworthy? He who loses his life shall find it, Lord. It is Thy promise to mankind which we cannot doubt. We know that all we long for, all we yearn to accomplish, can be achieved by the free sacrifice of every petty whim and self-seeking ambition. Guide us, Lord. Guide us. If we fail, it is because our weak human intelligence cannot compass Thy mighty motives."

Here Mr. Quimby was so overcome by emotion that he was unable to proceed in speech. Turning his back to his audience, he knelt again. Alec was frowning worriedly. Miss Irene fidgeted. The negroes opened their eyes boldly in wonder.

The Yankees, under a man named Warren, were crossing Gravelly Run. Lee, caught with so many of his harassed men, and no encampment, would not sleep that night. Was that the cause of this collapse of dignity in one accustomed to demanding awe? Mr. Quimby clasped his massive, withered hands, knotted his finger joints, and his whole stiffened body seemed to writhe. Was he weeping? His wife, depressed, detecting in him added signs of age, would have preferred to clear the room of all observers, but that she could not emphasize this moment of weakness.

Christ, hear me. Jesus, hear me. It's too hard, Lord. It did not come upon me till this morning, Lord. Is *that* the last thing you would have from me? Mr. Quimby, praying silently, felt cold, inquisitorial eyes upon him. It is an agony, he told himself, to be alone with God. I'm not strong enough.

The house they were in was on the Quaker Road, and on a slight rise of ground, so that it received the full impact of the wind. Mr. Quimby, as he felt the timbers shake, had to suppress involuntary heed to outward noises. At first the darkness had been filled by separated sounds: rattlings of tin on the roof, slapping of loose boards in a shed, dreary clatters from the old slaves' quarter, where the cabins, no more occupied, were about to tumble. Now the individual accents of that confusion were sinking away. Instead, there was a steady and profound sighing from the chimney, out of which the feathered ashes blew inward. Lightnings continued, but without the startling crackles of the thunder. When a blaze sprang from the shrouded heavens, it ran in an unsounded flood over the window, and burned, upon the deluged silver glass, the immovable outlines of trees and the distant roof of the kitchen. Through the pale impassivity of webbed panes, the illumined rainfall was visible, as if a billion silver ropes stretched tautly between new grass and dreary sky. On this watery harp, the flame itself, shivering the dulled clouds and making them glorious, ran softly downward.

Miss Irene, when the dense silence, more awful for the passing revelation, returned blackly to the window, and her whole thought was disturbingly filled with the pattering of endless raindrops on the top of the house, considered the 'poor, stricken soldiers without a shelter,' and wept quietly—not for them, but for Allan; and because such things as this could be.

Mr. Quimby, asking, Have I kept *this* good, because it *is* my only good, for myself, rose dumbly, indicating a dismissal of the company. Why, he questioned, when I tear myself apart, when I am ready to do what few men have done, do I feel such guilt? He looked at the others as from a long way off. He could not face his wife. He glanced at Alec sternly, furtively, almost hatefully. "Continue your prayers in your own rooms," he said. "And don't sleep

478

in your cabin, Jane and Ella. Stay here with my wife tonight."

Ella and Jane, though reverent of his fervour, were conscious of the indiscretion which their presence was. They rustled, curtsied, but were avid to withdraw. They walked quickly out. Alec, too, was glad to gain his feet. He wanted to continue reading Froissart's *Chronicles* which he would take to bed with him. When his grandfather showed more self-control, Alec liked him better. The piety of the grown people was forced on the boy.

As Miss Irene, clambering from her knees, rearranged her cap, and, attempting to revive the easy atmosphere of every day, went to poke the fire—because she was afraid Alec might misconstrue Mr. Quimby's peculiar excitement (*not that she herself knew what it meant*)—her husband addressed her suddenly.

"Don't let Alec leave the room, Irene," Mr. Quimby said sharply. And he turned to the boy. "I have something to say to you, and to your grandmother. She will reproach me now, perhaps, but later she will not. I have been in travail of mind for several days. I think God has given me the answer to my prayers, in a resolution I have just made—though it took this storm to arouse me to my shortcomings."

His eyes, with reddened lids, were vague and wild, peering down and avoiding them all, as though he did not hope that he could trust them, or aspire to their understanding of his determination. Impatient, Alec hesitated. Of his two guardians, he preferred his grandmother. In her face he could always read a constant attention to his likes and dislikes, to his moods and preferences. As she was, so he fancied, others ought to be.

Miss Irene carefully replaced the poker, with the bellows, by the mantelpiece. At the same instant, came another lightning flash. Since the window shutters were off the hinges, there was no refuge from the bright blindness that passed across their eyes. She waited hopefully for a further symptom of storm which would delay all talk. If her husband would only get to bed! When he was recumbent, and 'like a baby,' while she warmed his sheets, she felt no menace in him.

"Irene, we have petitioned God to help us, and we have offered, in testimony of our readiness to yield to his guidance, most of our worldly goods. What means most to us, what we prize the most of all that Providence has left us, we have *not* offered. Ask yourself

479

what we keep from God. You are even more responsible than I am. You know what it is."

Now he was staring at her almost fiercely. She should not make this suffering futile. Pity for self, in conflict with a simple duty, indicated spiritual feebleness. Anyhow, it was 'said.' If she obliged him to plead or argue—*O God, God, let not that woman argue*—he would not be able to control his temper. It had come upon him this very day that women did not need religion, had no love for 'right.' *She* would be satisfied to patch up this life as it was. *She,* after Allan's treachery to all he had been taught, could strive, with old, habitual fervour, to keep things merely 'going.' No agony could ever break her, could ever make her pleasure in trivial, mundane things grow any less. *I* have disappointed her, Mr. Quimby thought, yet, even though she takes so little joy in what I am, I am enough. She doles out her tributes. She wants to buy salvation piecemeal. As if any price could be too great to pay for Truth, for some release from *this.*

He did not 'criticize' his wife, did not 'condemn' her. She was less 'proud' than he. Perhaps it was her humility that he envied. O God, he prayed, as he gazed at Alec, let the boy see that I think first of his *final good.* Make me less envious. Help me to go on realizing what she does not feel, that there *is* a Good which is Thine above, and is *Absolute.*

Miss Irene cried, protectingly, "Alec!" and made a step toward the boy. What was she doing! Her husband, even if he *had* 'gone crazy,' could not disregard the welfare of a child. She felt so inadequate, so bereft of any power to anticipate, that she sat down quickly on the nearest chair. She said, irrelevantly, "I've always tried to do my best, Daniel, and now you seem to think I've failed. It hasn't helped Lee and the Confederate army to see us without sufficient clothing and not enough to eat." She listened for the thunder, felt the world was strange, and began to fan herself with her handkerchief. Could it *be* that her husband was suggesting that Alec go to war? *Then* she would be justified. No man could contradict her if, with *that* before her, she became her husband's enemy. The existence of a woman held two obligations: one toward her spouse, one toward her children and her children's children. Within the limitations of her 'duty,' she had served Daniel docilely. Rebellion now was something 'holy.' Was Alec man enough to be against her, too? Would she stand alone?

Mr. Quimby's tongue fumbled his dry lips, parted in his beard, Alec, wishing, simply, adults would not quarrel, waited restively for explanation. It seemed as if the thud of wind and rush of rain outside but emphasized the discomfort which each was undergoing separately. Mr. Quimby knew himself about to speak what was from his soul, and so hardest to say. To keep to the purity of an unapproved intention took ten years from the waning span left him. "Irene, you have already guessed what I want to do. Alec is not too young to enlist. It is the only expiation we can make for—for what has happened. He is going to fight for General Lee. I am going to take him to Lee's headquarters. He *must* go tonight."

Why had Mr. Quimby the impression in his own mind that a lie had been told? This joylessness in doing 'right' must be the penalty of timid conscience. He was wrestling as Jacob with the angel. Time seemed important. He was afraid of the calm that would come with morning, bringing an eternal hesitance.

Miss Irene's buoyant tact departed from her. Her features shrank, withered. Her stare grew mean with animosity. "You *can't* do it! You *shan't* do it! Alec is still a baby! You—you—" Her discreet silences of the past now appeared to her purposeless. "You've driven your own son from us for your—your *principles*. I—" She was dumb, rising, her whole face working as she sought control. She mustn't say too much.

"Alec *must* go." Obstinacy was the mask for emotions, needs, that Mr. Quimby had never attempted to interpret to her and never could. He made himself stone. O Absalom, Absalom, would that I had died instead of thee! If she had reviled him, her opposition would not have devastated him more. For forty years she had nagged him to resist the awful Might of Providence. She would go on denying him the relief of submission, always urging him to hold something back.

"But I'd *like* to go, Grandmother," Alec said suddenly. His eyes had furtively brightened. His attitude was eager. He thought, hungrily, I reckon Grandfather doesn't take me for such a ninny as she makes me believe he does. There was, also, this shameful 'secret' in the family. He would wipe it out.

"Alec, don't you care a button for your old grandmother? Don't you feel *anything* for me?" Miss Irene, crushed, watched him, and slyly added, "And on such a night! Why you'd be drenched to the skin before you got there, Alec, not to mention being killed."

Alec fidgeted his shoulders. Quiescence had always irked him. His grandmother would never guess how indifferent he was to her kindnesses. He was 'tired' of thanking 'them' for things he didn't want, just to prevent their 'being hurt.'

Mr. Quimby placed a cold hand on the boy's arm. "Alec knows he is not too young to give what he can to save Virginia."

There was silence. The steady lap of the rain seemed to grow louder. Again the window panes were drenched with silver, and the room darkened, while the trees, blackened by the evanescent brilliance, flashed mercurially. *Yankees crossing Gravelly Run, Yankees crossing Gravelly Run!* Alec sensed them going *on, on, on,* himself pursuing, *further, further, further* than he had ever dared to hope. The oppressions of obedience melted like weighty clouds from his mind. Just to be independent as he had not been before! He forgave his grandfather's former sternness. 'Grandfather,' after all, had 'understood' him better than 'Grandmother' did.

"Alec—I haven't anything to say. Your grandfather knows best—but don't it mean anything to you to have Grandmother and Jane and Ella wash and cook for you, make as many nice things as we can—now food's so scarce—and see that you have nice warm clothes in the winter—knit you a singlet—you remember the nice singlets I knitted you last winter—and love you and care for you? Nobody ull ever love you like your grandmamma does, darling. It isn't that I'd keep you—but I don't believe your grandpapa realizes how little used to hardships you are—that you are too young yet."

Alec pushed back his gold curls. A sullenness of depression came into his eyes. "Of course if you don't want me to leave you, Grandmother—" His voice broke, in its changing falsetto.

"No, no. I wouldn't be selfish. It's only for your own good." She felt malicious, driven always to that 'good, good, good'—*good of everybody—good of everything.*

"Pack a few things up. Pack your running bag. Charlie Sherry is going to give us some horses." Mr. Quimby pushed his wife, and gently forced Alec toward the door. As the boy, only perfunctorily reluctant, yielded, Mr. Quimby was conscious of a gauntness of spirit possible only to a soul starved of its communion with God. This gesture, as well as others, somehow failed.

Honestly, Miss Irene was bewildered. She believed that, when the two of them found out what a wretched night they had selected, they would return. Desperation made her wish to hoard such few odds and ends of existence as were left her. The same state seemed to throw Mr. Quimby 'off his balance.' It was not wicked, she decided, to pray that he might realize enough suffering to 'open his eyes.' God certainly promised repentant man forgive-ness if he promised anything.

IV

"And so I ask God to help us, and to keep us in such mind as to be always fit for His support."

The chaplain had to raise his voice to send it above the noise of the rain. On his final words, the men, who had been ordered to proceed, fell into marching step. The ambulance wagons were bringing up the rear. He waited, and watched the first ones pass. So difficult had been his position in the army, and so long his 'spiritual' struggle, in his effort to accept the shedding of human blood as 'right,' that, finding almost every one against him, he had condemned himself for 'cowardice.' It was therefore a relief to him to endure, like this, equally with officers and 'common' soldiers, the onslaughts of tempest.

The chaplain knew that General Lee had no intention of giving in, and tried to be glad that this was so. Some believed that the commander would advise the evacuation of Richmond. It was vaguely apparent, even to those partly excluded from army secrets, that Lee's intention of crossing the Roanoke River must be evidence of a plan to join Johnston in North Carolina, and, hence, the symptom of a desperation only hinted at. Danville, the chaplain had heard it rumoured, might be the next capital of the Confederacy. All this furtive gossip, coming to his ears, depressed him, for victory would show that God had smiled on his decision to give himself whole-heartedly to a partisanship in violent acts.

Scrupulously, the chaplain ignored what might be false report. He was stern with those who contemplated base desertion. He was stern with himself. *God will not abandon us, God will not abandon*

483

us, he kept on thinking, as the lightning, flashing, puddled gloomy sky in floating, watery earth, and he could see the looming wagons and the straining horses, plodding mildly past. 'Helplessly honest' as he was, he realized plainly that this was not a perfect world. If, in his sermons, he sometimes dwelt more on punishment than on reward, it was because, life being *this* and *that,* he found it a better thing to condemn mankind than to condemn his Omnipotent Creator. The chaplain was too modest to consider important in the Divine Plan his own sacrifice of fastidiousness and sensibility; but that these others, with lives spent and bodies exhausted, were striving to no 'blessed purpose,' he could not credit. *Am I then more reasonable than God,* he would ask himself bitterly, *and is my recognition of justice, my appreciation of heroic acts, more acute than His! Have I more compassion?* No, no, no, was the answer, and a thousand times no!

Of course there was the suffering of the Northern armies to take into account. As they had been, throughout the war, possessed of temporal powers superior to those of the South, the chaplain assumed that, naturally, they had 'more to learn.' The lesson of adversity, which he had conned so well himself, was something God had sent upon them for their benefit. Meanwhile, *he* rejoiced that 'duty' held him to his post. As much as he longed to escape this wretched spectacle, 'petty pride,' if nothing else, restrained him. He would be obliged to watch it to the end.

Nat Jenkins, a teamster, recognized in the lurid vagueness, the dripping figure in a sodden cloak, drew his pair to a momentary standstill, and, leaning from beneath the wagon hood, called, "You ain't much better at walkin' than I am, Chaplain. Come on, lemme give your bones a lift. Git in with us." Nat was a driver who had lost one of his legs at Gettysburg. Finding, he said, that 'a peg warn't much use at home,' he had rejoined the army some months before and resumed his old task of caring for the horses.

When the wagon rasped to a standstill, gloom was ascendant, and the chaplain, harassed by the threats, uttered in hoarse voices, of those whose progress was impeded by the incident, had to fumble for the muddy wheel, and hold it, as he placed one lifted foot upon the slimy hub. Nat tried to 'give him a hand.' They failed to reach one another. The chaplain slipped and half fell; when he was warned, by a sickly twinge in his ankle, that he had

484

received a sprain. Compressing his lips, as he at last succeeded in his effort to gain the driver's seat, he refrained from mentioning his mishap. But he wondered, as the team began to move again, if wounded soldiers left like this. He had contracted a cough, which shamed him very much; and the diet of musty meal and cabbage produced flatulence.

The road was so deep in invisible mire that the vehicles proceeded with sucking noises. Nat kindly pushed some old sacks toward the chaplain and told him to cover his knees with them. "Sheridan's gonta find his birds flew off," Nat observed, forcing his heavy accent to overtop the storm, as he blinked stolidly, with bright, revealed eyes, at the sudden, chalky clouds bristling so low and near the earth that they appeared to be only two or three hundred yards ahead of him.

The chaplain scarcely attended. Able to clench his teeth and endure pain for himself, he was almost maddened by the terrible groans of a man in agony who lay just behind him. When the thunder *diinged*, with a subdued clatter, he was glad to sense that other sound 'drowned out.'

There was something 'archaic' in this procession. For miles around, there in the dark, the pikes and lanes must be filled with this press of tramping infantry. Backward, as the chaplain's fancy penetrated the night left behind, he seemed to hear, repeated infinitely, the cries of torment to which he was obliged to listen. As much as he conscientiously abhorred a suicide who would leave his burden for another's bearing, the chaplain decided that it would not be altogether unforgivable to place beyond misery a man in such affliction as the one whose moans and oaths he could not evade.

Plum-*plump*, plum-*plump*, plum-*plump*. Another company was overtaking them. Nat drew up on the incline of a gully. The chaplain lurched. His ankle dartled aches. To suppress a groan, he bit his lips under his moustache. More and more—and they were marching on—to *what*, O God? In expression, the chaplain was a stoic, yet vicariously, from the gladdened tongues of comrades, he enjoyed shouts of triumph. Often he had imagined these 'brave boys' entering Richmond, crying *hallelujahs*, with the Yankees subjugate. Then flags would be flying, then banners would be waving, then ladies would be throwing flowers from their front

485

verandas. At the inauguration of President Davis, long ago, it had been that way. *Roo-oo-oom*, went the low reverberation over the sky. *Crickle-crackle*, threading in the burning silver bushes, went the lightning flash. In a daze, the chaplain saw the dim clouds vanish and the brilliant earth spring up. The heavens bent 'like a bow,' and from that bright-scarred universe, descended, in quick millions, all the glassy arrows of the rain. Every new twig and bough blossomed with metallic flowers. The trees, that were yet bare, stood forth nakedly in diamonds, and it was as if each bole, with its trickling wings of foliage, shed a winding sheet.

At the same moment that the landscape was born, vibrant upon a vanished dark, the glare blenched the huddled shoulders of the hastening soldiers, and exposed their eager, furtive faces, soddenly intent. As they marched, in jostling flame, away from him forever, the Holy Ghost seemed to be playing on each glistered rifle barrel.

"General Lee, I reckon he's a pretty fine old man," Nat was ruminating, in audible geniality. "Yes, suh, y'all won't find anybody no better to his men than yo' Uncle Robert. Plenty in a ticklish fix like this here ud take to the road 'thout no baggage—an' no wounded neither—leave them to the Yanks. Wouldn't blame him if he had. Guess after all we had to stand this winter *nobody* ud blame him. War ain't made these fellows mean, suh. If it's done anything to he'p these fellows use their brains, it's made 'em charitable. I figure sometimes that I don't blame nobody for anything, no matter what they do."

"Blame?" echoed the chaplain, doubtfully, attempting to distract his meditations from his swelling leg, yet revelling in the difficulty of mastering his discomfort. "I don't believe our forgiveness should be too wholesale, Nat. There's always the Devil to fight. We must keep on our guard against accepting *him*."

"I ain't lost my respect faw the Good Book, suh, an' maybe I'm goin' too far when I say it, but between you an' me, chaplain, I got my doubts o' that Devil."

This was a heresy which the chaplain would gladly have condoned. But six months before—*not now, not now*. Now he felt it an easy decision of a problem to forgive everybody. He was not one to treat as unimportant the convictions of untutored intellects. Even some of the great heroes of the Bible had been illiterate. Yet—without the Devil— Was agnosticism poisoning him? Had

486

he become infected with the malady of the age? He shuddered. "No, Nat. You are mistaken. The Devil is something we can fight. If he were an invention, as you seem to suppose, I would say that man invented the Devil in order to avoid sorrow. It would be a sadder world without the Devil, Nat. We would all be innocent, if that were so—and innocence, as we see among the savages, is a more hopeless state than sin. There is hope for the sinner. None for the innocent. You mustn't try to put your doubts into *my* mind. I couldn't face the pity that would mean, my man. Why, we *need* the Devil—need him as we need a God."

Nat was silent. The chaplain, in the lightning, relieved that the conversation was dismissed, watched the horses' bulky, rising, falling rumps.

V

Dere's buckwheat cakes an' Injun battah,
Makes y'all fat, an' a lil' mite fattah,
Den hoe it down an' scratch yo' grabbel,
To Dixie Lan' Ah's boun' to trabbel,
Then Ah wisht Ah was in *Dix-ie,*
Hoo-*ray!* Hoo-*ray!*
In Dix-ie Lan' Ah'll take mah stan'
To live an' *die* faw Dix-ie.
A-*way down Souf IN DIX-IE!*

Maude and Arthur, enjoying the sunshine and the happy morning after rain, clasped hands tightly, sang at the top of their voices, ran along the street together; and 'Miss Imogene' had to remind them they were on their way to church, and, finally, call them back to her side. Maude, with her puffed green silk showing her fat white arms, was very 'hoydenish.' By the time that they arrived at service she would have her leghorn hat on her shoulders where her corn-coloured hair hung down. Arthur, who was milder, more awkward when he romped, was very 'imitative.'

Even 'Aunt Imogene' was affected by the 'gleesome' weather, and could almost imagine that life in Richmond was like it 'used to be.' She had challenged, today, her own strict war-time convention of modest apparel, and had removed from moth balls her lilac brocade, though the end of the winter seemed an inappropriate time to don it. Her bonnet was 'out of fashion' and her gloves not new, yet, as she had glimpsed herself in the cheval glass before leaving home, she had felt, so she had told her niece and nephew, 'quite fine enough to attend a reception given by Mrs. Davis.' But social events at the Confederate White House were becoming more and more infrequent. The 'good old times' of lavishness and refined etiquette were passed. Would they ever come again? Miss Imogene breathed a little resigned sigh. Nobody knew how long this 'wicked' war would last. The Davis family—with the exception of the President—had quitted Richmond, 'for a visit.' It was most depressing. And 'the poor, dear girls' in the 'present generation' had no 'social life.' Well, to doubt General Lee would be a stupid sacrilege, and the President, despite the contumely that was being heaped on him by the jealous and the ambitious, bore all things 'nobly.'

Arrived before the church door, Miss Imogene confronted the familiar throng of entering worshippers, and felt much comfort in the sight. She was not considering the Eternity of God, but the permanence—*thank Heaven*—of customs, 'civilized usages,' reverences. Here were the same faces, the same sunshades, the same failing efforts to sustain the 'mode,' the same silhouettes of crinolines and hoops and beavers, the same tight trousers of the gentlemen, the same walking-sticks. Capitol Square, behind, in its flutterings of spring, breathed for her, from its dampened grass and walks, this prevalent, inspiring repetitiousness. 'Monroe' was dead. She had heard the message two years ago. Yet the butterfly awakened, little chickens hatched, and there was always 'promise.' Time had modified her sorrow for her 'awful loss.' She had begun, she fancied, to 'learn' from it. It was this appearance of the usual that decided her again, on each successive Sunday, to know God as 'Good.' With the enemy 'at the very gates,' not a Sabbath went by without a full attendance at the morning service. Nations might fail, she would say, with sad amusement at humility, but Maude and Arthur must be 'brought up nicely,' and must go to church.

As she was mounting the steps, picking her way discreetly, just the tips of her extended fingers elevating her flounces, while she admonished the children to quiet, her attention to them was deflected by the creak of carriage wheels, and by the stamps of horses. Feigning casualness, she glanced behind her guardedly. Ah, it was the President! She made a moue at Maude and Arthur, frowned on their giggles, and told them to wait here in the vestibule beside her that Mr. Davis might enter first. She was perturbed, she acknowledged to herself, to see him look so care-worn, yet she was somehow 'thrilled' by his air of dignity and self-engrossment, his 'unhappiness.' Of course Mrs. Davis does her best to comfort him, Miss Imogene thought. But it seems too bad, when you can see he has so much upon his shoulders, she is not beside him.

She lifted her own meek and unworldly face, and gave him a squinting smile. His mien was stiff. He walked with downcast eyes. Perhaps he had forgotten that she had ever been 'presented' to him. How she longed to express to him her indignation with all the members of his Cabinet, who, during this last hard winter, had criticized him 'treacherously'! Gripping her prayer-book feebly, she composed her hands upon her stomach, while she furtively cast a look behind her to be sure her dress 'hung right.' She could not 'pretend' to diagnose the real trouble in the President's quarrel with General Johnston, but that Mr. Davis had begrudged giving full military power to General Robert Lee, she did not believe. When a man is in the heyday of influence, he finds many friends, but it is a true adage, and a bitter one, that rats flee from a sinking bark, she thought.

Her flat mouth worked palely. In spite of this joyful morning, this 'hope'—and, with God's Grace, she *felt* it—of success for the 'Cause,' Mr. Davis's strange, stony ignoring of his acquaintances affected unpleasantly her most 'susceptible' nature.

She had watched Mr. Davis as he cautiously alighted from the carriage. Now she followed his every movement. A few addressed him. He responded distantly. She was so concerned for his popularity that she wanted to 'shake' him. He was 'a great man and a gentleman,' one that would never be appreciated in this 'faulty' life. His 'austere' features satisfied her utterly. He reminded her a little of Monroe. But the mass will never understand him, she reflected. He is an aristocrat to his fingertips. Lottie told me that his family in Kentucky did not stand very well, but I do not credit such stories.

Maude whispered, loudly, "Arty, Arty, that's the President!" Arthur whispered, yet more audibly, "Look, Maudie, look, Maudie. It's President Davis! It's President Davis!" Miss Imogene, experiencing a little tremor as Mr. Davis passed, blushed, both at their indiscretion, and because '*he*' did not speak.

Then she hustled the children through the padded door. Now that the President had gone before her, it seemed to her imperative that she follow closely. Her expression was solemn, unconsciously abstracted. If Mr. Davis could only realize how all depended on him to give them cheer and comfort! A man such as he was, 'born to command,' must affect the state of mind of all about. Lottie Price's conjecture that the President was breaking under the strain put upon him, did not, as Miss Imogene nursed charitably her injured self-esteem, seem too far-fetched. His 'eagle eye,' she felt, was 'blinded.' He seemed worn and full of doubt. Suppose—oh, suppose—that something really awful were about to happen!

Miss Imogene rustled hastily toward the 'Rolfe' pew, pushed Maude on ahead of her, and, clutching Arthur, jerked him roughly after. Then she subsided upon her knees, concealed her own face decorously, and immediately, as though the time were precious, began to pray for Mr. Davis.

The President, also, was praying. She could glimpse him kneeling, with his hat removed. The back of his thin neck was very plain to her. When he inclined himself, his elbow resting on the upright of the bench in front, and pressed his small, cold fingers on his brow, she wondered, almost feverishly, on what calamity his meditation concentrated. She asked the 'dear God Who rules over all things,' to revive in Mr. Davis his former buoyant spirit, to open his eyes to the loyalty he elicited, to make him more friendly, more winning toward his enemies.

Perhaps it was really *wrong* to ignore completely all alarming rumours. Perhaps General Lee really *was* retreating.

As a rule, it was very quiet in the church. Miss Imogene liked that quiet, in which, as she said, she found her 'refuge from the world,' while she admired the cleverness of little Evie Dillon, who could turn her dresses and dye her mantles and make them new again. Old Miss Georgia Rossiter was not looking so well today. It would be a pity if she did not live until the war was over.

Yet, the sad demeanour of the President made Miss Imogene so very nervous that her sanctuary was lost. Herself fidgety, she found that she had never heard so many 'graveyard coughs,' so

490

many rustling petticoats; nor had the thud of the feet of tardy arrivals at the service ever seemed so loud.

At last these signs of agitation subsided. Somebody tapped her on the shoulder. She started irritably, but controlled herself. Mrs. Emmet—'Miss Lizzie Emmet'—whose pew was to the rear, was whispering, "Have you heard the *terrible* news, Imogene? Just look at Mr. Davis, won't you! There must be some truth in it."

With the tidal groaning of the organ, Miss Imogene was exasperatingly prevented from inquiring what the news might be. The first bars of the processional crashed stalwartly. She was obliged to rise, and to give polite heed to the behaviour of Maude and Arthur, who, when they were not rigidly prompted, did not follow the rules for conduct very accurately.

It appeared that the end of the hymn would never come. Miss Imogene sang on, for her voice was 'trained,' and she always made it a duty to encourage the children musically. Though she kept her back straight, and her gaze was fixed resolutely on the dull glitter of the cross and the silver altar vases, she was in a fever of apprehension. It was a fact, then, what Lottie Price had heard— that Lee was retreating toward Carolina, and the authorities in Richmond were keeping the matter secret! How *could* Mr. Davis treat people so unjustly, holding them 'in the dark!' It was not *'right'* to do so. Her kindly opinion of him began to alter. Perhaps he had given her that snub upon the stairway *'purposely.'*

The evacuation of Petersburg was a 'blow'! She couldn't believe these things were truly happening.

Oh, what a long ritual! Two or three times, after the singing was done, and, with a reprimand to the inquisitive children, she had sat down tensely, and had craned her neck sidewise, and tried again to catch Miss Lizzie's eye. No interchange could be accomplished. To say *'that* much' and to add nothing more in explanation, was just like 'spite' on Miss Lizzie's part. Miss Imogene began to tremble. She could feel her dish face flushing miserably. She strained and strained to find a meeting glance. Miss Lizzie, wretchedly absorbed in other matters, remained inviolate.

Miss Imogene had a weak heart. Often, when disturbed, she had this 'queer' sensation. It was as if a dim river, storming through her eardrums, also drowned her sight. The weather out of doors must have continued bright, yet when she stared above her at a thunderous purple window with its gleaming angel, she fancied that the sun, eclipsed, was fading slowly. The odours of leather prayer-books, musty cushions, people's clothing, lilies on the altar, made her vaguely sick.

President Davis remained. He was still present, powerful, actual to her imagination, getting up and sitting down, as she was doing. He was 'high church,' just as she was, and, when the Sacred Name was spoken, bent his head. She approved him. Yes, she would not 'be shaken.' But would this awful service ever culminate?

She listened headily to the collect. The fierce gilt eagle swooping from the lectern unnerved her particularly. She was annoyed that the handsome purple ribbon in the Bible was growing frayed. Everything was becoming 'trivial—trivial and strange.' Even the 'Stars and Bars'—the dear flag that had seen so many battle-fields, after the ladies of Altar Guild had presented it.

Now the moment was one of silent adoration. There was a per-fect and unpremeditated hush. It was broken as the door into the vestibule whined softly on its padded hinges. Miss Imogene, shocked unreasonably, stretched her neck stealthily, and was aware, with a maddening sense that she invited comment, that other necks were stretched. Under the dim, glamourous seepage of day which fell through the bedizened windows, illumining the wax-gilt faces of the twelve apostles, the congregation crouched as under an inacceptable ban of disapproval. Sighs issued from its many lips unanimously. Restiveness was displayed. A boy was tiptoeing rapidly down the aisle. He was an awkward boy, bare-foot, dressed in homespun. Obviously, though he made almost no sound, he was abashed by his realization of an untimely intrusion, and by the attention he unwittingly attracted. A hundred pairs of eyes defined his appearance—and he knew it. A hundred minds, after the observation of a white piece of paper that he held in his hand (which might be a message, might be a letter) questioned what they saw.

So intense was the common interest in the advance of the strange boy along the aisle, that for several seconds the organ laboured with rheumy music, and those who were effacing themselves so piously forgot to rise to it.

Came a reluctant shuffling of hasty shoes and boots, an upheaval of slithering, rattling hoops and petticoats. This, too, was subdued, died away. The conspicuous boy had reached the President's pew. He was delivering his missive openly, and Mr. Davis, with discreet but agitated haste, was reading it.

Miss Imogene, confirmed in her alarm, felt 'ready to faint,' and fumbled stupidly the lace around her throat. If Miss Lizzie would only divulge the mystery to her! Miss Imogene, become stern in her determination, half faced about. Miss Lizzie, very fat and not given to vivid gestures, was prepared for the mutely worded question, and a series of round, exaggerated mouths expressed the sentence which it would be inappropriate to enunciate more loudly in the atmosphere of worship. Several times she wagged her head up and down, in severe emphasis, chin reproducing chin below it, in an inclination toward the distant President.

Song was no more than absent peeping from a few. The boy was departing. He braved an exposure meet for crime. He was almost running. As Mr. Davis returned to punctilious behaviour, the congregation, relieved, sensing a purer air, grew louder-voiced, quite resolute. There he stood like the very sign of faith, his slight, erect shoulders as indomitable as ever. The details of his small, clean profile, occasionally exhibited, indicated such staunch, accepted attributes of character that Miss Imogene was obliged to shed tears of penitence, and to wipe her nose elaborately. Oh, we have a strong man at the helm, she thought devoutly. Thank God for that. We poor women must depend on the men-folk entirely, and we have no right to suppose they will fail us. They need all the spiritual support we can give them. Poor Monroe!

Too avid her hope! Mr. Davis was bending carefully. Mr. Davis was lifting his 'stove-pipe' from the red plush cushion. Mr. Davis, with a tight, sardonic mouth, and furtive, brilliant, reserved eyes, was quitting the edifice of God. Why, indeed, Miss Imogene condemned resentfully, could he not considerately delay departure until the service ended! She could have screamed. Maude and Arthur, alive to a diversion, climbed on their knees, sprawled over the pew back rudely, and, with fingers poked deep in their wet, open mouths, looked after him.

Miss Imogene, twitching harshly Maude's exposed under-ruffles, drew the little girl to reversed position. Arthur, less docile, evaded the insistence and went on staring. His aunt was much too ill at heart to give further heed to him.

493

Again the organ swelled on the dimness, and seemed to measure, with its pauses, the distraction of the group below it. The minister, like a host who would gloss an offence to etiquette in his own establishment, climbed into the pulpit, and, with tactful ostentation, spread his sermon out.

His meticulously conned words penetrated, with peculiar detachment from their source, to the uttermost corners of the building; while his features bore an expression which showed his calm an effort; and, twice, as he reiterated his text, he repeated it wrongly, having to correct himself.

"Is it a mes-sage-a-bout *Lee?*" Miss Imogene mouthed sibilantly. She could no more listen to the preacher's declamation than she could 'fly.' Twisting her body, she glared a command to Miss Lizzie.

Mrs. Emmet remained obstinately correct. Her popped brown eyes, smoothly averted, form interrogation, saw, it appeared, nothing but the figure in the surplice, and heard only, "The fourth chapter of John and the third verse— 'and this is that spirit of antichrist whereof ye have heard that it should come: and even now it is already in the world,' " which the figure was announcing.

Mr. Caldwell was rising. Mr. Caldwell was recovering his hat softly from the place where he had laid it beside him. He had sidled into the aisle and was covering, guardedly, the length of velvet carpet that stretched to the door. Mr. Minnegrode was rising. He and Mrs. Minnegrode, with some remark made sotto voce as they passed Miss Imogene, were hurrying out. Mrs. Alderson had taken the chubby fists of Fanny and Adelaide, and was leading them with her. Mr. Smith Kirby Jones went by like a thief. Mr. Seddon got up stiffly and looked for his lavender gloves. Mr. Breckenridge stalked from his pew boldly, and, overtaking those who had been in advance of him, rushed on in an unmannerly way. All those who were in the church who were in any way associated with the Confederate government were rising. Miss Imogene observed it. Constantly was audible the squeaking of shoes, and the muffled thud of the door swinging back and forth reiterantly. Every time an exit was made, the door caught for an instant and permitted the flat glare of the Sunday street to break inward, always unexpectedly, and flood the interior with crudely different light.

494

The minister, Mr. Cushing, for some moments, continued his discourse. As the flutter and agitation of removals persisted, however, he broke it off shortly, and said, tremulously, "I do not know the exact nature of the crisis which is calling away from worship so many faithful members of this congregation. I am prepared to believe that it is something of importance, or the beloved President of our Confederacy, Mr. Davis, would not absent himself in the course of that service to which he has always devoutly adhered, even since we have been given no peace from the Yankee marauder. So I will not continue with my address. This flock is dismissed." And he held up his hand and faced the altar. " 'The Spirit of the Father, Son and Holy Ghost be with us all and forever more. Amen.' " On the 'amen,' his voice was husky. With head bent, eyes abased, and his robes switching clumsily about his hurried legs, he crossed the chancel quickly and disappeared into the hidden vestry.

The abrupt alteration in his manner, with the revocation of his intention to preach, brought to a temporary halt the stealthy preparations for leaving that many were engaged in. As if discovered in a naughtiness, they glanced at each other and did not know what to do. The building, without the minister, seemed empty. The unattended altar left them ill at ease. Everything beyond the chancel rail had become, suddenly, oppressively mysterious, almost menacing. It was like a place of doom in which they were all caught, and, in their 'Sunday best,' ridiculously.

The depleted choir was disbanding. Mr. Remington, the crippled organist, had joined the crowd below the stalls. There was the clatter of music racks being overturned.

The pack congested. The aisles filled with persons moving, as in a fire, or a panic, toward the entrance door. With fierce, quivering hands, Miss Imogene clutched her two children and assailed them with orders of despatch. Mrs. Emmet, waddling slowly and goutily, was not brought to account for her inconsiderateness. Rather she was evaded as one who might retard flight. Women who were well acquainted were gazing at one another as at strangers, being too obsessed by uncertainty to recognize the already known. It was impossible to proceed as briskly as one wished. Miss Imogene pushed on impetuously, was 'caught in the act,' and exercised an almost unendurable restraint.

The sunlight still sank gauzy bars of colour through the robes of the apostles. From the fiery glory of the spotless angel's gown coursed moted shafts of glare. Miss Imogene could not recover from a superstitious impression that Peter and Bartholomew and John, the Beloved Disciple, and the Reaper in the lily field were being abandoned. The church, gutted of humans, appeared indeed garnished for a Presence that inspired dread. Lo, He stands at the door and knocks, she seemed to read—and the angel in the lily field lays down his sheaves. No man knoweth when He cometh. No man is prepared. Be ye also prepared—*but not for this, for this.* She glanced about her at this awful Silence, that grew and grew, with the growing wedges of the sun, to a burden of alarm which she could not sustain.

The street! She fought for its dear commonplace; and was there at last. Carriages, in numbers, with the crazy glitter of great black-glossed spokes, were just driving off. The grass on the slope of the square was 'different.' She even saw its green as livid. People were rushing by, people were streaming by. The stone-blue sky might well have burst upon the hillside to shed in the park all the throng of excited humans who ran hither and thither. Deliriously she watched them, realized that *this* was Sunday.

"Richmond's abandoned! Richmond's abandoned! The Yankees are coming!"

Between tears and shouts, Maude and Arthur teetered on tiptoe, jerked at her arms, and were, obviously bewildered, anxious to dart away. She heard the calls, the cries, the echoes entering in the church behind. She was rooted to resist this wildness as she would a hurricane. If the Yankees came, the town would not be safe for any decent person. She must fetch the children home. She must find Miss Lizzie and try to borrow the 'Emmet' carriage. If only she had not been persuaded by Jessie Connor to sell the horses— even her riding-horse. The silver, the linen, it would all be rifled. Nothing would remain. With that terrible and solemn background she had this instant quitted, Miss Imogene longed not for the treasures that would not be corroded, but for something tangible, for something she could hoard and keep.

"Mr. Lindsay?" she shrieked. He turned, met her dry eyes, dis-tendedly wide and fixed, and said, as cursory advice, "It's the climax, Miss Imogene. They are moving the archives. Mr. Davis

496

has gone, they tell me, and a good many members of the Cabinet with him." Then Mr. Lindsay, defensive against her protestations of astonishment, sped beyond her.

The children lunged ahead of her. They pulled her and she did not prevent it. "The Yankees are comin'! The Yankees are comin'! President Davis is gone! Flee for your lives, all you Southern people! The Yankees are gonta take possession here tonight!" She heeded all the words of this madness, but as though trumpets deafened her. Her heart squeezed, clutched, squeezed, clutched. It was like a *thing* sucking, pumping dry streams for water. She ran. She continued to run. Home was down the hill—but that, also, an illusion. Where then? Where then?

VI

Chancey Harris had seen 'Miss Mabel' leave at twelve o'clock. All the valuables that she could not put into the buggy with herself and Jenny, she had confided to him. In particular she had cautioned him to guard the flag in her possession—the one that her husband, 'the General,' had carried with him through so many battles. Chancey's panic, inspired by her own, had led him to take refuge in the cellar. He had remained there for several hours, as in a dungeon, buried, while the crowds marched on in the street without.

On the upper floors of the dwelling it was very still. Chancey was interred beneath that strange and empty quiet as beneath tons of earth. Everything Miss Mabel had asked him to do he had promised. He had even offered to tell '*them*,' for her, that the house was dangerous because of the recent death of one of its intimates who had had 'the pox.' Beneath a heap of kindling behind a stack of empty boxes, he had secreted the flag very carefully. The story of 'the pox,' as his fancy elaborated it, began to affect him so strongly that he felt unclean. He could imagine himself here for ever. He spread out his big hands and scrutinized the pink palms doubtfully.

Chancey, growing hungry, tried not to think what it would be like down here when the evening came, and nothing had happened to change the cellar litter that was around him, but that the dim wing of sun, entering through the mean window, had swerved, first to the cobwebbed ceiling, later to a spot upon the window ledge,

497

then drawn away. He shivered when he anticipated his continued safety. No one would have believed that the excitement in the streets was not the signal of a jubilee. *He* was not necessary to that clamour. A mis'ble lil star would soon be there glinting upon him.

How does it feel when the sun shines down forever through one small and dustied window and steeps six feet of yellowed earthen floor in steady motes? Nobody in the town of Richmond knows who that fellow waiting to be forgotten is. *Chancey Harris, Chancey Harris,* Miss Mabel's Chancey. There ull be nobody left, in a year or two, kin recollec' a name like dat. How long a time 'fo' de Lawd call an' de Lawd take? Maybe Chancey Harris live so long ago de Lawd ain' callin' him. De Lawd fawgotten dat he evah took accoun' uv sech a niggah. Swing low, sweet chariot, pick us up, carry us along. Swing low, sailin', sailin', moonlight, starlight, grave-light—grave-light heah where de sun is shinin.' Ain' no Chancey lef'. Chancey ain' no mo'n dat fly buzzin'. Chancey ain' no mo'n dat lil spec' o' dust. Upstairs on de street, folks walkin', trampin', marchin' on. Grave dus'. Dey's mo'n mo' grave dust. Chancey Harris wanderin' off nowhere, 'cause he ain' pa'ticulah, 'cause he daid—daid an' gone away. All daid an' gone away an' lef' de empty house to Chancey Harris' ghos'.

When he had endured all of solitude that he could bear, he stole gently up the slowly creaking cellar stair. With bright eyes fixed, he gazed around him. He wanted to get away. How escape Chancey Harris, closed in like this? If de folks out dere in de street don' know no Chancey Harris, how will dey let him out? He couldn't leave all this stuff for the Yankees 'nohow.' Miss Mabel was gone, *ended.* Going away never ended. Up stairs, down stairs, in mah lady's chambah, goin', goin', goin'.

Chancey mounted through fathomless halls to 'de Gen'al's' room. There, as he recollected, the solid silver soup spoons had been hidden in a clothes-hamper. To reassure himself, he peeped beneath the mattress, found the silver serving-tray again. If he left, he ought to take all 'dis truck' with him. For what, for what, for what take *any* truck? Nobody need dis kind uv truck wha' all is goin' 'fo' it gits too late.

Three hours before there had been 'live people' alive in here. Now the clock ticking on the disordered mantel tapped marks for the final minutes before a burial. *Who* was to be buried? All were going to be buried, 'Norf an' Souf.'

A fly, flat on its belly on the ceiling, did not stir when Chancey made a foolish, barefoot leap at it. The closed blinds looked transparent and the strongest glare was on the crystal chandeliers that twinkled solemnly and brilliantly. Shouts, cries, calls, laughter, shuffling steps, he could hear; but in this place all that penetrated was a *doubt*. Shouts, cries, calls, laughter, and mourning *somewhere* for *somebody*. Dis heah's a *daid* house, Chancey Harris. De people pass an' de houses las'. Dis house daider dan de mausoleums in de cemetary.

Room after room he walked through. The beds had been stripped of linen, and the blue-striped mattresses suggested worms asleep. There was a wash-bowl filled with water on the marble slab of a dressing-stand. In the milky fluid of the basin lay the greasy, rotting soap. Worms workin', ev-yt'ing rottin', worms borin', borin' all de time. The walls, in their senseless figuring of gold and brown, were walls on which even the pictures didn't '*see* nothin'.' Everything in this house was 'jes' standin',' dreamin', sayin' to hitse'f, Tomorrow, tomorrow dere won' *be* no tomorrow. Tomorrow come already, come to stay. Y'all's caught in de deaf room, Chancey Harris, where de worms is thrivin' an' yo' soul deserted.

He was afraid to leave. It seemed as if he had become so accustomed to the silence that to abandon it would be to leave himself exposed. Completing his quick, stealthy survey of the upper premises, he began to *go* down—*down* where the heart lay in his boots. Be quiet, Heart, don' be kickin' up, Heart, y'all stopped yo' beatin' long ago. Y'all has to lie low where y'all gwineta go, and take account uv dis.

On a landing, he halted. He heard a noise. It was not a vague sound, loud and distant, from the moving crowd outside. It was not the summons that would come so thunderous that the house would crash. It was not the horns, the trumpets, and the angels blowing. *Tic-tic.* That was the clock. *The death-watch in the wall.* No, it was the clock, that, alone, and deathless, since it had no heart, would go on living.

Somebody was coming! Chancey waited. Come on, y'all, live man. See dis daid man standin' watchin'. See dis Chancey Harris. Ah don' like livin' noises in dis deadly house.

It was in the dining-room, where no cloth was laid. The sash was creaking. The sash was rattling firmly, sash was being lifted.

Chancey, descending from the landing yet another pace, pressed himself back, effaced himself on the cold mouldings of the stairway by the newel post. He yearned to be nothing. He that was nothing, yearned to efface this body which belied him. Couldn' nothin' git him in dis deadly house ef he had no body. Silver spoons in his pockets clicked together. No' mo' Chancey. No' mo' Chancey, carrying silvah spoons.

Somebody tiptoed. First there was the thud of a foot soft as his own and bare. Then tip*toe*, tip*toe*, still unseen, from the open window to the open door into the hall. He could tell, because the noise of crowds was louder, that the window remained open for the man's escape. Somebody was creepin', somebody was searchin', somebody, careful, 'jes' like Chancey,' searched the secretary. Somebody, 'lookin' in de sideboard drawers,' wanted to take the silver out.

There was a fanlight toward the street, and the strip of Brussels to the stairway seemed powdered with a gaudy dust. Gaudy in de graveyard, gaudy in de graveyard, flowers on de carpet, jes' de ghostest flowers, shet de cawpses out. Sun shed itself, shed *years and years*. Who cares how long, how long silver spoons stolen, lambs cryin' in de street?

The key to the front door hung on a nail outside the parlour. To fit the key into that twinkling lock would not take a minute. Life come inside, in frough de window, life gonta git him. Chancey was afraid, with the spoons in his pocket, of the glare and the shouts that would greet and pass over when his present ghost took flight.

Tic-tac, tic-tac. Nail hammers! One, two, free, nails driv' in de coffin. One, two, free nails. Nails is little but enough to hold dat sinful man. Don' need mo' dan two free nails when de coffin's set. *Tic-tac, tic-tac.* Time is speakin'. Y'all don' know his language. Time got hammahs.

Chancey made himself steal-silver-spoons *onward*. He had gone as far as the open door into the dining-room. He peered through the crack. Another, on the other side, was craning, looking. Eyeballs flashed. *Two* Chancey Harris faces stared. *Jimmie!* Chancey Harris started, trembled. Did Jimmie Harris call his own name to his mammy or did Chancey Harris say it? Jimmie! Daid, gone—gone aw daid—all de same. Jimmie Harris ran off to de Yankees. Jimmie Harris tuk Miss Mabel's plate. Jimmie Harris, in a Federal prison, maybe, died free years ago. Jimmie, Jimmie, how kin y'all come back?

"Jimmie?" Chancey hissed the loud, real name, Jimmie Harris. Jimmie Harris, ragged twin brother of Chancey Harris, cringed and shivered when his name was spoken, but *he* did not speak. Jimmie had the look of 'a mean niggah'! "How y'all come heah, Jimmie? What y'all doin' prowlin' in Miss Mabel's house? How y'all come heah limpin'? Yes, Ah sees y'all limp. Did a ball an' chain do dat? Git up off yo' hams an' quit yo' glarin', Jimmie. Dis yo' brothah. Don' y'all know me? Ah knows y'all 'dough, y'all shame yo' mammy. Ah ain' gonta condemn y'all, niggah. Ah 'membahs when y'all was small an' tiny an' would ask mah he'p."

Jimmie's gaze retained distrust preciously. His big mouth opened for, perhaps, a lying explanation; but he would not give it. Maliciously noting the empty house, his defiance increased. He sprang. He was like a cat. He had his cat paw, big and black and pink, on Chancey Harris's neck. Chancey, feeling his lungs full of straining, while his eyeballs bulged, struggled. He regretted he had been so tender. His fists crept jerkily behind him, and he sought in his pockets for the razor he had found upstairs. Chancey Harris *yelled* a thought. He was bowed, resisting the soft grip that enclosed his throat in iron, but he slashed instantly, brought his arm about, swung his fist sidewise, and slashed obliquely upward. It was easy, easy, all too easy. He and Jimmie 'usta play togethah.' He and Jimmie had nursed together the same mammy's breast. Jimmie Harris come heah in de dark an' cut Chancey Harris's neck. Da's how he done it. He come heah sneakin' an' he come heah prowlin' an' cut Chancey Harris's neck.

The clutch on Chancey's throat was released, and breath poured excitingly into his tightened chest. He staggered. He stooped. He drew himself labouredly aside. The big black man, fallen before him, humped inertly on the carpet. Jimmie Harris, big black thievin' niggah, git Miss Mabel's carpet dirty. Jimmie Harris, lying on the floor in dampish darkness, had a twisted look. His eyes were glaring. The dark was red. He was red inside, just as Chancey Harris was. He was bleeding *that*.

Chancey would not trust to luck. One time hit him. Next time hit's me. He bent and worked quickly with his sticky razor, slashing, in the slack wrist, above the weak, curled fingers, another artery. Jimmie was allus a stubbo'n, silent niggah, an' *now*— House won' speak. *Tic-tac, tic-tac.* House won't speak. Folks goin' by in de street. Nobody know who goin' by, who las', whose turn come tomorrow.

Chancey Harris rushed skilfully into the hall. Chancey Harris turned the key fitted into lock too small for heaven. But he went out. Nobody knew. Nobody noticed. He went out alive again. Daid man in house. Jimmy daid in house. What de house wants. House axes bofe uv us. Hit take Jimmie. Not till next time it take Chancey Harris. Live, livin', goin' down de green street callin', sayin' no' mo' deaf. Ah don' believe in no' mo' deaf. Ah's *live!* Livin'! Dis is *Me!*

VII

With the windows closed, the shades drawn, the three or four candles in bottles on the mantel fuming, and the air dense and gauzy with cigar smoke, the parlour was very hot. 'Miss Pearlie' was very uneasy. Though it was she who had ordered the transoms draped, and every sign of the life in the house disguised, she had stumbled to a shutter more than once and opened it a crack. Pandemonium entered through the merest slit. She put her eye there and saw, first, the glow in the sky made by the burning warehouses; then, though the street lamps were broken or extinguished, the roofs of the houses opposite looking all red and wet.

If, desperately, she leaned a little farther, and the cool air whetted on her shrunken throat, she beheld the bonfire flaring in front of Mahoney's Saloon, and the crowds of people tossing on below her in the semi-darkness. The mobs of hooligans had been like this the whole day through. Nobody in Richmond had been able to stay still. They had just marched up and down. The City Council had ordered all the drink in town destroyed. Dandy Parish had told Miss Pearlie that the niggers were out with mugs and pitchers and were scooping it up. Rosie said if a nigger touched her she would cut her throat. Miss Pearlie, not so used to niggers, did not feel very differently. Yes, the darkies were crazy. She did not know what they were expecting, but she was afraid. She was the 'madam' of a 'very select' establishment.

Peering down on the obliterated sidewalks, Miss Pearlie stared upon a thousand heads and shoulders. Rising from beneath, with varied murmur, came peculiar sounds of wordless boisterousness. Crouching, deaf to the congested noises in the room behind her, she hugged herself concealingly inside her shawl. There were girls who had asked for permits to visit camps right on the fighting line. She disapproved of their temerity. Miss Pearlie had cajoled her own into refusing such opportunities. It was through appeals to Dandy Parish's influence, that she had kept Rosie back. All for their own good anyway, Miss Pearlie was thinking. They wouldn't have been safe. Now, after she had angled for protection through these many months, she *could* not allow her plans to be defeated. She had fed her girls through all the time of scarcity, and at her own expense.

In the window beyond her own stood, silhouetted against a weakly background of candle glare on a dirty wall, the shapeless figure of a woman in a Mother Hubbard wrapper, leaning rugged elbows on an open sill, and calling out hilarious greetings to those who passed. "Come up and see me, honey? Y'all ain't gonta leave me lonesome, honey?" came the woman's bawling. Hoots and whistles of derision were the answers to her invitations. "Got some sho' 'nough money to spend tonight, ain't y'all?" she wheedled. And a man replied, "Yep, Lizzie, but if yo' company's the best the house can offah us, we'll do better somewhere else."

You'd be a fool, you would, to stop with *them* vermin in that bawdy place, Miss Pearlie thought, the reckless behaviour of her 'low-class' competitors offering her some consolation.

> "Tra-la, tra-la, tra, la, la, la, la,
> He is my on-o-ly joy!
> He is the dar-al-ing of my heart,
> 'Cause he's a so-jer BOY!"

screamed the siren in the wrapper, who must be drunk to call attention to herself like that. Miss Pearlie stared at her hatefully and enviously, hating the example of an idiocy which would take such risks. For her own part, if she had to leave the town she would, but it galled her to think of the possibility of meek submission to the looting of her goods. But for the roll of bills inside her dress, she would even now be beggared; and the Confederate money might be worthless. She felt grim pity for herself. Previously Dandy had been the channel of intercession with the powers reigning, but if the Federals were going to occupy Richmond by morning, and she to survive for a new régime she must rid herself of his dangerous patronage. Rose could manage Dandy if she had a little sense.

Miss Pearlie was small, with a strong, leathery countenance, a long, inquisitive nose. Her eyes, with their one thought that never altered, were ferrety and quick. She was daring, with a small, stupid daring, 'like a sickly bird.'

In dour eddies, like soot, clouds of burning moved in the sky over the throng. A senseless terror possessed her and she drew the blinds more narrowly.

> Oh, there was an ol' *so*-jer,
> He had a wooden *leg*,
> He had no tobacco,
> But tobacco he could *beg*.
> 'Nother ol' *so*-jer,
> Sly as an ol' fox,
> Always had enough tobacco
> In a ol' tobacco *box!*

Nonsensically, like happiness, the people below her were shouting songs. Two men, in altercation she could not distinguish, drew a circle of panic about them. One was swinging a bottle, gripping it fiercely by the neck, and expounding with it threateningly. An instant of expanded vision, and the aimless tide swam over the place of drama, jeering, lurching, scattering its infinity. Faint wafts, as of strayed, foolish gaiety, floated back.

Miss Pearlie had never seen niggers break loose, but there were niggers here, and she dreaded. It was a long time since any urge of other passion had inclined her to dissemble her covetousness. Rose, Lizzie, Sally she saw, not victims of herself, but of youth. Her dry mind saw them her captives by way of powers she had no time to question. If she was ready to sell virgins, it was not, simply, by reason of the malice of a procuress, or because of a lecherousness enjoyed at second hand. But she was not comfortable with purity. The strange state of innocence left her more than ever alone where

504

she was, with her own wits and money to live by. Dandy Parish flattered her. She knew it perfectly. To accept his flattery as genuine was her deliberate self-indulgence. She liked to have men turn to her for comfort. She liked to provide them with girls and 'love.' She liked the long, the hard-earned importance of being the mistress of her own house. In the menace constituted by the unleashed negroes, she felt the first awareness, in many a day, of her own body. Her age had lifted her above one vulnerableness, but, with this new aspect of possible brutality, timidity came back.

Morning—something just about to happen—stood above the housetops. Feeling its relentless approach, as it bore the undivulged solution of her crisis, she was tense and sullen. She closed the window briskly, tremblingly. She was determined that, when the Federal arrivals marched up this street, Dandy Parish (damning 'protector'), if the cause he favoured should be lost, must be out of sight.

The girls were drinking. Miss Pearlie did not drink. And on a night when 'influence' might be lost to her for ever she disapproved of it for them. It was Dandy Parish who had brought the liquor in from the débâcle of the storage warehouses.

He was at the piano, playing. Roy Peters, Careless Stratton, Lizzie, Belle, Sarah, Sally were gathered about him in a jubilant, defiantly unmindful group. Near them, a little excluded, was the man called 'Sergeant' Terry, who had just come in this evening. Belle, Sarah, and Rosie said he was a spy. But Miss Pearlie had looked at them very fiercely with her bony, little finger on her lips. "He's gonta stay right here with us and tell us how to act," she said. 'Sergeant' Terry, though he affirmed himself 'Confederate,' might have possessed the gift of prophecy, for he could tell them all that was going on in the Yankee camp. He had seen so much of the war that he had grown 'impartial,' he said. This did not explain the sad condition of his uniform, or why its braid and buttons had been ripped off. But Miss Pearlie needed a go-between. She was convinced that part of his narrative was true, that he did know officers in the oncoming crowd. She had the girls so trained, she said, to ignore the war, that when the soldiers came to visit her they forgot that the war was going on. And she added that the men were glad enough of it. When Rosie had declared that she wouldn't entertain that man for a 'Yankee dollar,' she had been reprimanded. "You can't have all your company fat, strappin' fellows like Dandy Parish," Miss Pearlie gibed. She had no patience with Rosie's docile infatuation for him. It interfered with a realization of the way to take in cash.

'Sergeant' Terry, though consoled by a toddy, looked 'lonesome.' "What's the matter with my Rosie? Ain't the girls bein' nice to you, Sergeant Terry?" Miss Pearlie asked, hobbling toward him in her angry, lame-dove manner, and standing 'bunched' (as Dandy called it) scrutinizing the fellow guardedly.

Even Miss Pearlie admitted that his base and crafty face was 'mean.' But who's got time to think of *that,* she demanded silently, in indignation. She began to call, in her cajoling voice, "Come here, Rosie. Come and talk to Sergeant Terry. You don't treat him nice."

He was smirking evilly, lingering over his toddy, smacking his lips, rising importantly upon his toes, then settling to his heels again. "If you'll excuse me, Miss Pearlie," he said, "I don't want none of the lady. She needs improvin'. To me she turns out to be a vixen. She's done slapped my face." And grinning, biding vengeance, he exposed his snaggled teeth.

"Why, Sergeant Terry! I'll see to her—if you ain't ready to bring her down a peg yourself." Miss Pearlie did not know whether to take the situation as a joke or not. It was true that Rosie had said that she wouldn't be 'lovin'.' to a man like that 'if he was Ulysses Grant.' Miss Pearlie had to restrain her irritation. She must remember she might *need* her Rosie.

In a plush chair in a corner, Rosie sat, in her frayed, wadded dressing-gown, and sulked, 'as if she were a little better than everybody.' Miss Pearlie was often lenient toward 'the high-and-mighty,' but there was a time and a place for it. A brisk, frowzy little figure with her cap awry, she approached Rosie determinedly, commandingly. "Rosie, see if y'all can't git Dandy Parish out o' the room with y'all. If the Yankees decide they got to clean us out he'll be the first one they'll arrest. The row he makes with that piany's gonta draw the crowd on us. It's risky for Dandy to set around here an' expose himse'f. It's for his own sake, honey. You can do more for him than anybody else." Miss Pearlie pleaded shakily, her voice syrupy in supplication, but her eyes cold. At this instant her 'gratitude' for Dandy's services was turned to hate. Dandy had a good record in the Confederate army, but that was no longer of any use. He had been the owner of a livery stable business until a few months past, when the government had confiscated his last horses. His habit of throwing money about 'like a drunken sailor' persisted, but Miss Pearlie conjectured that, despite his continued air of lavishness, his pockets must be nearly empty. In reckless expectation of his own ruin, he was ready to ruin her as well.

"I ain't gonta stay awake at night if Dandy gits arrested," Rosie protested. Miss Pearlie was baffled. "But he's such a handsome, strappin' fellow. It ud be a pity to see him in the jail," she said. The girls, out of hearing, made fun of Rosie's 'moonin'' after Dandy. If anybody spoke about it 'to her face,' she got 'mad' at once. Still Miss Pearlie hoped. "Go on, Rosie. Ain't I been just like a mother to you? Get him out o' this for me."

Rosie got up slowly. Dandy, in his shirt sleeves and a bright blue waistcoat, wore his hat. She took it off. He was sensitive of the growing baldness of his curly head. He snatched the hat and put it back again. Rosie tweaked his fine, sprawling black moustaches, and forced herself upon his knees. The tipsy girls around them screeched delightedly, "He'll catch cold, Rosie. He'll catch cold, Rosie."

"What's the matter with you? Are you sick, you bitch?" he muttered. He was annoyed with her as usual, but, when the others heard his words, he always spoke good-naturedly. "Set down in a chair."

Rosie rode heavily on his hunched knees while he trod the pedals stubbornly.

> Oh, don't you remember Sweet Betsy from Pike,
> Who crossed the big mountains with her lover Ike,
> With two yoke of cattle, a large yaller dawg,
> A tall Shanghai rooster, an' one spotted hawg!

Dandy pounded the tune jerkily. Careless Stratton, Roy Peters, and Belle and Sarah, embracing one another, yelled. Rosie bumped leadenly against him. One of her big, lethargic arms stole about his neck. Dandy knew what she was up to. Her hot face pressed his cheek, and the suffocating air in the crowded room seemed to grow a little worse. He liked the girls, but he never gave 'unneces-

507

sary' time to women. When Rosie had first begun to 'make up' to him, he had warded off her insistence by bringing her other 'callers.' He had told her he liked to see her have her 'pick.' "You act like you was doin' hawse-swappin'!" Rosie had said. Dandy had felt unwillingly flattered that she had grown so angry.

"The years are creepin' slowly by, dear Paul,
    The winters come and go;
The winds sweep by with mournful cry, dear Paul,
    And pelt my face with snow;
But there's no snow upon the heart, dear Paul,
    'Tis summer always there,
Those early loves throw sunshine over all,
    And sweeten memories dear!"

In falsetto, Dandy carolled in her ear. He wanted to give her something that she hated. When he glanced at her sidewise, her eyes were very close to his own, and gave out little sparks of malice, derision. Another expression lay under this quick surface. It was fear. She was afraid of him. His muscles tightened. His whole body was harsh, excluding contamination by her soft weight. (Why in hell, he wondered.) The look she had was the kind that obliged him to remind himself that Rosie was 'one of these here daughters of joy.' She was 'trash,' too. He knew all about her former home life and her family. She had told him. Dandy was thankful that he had spent a few years in the army. The kind of thing Rosie suggested to him had always tempted him too much. He was thirty-six, and had had a gay time in his 'day,' but he resisted getting 'soft.' True that the life of soldiering had proved too much for him, and that he had escaped nefariously, the call of the last draft. Yet if anybody reminded him that he was not completely patriotic, he wanted to break that fellow's head. Dandy had only to hear the name of General Lee to feel inclined to weep. That sort of 'healthy' sentiment did a strong man credit. It was a part of his dislike of Rosie that she gibed at this sincerity which she did not comprehend. Gambling, any kind of risk, was an evasion of 'the ladies.' When Dandy glanced again at Rosie's languorous, nearing eyes, he felt stupid, enraged that she suggested to him he was stupid. His elbows pushed her brutally, but he had no relief. "I don't want any lady-birds tonight," he sneered. He never let her guess how 'mad' she made him. It was only when the

508

warmth and softness of her enfolded him, that he felt completely dissatisfied with what he was. It was his desperate resistance to this heavy, clinging Rosie that made him callous of Miss Pearlie. He was in a mood to wish the whole house to be raided, Rosie bundled off.

"Don't quit playin', Dandy. Short life an' a merry one's our motto, but we don't want to hear no mo' about dear Paul. Give us somepin lively. Keep her up, ol' partner. Play lil shune Dixie died by." Careless, happily inebriate, slapped Dandy's shoulder broadly. Dandy winced.

He broke into the first notes of *Dixie*. Miss Pearlie, beside herself, came running to him. "Look here, Mister Parish, that's goin' just a little bit too far, even for me. You don't know who's out there can hear you!" She was quivering with vexation, bestowed on Rosie a malignant, sidelong glance, then, restraining her justifiable rage, added a wink of warning.

"Folks think y'all doin' this 'cause you're scared to death, Dandy," Rosie whispered. "Come on outa the room and leave these ijits alone. I allus thought you was the kind o' fellow ud do what you wanted to, no matter what happened. Come on out with me."

Miss Pearlie saw the passage of the whisper, saw Dandy flush, and, deciding to trust Rosie to decoy him, withdrew stumblingly again to 'cheer up' Sergeant Terry.

Dandy realized there was a plot between the women, but his conscience smote him for Miss Pearlie's sake. He put his hands under Rosie's armpits, and lifted her. Then he stood. His gesture invoked the clamour of a drunken protest from his audience, which he ignored. It was not Rosie's beguiling attitudes that unmanned him, but his feeling that this night of nights, this night of national crisis, was passing inappropriately. "Come on," he said to Rosie roughly. And he left the room. He wanted to leave the closeness of the house, get out into the air, the street. It shamed him that he had come here for a refuge, that he was not quite as brave in anticipation of the Yankee retribution as he wished to be.

Rosie followed him exultantly, but she did not intend to let him quit her. For one thing, if she could hold him back, it would satisfy a natural malice toward Miss Pearlie, who made use of everybody.

Seeing them depart (Dandy, dogged, florid with emotion, disgruntled, Rosie slyly pursuing), the madam's dry, insistent little mind went on with its self-centred scheming more comfortably, thinking, since an old woman's life went on privately (ignored, almost, by itself) she had a 'right' to what she got. In every detail of the girls' thoughts, gestures, bodies, the men were interested. If Miss Pearlie now and again envied them their apparent easy achievement, it was not often. Her desires were dead, slain long ago. Rebellion tired her. Like a nun, she enjoyed a sort of advantage, a security earned by willing self-immolation. She remembered the weaknesses of flesh, but not very well, though she could use the lessons of this faint memory to influence others. Dandy's male blandishments were a threat; his conceit robbed him of proper calculation. That was why she felt that handsome Rosie ought to handle him. Miss Pearlie would often watch, aghast, people 'in love.' You've got to learn that ain't the way to anything, she thought. Sergeant Terry, she could manage. He was like herself, her healthy enemy. Hugging the burning money in her bosom, but true to the caution her glimpses of the lawless street had inspired, she was already offering him bribery. "To be flat with y'all, ma'm," the sergeant was saying, "I think that present that you talk about sounds pretty niggardly." But he accepted another toddy smirkingly, and smacked his lips. Miss Pearlie was slightly bitter, stony, sterilely resigned.

In the dim hallway, Dandy halted. The house was sealed to sound and outer light, yet, suddenly, from the excluded distance, muffled waves of cheering broke upon it. Rosie shivered. "Come on, Dandy," she repeated. "You ain't gonta let that bawlin' out there make y'all lose yo' head. Come upstairs with me."

Rosie tried to keep her insolence. If Dandy guessed how she was feeling, he would never come. He was in a sweat of haste. The noises were, to her, hostile. She laid her fingers gently on his weighted hands, reclined her cheek upon his shoulders. "I'm feelin' awful lovin' tonight," she said. "Funny I can't pay no attention to that racket." His heart—it was pounding helplessly against her own. Oh, Lord, —— damn the man! If *she* had only made it beat like that! It wasn't the 'the life' she minded. That was easy—'too blamed easy.' It was Dandy, Dandy. But for him, the 'gentlemen' who called her form 'divine,' were all alike. He could beat her, he could kiss her. It was the same. He was driving her to drink. She looked up at him hatefully. She was 'wild' that he was careless of the power he had. What made fellows go into the army? What made them leave as on a quest for misery, for bodily discomfort, pain? Sluggishly, she had pitied the soldiers. But for Miss Pearlie, always 'at' her savagely, she might have refused, sometime, to accept their money. I ain't got nothin' seems worth holdin' back, she thought contemptuously. Dandy had poisoned her stolid generosity. He had robbed her of the privileges of immorality. She no longer luxuriated in its shamelessness. "Don't be listenin' to them —— rowdies, Dandy. What's the use pretendin' you got so much interest in that rumpus? The Yankees sho' will take y'all if they git a hint about you, an' the Confederates, since y'all skipped out o' that draft, are liable to git you, too. I know y'all don't care much about the lovin', but I'd do it just to show you ain't a coward!"

She was so upset that she accepted the challenge of the situation and became 'contrary.' If she 'riled' him enough for his 'hity-tity' notions he'd try his best to break her down, and then—— Her white bulk pressed him, her hands were teasing in his thinning hair. He stared at her blankly. Rosie said to herself that she would 'sho' go crazy' if she had to 'stand' that absent scrutiny much longer. Dandy had been willing, often enough, to pass his time with her; but the yearnings she aroused in him were transient, and he stubbornly 'forgot.' "Come on," she whispered spitefully. "Come on, y'all, you —— fool! Why, you ain't a man! You ain't good enough for a woman!" Rosie had little pride, yet she was bruised against his hardness. She was massively excited. The war, —— damn the war, damn their dirty politics! What in the hell was the war to her? What was it to him? His tearful talk about it was pretence, a plague. If he would make her jealous of some other woman, she would 'stick' her ground. There didn't nothin' matter to *her*, she hoped, but she could *hate* all right! State's Rights! Niggers! Mr.——Davis! How many niggers did Dandy own! He could call her a ——, and she'd *be* a ——! Yes, she knew which side her bread was buttered on—and so did *he!* The —— lousy hypocrite!

"Quit that, Rosie! Lemme go! I can't stand all this skulkin' any longer; I've damn well got to see what's goin' on outside!" He turned away. He had thrown her off.

She ran after him and pommelled weakly at his back. "I could stick a knife into your rotten guts!" Her complaint was heartfelt.

He unwound himself, again, from her arms, and with a brutality which gratified her. He could tell, when she let him see her eyes, that even decent anger, with her kidney, was a kind of trick. When she provoked him—better, when she caressed him, he was conscious of a well of weakness in his chest, of his veins that were warming, that were dilating, flowing tepidly with honey. His head inclined as he listened to the growing uproar in the street, and his florid face turned strangely white.

All the time that Dandy had been in the army, he had saved himself *with girls:* from fear, from monotony that dulled him, from subservience that cramped. But his self-respect would not permit him to show any gratitude to them. To hell with the ——, he told himself. He would not allow it that she tempted him. The faint glint of attention her blows had commanded faded from his eyes; and, cursing her aloud good-naturedly, he hurried down the hall toward the barred front door. He had to make some proof to her that she didn't count.

For an instant Rosie was too desperate to follow. "Yah, go on. Put yo' head in a rope!" she yelled. She lagged weakly. It don't make no difference anyhow, she stormed silently, insisting she had rather see that lunatic in jail than out. She *didn't* care. You could sell her naked on the block at the slave market in New Orleans, and she wouldn't 'turn a hair.' Nobody could keep *her* down, or keep her 'in her place.' She'd walk up and down Grace Street with her clothes off! Give 'em the stomachache. Tell all the quality she was low-down mountain trash and a —— besides! She was glad, *glad!*

Yet even to have her wrists secured in his hands relieved, ever so slightly, some of her demand for him. The sensation, thin as a trickle of moisture on parched lips in a desert, was humiliatingly precious. If she could only use what she knew against him to bind him to her! Or did he mean to flout the conquerors as well? He did not trust her, as she realized. He had always been secretive with her. If she lost him, if he went away, as he had hinted, horrible familiar deadness would descend upon her. If Dandy left

512

her now, he would leave her to a stupor. It was not pain she dreaded wordlessly, but boredom. Everywhere else, her appetites failed her. In the constant gestures of habitual invitation and bestowal, she received nothing. Bewildered, she resented even Miss Pearlie, who had cupidity to keep her soul awake.

Dandy was proceeding impetuously. "Come on, have a look," he challenged, shouting as he passed the parlour. Rosie, when she saw the others crowding in the parlour doorway, anxious to find out what was happening, gave in to her sickness, and ran cumbrously ahead of them to reach his side. "Yanks are here," he foretold bitterly. "Yanks are here! You won't find me stickin' in this corner any longer outa sight. To the devil with you all.".

Miss Pearlie was beside herself. She rushed into the hall, her dry, tight little face militant. "You big drunken son of a ——," she ordered shrilly, "I ain't gonta allow it!" Offhand, Dandy set her out of his way. Rosie, in the malice of frustrate possessiveness, was glad to help him to outwit the 'madam.' She thrust forth her 'flawless' arms inexorably, and held Miss Pearlie back.

Lizzie, Belle, Sarah, glancing at one another, were ready for any 'fun,' for catastrophe. They fled the ominous repressions of the parlour. Catching up their petticoats, they defied their mentor competitively. Dazed, Roy Peters debated, then followed, relieved, if for no reason. (Something momentous stood there in the street. Something, like a miracle, so long awaited, had to come at last.) Careless Stratton, reeling slightly, carried on the song that he had left:

> " 'Tis the song, the sigh of the weary,
>   Hard Times, Hard Times come again no more;
>   Many days you have lingered around my cabin door,
>   Oh, Hard Times, come again no *more!*"

Throatily he declaimed, annihilating melody, covering his drunkenness, which suddenly was frightening because of its inappropriateness. He had come here to escape all resolve. He was overtaken.

Only Sergeant Terry peered from retreat, too wary to risk exposure.

For five seconds, Miss Pearlie was a termagant. Her heavy, eager nostrils were large with anger, her shrivelled features bleared. She damned Dandy over and over again, hoarsely. "I'm ruined,"

513

she kept saying. "The house won't have a stick of nothin' left in it. I *got* to play 'possum till things settle down!" Her goat voice cracked. Her keen eyes glittered with thought single to thoughtlessness. As Rosie had beat at Dandy's chest, Miss Pearlie pounded it more viciously. He was not easy with her, but her leathery constitution seemed to feel no blows. At length, he and Rosie, between them, had her pinioned. A chain was grating, a key turning. The solemn door, released, stalked inward leaving a chilly orifice. Miss Pearlie, exhausted, submitted, cursing, and began to fan herself.

The nervous group, huddled behind him craning, fearful of Dandy's boldness, yet beguiled by it, were suddenly astonished; less by the spectacle of soldiers marching, than by the daylight, which, while the house, shrouded, had kept the false glimmer of candles as if perpetual, was burst so coldly and so differently upon the street. Faint *oh's* of awe echoed from lip to lip. Chests tightened, grudgingly, oppressively.

"By gosh, they *are* here!" In a more indefinitely engendered timorousness, Careless Stratton, no longer foolish, forgot personal caution and leaned weakly and openly on the door lintel.

Chill damp air was freshly insinuated on the ankles of the watchers. The soft touch of the wind was on their faces, dissipating the pent warmth of their feverish bodies.

Somehow the pavements had emptied of all but stragglers. The houses were dingy and still, displaying only a few murky lamps. Under the slaty sky, with its soaring glitter of coldness, the lines of slanting roofs remained dark, but were damp and bright, new-washed with desolation. In the breeze that was so vividly felt, the chalky clouds of day rested.

Racing beside the troops, a few shadowy little nigger boys pattered. A spiritless clatter of uniform marching seemed to explain the muteness that had come with an hour too dreary and too final to be endured. At intervals people, out of sight in windows, hissed.

All at once a fife began to trill. The raw, fragile sound, so much younger than any look of grey dawn or tired, stamping men, quivered hopefully, yet without conviction, through *Yankee Doodle*. At the silly wistfulness of the fife, eyes grew wet, unreflectively. Nothing could bear up against such a light sound. Flesh, already too-used, could not bear up under such insipid youngness.

514

The titter of the fife stabbed each heart with the specific pain of something it had lost, but of which it could not remember even the name—something, maybe, that it had never had. Having to bear, together, dour morning, silence, and frail melody was a gratuitous injustice against which each listener writhed. Rosie looked at Dandy, standing like a statue, the wind bellying his white shirt sleeves, ruffling the fine curls on his forehead, while his eyes remained almost sightlessly brilliant. In some stupid way, she realized that he was never farther off than now. Tears ran down her cheeks. The fife pierced her and she hated it. She was glad when the music ceased.

"Hurrah!" shouted Belle and Lizzie hysterically. Miss Pearlie, a wooden, vindictive stoic, hushed them viciously. A flag bearer had just obtruded, above the weary mass, the foreign Stars and Stripes. The unfamiliar banner, succeeding on the cajolery of the fife, left all disconcerted, insecure.

Prisoners! More and more prisoners! Yet the clothes of all were so dull and patched and shapeless, it was difficult to distinguish blue from grey. Dandy was so engrossed that he was not aware that Rosie gripped his arm.

"Glad to see you home, boys! Three cheers for you and your Uncle Robert!" Dandy, astonished at his own temerity, felt the peace of abandoned calculation. His defiance came as a blessedness to everybody. Careless smiled witlessly. Lizzie smiled. The cheers, hesitant but gathering, went up and down the block. Voice repeated voice with strengthening bravery.

Dandy waved his hat. One of the prisoners, his pallor making him distinct in these acrid rays of reluctant morning, removed a crushed cap and shook it in fatigued appreciation. "You done your durndest, fellows!" Dandy shouted. The ecstasy of sickly enthusiasm burst in a last clamour, then waned. Belle and Lizzie sobbed unreasoningly on one another's bosoms. Careless Stratton sobbed with open countenance. Roy Peters, unable to sob, showed a rigid face.

"Nobody can lick Virginia!" muttered Dandy.

Miss Pearlie only, stony in her doubt, creased her skirt nervously and tried to decide what the next move should be.

Rosie swore at herself. Looking up at Dandy, she knew defeat. If Dandy had to stand what *she* did, he'd cut his throat. Staleness was like an evil taste drawing her throat close. Her fingers on him were a beggar's. The pride went out of her flesh. Allus the same ol' thing, same ol' thing. I don't mind tellin' lies if it does 'em good, but what's the use? She was in this waste, which was her own heart. Dandy had something to live for. He always would have. As for her—Federals, Southern—even if he told her that he loved her, she'd only get the same old bosh!

Sunshine was laying barrenness on the crowded scene.

"Well, we ain't been fired at. Let's have another drink," Careless suggested. He drew away from the door, swaggering.

The others were glad of his hint. Something they had listened to—not the fife alone—wanted to be drowned out. They were furtive, hasty, anxious to refasten the door, anxious to feel the staleness of the night retrieved and permanent. Rosie, staring at Dandy, who delayed, regardless, thought that, 'pretty soon,' she'd be doing 'somethin' awful' to herself.

XVIII

IT was a pitch-black march. The men, passing through Chester-
field Court House, were there joined by Ewell's forces from
beyond the James; but the agglomeration of new contingents did
not exhilarate. In the dark none were certain whether their
trudging was toward defeat or adventure. Even some of the least
among the soldiers knew that the Southside Railroad, of desperate
importance, was in Federal hands, and that all attempt to hold
Petersburg longer had been abandoned. That Davis had fled Richmond was kept officially from their ears, yet gossip had already
broadcast it. Where was the President, was being asked. No one
could answer. But this portion of the army remained intact, and
recognized itself as more important than the flight of any cabinet.

To the frustrate pilgrims, no landmarks were discernible. Along
the road they descended or mounted, nothing was visible but the
vast shadow of the earth, as it sometimes rose, in the summit
of a hillside, to the star-sprinkled sky. As they tramped out of
a depression and up rising ground, they might have been hastening
on right over into nothingness. Occasionally trees, in bulky masses,
stood apart, and there was the little sound of leaves blowing. The
heavens were a dense transparence. For a long time Oscar kept
his gaze steady on one larger planet which, for what seemed
hours, flashed on him the same lustrous, spidery signal. How
far away do they say them things are, he wondered. To reckon such
a distance was beyond him. Just to approximate a calculation like
that extended his fatigue to the never-ending, and his curiosity
as to other worlds finally blurred to an impression of little twinkly,
gold beads, some as fine as dust, raining their uncountable numbers upon his dazed eyes, burning his heavy eyelids as they
drooped despairingly on his exhaustion.

Now and then blotchy groups of houses appeared. Lamps
brindled the shadows. Or lamps in the upper story of a house

went out as they approached. People, fearing them, preferred to extinguish every glow of hope, and to subside profoundly into the privacy of the dwellings.

It was not always like that, of course. Sometimes a door would be thrown open, a dog would bark, and strange, cheery voices of encouragement would echo down the road. Once Oscar was allowed to stop for a drink of water. But by and by the lamps grew less. Some of the villages had been burned, or razed. And, more and more frequently, the inmates in such as stood unscathed, seemed to have gone to sleep. The night was left entirely to the men, who were wearied by the very realization of the spaces accorded them.

The troops skirted a damp-smelling orifice that was a pond. They were called to halt, and when the clatter made by the falling to rest of all their arms had ceased, the high, vibrating blare of singing frogs gave some uncouth omen. In the dark the smell of spring, of grass, of dew, was everywhere, mingled, at intervals, with murkier emanations of stirred dust. Here perhaps it had rained. A sweet moisture was distilled with the sudden scent of fields, the honeyed smell of an orchard. Rifle barrels felt greasy. The horny, lapping shapes of bats darted restlessly over the heads of the groups along the highway, and the soldiers were almost eaten by the young mosquitoes.

"At-ten-tion! Shoulder arms! Right about, *face!* For-ward march!" *Left*-right, *left*-right, *left*-right, *left*-right!

Oscar went on, his whole attention occupied with the thought of morning, a goal which he anticipated absorbingly behind what should prove to be the last hill. Meditation had now become no more than a muttering of his consciousness, a sluggish resumption of the need to keep alive, to keep going, to get *somewhere*, no matter where, before he went to sleep. To be reprimanded threateningly jerked him up. He was glad of every curse, of every nudging blow from a comrade, which persuaded him, more through the domination of instinct, than through will, to continue as he was, jogging up the long incline, and hurtled resistlessly down it by the impetus of other trotting men who kept with him. Sleep cajoled him. Sleep nourished all the labour of his thoughts, and he was about to abondon himself to it gratefully, to sink down, amidst weighty equipment, never to rise, never caring to rise—when

518

the day broke unexpectedly with the speedy retrogression of the sky, with the blackening and waving and scintillating of the scraping branches just ahead of him.

The company, straggling along a gleaming railway line, was instructed to halt and to stack arms. The men, all laggard, blinking, obeyed without surprise. As they sank, more than idle, in the grassy dust of the embankment, the sun, like an icy plaque, rode over the horizon and tilted down on them. They had been thirty-eight hours in motion. Oscar sat there and wondered how he had come and where he was going. Wonder was trivial in comparison to this awful lust for indolence. His dead body demanded so little of him that he could almost ignore it, could fling himself, at length, on his side, on his elbow, and, propped so, regard the phantasmagoria of the day as one regards a panorama left behind.

For some reason, relief was almost too much. Oscar wanted to cry. Up the purpled silver of the track, the sun rushed to a converging point which was a dazzle. From down there supplies would be coming soon. He thought about the good breakfast all of them were going to have, and he could bear it no longer. He rolled over on his stomach, and, his face hidden in his sprawled arms, felt the hot tears run along his nose and into his mouth and collar, while his shoulders shook.

Mark Pettis must have noticed that he was crying. Oscar could hear the thumping of Mark's footsteps in the sod, and knew, in a minute, that Mark was squatting at his ear. "Y'all ain't lookin' very thrivin', Oscar," Mark said.

Mark was one of those fellows who never complained about his own troubles. His voice was very kind. Neither was Mark very respectful of 'Uncle Robert,' whom he called 'Old Lee.' Yet Oscar, in defiance of any inward jealousy, respected Mark. When Mark had been asked by some one why he did not desert, he had 'let fly a string of cusswords that would make an ordinary soldier feel ignorant.' Oscar had once suspected Mark of 'puttin' on,' but had long ago renounced criticism. Mark's gift of silence, and his equal talent for profanity, Oscar revered, aspired to accomplish. They were the symptoms of Mark's rectitude. Oscar could not always 'stand up' for himself, but he could defend Mark. It was as if the preservation of Mark's image intact were Oscar's own self-justification.

This was, maybe, the hundredth time that Oscar had succumbed to his limitations in endurance, and had thrown himself, as it were, upon Mark's mercy. And Mark, as usual, was very lenient. Oscar could not allow himself to believe that what he lost in self-esteem, Mark, as his comforter and mentor, gained. Though now and then it felt like that.

Oscar moved his chin slowly out of the grass and lifted it. "You're tuckered out, and no mistake, boy, but you ain't licked," Mark admonished. He was squatting on his hams. Oscar saw that his legs that were supporting his bent body trembled a little. Mark's bearded face was as white as dough. His jaw was hard, 'like his teeth was gritted.' His eyes glittered peculiarly and he looked at Oscar strangely. Oscar saw that Mark, also, was 'all tuckered out.'

But they could not loll there and observe each other. Some officials who had come up from the road were moving down the track. Man after man climbed wearily to his feet and offered a half-hearted salute. Mark rose woodenly, and Oscar was obliged to follow. Oscar's heart leaped in astonishment. "It's the old son of a gun himself!" he whispered. Mark nodded.

As the two waited, in polite attention, Lee drew nearer. He was walking with several others, heavily, and his shoulders drooped. "This here's tellin' on him," Mark whispered.

There was a silence. The 'boys,' grudging and obedient, stood there in unnatural postures of respect, and, as desultory chatter ceased, the morning was so still that the tramping of the officers along the railway line could be heard by everybody. Mark's dry, bearded, dust-caked lips mumbled an insistent suggestion. "Come on, Oscar. Give him a send-off. See ef y'all can't work up a little enthusiasm. Looks like he needed it."

Oscar felt hatred for the effort, but glanced at Mark's eyes. There was something frightening, something almost malicious in their hunted sparkle. Mark looked as if 'he couldn't hardly keep goin' himself.' Mark looked almost desperate, as if he hated Oscar, hated General Lee, and hated everybody. But he kept right on 'cussin',' urging Oscar to yell, to make a noise, to do something. And finally a few scattered ejaculations of cheering did run along the line. Mark called out loudest of all, "Three cheers for Uncle Robert! *Rah!* Rah, rah, rah!" And Oscar cheered, also, but felt

520

foolish, the sounds thick in his throat, and shameful, as if he were doing something inappropriate. Lee acknowledged the greeting perfunctorily.

"God damn it! He don't seem to care a —— damn *how* we feel!" Oscar said, sotto voce, when Lee had passed, and he was able to sit on the grass again. Mark did not pay any attention to this; but Oscar, with the keen gaze of resentment, noticed nervous tremors.

There was a rumbling in the distance. The noise grew louder as every face was turned toward it. The soldiers, languid to the presence of their commander-in-chief, roused themselves spontaneously, and began to laugh and to call out in expectation. The bulging front of an engine was growing out of a squat speck low on the landscape. The young weeds in the track still waved gently as in an abandoned garden, but the headlamp grew, paled by the sun, until, from the minute vortex, which seemed to whirl as the train came closer, wider and wider black-razzled circles spread over the day.

With its funnel spinning the smoke backward in a dingy torrent, and a little banner of milder vapour fluttering over the whistle, the train, shrieking an announcement of its approach, slowed the revolutions of its wheels, and was still, its greasy shape prominent in the centre of the dew-rimmed fields, bathed in the damp purity of the morning, across which it had cast, but an instant before, the sooty, gliding shadow of pollution.

"Three cheers for the dinner wagon!" an exuberant man decided. And *halloos* rang incongruously. The men were in disorder and weak uproar. The haggard countenances were radiant with distorting smiles. Some ran up the track, and, careless of disfavour, intruded on the scene of disembarkment. "Supplies from Danville! Supplies from Danville!" was repeated over and over, in senseless accents of repetitious joy. Ragged coats waved, caps went into the air, and cluttered the grass. The officers looked 'fussed,' and tried to remain oblivious to the clamorous approbation of the soldiers. From the cab of the engine a white cloth was flickered. It was a train of peace, all right.

The train consisted of the engine, a tender, and a freight car. Several armed men could be seen aboard it. Rifles bristled from the open door of the car, and, as the whole creaked to thudding rest, a civilian carrying a bayonet sprang to the ground. He went up to General Lee, and talked to him eagerly, while the train crew craned, and appeared to listen and to interject comment. The soldiers who had not drawn sufficiently near to understand what was being said fidgeted impatiently, or distracted themselves with shouted remarks that ridiculed the bandit-like appearance of the engineer and firemen, who, their faces muffled and half-concealed by handkerchiefs, wore pistols in their belts.

The train continued to stand there, smoke faintly exhaled from the broad triangle of stack. Once the engine moved, the piston went up and down slowly, and thrust on the reluctantly turning wheels; but was still again. Beyond the worried conversation in which crew and officers were still engaged, nothing happened. Nothing could be heard but the beating of the steam, like the thump of a heart, and the lisp of a breeze in the woods by the track.

"No bacon an' fried eggs for us this mawnin', partners! The provision agent must 'a' been asleep at the switch!"

"Well, they ain't much you kin beg, er borrow, aw steal in *this* neighbourhood."

These conclusions, reluctantly arrived at, were passed from lip to lip, in a murmur of furtive protest and of disappointment; while the eyes of the watchers were suddenly intently fixed on the minutest gesture of General Lee and his associates.

A youth who had loitered within earshot of the consulting authorities, now ran to join his comrades, and, as he passed them, cried, "Hell to pay this time, sure 'nough, friends! Uncle Robert standin' on his hind legs rowin' that nincompoop come up with the switch engine says the stuff from Richmond ain't never come through. We gotta hustle an' find somepin faw ourselves in this Gawd-fersaken place!"

The train was churning again. It jetted large darkness on the soaring sun, and began to roll on smoothly, while the individuals who, a few minutes ago, had descended from it, ran to hop aboard.

Lee, left exposed by the disappearance of the car, hastened once more up the track, and was reviewed silently by the same troops who had cheered him.

From the spectacle of his embarrassed commander, Oscar averted his eyes. Well, what the hell—he *oughta* be ashamed, Oscar thought. For his own part, the discouragement of this incident left him with all the impressions of his exhaustion renewed. The empty place inside him that was the pit of his stomach, burned as if he had swallowed raw whisky, and he felt dizzy. Every muscle in his body ached. A kind of hollow gripes tormented his vitals. That any one should, for any reason, demand another ounce of effort from him, struck him as so outrageous that only a lunatic yelling could have expressed the mindless violence of his chagrin. Aloud, he said, "Well, what the hell do these folks think we *are*, anyway!" His resentment of Mark grew with his rage at Lee, and his sickness under the onslaughts of the sun, and the complete vacancy of the country scene. Not even no water here, he thought, glancing about, but hardly able any longer to distinguish anything. Just the trees waving, and the long, brilliant desolation of the empty track.

Most of the soldiers were past profanity. They sat down, or laid themselves despondently on the ground, while the augmenting glare burst ruthlessly upon their uplifted eyes.

"Don't get soft, old Oscar," Mark said, as Oscar threw aside his belongings, and rolled, with the others, in the only comfort of a little shade just below the track.

Oscar opened his hot eyes and stared helplessly, no longer suppressing the animosity these condolences aroused. *Give* up! Fer Christ's sake, why can't he *give* up! Oscar abused him in his mind, at the point for railing speech, but still, for the moment, controlled by habit. "What kind of a god-damned jackass do you take me for?" he demanded. His head felt swollen as by a contusion, but all with this terrible ache of weakness. His feet were sore and like a fever in his torn boots. This was a disease for which no cure existed.

All at once something occurred to him, something unprecedented, which he had observed a quarter of an hour—half an hour before —but to which he had accorded no significance. Oscar sat up, crouched on his knees, and said, boldly, "Mark, I noticed somethin'—I noticed somethin' I bet y'all didn' notice 't'all!" Oscar was frightened. Why hadn't he seen what it meant the first minute! And the wave of nausea which flooded his brain with black came again in a more obliterating tide. But his mind was alive and keen with this new alarm, which insisted that he should not be tired, that it was dangerous to be tired. "Mark, did y'all notice what I noticed?"

Mark, squatting as previously, picked at a grass blade. He kept his gaze away, on the ground, and Oscar could have smacked him square in the face. (*Now* will he quit all this 'put-on' stuff!) "Well, what did y'all notice?" Mark said. "I notice a heap I don't talk about, Oscar. Sometime when y'all take notice like I do, the best you can do faw yo' friends is to keep yo' mouth shut about it."

Oscar realized that Mark was going to leave *him*—as usual—to confess such danger as there was. He grew cold, and calmer, too, with despair. (Only if Mark don't carry on about it, maybe I'm a fool, and he can call me a fool in his mind like he always does.) "Mark, did y'all notice Uncle Robert's dressed up like Sunday? Did y'all see that brand-new uniform he's got on, an' everything shined up like the chin of a nigger been eatin' greasy 'possum? He's got his dress sword on, too," Oscar whispered rapidly. Though he denied it, this observation made to his friend was like the denial of a pact that he and Mark had always kept.

Mark rooted among the grass blades where a beetle was running, poked it with his finger, and turned it over. "Yeh—I noticed it," Mark answered very deliberately. There was a fine edge to his voice that rasped Oscar's nerves as if a thin knife had been run keenly over him. "Looka here, Mark, god damn it!"

Mark's chin jerked and he glanced around quickly. Two pairs of militant eyes encountered. Oscar's were bitter with fear. "Well, what 'che think about it?" His tone was cutting.

"Reckon Uncle Robert put his new suit on to keep his dander up," Mark answered sullenly, his face crimson. Anybody would think the reply disgraced *him!* Oscar would not let him 'get off.'

"Mark—what if this here war was to—to end? Would y'all *care?*"

All at once Mark ducked his shoulders, and pretending to stoop, covered his face with his two thin, enormous hands. "What the hell are y'all talkin' about!" he kept saying. "What the hell are y'all talkin' about? I got a wife and four chillun in Alabama. What the hell are y'all talkin' about?"

"Say, shut up, Mark. Faw Christ's sake! Faw the love o' Moses, Mark. Rip's lookin' at y'all. Lute's lookin' at y'all!"

"Well, get the hell out o' here. *You* get the hell outa here!"

Mark was grumbling fiercely, but the sobs, half concealed by his undertone, were still apparent. He had glanced at Oscar murderously.

A lump constricted Oscar's throat. If Mark believed Uncle Robert was going to surrender, then Uncle Robert was *going* to surrender. Oscar felt Mark—Mark the invincible, Mark the swindler, Mark the patriot—forcing on *him*—Oscar didn't really think so, *hadn't* thought so—why, good God, certainly he hadn't thought so! It was only one of those funny notions that go through your mind—why, Mark, for Christ's sake, why, Mark—

It was here that all Oscar's long respect for Mark became a burden. Mark can go to —— —— hell, Oscar thought. But why was it so hard, after four years, just to think of Uncle Robert— and the whole time for nothin'? That was what—well, god damn Mark, it couldn't be, the railway and the track and the ambulances standin' over there in the shade with the mules out and last night and how tired I am and I'm so tired justa *think* o' victuals makes me wanta puke, just to think o' victuals makes me wanta puke, but why did he have to go and put on them clothes and that sword why did he justa think o' victuals makes me wanta puke.

Mark was glad that the war was over. Oscar watched him and wondered. The men wallowing on the ground, the men stretched out like they didn't have any more life in 'em, the men stretched out, and some cavalry horses not tethered, cropping so they had wandered in amongst the men, and the sun shining down on the long track. And Mark straightened up, and he said, "Talk about the weather, talk about any fool thing that comes into yo' head aw I'm through with y'all. I can't stand no mo' of this." And he walked off a little way, as if he would never forgive Oscar.

And Oscar felt as if his eyes were gonta bug out of their sockets, he was so hot and dry and the glare hurt him so, and he didn't have the will to move up off the ground where it was so still and grasshoppers ticking, and his whole body was one lump of misery, and his insides were a sickness, and he did not remember that it had been much worse when he had been severely wounded two years ago. But for '*nothin*'! This crowd o' ragpickers, and farmers' scarecrows. This bunch of famine sufferers that had been stickin' together doin' a little fightin' all through the winter until spring come—and now, for what? But old Lee oughtn'ta 'a' worn his new sword and his new suit. If his eyes ached like this and his belly ached like this he wouldn't 'a' worn his new suit. He wouldn't let all this go for nothin'. There wouldn't be any Yankee this side of Kingdom Come could make him believe that all this went for nothin'! But Mark wanted the war to be over. Mark had a wife and four children. He wanted the war to be over. God damn it, we all wanted the war to be over, but not with this kind of insides, not when your mouth felt like a wad of cotton, not when Uncle Robert put on a new uniform and his best sword.

. . . .

To the front attack Ewell had arranged a quick defence. But the engagement was not long under way when he realized that his men would not have the endurance to resist superior forces to any conclusive end. Lieutenant Garfield had a message to Faraday instructing him to begin the retreat imperceptibly by drawing off several companies from the rear, while the manoeuvre would be concealed by the firing of the lines in front. Then, as soon as the withdrawal was under way—but not so rapidly executed as to leave the vanguard entirely unprotected—the remainder would be able to follow.

Garfield had galloped some little distance, and was just feeling relief in finding himself removed from actual scenes of stress, when a young man whom he did not know, but whom he believed he had been introduced to as somebody's aide, rode up beside him, gesticulating excitedly and, even before close enough for speech to be plain, uttering some phrase that sounded warning.

"Surrounded!" He was out of breath and could scarcely speak. "Federal cavalry coming up on the rear. Notify General Ewell! We are doing everything possible but the situation could hardly be worse." He stuttered slightly, and kept gasping, as though about to suffocate, choked by his collar.

The two gazed at one another, while their horses stamped and backed, drawing them apart. For how long, Garfield wondered, would he be obliged to see that look in everybody's eyes. The young arrival's glance was strained, fearful; and the announcement that he made was like a challenge. In these days, all in positions of responsibility regarded one another oddly, pugnaciously, in attitudes of obscure hostility.

526

Garfield, resisting this general hysteria which he had encountered everywhere, answered as calmly as he could.

"I was just bringing instructions for the revision of our position," he said rather coldly. "Here's the memorandum." And he offered the note that General Ewell had entrusted to him. "I advise holding those orders in abeyance until I can take your message and you get the general's emendations." Garfield's voice quivered with contempt. All at once he was enraged, feeling as if he had received some vague insult. Why did the ass keep staring at him! Manners —oh, yes, he remembered now, Manners was the young man's name. A fop and an ass if ever there was one. And a man like that, a perfect lady-killer, he had heard, was the person you must deal with, in a crisis, as an equal! In order to prevent himself from indulging in superfluous rudeness toward this individual whom he had seen but once or twice before, and whom he suddenly hated —if for no other reason than that he was sitting there gaping at him and had just told him bad news—Garfield dismissed the conversation peremptorily, clicked to his mare, turned her head, and cantered briskly away. Thank God, to be left by himself—at least until he could get this information back.

The morning, so welcome after the long, restless night, was still and brilliant. Cataracts of rattly, far-off noise from the front extended, rather than diminished, Garfield's sense of the day's spaciousness. Thick pops in the sky shed their echoes so remotely that the sounds must have carried to some fifty miles off. It was an immense world, filled with pungent, tepid scents, and the acres of air were only lengthened by that vague, elongated hiccup. *Ploo, ploo.* The lava deluge splattered the blue, garnished horizon; but it left no trace. Spring trees and bushes billowed daintily across the green and tousled fields. If the force impinging on the rear were of sufficient numbers, a surrender wholesale might be the only answer to the problem. Garfield was old enough in army life to view the prospect with a practical acceptance of its limited possibilities. At the same time, with the gentle, barren heavens flung illimitably above him, from hill to hill, and on, and the fresh, gentle wind vivid in his nostrils, he could not accept flatly the preposterous statement that he and the other men and officers were 'hemmed in.' Indecision caused in his mind a struggle that was like a new courage. Why, we *can't* surrender, he thought dully, listening to the

527

faded *bon-ga, bon-ga* that rolled invisibly upon the light, pushing the way to another, higher zenith, and scattering the sunshine more brilliantly over trees, and grass, and farther, swiftly moving figures. He exulted. Why, he had a crazy feeling—damn those Yankees— that there was too much *room* out here for a surrender!

.   .   .   .

At the next village the first lot of supplies to arrive from Lynch-, burg were to be distributed. The good news that food was awaiting had spread through the ranks quickly. A few of the fellows were enough enlivened by it to indulge in jokes. When Jake heard the other boys 'carrying on,' he smiled vaguely, approving them and trying to keep up his end of things. But the anticipation of a meal absorbed him to a degree which he felt as 'unnatural,' and he could not think collectedly of other matters. All yesterday, he and Si McKee had chewed bark and sweet gum, trying to 'git a little juice' in their 'stummicks.'

As they reached the outskirts of the town, the sun was coming up. Its flickering rays bestowed on the straggling cottages and shanties a background of vivacity of which the tin roofs and the shingles would not partake. A woman or two was awake, a few people bent or moved about in the fields and gardens, as the soldiers passed, desisting from the pursuance of their occupations. A girl in a long calico wrapper shaded her eyes with her hand, and seemed, as she stood under some blossoming fruit trees, to specu- late stolidly on this invasion of the place by strangers.

The 'Square' was not much more alive. A general store was closed. The shutters were down in the windows of the post office. An old man leaning on a stick seemed left the single citizen to greet the peaceful invaders. About the overflow from a wooden drinking trough for horses, three thin, black bristle-backed hogs grunted ceaselessly. Chickens that were only half awake ruffled their feathers on the deserted veranda of a small house before which a sign, *'Justice of the Peace,'* swung out. And in this blighting quiet, more conspicuous than that of the night or the lonely country, everything twinkled, everything shone, the dew sparkled and whitish emanations mixed of fog and sun hung over the gardens and the patches of grass and young weeds. Jake discovered such familiarity in the scene that he could not but think his mood of the day previous, his distrait mood of the night before, altogether the product of illness and delusion. Me an' Si wasn't in a reasonable frame o' mind yistiday, he decided, his uneasiness placated. Seems like I can't recollect thinkin' nothin' ordinary.

But the aspect of hilarity which truly astonished him was to be met with on the farther side of the village. Here was in progress an activity independent of the lean and indifferent welcome of the townsfolk. Several army wagons, arrived by some other route than the one traversed by Jake, had drawn up at the border of the highway, and from these rations were being distributed. With great clatter and excitement tin plates and cups were produced. Jake got his out but held it rather nervelessly. "Uh-huh, reckon I ain't woke up yit," he admitted to a hectically jovial comrade who pressed him to take more interest in what was going forward. "Seems like I'm 'fraid to count on gittin' a real bellyful." He gulped, his Adam's apple lumping drily in his tight throat. He felt cold. Funny how he kept on feelin' just as cold now that the sun was out. I must look kind of onery, he said to himself. His feet were entirely free of his relics of shoes. His pants were frayed. His coat was split across the shoulders, and his chest was not protected by a shirt. A barefoot child, neat in a clean apron and pantalettes, had strayed into the throng of soldiers and was gaping at them timidly, twisting her fingers in her frock, then tiptoeing and leaning her elbows on a barrel against which she supported herself. What's that little gal figurin' out about me, Jake wondered. I reckon all o' them thar look jist as funny as I do.

But he could not be certain. Sickness and faintness were strange and particular, he fancied, to himself, and he could but conjecture some special, unshared oddity as their outward sign.

In the long queue formed to reach the wagons, he shuffled slowly. He was 'tired to death.' Well, he thought, we got into it, an' we gotta git out some way aw 'notha. No use to git het up.

Some cavalry horses, unsaddled near him, had been given some straw and were chewing it methodically, dribbling saliva and stamping. What does that stuff taste like to 'em, Jake questioned, a flush warming his gaunt cheeks, as he imagined their pleasure and felt a sensual anxiety for vicarious participation in it. When a horse reared its coarse plume of tail and spilled droppings in the road, that stimulated Jake's curiosity. He was preoccupied with all natural processes. Yeh, they're workin' yit, he exulted. It's jist as usual with them!

When, by retarded stages, he had reached the food van, and could observe the biscuits and parched-meal coffee bestowed on the man ahead, Jake's quiverings grew acute. He became abruptly sick. What's the matter with me, he meditated in alarm. I ain't done nothin' but dream about this mess all night!

His turn had arrived. Avid to waste nothing, he humbled the tempest in the pit of his stomach, and held out his plate. He was so shaky that the extended plate wavered. This surprised him, made him want to hide. He looked down on the bony arm, half naked, greyed with dusty hair, as it protruded from the rent sleeve. Ain't much of a arm, neither, he thought, dubious of this 'carcass' of a body that provided his only dependence in the fight for life. Regular old rag-bag, he thought of his coat and his whole person. In a sombre doubtful fashion, this tickled his fancy. Blamed ef I ain't the wust ol' scarecrow I ever seen! He laughed uncertainly, aloud; but was immediately fearful of the criticism of the man in front.

Biscuits and jerked meat had been laid in his tin salver. As he was ordered to move on, he made a miserly gesture of distrust and tried to stuff meat and biscuits together into his mouth. But they did not taste good. He gulped.

The coffee was scalding, pale amber-brown, and more lucid than coffee should be. It sloshed on his shaking hand and burned him. But he could not wait for the taste, for the wet heat; and drank until he coughed, and the tears came into his eyes, and perspiration started all over his forehead and his itching scalp. God-A'-mighty, what good stuff! Prowling on, seeking privacy for his enjoyment, he drank as he walked, the plate rattling in his hand, and the coffee dribbling from his eager mouth. Glancing to one side, Jake's gaze met that of another soldier, a man who was guzzling as hungrily as he was, and the two, like boys detected in enjoyable misdemeanour, smiled and interchanged guilty delight.

Jake was as dizzy as if he were drunk. His throat kept closing on the food, and half rejecting it; but his will to make the most of his opportunity conquered this strange repugnance. On his tongue everything was tasteless, but in his vitals there was a glorifying warmth. He felt 'kinda crazy,' but benevolently so.

530

All these fellahs got theirs, too, Jake thought. All goin' down the little red lane. Now if folks was made different they wouldn't have to eat. There's Phil Cross never got no further thin Amelia Court House. He laid down in his tracks and give up the ghost. Rations wouldn't 'a' done him no good if he'd got 'em. An' by the time he's been a week aw so underground, them worms an' critters ull make a meal outa *him*. Then the worms git cotched by the birds and digested, an' so on. An' if we all's spry we gits the birds. What ain't needed faw the system goes to make the crops. Funny, I call it.

His obsession as to the importance of food made it a holy obligation that he consume all he had received. If he didn't eat it *quick,* he was going to lose it. The boys were a good lot, but some people get kind of out of their heads when they're as hungry as this, and they don't know what they're doin'. Jake crammed his mouth with the last crumb, tilted his mug and licked at the final drop of moisture now tepid. He wanted to go on eating forever. If he left off, the sickness and the vagueness might come back, like a spell laid on his mind. He was weak enough to die, but he wasn't ready to die.

That's safe, he thought, as he stood up from the log on which he had been squatting, and rubbed his belly. That's inside me anyhow. He surveyed his engrossed companions and was glad that none of them were giving heed to him. He liked his partners, yet he felt triumphant toward them. He had outwitted them. What he got, he got. It was stowed away 'snug.' Jesus, what does anything matter when eatin' is as good as that, he thought. A cloud had passed from his brain and eyes.

But, shambling toward the horse trough to wash his vessels, his exhilaration was offered a shock. Pain suddenly drew a tight knot under his breastbone, and these devious knife thrusts as from a foe were followed by paralyzing gripes. Terrified by these unexpected symptoms, he halted, and, like a panic-stricken child seeking adult aid, looked all around him with a mute, beseeching glance of complete helplessness.

At this moment, Ray Williams also approached the horse trough. Jake rallied. He hated to acknowledge defects resulting from the consumption of a meal, yet he despaired of moving. "Did that there hardtack pison y'all, too, Ray?" Jake asked ambig-

531

uously. "My stummick feels like it had a knot in it big as a watermillion."

Ray, whose appetite was still unappeased, was cross, and regarded Jake sulkily. "Naw, you dern fool! Y'all got weak, that's all. Yer insides git lazy whin they ain't got nothin' to work on. Brace yerse'f up an' quit huggin' yer miseries. We got enough to worry about. I could eat ten times as much as that."

Jake felt indignant. "Y'all et somepin already. I seen that woman give y'all sompin down that road where we all stopped faw water." Physical discomfort was intensifying, and it was somehow insulting that Ray should hint at retribution—as though Jake were being punished for failing in appreciation of food's benefits.

"Aw, she gimme some raw potatoes."

"I ain't noticed y'all shared 'em up with anybody."

"Aw, go to hell! She'd 'a' give y'all some if you'd axed her."

Jake, in the sunlight, was in half-darkness, inundated by waves of opaque nausea. Christ, what was happening to him! "That's a damn lie. Folks in them houses run off when they seen us comin' an' hid all the victuals they had. Didn' y'all hear that gal cussin' us, sayin' we was like a swarm o' locusts in the Bible come an' took everything people roun' here raised—

"Y'all ain't got the sense y'all was bawn with, Jake. Si an' me snook ahead las' night an' come down on them folks an' put a pistol to they heads. They didn' make no mo' bones 'bout the raw taters then."

"If y'all got reported missin', how much ud them taters be wuth?"

"Aw, I don't care. Let 'em report us missin'. We come back, didn't we? Anyhow, everything's gone to hell. They give up tryin' to keep discipline in this company long ago."

The pain in Jake's insides was something awful. It was so bad that his wit was dissipating. Still protecting that lost pleasure in the breakfast, he controlled symptoms of anguish, and allowed Ray to slosh his mug and pan in the greasy trough water and walk off.

But no more could be borne. Jake would have to take to the woods, or somewhere. His chest tightened. The pit of his stomach was gnawed by a fanged anguish. Then, abruptly, all the precious food, which now seemed to include his entrails, rose, disgorged.

532

Horrified by the easy regurgitation, he yielded, dizzily watched himself in this humiliating process in which he not only defiled the earth, but submitted, after long struggle, to an abrupt defeat. He waved his feeble arms, he staggered. The pigs ran about grunting, frightened by the sounds of retching; and he hated their health.

It was his impulse, when the act was finished, to take flight and conceal the chagrin that brought weeping. Oh, the pity of it! The pity of it! What irked him most was that the mess he was making revolted him as it did others. If I was a dog—

"Don't be so wasteful, Jake!" Ray was repassing. Other men passed and hurried on. Jake leaned limply by the trough. Gone! An' God knows when you'd get any more. This was the greatest of all despair. It was not that his bowels were chilled, that his tongue was thick and felt grey, that the knife probes under his wishbone, while more tentative, continued. It was not that—

Came the peremptory clarion of the bugle. Habit made Jake start, straighten himself. He bent spiritlessly to collect his pan and mug. The fellows were all hurrying along. Some delayed for a hasty dipping of receptacles in the running water. Shouts were exchanged. "Sheridan ain't far off now!" They were herding in the street. The rejuvenated lines were already reforming with that sudden, miraculous order imposed by relentless authority. Jake had to go too. He had to ignore every spontaneous inclination, while he collected his belongings and hastened after the rest.

Wonder at himself did not quit him. He hurried on lamely, and thought. They all gotta eat. We gotta eat.

It was strange, like discovering some mystical phenomenon, and stirred him to a sickly, voluptuous trouble. He never seemed to have realized it before. Goats, donkeys, mules, officers, privates, everybody. It was as if he were initiate in an unshared esotericism. Lights, liver, all them things inside of 'em workin', controllin' everything—and people talkin' like they didn't know it.

If he didn't get something in him again by noontime he was going to give up. What was the use of being afraid of the sergeant or the captain or anybody? Here they were, tramping all over the world, and getting nowhere at all, clattering along like a lot of sheep and getting nowhere at all. Lookin' for food, they were.

"April 7th, 1865.

"General R. E. Lee, Commanding C. S. A.
"General,
  "The result of the last week must convince you of the hopeless-ness of further resistance on the part of the Army of Northern Virginia in this struggle. I feel it so, and regard it as my duty to shift from myself the responsibility of any further effusion of blood, by asking of you the surrender of that portion of the Con-federate Southern army known as the Army of Northern Virginia.
      "Very respectfully, your obedient servant,

                        "U. S. GRANT,
                      "Lieutenant General
                "Commanding armies of the United States."

                              "April 7th, 1865.

  "General,
  "I have received your note of this day. Though not entirely of the opinion you express as to the hopelessness of further resistance on the part of the Army of Northern Virginia, I reciprocate your desire to avoid useless effusion of blood, and therefore, before con-sidering your proposition, ask the terms you will offer on condition of its surrender.
            "Your obedient servant,

                        "R. E. LEE,
              "Commanding Confederate Forces."

                              "April 8th, 1865.

  "General,
  "Your note of last evening, in reply to mine of the same date, asking the conditions on which I will accept the surrender of the Army of Northern Virginia, is just received. In reply, I would say, that peace *being my great desire, there is but one condition I would insist upon, namely: That the men and officers surrendered shall be disqualified for taking up arms against the Government of the United States until properly exchanged. I will meet you,*

534

or will designate officers to meet any officers you might name for the same purpose, at any point agreeable to you, for the purpose of arranging definitely the terms upon which the surrender of the Army of Northern Virginia will be received.

"Very respectfully, your obedient servant,,

"U. S. GRANT,
"Lieutenant-General."

"April 8th, 1865.

"General,

"I received at a late hour your note of today. In mine of yesterday, I did not intend to propose the surrender of the Army of Northern Virginia, but to ask the terms of your proposition. To be frank, I do not think the emergency has arisen to call for the surrender of this army; but as the restoration of peace should be the sole object of all, I desire to know whether your proposals would lead to that end. I cannot, therefore, meet you with a view to surrender the Army of Northern Virginia, but as far as your proposals may affect the Confederate States forces under my command, and tend to the restoration of peace, I should be pleased to meet you at 10 a. m., tomorrow, on the old stage road to Richmond, between the picket lines of the two armies.

"Your obedient servant,

"R. E. LEE, General."

"April 9th, 1865.

"General,

"Your note of yesterday is received. I have no authority to treat on the subject of peace. The meeting proposed for 10 a. m. today would lead to no good. I will state, however, General, that I am equally anxious for peace with yourself, and the whole North entertains the same feeling. The terms upon which peace can be had are well understood. By the South laying down its arms it will hasten that most desirable event, save thousands of human lives, and hundreds of millions of property not yet destroyed. Seriously

535

hoping that all of our difficulties may be settled without the loss of another life, I subscribe myself, etc.

"U. S. GRANT, *Lieutenant General.*"

(From a letter said never to have reached Lee's hands.)

This letter is quoted with verbal differences by U. S. Grant in his "Personal Memoirs." With it he gives an answer from Lee acknowledging receipt of this.

III

The bonfires sprang glossily upon the night, which then became a darker cushion for the enormousness of light. The fires were at intervals all along the edge of a wood. Poppings and comfortable explosions sounded for a mile or more. Fresh odours of burning were bitter in the soft air.

During the last few days the opposing armies had scarcely been out of earshot of one another. There was little effort to disguise positions. At twilight of this very evening a peppering from musketry had warned the Confederates of new arrivals to swell enemy forces. This meant that the supplies so imperatively needed would again be intercepted. Bad luck, so repeated, brought to many, and even to some leaders, a callous mood. Those whom privation had not made ill, were in a state for feeble roistering. The trees were in such faint leafage as scarcely to obstruct visions of the stars, but it was warm, after some showers, and there were heady intimations of spring in the smell of the country.

Longstreet, Gordon, and Fitz-Lee had just been advised of the temper of 'Uncle Robert's' correspondence with Grant. The theme of those recent letters obliged discussion of a painful topic. Inside the crowded, glowing tent, with its flap gratefully open on the dark, a brief, awkward silence followed argument a little indiscreet. General Lee, with that persistent calm which, for some reason, aroused in his inferiors an unwilled, and even disrespectful, pity, cleared his throat slightly, and said, "Then you all agree with me that Sheridan's cavalry constitute no insurmountable difficulty?"

The officers fidgeted. Lee's kindly, rather chilling eye rested, specifically, on nobody, yet he interrogated all, and with that

536

naïvely disguised eagerness which made all hesitate guiltily before replying, since they could not honestly concur in the utterance of even this temperately hopeful opinion.

Gordon was ashamed to feel sorry for Lee. It was unwarrantable presumption when the little fry pitied the great. But that was the fact. Lee's conscientious tenacity in these last weeks had made them all marvel. Some had been annoyed with him. Yet to criticize such firmness of purpose was tantamount to the meanest self-interest. Gordon reserved his own emotions and spoke quizzically to his commander. "I don't think we need regard our enemy the Irishman any more timorously than we have heretofore, General. Except when the odds were overpoweringly on his side he has never been able to do anything to seriously molest us, and the advantages now are not so much with him that we need to give up hope."

Gordon was moved by Lee's effort to smile, which did not disguise depression or conceal any of the haggard traces of fatigue. The general's scrupulousness was becoming equivalent to self-flagellation. In the scarcity of food, he went out of his way to create, in deprivation, an equality with the men. Gordon had observed this wonderingly, and, while he did not comment—Lee's own attitude allowed no comment—did not approve. It is as if he were undergoing some kind of voluntary penance, Gordon would think, and would feel vexed. The common sense of warfare did not allow for that kind of stuff. General Lee would not touch any meat if any was to be had. And, as he had always been a teetotaller and did not use tobacco, it was incredible what his nerves and his physique endured while he said nothing about it, keeping the same equable temper with everybody.

It was very recently that Gordon had made his escape from the foray in which most of his men had been lost, and an impression that success could ultimately be had on a very narrow margin of advantage was still strong with him. If there was any excuse for optimism now, he would certainly take it. Nobody dared to tell General Lee just what the possibilities against achieving a spectacular retreat were. It was peculiar that Lee—upon whose clear-minded fortitude all associated with him had hitherto depended, Lee who was the most revered of all officers—should, at this moment, appear in the light of one too weak to listen to plain truths. I don't know that he takes it any harder than the rest of us, either, Gordon thought, puzzled.

All that could be definitely planned had already been agreed upon. Longstreet was undisguisedly ready to leave, and got up from the cot where he had been sitting, bolt upright, and with an expression of acute worry of which he was unaware, but which, in its origin, was presented to him as impatience with everything and everybody present—General Lee, of course, excepted. However, when he had made the initial gesture toward a departure, the others showed an untactful alacrity to follow.

Why did they wish to leave Lee alone? All were devoted to him. "My God, I wish I could take on his burdens," Longstreet had said, and with honest impetuosity.

Fitz-Lee thought it, perhaps, a duty to linger. He made his respectful signal of departure, but, reaching the first step in the out-of-doors, held back. "Fine spring weather anyway," he said.

General Lee appeared to realize an uncomfortable atmosphere of some sort, for he came outside the tent with them, and stood there, remarking absently on the stars. Gordon asked him if he believed that their mutual friend, Scarborough, had fallen from the good graces of Davis, and in that way lost his pre-eminence as an unofficial influence with the War Department. But the remark was awkwardly made. Lee was abstracted, and Gordon suddenly unhappy as to the whereabouts of the President, who soon must be in the humiliating position of a fugitive from Federal, 'so-called' justice. There was no topic you could bring up which would not yield some fruit of discouragement. Gordon thought bitterly that it would be better if they had all been born dumb. General Lee's attitude toward them was that of a meticulous host speeding parting guests. But it was a shame to pity a great man anyway. It made you hate yourself. Gordon felt he would rather, ten times, it had been himself convicted of this wavering, ill-judged optimism, than the man whom all had worshipped during the last four years, who had held the whole army together by his temperateness, his charity and his good sense.

The three officers, not so much younger than Lee, either, made faintly childish salutes, and started off into the night. They had been called there on purpose to argue what should be done, yet took their departures feeling all the guilt of intruders. Lee had never been kinder or more—well, one could hardly say "affectionate," of him—but never milder or more earnestly interested in the suggestions they had to offer. That was the whole thing. They missed a customary obstinacy under his quiet manner. He was not dogmatic in general matters, but as regards accuracies of military plan or manoeuvre he had never before invited a contradiction. The three men assumed a cheerfulness which was insincere. Lee, also, as he said good night to them, spoke cheerfully.

They had taken only a few steps when he called them back. "Then we are agreed," he said, "to sweep the cavalry of Mr. Sheridan out of the way and go on toward Lynchburg? Unless we find the mass of the enemy behind Appomattox Court House turns out to be too imposing. In that case a flag of truce will have to go forward to General Grant and we can ask for an interview."

"I don't think it will come to that, General," Longstreet said hastily, drawing attention from something that should not be mentioned.

Lee was holding some papers which fell to the ground. He leaned to secure them. Gordon offered to be ahead of him, and also stooped. As he returned the rumpled documents, he noticed with what an aged inclination Lee had bent toward the earth. But the resonance of Lee's voice, as he said the second good night, defied any impulse to sympathize. "Good night, God bless you. And as much rest as is possible under the circumstances," Lee said. Gordon could not refrain from offering his hand respectfully. Then felt ridiculous.

He found an excuse to make his path diverge from that of the others. Fitz-Lee noticed, of course, he was saying to himself, and Longstreet. Gordon resented this. He wanted, jealously, to protect Lee from their observation. He was angry with himself, with all of them, because, in their hearts, while Lee needed them, they had already given up. But with two corps left—Longstreet's and my own—there's not a chance! My Lord, *ought* we to tell Lee that! Longstreet's as much of a coward as I am.

He found his horse, found Sublieutenant Smith and the horse and the darky servant who had come with them. But, as he mounted, and rode down the camp, seeing at a little distance the sinking fires and the men who, some of them in the open, were already sleeping, he knew that he was not going to close his eyes for the rest of the night, because he would remember Lee standing there in front of the tent looking so courtly, so meticulously considerate of them all, yet so broken. It was painful to Gordon's own self-love that he could not verbally agree with Lee, whose judgment he had always extolled to everybody.

Lee went indoors and thought he would unbuckle his sword-belt and lie down awhile. He told the servant to put out the lamp, and go away to rest; and that left long-anticipated solitude, and no light but that which entered as the tent-flap was left wide. Through this space, he could see the stars, sown as if in water, above a dense rampart of hills, fields and trees soaked in dark. He sat down on the edge of a cot without coverings, and remained still there for several minutes. No, if he reclined here for so much as an instant, he would never have the strength to get up again.

And I am not a proud or extra vain man, either, he thought. It shocked him a little when he had, as now, to face it, to find out how much he had depended on the comfort of public approbation. Yes, that humbled the spirit. That brought a man low and humiliated him before God, perhaps a necessary experience. They will never understand how inevitable these last steps have been, Lee said to himself.

It was this that made him unutterably weary—that the cause and effect of these Providential events would never be apparent, clearly, to any but those involved in final plans and decisions. To the rest, any apology he or his staff could make would be useless.

Here was a weakness he might be really ashamed of. Ambition was a poison. It levelled, but it did not exalt. The ambitious were defeated, not when they failed to achieve success (did not fulfil their boasts) but when they found themselves all at once susceptible to the whims of those whom their judgment despised, when such honours as they accepted could have no permanence, when their hearts were not in accord with what their lips uttered, and they bowed to their inferiors in order to receive the cheapest adulation.

My God, I do not think I have been ambitious, he thought. The very suggestion of this frightened him. Where did escape lead if the contamination of a yearning for indiscriminate praise went with it! Yet most circumspectly could he say for himself that he had done his duty. It even pleased him that that duty had been so hard. Yes, that was the one solace offering him the restoration of his self-esteem. It was a temptation to blame Richmond, but he would not do so—this question of supplies and provisioning—and his own advice had not always been listened to respectfully. But he would not blame Davis. Davis was in the last throes of a calamity. O God, help me not to blame Davis— not to blame anybody. Give me the courage to acknowledge my own faults and bear my own burdens, Lord.

It seemed to Lee that, for the first time, he could see clearly just what *had* taken place during the last four years, and before that—long before that. His attitude toward slavery had not entirely altered. The abrupt liberation of thousands of ignorant negroes was going to create a situation that would menace both them and people of property and education. Yet, as far as he was concerned, he was through with any more attempts to interfere with the future. No doubt an odd fellow like Lincoln would take to himself the credit for having inaugurated an epoch—for having salvaged a whole race. And this while the difficulties of the South continued—increased, as far as that went.

Lee's depression became torpor. He could not see any relief from anxiety and self-reproach, unless he would be able to give up his own will entirely, and trust all to God. This awful physical exhaustion was simply taking all the spirit out of him. And it worried him that his nature was not more one for self-abasement. He had to get over any tendency to be fastidious. An ignorant old mountaineer whom he had seen confessing Christ at a camp-meeting was more courageous. Yet Lee did not believe that the mental habits of refinement were wasted. Devotion to privacy did not need to be excused. Only he was upset that it required such a real effort of him when he mentioned religion in public and tried to make apparent to the veriest private in the ranks what its benefits were. On that account if no other I ought to remember old Jackson as a better man than myself, Lee thought; but it was more a self-chastening and half-whimsical conclusion than any-

541

thing he actually believed. Vanity, vanity, all was vanity. This was an hour when, if ever, he should have been praying; but he did not have the heart. Recognition of God's greatness and man's insignificance he had to the full, but it was not bringing him the comfort he had honestly so often found in that reflection. Was it age that made him feel like this? Was it the approach of his own physical decay that made him petty for praise and for all the trivial enjoyments of life?

With an involuntary groan, he did lift up his booted feet and stretch himself at full length on the cot. He was ashamed of the grunts that uttered the aches in his bones. They were not half so bad as the soreness of his spirit. He was a doomed man—as complete a failure as the world had ever known. He did not feel so much weak as deadened. He was completely inert and dead to all the fine impulses—to all matters of principle, devotion to truth, self-sacrifices, self-immolations for the good of the State. He even suspected the motives which had led him to accept the command —though Heaven knows he had played no politics to get himself to the front.

Certain members of his staff occupied another tent lashed to his own. He feared they had overheard his mumbled ejaculations, and he repressed them, trying to contain himself, to control his restlessness, and lie very still. He stared out of doors.

There were the trees as before, gaunt and stony with their ruffles of deep boughs. He could smell evergreens. The woods out yonder—*seen as through a glass, darkly*—they contained all the people who would go down as he would go down—all the lives, mysteries of universes. . . . Stars seemed blown toward him on the soft throb of the wind, and to bear toward him a message from some life not shared by humans. *By the blast of God they perish, and by the breath of His nostrils are they consumed. . . . Now a thing was secretly brought to me, and mine ear received a little thereof.* Tremulous, with its millions, the shaky glitter of the night rolled on. A horny planet, flapping a strange, insipid radiance on him, speared his eyes with its bluish brambles. The Milky Way spread very distantly like a fog, in which speckled crustings were no more than gilt shadows under the far-off vapours. It was as though the sky nursed secretly its own unpenetrated glitter, and the faceless lights flashed grudgingly.

Lee raised himself on his elbows, pushed himself up to a sitting posture; then sprang resolutely to his feet. No use denying it, he was too perturbed to rest. Virtue had gone out of him. Had the whole effort from the beginning been misguided? That was what worried him. Was the intention of the South itself unjustified? Or had a growing prejudice against Jeff Davis's inconsistencies warped his own judgment of the profounder issues at stake? Should there have been no war? How can the commander of an army evade burdens of responsibility beyond the power of any single man to bear, if he does not see that mankind has little or no choice of action, and that even the most glorified decisions made by man have little or nothing to do with his freedom of selection? Yes, Lee admitted, as he sat upright again and hung his tired legs over the cot, certain common-sense aspects of life are repulsive to me, have always been. There were many details of the war that he had been satisfied to leave to the consideration of others. But success would alter things. It was no niggling hunt for fame, before God it was not, that made him long so desperately to discover some other way out of the present dilemma than that offered him now.

There was a sentry outside. Lee noted absently the intermittent thuds of his pacing feet. You had to keep up a front even before *that* man. Slowly he got up, smoothed down his hair and beard, and walked out of doors. Fryth and Lockhart were not asleep either. There was a candle burning, making a small shadow of itself on the dimmed, obtrusive slope of their tent. Lee drew nearer and called, softly, "Fryth?" A low murmur of conversation went on uninterruptedly inside the tent. They had not heard him. "Fryth!" he called again.

A hush came, as of dismissed confidence, the shuffle of boots, and Fryth, wearing his sword but without his coat, appeared in silhouette through the open canvas. He was upset. "A thousand apologies, General!" And he held together the band of his shirt, which was unfastened at the neck.

Lee might have commanded his servant who was only a stone's throw away, sleeping on the ground, but he would rather keep the darky in ignorance of the restless night he was passing. His kindness to the lowly was invariable, but it was combined with an extreme repulsion to the mere thought of having them surprise him at any disadvantage so that he would be unable to condescend to them. It was difficult enough to face Fryth.

Lee said, "This is an eleventh-hour intrusion on well-earned leisure, but you don't seem to be sleeping anyhow. I've let my light go out, and it seemed too bad to wake Henry—nobody enjoys a sleep as a nigger does. I want to send a message to General Gordon. Henry expects us to move tomorrow and I can't find anything to write on."

"Why, of course, General. Lockhart, have you got some writing paper and a pen handy? Won't you come inside, General? The candle has been burning at both ends—I mean something went wrong with the wick and we found another one at the other end. Lockhart, will you push that goods box right side up where it is cleaner so General Lee can sit on it?"

Lee felt bruised at heart, timid, aware of this craven second-nature in him that made him want to come in here with these young men to whom he could not speak a word frankly, and who would not be able to give him any comfort if he did. He saw them waiting on him with that pleasant deference which he usually found agreeable, but which, tonight, made his hand tremble on the paper. It was as if they expected something of him that he could not give, as if they were cruel toward his maturity, and did not realize that strength, even for the strong, has its limitations —that, in the end, a man goes to God rather than to his commander-in-chief—as if his bones would not also lie finally mouldering in the ground. Literal death was however, something too unclean to contemplate.

Lee wrote very hurriedly. Unwarrantably it seemed to him imperative that the note be sent to General Gordon without a second's delay. When Lockhart could not find an envelope, Lee did not wait for it. His calligraphy was unsteady.

"Dear Gordon," the note explained, "this epistle is the result of midnight meditations. As I suspect you are not sleeping either, I want to have again, and more exactly, your opinion of the probability of success in case we take the bull by the horns and do attack. I would also like to know in more detail the condition of your own corps and just how much you think can be got out of it in offensive action." Lee signed it, and folded it rapidly, foolishly suspicious that the words, almost puerile, might be glimpsed over his shoulder—though he was quite ready, certainly, to tell Fryth and Lockhart of his own accord what was in the letter.

It was after all Colonel Fryth's servant who was roused and sent to fetch a messenger. Lee, to conceal his impatience, quitted the tent for the dark. But neither Fryth nor Lockhart felt it etiquette to retire without his suggestion, and came out of doors with him—Fryth waiting a little behind while Lockhart talked to the servant, and both not far from General Lee as he hesitated between an agonizing desire for solitude, and a frank wish for their presence, which would distract him from the foolhardy eagerness with which he was looking forward to Gordon's reply. All talked laconically and were fidgety.

It was at least an hour or two before dawn, yet there was already apparent a kind of thinning of the night. It was possible to see objects very distinctly. Here and there a camp fire beamed in rayless embers, sending a faint rosiness toward the trunks of trees. A man was asleep on the ground not twenty feet off.

"Do you think you can make out the time by that light, Colonel Fryth?" Lee asked, after a brief pause which seem interminable. The messenger had gone away, and his departure had left for those behind a dreary accent of sleeping presences.

Fryth retreated a step and, by the grisly illumination from the tent, took out his watch, holding its glinting face obliquely. "Just after three o'clock, General. Three—yes, three-fifteen exactly."

From Lee, unnoticed by himself, came a deep audible sigh. He made no comment on the time, and Fryth and Lockhart did not know what to say. They could hear an owl calling. The moan, as from a spirit rarer than flesh, came twice through the wood. The man on the ground snored, with a choking noise in his throat. Stars near the horizon had grown larger, but those higher up seemed to fade away in twinkling dust in the brightening sky. As a rule, Lee would fill all embarrassing silences. He never discussed himself personally, but showed a tactful interest in the welfare of the men. Fryth and Lockhart wanted to go to bed, but wondered if General Lee still desired something of them. Fryth was very fond of a cigar, and it seemed to him, at this moment, while he regarded the vague shape of Lee, that no price for a smoke would be too much. But the general was an abstainer from tobacco, and the stale cigar which Fryth was treasuring to soothe his resentment of a bad diet remained in his pocket.

The quiet was becoming so oppressive that the trudging of the sentry rang like beating on an anvil on the hardening earth. Through the shadows, Fryth glanced at Lockhart and Lockhart at Fryth. Fryth coughed. A twig snapped. The man on the ground called out unintelligibly in his sleep. General Lee sighed again. The earth began to flash black, and the sky to show more plainly. A horrible greyness stole through the trees. Fryth thought that if this went on they were all going out of their minds.

Then, thank Heaven, there was a *thump-thump*, loud on the empty path, and the messenger, who had gone away on horseback, loomed, on a white mare, returning mutely under the black boughs from which the dew dripped. The dawn was like some obscure fluid saturating every object. Man and horse seemed preternaturally large, but indefinitely vivid, like ghosts.

Lee stepped forth a little from the shadow, but did not allow himself to anticipate the man's approach. He felt as if he had been waiting for hours in some unbearable dream. But I must not take Gordon's opinion too seriously, he was saying to himself, forewarningly. After all, his judgment is fallible, and I do not need to act on it. Though he had so longed for the messenger's arrival, he had a distinct repugnance to taking the letter which the man presented. It was produced, when the man had dismounted, after hurried, ostentatious fumblings in his pocket. Fryth was wondering what the devil Lee had written to Gordon about.

Lee moved to the flap of the tent and read, "My old corps is reduced to a frazzle. I should have said more about it last night. Unless I am supported by Longstreet heavily, I do not think we can do anything more." It was not necessary to see the remainder of the note. It seemed to Lee, shakily refolding the paper, that its content was a deserved punishment for something or other. (Thy Will be done.) What had he expected anyhow? All had been discussed at sufficient length at the interview the evening before. Well, he gave up. Misery now came on him with cathartic intensity. Fryth and Lockhart were staring at him. He owed them some explanation of his peculiar behaviour. He could not give it.

546

"I seem to have abused the good nature of you gentlemen," he said. "I'm afraid your night's rest is gone."

He wanted to get away from them as quickly as he could, and started toward his own quarters. He did not want anything more for himself—*no, God, no more while he lived.* He was through. Or had it been entirely for himself? Was he more wicked than he once had thought himself, or had he suddenly become more honest? But it was not in the power of any human man to decide. That was the only thing that made the situation bearable. He was willing to renounce interest in the whole affair—praise, blame, everything. But only if some compensation were allowed him—if every connection with public affairs were severed— Then a man might treat his own sores privately. Petty irritations stung him. Only to get those two out of the way. "Good night, gentlemen," he said, again, pointedly.

He walked rapidly to his tent. Soon, in an hour, when the sun was up, something more could be decided, something more could be thought out. Why had he ever sent an impetuous note to Gordon? What weakness in himself suggested to him that Gordon be allowed to decide what no one other than the commander *could* decide? The impossibility of communication with Richmond—the disintegration of morale—who was there to turn to? But if I am obstinate, Lee thought, it is because I cannot but feel that the least man in my own forces had rather stand out until there is no hope at all. I'm not acting for myself and never have.

He had taken the first step indoors when he was crushed by a new realization that he might, after all, be obliged to yield to the facts as Gordon and others saw them. He halted. "Gentlemen," he said to Fryth and Lockhart, who were still looking at him furtively, "I think I ought to be frank with you. I'm afraid there's nothing left for it but to go to General Grant."

They thought that his voice sounded thin, high and almost accusing. Both of them, in their curiosity as to his agitation, sobered. What was there to remark?

Lee knew they had expected this, and felt his first strong resentment of them—as though they had taken advantage of his self-exposure. He said, harshly, expecting their contradiction,

"But if I can find any concurrence with my judgment, that won't happen yet."

Fryth's only answer was, "Are you feeling ill, General?" Lee did look most exceptionally pale and old, and the two made, simultaneously, a step to his side, wondering if he were about to faint. Also, they wished to cover, by this gesture, their embarrassment before his condition and the bad news.

He fled from them into the tent, and they remained looking after his bowed shoulders as he disappeared.

Now, sharing the secret of a defeat, they were ill at ease with one another. "There is certainly no comparison in the qualities of the two men—General Lee and General Grant," Lockhart commented irrelevantly, in a hushed voice.

"Yes," said Fryth, "Grant's callous, absolutely callous." And, only feigning discretion, they continued, as they retraced their way, to discuss the comparison. Lockhart expatiating on the commander while his adjectives grew.

By the time they were under shelter, they felt quite encouraged. The war was arriving at a disastrous termination, yet the best of its experiences they owned. "Nearly as perfect as a man can be, Fryth," Lockhart was saying. "Why, who can tell what strain he's been under? It's frightful, simply frightful—to any one so conscientious, with his sensibility. No, it's God's truth, if the worst does come to the worst, I'll be *proud* to surrender under him."

IV

Memories scattered in the night. Stars swerved under flying hoofs; and the cold rider passed on, leaving behind him an empty road.

Davis, in bed, in the house of the farmer who had befriended him, heard that sound of pursuit leaving his dreams, leaving him inescapably free of his dreams, unable to return into them and wrap himself in their perfection. He was safe enough here, in body. Even should they surprise him, it was not for the flesh he feared. He was afraid, rather, of some grotesque joke—of what they were already saying of him, he, the man who had tried to found an empire, who had taken the loose fancy of a generation of pretentious

548

Southerners and had made it his own, and had founded, for its realization, a new government.

Pride wounded was like a burning forever of the flesh. There was an incurable night on his mind. He wanted to die, but if he died, if he went away too utterly far, to Brazil or the Argentine, or some place like that, who would deny all the charges and the arguments convicting him, who would defend, not the act of the Secessionists, but the act of Davis?

The great man's name was his nakedness. Once it had emerged from the dark, there was no cover. The great man's name was there like a proud target for the Lilliputian arrows. Davis had reduced the barrier between himself and others for nobody. Yet his name was before him and before the world as nude as Christ.

In the strange room a window was open. Pride fretted, fretted, like foam at the cliff, at the open window on the night. But pain, in the heart of the man himself, was a citadel that would not fall. He groped for a blind man's eternity. If there were only the chilly invisibility to be conquered! After writing pamphlets, making speeches, tossing the garlands of his oratory across the universe, he was reduced to the smallest grain of the smallest dust, no more than a mote in the eyes of his disciples, hampering their selfish search for benefits.

Toward the oblivion that would not come, he stared with a stiff face, feeling the shadow of the apple tree screening the window his one friend; his critic, the rag man at the corner. Oh, for death unmenaced by the promise of a resurrection! To be a dust unpolluted by a mingling with the other dust! Since there was nothing to assure a man that he would not live, there was nothing to assure him that defeat and the shame that was his burning cloak would not bide eternally.

Loneliness should have been cool, yet, in the bedsheets, he trembled like a runner in the heat. Pain would not make a light for him. He could see nothing at all but the next future that was the next day. Not even his wife and his daughters, so compliant to his every wish, could pity Davis. God could not pity Davis, for, with Davis, God was buried.

The hours that were waiting on something merciful seemed to take a long time. What the flight from Richmond had meant to the rest did not matter, only what it had meant to himself.

549

How could he lie there and endure to remember the shock of the message received in church, the humiliation with the shock, because, all along, he had anticipated, he had prepared—the significance of his resolution unacknowledged, he had kept the horses fed and watered, waiting for harness, certain in himself that what had happened now, even then, was to happen, but excusing himself, saying to himself that the despair he felt was for his family, and that his cautious planning of escape was for their sake.

A law was a snare. It was not made for the makers of law. In Washington, when deep in national politics, he had felt a rage for the condition to which intelligence reduced him. Fatuous liars had wished to make him their dupe. He had resisted. He had used against them their own methods. But they had an advantage. They were men who believed in their own chicanery. He wanted the highest thing, something to which he could give himself wholly, without embarrassment to his mind, something constructed wholly out of his own heart and bowels. The South, then, had been no better than the North. But the South, agriculturally so settled, was politically unformed. It offered to the vast imagination something that the North did not.

Davis admitted silently that he was vain. Yes, but with the difference that his vanity reached such dimensions as exceeded any reckoning in THEIR *small scope. They thought him cold. He was cold because he could love. Once in his life love had deceived him. It had insulted him, dragging him to the weak level of all its intimacies. That had been with his first wife. He was not intimate with his second wife. He was scrupulous with her, loving her in her own way, doing his duty by her with far more arrogant correctness than she could ever guess. People considered them ideally mated. They were ideally mated. He had determined they should be. His wife should have not one iota less deference than his wife should have. Not one obligation imposed by others did he accept, and there was the more on his mind—because there must not be one crack, one crevice left through which they could enter on his inner life and crumble him.*

O God, this barren failure! He loathed the star, looking in through the apple flowers. There was his own face, exposed, and all the million faces unseen, observing, abhorred. Be still, my heart, be a grave. The grave they cannot discern. There is always quiet under sound, under the hastening feet. But the night would not take him. Whatever he tried to think made an opening always inward, to a silence and a silence, and another silence within that. But it was not still enough. Somewhere, there was light. But there was also—nothing. Men, rushing after their own shadows, did not trample him. They rushed on. He longed to transfer to them this feeling that would not be quieted, that they had aroused because they were less. Beaten to heel by his wit, held in the noose with which his oratory could bind them, they had done as he demanded. But he would not give one of them thanks. It was shown now that what they had acknowledged had not been out of any instinct to appreciate him, but because, without convictions, they had yielded to a stronger will.

He gloried in his will, but not in any tolerance born of compulsion. What he was ashamed of now was not his failure to make friends, but that he had indeed made a few. Every friend a man owns is an indication that he cannot live without flattery. Humble people do not hate the mob, because they think and feel in the terms of the mob. Oh, it made him hate the mob that blamed him because he could not love it on its own plane. He who was called cold could endure coldness least of all. Either people had to believe in him completely, or he went through such torment, in his fear of being made absurd, that he longed to die. When a man has a dream, an ambition, and it is not yet realized, that dream, in view of the facts, is always absurd. He cannot be grateful enough to those who, if they do not see eye to eye with his faith, and discern his ridiculousness, ignore it. For it is through overlooking all absurdity that the dream sometimes comes true. Kindly eyes that are familiar with you are the worst of all, for they know the fact too well to be able to understand the dream.

Davis lay there and clenched his small, harsh fists, staring up into the dark with his one good eye, trying to make both eyes the same—stone. Let him be like a stone, clean and unfeeling, he, the grotesque man lying here in a nightcap and the farmer's borrowed shirt, a stone, deader and older than the graves of Indians back of the farmer's house. Time, as he waited for them not to forgive, could no longer bruise him. A free man could not sin. Was he a man who made ignorant blacks equal by the mere gift of a vote? Was he a man who, in a world chained with its own credences,

551

made any one free? What he must school himself to learn was this long story of oblivion only just begun. O God, God, to be young enough to live another life, a life to contradict the present! He was caught here like a rat in a trap, as if to give his enemies the pleasure of knowing that he suffered. Every pale drama he had enacted was caught here in his mind to be gone over and over, sentient in his abased heart. How could a stolid population demand of him, the damned, such writhings as were beyond the measure of its comprehension?

He had slipped away out of Babel—yes—into an age too old for change. The nevermore lay on his fretting spirit, and he was tired of his struggle to lift it. The days in Montgomery seemed so puerile that he wondered at the triviality which had made him glow with the admiration they had afforded. The past was like a satire written to prophesy today. He was humble. They would never conquer him, never see him bowed down. He was all!—and humble. Turning toward the night as toward a mirror he was sick of evading, he seemed to himself coming out of the sleep that had lingered, even while he could see the fruit bloom and the tree and the window. Never, never, never. The orgy of torment abated. Small, secret things took him. In the sear light of the dawn stalking brittle through the twinkling boughs and twigs, he allowed his impotence. (Thunderer, now, for the first time, you are in your place.) And so he thought he was, he, the small man, the small flower in the vast field. He cried a little. But he knew that this mood was only the consequence of his sleepless hours, and that by and by, when he was stronger, he would begin once more to scourge himself. For it is seldom that a man who aspires to greatness can die happy. Nothing but the treachery of death could crumble the head, the heart, the firm lips. Or would it be only death? Was the body a louder cry than death? When the two silences of man and death lie breast to breast, is there born another silence yet more terrible? Can a man's life indeed be finished and he live? Oh, let the smallness draw him! Let the smallness draw him and shrivel him away out of every memory. If death would only drench him with its white, he felt; but first, before death and before dying, blot out all their knowledge of him. That was the revenge he longed to have on them, that they should not remember him.

V

Lee had conquered the mood of the night, but it was just as if he were recovering from a beating. His bones ached and he felt bruised physically as well as mentally. It was a fine day, which gave him an awful longing to cast aside all the affairs of an army, as if there were some virtue in selfishness after all, as if it pointed the only way man should live, proving all his efforts to right theoretical wrongs presumptuous and unimportant. Was there anything that could justify the wholesale slaughter of human beings? As a soldier he had long ago abandoned meditation on that, and of course his intelligence told him that men could not live for the security of pigs in a pen. He had a very honest respect for the man who, performing his duty selflessly, never questioned the right of his superiors to ask it of him.

Just the same, the April morning, with so much beauty, gave him a feeling of age and impotence, convinced him of his own folly, and that to fail in any undertaking is the highest immorality. Yes, he felt bitter, wondering that God had endowed such feeble creatures as human beings with anything like a soul. The sky was a very damp and lucid blue, and, as he rode along, he saw the fields glittering with a green so tender and barely perceptible that it would have seemed a crime to tread on it. The sparrows were talking together with minute chirps, and would flutter down in front of the horses, and wait, rather like pigeons, until they were almost ridden upon; then bounce up and sail away. Traveller seemed to be in fine fettle, prancing a little, if sedately, and sometimes flinging up his head impatiently. If a man is not humble he cannot be kind, Lee thought. But that made it all the more incredible that he was where he was, still leading this army which now comprised only eight thousand men, all the rest having been sacrificed.

Fitz-Lee's cavalry constituted the vanguard. There were two thousand sabres. The mild, delightful weather reanimated even the thin animals of the riders. The tired men were, as if despite themselves, in better spirits than usual. Perhaps they were ashamed of the jauntiness they assumed involuntarily. Not a word was said as to the real seriousness of what the day was almost certain to

553

bring forth. The wind was honeyed in the nostrils. All breathed it with a greediness that seemed guilt. To enjoy life had become irresistible, and no effort of imagination could overcome the faint, pleasantly melancholy exhilaration of a canter down a road still foggy with refreshing dews and brooded over by such a joyous mounting sun. But this voluptuous expectation of the flesh itself drew and gathered together a greater horror, when Lee compelled himself to realize that no new opportunity could come to make this vigour count.

When he pulled up to review the assemblage, and remained out of the turmoil waiting for Colonel Carter's artillery to follow the horses, the prospect lost some of its illusory gaiety. And when, with the trains, placed to come between the artillery and the remainder of the active infantry, appeared droves of unarmed stragglers, barefoot, ragged, showing in their dull faces the stoic despondency of great suffering, Lee rebuked himself for taking any pleasure at all in life. That spiritless crowd, doggedly following the mass, obviously resented every demand that made it move and persist in moving for its own safety. By now, the freshest hours of the day were gone. Vaporous dust hung over the stone walls and fences. Clouds lurked about the sun, and the morning was humid and discomfiting.

Lee, when a group came to a halt near him, felt that he should have been ready with some encouraging address. But he could not say anything. Like every other gesture made, words seemed futile, and to speak at all tormented his self-respect. The fatigue resulting from not having slept for some nights became more and more a weight on his mind, and it was all he could do to attend to his duties. His very surroundings of the moment grew vague like a fading memory. Fruit trees of an orchard in which he and Traveller rested were no nearer than the sky itself. He could not shake off the conviction that a long, long sleep was due him, and that, if he could indulge in it, he would awaken to some happier realization of things than the spectacle of these dingy, monotonous figures dragging through the warm sunlight could ever convey. After life's fitful fever, he thought. But this was treachery to his obligations. Yet why not? He conceived of all the men who were going by longing, as he did, for the same thing, so that it became actually sanctimonious to really pity the dead.

554

Somewhat apart, he had selected this position because it commanded a fair view of distant operations. The cavalry was out of sight, having taken the direction of Appomattox Court House, when a heaving of the air in the distance brought the message that Sheridan had been encountered. The shooting, at first, sounded sporadic, and of course gave no indication of what the cavalry charge itself might be. Lee found attention to those far-off splutters intolerable. But it was his premonition of futility that was wicked. When Colonel Lockhart rode up with the boastfully uttered news that a message had come to say Sheridan was falling back, Lee only answered, "Yes, yes, well," quietly, and was rebuked by Lockhart's evident delight. How long would it go on? Muteness was killing him. Everything he felt, fixed in his heart, made a self-persecution which was necessary to bring him to heed at all. His officers, he could detect, were surrounding him kindly with a false atmosphere of faith. They wanted to cheer him. He did not permit himself to resent this, but did so despite the inward effort to the contrary. Tears came to his eyes, and his very acute consciousness of their varying states of mind seemed a part of the penance he exacted of himself to go through this whole proceeding without once sharing his thoughts or his depressing emotions with anybody.

For an hour, the Federal forces retreated. Lee's servant brought him a bowl of cabbage soup which he ate, sitting on a log, when he had got down off his horse. It was repugnant to him that he had to consider his own bodily appetites, keep himself going. The bees burred glossily in the peach trees, clung stickily to the flowers, and gave to the boughs the appearance of a myriad activity, newly inspired after the somnolence of winter. Grass, close to the earth, which was visible beneath it as through a green powdering, wavered in the breeze. The clouds that sometimes came over the sun were deep-bosomed and very still.

Lee's staff was in frantic anxiety to crack jokes. It was as if they saw, tacitly, that Lee, having assumed major responsibility, bore the burden of the approaching dénouement. They, involved only because of him, resisted the future and possible condemnations. Thus, in showing him, more plainly than they had ever done, the reverence, the esteem they had for him, and in refusing to criticize him or be depressed, they escaped their own burden. The war was his. They made him a present of it—and consoled him for the gift. He did not quite admit all this, but he was very definitely exasperated as, one after another, they presented the situation to him in, as it were, the best light. He had never felt so helpless and alone.

But they stirred him up. Annoyed and determined to believe that the end had to come at once, and the more quickly the better, he was affected by their gadfly insistence on hope. His face lost the grey pallor that had, earlier, spread over it. And he felt nervous, under his repression, almost apoplectically excited. To keep them from guessing that their persuasions counted, he allowed them to suppose that he had certain plans which he had not openly committed to them that required his closer inspection of the actual fighting. And he mounted again and rode down almost perilously near the front of things.

His own forces had certainly advanced for over half a mile up the road. Sheridan's cavalry, just distinguishable beyond the faint haze crawling low over the heated artillery that was at last in position and in use, did seem to be making off. Lockhart handed Lee his glasses and the general stared a long time over the arrested ranks of his own men.

When he handed the glasses back, Lockhart saw that the hands that presented them were a little tremulous. "Your observation must have missed something, Lockhart." General Lee's tone seemed, painfully, to express triumph.

Lockhart, in his turn, looked. He had been offended by the commander's unappreciative manner, but was now aghast. "Why —why—where are they all coming from! Why there are millions of them, General!"

Lee's mouth, twisted in his beard, was slightly sardonic. "Not quite that," he said.

But they did seem to be innumerable. "Have the goodness to call Fryth and Wilson up," Lee ordered. That one glance of exultance had dimmed. His eyes resumed their dreary stare of patience.

Lockhart was glad enough of anything that would get him out of a silly fix. He had never seen as many Yankees in his life. The Confederate forces were concentrated, more or less visibly, in a kind of amphitheatre. The morning's fighting had been through one or two channels of approach only. Now, suddenly,

556

thousands of infantry, and, behind these, one estimated, other thousands, sprang, like the sown teeth of the dragon not from choked thoroughfares alone, but from every encompassing field and wood and hilltop, so that the entire dizzy, sunny landscape, under its gliding, moulting shadows of passing cloud, took on a new character, and was completely alive with moving specks of contradiction, the human, growing masses articulating, as separating space diminished and they enlarged, definite figures of men and little twinklings of arms and armament like bits of broken mirror multifarious in the dim spurts of trees.

Lockhart met Fryth and Williams only a few paces on, and the three rode back together, making, shortly, with others, a group of perturbed persons who spoke volubly, or else were silent as if struck dumb by amazement. Nobody was able to come to any decision as to what this meant. All waited for Lee to announce what was in each heart. Thank God the morning was over.

He said, "We must dispatch a truce to Grant at once and ask him to treat. I do not see how our duty will let us do anything else. Somebody must find Gordon and tell him to display a white flag."

When Lee spoke he did not look at anybody. He was very abrupt. The officers coughed or glanced at each other. Some wanted to cry, though not exactly through wretchedness over the defeat. They hated the general a little. His presence with them made it harder for them to get through the next few hours, hard in any case.

There was uncertainty in the road. A man on horseback, sent by someone or other, and leaving the body of troops, was galloping toward them. He looked frantic, as if he had received some terrible shock and were fleeing for his life. Yet the actual encounter appeared done with. There were some sporadic burbles of shot, but you could not say who fired or from which side. Wonder had paralyzed the whole agglomeration of troops and officers. And meanwhile, the Federals, in implacable numbers, veered toward the focus of this scene, and it was impossible to say how many were still to come or what they intended. It was as if *the* moment had arrived. There was something gala in the aspect of a whole world wrested, as it were, from Nature, and given over to human affairs of overpowering importance. Shouts, muffled orders,

557

even drifts of casual conversation, echoed upward from the ranks of the besieged. The thud of hoofs was distinct, as separated riders passed along the road or crossed the field to reach the commander-in-chief and his party. But those thousands who engrossed the eye, and occupied the whole landscape, so that it was as if their gestures were reflected in the very sky, they made no sound at all. They were still too far off for more than the faintest murmur of disturbance to emanate from their infinite, meandering lines. And so the two armies, one forming on the hills, the other huddled in its nest in the valleys, waited on each other. From amidst the lower, smaller herd of men a few martial-looking banners protruded. These seemed inappropriate. Rather did the insolence of conspicuous flags belong aptly to the mobs of men on the remote slopes. In realizing this, the tricked beholders felt a kind of nausea. But they had ceased to be frightened. The impossibility of contesting the ground against such superior attack left them free of all obligation, all responsibility. They became childish, like schoolboys, and did not know what to do with themselves. It was like a holiday in school, except for those who, ill or wounded, had become indifferent to holidays.

The officers did not feel quite the same. Since there was no fighting to direct, they were even more in the limelight than at other times, and, under the circumstances, they could not hope to appear very well. Mingled with gratitude that, the war thus suddenly—at least in all probability—ended, they were alive, was disappointment that they had not accomplished more, that the opportunities for distinguished promotions were past. In some there was a real sense of tragedy. What was to become of the South? But all looked to Lee as to the one who, representing them, would, they entreated silently, make the most of a final opportunity. A few, like the general himself, had been, for long, so sick and disheartened that they could not be anything but glad of this respite. Yet it was an imperfect relief. Most of them were convinced that not a leader on the Northern side was to be trusted.

*   *   *   *

The ruse had worked. Sheridan, who, to gain an eminence, had sheered off the road, was now mopping his forehead with his handkerchief, and, in a sweat of excitement as to what the next move would be, saw the flag of truce; very significantly prominent, elevated below him. His heart turned over a beat. Of course there was nothing else for them to do, and yet he had not been absolutely certain of them until it had happened. As on another occasion, he made that favourite gesture with his fist, thrusting out a gauntleted hand and contracting the fingers tightly. "I've got 'em!" he exclaimed to Hackett (his second in command). "Like *that!*"

Hackett, a little jealous of these superlatives, nodded sedately. "The neatest trick ever turned!" Sheridan persisted, and wondered why Hackett, as if embarrassed, did not echo the self-approval. None of Sheridan's friends were lavish of their commendation. What he said when he was in the highest good humour always seemed to turn them a trifle cold. He could not understand their 'nasty' reserves. Envy of course, pure envy. If I stopped to get to the bottom of all this carping, Sheridan thought, I'd bring myself right down to their level. Why, there ought to be a national acknowledgement of what I've done. They ought to strike a medal in my honour the way they used to for the old Romans. Grant wouldn't get where he is going without me.

And, as he began again to talk and bluster loudly, drowning out all this 'high-toned moderation,' an opaque attitude toward his surroundings returned. He saw those little knots of men beneath him—only a fragment of an army—and, everywhere, ornamenting, with signs of triumph, every mile of advantageous ground visible, his own forces. A sight for sore eyes, sure enough! The end of a great business! Nothing to outdo it in history! "Never saw people as thoroughly licked," he kept repeating, his little eyes self-centredly keen in survey, his goodnature bellicose. "Never saw people so thoroughly licked. It ull take 'em fifty years to get over this!" But his companions were as cold as ice. He felt he would like to pick up Hackett by the scruff of the neck and *shake* some enthusiasm out of him. The man didn't know what a great moment in history was!

559

VI

"Appomattox Court House, Virginia,
"General,   "April 9th, 1865.

"In accordance with my letter to you of the 8th instant, I propose to receive the surrender of the Army of Northern Virginia on the following terms, to wit: Rolls of all the officers and men to be made in duplicate, one copy to be given to an officer designated by me, the other to be retained by such an officer or officers as you may designate. The officers to give their individual paroles not to take up arms against the United States until properly exchanged; and each company or regimental commander to sign a like parole for the men of their commands. The arms, artillery, and public property to be parked and stacked, and turned over to the officers appointed by me to receive them. This will not embrace the side arms of the officers, nor their private horses and baggage. This done, each officer and man will be allowed to return to his home, not to be disturbed by the United States authority so long as they observe their paroles and the laws in force where they may reside.

"Very respectfully, your obedient servant,
"U. S. Grant, *Lieutenant-General*."

In the complete silence preserved by those who were attending, Grant had been writing for several minutes. His letter contained only phrases conned in advance, and yet his stiff fist, always awkward with a pen, moved with cramped hesitance, and he felt an abashed presentiment that his small, wavering calligraphy would not be easily deciphered. When he had done, he rose from the table, and, boldly determined to be impeccably polite, made a slight bow, curt and uneasy, and offered the page for General Lee's perusal.

General Lee also inclined his head, and, with a brief apology, stepped toward the window, explaining that the light was bad.

It was not a very bright day. Rain was gathering. The glare was stale and chilly. A hen was chuckling in the yard. The two parties accompanying the commanders were self-conscious with one another and overconsiderate. The Federals wondered what the Confederates were thinking, and the Confederates appraised their vis-à-vis with a prejudiced eye. The farmhouse parlour did not contain very much furniture, and what was there was very stuffy. All the gentlemen remained standing.

General Lee scrutinized every word so slowly and with such exacting attention that Grant's face became flushed and his heartbeats rather loud and angry, as he asked himself if even *this* generosity had failed to convince Lee that he, too, was dealing with a gentleman and a man of far-seeing imagination.

But at length Lee seemed satisfied. He looked up from the paper and the two pair of eyes met.

It was now Lee's turn to feel disturbed. The strangely open expression, rebukeful and even trusting, and at the same time demanding, which he observed on Grant's face, and which suggested the anxiety of a child, was something that the Confederate general could not interpret. What he saw was a stocky, carelessly mannered, emphatic figure, in a handsome bebraided coat too large for it, and, above the gilt-edged collar, features somewhat younger than his own, a full beard, greying hair—nothing very dignified or important there beyond the borrowed importance of gold-starred shoulder straps. Yet it was as if that small, brusque, silent man were trying to ring from Lee a personal admission of some kind, as much as to say, for instance, that both of them had had a hard time, or that what was occurring at this moment ought not to be counted an individual matter.

Lee shrank from the intimacy with which he was being observed. It seemed to him that *his* humiliations should be apparent enough already. When Grant indicated to him the vacated chair by the table, Lee felt a faint, unreasonable disgust for the, "At your discretion, General," and the tone in which it was uttered, just as he strongly disliked accidental meetings of eyes, and half suspected that an apparently sincere deference masked self-congratulation of some sort.

He wrote with a more brisk and florid stroke and more quickly than Grant, and the compulsion to brevity seemed to him so obvious that he had scarcely premeditated the wording of this letter. He did not wish to be rude—could not, in fact, in his position, allow himself to be. But he would not be able to quit this place fast enough. He hoped he was not arrogant in feeling that even terse sentences conveyed to the appreciative mind the devotion to a trust that could lie equally behind a victory and a surrender. This miserable half-hour was another exercise in self-control, and he had no doubt, he told himself, that he needed it.

> "Head-Quarters, Army of Northern Virginia,
"General,   "April 9th, 1865.
"I have received your letter of this date, containing the terms of the surrender of the Army of Northern Virginia, as proposed by you. As they are substantially the same as those expressed in your letter of the 8th inst., they are accepted. I will proceed to designate the proper officers to carry the stipulation into effect.
> "Very respectfully, your obedient servant,
> "R. E. LEE, *General.*"

He blotted the paper neatly, passing the blotter over it several times, as he found himself reluctant to give it up. The tips of his fingers pressed forcefully and precisely upon the paper. He did not believe that he was showing anything that he ought not to show. His hand felt to him steady. His own gravity weighed him down so that it was hard to bear. But he must remember that all this had really happened yesterday. It was too late to regret it—if one ever should regret. Regret might be considered blasphemous.

Again he had to encounter that wretched, seeking stare from that little man dressed in the clothing of his elder brother. Lee allowed it. He would not give glance for glance, but Heaven knew there could be no dignity in pretence at this stage. How he was feeling must be written all over him, and the right kind of pride might as well confess it. He could feel the sting of tears in his eyes. There was more submission in prominence than in obscurity. Oh, to get away, get away—anywhere!

"It seems to me that is all, General," he said to Grant coldly, "until I can send you the amplifying details that will be necessary."

Grant, for some motive that he could not admit, was loath that the interview should terminate. "Yes," he conceded, musing over the paper he held, and unable to marshal further excuses for prolonging this wooden conversation, "it seems to me that we have come to as satisfactory a conclusion as may be under the circumstances. I wish you a very good day, General."

There were other murmurs of respect, a cautious interchange of salutes, and the visitors, as Grant's attendants retreated politely to permit them a more spacious exit, left the room.

Grant stood there thinking, So that's all there was to it. He felt baffled.

The Federals were glad to have the defeated out of the way. Their presence had imposed a most oppressive restraint. Nobody enjoyed solicitous hypocrisy, yet all congratulated themselves that they had done very well. They regarded Grant with renewed approval. Lee's 'mob' could have asked for nothing better than they had received.

Grant did not wish to give the scene just terminated too much importance, and immediately returned to his desk to go through other business. He had, however, scarcely reseated himself, when he was shocked by turgid rumbling made by three successive cannon booms, the startling sounds followed by roistering cheers not far away.

Good Lord! Had he ordered that! Of course salutations would be fired endlessly all over the country as soon as the telegraph grew busy. But this was in earshot of Lee's own lines. It must not be repeated. Everything that he had carefully arranged, the whole effect that he had aimed to produce, was jeopardized. Damnation!

Major Dewey was still present and turned away from the window pleased. "The boys were instructed to celebrate and I don't suppose they'll need any urging," he remarked, facing Grant with a smile.

Grant thumbed some papers uncomfortably, turning his cheek to the other and half pretending to resume his writing. "Well, have it stopped," he said gruffly. "It's no way to take this situation. Give the ink time to dry."

Of course Dewey must have been surprised, but Grant would not even notice him. If I ever could afford to have things my own way, I can now, Grant thought heatedly. Let them grumble. I'll have enough liquor rationed out to put them in a good humour if that's what they want. He said, "Do you know whether my instructions to issue rations to the Confederate ranks have gone out or not?" To prevent any remark from Dewey—and, if he knew on which side his bread was buttered he would not offer any—Grant went on talking. Why should a man have to apologize for generosity when generosity could so well be afforded! Damn it, you are never safe from pettifoggers! Now Lee's licked they want me to insult him.

But the rôle of large forgiveness was not easy. It's the vanquished who are not generous, Grant thought, considering what he was going through. A damned crabbed lot, Lee and his blithering cohorts! The confounded blockheads are so proud of themselves that they'd *rather* be hated. I'm sticking to all this to satisfy myself—not *him,* damn his hide! And this is the last time I'll ever waste my precious energy on the fools.

XIX

THOUGH a glance at the clock might have told them of the ample time at their disposal, Mrs. Sutter and Jemima were in a fever of haste. When they were alighting from the hired hack, Mrs. Sutter, who had taken off her long, white, kid gloves superfluously, and was just putting them on again, was awkward enough to drop one in the muddy gutter. "Oh, *Ma,* you *are* upset!" Jemima cried petulantly, for she could not bear it that even so mean a person as the negro coachman detect her mother's social clumsiness.

The glove was quickly recovered, and the two women, hurriedly lifting their skirts in front, but dragging them behind, made their way up the shallow steps that led to the entrance of the theatre. The lobby was very well lighted with gas, and numerous ladies in expensive mantles and gentlemen in high hats and capes were loitering expectantly outside the ticket gate. Jemima was secretly impatient to enter, as she could not bear to stand about in a throng in which nobody knew her or would bow to her. At the same time, it would be horrible to be the first inside, so she delayed her mother and called attention to a handsome painted likeness of Miss Laura Keene, hanging just beside the window at which seats were sold. Mrs. Sutter, who could be easily distracted and might even forget to be on her best behaviour, hesitated in front of it and said, "Is *that* what she looks like! That dress does not look to me in the fashion at all. Why, she looks almost as old as I do."

Again Jemima was discomforted, for she was already regretting the temerity which had led her to agree to come to the theatre without the protection of a male escort. It appeared to her that all of the really fashionable young ladies she saw had with them either fathers or brothers, or else, if they were chaperoned, gentlemen to whom, probably, they were affianced. She supposed that everybody would imagine that *she* was without an interested suitor, to hand her in on his arm, or carry her reticule for her, or take her mother's wraps. "It is too bad that Homer has not been returned home yet," she remarked very loudly, wishing to be overheard, but going rather blind as she felt she attracted attention to herself. "He likes a good play so much, and he will be especially put out when I write him he has missed Miss Keene. But very likely the *officers* will be the last who are allowed to come home. The fact that he has several badges of courage doesn't seem to earn him any privileges."

As Jemima said this, she patted stealthily the wreath of fuchsia that crowned her neat hair, and hoped the tulle that was laid about her naked shoulders had not become too mussed by her cloak. She was *so* relieved that her mother, also, had worn décolleté, after protesting that she was sure it was not like an opera and that you need not present yourself in a low-necked dress. Mrs. Sutter, Jemima thought, was the most contrary woman alive. How she ever expected her daughter to reach the highest place in Washington society when she herself was always forgetting correct behaviour, Jemima could not fathom.

At last it seemed time to go in. Or at any rate, if they lingered any more people would think they were not used to coming here. To judge by the 'mob' they had watched file in ahead of them, they should have found the theatre filled. To their great astonishment, it was, as yet, almost entirely empty, and even gloomy, so that, when Mrs. Sutter declared vexedly that they were early after all, her voice echoed loudly and conspicuously through the auditorium. "Don't be so vulgar, Ma," Jemima had to whisper fiercely, tweaking her mother's gown. The usher who wore white cotton gloves and took them to their seats, glanced in such a perfunctory way at the numbers of their tickets, and seemed in such unwarranted haste to be off to gossip with his idling companions, that Jemima could not but fancy that he, also, was contemptuous of their unaccustomedness to their surroundings. "Why," said Mrs. Sutter, turning about and seeing the dimness that enveloped their arrival, the dingy forefront of the unillumined stage, the piano, shapeless in a felt cover, below the pit, "I had a notion that with the relief everybody feels to have the war done, and the President coming, too, the place would be packed—quite a gala night."

"*Pscht!*" ordered Jemima, involuntarily. But her exclamation of caution could not drown the awful clatter made by the plush seats as they were lowered, dropping into position with such startling bangs, that the noise was quite as arresting as pistol shots.

There was the offensive usher rushing off before he had even given a playbill to them. Mrs. Sutter, once she had struggled through the difficulties of crushing her hoops to the correct angle for permitting her to remain comfortably where she was, refused to budge, insisting to Jemima, with unnecessary sibilance, "Don't make him come all the way back here, Jemima. Why on earth did you forget to ask him? What will he think of us!"

Jemima, however, considered it would be too horrible to go through the evening ignorant of what was supposed to be taking place on the stage, and not knowing the names of the actors and actresses. If that employé of the theatre believed that he could treat her 'any old way' she would teach him his manners. So, again, labouring with the stiff widths of muslin that she must not spoil, she stood up and called out, quite peremptorily, "Usher—usher! Will you *please* pay attention! You have forgotten to give us a playbill, *if* you please!"

He was some distance behind them, and up the aisle, and he surveyed them, surprised. But when he saw what was the matter he came running, such a smirk on his face that Jemima felt tempted to 'slap' him. They were much too 'know-it-all,' these menials.

Now she had secured the bill, she was in so much exasperation, and so certain that all the people who were coming in were watching her and her mother, and perhaps smiling, too, at an incident which was not at all her fault (but the man's rudeness and stupidity) she could not read, and handed the miserable printed slip over to Mrs. Sutter at once.

"*Ford's Theatre*," Mrs. Sutter began. "Um—um—*Friday evening, April 14th, 1865. Benefit and Last Night of Miss Laura Keene—One Thousand Nights—Our American Cousin.*"

"We *know* all that, Ma," Jemima interrupted, fiercely and snappishly. And *why*, for gracious sakes, need her mother read so audibly!

"*Florence Trenchard, Miss Laura Keene. Abel Murcott, John Dyott. Ash Trenchard, Harry Hawk. Um—um.*"

"Oh, *Ma!*" Jemima fretted.

567

Then she heard her mother saying, with altered voice, "Look, look, Jemima! There's Mr. Lincoln's box all ready for him! See the flag on it! I told you you would be much better able to see him here than if we had sat in the dress-circle."

Jemima's curiosity was a temporary salve to her distress, as it took her mind off things—off the way the theatre smelled of peanuts, and how her slippers hurt her, and how she ought at least to *pretend* that she knew somebody here. She agreed with her mother that the last time they had seen the 'First Lady of the Land' out driving, she had appeared much stouter than in the first year of her residence at the White House, and that the proportions of her figure were not at all becoming. "They are such plain people." Jemima stated antagonistically. "Of course Mr. Lincoln is a very good man, but Adelaide Whitehall, who knows simply *everybody*, says that Washington society has deteriorated unmentionably since they became its leaders. In the beginning Mrs. Lincoln hadn't the least idea how to behave herself, and she overdresses terribly and is *so* affected, while Mr. Lincoln't manners are as plain as his face."

Mrs. Sutter raised her eyebrows, primmed her mouth, and admonished. "Hush, Jemima. Hush. If people hear you criticizing the President and his family they'll think we're unpatriotic. Mr. Lincoln's quite a hero now—with the Emancipation Act and all."

"Well, he's not *my* notion of a hero. Think of *waltzing* with a man like that."

The faint radiance in the theatre was fast becoming a glare, as a man with a taper in his hand passed along the side aisles igniting other gas jets near the boxes. Several stooping gentlemen in black coats and broad white vests were crawling from the abyss beneath the stage. "A harp, two fiddles, and the piano," murmured Mrs. Sutter. "The concert part is to be something extra because the President's here."

Quite a numerous audience had assembled, and a languid buzz of conversation filled the stale air. There was a smell of heavy perfume, of powder, and a closeness indefinable. Mrs. Sutter longed for her bottle of salts. And Jemima felt that a press like this put every tax upon a lady's obligation to remain 'dainty.' Mother and daughter were uneasy. The heightened artificiality of their surroundings left them burdened by their unwilling awareness of weaknesses of the flesh, among these a tendency to perspiration under the armpits, and the perversity of their pomaded curls which would not stay in place.

Yet there was a hint of excitement which lifted them above the personal matter of appearing at home, and of making loud, blank remarks to the effect that the lady in the upper box above the President's must be Mrs. So-and-So, implying familiar acquaintance with her. Under the flat, ambiguous expanse of the curtain, which was painted to imitate folds of scarlet velvet held in tasselled loops, showed, inadvertently, a pair of shanks in overalls, with the blond edge of a frowzy broom a man was swishing back and forth. Jemima was in ecstasies at the crude spectacle. Even that glimpse of dirty boards, vanishing, in lines of parallel cracks, behind the canvas which the unseen stage-hand was oscillating, gave her a thrill that permeated her very marrow. And she said to herself that if the stage but offered a more ladylike career she would rather be an actress than anything in the world. Women like Miss Keene were of quite good standing and accepted almost on an equality by everybody. Jemima did not state her conclusion in so many words, but she did not find it quite fair that a woman could put herself so in the limelight, receiving, no doubt, even the addresses of utterly strange men who admired her, and not have to pay any penalty for her advantage. She began to dislike Miss Keene a little. Yet if I were only she, Jemima thought—but I suppose if I were I could not marry well. How do they dare take such risks?

The violinist was wiping his brow with his handkerchief. People continued, constantly, to sidle between the rows of seats, in their passage making one another very uncomfortable. The dress-circle presented an elegant array of velvets, brocades, and satins, an exposition of round-cut bodices revealing plump or meagre shoulders emerging with discreet nudity from lace berthas, ribbon ruchings, starched drapings of tulle, or meticulous arrangements of wax or silken flowers. Now and then a twanged reverberation from some musical instrument suggested either that it had been dropped on the floor and quickly recovered, or that the musicians were uttering notes of warning. The smoky, rose body of the bass viol leaned above the parapet of the stage and was like a protruding spinal column. The square piano was an onyx table that issued disjointed trills. A fiddle squeaked languidly; and this first note of tightened anguish was followed by an arpeggio drawn tinnily from the harp.

Every instant, Mrs. Sutter kept her gaze fixed on the President's box, as she attempted to peer behind the looped chenille curtains to discover how many chairs were placed there, hoping to deduce therefrom how many individuals might be expected in the President's party. The 'tuning up' had suddenly become more brisk and businesslike. So they were going to be *late!* The auditorium would be dark and nobody would be able to see anything after all. Mrs. Sutter clicked disgustedly. It was outrageous the way people who wanted to be in the fashion came in after a performance was started and made all those who really wanted to see the play lose half of it. It was not cordial to the public either. Mrs. Lincoln must have become as 'stuck-up' as her enemies reported her. I suppose she thinks she can behave just any way she likes, Mrs. Sutter thought, with a grudge in her heart. To conquer an unworthy annoyance, she took up her playbill again and droned out to Jemima a verse printed at the bottom. *Patriotic Song and Chorus, Honour to Our Soldiers.* By the time she had reached the final lines, her voice was thick and throaty with emotion, and, as it almost broke, she covered her dilemma by hastening to announce abstractedly, *"Benefit of Miss Jennie Gourlay, in the great sensational drama, The Octoroon,"* perhaps not a nice play for Jemima to see.

Jemima was as much moved as her mother. One did not need to seek only in the theatre and in the frivolous reading of novels for the fine and noble things in life. Heroism, sensationalism were everywhere, and today. They were silent, wrapped in a glamorous melancholy, enhanced by the anticipation of the play to which they looked forward with all the voluptuary's delight in emotions he can enjoy without self-commitment. Hair pomade, bay rum, patchouli, and the perfume of some natural violets worn daringly by a lady near them, left them with every perception calmed and every sense stimulated. " 'The play's the thing,' " quoted Jemima. "Oh, Ma, I do so worship the romantic!" She did not take very kindly to it when the musicians struck up an air. They played, *"For we are so awfully clever,"* and Jemima and her mother both knew the refrain so that it interfered a little with the languorous mood of waiting for an event.

570

Still more disagreeable to their unpreparedness was the late arrival of a very large woman with her husband, these two wedging themselves along between the Sutters' row and the next, while Jemima and her mother, bending their knees unwillingly and protecting defiantly their tip-tilted hoops and mussed petticoats, refused to get up. They felt all the more justified in their obstinacy because 'the dowager,' as Jemima abusingly called her, while she discommoded them, kept her own face turned to the stage, which she concealed completely, and this at the very moment when the curtain might rise. Mrs. Sutter grimaced curtly. Jemima's nose was tickled by a fur tippet, the tails of the lady's pelisse flapped on her mouth, and she was so inundated by material emanations from this heaving female presence that she was revolted and could have wished herself at home. In the predominance of smells all around there was a positive indecency, as if people had no right to congregate themselves in such intimacy. The odours of scent were as pronounced and repulsive as the less mentionable impressions.

At last a bell did flutter glassily. A furtive usher was observed, turning off gas jets quickly; and only the plank floor of the rostrum remained aglow and distinct, while the curtain, with its radiant edge, was being wafted, slowly, mysteriously, upward.

This centre as of a holy conflagration reflected upon the features of the audience, now gleaming palely, and the people themselves gained, from the gloom, something mystic, as a twinkling ornament, a jewelled hair comb, a bracelet, a ring, or the tinsel on a dress stood out prominently. In the veiled recesses of the President's box, one lowered gas jet burned, blue and apart. But those who had prepared for his presence were compensated and revenged themselves with indifference to his delinquency. All was indeed set for the fine comedy Miss Keene would act. Jemima, whose gloves were clammy, grasped her mamma's plump wrist and squeezed it impetuously. "Ma," she whispered, "I really think nothing is so much an art as a fine theatrical. I feel transported already. But I could wish the play was not so funny as they say it is in part. I suppose it is because Mr. Lincoln is so humorous that he prefers a piece like this. What I like best is to be taken right out of myself by something that has sentiment and is stirring, too."

"Psch!" said Mrs. Sutter, annoyed to have to think of anything at all. Her face was stolid, but a delightful weakness permeated her whole body, and was accompanied by a feeling of generosity toward the actors, whom she depended on guilelessly to shake her with sobs or propel her to mirth, either course being acceptable to her. And she settled herself more comfortably. Her ruchings would soon be a wreck, but what did it matter—for once, what did it matter?

In direct contradiction of her earlier interest in the President's visit, she felt almost spiteful toward him when, near the end of the second act, the spell was broken and the play stopped completely, scattered gas jets flaring into temporary prominence while the orchestra struck up boldly, *Hail to the Chief*, and, with an example which she was reluctantly obliged to follow—spilling her wraps, her playbill, her reticule and handkerchief—the whole audience stood up. It made her quite giddy to have all the lights on again, and the stage just as before, the curtain remaining elevated. The modesty of the actors was perfect. You would have thought, she said, that people had come to see Mr. and Mrs. Lincoln, and not Miss Keene. For the nonce, attention was given entirely to them. Such a fuss and rustle! It took quite a while for the presidential party to ensconce itself in the box, and Mrs. Sutter was aggrievedly aware that, through this delay, after the music had ceased, and the polite quiet was only broken by coughs, whispers, and the rattle of crinolines being rearranged, something precious, like a rare aroma, was being dissipated from her own mind. It would be 'thanks' to the President if she could not recapture it. She was not inclined to yawn, yet, as she crowded herself down into her chair, her sensations, those of some one thrown back, at an unpropitious moment, on his own resources, were a trifle sickly. The deadliness of the ennui which she and Jemima had suffered from during the time in which the war had deprived them of all their usual amusements seemed stealing on her again. "Mrs. Lincoln cannot *compare* with Miss Keene!" Mrs. Sutter hissed loyally. "She's the most commonplace woman I ever saw in my life. I have no *patience* with her. And as for the *President*—he is well enough, I know—but did you ever see *plebeian* so written all over a man! If he hadn't managed to make himself president nobody would ever give a second thought to him. (I can't *abide* that lilac dress.) And imagine being married to him, imagine a man like that making *love* to you."

Jemima remained more successfully immersed in the play. She was not going to allow the intrusion of the President's party to defeat her. She could not witness any sort of drama interpreted by a handsome woman of fashionable appearance without, immediately, conceiving of herself in the same part and wondering if she could not do it better. She said, "Oh, *bother* him, *Ma!* Don't you agree, now, that Homer is *just* as handsome as Miss Keene's lover? *Don't* you, Ma? There are a great many people with a fine presence who are not on the stage at all, and I do believe that some of them, if they had the chance, could act Miss Keene's part more dramatically."

Mrs. Sutter sighed deeply, envious of Jemima's valiant wholeheartedness, and of her self-confidence. Well, she herself would guard her pleasure preciously. It was so seldom she and Jemima had any 'distraction.' And resolutely, as one settling in a tepid bath, secure though ready to be undone, she resumed concentration on the actors, so disturbingly *more* than real, with their crimson-splashed cheeks, their lashes rayed like those of dolls, their glinting eyes which softened to none of the emotions they declaimed, and their careful voices, seeming, by an odd, emphatic accent, to direct, at intervals—*Ha! Thus!*—what she *should* think and feel! She was not going to be indulged with a good cry, but with laughter, tears only slightly, now and again. Jemima was 'ravished,' termed Miss Keene 'divine.' Mrs. Sutter thought that a little harmless theatre-going made every day easier to bear.

.   .   .   .

Just before the beginning of the third act, Mrs. Lincoln expressed a desire for a drink of water, and Major Rathbone gallantly offered to go and fetch it. Mrs. Lincoln was very handsomely gowned, the deep low-neck of her costume finished with a bertha of real Venetian, while the purple velvet of her draped overskirt, magnificently distended by her hoops and caught on the sides with knots of expensive velvet, fell over a lilac taffeta petticoat with a pleated flounce. When Major Rathbone returned in the company of a page boy who was bringing the glass of water on a salver, the two, to reach her, had to pass in front of Miss Harris, who sat nearer the stage. Mr. Lincoln saw that the sweep of his wife's garments left little room for feet, and he leaned forward and twitched a fold of the underskirt out of the way. "Oh, the fol-de-lols, the fol-de-lols," he said. "No man would have the courage to endure the martyrdom the ladies submit to almost every minute of their miserable lives."

When he made this observation, Mrs. Lincoln turned her short, fleshy neck, and her insipid, plump-cheeked face offered him a look that mingled doubt, incomprehension, and reproach. He treated her so much like a child who requires indulgence that she would vacillate between a slow chagrin at the suggestions which undermined her self-confidence, and sentimental abandon to the relief she always felt in his strong, protective companionship. Every epoch marking the progress of his success she had enjoyed from the bottom of her heart. And she would often tell him, with quiet tears in her eyes, that if she was a little vain of his position, she had a right to be. "You did not use to be so reserved with me, Abe," she would also say. Yet, actually, that very unresponsiveness of his provoked her to gratitude, releasing her as it did from the effort to appear constantly understanding of a man so whimsical. If she felt more and more the need to fortify herself with the show of society, it was a longing which was natural to a woman bereft of one of her children—of more than one, if you looked backward far enough—and, in a sense, through the horrors of war and the exalted burdens distracting Mr. Lincoln from his homelier duties, deprived of intimacy with him whom she was 'humbly proud' to acknowledge her lord and master. She gave little fatuous sighs whenever she thought of the sacrifice undreamt of demanded of a great man's wife. The President's aloofness was a trouble to her, but it was also the reason for a boast, and she was accustomed to speak rather contemptuously of the women who had their men too much in their single company. 'Abe' was, at bottom, a family man, but she could not pretend to require it of him that he be satisfied to hide his light under a bushel and exist entirely for such a 'humdrum' person as herself. "I have no patience with ladies who hamper the careers of their husbands," she would remark firmly.

While the page boy remained erect beside her, and held the salver, she sipped self-consciously, her fat little finger delicately crooked, for she was always obsessed, and, indeed, upset, by the

574

notice directed toward her when she made a public appearance. She wished that Abe had not developed such an air of grimness, and that he would give more heed to the people in the audience, who would certainly appreciate a look from him.

"How do you like the play, Mr. Lincoln?" Miss Harris inquired brightly; and again Mrs. Lincoln darted a swift glance over the edge of her glass, for she and Miss Harris got on 'so amiably,' and it did seem most genteel of Miss Harris to overlook all Abe's small peculiarities and seem so fond of him. Most pretty ladies Mrs. Lincoln did not trust, but Miss Harris was so 'tactful.' She never forgot to be kind and always did the proper thing. Mrs. Lincoln could wax most enthusiastic about her, 'the dear,' and now that she and Major Rathbone had become engaged it was all so 'lovely, so appropriate.'

Mr. Lincoln was sitting in a plush-upholstered armchair, and had his long legs awkwardly crossed and his gaunt arms folded on his chest. His slight frown was languid rather than vexed, a matter of habit, and he had one eyebrow, the right, cocked higher than the other. How his wife knew that symptom of fantastic moods—though tonight he was being rather well-behaved. She could catch glimpses of his full face as he would glance toward the stage, his sagging mouth, his thick lower lip thrust out petulantly, but not ill-humouredly, his thin upper lip compressed, Mrs. Lincoln had heard it expressed that Mr. Lincoln's mouth was cruel, contemptuous; but to her that sardonic intimation, composed of smile and weary sneer, indicated no more than the fatigue and self-absorption of which she was jealous. His eyes were very sad. There were times when, in privacy, he disparaged himself. Then he made her almost hate him, and want to cry. If he had not, in the beginning, intended to free *all* the negroes, she did not see how that made any difference in the final result of things. He *had* drafted the Emancipation Act, and he *had* done very nearly everything in making the nation keep its head in a time of unprecedented stress. Even his worst enemies admitted that his temperateness had done more to save the Union than all the hullabalooing of the Abolition people, and even than—than Secretary Stanton himself! Mrs. Lincoln could not abide that Secretary Stanton. He snubbed her husband right and left, issued ultimatums as if they came from the Presidential chair, and was the most obnoxious person she ever saw in her life. Abe was not only 'ironical,' as some had called him—she was in doubt of the term—he was downright perverse. He was the most egotistical man she had ever seen, and, with all that, he actually seemed to take pleasure in letting Stanton have everything his own way—and get all the credit, too. Now what was he thinking about? Mystification, that was what he liked. But no man ought to try to mystify his own wife, especially when she has shared so much he has been through that she knows him inside out, like a book, and he cannot keep anything from her.

"Why, it seems to me a capital evening's entertainment, Miss Harris," Mr. Lincoln was saying. "I don't know as anybody could give me a prize as a critic of acting, but Miss Keene seems to me to do her part in fine style, and I have had some laughs as good as any I ever had in my life. The ladies don't get all the laurels, either. The gentlemen are pretty good, too." Mrs. Lincoln, the page dismissed and Major Rathbone returned to his chair, heard Abe's drawling voice complacently, but she did wish that he might have learned to sit up straight. Miss Harris had that 'soft, Southern accent' that people talked about so much. It was nice, and yet—

Miss Harris often professed that she was quite fond of the President, and that she sympathized with his quaint ways perfectly. The gravity of her regard for him was not, she felt, contradicted by her 'mild amusement' at his oddities. When they were in a company like this, she always conversed with him very pointedly. Mr. Lincoln was one of those men of whom no other man need be jealous, she had assured her fiancé, and he, with slight reluctance, had agreed with her. She had never made plain to Major Rathbone the strange impression which, however, she always had as she allowed herself to gaze directly into Mr. Lincoln's eyes. He was a man that 'piqued' her. She supposed it must be the quality of 'greatness' which she felt, looking out at her from that extraordinarily rugged face. It could give her quite a 'thrill.' And 'dear little Mrs. Lincoln' must, after all, be a most unsatisfactory mate for him. No doubt really a tragedy, though you would never guess it. The President certainly was not polished, but he was the soul of gallantry. She admired him 'hugely,' as if he were her father. No, really, at times she had an intuition of such 'strength of character' concealed in his ungainliness that—

576

that—well, she hardly knew what to do about it. But there was a stringiness in his throat, a withered, ageing look to his features, a something in his person so graceless that, though he was gracious enough with a speech, he repelled her. And this 'tiny, tiny' repugnance to his physique, something so small that it hardly seemed worth considering, made her all the more appreciative of her own strong, youthful lover. She would not have blamed Mrs. Lincoln very much if she had shown herself unhappy with Mr. Lincoln. He was so—so 'cryptic.' "Beauty and the Beast," Major Rathbone had whispered into Miss Harris's ear, as she had sat with Mr. Lincoln at a banquet just the other night. "Don't deny that you have made a conquest of him." She *did* deny it. Oh, she did, she did deny it! That would be too embarrassing—and, besides, he was 'such a *nice* old bear,' and Mrs. Lincoln, too.

She said, "I believe you grudge us our triumphs, Mr. Lincoln. You will have to admit that in the art of the theatre, anyhow, women, from Peg Woffington on, have cut the finest figure."

"Oh, as to *figure*," Mr. Lincoln answered, smiling at her, "I did not say there was much to be compared. There would not have been, for instance, much of a choice between the elder Booth and Miss Charlotte Cushing—and if there had been any little altercation behind the scenes when both of them were present I would bet my money on Miss Cushing as having the best chance to win."

"For shame, Mr. Lincoln!" Mrs. Lincoln remonstrated, shifting her bland, nervous little grimace of affable apology to a focus upon Miss Harris, who was, nevertheless, laughing unrestrainedly. Mrs. Lincoln hoped that, by now, people understood 'Abe's naughtiness,' but gracious only knew.

As the lights were going out again, after the intermission, Lincoln stirred, cramped by his chair, and refolded his arms. He did not know whether he most admired or most resented Miss Harris. But he liked her company and would always give her 'as good as she sent.' He had a great deal of respect for her. She was considerably less boring than 'most gals' of her age. His remark just then put him in mind of a conversation he had had, just the other day, with the son of the old Booth whose reputation had been so great, and he had not liked this 'younger version,' self-conceited, soured—the reason being, probably, that he had not achieved a fame equal to his father's. He had been actually rude.

577

Even in retrospect, Lincoln resented it. Why should a man seek for an introduction on purpose to vent his spleen on *you*, a stranger! The fellow must be an unfathomable 'crank'! But Lincoln dismissed the memory. He thought too much of himself to let that riff-raff disturb him. The older he grew, the more firmly settled in power, the more it pleased him to offer to the world a mode of treatment exactly contradictory to that which, in his early life, it had offered him. He liked to be as generous as the others had been 'measly.' Yet he had to recognize that he was not, for that, any the readier to 'eat humble pie.' In general, toward people who did not show him respect, he was thoroughly ready to be vengeful. He was not going to deceive himself on that point. Any apparent inconsistencies were not real. He had made use of Stanton and of several more, and they would never know it. He even allowed them rope to hang themselves, if that was what they wanted. Though he did not feel inclined to do it for them. He had profited too much by their experience.

Well, he thought, Tad need not feel about me the way Booth feels about his father. I have left my son plenty of room to improve on my career. If he can't do any better than I have, there's not much hope for him. Good God, if I look to any man of brains the way the men now in public office and in the public eye look to me—well, I am glad I'm not the Lord Almighty. I would hate to be responsible for the crew. The joke is always on the fellow who thinks he's doing right. The damn fool who has no sense and no moral ideas can be forgiven if he's wrong—but think of the rest of us!

It did seem lately as if the bottom had dropped out of everything. No accounting for it—unless age— Or was it this girding habit of caution? Lincoln knew he would always have to look ahead and see what was common sense, and the things that had affected him the most, that he felt most deeply, and could not explain by any reason—he was ashamed of them. He had never even mentioned them—not once in his whole life—not directly. Or did he 'fool' himself that he had any deeper side? No, by God, he did *not* fool himself. This obstinacy was a pain. But calculation, also, was a pain. It made all he touched barren. And he would never be able to get over it. He *was* convinced that he was a great man, though every plaudit from the public failed as true appreciation. Then for what did he wish to be admired? For being as unlike them as possible, as unlike, say, that petty-spirited, revengeful son of Booth. Yet was he? The confession that 'we are all poor critters' was never made in the right way. It degraded those who made it because of the style in which they made it.

His gnarled fingers resting, with determined nonchalance, in his lap, Lincoln swung one foot stolidly, nervously, and said, "I appreciate any acting that's not too intelligent, Rathbone. Anything that don't make me think. It's the folly of wise men to figure out that, by tying their brains into knots, they're helping on the progress of a nation."

"You surely can't convince anybody nowadays that you haven't done so, Mr. Lincoln," Major Rathbone replied with speckless politeness.

"No, I can't," rejoined Lincoln, harsh and affable, "because I'm not going to try. Whatever profit I get from mankind's illusion in regard to me, I've earned. And I won't say it's altogether illusion, either. I've told the truth as often as I dared to, Rathbone, and I prefer it—in general—and that's a good deal more than can be said of most men who begin life in a legal way. I still believe in myself. Don't misunderstand that. But I don't know why I do. No man with anything more than sawdust in his cranium can believe in the value of his own efforts for any *reasonable* reason. But if he's done the best he knew how according to his own onery lights, I guess that will have to do for him. Now I'm quitting judicial meditations and beginning to enjoy myself. It's time—as Mrs. Lincoln will tell you."

"You will always be a great moral force for the nation, whether you acknowledge your power or not, Mr. Lincoln."

"Will I? Heaven forbid, Rathbone!" The President straightened himself suddenly. "On with the play then, as our friend Shakespeare says somewhere. You know there's only one kind of morality, anyhow—or all brands boiled down come to the same thing: Don't judge your neighbour. You may be just like him. I learned that in Kentucky when the ugliest folks of my acquaintance used to tell Pa what an unprepossessing boy I was. One thing you can put down for certain, however, is that I'm not tolerant. Whenever I catch anybody indulging in the kind of religion I don't agree with, I want to break his neck."

Mrs. Lincoln lifted her pearl-spoked fan and gently tapped his arm. "Abe, don't talk so loud. We're so conspicuous up here nobody will forgive you for distracting attention from the stage."

"Who says I'm not selfish, self-obsessed, and self-centred, Rathbone?" Lincoln whispered back over his shoulder.

Major Rathbone, smiling in a discreet silence, shook his head. There was a subdued tap on the door of the box. The major half rose in annoyance, when the same page who had brought Mrs. Lincoln the glass of water entered soundlessly.

The major hastened over the dim carpet and intercepted the boy as he approached the group. "What's this? Don't you know this is no time to interrupt us!"

On the stage, an absorbing dialogue was in progress between *Florence Trenchard* and *May Meredith*. Miss Keene's 'perfectly modulated' voice floated distinctly past the proscenium, and her clear tones seemed to occupy, as with a disembodied extension of her presence, every corner of the gloomy auditorium. The gas footlights were sizzling gently, and, behind their glazing radiations, the figures of the two actresses seemed *en bloc* with a vivid, glassy atmosphere, self-contained like the glass box of an aquarium. In their intimate apartness, the two women, luridly perceived, exposed, with monstrous impersonality, tense thoughts and feelings. The hushed listeners, equally without decency, were the passive party to all this stimulation of emotion done for effect. It had just occurred to Mr. Lincoln that people liked to see hearts broken and lives wrecked, even without the perfunctory reconciliations and amendments of the play, provided that in the case of real life, also, they have no responsibility for facing what comes after. No, he would probably go on until he died, like the old mare who went on forever in the shade of the same tree. He could not be spectacular. That someone called Lincoln had become so, left him not knowing where to turn. He was afraid of this thing.

The whisperings of Major Rathbone attracted his interest and he craned away from the brilliant simulacrum of an enclosure which held the two stilted actresses. What were Rathbone and that page 'gabbling' about?

The theatre was perfectly and oppressively still. From the blurred row-on-row of barely perceptible countenances, rigid in attention, emanated something avid, consuming, something which drew to itself ruthlessly all the spent energy of the play's performers, something which fed, parasitically, on torments it did not endure, on laughter that its dissolute, enormous passiveness could never generate. Mr. Lincoln had no exact name for the impression he was receiving, but it made him restless. He was too factual, too bleakly critical, and searching for the plain truth, to be able to get entirely inside this feeling. Except when witty remarks were spoken, he could not 'see much in it.' Yet it was there—something he found vaguely disturbing and offensive, in pleasure pursued too much like an earnest occupation, and for its own end. He could make out, in a seat just below him, a fat woman, staring, her mouth slack, her eyes made dazed and prideless by emotion. She would have been in more becoming surroundings, he thought, if she had been at home, sitting by the parlour lamp and doing knitting for her children. The thin one in muslin, giving the same rapt, self-exposing concentration to the stage, was certainly her daughter. Lincoln's underlip twisted rather cruelly, and he said to himself that both of them gave him the feeling of having detected them through a keyhole in some private act. He could not help resenting them. If he were able to feel as much as that—*if* he were able, any longer, after some years of hell that he remembered indistinctly, sentimentally—it would be in some mighty private place.

"Yes, sir, I know, sir. But he was so persistent, sir. I says to him I'd give you his card and you would know whether the President was receiving anybody or not."

Major Rathbone, talking *sotto voce*, had edged, on tiptoe, to the door, in which was cut a small, round hole that admitted a seepage of further light from the corridor. In the roseate semi-secrecy of the curtained box, he stood there peering, turning over the visiting card with which the page had presented him. "*Mr. John Wilkes Booth,*" he read, and, in decorous fury to the attendant whispered, "*Certainly* the President isn't receiving now! The man must be a fool. I never heard of such presumption in my life. What kind of an idiot are *you* to bring such a message—in the middle of the play, too!"

"I don't blame you, sir. But I don't know what to tell him, sir. I don't believe he's in his right mind, sir. He won't listen to nothin' and I says—"

The major interrupted. "Tell him anything you want to. Tell him he can go to the devil. *Damn* his presumption! He'll be *kicked* out if you can't get rid of him any other way. And you, too, mind you, boy. Why, it's perfect lunacy—and in the middle of a theatrical performance, for *this* triviality! He may thank his stars that the President merits some respect and that there are ladies present!"

Rathbone was so angered toward that 'upstart, that worn-out, third-rate actor, that poseur, Booth,' who had got himself introduced at the White House recently at a more or less public reception—'God knows how'—that he stumbled over a chair. The page boy darted out stealthily, no doubt escaping one wrath to encounter another. Rathbone returned to the sofa along the wall back of Miss Harris. From this deferential retreat he could study, at his leisure, his fiancée's 'striking' profile, under the wreath of smilax on her bandeaued hair. With a kind of modest enthusiasm she was watching the play, her lips parted, her beauty a delicately chiselled relief against the artificial brightness beyond her. Rathbone sighed correctly. She was undoubtedly the most charming and provocative woman in the world. And to think that miserable Booth expected to nose himself into *her* society. The man was a miserable cur who ought to be shot. His manners were so insufferable that no decent woman could afford to speak to him. And his opinions were treasonous—the mixture of effrontery and favour-seeking! But *look* at that girl—totally unconscious that I am feasting my eyes on her, Rathbone thought. She is as innocent as a child of ten and a brilliant little woman of the world, too. What a relief it will be when I am in a position to protect her! Oh, to hell with these petty interruptions! Even for the sake of President Lincoln I cannot waste time on these sordid incidents. Oh, if we were only alone! If the play would only last forever and I could see her looking like that—there—like she is now, with her hand pressed to her bosom—until my dying day!

.   .   .   .

In the corridor, Booth, fearful that he might be conspicuous to the theatre audience, had remembered to remove his hat. Now he was in an angle out of sight he put the hat on, to get it out of the way. But that did not suit him. His strong sense of the appropriate demanded it of him that he discard the grotesqueness of headgear, and go on to the deed he was about to perpetrate with brow bared as for some holy office.

To be rid of the page boy had required manoeuvring, and to coax the puzzled youth to let him wait here had cost just the sum that would buy privilege without arousing suspicion. The passage in which Booth stood led narrowly, with the illumination of two gas jets both turned very low, directly to the President's box. Surveying the whole ground, on first entering, behind the dress-circle, Booth had seen how he would plan this exactly. Softly, he advanced some paces. His shoes creaked disconcertingly.

At the saloon next to the theatre, he had taken, in the last hour, several drinks. Even these seemed to have ill prepared him for his enterprise. As many times as he had rehearsed his course, making certain of the very words he intended to shout out to the observers when the blow was struck, he could not overcome an impression of the oddity of the circumstance he was in, could not make himself familiar with his rôle. No, he could not believe—could not actually convince himself—that the hour had sounded which would commit him to murder—*the* murder—the *real* murder. Originally he had premeditated the assassination as occurring just as the President should be leaving the lobby to enter his carriage. The alteration in the decision put everything out.

Booth walked on, on tiptoe, once or twice glancing behind him to the closed door which gave egress to the auditorium. He could not sustain this caution. Either he must act recklessly, ignoring dangers and consequences, or he must give the whole thing up.

To admit that, already, the behaviour conditions demanded of him was that of a criminal, brought to an unendurable sum a list of humiliations extending far into the past. His talents slurred, the importance of his individuality treated as nothing, his conscientious effort to gain the prominence his worth deserved become excuse only for the gibes and triumphs of his inferiors, his longing for self-assertion had grown, as he was willing to admit to himself, fanatical. There were others whose early slights history recorded, who, by gestures against tyranny such as this he was contemplating, had forced public recognition, commanded an acknowledgment of their merits.

Several times, recently, various persons had tried to tell him of incidents that were to President Lincoln's credit. Booth had flown into a passion. The spectacle of Lincoln's power had demoralized the minds of the critics. Booth felt that he knew the world. He had conned all its hard lessons. And he had never seen any man rise to a position of despotic prominence through the approbation of a mob—and all crowds were 'mobs'—except by guile. Lincoln was not ingenuous. He had not been lifted to fame on the shoulders of others merely by serving a purpose which he did not suspect. Every step in his career, when examined, revealed the cautiousness of a shrewd mind. He had not been among the first to violently oppose Southern interests. Not he. Even after the war was a fact, he had remained reserved as to his personal bias toward its issues. But once those, whose idealism for the South exceeded the mean impulses of common sense, had thrown down the gauntlet, Lincoln had come forward just in time to benefit, through sage utterances entirely trite, from the follies of those higher-minded. Look at his shilly-shallying in the beginning! McClellan was half a Southerner in his beliefs anyhow. Had Lincoln dismissed McClellan peremptorily when the provocation had been ample, then the absolutism of his later behaviour might be said to have evolved consistently from his honest prejudices. But that was not the case. For at least two years, Lincoln had played at the game of war; and not until he had been forced to recognize the breach between North and South as final, and no gain to be had from straddling their view-points, the intolerance of both sides making compromise perilous—not until this state of affairs had developed had he shown anything like frankness or decisiveness.

Lincoln was now the hero of the emancipators; but where, in the entire course of Lincoln's career, had he displayed any of the mad sincerity of a John Brown! He had needed to be convinced that the South never would bear with him, before he had risked what he might have profited in that quarter, and come out baldly with the no-slavery slogan. He was the friend of the afflicted, was Mr. Lincoln—the new Immanuel, a second Christ! When Booth thought of the hideous, sacrilegious tributes now offered so fluently by the newspapers, his blood turned fiery. Did Jesus Christ, or would a true follower of Jesus Christ, sit by in all the comfortable security of a Presidential mansion, and see hundreds of thousands of lives destroyed, homes wrecked, innocent people left without any hope of sustenance! Had Jesus Christ been wor-

584

shipped by a Sherman or a Sheridan! Ah, yes, *they* worshipped Jesus Christ! They worshipped him as they revered a Lincoln! Farms burned, plantations uprooted, generations of toilers put at naught, men hanged or shot as spies for refusing to play traitor to all their loved traditions, women slain as well, virtue despoiled —and the Yankee soldiers, themselves no more than cannon-food for Grant's implacable ambition—that was the fact behind the program of regeneration! To hell with those who did not lick the boots of the Republican administration that had split a peaceful nation in two! Did Jesus Christ achieve the successful career of the American poor-white who climbs up to the top? *Did* he, I ask you, O my sapient friends and fellow countrymen? Did he propitiate this one and the other one? Did he sway gatherings, *not* by honest passion, nor by reason, but with mob oratory, cheap appeals to the 'honest' hearts of 'plain' men, funny stories, barroom anecdotes dressed up as parables? Far from being an example of the Master's teachings, he is not even a frank Pontius Pilate. It would lose him his position, if he washed his hands too openly! And this is no exaggeration, so help me God, Booth said to himself as he clenched his hands. Hate, hate, hate, and hate was courage. It was no shame to hate Lincoln, hate the very breath he breathed, for such hate as this was almost holy and made even murder 'right.'

Booth had exhausted himself with the meditation that, lasting seconds, had the importance of a century. He drove his nails into his palms, closed his eyes wearily, and leaned against the wall a space. But that very fickleness of public opinion, veering with each bombastic influence, how easily it could be turned against him now! What power these devilish people had! Fools were the rulers, fools always the tools of fools. Had they hearts? O God, God, God, had these people hearts—hearts for ever sealed against him in a stoniness of indifference that he could never penetrate? Through all of his years as an actor, he had tried to move these people. Now he *would* move them; by God, he would move them! He would slay their Lincoln! He would astonish them. He would arrest them. He would make himself memorable. If this is your idol, I destroy your idol! See—I spit on it! Death was too good for the man—and hatred—this hatred for an individual Booth had conversed with but once—approached sublimity. He was himself astounded by it. Its magnitude re-established him in his own

585

eyes. But he grudged Lincoln the fine end. These hands, these hands, these hands, he thought, looking down at his own hands, to be demolished, to leave themselves sacrifice—as if Lincoln and himself might be embraced together in one cavernous darkness. Yet he *had* to do it! Other men had come into recognition easily. Only of John Wilkes Booth had Fate, like a Shylock, required the last drop of blood in payment. And the soul spread out, for all the leering eyes, in awful nakedness.

Again time had only been a few minutes. It seemed to Booth that the cycles of years of misery dragged with him through the corridor. Had he made a mistake to swallow so much whisky? Was the false courage it engendered betraying him? Was he, who had never done a single soul a vital injury, to bear the penalty for every outrage left unpunished in the war? There was one way, one way. He must pretend that there was one way—that ahead. If these were his last moments they could not be soothing. He had to hug, not solace, but wretchedness and frenzy. It needed the fullest realization of the poor end left for his career. If he allowed himself to remember anything lovely, anything that might make life precious, he would recant everything and flee.

He was so giddy that the gas, flittering on the red wall, went for an instant, completely dark. He was alone in this darkness. He had always been alone. And this nakedness, which no close friendship protected, was what he must leave himself with before the crowd. For weeks, as he designed this, he had been obliged to act the part of the cold schemer, the wily hypocrite. And his mother might believe, if no one else did, that his longing, since childhood, had been to portray the *great* rôle, the fine rôle, the rôle in harmony with his self-esteem, despising cruelty, revering integrity.

"He that trusts to you, where he should find you lions, finds you hares; where foxes, geese." That was the mob, the typical audience; docile, chanting psalm-singers, prating from the gospels while they destroyed what they could never re-create! Lincolnites, damn them! Lincolnites! The 'demi-Atlas of this earth,' is he! Ha, Mr. Lincoln, you build your towers upon shifting sands! What I do for you today, they will do for your memory tomorrow—yea, as for *mine*, for *mine*. But you shall not be alone. We will be together, wiped out by Times's obliterating mark. Insulted by your *plain* men, your *common* men, your men with hearts of gold! The viler the object of your compassion, the more perfect the security from which you reach to extend your pity. You showed none for me, nor do I require your lenience. I am one of Nature's aristocrats! Your sheep, sprung full-fledged from the sheepfold—with rings in their noses for you to lead them by, they will have none of me. Their applause is something I can do without. I do not seek it now. Rather I seek their animosity. They cannot deny me their animosity. They have denied me a great deal, half starved me, made me ridiculous, odious, derided my exceedingly foolish desire to give them the best fruits of a long experience. But hatred they will give me in a plenty. I am an aristocrat, *not* through inherited privilege, not through the wielding of power and that accumulation of wealth by which you hope to make your children just the opposite of what you are yourself, the *common* man—but I am an aristocrat because it pleases me to be so. Because I would rather die—as I may die, O God, may I not die—and there are more, others, my friends in the South. Somewhere are those who will say Booth did nobly—some who love Booth, who will let Booth rest— in memory, memory—I am going under—will let Booth— But without any of your damned, sentimental pity! *Damn* your equals! He who is alone as I am *has* no equals. Damn those who parade equality, who cannot rise above your cloddish justice that levels, never lifts, but levels.

Booth staggered a little. He was almost at the end. The door of the box was straight before him. On the other side of the door was the stage, in progress on it the drama of a trivial comedienne, Miss Laura Keene—*Our American Cousin*—in the third act. Booth's skin was chill and damp. Soon he would be bereft of reason— *they*, waiting there to seize him, to carry reason away. The closer he drew—here—toward the conclusion of what had begun, the less he was attentive to Mr. Lincoln's hidden presence. The affair shrank—or expanded. There were two combatants: that familiar, faceless audience, of which Booth was becoming more and more agonizingly aware, and a figure apart, his own, that he saw distinctly as if before him, while it leaped from the box into the limelight not intended for it. Watching, watching, its inertia perfect, as incomprehensible to him today as at his tragic début before it, was the monster in the dim pit. Not one there would be for him. All were against him. He was so accustomed to expect that. There was a poison in his veins. *The poisoned Hercules,* he thought, and imagined the hairy cloak stripped from the defiled flesh, leaving the hero a thing of loathing. In the innocence of his early youth he had assumed in these people possibilities of comprehension. Since his first part taken, as a juvenile, in one of his father's plays, nothing he had ever had from them but had been bought with blood. The hollow character of that applause which had complimented his father's genius on so many nights, John Wilkes had once worshipped. But he had meant to exceed his father. He had tortured himself to *feel* more, to give to a rôle the very breath of his own existence. If sincerity is not genius, what *is* genius, he had thought. To realize that talent was a trick, that talent was specious, that talent considered the spectator always, played on him for an effect—that was not bearable. That made reward itself worthless, and for the shrewd, not the great. So fame was parcelled out. He knew it at last. He had been a fool. He who refuses to be base is a fool. He who rejects apprenticeship to claptrap is a fool. Suffering has no sanctification. The crowd asks not for genius but for amusement, for clowns , not actors. As art holds the mirror up to Nature, the crowd will shatter the glass that shows it its own image!

Booth halted. He stood on his toes, and gazed, through that little round of window in the door, at the back of some one's neck. It was the silhouette of Mr. Lincoln's head. Beside it, a little lower, were Mrs. Lincoln's broad, sloping shoulders, bare and pallid. Vaguely, somewhere over to the right, were other people— Major Rathbone, Miss Harris—the page had disclosed the names.

It was the stage that held Booth, and the wooden posturings of the two fashionably gowned women who occupied its centre. *He* could pour into a gesture, an assumed character, all the vivid elixir of misery! *He* did not need the latest Paris style to make a *man* of him!

In quick, bewildered retrospect, he turned to this and that evening when, even by violence, since he could not stir their sluggish souls in other ways, he had tried to compel *them* to admit that they were witnesses to *real* suffering, *real* pangs of sentiment. His sensibilities had always been his curse. In his boyhood, it had been his mother who had comforted him in his too great feeling.

"There's a great spirit gone! Thus did I desire it; What our contempts do often hurl from us, we wish it ours again." But they will never say that of me, he thought. No. I cannot wish it. Unless I despise the world utterly, I am unworthy of myself, unworthy of what I have to do, and I shall not be able to do it. "Conscience is but a word that cowards use . . . to keep the strong in awe. He was a fool for he would needs be virtuous. . . Fling away ambition. By that sin angels fell. . . . Now I am past all comforts here, but prayers."

His heart beat with dead, loud strokes, very briskly, as if the persons on the other side of the partition ought to hear it. And if nobody should ever know how it was with him, why do it, why destroy every last hope? What has got into a man when obscurity becomes humiliation? He could no longer understand people who lived on to the obscure grave with no desire for importance in the eyes of others. What curse was it that made a man care for accomplishment when every wit he had told him that his insignificance in the end was as sure as death itself, such men as he was never being at heart's ease while they beheld one greater than themselves. No—that was not the reason. It was certainly the lie he hated. His modesty was fierce now, like a flag. It was that they must respect—his modesty and his sincerity—if they accorded him nothing else. It was a poor thing to die for, he thought, that failure be not insulted. As time goes on, we propitiate. We take a little more, and a little more from our first perfect aspiration. " 'Tis slander whose edge is sharper than the sword." I could cut my own throat, he thought, and it would be all over—an honourable suicide. Oh, the fool, the fool, the fool! Their comment on him would never be any different. The *fool*, to feel. The *fool*, to admit feeling. The *fool*, to die singly for a defeated South. Yes, he had almost forgotten the South.

One, two, *three!* I must open the door. *I!* I am dying—in order that I make a clod immortal! If I did not kill him— Mother, mother! I can't do it! I can't do it! She's the only one who *would* know the things I loved and that they are none of them to be despised.

How often he had thought, If I had never cast these pearls before the swine that fill the theatres! If no one had ever heard the name of John Wilkes Booth! Was it this willless thing, an audience, that *made* a man, that confirmed him, so that until that confirmation was received the man was *not!* Was goodness, beauty, all comparable, all subject to the whim of a decision? Had a man nothing more than the fancies of numbers to live by? Was a god dependent on his congregations for the form he took?

He shivered superstitiously. Yes, God he himself did not question. He was *there*—between Mr. Lincoln and a cold infinity—must be. God, God, God, pity this 'assassin.' The word was murk in his mind. He heard it quoted. It impelled him to fling back the door and not hesitate any longer. A fatuous, artificial laughter—chimeric sound—gave him the proper conviction that this was a play without consequences. True, true, this was a world to be shunned—yet, *if* shunned—*what other?*

He pushed the door inward. It creaked slightly. The bleared, waiting audience was visible. It obliterated, with its inanition, JOHN WILKES BOOTH. This was indeed a fight for life. Booth was just behind the longish back of Lincoln's head. Shall I resign this flesh *to* you, and *for* you, he asked silently, trying to work himself up again to the same pitch. There is a power in wretchedness—there is a majesty in loathing—

But how was it to be done! Which hand first! Where was the pistol! If he aimed this close, he might shatter the man's whole skull. Or have you forgotten your own first days of ignominy, Mr. Lincoln? An empty belly is something none of us would boast about. Well, *I* boast about it! Do you hear me? Your vanity is pretty enough to screen itself. You can live *without* all the lickspittle admirations that are food and drink to you, can you! There are no closeted hours of writhing and agony for *you!* Nothing *you* would hide. How's that silly woman with you for the 'First Lady in the Land?' Your shame has to be complimented as well as your pride. I'm to kotow to *her* ilk, and bend the knee, am I! An uncultured oaf is to smirk his condescension on those that have served a Muse, and on the South where at least the Muse has been nurtured by lavish prosperity.

Booth could imagine how he looked, his hat—he had dropped his hat somewhere—his hair in a ragged mop, his eyes glittering. Crazed, crazed, they would think him crazed. But how to convey the dignity represented by this mad appearance. His consciousness of himself interfered with his motions. He was tortured by it,

590

brought risk by delay, did not know what to do next, and wished that some one were there to tell him if the time had come to fire the shot.

The shot, once it sounded, would bind him to haste. There would be no more hesitance—*never, never, until the grave received him, any more time for hesitance.* It would take people a second to digest the occurrence, when, with his knowledge of the theatre, he might, leaping to the wings, reach the street in safety. At the corner, just behind the stage door, he had left his horse tied. Payne, Atzerodt, Herold, Arnold, O'Laughlin, Dr. Mudd and Mrs. Surratt—Booth had plenty to co-operate with him in his escape. He would have preferred to do without them. Now he was glad. Out of a world in which lights would be quenched, there would still remain a few faces. He tried not to see them as unequal to great company. Herold would be waiting for him.

He entered the box. Then the one-minute before the too-late rose like a tangible thing in front of him and the next step to take. Nobody was aware of him. Too late, *for me, for me, for me*—he did not think about Mr. Lincoln. It was odd to be two: to be mad, and to contemplate one's madness. He had taken his pistol out and held it ready. For the longest moment on earth he was holding it before him, hearing, off somewhere, the tick of the trigger, and, simultaneously with the small noise, the brief *ploff* of report. The box was filled with smoke.

Booth ran to the front of the box. He had noticed, surely, Mr. Lincoln topple forward, and was astonished that nobody attempted to halt the assailant. Everything took a long time. It took a long time for people in the box to rise. He had placed his hand on the box-rail and braced himself for a vault over its side, when a woman not a foot away began to shriek at the top of her voice. Somebody else, with the grip of a man, caught hold of his arm. He jerked his stiletto—he had once meant to do the deed with this—out of his waistcoat pocket, and slashed with it at the awful hand—that was as if all of *them* were trying to hold him. It let go, and he jumped, just as he had meant to, but not caring where he landed. The pull of terror on his mind took every bit of sense of anything out of him. When he hit the stage, on his knee, the woman was still screaming. It was her cries that set him wild, every nerve of him demanding if anybody only *would* stop her, for God's sake stop her. It was then, to defy her, before she could make him lose his wits, he remembered to call out, "Sic semper tyrannis!" in a very loud voice, and felt heartened, as by something miraculous, that he could speak so clearly, could hear himself speaking so clear, despite all of them, despite any effort they could make to prevent the business, or keep him from driving into them, into their dull guts, all of its meaning. His right foot hung somewhere. He could not undo it. When he looked around, certain that nothing existed but the space in which he lay, the smell of dirty planks, the footlights that sputtered near him, he saw that what wrapped his foot and would not be kicked off was the flag hanging from the President's box. It was this noose of cambric that had made him fall so that he was almost on his face. He had to gain a little time, make himself think of doing something—that he was still moving and not lying here—and he shouted out, "Revenge for the South!"

The parquet below him had come to life. "Catch him! Hang him!" they were crying. And again, "Hang him! Hang the traitor!" His mind seemed to grow weak and all its visions pale, as he kicked with his leg hung above him in the loop. There was nothing more to think about, ever, than that damned cotton holding him to judgment. The stage seemed to become crowded, and there was shrill chattering; but nobody came nearer. Then he knew they *were* coming near him. Trains of women's skirts brushed in a silk foam very close, level with his eyes. Feet were running. The auditorium was filled with the blurred discourse of many speaking together. A shout from the gallery came down like a hoarse waft from a bellows. "Grab him! Hang the skunk!" Multitudes were talking under a dark sea. They were talking around him. The black tide of their mingled voices inundated him, leaving him mysteriously unscathed. As the tumult grew into a very soaring, some scattered lights blazed to the left, to make the distance vaster, his place here on the footboards more remote. The screams of the woman in the box persisted. They shrilled in his brain and made little specks of bright, piercing attention in the undifferentiated sense of an agglomerate. A pain clutched him in the knee and hip. He pushed his foot out with a lunging motion, and the cloth tore. The hurt to his leg made him faint, but something stupid, more intense than pain urged him to despise the leg, to let his will ride high on its very injury.

592

Stilted on the pain, he darted toward the wings. People did not pursue him, *things* pursued him. He saw a vacancy—*door*. There was the limed, brick wall of another corridor. As though his own excitement were the contagion that spread, that woman, stabbing his soul with her cries, was joined by other women. "Hang him! Hang him! Oh, the beast! The coward!" The cries flew along in the corridor, the damned things echoing fainter in the corridor that was of white, blind brick, and smelt dusty like a vault. But he found a second-self, hiding in the old one, and it made the miracle of his dead leg bending and running, of his face that he had almost forgotten the look of, but must be queer with the dirt of the floor all over his clothes. The damned women wailed farther off, and the turgid rage of the men muttered farther off, and he went down some dirty steps, and there was a split-bottomed chair at the door which frightened him by being empty—he had expected the doorkeeper—and he went into the street, out of *hell*.

The street was like death. Just around the corner were some horses, were two or three carriages, the coachmen somewhere while the play was on. The slight trees waited ahead of him, waiting stiffly for him to run by. The stars were yonder, shining over the country, waiting for him to find Herold with the horses and ride out into the country. But nothing was the same. Something regretted stayed there behind him in that clamorous house. His right to freedom—nobody had ever dared, technically, to bring a thing against him—stayed there in the theatre. They had robbed him. Even here at last they had robbed him. Lincoln was, by this, surrounded by commiserators. Was that man never to pay *anything* for what he had got? Booth's leg was a torture so long drawn he could not conceive of ever escaping it. Maybe they would take his life, as well, sparing him not so much as *that* wretched remnant. Always, they had had the whole; he, nothing. The nothing was laid before him in the dull lane of the street, the houses, that had nothing for him, warm with their lamps shining out on the spring night. The nothing was so immense that the distance of the stars did not impress or comfort, did not so much as diminish *them*. If Lincoln was *dead*, they would acclaim him. Or was he dead? Booth could not be certain. All had transpired too quickly. Yet that was the most he had to carry with him for hope, as he sped the length of the block and turned around the corner. He was not thankful for Herold's presence. What good did that do? He was alone with the one preciousness of his own life to guard for what it was worth. And that so little, little. How could revenge be sought upon a man whose life was worth so little? His limp seemed to him to conclude the rest despicably. But, because it would please *them*, because *he* was what they hunted, the distraught beasts, he was not going to yield. Nobody was going to see *him* die. See *him, John Wilkes Booth*, while the image of their Lincoln stood between him and them and protected his privacy. If he had a chance, he would write his story down. Then somewhere an eye—looking out with pity—or *contempt*—rather be forgotten than brave the contempt—would read—oh, God knows what! God knows what—what is? Anyway it would not be as *they* set forth the truth. It was worth that— JOHN WILKES BOOTH—like a word of loathing, blazoned on their minds, on the noncommittal sky. Trapped as a rat he might be, but the death-blow that could come from his own hands did not frighten him so much. Until then—*then*— Christ, his leg was aching! He had never been very good at bearing bodily pain. But he was too good to go under—not without fight.

XX

*THE Emperor Napoleon, who is now on a visit to Algeria,
expressed himself as greatly pleased by the peaceful and
prosperous conditions in the colonies, and has issued a proclamation to the Arabs containing instructions to duty and submission
based on the teachings of the Koran.*

*Mr. Jefferson Davis, one-time president of the Confederate
States of America, has been surprised in hiding and captured by
a contingent of Federal cavalry, who, under instructions from
those suspecting his whereabouts, came upon him in a farmhouse
near Irwinsville, Georgia. Accompanied by his family, he has been
concealed there for many weeks, his identity screened by the connivance of a small group of sympathizers with his vanquished
cause. These, as well as Mr. Davis, are now under arrest and await
trial on a charge of treasonous conspiracy against the United States
Government.*

*This morning, at eighteen minutes past one o'clock, her Royal
Highness the Princess of Wales was safely delivered of a son who
is to be called Prince George.*

*The last of the Confederate generals, Kirby Smith, has now
surrendered, and his delayed submission has brought the war of
secession to its final chapter.*

*In the railway accident between Shrewsbury and Chester, imme-
diate assistance was given to the wounded passengers by those who
avoided injury in the catastrophe. Mr. Charles Dickens and Mr.
S. Rea of the "Illustrated News" were among those well known
persons who volunteered aid to the more unfortunate.*

*Earl Russell let it be known to the Geographical Society that
Mr. Baker had succeeded in discovering the second great source of*

595

*the Nile, not less important than the Victoria Nyanza of Speke.
. . . This second and main source of the Nile is at Lake Albert
Nyanza, north latitude 2° 17'. . . . The business of its location
which has engaged our explorers over such a long period will give
those who have succeeded a just fame. . . . As the confirmation
of each successively conjectured fact removes some of the glamour
from the romance of antiquity, it brings compensation in opportunity for the dissemination of peaceful arts and cultures. Our
grasp on the realities of the known world is constantly and rapidly increasing. Even the dream of discovering the poles begins to
seem to us a likely achievement. Scientific exactitude combined
with pluck and the spirit of adventure are working in unison to
establish for man that familiarity with the surrounding earth which
abolishes superstition. The conquest of wild Nature with the understanding of her laws supply the firm base for racial concords.
We begin to look forward with assurance on an epoch of peace
and good will among nations. Certainly, in contradiction of the
dogmatic controversies that have stirred England during the last
decade, evidence of an All-Wise Intelligence is much clearer now
than it was a generation ago, when the desire to locate causes,
whether of the flow of the Nile or of the forces which propel mankind to action, was condemned as an urge from the promptings of
his Satanic Majesty. . . .*

II

Harry must have been in great pain. It had come upon her as
a shock. She had concurred in his suggestion that she sleep alone,
and had been resting on the green baize sofa in the parlour, did
not mind a bit. But she had been aroused in the small hours of
the morning by Harry's groaning. "Harry!" she had cried, her
heart tightening with a kind of resentment that, before she had
come in here to sleep, he had made so light of his condition. "What
is it, Harry?" she had called. He had been slow to answer, and she
had not waited to find her slippers. She had not been able to find
the candle or the matches, either. And when at last she did, and
the candle flame made his huddled body frighteningly distinct, he
must have pretended sleep. "Were you groaning, Harry?" "No,"
he had said, crossly, "I wasn't groaning. Why did you wake
me up?"

596

"You *were* groaning," she had said. But he had answered that it was a bad dream, he guessed.

Harry had always told Midge that she was 'sensational.' Remembering that, she had gone back to the sofa, shamed, and had tried to quiet her uneasiness. It was so wonderful to have him home again. She meant to do every single thing that would please him. In the past she had not always been so conciliatory. But she had learned her 'lesson.' Harry really underrated her. He did not know how much she loved him. She was going to show him that the harassing experiences of the years of war had made her adult and responsible at last.

Yet she had lain awake, wondering. Yesterday, when the doctor had talked to Harry, he had asked her to leave the room. No, he was groaning again. She was certain! But she was afraid to return there to disturb him. And she was afraid to go to sleep. It seemed wicked to go to sleep. She wanted to be his 'noble little comforter.' He had once called her that. O Harry, Harry, Harry, she had cried, sobbing and pitying herself, I want to be your noble little comforter!

Daylight arrived at last. Midge had waited for it until every bone ached. She was so tired that she could have wailed in misery. Harry must have rested after all, he had, during the last hour, breathed so quietly. She wanted to hide herself from the slow sun as it tingled on the parlour wall. Duty would not permit it. She must make Harry comfortable, make every sacrifice.

When she had risen and put on her puce, trying to look neat for him, and had smoothed her hair, she went, not even stopping to wash her face—more virtuous because she did not wash her face—into the bedroom; and to the bed. Harry was sitting up. His face looked drawn, but he smiled. Yet she could not get over the suspicion that he was being secretive. If he had not been ill, she would have reproached him. Surely she had not deserved to lose his confidence!

Her love was just more than she could bear. That was the truth. She went about the house, and to the kitchen to prepare the breakfast, and every minute she had to fight against the desire to burst into tears, to abandon all effort and cry and cry—or to go to sleep again. Harry did not understand her. By being mysterious about his state of health, he increased her anxiety. It was the same about money. She knew he must be worrying about that.

At twelve there was the visit of the doctor again. He came in gruffly. His rather cross manner shook the last of her self-reliance. She was bearing more than anybody ever had in the world, and even the doctor had no consideration for her. In a sense, she had more to bear than Harry. Harry was incapable of doing anything for himself, and had nothing to do but to lie there and be ill. Oh, it was selfish, it was selfish! But she wished that she were ill, to lie there by Harry. She wanted to lie down close to him, resting peacefully, breathing his breath, leaning upon his breast, and trusting to him completely as she had been used to lean.

The doctor stayed a long time. When he was leaving, he called Midge from the dining-room. He wanted to speak to her. He was more deferential to her now. He looked at her coldly and professionally, but rather pityingly. She hated him. His compassion, so grudging, was the symptom of some power he had over her, over Harry's life. But she was obliged to listen. She gazed downward at the carpet and bit her lips.

"Mrs. Lamb, I don't think you ought to be kept in the dark as to your husband's real condition any longer. I don't think you should dissuade him from going to the hospital. He holds out against an operation so far, but if you don't do your best to make him have it, I can't answer for the result."

Midge was offended, terribly offended, for Harry had never spoken to her frankly. Of course when the case was put to her like this she would urge him to go. She was enduring such agony as this cold, hard man could never dream of, but for Harry's recovery she was willing to make any sacrifice.

When the doctor had departed, Midge retired to the kitchen again, and had her 'good cry.' Nothing would matter, no loneliness, no disappointment, if she could save Harry.

She was weak when she saw him, but concealed it. Approaching the bed, she patted his arm. She wanted to tell Harry that he must have the operation, but she did not know how to bring it up. "Harry," she said, after a while, "you must not be stubborn. The doctor has told me you must have that operation. You mustn't keep things back." And she glanced at him a little guiltily. She could see that he was angry because the doctor had appealed to

598

her. That made her glad. Harry, Harry, she was thinking, you must get well! No doctor, no dictate of science, could keep them apart. She was very gentle with him, smoothing his pillows, urging him to drink his broth. But when she became too attentive, too solicitous, he grew irritable. He was cross, then apologized. At last he said he wanted to be alone. He wanted to sleep a little. She went away and left him, and let him sleep. But when she peered through the opened door into the darkened room, some time later, she was certain, though she did not dare to ask him, that he lay awake.

When she came back after a couple of hours, he said, "Well, I suppose you and Dr. Smith are right, Midge. I'll have the operation. We'll make the arrangements when he comes tomorrow, but let's don't talk about it now. I know I'm hard to live with, but when I'm well again, my poor little girl, you'll find I'm just as nice as I used to be."

Midge knelt beside him and embraced him. How could he imagine that she ever doubted him! She showed him the love in her tearful eyes. "Darling, darling Harry! I shall be very angry if you talk like that. You don't know what heaven it is to have you back!"

He answered her brave smile, but his brows twitched nervously. She was uncomfortable. Perhaps he lacked the strength for the ardent caresses she still demanded. She felt ashamed, and went away again. No, she would not resent. She fought with herself, with the hurt in her heart. No, she would not resent it. And she remained very resolute about the hospital.

Three days later, all had been arranged, and Harry was prepared to go. She hoped, sadly, that the doctor realized what her courageousness was costing her. But *he* saw the matter only professionally, and of course would not. A carriage came to take Harry away. Before the parting, there was a tender passage between them. "I wouldn't have the grit to go through with it if it wasn't for you, darling," Harry said. "The last year has worn me out. I don't think I'm any weaker fibred than the others, but the last part of the war used me up. And this thing is the result of the bullet they couldn't find, of course. Well, if I ever do get well, I'll want to spend my last days in peace—peace with you, Midge. But don't come with me to the hospital, Midgie," he had added.

599

"This time I've got to be selfish. I won't have an ounce of energy to spare, and can't even give the proper thought to you. Heaven grant that you get along all right without me."

She smiled at him. All through that last hour she smiled at him, forgetting, however, to answer his words, not hearing half he said, only seeing that Harry, Harry was going from her—and perhaps forever. But she would not say it was forever. She would not believe that. To admit even such a possibility seemed treacherous. Harry had said that her faith in him, in his return, had taken him through the war.

Oh, the war, the war, how she had hated it! And now, thank God, the war was ended. Harry had come back!

Yet in the final moment, at the door, after she had carried the pillows to the carriage, and had helped Harry in—poor Harry whom she had always thought so strong, and who was now so weak—she had to flee from the spectacle of his departure. In the midst of the gesture of waving, while she tried to leave him with a cheerful impression of her—as though her heart were not broken and this hell—she had lost her self-control utterly. She had not been able to call 'Good-bye.' Despite everything she had intended, he had seen how much she was affected, and had gone away with *that!* She was in such utter misery when she was left alone that she wanted to die. O God, O God, let Harry live!

She could not endure being alone. She put on her shawl and bonnet, and, excusing herself, because Harry did not like to have her talk about his illness, she went out. She went to see Cora Spearing, Dulcey West and Fanny McCarthy. She had to talk about Harry. She could feel her eyes burning with a queer, prickly brilliance, and realized that she was feverish. It was as if she expected her friends to *do* something—save her, save Harry. As she discussed the matter with them, and they were all politely sympathetic, she was convinced that they did not comprehend her, that they did not know what she meant. She went home. She was humiliated, having exposed to others something private, something they must find incredible. But she was *not* hopeless. She knelt down by the bed and prayed. It was God that people went to in these awful troubles. God must understand her. And as she prayed, and prayed, petitioning God in a very heart-felt way, she felt a sudden leap of hope.

Afterward, she rose and threw herself upon the coverlids and pillows Harry's form had pressed. They were cold, yet, in them, she discovered the faint scent of his body. She hugged the pillows to her, wept in them voluptuously. Then she went to sleep.

In the morning, when her eyes had opened of themselves, she was conscious, instantly, of a menace. She could not remember what it was that threatened. She *would* not remember. She tried to draw numbness again upon her. But it was impossible. Sleep left her like a blessing gone forever, and the facts presented themselves unequivocally. Harry was in the hospital. This was the day for Harry's operation. By the evening, perhaps the doctor would be able to tell her whether Harry would get well or not.

She tried to eat her breakfast. No use. There was very little money in the house, very little in her purse. The sum from the bank was running very low. She had refused to tell Harry. She had wished, maybe, to martyrize herself a little. Anyway, she couldn't eat. Noon came and food sickened her more than ever. Then began a kind of pressure on her mind. She had thought all there was to think, all that she could bear to think—and she went on thinking. All at once she cried aloud. Her fists were clenched. She struck at her forehead and beat her bosom, and felt a kind of stolid wonder at the way she was behaving. "God," she insisted, calling aloud, *"don't* let me think!" She wanted to send a messenger to the hospital and she did not dare.

At three o'clock, when she had decided to go herself, there was a knock at the door. A boy sent by Dr. Smith had brought a note. She took it avidly, then slammed the door on him. When he had departed, she regretted this. Perhaps an answer would be needed. She must call him back.

Then she read the message. The operation was over. Harry was resting fairly comfortably. But she had better wait until the next morning before she went to see him.

She sat a long time with the message in her lap. Sometimes she would feel that she couldn't understand it, sometimes that it meant one thing, again, another. And how could she bear it till the morning—bear another night! Yet for three years of the war she had borne this, borne constant anxiety. And Harry had been wounded once. She had been obliged to think of him away from her in the Libby Prison. Then the end of the war had come, he had been liberated. No joy could equal what she had felt on seeing him once more. As he had recounted to her the horrors of his experience, what he had been through had only seemed to enhance the miracle of his survival. In the Libby Prison there had been three hundred and forty-four deaths in one month. The water the prisoners had to drink had been full of garbage. She had been able to imagine the three-story brick warehouse, the barnlike rooms—whole companies packed together, not space to walk about in comfortably or to sleep in at night, the open sink in the floor in its puddle of filth. Harry had survived all that. She had to be hopeful.

That night, Midge went to bed very early, almost as soon as it was dark. Sleep would not come. There was a grey, taut aliveness in her mind. Horrible impressions moved there. She drew together her eyelids, as if, drawing the blinds of a habitation, she shut everything out. She couldn't sleep. At moments she was languorously certain of Harry's nearness. She believed he was beside her on the bed, and that she might stretch forth her hand and feel his arm. But that was not true.

Before the sun was up the next day, she had risen and dressed herself. It was wonderful to ascertain, as she did now, surely, that she had not a single thought or desire in the world which exceeded her longing for Harry's recovery. The completeness of her wish, excluding all others, made her think she must have become worthy of an answer to her prayers. God would help her.

Overcoming even her fears for his safety, her desire to see him and be with him made her happy as the hours passed. She would see him soon, and that was all she cared about.

She had just stepped out on the porch, when she saw a man walking quickly along the street, which had, as yet, few passers-by. He veered and, to her surprise, came into the yard. "Mrs. Lamb?" he asked. She had waited for him stupidly, hating to see him come, refusing to ponder on why he came. She could not speak to him. Terrible shame of her weakness, of the foolish state of her emotions, made it impossible for her to say anything to him. He handed her a folded paper. She took it and learned that she was to come to the military hospital at once. Harry was worse. The man who delivered the message had, she thought, looked at her queerly. And he seemed anxious to get away.

She allowed him to pass out of her sight. Then she rushed to lock the house, and to hasten as quickly as she could after the man. As she went along she was furtive, dodging the expectation of meeting any one who knew her. No, certainly, she could not bear this any more. Her legs were about to sink under her. Her whole thought was one moan of protest against being required to suffer any longer. She had no clear meditations of any kind.

How she hated the hospital lawn, the clean path, the wide steps! She opened the glass front door as if it were against her will, as if she were doing something that every atom of her being protested against. Yet she was going to Harry. She wanted to ignore all intermediaries and run past every one, up the stairs to the floor above, to the room where she thought he must be. She wanted Harry to live, but herself to lie down at his feet and die, if need be, that she might rest. Oh, to see Harry living, warm, ready to embrace her—and never to think again! How could she keep cold and composed, even if she saw him? How could she, as she suspected he wished, demand nothing of his failing energy? He *must* still yield to her the strength to give her just a little, little comfort.

A man in a white jacket stopped her. She had to sit down on a stiff chair and wait and wait, while people talked about her. She had nearly collapsed. Then she saw Dr. Smith coming down the stairs. Her hatred of him flared up, and she felt the indignity of having to restrain herself meekly to hear whatever he had to tell her—*first*, before she had seen Harry.

He approached her very slowly. He took a year to cross the hall. In her impatience she started up. Whatever he said—it would kill her.

"My dear madam—my dear Mrs. Lamb—I regret to tell you— I am sorry to say—" And he finished, lamely, as if embarrassed, "Your husband did not rally as we had hoped, ma'm. He just passed away—very quietly. Thank Heaven, the introduction of ether has saved a lot of unnecessary suffering." He stopped.

Midge did not understand him at once. Then it came over her gradually, the meaning of all his cold, hateful face. She decided to kill herself—as if that settled it. But she was too weak. She sat down on the edge of the chair. She tried to ask him some questions. She was too ashamed, the tears at last brimming over her eyes.

Harry was upstairs. That was the fact that came through at last.

Harry was upstairs, and she must see him. She demanded it. She suspected it of the doctor that he would not allow her to see Harry. He bowed gravely. Several hospital attendants were in the hall. They were watching her. She refused to care or to be deflected. The doctor called to some one and asked him to show her upstairs. To her astonishment, the doctor seemed grieved. His face was honestly troubled. She was jealous of that. He had no right to be. Something upstairs was somehow to contradict everything the doctor said.

On the way, she was faint again. And when they came to the open door of the room, *his* room, she thought—NO! And there was a terrible cry in her against thinking or accepting at all what she had to see or these others say to her. She went in. Somebody was under the cover. His face was not covered and he looked as usual—almost. She went up to him. Harry, Harry, Harry! It was true. She had seen it! Oh, if only she had not come! If only she could go back and live everything over so that this need not happen! Harry, Harry, Harry! She gazed at him. She knelt, quivering, put her hand out and touched his. What was the matter with him! He gazed at her as through a silken veil. What had they done to him! She wanted to help Harry. He must not be dead. He was too calm.

They were making her betray him, because he was like this. She did not want to leave. The attendant spoke to her, but she would not leave. She clung with both her hands to the cold one that did not respond, that was not as stiff as she had heard the hands of dead people would be. She wanted to creep into the bed beside him. All the times she had lain beside him and he had made her warm, because she had trusted him so. All through the war she had kept her faith that he would come back sound. She had not dared to lose it. "Harry!"

The attendant believed she should go. They half carried her away, but her whole being and everything that desired life stayed behind. What did it mean? What, *what* did death mean? It meant so nearly nothing at all. It was so senseless. She wanted to be unconscious. But then they might never let her see Harry again. In the end she must have fainted.

When Midge was at home, after the nightmare, after the delirium, she thought, And Harry was three years in the war. This
604

might have happened at any time. But it hadn't happened. Then why had it happened now?

Dulcey West came to sit with her. Harry's body was downstairs, but Midge did not rise to see it. She lacked the strength to do so. And it was terrible to have Dulcey there all the time, watching, kind, considerate, more affectionate than she had ever been, and so, in some especial way, confirming *it*—it *was* so. Midge would moan, when Dulcey left the room, hoping that Dulcey would not come back. But the bond between Midge and Harry was stronger than ever. His death had made everything between them real and almost violent. A spiritual emanation from the body below associated itself with everything she and Harry ever had said or thought. When Dulcey came in, Midge turned her face from the light. There was something luxurious in grief. She wanted it alone. She wanted to live completely in her private thought of Harry and no other.

The funeral, she dreaded. She tried to shut out from her mind her knowledge that it was going on. That was impossible. People walked about downstairs. There was a sound of singing. My God, it *was* a fact!

She sprang from the bed, tried to reach the door, screamed. Dulcey heard her. Dulcey was there holding her. Midge wanted to sink through the floor. Why won't she leave me! Oh, don't she see, *see* that I can't bear it! But Dulcey was only trying to be kind.

Midge lay down again, quietly. They are taking him out, she thought. They are in the hall, at the front door, on the porch! Her nails dug through into her palm. She felt the hurt and wished it more. Her head, thrown back on the pillow, moved from side to side. Then she was still. *All* gone. But the war was over. It couldn't be!

Suddenly, she was angry. All these four years they'd been killing people, and not before had she been allowed to comprehend what they were doing. She lay there years. Dulcey lifted the shades a little—as if it were *safe*, now, to let her look out. "Dear Midge, if there is anything I can do for you, I will be downstairs."

Midge did not answer. She lay there weak.

Another day and another day passed. No use protesting. He was buried. They had put him in the earth that crumbled with him, that mouldered—until he vanished. But she herself, she considered amazedly, would sometime come to that, too. Then she was so afraid that she scarcely dared stir. And of what use the long effort to live with death the only answer, the irrefutable answer. Trying to imagine herself dead, she fretted. She could not. Only there *was* a creeping horror. That was true. The horror stood just there. She might pretend all her life to ignore it, but it was waiting for her. Then how was it people dared to think of other things, and to pretend? Lincoln was dead. Lincoln had been assassinated. That had made small impression on her. Now it meant something. Was he with Harry? And all the soldiers that the war had killed, were they with Harry? All the men who had died in Libby Prison, were they with Harry? The number of the dead became so vast that she was resentful of it, of this solemn ambiguity which Harry could interpret—she, *never*.

Because she could not apperceive death, organize it, relate it to anything else—even her own mood being too large and vague—she took to discounting its presence. A week went by, and she was still occupied with her grief. It left her no energy for another thought. Dulcey had moved over temporarily and kept house for her; but Midge was too indifferent to show more than a perfunctory gratitude. Harry, darling Harry! Protecting herself and defying death, Midge indulged her memory. She and Harry were the dearest lovers ever had been. No two people had ever been such dear good lovers or loved each other so. She tossed, because she could not sleep, and made the pillows hot. Yet it was very satisfying to lie as she did without a shadow or cloud on all her recollections. She fed memory so lavishly that the past was keener than the present. She never wanted to rise from her bed again. Sometimes a smile lay on her hot, parted mouth. But she was jealous of the years he had spent in the war. She used to hate them. She hated them more every day. That was the one time that she could not remedy. Still, *she* had conquered. The commanders of Harry's regiment had received only his proud gestures of submission to duty. The rest belonged to her. After a while, even the body in the grave did not trouble her very much. Harry was in the cemetery sleeping, dreaming of her as she of him. They were both sleeping. The world itself, with its crazy dreams, was only asleep. And later, in the dimness of her mind where lay the future, they would both wake up.

Three weeks after Harry's funeral, Dulcey resigned the housekeeping and went home to her husband. He and she, Dulcey said, were worried about Midge. A lawyer had come after Harry had been buried, and had read the will. There was not much money in the bank. The house that Midge was residing in was mortgaged. Hating them all for reminding her that she had to live again, Midge got up.

Why had they not allowed her to fade away peacefully?

Harry had certainly left her very little. She was surprised that he had not provided for her any better. It seemed that *he* might have thought ahead and have allotted her the money to sustain her while she indulged her sorrow. The lawyer assured her that, as a soldier's widow, the widow of Lieutenant Harry Lamb, she would receive a pension. But the payments hung fire. There was much red tape. Dulcey suggested that, to make her living, Midge try dressmaking. Midge felt it unkind of Dulcey to insist on effort of any kind. People did not realize what grief did to you. Dulcey was irritated. Midge, she said, was growing selfish in her sorrow. They quarrelled acidly with one another. Dulcey went away. Afterward, she wrote a note, and apologized to Midge. But the apology was rather stilted. Midge was in the wrong. Dulcey pitied her, but took nothing back.

And Midge began to get up and go to bed and do her housework wearily, having now so much less time to devote to thoughts of Harry.

One day she had a relapse. A fleshly sense of Harry's presence and his old attraction for her became so dominant that it was, she understood, indecent. It seemed to her that she was going mad. She saw that she could not be responsible to the proprieties if he did not come back.

This, also, passed. But Harry had loved her. Even while at war he had protected her. There were bills to pay. The government still delayed the pension. It did not seem to comprehend what she had given up for it.

Having to confront creditors, Midge felt degraded. Harry had not left her enough to allow her to make her regret for him entirely beautiful. Grief was disturbed, her mood was distorted by these leering mundane intrusions.

In June, she had made no further attempt to secure dressmaking. She had scarcely the money to buy her food; and she decided for the second time that she would kill herself. Yet she could not bring herself to do so. Harry's memory was lovely. Her feeling for Harry was still so lovely. When she contemplated a violence against her person all became too grotesque.

There was Harry's Uncle William Logan. He and Harry had quarrelled about the issues of the war, and, Harry admitted, they had insulted one another. Uncle William Logan wrote Midge a letter of commiseration. He offered Midge his hospitality. He ignored it that Harry had called him a 'devious old skinflint,' and had expressed a determination never to see his face. Uncle William had not wished Midge and Harry to be married, either.

But, when she read the letter, she forgave him. She had no family of her own, and she required *somebody*. She prayed all the time that Harry would understand her motives and that he would forgive her for not resenting Uncle William more. But she was too weak to earn her living—oh, so very weak! And she could not resent. So much of her strength had gone to loving Harry that she could resent nobody. Uncle William wanted to come to see her. She wrote and told him that she would be very pleased to see him. She felt very guilty. But she was so tired that she was nearly dead, and could hate nobody.

Uncle William was the only one who offered her a home. The house she was in, alone, seemed filled with the life that she and Harry had once lived in it. It was more than she could bear. If she were ever to be able to exist again, she must leave this house.

The day Uncle William was expected, she was more nervous than usual. And she was so sorry for herself that she wept constantly and silently. She wondered how, when she had to speak to him of Harry, she would ever be able to control her voice. Harry was so proud, so reserved, so obstinate in his opinion. Would he have rebuked her for admitting Uncle William? She would not allow it. The meeting with Uncle William, whom she needed, should not destroy the blessed harmony and sacredness of all she felt for Harry.

Uncle William was expected at one o'clock. She had not gone to the depot to meet him, but she was on the porch when he appeared. And she had tried to make her mourning neat and attractive. He must not suspect that she held it against him that he had disagreed with Harry.

It was a bright, still day in June. Uncle William did not come from the station in a hack, but came into view walking, carrying his carpet-bag himself. Harry had always said that Uncle William thought more of the money he was losing in the war than of wrong or right. Unlike so many Northern manufacturers, Uncle William had lost money. But he had no family, and he had enough. Midge, as she hesitated, watching his approach, was determined to feel no repugnance to him or his point of view. He was blunt, and honest, if not, like Harry, altogether noble.

She met him at the gate. He glanced at her mourning, as if seeing it apart from her; and seemed confused. But she smiled. She appreciated his kindness to her; and because he seemed to regret the harshness he had shown to Harry, she determined to be good to him.

It was not until she had served his dinner to him, that they spoke of money. Then he brought it up. "From what I can hear, Harry didn't leave you very well provided for," Uncle William said. "His country owes you a lot of money, but from what I can learn of government tactics in such matters you will have to wait to get it. So that's why I wrote to you with the suggestion you keep house for me. You can stay on if you like it, and if you don't, when you get your pension started or some work to do, you can give it up. Harry, I believe," Uncle William added sourly, "thought you never ought to learn to work."

She braced herself to withstand, and not to be entirely thrown off her balance by his ungracious manner. He had a hard, curt face, but his eyes, as she realized them scrutinizing her sharply, did not look unkind. She said, "I have decided to accept your offer, Uncle William. I *must* do something to support myself. There's no question of that."

She felt her own pathos strongly, but she saw, in an instant, that he was much too calloused to be rebuked by it.

When all had been discussed between them, circumspectly, and Uncle William had gone to his room to take a nap, she went to her room. Then she saw that, greater than her fear of death, was the fear that Dulcey's words had given her of being poor and hungry. Harry had always called her charming, always called her pretty, always called her dainty. And if she became a drab, if she slaved, if she went on from irksome day to irksome day, in this obscurity, she gave Harry up. Harry loved her. He wanted her to be happy. She would not be pleasing her beloved Harry if she clung to misery. And, oh, the blessed relief of a soul to turn to—even Uncle William!

She lay down on the bed and thought a minute. Then she sprang up. She was mad. Because she could not remain alone in this house with her grief forever, she had accepted readily the overtures of an Uncle William who was Harry's enemy, who hated him, wanted to use her, and came here to gloat. But, for a mere occupation, merely to earn her bread and butter, she had not the courage to live. She could not be alone any more. She, who had been accustomed to so much love, she could not go on destitute in this empty universe. She loved Harry, she loved Harry. No one need dare imply to her that she did not love him just as ardently. It was a horrible revelation. She loved Harry, and yet, for the sake of her own flesh, her fear of hunger, her own physical indulgence, she would sell herself to Harry's enemy. She had never felt truly religious before. If this were all— Harry was more than that! Or she was, then, so much less than Harry? Her love was spoiled. Her love was ruined. She had outraged love. She had insulted it.

But, all the time, while she protested, she knew that she was going. Her grief had consumed her, and she would be dead if she stayed in this house of misery for another two months. Oh, the luxury of a dependence, the luxury of a dependence, the luxury of somebody to whom she could talk! To talk to somebody, to rest on the will of somebody, she would betray Harry.

Either they're mad, or I'm mad, she thought, as she remembered the war and the high-flown talk about it. It was as if she had just understood the Libby Prison. If men were like this—if men were like herself—they were not worth saving.

She kept beating with her mind, pressing on this fact of the Libby Prison—all the other facts that had meant so little to her— and they were now hard and true, like the new fact of herself, on which her heart, as if not already broken, seemed to burst again. She was crazy. This dull impression of her sanity must be just craziness. Either she was mad or the rest were mad. They did not believe in death. Then what was it that had been done to her alone, that obliged her belief? She, who had the greatest reason of them all for not believing? But it was just the reason that had convinced her. She had lost Harry. It came over her again fresh, as if she had never comprehended it before. She had lost her Harry. There was no waking up.

The world was like Gomorrah burning. If she had a voice that could go farther than other voices! If her mind could only send forth what it felt, that was not so much hatred for all this horror, as something to stir them, something to help her, so that they would be obliged to feel as she was feeling! So she need not be alone so utterly!

It would be so simple to live—even without Harry. If she had never known Harry. But with Harry death had come to stay. Now she had a *real* grief to speak, it ran too deep. Or had the others no real griefs? Had some fantastic accident of her mind made her unique?

She wanted to be buried, not in the earth, but in some place that would hide this loathly difference, barring her from those who were happy. Harry was buried in the kind grey woods. Harry was under the quiet leaves. He was where the mouldering foliage did not make even a rustle. But she wanted to be buried deeper— not a whisper. She wanted Harry to forget everything that she had said to him. Because she could not live utterly alone without any hope, and because even the meagrest charity from Harry's despiser was something she clutched at helplessly. There was no dignity left in her at all. And because that was true, she denied it to others, denied that grief had robbed them and they remained any nobler, any more courageous than herself. If they were braver, if they assumed their duties more complacently, it was because they did not feel grief.

She lay down on her side, stretched on the bed abandonedly, and thought of Uncle William in the next room, appraising her, wondering how much he could get out of her if he offered her this semi-sanctuary of his home. She wanted to go to sleep. As in the past, she longed to creep into a doze that would hide her from herself. But the half-sleep that was exhaustion was like a nightmare. Little devils with horned wings made nests in the ceiling. Red roots that were a slimy coral twined to harbour them. Filthy with a green and ghastly lechery the little gnats infesting brothels she had only read about gnawed their way up to heaven. A woman with a male hide stamped, inflating her belly. Because nothing was done here but for pay. The archangel, that was *not* Harry, but was her memory of Harry, sprang to the circle of the ring. His pinions flamed. Murderers enjoyed his wrath. There was nothing more to learn. Only the wild white mares poured through the forest, clattering through the dark and not able to escape. On stale pinions, over the broken prow of the ship, floated THE VOICE. And under all this, like a black river, her grief kept running, carrying no part of the turgid sounds and shapes. That was the war. The war was over. But she knew in her heart that she did not want to be faithful. The very love she had felt for Harry tired her out, and made her want to leave it behind her, find something hard, cold, hateful, undemanding. She wanted to lead a hard, mercenary life. And perhaps when she found a man who would give her everything, to whom she owed nothing, she would marry again. In the meantime, she wanted to make the most of Uncle William.

But why did they have the war? She roused and looked about the room, looked all about her—feeling that the room ought not to be here, ought not to be the same, and people wearing hoops, bonnets, dresses, behaving as if that covered what was underneath, what she felt and could not survive. If false words could fall anywhere, they ought to bury everybody. And in a desert red as a funeral pyre.

She *must* have a God! In this mean life which could not save her grief, in this life which made even grief mean, she *must* have a God! She tried to think what God must be like to be fit to save her—a God compassionate, beautiful—like Harry. It was sacrilege, but it was the best she knew. *Like Harry.* A God that was good, that was kind, perpetually kind. She did not care much what her God would be like, if He would be as good as Harry was. Oh, that was what everybody needed, and after the war, too—a kind God. Oh, good kind God, she sobbed to herself, and began to weep. At last knowing what God was to be like, she felt very humble. She was almost happy. She knew Him well. He was not so awful as *they*— the others—had made Him out. But her mind wanted her to die. Her mind was less afraid than her heart. It wanted her to die.

III

On the lawns and before the houses that abutted on the street, seats had been erected. Mrs. Deering and her niece, Mildred, had one of the best vantage points on Pennsylvania Avenue. And the day was so lush, the sunshine so heavy on grassplots dappled with yellow mats of dandelions, that the impression made on both ladies bereft them of any criticism of life. "What a heavenly day!" Mrs. Deering would exclaim continually. "What a heavenly day!"

Just to watch the gay crowds moving, before any soldiers or procession appeared, brought a kind of happy exhaustion. The languor of full summer was already pervasive. Muslins, straw bonnets, and transparent mitts had taken the place of the sober wrappings of winter. Carriages rolling ostentatiously by were filled with fair female occupants, who sat daintily upright amidst billowings of lace and roulades of diaphanous flouncing, and turned on the idlers who sometimes impeded the lively horses, smiling faces paled or rosied by the green, the lilac, the ruby tints lining the small, tilted sunshades. A kind of somnolent chatter, a droning, like the mumbling of a fluctuating swarm of bees in a close garden, flowed from the lips of the throng. Girls tittered confidently. Their young male escorts laughed boisterously. Children's voices broke the merged sounds with shrill interludes of eager altercation. A baby of two, chubby, with bare arms and blue shoulder knots, became conspicuous when it toddled beyond a curbing and was threatened by the hoofs of a span driven in a fine landau. The negro coachman in his slick hat pulled up abruptly, and a young hero of sixteen or seventeen rushed out to snatch the infant from before the plunging feet. Cheers for his deed showed the exuberance of general goodwill. The mother scolded and slapped the child. But its wails were drowned in the echoes of happiness, and hero and victim passed out of sight.

Noontime had come. Mrs. Deering and Mildred began to feel aches in their backs. The trees languished. Waves of heat trembled liquidly in the still air which looked blown. The hard bench on which they were resting became too substantial. Occasional half-movements in the crowded foliage, which somewhat impinged on their view of what would be the line of march for the awaited regiments, soothed the ladies into longings for a nap. Mrs. Deering fought against the desire for 'a siesta' almost uncontrollably. Her lids drooped agreeably, her body sagged. Then she would realize herself and bounce to an attitude of expectation, fearing that, in her dozing, she had missed something. The day was too precious to waste in unconsciousness, even these exhausting final minutes.

She and Mildred missed, unconfessedly, the usual dinner at home. They had brought a cold luncheon with them, in a pasteboard box, and had partaken of it decorously, a trifle prematurely. Mrs. Deering began to think of hot greens, and then to consider the dandelion salad spread for somebody's picking. But she would like *her* greens not cooked with middlin', but prepared with a 'rue —a roue—something like that,' as the Creoles did it in New Orleans. Dear, dear, dear, OH, dear, dear, dear, it was very warm!

She was irritable. Mildred, when glanced at, also showed a fidgetiness that revealed irascibility. The steady glare beat like the drizzle from a furnace, on the napes of their necks. People all about looked suffering. "Looks to me like they are never coming. They've no right to set one time and then come at another," a lady on the bench below remarked indignantly to a companion. And the girl who was with her, eyes glazed by a drowsy ennui, replied, petulantly, "Yes, it's a shame the way these things are run in Washington. It's a downright imposition. And they know it when they sell the tickets!"

Mrs. Deering silently agreed. She felt especially privileged to object, for she was one of the poor mothers who had lost sons in the war. These several exasperating hours which she must sit through to render tribute to the soldiers seemed a slight to the deep black which she had kept on wearing, though Lewis and Ferdinand had been dead two years—since Gettysburg.

She and Mildred had swallowed their morning coffee, and eaten their pancakes in a haste bad for the digestion. Now that the stimulation of the lunch, also, was wearing off, a kind of sickly commonplace, which grew in the veins as with the effects of fatigue, began to be apparent in all that they were regarding. The locusts silent, the trees themselves began to buzz, and to sway a little. But the hot air that stirred was unrelieving. How dazzling the avenue! Speckled and blotted with aimless persons, their drifting shapes appeared compressed to insignificance beneath some torrid

614

glass. Those assembled were not talking so much. Yawns took the place of comment. Voices, when overheard, were shrill and unlovely. The respirations of a wind without humidity rasped the cloudy branches. An odour of noon was represented by a compound scent of horses, humans, dyed clothing and a sweetness from a hedge of flowering shrubs, suddenly become repellent.

In the first lapses of time, the passage of civilian vehicles crammed with merry-makers in gala atire had heightened anticipation. Diversions, as the preamble to certain enjoyment, had been almost welcome. Now these appearances became an affront. Each derangement of the multitude, as it overflowed the sidewalks, aroused a hope that the climax had come. But this momentary distraction from the monotony of pedestrian antics, despite the misleading intrusion of a policeman or two, or of some official on horseback, always proved to be unassociated with the main object of the assemblage. Compelled to remain passively upon these 'horrid' elevated seats, Mrs. Deering felt perfidious weakness in the pit of her stomach. Mounted gentlemen in a regalia of badges and sashes only awakened her ire.

As the effort to continue keen grew more prolonged, her eyesight seemed failing. Things far away retreated, drunkenly, to yet farther distance, and there was no more will in her that would draw them near. Unpleasant obtrusions, she sensed accurately. A woman in front of her, exposing, now and then, a bulbous, raddle-cheeked profile with huge sweat-greased nose, was fanning, heavily, methodically, with a newspaper, beating her fat breast with it steadily. A boy of six or eight, knocking a *rat-a-tat-tat* on the stand with his swinging heels and blumping legs, made the whole structure shake. When his querulous mamma tried to pacify him, giving him a banana from a rattling sack, and he stuffed his mouth unctuously with smeary, oozing pulp, Mrs. Deering was obliged to avert her thoughts from him.

It was just as this stagnance of interest had begun to breed, in resultant dizziness, a sort of animosity toward all its accompaniments, that Mildred, whose youth gave her greater hardihood, stirred in her seat, fluttered her crumpled handkerchief ecstatically, and, half rising to her feet, cried, "They're coming, Aunt Myra! At last they're coming!"

Mildred was vain that she had been the first to note the advancing parade. Several persons scrutinized her, piqued, examining her enviously before they would look at the street. Finding herself the cynosure of so many eyes, she overcame her excitement, recovered a demure posture, and thought particularly of a young man three steps down who had stared at her steadily and had not yet left off. Her pride in what was to occur was quite equal to Mrs. Deering's, but her sentimental enthusiasm for 'the soldier boys' had none of the painful associations felt by her aunt. She simply felt important in having anticipated the discovery all sought. For several seconds after her triumphant ejaculation, she was so engaged with self-consciousness of a satisfactory nature that she saw nothing at all. Indeed, the first to detect the marchers, she beheld them last. Concern as to the possible becomingness of her new 'chip' left her exteriorly blind. And then there was the sensation, almost anticlimactic, which she experienced when she realized that her little outburst had been at once dismissed. Rousing from self-communion, she was obliged to feel that, instead of continuing to command attention, she had put herself in the position of being peculiarly alone. All apart, and by herself, she had to go back over her recent meditations and resume the animation of which the shock of notoriety had deprived her. The young man had evidently forgotten her existence, and she quickly glossed over her admission that *she* had recognized him. After all, *he* was not her absorbing interest. But she was ashamed. She looked distastefully at her lace-enveloped fingers. When the first flag tilted jauntily above the dispersing masses yet clotting the road, and advance officials on horseback began to drive men, women and children before them, and with a ruthlessness equivalent to hostility, Mildred felt less inclined to shout *bravos* than to weep. She had endured suspense here much too long. It would have been more pleasurable to stay at home where she was comfortable and 'appreciated.'

Mrs. Deering, rejuvenated, and very possessive toward the nation, was bolt upright, her black-mitted hands gripped tightly together. She, too, had glanced around her, expecting, for some reason, that the fact that she was in mourning would force heed to herself. She *did* notice, however, that the signals of bereavement were not unique. There were many, even in her own grandstand, also dressed in crêpe. At least the exhibition of her loss—and she had demurred about it—was not indiscreet. Ah, well, she thought, *they* know. It is the mothers who have given most to make this fine day possible.

She was not jealous of those others. Rather she felt it meet that some sign of comprehension pass between her and them. I have lost *two* sons—my all and only, she told herself defiantly. Could any mother on this earth give more than that!

But these personal reflections which made her tremble a little in her importance were soon swept, mercifully, right out of her brain. There was the *boom* of a signal gun. General Sherman, on a bay horse, was already approaching, riding in front of his men. Mrs. Deering felt, as she watched him, that she almost loved him. She liked his 'little martinet' bearing. His oldish appearance, his insignificance, were, in a way, disappointing. Yet he looked 'fatherly.' He had a short, stubbly, whitish beard, and his small, keen, deep-set eyes were full of humour. There was something altogether delightful to her in the heart-felt manner in which, overcome as he seemed by his weighty uniform and his decorations, he bowed, removing his broad hat and waving it again and again.

She could just see his whole career from start to finish, and imagine how he had made himself just what he was. Nothing could be more 'forthright' than his dry, rugged face, hook-nosed and, she conceded, somewhat inexpressive. But *think* what he had done! Think of his march to the sea! He was a man it would be very hard to 'fool,' Mrs. Deering thought, and any mother ought to be 'proud and relieved' to trust her sons to him. She surveyed her associates aggressively, mutely demanding of them a militant agreement with her approval.

Mrs. Deering was 'moved.' It was plain that Mildred was, too. And the elder lady patted her lids with her handkerchief. She had not seen the parade yesterday, and, in consequence, had not seen General Meade and those commanders more nearly related in the fate of her sons. But that was because, at the ticket-sellers', there had been such a mob no places were to be had. She felt, therefore, some condescension toward this half of the army which derived from other portions of the country. But Mildred had three *own* cousins under General Sherman, and must enjoy this most. Dear little Mildred, Mrs. Deering thought. Would the child break down?

It was strange that, as the 'boys' surged on, the high glare seemed to cool, and the perspiration dewing every forehead to become refreshing. For a few seconds, as the throng sank backward to give space to soldiers, there was a sensible and exhilarating stillness, expanded by the rhythmic thump of boots. The men had halted to mark time. *Tum-tump, tum-tump, tum-tump.* Mild cheers greeted them. The flexed legs flashed in some endless, mechanistic design made of the bright braid bending along the seams of the blue trousers. The rows of hardy, sunburned faces showed chins at one level, eyes stoically fixed on one distance. Their pretended obliviousness to expletives of praise was itself 'inspiring.' The spectators, before this brilliant uniformity, felt individual, and weak.

Mrs. Deering said to herself, I never saw a sturdier, finer-looking set of young men—or old ones either. In all this compact of united motion, she realized, vaguely, something protective risen between herself and—and *what?* Southerners, for one thing. She had lived in Washington for many years, but she had never liked the South. As a matter of fact, she never had 'understood the war very well.' Sometimes, when 'Ferd' and Lewis had talked to her, she had thought it was all about slavery. Again it was State's Rights, or Fort Sumter or something else. With this magnificent organization to defend her, her meek conjectures of the past seemed worse than useless. They seemed presumptuous. She felt like crying—she, such a 'poor old nonentity,' but her *boys,* her dear and beloved sons, they had shared in this! She fidgeted uneasily. I must be brave, she insisted to herself. I mustn't lose my grip. But she reached over covertly, and caught Mildred's hand. After all, Mrs. Deering was sixty-two, and it was hard to sit here in the sun for hours, and then—she had loved those boys, yes, she'd loved those boys so—*too* much, Mr. Slaughter, her minister had told her, oh, far too much. But now that she saw what a fine, grand thing the army was—*her* army—refuge of her boys,—she would never lift her voice to protest again. This just showed what 'duty' was, and selfishness so 'ignoble and ugly.' What could she have ever done for her boys, if they had lived, that could have equalled *this!*

Somebody called an order. When Mrs. Deering saw all those simultaneous legs stiffen at once, her heart swelled and tapped in her breast. She was awed. *Our* army, she whispered to herself, *our* army! I must remember that. "Isn't it beautiful?" she muttered to Mildred.

Abruptly, the monstrous ONE began to move like a millipede,

618

and in its numbers she saw boys like her own. A band suddenly flashed chords on the tense air. The bright sound crowded to the tops of the trees and the blue sky above them. The blare of the instruments was one joyous breath, stifling, breathed from every throat. And this, also, became accent, was measured with strength. Plum-*plump*, plum-*plump*, plum-*plump*. There was a monotonous, disturbing brushing of hundreds of boots stamping the road. The bandsmen walked mincingly, sedately, like-ladies, their hips swinging, tight in their close trousers, their heads a little cocked as they blew steadily, with stuffed, empurpled cheeks, into their sparkling horns. Flags, resting on their thighs, dipped stiffly, swung gigantic folds, and seemed to sweep, with a kind of pride, unmoved over the noise. The bandsmen were heated and some wore handkerchiefs draped on their heads beneath their caps, protecting their necks. Their faces grew swollen and expressionless. The horns were like flaring mirrors.

The din they made lifted a multitude on tiptoe: Mrs. Deering half rising from her place on the bench, Mildred rising, pale. Contradicting yet assisting the chortle of the brasses, the drumsticks bounced profoundly. The stretched drums and the heavy sticks—drums round and ghostly in the sun—walked heavier than the thunderous feet. The musicians proceeding, glanced about with roving, enchanted eyes. The listeners had received all they could endure, sought for release. It came. The tune was familiar. Stunned by the dizzying aspect of its presentation, they had not, at first, recognized it. Affirmation must be affirmed. Concordant acclamations became, unpremeditatedly, the very melody itself, accepted, driven home by the drum taps. The crowd found now but a single voice for its unanimity, its triumph. It began to sing.

> Bring the good old bugle, boys,
>   We'll sing another song,
> Sing it with a spirit
>   That will start the world along,
> Sing it as we used to sing it,
>   Fifty thousand strong,
> While *we* were *march*-ing *through Geor-gia!*

The song was not a year old. Yet it seemed to be old with something they had all felt before. Its triumph pressed in their throats.

They sang raucously. They sang out of time. They yelled and cried aloud.

> Hur-*rah*, hur-*rah*, we bring the *ju*-bi-*lee!*
> Hur-*rah*, hur-*rah*, the *flag* that makes you *free!*
> So we *sang* the *cho*-rus from *At-lan-ta* to the *SEA*,
> *While* we *were* march-*ing* through *Geor-gia!*

Men's hats tossed into the air. Out of the rackety chant came an impression, with the madness, with the elation, of an almost unbearable seriousness. It was conveyed, mostly, by the sheer ponderousness of many. The universe of the street fluttered and resounded with the stentorian bawling. The trees, the buildings were unimportant to a world so in flood. Cheers rose into shrieks, bellows. Women near Mrs. Deering burst into tears and laughed wildly. A kind of moaning of delight rent their breasts. They saw one another dimly, but had ceased to be ashamed.

Voluptuously, fearful of this insanity, yet glad, Mrs. Deering relinquished her will to the vast, foolish impetus of pride, of delight. It was but once in a lifetime that you had the privilege of beholding a nation moved. The 'brotherhood' that had come out of the experiences of war was now very clear to her. If Lewis and Ferdinand could only rise to hear! Could know her unabashed vanity in her memory of them—she who had no more to give to any future victories of right. Beaming through tears, she craned her head in glad bewilderment, and corroborated, in the expression of each face near her, her own orgiastic fervour. Hats were still hurtling toward the trees, and making small, heavy whirlwinds, dark in the glitter of the sun. Sky and trees brushed lightly over the scene. Shadowy fountains of fresh green leaves blenched. At the summit of this unearthliness, the dome of the Capitol swelled in a white bubble, carrying uplifted feelings solidly to heaven.

It seemed to Mrs. Deering that, up to this instant, she had led a mean, crabbed, and uneventful life. Conscientious as she had been all of her days, hard as had been her widowed struggle for her children, she had never, until now, experienced a really noble and selfless emotion. It's not the decisions of the wiseacres that make nations great, she decided, but big, generous, unashamed *feeling*—that's what it is! In the days when she had been courted by her husband, she had believed herself in the throes of sublime romance. And so she had been. But what did love for any one human, love between any two humans, amount to, compared to sensations that burst the heart and were bigger than men themselves, did not consider men as men apart? Fear dogs our footsteps every day of our lives. Fear of poverty, fear of the opinions of our neighbours, fear of this and that. Save *here*, O God—here, where *all* approve, and approve without petty reflection! Contemptible indeed is the spirit that persists in isolating itself in the midst of a gladness so general that no babe in swaddling clothes, no decrepit old man is immune to its contagion! Why the very birds of the air must rise in ecstatic flight under the influence of these blended voices, the mighty sound of these many feet! Mrs. Deering could not understand how she had lived all these years and never known what it was, really, to be a member of the human race, received here and anointed one of them, as by God in a church.

"*Sing*, Mildred!" she ordered. "Shout! Say 'Hurrah!' I can't keep quiet. I can't keep my mouth shut!" And, while the tears were running, she was swaying slightly, almost ready to dance.

Mildred, bereft of her usual awareness, turned on her aunt eyes opaque and brilliant as those of a roused sleeper. Her lips quivered. She smiled strangely, as if she only, living, smiled on the dead. Her aunt could see that she was 'a long way off.'

The little boy on the grand stand—the one who had first attracted Mrs. Deering's notice when he was given a banana—now suddenly took fright from the riotous behaviour of the adults around him, clutched at his mamma's skirts, and, finally, finding them too voluminous to be encompassed, threw his arms about her spindling waist, leaned frantically on her, and screeched, "Ma, Ma! What's the matter, Ma? I'm scared, Ma! Please look at me, Ma. I'm here, Ma! Please don't act like that, Ma!"

His mother, teetering on the bench to which she had mounted, turned on him a stare as wild and dreamy as Mildred's, and did not answer for a space. A silly smile on her parted mouth, her cheeks were wet. When she came to herself and could comprehend what he was saying, she felt that he had spoiled something, and slapped him rudely several times, and with a drunkard's irrational irritability. "Willie! How dare you! Don't you see folks are *looking* at you! Can't you be glad like everybody else that the war is over and the soldiers home? Can't you *behave* yourself!"

He was reassured by her anger, and rubbed his fists with perfunctory forlornness into his eyes, but she snatched his sticky hand away. "Don't do that!" Her heart was like 'sweet bells jangled out of tune.' She had never *seen* such an exasperating child! Flirting out her ruffles, smoothing their folds to hang equally, she climbed down on the seat again, not forgetting, as she did so, to jerk Willie, roughly, closer to her, assuring herself that he had resumed, decorously, his place at her side, and assuming over him, thereafter, a severe, vindictive espionage. That was the lot of a mother—never a moment to think of herself! But Mrs. Deering, who, in a wave of sentiment, had forgiven the banana, felt differently. Poor little fellow, she said to herself, seeing how badly cut his baggy breeches were, and that his jacket was pulled all awry; and, in a faint way, she pitied the unlovely mother who was not yet mature enough to know the élan that came so devastatingly with perfect sacrifice.

Regiment was succeeding regiment. 'Fighting' Johnny Logan, 'Fort McAllister' Hazen, 'Susan' Wood, 'Allatoona' Corse, Frank Blair, Leggett and Force—heroes of Vicksburg. Mildred had read the newspapers and knew the names of most of them. There were ambulances at the rear of the seventeenth corps. General Slocum, less whiskered, looked younger than the others. Some girls pushed out of the crowd to meet him and gave him flowers. He carried the bouquet on his saddle bow, gallantly, while a single rose he thrust into his hat. His staff was on his right: Major R. P. Dechert, Lieutenant Colonel E. W. Gridon—Mildred could not remember the names of the others. She had detected, in the audience with her, a dapper man holding eyeglasses to his eyes, and thought he must be the attaché at some foreign legation. She was annoyed with him when he did not clap enough. It was said that the world was envious of the United States. It had not believed that a democratic nation could produce such an army. Mildred glowed, as with vengeance, on the attaché. Oh, his temerity.

The crowd was now very quiet, though cheeks remained wet. Flagging of appreciation this was not, but fatigue. Yet it brought a troubled conscience, and the applause came dutifully, in little flutters. There was a hardier hullabaloo in the distance. Grant was receiving there a boisterous reception. Sherman, later, it might be supposed, was joining him in the reviewing stand. The armies marched in close column, with their lines well dressed, their bayonets at shoulder-arms. People seated at a disadvantage could see, by elongating their necks, that Grant, off yonder, was being saluted by the lowering of colours, and heard a ruffle of the field music.

Mildred was expatiating politely on the beautiful, restless look of the horses in a body of cavalry, and Mrs. Deering was thinking that she would remember her own feelings at the supreme moment of this pageant till her 'dying day.'

At the end of the procession came several carts filled with humourists who had decorated their nags with carrots, wreaths of onion and turnip, armourings of pots and pans and other twinkling plate. *Sherman's Army,* was painted crookedly on a cardboard sign. The plethora of excitement had left the observers indifferent to novelty, yet this twisted echo of their first strong impression was received appreciatively. They were glad that nothing more violent than laughter would now be required of them. The sun had grown suddenly hot again. Even the antics of these clowns at the end could not disguise the fact that delirium had completed its moment. The hour had become empty, fit to be devoted to consideration of the weather, the time to go home.

In the grandstand, people, impatient of the further attention demanded, had already begun to rise; ladies to collect their parasols and their belongings, children to fret. And the avenue, before the mock regiment could get properly out of the way, was trickling once more flowered head-gear of women, top-hats, sunshades. Like the roar of a tide that has swept on to other strands, came mingled vibrations from that barricaded distance where were others beholding freshly the visions that, here, were past and stale. But it did not disturb the present's business. The music of bands tingled in people's heads. You did not know whether you were actually listening to tunes played farther off, or merely attended trapped echoes. *Marching Through Georgia* thumped vapidly in a hundred minds. Some boys on the pavement began to whistle it.

Mildred, helping her aunt to collect handkerchief, reticule, purse, felt, limply, a great, rewarding peace. She had the sense of some enormous accomplishment. She was ready to go home as to a rest well earned. Her new muslin had been worn for its occasion, and, conscious now only of its crushed ruffles, she longed to take it off. In the house it would be so cool, so blessedly private. She did not again resent the crowd, but she was finished with it, as it with her. She wanted to be alone to digest her impressions of a cortège that she would probably describe to her children and her children's children. Oh, it was wonderful, she thought. Had she fought the war herself, she would not have felt more patriotic. She was grateful, as if something extraordinary had been given to her—and by the 'boys,' the soldiers, by these throngs of people whom she did not know. Her future seemed to her larger than it had been six hours ago. She thought fantastically of all the elevating situations it might contain. Perhaps it had been too much for 'poor Aunt Myra.' Her gestures were a little shaky.

The avenue was filled with carriages. Every black wheel that turned burned with a thousand rays like a disk of sun. Hundreds of revolving, mirrory rockets flashed along the street. The droning of a vast chatter had diminished. Instead, marked and irregular noises became more prominent. Hoofs clattered, axles squeaked. A wagon passed incongruously. The weary, nasal invitation of a peanut-vender floated, in a singsong, from the curb below. Dressed in an old, greenish coat, and a shapeless beaver too large for him, a man selling toy balloons threaded, with his furtive expression of anxiety, in and out amongst stragglers. The balloons, in their fat, glistening clusters, floating flamboyantly, with laggard irregular resilience, over the hats of the passers-by, were like pursy haloes, red and blue. Shouts of trade were perpetual. A bladder wheezed stridently in the hands of the child who had inflated it. "Pop-corn! Cold lemonade!" People hurried. A woman ran along the street trying to catch up with somebody, and every moment calling, "Rosie, Mamie! Don't you run like that!" Boys were taunting one another. The disintegration of the populace from its singleness of interest was rowdy, discouraging, persons hastening in opposite directions retarding one another. There was a general air of frustrateness.

Obviously, Mrs. Deering had felt the strain too much. Mildred was alarmed. The elder lady, supported by her niece, had taken several steps toward the crude, unpainted stair, when feebleness overcame her. She sat down quickly on the nearest abandoned chair, panting, fanning herself. Mildred was shocked to see the

624

kindly, wrinkled face all at once ghastly. "Auntie!" Mildred cried, bending to assist her. "Auntie! The heat! The excitement! It has been too much!"

Mrs. Deering was humiliated. With a desperate fist she battered her slack lap limply. Her eyes rolled drearily, in a gaze that gave her an unwonted air of ancientness. "It's the boys, Mildred," she groaned. "It's like I didn't seem to realize before—and the war— all we've read about it these years. I had a terrible feeling—just like I was going to faint." She pulled herself together. "No—I'm better now. No, don't bother about me." And she pushed her niece off.

Patting her eyes, Mrs. Deering stood up, smiled wanly. "Just too silly, ain't it!" she said stoutly. "This is a glorious recompense. I'm not denying that."

Well—the grandstand was becoming a skeleton, unclothed. A man in shirt sleeves was removing some chairs that had been placed, at the last minute, along a rear ledge of the platform. The street was returning to the ordinary. A humming, far away, indicated that there was still a mass of humans in another street, another planet; but here a tide of desolation encroached. Even Mildred was feeling discontentedly the 'poky,' aimless look of everything. Seemed like a Sunday. Over the light-bristling trees the sun still reared in the faded sky. The remote façade of the Capitol looked almost deathly in its air of permanence.

"Aunt Myra," Mildred said, "I'm going to treat you like a little girl. I'm going to march you home just as fast as I can and make you lie down. We'll try to find *somebody* with a hack to rent us."

It was an awful extravagance, but, for once, Mrs. Deering did not feel like making an objection. Drudge, save, scrimp—and yet—today! Oh, what a pity we cannot always live on the plane of our finest moments! What she had felt when the salute had sounded and General Sherman appeared must be the real truth of things. And now—as with her boys—she could only feed on memory.

"It's the sun, Mildred. My, how I wish I'd had some foresight and brought my smelling salts! I'm real faint yet. Goodness, I'm faint! Ask that man down yonder with the lemonade if he'll sell a glass of water."

THE END

Cassis-sur-mer, 1926,
Montreal, 1928.

$\mathcal{V}$OICES OF THE $\mathcal{S}$OUTH